ILIUM

ILIUM

DAN SIMMONS

An Imprint of HarperCollins*Publishers*

Grateful acknowledgment is made to the following:

Random House to reprint from *Remembrance of Things Past: Volume 1* by Marcel Proust, translated by C. K. Scott Moncrieff and Terrence Kilmartin, copyright © 1981 by Random House, Inc., and Chatto & Windus. Used by permission of Random House, Inc.

University of Chicago Press to reprint from *The Iliad*, Book IX, translated by Richard Lattimore, copyright 1951, by the University of Chicago Press. Used by permission of University of Chicago Press.

HarperCollins books may be purchased for educational, business, or sales promotional use. For information please write: Special Markets Department, HarperCollins Publishers Inc., 10 East 53rd Street, New York, NY 10022.

FIRST EDITION

Designed by Mia Risberg

Printed on acid-free paper

Library of Congress Cataloging-in-Publication Data
Simmons, Dan.
Ilium / by Dan Simmons.—1st ed.
p. cm.
ISBN 0-380-97893-8
1. Imaginary wars and battles—Fiction. 2. Mythology, Greek—Fiction. 3. Gods, Greek—Fiction. 4. Mars (Planet)—Fiction. I. Title

AUG 5 2003   PS3569.I47292 I45 2003
       813'.54—dc21   2002044791I

03 04 05 06 07 JTC/QW 10 9 8 7 6 5 4 3 2 1

This novel is dedicated to Wabash College—
its men, its faculty, and its legacy

Mean while the Mind, from pleasure less,
Withdraws into its happiness:
The Mind, that Ocean where each kind
Does straight its resemblance find;
Yet it creates, transcending these,
Far other Worlds, and other Seas;
Annihilating all that's made
To a green Thought in a green Shade.
    —Andrew Marvell's "The Garden"

Of possessions
cattle and fat sheep are things to be had for the lifting,
and tripods can be won, and the tawny high heads of horses,
but a man's life cannot come back again, it cannot be lifted
nor captured again by force, once it has crossed the teeth's barrier.
    —Achilles in Homer's *The Iliad*,
    Book IX, 405–409

A bitter heart that bides its time and bites.
    —Caliban in Robert Browning's
    "Caliban upon Setebos"

Acknowledgments

While many translations of the *Iliad* were referred to in preparation for the writing of this novel, I would specifically like to acknowledge the following translators—Robert Fagles, Richmond Lattimore, Alexander Pope, George Chapman, Robert Fitzgerald, and Allen Mandelbaum. The beauty of their translations is manifold and their talent is beyond this writer's comprehension.

For ancillary poetry or imaginative *Iliad*-related prose which helped shape this volume, I would especially like to acknowledge the work of W. H. Auden, Robert Browning, Robert Graves, Christopher Logue, Robert Lowell, and Alfred, Lord Tennyson.

For research and commentary on the *Iliad* and Homer, I would like to acknowledge the work of Bernard Knox, Richmond Lattimore, Malcolm M. Willcock, A.J.B. Wace, F. H. Stubbings, C. Kerenyi, and members of the Homeric *scholia* too numerous to mention.

For insightful commentary on Shakespeare and Browning's "Caliban upon Setebos," I gratefully acknowledge the writings of Harold Bloom, W. H. Auden, and the editors of the *Norton Anthology of English Literature*. For an insight into Auden's interpretation of "Caliban upon Setebos" and other aspects of Caliban, I refer readers to Edward Mendelson's *Later Auden*.

"Mahnmut's" insights into the sonnets of Shakespeare were largely guided by Helen Vendler's wonderful *The Art of Shakespeare's Sonnets*.

Many of "Orphu of Io's" comments on the work of Marcel Proust were inspired by Roger Shattuck's *Proust's Way: A Field Guide to* In Search of Lost Time.

To readers interested in emulating Mahnmut's Bardolotous love of Shakespeare, I would recommend Harold Bloom's *Shakespeare: The In-*

vention of the Human, Herman Gollob's *Me and Shakespeare: Adventures with the Bard*, and *Shakespeare: A Life* by Park Honan.

For detailed maps of Mars (before the terraforming), I owe a great debt of gratitude to NASA, the Jet Propulsion Laboratory, and *Uncovering the Secrets of the Red Planet*, published by the National Geographic Society, edited by Paul Raeburn, with forward and commentary by Matt Golombeck. *Scientific American* has been a rich source of detail, and acknowledgment should go to such articles as "The Hidden Ocean of Europa," by Robert T. Pappalardo, James W. Head, and Ronald Greeley (October 1999), "Quantum Teleportation" by Anton Zeilinger (April 2000), and "How to Build a Time Machine" by Paul Davies (September 2002).

Finally, my thanks to Clee Richeson for details on how to build a homemade casting furnace with a wooden cupola.

Author's Note

When my kid brother and I used to take our toy soldiers out of the box, we had no problem playing with our blue and gray Civil War soldiers alongside our green World War II guys. I prefer to think of this as a precocious example of what John Keats called "Negative Capability." (We also had a Viking, a cowboy, an Indian, and a Roman Centurion flinging grenades, but they were in our Time Commando Platoon. Some anomalies demand what the Hollywood people insist on calling a backstory.)

With *Ilium*, however, I thought a certain consistency was required. Those readers who teethed, as I did, on Richmond Lattimore's wonderful 1951 translation of the *Iliad* will notice that Hektor, Achilleus, and Aias have become Hector, Achilles, and Ajax (Big and Little). In this I agree with Robert Fagles in his 1990 translation that while these more latinized versions are farther from the Greek—Hektor versus Akhilleus and the Akhaians and the Argeioi—the more faithful version sometimes sounds like a cat coughing up a hairball. As Fagles points out, no one can claim perfect consistency, and it tends to read more smoothly when we return to the traditional practice of the English poets by using Latinate spellings and even modern English forms for the heroes and their gods.

The exception to this, again as per Fagles, is when we would have Ulysses instead of Odysseus or, say, Minerva replacing Athena. Alexander Pope in his incredibly beautiful translation of the *Iliad* into heroic couplets had no problem with "Jupiter" or "Jove" ripping Ares (not Mars) a new one, but my Negative Capability falters here. Sometimes, it seems, you have to play with just the green guys.

Note: For those readers who, like me, have problems in an epic tale telling the gods, goddesses, heroes, and other characters apart without a scorecard, I would refer you to our dramatis personae *beginning on page 573.*

ILIUM

The Plains of Ilium

Rage.

Sing, O Muse, of the rage of Achilles, of Peleus' son, murderous, man-killer, fated to die, sing of the rage that cost the Achaeans so many good men and sent so many vital, hearty souls down to the dreary House of Death. And while you're at it, O Muse, sing of the rage of the gods themselves, so petulant and so powerful here on their new Olympos, and of the rage of the post-humans, dead and gone though they might be, and of the rage of those few true humans left, self-absorbed and useless though they may have become. While you are singing, O Muse, sing also of the rage of those thoughtful, sentient, serious but not-so-close-to-human beings out there dreaming under the ice of Europa, dying in the sulfur-ash of Io, and being born in the cold folds of Ganymede.

Oh, and sing of me, O Muse, poor born-again-against-his-will Hockenberry—poor dead Thomas Hockenberry, Ph.D., Hockenbush to his friends, to friends long since turned to dust on a world long since left behind. Sing of *my* rage, yes, of my *rage*, O Muse, small and insignificant though that rage may be when measured against the anger of the immortal gods, or when compared to the wrath of the god-killer, Achilles.

On second thought, O Muse, sing of nothing to me. I know you. I have been bound and servant to *you*, O Muse, you incomparable bitch. And I do not trust you, O Muse. Not one little bit.

If I am to be the unwilling Chorus of this tale, then I can start the story anywhere I choose. I choose to start it here.

It is a day like every other day in the more than nine years since my rebirth. I awaken at the Scholia barracks, that place of red sand and blue sky and great stone faces, am summoned by the Muse, get sniffed and passed by the murderous cerberids, am duly carried the seventeen vertical miles to the grassy summits of Olympos via the high-speed east-slope crystal escalator and—once reported in at the Muse's empty villa—receive my briefing from the scholic going off-shift, don my morphing gear and impact armor, slide the taser baton into my belt, and then QT to the evening plains of Ilium.

If you've ever imagined the siege of Ilium, as I did professionally for more than twenty years, I have to tell you that your imagination almost certainly was not up to the task. Mine wasn't. The reality is far more wonderful and terrible than even the blind poet would have us see.

First of all there there is the city, Ilium, Troy, one of the great armed poleis of the ancient world—more than two miles away from the beach where I stand now but still visible and beautiful and domineering on its high ground, its tall walls lighted by thousands of torches and bonfires, its towers not quite as topless as Marlowe would have us believe, but still amazing—tall, rounded, alien, imposing.

Then there are the Achaeans and Danaans and other invaders—technically not yet "Greeks" since that nation will not come into being for more than two thousand years, but I will call them Greeks anyway—stretched mile after mile here along the shoreline. When I taught the *Iliad*, I told my students that the Trojan War, for all its Homeric glory, had probably been a small affair in reality—some few thousands of Greek warriors against a few thousand Trojans. Even the best informed members of the *scholia*—that group of *Iliad* scholars going back almost two millennia—estimated from the poem that there could not possibly be more than 50,000 Achaeans and other Greek warriors drawn up in their black ships along the shore.

They were wrong. Estimates now show that there are more than 250,000 attacking Greeks and about half that number of defending Trojans and their allies. Evidently every warrior hero in the Greek Isles came running to this battle—for battle meant plunder—and brought his soldiers and allies and retainers and slaves and concubines with him.

The visual impact is stunning: mile upon mile of lighted tents, campfires, sharpened-stake defenses, miles of trenches dug in the hard ground above the beaches—not for hiding and hunkering in, but as a deterrent to Trojan cavalry—and, illuminating all those miles of tents and men and shining on polished spears and bright shields, thousands of bonfires and cooking fires and corpse fires burning bright.

Corpse fires.

For the past few weeks, pestilence has been creeping through the Greek ranks, first killing donkeys and dogs, then dropping a soldier here, a servant there, until suddenly in the past ten days it has become an epidemic, slaying more Achaean and Danaan heroes than the defenders of Ilium have in months. I suspect it is typhus. The Greeks are sure it is the anger of Apollo.

I've seen Apollo from a distance—both on Olympos and here—and he's a very nasty fellow. Apollo is the archer god, lord of the silver bow, "he who strikes from afar," and while he's the god of healing, he's also the god of disease. More than that, he's the principle divine ally of the Trojans in this battle, and if Apollo were to have his way, the Achaeans would be wiped out. Whether this typhoid came from the corpse-fouled rivers and other polluted water here or from Apollo's silver bow, the Greeks are right to think that he wishes them ill.

At this moment the Achaean "lords and kings"—and every one of these Greek heroes is a sort of king or lord in his own province and in his own eyes—are gathering in a public assembly near Agamemnon's tent to decide on a course of action to end this plague. I walk that way slowly, almost reluctantly, although after more than nine years of biding my time, tonight should be the most exciting moment of my long observation of this war. Tonight, Homer's *Iliad* begins in reality.

Oh, I've witnessed many elements from Homer's poem that had been poetically misplaced in time, such as the so-called Catalogue of Ships, the assembly and listing of all the Greek forces, which is in Book Two of the *Iliad* but which I saw take place more than nine years ago during the assembly of this military expedition at Aulis, the strait between Euboea and the Greek mainland. Or the *Epipolesis*, the review of the army by Agamemnon, which occurs in Book Four of Homer's epic but which I saw take place shortly after the armies landed here near Ilium. That actual event was followed by what I used to teach as the *Teichoskopia*, or "View from the Wall," in which Helen identifies the various Achaean heroes for Priam and the other Trojan leaders. The *Teichoskopia* appears in Book Three of the poem, but happened shortly after the landing and *Epipolesis* in the actual unfolding of events.

If there *is* an actual unfolding of events here.

At any rate, tonight is the assembly at Agamemnon's tent and the confrontation between Agamemnon and Achilles. This is where the *Iliad* begins, and it should be the focus of all my energies and professional skills, but the truth is that I don't really give a shit. Let them posture. Let them bluster. Let Achilles reach for his sword—well, I confess that I'm interested in observing that. Will Athena actually appear to stop him, or was she just a metaphor for Achilles' common sense kicking in? I've waited my entire life to answer such a question and the answer is only minutes away, but, strangely, irrevocably . . . I . . . don't . . . give . . . a . . . shit.

The nine years of painful rebirth and slow memory return and constant warfare and constant heroic posturing, not to mention my own enslavement by the gods and the Muse, have taken their toll. I'd be just as happy right now if a B-52 appeared and dropped an atomic bomb on both the Greeks and the Trojans. Fuck all these heroes and the wooden chariots they rode in on.

But I trudge toward Agamemnon's tent. This is my job. If I don't observe this and make my report to the Muse, it won't mean loss of tenure for me. The gods will reduce me to the bone splinters and dusty DNA they re-created me from and that, as they say, will be that.

Ardis Hills, Ardis Hall

Daeman faxed into solidity near Ada's home and blinked stupidly at the red sun on the horizon. The sky was cloudless and the sunset burned between the tall trees on the ridgeline and set both the p-ring and the e-ring glowing as they rotated in the cobalt sky. Daeman was disoriented because it was evening here and it had been morning only a second before when he faxed away from Tobi's Second Twenty party in Ulanbat. It had been years since he visited Ada's home, and except for those friends whom he visited most regularly—Sedman in Paris, Ono in Bellinbad, Risir in her home on the cliffs of Chom, a few others—he never had a clue as to what continent or time zone he would find himself in. But then, Daeman did not know the names or positions of the continents, much less the concepts of geography or time zones, so his very lack of knowledge meant nothing to him.

It was still disorienting. He had lost a day. Or had he gained it? At any rate, the air smelled different here—wetter, richer, wilder.

Daeman looked around. He stood in the center of a generic faxnode pad—that usual circle of permcrete and fancy iron posts topped with a yellow crystal pergola, and near the center of the circle the post holding the inevitable coded sign that he could not read. There was no other structure visible in the valley, only grass, trees, a stream in the distance, the slow revolution of both rings crossing above like the armatures of some great, slow gyroscope.

It was a warm evening, more humid than Ulanbat, and the faxpad was centered in a grassy meadow surrounded by low hills. Twenty feet beyond the pad circle stood an ancient two-person, one-wheeled, open carriole, with an equally ancient servitor floating above the driver's nook and a single voynix standing between the wooden tongues. It had been more than a decade since Daeman had visited Ardis Hall, but now he remembered the barbaric inconvenience of all this. Absurd, not having one's home on a faxnode.

"Daeman *Uhr*?" queried the servitor, although it obviously knew who he was.

Daeman grunted and held out his battered gladstone. The tiny servitor floated closer, took the luggage in its padded cusps, and loaded it in the carriole's canvas boot while Daeman climbed aboard. "Are we waiting for others?"

"You are the final guest," replied the servitor. It hummed into its hemispherical niche and clicked a command; the voynix clamped onto the carriole tongues and began jogging toward the setting sun, its rusty peds and the carriole's wheel raising very little dust on the gravel roadway. Daeman settled back on the green leather, rested both hands on his walking cane, and enjoyed the ride.

He had come not to visit Ada but to seduce her. This is what Daeman did—seduce young women. That and collect butterflies. The fact that Ada was in her mid-twenties and Daeman was approaching his Second Twenty made no difference to him. Neither did the fact that Ada was his first cousin. Incest taboos had eroded away long ago. "Genetic drift" was not even a concept to Daeman, but if it had been, he would have trusted the firmary to fix it. The firmary fixed everything.

Daeman had been visiting Ardis Hill ten years earlier in his role as cousin—and trying to seduce Ada's other cousin, Virginia, out of sheer boredom since Virginia had all the attractiveness of a voynix—when he had first seen Ada nude. He had been walking down one of the endless Ardis Hall corridors in search of the breakfast conservatory when he had passed the younger woman's room, the door was ajar, and there reflected in a tall, warped mirror was Ada, bathing from a basin with a sponge and wearing only a mildly bored expression—Ada was many things, but overly hygienic was not one, Daeman had learned—and her reflection, this young woman just emerging from the chrysalis of girlhood, had arrested him, this adult man just a bit older then than Ada was now.

Even then, with the puffiness of childhood still present in her hips and thighs and bud-nipple breasts, Ada was a sight worth stopping to appreciate. Pale—the girl's skin stayed a soft, parchment white no matter how long she stayed outside—her gray eyes, raspberry lips, and black-black hair was an amateur eroticist's dream. The cultural mode had been for women to shave their armpits then, but neither young Ada nor—Daeman sincerely hoped—her adult counterpart had paid any more attention to that than she did to most other cultural modalities. Frozen in the tall mirror then (and pinned and mounted in the collection tray of Daeman's memory now) was that still-girlish but already voluptuous body, heavy pale breasts, creamy skin, alert eyes, all that paleness punctuated by the four dashes of black hair—the wavy question mark of hair she kept carelessly pinned up except when she played, which was most of the time, the two commas under her arms, and the perfect black exclamation mark—not yet matured to a delta—leading to the shadows between her thighs.

Riding in the carriole, Daeman smiled. He had no idea why Ada had invited him to this birthday celebration after all these years—or whose Twenty they were celebrating—but he was confident that he would seduce the young woman before he faxed back to his real world of parties and long visits and casual affairs with more worldly women.

The voynix trotted effortlessly, pulling the carriole with only the gravel-hiss underped and the soft humming of ancient gyroscopes in the carriage body. Shadows crept across the valley, but the narrow lane went up over a ridge, caught the last bit of the sun—bisected as it was on the next ridge west—and then descended into a wider valley where fields of some low crop stretched out on either side. The tending servitors flitted above the field, Daeman thought, like so many levitating croquet balls.

The road turned south—left to Daeman—crossed a river on a wooden covered bridge and then switchbacked up a steeper hill and entered an older forest. Daeman vaguely remembered hunting for butterflies in that ancient forest ten years ago, later on the day he had seen young Ada nude in the mirror. He remembered his excitement at collecting a rare breed of mourning cloak near a waterfall, the memory mingling with the excitement at seeing the girl's pale flesh and black hair. He remembered now the look Ada's reflection had given him when the pale face looked up from her ablutions—disinterested, neither pleased nor angry, immodest but not brazen, vaguely clinical—looking at twenty-seven-year-old Daeman frozen by lust in the hallway much the way Daeman himself had studied his captured mourning cloak.

The carriole was nearing Ardis Hall. It was dark under the ancient oaks and elms and ash trees nearing the top of the hill, but yellow lanterns had been set along the roadway and lines of colored lanterns could be glimpsed in the primeval forest, perhaps outlining trails.

The voynix padded out of the woods and a twilight view opened up: Ardis Hall glowing on its hilltop; white gravel paths and roads winding away from it in every direction; the long, grassy sward extending down from the manor house for more than a quarter mile before the greenway was blocked by another forest; the river beyond, still glowing, reflecting the dying light in the sky; and through a gap in the hills to the southwest, glimpses of more forested hills—black, devoid of lights—and then more hills beyond that, until the black ridges blended with dark clouds on the horizon.

Daeman shivered. He hadn't remembered until that minute that Ada's home was somewhere near the dinosaur forests on whatever continent this was. He remembered being terrified during his previous visit, although Virginia and Vanessa and all the rest had assured him that no dangerous dinosaurs were within five hundred miles—all the rest being reassuring, that is, except for fifteen-year-old Ada, who had merely looked at him with that calculating, mildly amused look he soon learned was her habitual expression. It had taken butterflies to get him outdoors for a walk then. It would take more now. Even though he knew it was perfectly safe with the servitors and voynix around, Daeman had no urge at all to be eaten by an extinct reptile and to wake up in the firmary with the memory of that indignity.

The giant elm on the downhill side of Ardis Hall had been festooned with scores of lanterns; torches lined the circular drive and the white-gravel paths from the house to the yard. Sentinel voynix stood along the driveway hedges and at the edge of the dark woods. Daeman saw that a long table had been set out near the elm tree—torches flickering in the evening breeze all around the festive setting—and that a few guests were already gathering there for dinner. Daeman also noted with his usual hint of pleased snobbery that most of the men here were still dressing in off-white robes, burnooses, and earth-tone evening oversuits, a style that had gone out of fashion months ago in the more important social circles Daeman inhabited.

The voynix padded up the circular drive to the front doors of Ardis Hall, stopped in the shaft of yellow light from those doors, and set the carriole tongues down so gently that Daeman did not even feel a bump. The servitor flitted around to fetch his bag while Daeman stepped down, glad to feel his feet on the ground, still feeling a bit lightheaded from the day's faxing.

Ada swept out the door and down the stairs to greet him. Daeman stopped in his tracks and smiled stupidly. Ada was not only more beautiful than he remembered; she was more beautiful than he could have imagined.

The Plains of Ilium

The Greek commanders are gathered outside Agamemnon's tent, there is a crowd of interested onlookers, and the brawl between Agamemnon and Achilles is already picking up steam.

I should mention that by this time I have morphed into the form of Bias—not the Pylian captain of that name in Nestor's ranks, but the captain serving Menestheus. This poor Athenian is ill with typhoid during this period and, though he will survive to fight in Book 13, he rarely leaves his tent, which is far down the coast. As a captain, Bias has enough rank that the spearmen and curious bystanders give way for him, allowing me access to the center circle. But no one will expect Bias to speak during the coming debate.

I've missed most of the drama where Calchas, Thestor's son and the "clearest of all the seers," has told the Achaeans the real reason for Apollo's wrath. Another captain standing there whispers to me that Calchas had requested immunity before speaking—demanding that Achilles protect him if the assembled crowd and kings disliked what he had to say. Achilles has agreed. Calchas told the group what they half suspected: that Chryse, the priest of Apollo, had begged for the return of his captured daughter, and Agamemnon's refusal had infuriated the god.

Agamemnon had been angry at the Calchas' interpretation. "He shit square goat turds," whispered the captain with a wine-scented laugh. This captain, unless I am mistaken, is named Orus and will be killed by Hector in a few weeks when the Trojan hero begins massacring Achaeans by the gross.

Orus tells me that Agamemnon agreed just minutes ago to give back the slave girl, Chryseis—"I rank her higher and like her better than

Clytaemnestra, my own wife," Atreus' son, Agamemnon, had shouted—but then the king had demanded recompense in the form of an equally beautiful captive girl. According to Orus, who is three sheets to the wind, Achilles had shouted—"Wait a minute, Agamemnon, you most grasping man alive"—pointed out that the Argives, still another name for the Achaeans, the Danaans, the damned Greeks with so many names, were in no position to hand over more booty to their leader now. Someday, should the tide of battle turn back their direction, promised the man-killer Achilles, Agamemnon would get his girl. In the meantime, he told Agamemnon to give Chryseis back to her father and to shut up.

"At that point Lord Agamemnon, Atreus' son, began shitting whole goats," laughs Orus, speaking loudly enough that several captains turn to frown at us.

I nod and look at the inner circles. Agamemnon, as always, is in the center of things. Atreus' son looks every inch the supreme commander—tall, beard rolled in classic curls, a demigod's brow and piercing eyes, muscles oiled, dressed in the finest gear and garb. Directly opposite him in the open bull's-eye of the circle stands Achilles. Stronger, younger, even more beautiful than Agamemnon, Achilles almost defies description. When I first saw him at the Catalogue of the Ships more than nine years ago, I thought that Achilles had to be the most godlike human walking among these many godlike men, so imposing was the man's physical and command presence. Since then I've realized that for all his beauty and power, Achilles is relatively stupid—a sort of infinitely more handsome Arnold Schwarzenegger.

Around this inner circle are the heroes I spent decades teaching about in my other life. They do not disappoint when encountered in the flesh. Near Agamemnon, but obviously not siding with him in the argument now raging, is Odysseus—a full head shorter than Agamemnon, but broader in the chest and shoulders, moving among the Greek lords like a ram among sheep, his intelligence and craftiness visible in his eyes and etched into the lines on his weathered face. I've never spoken to Odysseus, but I look forward to doing so before this war ends and he leaves on his travels.

On Agamemnon's right is his younger brother Menelaus, Helen's husband. I wish I had a dollar for every time I've overheard one of the Achaeans gripe that if Menelaus had been a better lover—"had a bigger cock" was the way Diomedes crudely put it to a friend within my earshot three years ago—then Helen wouldn't have run off with Paris to Ilium and the heroes of the Greek isles wouldn't have wasted the past nine years on this accursed siege. On Agamemnon's left is Orestes—not

Agamemnon's son, left at home and spoiled, who will someday avenge his father's murder and earn his own play, but only a loyal spear-carrier of the same name who will be slaughtered by Hector during the next big Trojan offensive.

Standing behind King Agamemnon is Eurybates, Agamemnon's herald—not to be confused with the Eurybates who is Odysseus' herald. Next to Eurybates stands Ptolemaeus' son, Eurymedon, a handsome boy, who is Agamemnon's charioteer—not to be confused with the far-less-handsome Eurymedon who is Nestor's charioteer. (Sometimes here I admit I'd exchange all these glorious patronymics for a few simple last names.)

Also in Agamemnon's half of the circle tonight are Big Ajax and Little Ajax, commanders of the troops from Salamis and Locris. These two will never be confused, except by name, since Big Ajax looks like a white NFL linebacker and Little Ajax looks like a pickpocket. Euryalus, third in command of the Argolis fighters, is standing next to his boss, Sthenelus, a man who has such a terrible lisp that he can't pronounce his own name. Agamemnon's friend and the ultimate commander of the Argolis fighters, plain-speaking Diomedes, is also here, not happy tonight, glowering at the ground, his arms folded. Old Nestor—"the clear speaker of Pylos"—stands near the halfway point of the inner circle and looks even less happy than Diomedes as Agamemnon and Achilles raise the level of their anger and abuse toward one other.

If things go according to Homer's telling, Nestor will make his big speech in just a few minutes, trying in vain to shame both Agamemnon and the furious Achilles into reconciling before their anger serves the Trojans' aims, and I confess that I want to hear Nestor's speech even if just for his reference to the ancient war against the centaurs. Centaurs have always interested me and Homer has Nestor speak of them and the war against them in a matter-of-fact tone; centaurs are one of only two mythical beasts mentioned in the *Iliad*, the other being the chimera. I look forward to his mention of the centaurs, but in the meantime, I stay out of Nestor's sight, since the identity I'm morphing—Bias—is one of the old man's subordinates, and I don't want to be pulled into conversation. No worry of that now—Nestor and everyone else's attention is focused on the exchange of harsh words and spittle between Agamemnon and Achilles.

Standing near Nestor and obviously allying themselves with neither leader are Menesthius (who will be killed by Paris in a few weeks if things proceed according to Homer), Eumelus (leader of the Thessalians from Pherae), Polyxinus (co-commander of the Epeans), Polyxinus' friend Thalpius, Thoas (commander of the Aetolians), Leonteus and Polypoetes in their distinctive Argissan garb, also Machaon and his brother Podalirius with their various Thessalian lieutenants standing behind them, Odysseus' dear friend Leucus (fated to be killed in a few days by Antiphus), and others I've come to know well over the years, not just by sight but by the sound of their voices, as well as by their distinctive modes of fighting and bragging and making offerings to the gods. If I haven't mentioned it yet, the ancient Greeks assembled here do nothing in a half-assed way—everything is performed to the full extent of their abilities, every effort running what one twentieth-century scholar called "the full risk of failure."

Opposite Agamemnon and standing to the right of Achilles is Patroclus—the man-killer's closest friend, whose death by Hector's hand is fated to set off the true Wrath of Achilles and the greatest slaughter in the history of warfare—as well as Tlepolemus, the mythic hero Herakles' beautiful son who fled his home after killing his father's uncle and who will soon die by Sarpedon's hand. Between Tlepolemus and Patroclus stands old Phoenix (Achilles' dear friend and former tutor) whispering to the son of Diocles, Orsilochus, who will be killed by Aeneas soon enough. To the raging Achilles' left is Idomeneus, a far closer friend of the man-killer's than I had suspected from the poem.

There are more heroes in the inner circle, of course, as well as countless more in the mob behind me, but you get the idea. No one goes nameless, either in Homer's epic poem or in the day-to-day reality here on the plains of Ilium. Every man carries his father's name, his history, his lands and wives and children and chattel with him at all times, in all encounters both martial and rhetorical. It's enough to wear a simple scholar out.

"All right, godlike Achilles, you cheater at dice, you cheater at war, you cheater with women—now you are trying to cheat *me*!" Agamemnon is shouting. "Oh no you don't! You're not going to get past me that way. You have the slave girl Briseis, as beautiful as any we've taken, as beautiful as my Chryseis. You just want to cling to your prize while I end up empty-handed! Forget it! I'd rather hand over command of the army to Ajax here . . . or Idomeneus . . . or crafty Odysseus there . . . or to you, Achilles . . . *you* . . . rather than be cheated so."

"Do it then," sneers Achilles. "It's time we had a real leader here."

Agamemnon's face grows purple. "Fine. Haul a black ship down to the sea and fill it with men to row and sacrifices for the gods . . . take Chryseis if you dare . . . but *you* will have to perform the sacrifices,

Achilles, O killer of men. But know that I'll take a prize as recompense—and that prize will be your lovely Briseis."

Achilles's handsome face is contorted with rage. "Shameless! You're armored in shamelessness and shrewd in greed, you dog-faced coward!"

Agamemnon takes a step forward, drops his scepter, and puts a hand on his sword.

Achilles matches him step for step and grips the hilt of his own sword. "The Trojans have never done us any harm, Agamemnon, but you have! It wasn't the Trojan spearmen who brought us to this shore, but your own greed—we're fighting for you, you colossal heap of shame. We followed you here to win your honor back from the Trojans, yours and your brother Menelaus', a man who can't even keep his wife in the bedroom . . ."

Here Menelaus steps forward and grips *his* sword. Captains and their men are gravitating to one hero or the other now, so the circle is already broken, turning into three camps—those who will fight for Agamemnon, those who will fight for Achilles, and those, near Odysseus and Nestor, who look disgusted enough to kill both of them.

"My men and I are leaving," shouts Achilles. "Back to Phthia. Better to drown in an empty ship heading home in defeat than to stay here and be disgraced, filling Agamemnon's goblet and piling up Agamemnon's plunder."

"Good, go!" shouts Agamemnon. "By all means, *desert*. I'd never beg you to stay and fight on *my* account. You're a great soldier, Achilles, but what of it? That's a gift of the gods and has nothing to do with you. You love battle and blood and slaughtering your enemies, so take your fawning Myrmidons and go!" Agamemnon spits.

Achilles actually vibrates with anger. It is obvious that he is torn between the urge to turn on his heel, take his men, and leave Ilium forever, and the overwhelming desire to unsheath his sword and gut Agamemnon like a sacrificial sheep.

"But know this, Achilles," Agamemnon goes on, his shout dropping to a terrible whisper that can be heard by all the hundreds of men assembled here, "whether you leave or stay, I will give up my Chryseis because the *god*, Apollo, insists—but I will have your Briseis in her stead, and every man here will know how much greater man is Agamemnon than the surly boy Achilles!"

Here Achilles loses all control and goes for his sword in earnest. And here the *Iliad* would have ended—with the death of Agamemnon or the death of Achilles, or of both—and the Achaeans would have sailed home and Hector would have enjoyed his old age and Ilium would have remained standing for a thousand years and perhaps rivaled Rome in its glory, but at this second the goddess Athena appears behind Achilles.

I see her. Achilles reels around, face contorted, and obviously also sees her. No one else can. I don't understand this stealth-cloaking technology, but it works when I use it and it works for the gods.

No, I realize immediately, this is more than stealth. The gods have frozen time again. It is their favorite way of talking to their pet humans without others eavesdropping, but I've seen it only a handful of times. Agamemnon's mouth is open—I can see spittle frozen in midair—but no sound is heard, no movement of jaw or muscles, no blinking of those dark eyes. So it is with every man in the circle: frozen, rapt or bemused, frozen. Overhead, a sea bird hangs motionless in mid-flight. Waves curl but do not break on the shore. The air is as thick as syrup and all of us here are frozen like insects in amber. The only movement in this halted universe comes from Pallas Athena, from Achilles and—even if shown only by my leaning forward to hear better—from me.

Achilles' hand is still on the hilt of his sword—half drawn from its beautifully tooled scabbard—but Athena has grabbed him by his long hair and physically turned him toward her, and he does not dare draw the sword now. To do so would be to challenge the goddess herself.

But Achilles' eyes are blazing—more mad than sane—as he shouts into the thickened, syrupy silence that accompanies these time-freezes, "Why! Damn, damn, why now! Why come to me now, Goddess, Daughter of Zeus? Did you come to witness my humiliation by Agamemnon?"

"Yield!" says Athena.

If you've never seen a god or goddess, all I can do is tell you that they are larger than life—literally, since Athena must be seven feet tall—and more beautiful and striking than any mortal. I presume their nanotechnology and recombinant DNA labs made them that way. Athena combines qualities of feminine beauty, divine command, and sheer power that I didn't even know could exist before I found myself returned to existence in the shadow of Olympos.

Her hand stays wrapped in Achilles' hair, bending his head back and making him swivel away from frozen Agamemnon and his minions.

"I'll never yield!" shouts Achilles. Even in this frozen air that slows and mutes all sound, the man-killer's voice is strong. "That pig who thinks he's a king will pay for his arrogance with his life!"

"Yield," says Athena for the second time. "The white-armed goddess Hera sped me down from the skies to stop your rage. *Yield.*"

I can see a flicker of hesitation enter Achilles' crazed eyes. Hera,

Zeus's wife, is the strongest ally of the Achaeans on Olympos and a patroness of Achilles since his odd childhood.

"Stop this fighting *now*," orders Athena. "Take your hand off your sword, Achilles. Curse Agamemnon if you must, but do not kill him. Do what we command now and I promise you this—I *know* this is the truth, Achilles, just I see your fate and know the future of all mortal men—obey us now and one day glittering gifts three times this will be yours as payment for this outrage. Defy us and die this hour. Obey us both—Hera and me—and receive your reward."

Achilles grimaces, twists his hair free, looks sullen, but resheaths his sword. Watching Athena and him is like watching two living forms amidst a field of statues. "I can't defy both of you, Goddess," says Achilles. "Better if a man submits to the will of the gods, even if his heart breaks with anger. But it is only fair then that the gods hear the prayers of that man."

Athena twitches the slightest of smiles and winks out of existence—QTing back to Olympos—and time resumes.

Agamemnon is ending his harangue.

Sword sheathed, Achilles steps into the empty circle. "You drunken wineskin of a man!" cries the man-killer. "You with your dog's eyes and your deer's heart. You 'leader' who's never led us into battle or gone into ambush with the best of the Achaeans—you who lack the courage to sack Ilium and so must sack the tents of his army for plunder instead—you 'king' who rules only the most worthless husks among us—I promise you this, I swear a mighty oath this day—"

The hundreds of men around me take in a breath almost as one, more shocked by this promise of a curse than if Achilles had simply cut Agamemnon down like a dog.

"I swear to you that someday a great yearning for Achilles will come to all the sons of Achaea," shouts the man-killer, his voice so loud that it halts dice games a hundred yards away in the tent city, "to all of them, throughout your armies here! But then, Atrides, stricken to your soul though you'll be, *nothing* you do will save you—scythed like so much wheat by the man-murdering Hector. And on that day you will tear out your own heart and eat it, desperate, raging that you chose to do such dishonor to the best of all the Achaeans."

And with that Achilles turns on his famous heel and strides from the circle, crunching across seashore gravel back into the darkness between the tents. I have to admit—it was one hell of an exit line.

Agamemnon crosses his arms and shakes his head. Other men speak in shocked tones. Nestor steps forward to give his in-the-days-of-the-centaur-wars-we-all-pulled-together speech. This is an anomaly—Homer has Achilles still in the argument when Nestor speaks—and my scholic mind makes note of it, but most of my attention is far, far away.

It's at this instant, remembering the murderous gaze that Achilles had turned on Athena in the instant before she wrenched his hair back and cowed him into submission, that a plan of action so audacious, so obviously doomed to failure, so suicidal, and so wonderful opens before me that for a minute I have trouble breathing.

"Bias, are you all right?" asks Orus standing next to me.

I stare blankly at the man. For a minute I cannot remember who he is or who "Bias" is, forgetting my own morphed identity. I shake my head and push my way out of the circled throng of glorious killers.

The gravel crunches under my feet without the heroic echo of Achilles' exit. I walk toward the water and once out of sight, throw off the identity of Bias. Anyone seeing me now would see the middle-aged Thomas Hockenberry, spectacles and all, weighted down in the absurd garb of an Achaean spearman, wool and fur covering my morphing gear and impact armor.

The ocean is dark. *Wine dark,* I think, but fail to amuse myself.

I have the overwhelming urge, not for the first time, to use my cloaking ability and levitation harness to fly away from here—to soar over Ilium a final time, to stare down at its torches and doomed inhabitants a final time, and then fly south and west across that wine-dark sea—the Aegean—until I come to the not-yet-Greek Isles and mainland. I could check in on Clytaemnestra and on Penelope, on Telemachus and Orestes. Professor Thomas Hockenberry, as both boy and man, always got along better with women and children than he did with male adults.

But these proto-Greek women and children here are more murderous and bloodthirsty than any adult males Hockenberry had known in his other, bloodless life.

Save the flying away then for another day. In fact, put it behind me altogether.

The waves roll in one after another, reassuring in their familiar cadence.

I will do this thing. The decision comes with the exhilaration of flying—no, not of flying, but in the thrill of that brief instance of zero gravity one achieves when throwing oneself from a high place and knowing that there is no going back to solid ground. Sink or swim, fall or fly.

I will do this thing.

Near Conamara Chaos

Mahnmut the Europan moravec's submersible was three kilometers ahead of the kraken and gaining, which should have created some sense of confidence in the diminutive robotic-organic construct, but since kraken often had tentacles five kilometers long, it didn't.

It was an aggravation. Worse than that, it was a distraction. Mahnmut had almost finished with his new analysis of Sonnet 116, was eager to e-mail it to Orphu on Io, and the last thing he needed now was to have his submersible swallowed. He pinged the kraken, verified that the huge, hungry, jellied mass was still in flagellant pursuit, and interfaced with the reactor long enough to add another three knots to his ship's speed.

The kraken, which was literally out of its depth here so close to the Conamara Chaos region and its open leads, flailed to keep up. Mahnmut knew that as long as they were both traveling at this speed, the kraken would be unable to extend its tentacles to full reach to engulf the submersible, but if his little sub were to encounter something—say a big wad of flashlight kelp—and he had to slow, or worse yet got fouled in the glowing strands of goo, then the kraken would be on him like a . . .

"Oh, well, damn," said Mahnmut, abandoning any attempt at simile and speaking aloud to the humming silence of the submersible's cramped environmental cavity. His sensors were plugged into the ship's systems and virtual vision showed him huge clumps of flashlight kelp dead ahead. The glowing colonies were floating along the isothermal currents here, feeding on the reddish veins of magnesium sulfate that rose to the ice shelf above like so many bloody taproots.

Mahnmut thought *dive* and the submersible dived twenty klicks deeper, clearing the lower colonies of kelp by only a few dozen meters.

The kraken dived behind him. If a kraken could grin, it would be grinning now—this was its killing depth.

Mahnmut reluctantly cleared Sonnet 116 from his visual field and considered his options. Being eaten by a kraken less than a hundred kilometers from Conamara Chaos Central would be embarrassing. It was these damn bureaucrats' fault—they needed to cull their local subseas of monsters before they ordered one of their moravec explorers back to a meeting.

He could kill the kraken. But with no harvester submersible within a thousand klicks, the beautiful beastie would be torn to shreds and devoured by the parasites in the flashlight kelp colonies, by salt sharks, by free-floating tube worms, and by other kraken long before a company harvester could get near it. It would be a terrible waste.

Mahnmut pulled his vision out of virtual long enough to look around his enviro-niche, as if a glimpse of his cluttered reality could give him an idea. It did.

On his console desk, along with the leather-bound volumes of Shakespeare and the Vendler printout, was his lava lamp—a little joke from his old moravec partner Urtzweil almost twenty J-years ago.

Mahnmut smiled and re-engaged virtual along all bandwidths. This close to Chaos Central there would have to be diapirs, and kraken hated diapirs . . .

Yes. Fifteen klicks south by southeast, an entire belchfield of them, rising slowly toward the cap ice just as languidly as the wax blobs did in his lava lamp. Mahnmut set his course to the nearest diapir rising to a lead and added five more knots just to be safe, if there was such a thing as safety within tentacle range of a mature kraken.

A diapir was nothing more than a blob of warm ice, heated by the vents and gravitational hot zones far below, rising through the Epsomsalt sea toward the ice cap that had once covered 100 percent of Europa and which now, two thousand e-years after the cryobot arbeiter company arrived, still covered more than 98 percent of the moon. This diapir was about fifteen klicks across and rising rapidly as it approached the surface cap.

Kraken did not like the electrolytic properties of diapirs. They refused to foul even their probe tentacles with the stuff, much less their killing arms and maws.

Mahnmut's sub reached the rising blob a good ten kilometers ahead of the pursuing kraken, slowed, morphed its outer hull to impact strength, pulled in sensors and probes, and bored into the glob of slush. Mahnmut used sonar and EPS to check the lenticulae and navigation leads still some eight thousand meters above him. In a few minutes the diapir itself would mush into the thick cap ice, flow upward through fissures, lentinculae and leads, and bubble slush ice in a fountain a hundred meters high. For a short time, this part of Conamara Chaos would look like Lost-Age America's Yellowstone Park, with red-sulfur geysers geysing and hot springs boiling. Then the spray trail would disperse in Europa's one-seventh Earth gravity, fall like a slow-motion slushstorm for kilometers on either side of each surface lenticula, and then freeze in Europa's thin, artificial atmosphere—all 100 millibars of it—adding more abstract sculptural forms to the already tortured icefields.

Mahnmut couldn't be killed in literal terms—although part organic, he "existed" rather than "lived," and he was designed tough—but he definitely did not want to become part of a fountain or a frozen chunk of an abstract sculpture for the next thousand e-years. For a minute he forgot both the kraken and Sonnet 116 as he worked the numbers—the diapir's ascent rate, his submersible's forward progress through the slush, the fast-approaching cap ice—and then he downloaded his thoughts to the engine room and ballast tanks. If it worked right, he would exit the south side of the diapir half a klick before glob impact with the ice and accelerate straight ahead, doing an emergency surface blow just as the tidal wave from the diapir fountain was forced down the lead. He would then use that 100-klick-per-hour acceleration to keep him ahead of the fountain effect—essentially using his submersible like a surfboard for half the distance to Conamara Chaos Central. He'd have to make the final twenty klicks or so to the base on the surface after the tidal wave dissipated, but he had no choice. It should be one hell of an entrance.

Unless something had blocked the lead ahead. Or unless another submersible was coming out-lead from Central. That would be embarrassing for the few seconds before Mahnmut and *The Dark Lady* were destroyed.

At least the kraken would no longer be a factor. The critters refused to rise closer than five klicks to the surface cap.

Having entered all the commands and knowing that he'd done everything he could think of to survive and arrive at the base on time, Mahnmut went back to his sonnet analysis.

Mahnmut's submersible—which he had long ago named *The Dark Lady*—cruised the last twenty kilometers to Conamara Chaos Central down a kilometer-wide lead, riding on the surface of the black sea beneath a black sky. A three-quarters Jupiter was rising, clouds bright and cloud bands roiling with muted colors, while a tiny Io skittered across the rising giant's face not far above the icy horizon. On either side of the lead, striated ice cliffs rose several hundred meters, their sheer faces dull gray and blunted red against the black sky.

Mahnmut was excited as he brought Shakespeare's sonnet up.

SONNET 116

Let me not to the marriage of true minds
Admit impediments; love is not love
Which alters when it alteration finds,
Or bends with the remover to remove.
O no, it is an ever-fixed mark
That looks on tempests and is never shaken;
It is the star to every wand'ring bark,
Whose worth's unknown, although his height be taken.
Love's not Time's fool, though rosy lips and cheeks
Within his bending sickle's compass come;
Love alters not with his brief hours and weeks,
But bears it out even to the edge of doom.
    If this be error and upon me proved,
    I never writ, nor no man ever loved.

Over the decades he had come to hate this sonnet. It was the kind of things humans had recited at their weddings way back in the Lost Age. It was smarmy. It was schlocky. It wasn't good Shakespeare.

But finding microrecords of critical writings by a woman named Helen Vendler—a critic who had lived and written in one of those centuries, the Nineteenth or Twentieth or Twenty-first (the record timestamps were vague)—had given Mahnmut a key to translating this sonnet. What if Sonnet 116 was not, as it had been portrayed for so many centuries, a sticky affirmation, but a violent refutation?

Mahnmut went back through his notated "key words" for support. There they were from each line—"not, not, no, never, not, not, not" and then in line fourteen—"never, nor," and "no"—echoing King Lear's nihilistic "never, never, never, never, never."

It was definitely a poem of refutation. But refutation of what?

Mahnmut knew that Sonnet 116 was part of "the Young Man" cycle, but he also knew that the phrase "the Young Man" was little more than a fig leaf added in later, more prudish years. The love poems were not sent to a man, but to "the youth"—certainly a boy, probably no older than thirteen. Mahnmut had read the criticism from the second half of the Twentieth Century and knew these "scholars" thought the sonnets to be literal—that is, real homosexual letters from the playwright Shakespeare—but Mahnmut also knew, from more scholarly work in previous eras and in the later part of the Lost Age, that such politically motivated literal thinking was childish.

Shakespeare had structured a drama in his sonnets, Mahnmut was certain of that. "The youth" and the later "Dark Lady" were characters in that drama. The sonnets had taken years to write and had not been produced in the heat of passion, but in the maturity of Shakespeare's full powers. And what was he exploring in these sonnets? Love. And what were Shakespeare's "real opinions" about love?

No one would ever know—Mahnmut was sure the Bard was too clever, too cynical, too stealthy ever to show his true feelings. But in play after play, Shakespeare had shown how strong feelings—including love—turned people into fools. Shakespeare, like Lear, loved his Fools. Romeo had been Fortune's Fool, Hamlet Fate's Fool, MacBeth Ambition's Fool, Falstaff . . .well, Falstaff was no one's Fool . . . but he became a fool for the love of Prince Hal and died of a broken heart when the young prince abandoned him.

Mahnmut knew that the "poet" in the sonnet cycles, sometimes referred to as "Will," was not—despite the insistence of so many of the shallow scholars of the Twentieth Century—the historical Will Shakespeare, but was, rather, another dramatic construct created by the playwright/poet to explore all the facets of love. What if this "poet" was, like Shakespeare's hapless Count Orsino, Love's Fool? A man in love with love?

Mahmut liked this approach. He knew that Shakespeare's "marriage of two minds" between the older poet and the youth was not a homosexual liaison, but a true sacrament of sensibilities, a facet of love honored in days long preceding Shakespeare's. On the surface, Sonnet 116 seemed to be a trite declaration of that love and its permanency, but if it truly was a refutation . . .

Mahnmut suddenly saw where it fit. Like so many great poets, Shakespeare began his poems before or after they began. But if this was a poem of refutation, what was it refuting? What had the youth said to the older, love-besotted poet that needed such vehement refutation?

Mahnmut extended fingers from his primary manipulator, took up his stylus, and scribbled on his t-slate—

Dear Will—Certainly we'd both like the marriage of true minds we have—since men cannot share the sacramental marriage of bodies—to be as real and permanent as real marriage. But it can't be. People change, Will. Circumstances change. When the qualities of people or the people themselves go away, one's love does as well. I loved you once, Will, I really did, but you've changed, you've altered, and so there has been a change in me and an alteration in our love.

Yours most sincerely,
The Youth

Mahnmut looked at his letter and laughed, but the laughter died as he realized how this changed all of Sonnet 116. Now, instead of a treacly affirmation of unchanging love, the sonnet became a violent refutation of the youth's jilting, an argument against such self-serving abandonment. Now the sonnet would read—

> *Let* me *not to the marriage of true minds*
> *Admit (these so-called) "impediments": love is* not *love*
> *Which "alters when it alteration finds,"*
> *Or "bends with the remover to remove,"*
> *O* no!

Mahnmut could hardly contain his excitement. Everything in the sonnet and in the entire sonnet cycle now clicked into place. Little was left of this "marriage of true minds" type of love—little except anger, accusations, incriminations, lying, and further infidelity—all of which would be played out by Sonnet 126, by which time "the Young Man" and ideal love itself would be abandoned for the slutty pleasures of "the Dark Lady." Mahnmut shifted consciousness to the virtual and began encoding an e-note squirt to his faithful interlocutor of the last dozen e-years, Orphu of Io.

Klaxons sounded. Lights blinked in Mahnmut's virtual vision. For a second he thought—*the kraken!*—but the kraken would never come to the surface or enter an open lead.

Mahnmut stored the sonnet and his notes, wiped the e-note from his squirt queue, and opened external sensors.

The Dark Lady was five klicks away from Chaos Central and in the remote control region of the submarine pens. Mahnmut turned the ship over to Central and studied the ice cliffs ahead of him.

From the outside, Conamara Chaos Central looked like most of the rest of the surface of Europa—a jumble of pressure ridges thrusting ice cliffs up two or three hundred meters, the mass of ice blocking the maze of open leads and black lenticulae—but then the signs of habitation became visible: the black maw of the sub pens opening, the elevators on the cliff face moving, more windows visible on the face of the ice, navigation lights pulsing and blinking atop surface modules and habitation nodes and antennae, and—far above where the cliff ended against black sky—several interlunar shuttles storm-lashed to the landing pad there.

Spacecraft here at Chaos Central. Very unusual. Even as Mahnmut finished the docking, set his ship's functions on standby, and began separating himself from the submersible's systems, he was thinking—*What the hell have they called me here for?*

Docking completed, Mahnmut went through the trauma of limiting his senses and control to the awkward confines of his more or less humanoid body and left the ship, walking into blue-lighted ice and taking the high-speed elevator up to the habitation nodes so far above.

Ardis Hall

A meal for a dozen people at the table under the lantern-lit tree: venison and wild boar from the forest, trout from the river below, beef from the cattle herds pastured between Ardis and the farcaster pad, red and white wines from Ardis vineyards, fresh corn, squash, salad and peas from the garden, and caviar faxed in from somewhere or the other.

"Whose birthday is it and which Twenty?" asked Daeman as servitors passed food to the dozen diners at the long table.

"It's my birthday, but not my Twenty," replied the handsome, curly-haired man named Harman.

"Pardon me?" Daeman smiled but did not understand. He accepted some squash and passed the bowl to the lady next to him.

"Harman is celebrating his annual birthday," said Ada from her place at the head of the table. Daeman was physically stirred by how beautiful she looked in her tan and black silk gown.

Daeman shook his head, still not understanding. Annual birthdays were not noted, much less celebrated. "So you're not really celebrating a birth Twenty tonight," he said to Harman, nodding at the floating house servitor to replenish his wineglass.

"But I *am* celebrating my birthday," Harman repeated with a smile. "My ninety-ninth."

Daeman froze in shock and then looked around quickly, realizing that it must be some kind of joke peculiar to this crowd of provincials—but certainly a joke in bad taste. One did not joke about one's ninety-ninth year. Daeman smiled thinly and waited for the punch line.

"Harman means it," Ada said lightly. The other guests were silent. Night birds called from the forest.

"I'm . . . sorry," Daeman managed to say.

Harman shook his head. "I'm looking forward to the year. I have a lot of things to do."

"Harman walked a hundred miles of the Atlantic Breach last year," said Hannah, Ada's young friend with the short hair.

Daeman was sure that he was being joked with now. "One can't walk the Atlantic Breach."

"But I did." Harman was eating corn on the cob. "I only did a reconnaissance—just, as Hannah says, a hundred miles in and then back to the North American coast—but it certainly wasn't difficult."

Daeman smiled again to show that he was a good sport. "But how could you *get* to the Atlantic Breach, Harman *Uhr*? There are no faxnodes near it." He had no idea where the Atlantic Breach *was,* or even what constituted North America, and he wasn't quite sure about the location of the Atlantic Ocean, but he was certain that none of the 317 faxnodes were near the Breach. He had faxed through each of those nodes more than once and had never glimpsed the legendary Breach.

Harman put down the corn. "I walked, Daeman *Uhr*. From the North American eastern coast, the Breach runs directly along the fortieth parallel all the way to what the Lost Age humans called Europe—Spain was the last nation-state where the Breach comes ashore, I think. The ruins of the old city of Philadelphia—you might know it as Node 124, Loman *Uhr's* estate—is just a few hours' walk from the Breach. If I'd had any courage—and packed enough food—I could have hiked all the way to Spain."

Daeman nodded and smiled and had absolutely no idea what this man was babbling about. First the obscenity of bragging of his ninety-ninth year, then all this talk of parallels and Lost Age cities and walking. No one walked more than a few hundred yards. Why should they? Everything of human interest lay near a faxnode and those few distant oddities—such as Ada's Ardis—could be reached by carriole or droshky. Daeman knew Loman, of course—he had recently celebrated Ono's Third Twenty at the extensive Loman estate—but all the rest of Harman's soliloquy was gibberish. The man had obviously gone mad in his final days. Well, the final firmary fax and Ascension would soon take care of that.

Daeman looked at Ada, their hostess, in hopes that she would intervene to change the topic, but Ada was smiling as if agreeing with everything Harman had said. Daeman looked down the table for help, but the other guests had been listening politely—even with apparent interest—as if such babble were part of their regular provincial dining repartee.

"The trout is quite good, isn't it?" he said to the woman on his left. "Was yours good?"

A woman across the table, a heavyset redhead probably deep into her third Twenty, set her most prominent chin on her small fist and said to Harman, "What was it like? In the Breach, I mean?"

The curly-haired, deeply tanned man demurred, but others along the table—including the young blonde woman about whose trout Daeman had inquired and who had rudely ignored the query—all clamored for Harman to talk. He finally acquiesced with a graceful motion of his hand.

"If you've never seen the Breach, it's a fascinating sight just from the shore. It's about eighty yards wide—a cleft going east as far as one can see, becoming more and more narrow toward the horizon, until it seems just a slice of brightness inset along the line where ocean meets sky.

"Walking into it is . . . slightly strange. The sand along the beach is not wet where the Breach ends. No surf rolls back into it. At first, all of one's attention is focused on one or the other of the edges—walking in to wading depth, you notice the abrupt shear of water, like a glass wall separating the walker from the curl and roll of tide. You have to touch the barrier—no one could resist. Spongy, invisible, very slightly yielding to heavy pressure, cool from the water on the other side, but impenetrable. You walk deeper on dry sand—over the centuries the sea bottom has felt only the moisture of rain, and so the sand and dirt are solid, the remaining sea creatures and plants there dried out, desiccated almost to the point of appearing fossilized.

"Within a dozen yards, the sheared walls of water on both sides rise far over your head. Shadows move within. You see small fish swimming near the barrier between air and sea, then the shadow of a shark, then the pale glow of jellied, floating things you can't quite identify. Sometimes the sea creatures approach the Breach barrier, touch it with their cold heads, and then turn away quickly, as if alarmed. A mile or so out and the water is so far over your head that the sky above grows darker. A dozen or so miles out and the walls of water on either side rise more than a thousand feet above you. The stars come out in the slice of sky you can see, even in daylight."

"No!" said a thin, sandy-haired man far down the table. Daeman remembered his name—Loes. "You're joking."

"No," said Harman, "I'm not." He smiled again. "I walked for about four days. Slept during the night. Turned back when I was out of food."

"How did you know whether it was night or day?" asked Ada's friend, the athletic young woman named Hannah.

"The sky is black and the stars are out in the daytime sky," said Harman, "but the slices of ocean on either side hold the full band of light, from bright blue far above, to murky black along the bottom at the level of the Breach walkway."

"Did you find anything exotic?" asked Ada.

"Some sunken ships. Ancient. Lost Age and earlier. And one that might be . . . newer." He smiled again. "I went to explore one of them—a huge, rusted hulk emerging from the north wall of the Breach, tilted on its side. I entered through a hole in the hull, climbed ladders, made my way north along tilted floors using a small lantern I'd brought along, until suddenly in one large space—I think it was called a hold—there was the Breach barrier, from the ceiling to the tilted floor, a wall of water, alive with fish. I set my face against the cold, invisible wall and could see barnacles, mollusks, sea snakes, and life-forms encrusting every surface, feeding on one another, while on my side—dryness, old rust, the only living things consisting of me and a small white land crab that had obviously migrated, as I had, from the shore."

A wind came up and rustled the leaves in the tall tree above them. Lanterns swayed and their rich light played across the silk and cotton clothing and hairdos and and hands and warmly lighted faces around the table. Everyone was rapt. Even Daeman found himself interested, despite the fact that it was all nonsense. Torches in braziers along the walkway flickered and crackled in the sudden breeze.

"What about the voynix?" asked a woman sitting next to Loes. Daeman could not remember her name. *Emme*, perhaps? "Are there more or fewer than on land? Sentinels or motile?"

"No voynix."

Everyone at the table seemed to take a breath. Daeman felt the same sudden surge of shock he'd experienced when Harman had announced that it was his ninety-ninth year. He felt a surge of vertigo. Pehaps the wine had been stronger than he'd thought.

"No voynix," repeated Ada in a tone not so much of wonder but of wistfulness. She raised her glass of wine. "A toast," she said. Servitors floated closer to fill glasses. Everyone raised his or her own glass. Daeman blinked away the dizziness and forced a pleasant, sociable smile into place.

Ada did not announce a toast, but everyone—even, after a moment, Daeman—drank the wine as if she had.

The wind had come up by the end of the meal, clouds moving in to obscure the p- and e-rings, and the air smelled of ozone and of the curtains of rain dragging across the dark hills to the west, so the party moved inside and then broke up as couples wandered off to their rooms or to various wings and rooms for entertainment. Servitors produced chamber music in the south conservatory, the glassed-in swimming pool to the rear of the manor attracted a few people, and there was a midnight buffet laid out in the curved bay of the second-floor observation porch. Some couples went to their private rooms to make love, while others found a quiet place to unfold their turins and to go to Troy.

Daeman followed Ada, who had led Hannah and the man named Harman to the third-story library. If Daeman's plan of seducing Ada before the weekend was over was to succeed, he had to spend every free minute with her. Seduction, he knew, was both science and art—a blend of skill, discipline, proximity, and opportunity. Mostly proximity.

Standing and walking near her, Daeman could feel the warmth of her skin through the tan and black silk she wore. Her lower lip, he noticed again after a decade, was maddeningly full, red, and meant for biting. When she raised her arm to show Harman and Hannah the height of shelves in the library, Daeman watched the subtle, soft shift of her right breast under its thin sheath of silk.

He had been in a library before, but never one this large. The room must have been more than a hundred feet long and half that high, with a mezzanine running around three walls and sliding ladders on both levels to give access to the higher and more remote volumes. There were alcoves, cubbies, tables with large books opened on them, seating areas here and there, and even shelves of books over the huge bay window on the far wall. Daeman knew that the physical books stored here must have been treated with non-decomposative nanochemicals many, many centuries before, probably millennia ago—these useless artifacts were made of leather and paper and ink, for heaven's sake—but the mahogany-paneled room with its pools of source lighting, ancient leather furniture, and brooding walls of books still smelled of age and decay to Daeman's sensitive snout. He could not imagine why Ada and the other family members maintained this mausoleum at Ardis Hall, or why Harman and Hannah wanted to see it tonight.

The curly-haired man who claimed to be in his last year and who claimed to have walked into the Atlantic Breach stopped in wonder. "It's wonderful, Ada." He climbed a ladder, slid it along a row of shelves, and reached a hand out to touch a thick leather volume.

Daeman laughed. "Do you think the reading function has returned, Harman *Uhr*?"

The man smiled, but seemed so confident that for a second Daeman half expected to see the golden rush of symbols down his arm as the reading function signaled the content. Daeman had never seen the lost function in action, of course, but had heard it described by his grandmother and other old folks describing what their great-great-grandparents had enjoyed.

No words flowed. Harman pulled his hand back. "Don't you wish you had the reading function, Daeman *Uhr*?"

Daeman heard himself laughing yet again on this odd evening and was acutely aware of both of the young women looking at him with expressions somewhere between bemusement and curiosity.

"No, of course not," he said at last. "Why should I? What could these old things tell me that could have any pertinence to our lives today?"

Harman climbed higher on the ladder. "Aren't you curious why the post-humans are no longer seen on Earth and where they went?"

"Not at all. They went home to their cities in the rings. Everyone knows that."

"Why?" asked Harman. "After many millennia of molding our affairs here, watching over us, why did they leave?"

"Nonsense," said Daeman, perhaps a bit more gruffly than he had intended. "The posts are still watching over us. From above."

Harman nodded as if enlightened and shuffled his ladder a few yards along its brass track. The man's head was almost touching the underside of the library mezzanine now. "How about the voynix?"

"What about the voynix?"

"Did you ever wonder why they were motionless for so many centuries and are so active now?"

Daeman opened his mouth but had nothing to say to that. After a moment, he managed, "That business about the voynix not moving before the final fax is total nonsense. Myths. Folklore."

Ada stepped closer. "Daeman, did you ever wonder where they came from?"

"Who, my dear?"

"The voynix."

Daeman laughed heartily and honestly at this. "Of course not, my lady. The voynix have always been here. They are permanent, fixed, eternal—moving, sometimes out of sight, but always present—like the sun or the stars."

"Or the rings?" asked Hannah in her soft voice.

"Precisely." Daeman was pleased that she understood.

Harman pulled a heavy book from the shelves. "Daeman *Uhr*, Ada informs me that you are quite the lepidopterist."

"I beg your pardon?"

"Butterfly expert."

Daeman could feel himself blush. It was always pleasing to have one's skills recognized, even by strangers, even by less-than-sane strangers. "Hardly an expert, Harman *Uhr,* merely a collector who has learned a bit from his uncle."

Harman came down the ladder and carried the heavy book to a reading table. "This should interest you then." He opened the artifact. Page after glossy page showed colorful representations of butterflies.

Daeman stepped closer, speechless. His uncle had taught him the names of about twenty types of butterflies and he had learned from other collectors the names of a few of the others he'd captured. He reached out to touch the image of a Western Tiger Swallowtail.

"Western Tiger Swallowtail," said Harman and added, "*Pterourus rutulus.*"

Daeman did not understand the last two words, but he stared at the older man in amazement. "You collect!"

"Not at all." Harman touched a familiar gold and black image. "Monarch."

"Yes," said Daeman, confused.

"Red Admiral, Aphrodite Fritillary, Field Crescentspot, Common Blue, Painted Lady, Phoebus Parnassian," Harman said, touching each image in turn. Daeman knew three of those named.

"You know butterflies," he said.

Harman shook his head. "I've never even really considered that the different types have names until this minute."

Daeman looked at the man's blunt hand. "You have the reading function."

Harman shook his head again. "No one has that palm function any longer. No more than they have comm function or geo-positioning or data access or self-fax away from nodes."

"Then . . ." began Daeman and stopped in true confusion. Were these people taunting him for some reason? He had come to spend the weekend at Ardis Hall with good intentions—well, with the intention of seducing Ada, but all in good humor—and now this . . . malicious game?

As if sensing his growing anger, Ada put her slim fingers on his sleeve. "Harman doesn't have the reading function, Daeman *Uhr,*" she said softly. "He has recently learned how to *read.*"

Daeman stared. This made no more sense than celebrating one's ninety-ninth year or babbling on about the Atlantic Breach.

"It's a skill," Harman said quietly. "Rather like your learning the names of the butterflies or your fabled techniques as a . . . ladies' man."

This last phrase made Daeman blink. *Is my other hobby so well known?*

Hannah spoke. "Harman has promised to teach us this trick . . . reading. It might come in handy. I need to learn about casting before I do more of it and burn myself."

Casting? Daeman knew fishermen who used that word. He could not imagine how it could have anything to do with burning onself or acquiring the reading function. He licked his lips and said, "I have no interest in these games. What do you want from me?"

"We need to find a spaceship," said Ada. "And there's reason to believe that you can help us."

6

Olympos

When my shift ends on the night of Achilles' and Agamemnon's confrontation, I quantum teleport back to the scholic complex on Olympos, record my observations and analysis, transfer the thoughts to a word stone, and carry it into the Muse's small white room overlooking the Lake of the Caldera. To my surprise, the Muse is there, talking to one of the other scholics.

The scholic is named Nightenhelser—a friendly bear of a man who, I had learned over the last four years of his residency here, lived and taught college and died in the American Midwest some time in the early Twentieth Century. Seeing me at the door, the Muse finishes her business with Nightenhelser and sends him away, out her bronze door toward the escalator that spirals its way down off Olympos to our barracks and the red world below.

The Muse gestures me closer. I set the word stone on the marble table in front of her and step back, expecting to be dismissed without a word, as is the usual dynamic between the two of us. Surprisingly, she lifts the word stone while I'm still there and closes her hand around it even as she closes her eyes to concentrate. I stand and wait. I confess that I am nervous. My heart pounds and my hands, clasped behind my back as I stand in a sort of professorial parody of a soldier's "at ease" position, are sweaty. I decided years ago that that the gods cannot really read minds—that their uncanny perception of mortals' thoughts, heroes and scholics alike, comes from some advanced science in the study of facial muscles, eye movements and the like. But I could be wrong. Perhaps they are telepathic. If so—and if they bothered to read my mind during my moment of epiphany and decision on the beach after Agamemnon's and Achilles' showdown—then I am a dead man. Again.

I've seen scholics who displease the Muse, much less the more important gods. Some years ago—the fifth year of the siege, actually—there was a scholic from the Twenty-sixth Century, a chubby, irreverent Asian with the unusual name of Bruster Lin—and even though Bruster Lin was the brightest and most insightful scholar amongst us, his irreverence was his undoing. Literally. After one of his more ironic comments—it was about the *mano a mano* combat between Paris and Menelaus, winner take all, that would have settled the war on the outcome of that single combat. The one-on-one fight to the death between Helen's Trojan lover and her Achaean husband—although staged in front of two cheering armies, with Paris beautiful in his golden armor and Menelaus fearful with his eye full of business—was never consummated. Aphrodite saw that her beloved Paris was going to be hacked into worm meat, so she swooped down and spirited him off the battlefield back to Helen, where, like effete liberals in every age, Paris was more the happy warrior in bed than on the battlefield. So it was after one of Bruster Lin's amusing comments on the Paris–Menelaus episode, that the Muse—not amused—snapped her fingers and the billions upon trillions of obedient nanocytes in the hapless scholic's body aggregated and exploded outward in one giant nano-lemming leap, shredding the still-smiling Bruster Lin into a thousand bloody shreds in front of the rest of us and sending his still-smiling head rolling toward our feet as we stood at attention.

It was a serious lesson and we took it to heart. No editorializing. No making merry with the serious business of the gods' sport. The wages of irony is death.

The Muse opens her eyes and looks at me now. "Hockenberry," she says, her tone that of a personnel bureaucrat from my century about to fire a mid-level white-collar worker, "how long have you been with us?"

I know the question is rhetorical, but when queried by a goddess, even a minor goddess, one answers even rhetorical questions. "Nine years, two months, eighteen days, Goddess."

She nods. I am the oldest surviving scholic. Or, rather, I am the scholic who has survived the longest. She knows this. Perhaps this official recognition of my longevity is my elegy before explosive termination by nanocyte.

I had always taught my students that there were nine Muses, all daughters of Mnemosyne—Kleis, Euterpe, Thaleria, Melpomene, Terpsichorde, Erato, Plymnia, Ourania, and Kalliope—each one granted, at least by later Greek tradition, control of some artistic expression such as flute or dance or storytelling or heroic song—but in my nine years, two months, and eighteen days serving the gods as observer on the plains of Ilium, I've reported to, seen, and heard of only one Muse—this tall goddess who sits in front of me now behind her marble table. Still, because of her strident voice, I've always thought of her as "Kalliope," even though the name originally meant "she of the beautiful voice." I can't say this solo Muse has a beautiful voice—it's more klaxon than calliope to my ear—but it's certainly one I've learned to jump to when she says "frog."

"Follow me," she says, rising fluidly and walking out the private side door of her white marble room.

I jump and follow.

The Muse is god-sized—that is to say, over seven feet tall but in perfect human proportions, less voluptuous than some of the goddesses but built like a Twentieth Century female triathlete—and even in the lessened gravity here on Olympos, I have to scramble to keep up as she strides across the close-cropped green lawns between white buildings.

She pauses at a chariot nexus. I say "chariot" and it is vaguely chariotlike—low, roughly horseshoe shaped, with a niche in the side allowing the Muse to step up into it, but this chariot lacks horses, reins and driver. She grips the railing and beckons me up.

Hesitantly, heart pounding wildly now, I step up and stand to one side as the Muse taps her long fingers across a gold wedge that might be some sort of control panel. Lights blink. The chariot hums, crackles, becomes suddenly girdled by a latticework of energy, and rises off the grass, twirling as it climbs. Suddenly a holographic pair of "horses" appears in front of the chariot and gallop as they seem to pull the chariot through the sky. I know that the holographic horses are there for the Greeks' and Trojans' need for closure, but the sense that they are real animals pulling a real chariot through the sky is very strong. I grab the metal bar along the rim and brace myself, but there is no sense of acceleration even as the transport disk jigs and jags, swoops once a hundred feet above the Muse's modest temple, and then accelerates toward the deep depression of the Lake of the Caldera.

Chariot of the gods! I think and blame the unworthy thought on fatigue and adrenaline.

I've seen these chariots a thousand times, of course, flying near Olympos or above the plains of Ilium as the gods shuttle to and fro on their godlike business, but I've always seen them from my vantage point on the ground. The horses look real from that angle and the chariot itself seems far less substantial when you're in one, flitting a thousand feet above the summit of a mountain—volcano, actually—that itself rises some 85,000 feet above the desert floor.

The summit of Olympos should be airless and ice-covered, but the air here is as thick and breathable as it is some seventeen miles lower where the scholic barracks huddle at the base of the volcanic cliffs, and rather than ice, the broad summit is covered with grass, trees, and white buildings large enough and grand enough to make the Acropolis look like an outhouse.

The figure eight of the Lake of the Caldera at the center of the summit of Olympos is almost sixty miles across and we zip across it at near-supersonic speed, some forcefield or bit of godly magic keeping the wind from tearing our heads off at the same time it muffles the sound. Hundreds of buildings, each with acres of manicured lawn and gardens around it, gods' homes, I presume, surround the lake, while great three-tiered autotriremes move slowly across the blue waters. Scholic Bruster Lin once told me that he estimated that Olympos was the size of Arizona, its grassy summit equaling approximately the surface area of Rhode Island. It was strange to hear of things here being compared to states on that other world, in that other time, from that other existence.

Clinging to the thin railing with both hands, I peek out beyond the mountaintop. The view is breathtaking.

We are high enough that I can see the curve of the world. To the northwest, the great blue ocean extends to that inverted cusp of horizon. To the northeast runs the coastline, and I fancy that even from this distance I can see the great stone heads that mark the boundary between sea and land. Due north is the scythe of the unnamed archipelago just visible from the shoreline a few miles from our scholic barracks, then nothing but blue again all the way to the pole. To the southeast I can see three other tall volcanic summits thrusting above the horizon, obviously lower than Olympos's summit but, unlike climate-controlled Olympos, white with snow. One of them, I guess, must be Mount Helicon, home to my Muse and her sisters, if sisters she has. To the south and southwest, for hundreds of miles, I can make out a succession of cultivated fields, then wild forests, then red desert beyond, then perhaps forest again, until land blends with clouds and haze and no amount of blinking or rubbing of eyes can resolve the detail there.

The Muse sweeps our chariot around and descends toward the west shoreline of the Lake of the Caldera. I see now that the white specks I noticed during our crossing of the lake are huge white buildings, fronted with columns and steps, graced with gigantic pediments, and decorated with statuary. I am sure that no scholic has seen this part of Olympos . . . or at least seen it and lived to tell the rest of us about it.

We descend near the largest of the giant buildings, the chariot touches down, and the holographic horses wink out of existence. Several hundred other sky chariots are parked helter-skelter on the grass.

The Muse removes what looks to be a small medallion from her robe. "Hockenberry, I have been ordered to take you somewhere where you cannot be. I have been directed by one of the gods to give you two items that might keep you from being crushed like a gnat if you are detected. Put these on."

The Muse hands me two objects—a medallion on a chain and what looks to be a tooled-leather hood. The medallion is small but heavy, as if it is made of gold. The Muse reaches forward and slides one part of the disc counterclockwise from the rest. "This is a personal quantum tele-porter such as the gods use," she says softly. "It can teleport you any place you can visualize. This particular QT disk also allows you to fol-low the quantum trail of the gods as they phase-shift through Planck space, but no one—except the god who gave me this—can trace your path. Do you understand?"

"Yes," I say, my voice almost quavering. I shouldn't have this thing. It will be my death. The other "gift" is worse.

"This is the Helmet of Death," she says, tugging the ornate leather headpiece over my head, but leaving it folded around my neck like a cowl. "The Hades Helmet. It was made by Hades himself and it is the only thing in the universe that can hide you from the vision of the gods."

I blink stupidly at this. I vaguely remember scholarly footnotes about "the Helmet of Death," and I remember that Hades' name itself—in Greek, Äidès was thought to mean "the unseen one." But as far as I knew, Hades' Helmet of Death was mentioned only once by Homer, when Athena donned it to be invisible to the war god, Ares. *Why on earth or Olympos would any goddess loan this thing to me? What are they setting me up to do for them?* My knees go weak at the thought.

"Put the helmet on," orders the Muse.

Clumsily, I tug up the thick leather. There are devices embedded in the material, circuit chips, nanotech machines. The helmet has clear, flex-ible eyepieces and mesh material over the mouth, and when I've pulled on the full cowl, the air seems to ripple strangely around us, although my sight is otherwise unaffected.

"Incredible," says the Muse. She is staring right past me. I realize that I've achieved the goal of every adolescent boy—true invisibility, al-though how the helmet shields my entire body from sight, I have no idea. My impulse is to run like hell and hide from the Muse and all the gods. I stifle the impulse. There has to be a catch here. No god or goddess, not even my minor Muse, would give a mere scholic such power without safeguards.

"This device will shield you from the sight of all the gods except the goddess who authorized me to give it to you," the Muse says quietly, staring at the empty air to the right of my head. "But that goddess can see and track you anywhere, Hockenberry. And although sound, scent, even heartbeat is muffled by the medallion, the gods' senses are beyond your understanding. Stay close to me in the next few minutes. Tread lightly. Say nothing. Breathe as lightly and shallowly as possible. If you are detected, neither I nor your divine patroness can protect you from the wrath of Zeus."

How do you breathe lightly and softly when you're terrified? But I nod, forgetting the Muse cannot see me now. When she waits, still staring slightly askance as if seeking me with her divine vision, I croak, "Yes, Goddess."

"Put your hand on my arm," she orders brusquely. "Stay with me. Do not lose contact with me. If you do, you will be destroyed."

I put my hand on her arm like a timid debutante being escorted at a coming-out party. The Muse's skin is cold.

I was once in the Vehicle Assembly Building at the Kennedy Space Center in Cape Canaveral. The guide said that clouds sometimes formed under the roof hundreds of feet above the concrete floor. You could take the VAB and set it in one corner of this immense room we find ourselves in now and you'd never notice it sitting there like a cast-off child's toy block in a cathedral.

One says "gods" and you think of the meat-and-potato gods, the main gods—Zeus, Hera, Apollo, and a few others—but there are hundreds of gods in this room and most of the room is empty. Seemingly miles above us, a gold dome—the Greeks had not discovered the principles of a dome, so this was in contrast to the classically conservative architecture of the other great buildings I have seen on Olympos—acoustically directs conversation to all corners of the breathtaking space.

The floor looks to be made of hammered gold. Gods lean on marble railings and look down from circling mezzanines. The walls everywhere sport hundreds upon hundreds of arched niches, each holding a white marble sculpture. The statues are of the gods present here now.

Holograms of Achaeans and Trojans flicker here and there, many of them showing life-sized, full-color, three-dimensional images of the men and women as they argue or eat or make love or sleep. Near the center of the room, the gold floor steps down to a recess larger than any combination of Olympic-sized swimming pools, and in this space flickers and floats more real-time images from Ilium—broad aerial views, close-ups, panning shots, multiple images. One can hear the dialogue as if the Greeks and Trojans were in this very room. Around this vision pool, sitting in stone thrones and lounging on plush couches and standing in their cartoonlike togas, are the gods. The important gods. The meat-and-potato, known-by-grade-schoolers gods.

Lesser gods move aside as the Muse approaches this center pool, and I hurry to stay with her, my invisible hand tremulous on her golden arm, trying not to squeak my sandals or trip or sneeze or breathe. None of the deities seem to notice me. I suspect that I will know very quickly if any of them do.

The Muse stops a few yards from Pallas Athena and I stay so close to her that I feel like a three-year-old child hugging his mother's skirt.

There is a fierce argument under way, even as Hebe—one of the minor goddesses—moves among the others, pouring some sort of golden nectar into their gold goblets. Zeus sits on his throne and it is obvious to me at a glance that Zeus is the king here, he who drives the storm clouds, god among gods. No cartoon image, this Zeus, but an impossibly tall reality whose bearded, oiled, and palpably regal presence makes my blood turn to frightened sludge.

"How can we control the course of this war?" he demands of all the gods even while he stares daggers at his wife, Hera. "Or the fate of Helen? If goddesses such as Hera of Argos and Athena, guardian of her soldiers, keep intervening—such as this stopping Achilles' hand in the act of drawing the blood of the son of Atreus?"

He turns his storm-cloud gaze on a goddess lounging on purple cushions. "Or you, Aphrodite, with your constant laughter, always standing by that pretty-boy Paris, driving away evil spirits and deflecting well-cast spears. How can the will of the gods—and more important, of Zeus—be clear, even here, if you meddling goddesses keep protecting your favorites at the expense of Fate? Despite all your machinations, Hera, Menelaus may yet lead Helen home . . . or perhaps, who knows, Ilium may prevail. It is not for a few female gods to decide these things."

Hera folds her slender arms. So frequently in the poem is Hera referred to as "the white-armed goddess" that I half expect her arms to be whiter than the other goddesses' arms, but although Hera's skin is milky enough, it's no visibly milkier than that of Aphrodite or Hera's daughter Hebe or any of the other female gods I can see from my vantage point here near the image pool . . . except for Athena, that is, who looks strangely tanned. I know that these descriptive passages are a function of Homer's type of epic poetry; Achilles is referred to repeatedly as "swift-footed," Apollo as "one who shoots from afar," and Agamemnon's name is usually preceded by "wide ruling" or "lord of men"; the Achaeans are "strong-greaved" and their ships "black" or "hollow" and so forth. These repeated epithets met the heavy demands of dactylic hexameter more than mere description, and were a way for the singing bard to meet metric requirements with formulaic phrases. I've always suspected that some of these ritual phrases—such as Dawn stretching forth her rosy fingertips—were also verbal placeholders, buying the bard a few seconds to remember, if not invent, the next few lines of action.

Still, as Hera begins to retort to her husband, I am looking at her arms. "Son of Kronos—dreaded majesty," she says, white arms folded, "what in the hell are you talking about? How dare you consider making all of my labors pointless? I'm talking *sweat* here—immortal sweat—poured out launching Achaea's armies, stroking these male hero's egos just to keep them from killing each other before they kill Trojans, and taking great pains—*my* pains, O Zeus—in heaping greater pains on King Priam and the sons of Priam and the city of Priam."

Zeus frowns and leans forward on his uncomfortable-looking throne, his huge white hands clenching and unclenching.

Hera unfolds her arms and throws up her hands in exasperation. "Do what you please—you always do—but don't expect any of us immortals to praise you."

Zeus stands. If the other gods are eight or nine feet tall, Zeus must stand twelve feet high. His brow is more folded than furrowed now, and I am using no metaphor when I say that he thunders:

"Hera—my dear, darling, insatiable Hera! What has Priam or the sons of Priam ever done to *you* that you have become so furious, so relentless to bring down Priam's city of Ilium?"

Hera stands silent, hands at her side. This seems only to increase Zeus's royal fury.

"This is more appetite than anger with you, Goddess!" he roars. "You won't be satisfied until you knock down the Trojans' gates, breach their walls, and eat them raw."

Hera's expression does nothing to deny this charge.

"Well . . . well . . ." thunders Zeus, almost spluttering in a way all too familiar to husbands across the millennia, "do as *you* please. But one more thing—and remember it well, Hera—when there comes a day that *I* am bent on destroying a city and consuming its inhabitants—a city *you* love, as I love Ilium—then don't even think about attempting to oppose my fury."

The goddess takes three quick steps forward and I am reminded of a predator pouncing, or some chess master seeing his opening and taking it. "Yes! The three cities I love best are Argos and Sparta and Mycenae of the wide ways, its streets as broad and regal as ill-fated Ilium's. All these you can sack to your vandal's heart's content, My Lord. I will not oppose you. I will not begrudge your will . . . little good it would do me anyway, since you are the stronger of us two. But remember this, O Zeus— although I am your consort, I am also born of Kronos and thus deserving of your respect."

"I never suggested otherwise," mutters Zeus, taking his hard seat again.

"Then let us yield one to the other on this point," says Hera, her voice audibly sweeter now. "I to you and you to me. The lesser gods will comply. Quickly now, my husband! Achilles has left the field for now, but a mewling truce makes quiet the killing ground between Trojans and Achaeans. See that that the Trojans break this truce and do first injury, not only to their oaths, but to the far-famed Achaeans."

Zeus glowers, grumbles, shifts in his chair, but orders the attentive Athena—"Go quickly down to the quiet killing ground between Trojans and Achaeans. I order you to see that the Trojans are the first to break the truce and do injury to the far-famed Achaeans."

"And trample on the Argives in their triumph," prompts Hera.

"And trample on the Argives in their triumph," Zeus orders wearily.

Athena disappears in a QT flash. Zeus and Hera leave the room and the gods begin to disperse, speaking softly amongst themselves.

The Muse beckons me to follow with a subtle flick of her finger and leads me out of the assembly hall.

"Hockenberry," says the Goddess of Love, reclining on her cushioned couch, the gravity—light as it is—giving emphasis to all her silky, milky-weighted voluptuousness.

The Muse had led me to this other room in the Great Hall of the Gods, this darkened room with only the double glow from a low-burning brazier and from something that looked suspiciously like a computer screen. She had whispered to me to remove the Helmet of Death and I was relieved to take the leather hood off, but terrified to be visible again.

Then Aphrodite had entered, assumed her position on the couch, and said, "That will be all until I summon you, Melete," and the Muse had stepped out through a secret door.

Melete, I thought. Not one of the nine muses, but a name from an earlier era, where the muses were thought to be three: Melete of "practicing," Mneme of "remembering," and Aoide of . . .

"Hockenberry, *I* was able to see you in the Hall of the Gods," says Aphrodite, blinking me out of my scholic reverie, "and if I had pointed you out to Lord Zeus, you would be something less than ashes now. Even your QT medallion would not have allowed you to escape, for I could follow your phase-shift path through time and space itself. Do you know why you are here?"

Aphrodite is my patroness. She's the one who ordered the Muse to give me these devices. What do I do? Kneel? Prostrate myself on the floor in the presence of divinity? How do I address her? In my nine years, two months, and eighteen days here, my existence has never been acknowledged by a god before, not counting my Muse.

I decide to bow slightly, averting my eyes from her beauty, from the sight of pink nipples showing through thin silk, of that soft cusp of stomach sending shadows into that triangle of dark fabric where her thighs meet.

"No, Goddess," I say at last, all but forgetting the question.

"Do you know why you were chosen as scholic, Hockenberry? Why your DNA was exempted from nanocyte disruption? Why, before you were chosen for reintegration, your writings on the War were factored into the simplex?"

"No, Goddess." *My DNA is exempt from nanocyte disruption?*

"Do you know what a simplex is, mortal shade?"

Herpes virus? I think. "No, Goddess," I say.

"The simplex is a simple geometric mathematical object, an exercise in logistics, a triangle or trapezoid folded on itself," says Aphrodite. "Only combined with multiple dimensions and algorithms defining new notional areas, creating and discarding feasible regions of n-space, planes of exclusion become inevitable contours. Do you understand now, Hockenberry? Do you understand how this applies to quantum space, to time, to the War below, or to your own fate?"

"No, Goddess." My voice does quaver this time. I can't help it.

There is a rustling of silk and I glance up long enough to see the most beautiful female in existence rearranging her fair limbs and smooth thighs on the couch. "No matter," she says. "You—or the mortal who was your template—wrote a book several thousand years ago. Do you remember its content?"

"No, Goddess."

"If you say that one more time, Hockenberry, I am going to rip you open from crotch to crown and quite literally use your guts for my garters. Do you understand *that*?"

It is hard to speak with no saliva in your mouth. "Yes, Goddess," I manage, hearing the dry lisp.

"Your book ran to 935 pages and it was all about one word—*Menin*—do you remember now?"

"No, Go . . . I'm afraid I don't recall that, Goddess Aphrodite, but I am sure that you are correct."

I look up long enough to see that she is smiling, her chin propped on her left hand, her finger rising along her cheek to one perfect dark eyebrow. Her eyes are the color of a fine cognac.

"Rage," she says softly. "*Menin aeide thea* . . . Do you know who will win this war, Hockenberry?"

I have to think fast here. I would be a pretty poor scholic if I don't know how the poem turns out—although the *Iliad* ends with the funeral rites for Achilles' friend Patroclus, not with the destruction of Troy, and there is no mention of a giant horse except in Odysseus' comments and that from another epic . . . but if I pretend to know how this *real* war will turn out, and it is obvious from the argument I have just overheard that Zeus's edict that the gods must not be informed of the future as predicted by the *Iliad* is still in effect—I mean, if the gods themselves do not know what will happen next, wouldn't I be putting myself above the gods, including Fate by telling them? *Hubris* has never been an attribute gently rewarded by these gods. Besides, Zeus—who alone knows the full tale of the *Iliad*—has forbidden the other gods from asking and all of us scholics from discussing anything except events that have already occurred. Pissing off Zeus is never a good plan for survival on Olympos. Still, it seems I'm exempt from nanocyte disruption. On the other hand, I believe the Goddess of Love completely when she says that she will wear my guts for garters.

"What was the question, Goddess?" is all I can manage.

"You know how the poem the *Iliad* ends, but I would be defying Zeus's command if I ask you what happens there," says Aphrodite, her small smile disappearing and being replaced by something like a pout. "But I can ask you if that poem predicts *this* reality. Does it? In your opinion, Scholic Hockenberry, does Zeus rule the universe, or does Fate?"

Oh, shit, I think. Any answer here is going to end up with me being gutless and this beautiful woman—goddess—wearing slimy garters. I say, "It is my understanding, Goddess, that even though the universe bends to the will of Zeus and must obey the vagaries of the god-force called Fate, that *kaos* still has some say in the lives of both men and gods."

Aphrodite makes a soft, amused sound. Everything about her is so soft, touchable, enticing . . . .

"We will not wait for chaos to decide this contest," she says, her voice shedding all sound of amusement. "You saw Achilles withdraw from the fray this day?"

"Yes, Goddess."

"You know that the man-killer has already prayed to Thetis to punish his fellow Achaeans for the shame that Agamemnon has heaped on him?"

"I have not witnessed this prayer, Goddess, but I know that it follows the path of the . . . the poem." This is safe to say. The event is in the past. Besides, the sea goddess Thetis is Achilles' mother and everyone on Olympos *knows* that he has called for her intervention.

"Indeed," says Aphrodite. "That roundheeled bitch with the wet breasts has already been here to the Great Hall, throwing herself at Zeus's knees as soon as the old fool returned from his debauching with the Aethiopians at the Ocean River. She begged him, for Achilles' sake, to grant victory after victory to the Trojans, and the old sod agreed, thus putting him on a collision course with Hera, chief champion of the Argives. Thus the scene you just witnessed."

I stand upright with my arms down, palms forward, head slightly bowed, all the while watching Aphrodite as if she were a cobra, but still knowing that if she chooses to strike me, the strike will come much faster and more lethally than any cobra's.

"Do you know why you have survived longer than any other scholic?" snaps Aphrodite.

Unable to speak without condeming myself, I shake my head ever so slightly.

"You are still alive because I have foreseen that you can perform a service for me."

Sweat trickles down my brow and stings my eyes. More sweat forms rivulets on my cheek and neck. As scholics, our sworn duty—my duty for the last nine years, two months, and eighteen days—is to observe the war on the plains of Ilium without ever intervening, observing without ever committing any act whatsoever that might change the outcome of the war or the behavior of its heroes in any way.

"Did you hear me, Hockenberry?"

"Yes, Goddess."

"Are you interested in hearing what this service will be, scholic?"

"Yes, Goddess."

Aphrodite rises from her couch and now I do bow my head, but I can hear the rustle of her silken gown, hear even the gentle friction of her smooth white thighs rubbing softly as she walks closer; I can smell the perfume-and-clean-female scent of her as she stands so close. I had forgotten for a moment how tall a goddess is, but I'm reminded of our respective heights as she towers over me, her breasts inches from my downturned face. For an instant I must fight the urge to bury my face in the perfumed valley between those breasts, and although I know well that this would by my last act before a violent death, I suspect at this moment that it might be worth it.

Aphrodite sets her hand on my tense shoulder, touches the rough leather embroidery of the Helmet of Death, and then moves her fingertips to my cheek. Despite my fear, I feel a powerful erection stirring, rising, standing firm.

The goddess's whisper, when it comes, is soft, sensual, slightly amused, and I am sure that she knows the state I am in, expects it as her due. She lowers her face and leans so close that I can feel the heat of her cheek radiating against mine as she whispers two simple commands in my ear.

"You are going to spy on the other gods for me," she says softly. And then, barely audible above the pounding of my heart, "And when the time is right, you are going to kill Athena."

7

Conamara Chaos Central

Counting Mahnmut, there were five Galilean moravecs in the pressurized gathering chamber atop the slab zone. The Europan construct was familiar to him—Pwyll-based prime integrator Asteague/Che—but the other three were more alien than krakens to the provincial Mahnmut. The Ganymedan moravec was tall, elegant as all Ganymedans, atavistically humanoid, sheathed in black buckycarbon and staring through his fly's eyes; the Callistan was more Mahnmut's size and design—about a meter long, only vaguely humanoid, showing synskin and even some real flesh under clear polymide coating, massing only thirty or forty kilograms; the Ionian construct was . . . impressive. A heavy-use moravec of ancient design, built to withstand plasma torus and sulfur geysers, the Io-based entity was at least three meters tall and six meters long, shaped rather like a terrestrial horseshoe crab—heavily armored, with an untidy myriad of morphable appendages, thrusters, lenses, flagella, whip antennae, broad-spectrum sensors and facilitators. The thing was obviously used to hard vacuum; its surface was pitted and sanded and repolished, then repitted again so many times that it looked as pockmarked as Io itself. Here in the pressurized conference room it used powerful source-repellers to keep from gouging the floor. Mahnmut kept his distance from the Ionian, taking a place across the communion slab from it.

None of the others introduced themselves via either infrared or tight-beam, so Mahnmut followed suit. He connected to nutrient umbilicals at his slab niche, sipped, and waited.

As much as he enjoyed breathing when he had the luxury of doing so, Mahnmut was surprised that the room was pressurized to 700 millibars—especially with the nonbreathing Ganymedan and Ionian in attendance. Then Asteague/Che began communicating through micro-modulation of pressure waves in the atmosphere—speech, Lost Age English no less—and Mahnmut realized that the room was pressurized for privacy, not for their comfort. Sound-speech was the most secure form of communication in the Galilean system, and even the armored, hard-vac Io worker had been retrofitted to accommodate it.

"I want to thank each of you for interrupting your duties to come here today," began the Pwyll prime integrator, "especially those who traveled from offworld to be present. I am Asteague/Che. Welcome, Koros III of Ganymede, Ri Po of Callisto, Mahnmut of the south polar prospect survey here on Europa, and Orphu of Io."

Mahnmut cycled in surprise and immediately opened a private tight-beam contact. *Orphu of Io? Are you then my longtime Shakespearean interlocutor, Orphu of Io?*

Indeed, Mahnmut. It is a pleasure to meet you in person, my friend.

How strange! What are the odds of us encountering each other in person this way, Orphu?

Not so strange, my friend. When I heard that you were going to be invited on this suicide expedition, I insisted on being included.

Suicide expedition?

". . . after more than fifty Jovian years without contact with the post-humans," Asteague/Che was saying, "some six hundred Earth years, we've lost track of what the pH's are up to. It makes us nervous. It is time to send an expedition in-system, toward the campfire, and to find out what the status of these creatures has become and to assess if they are a direct and immediate threat to Galileans." Asteague/Che paused a moment. "We have reason to suspect that they are."

The wall behind the Europan integrator had been transparent, showing the bulk of Jupiter above the starlit icefields, but now it opaqued and then displayed the various moons and worlds moving in their stately dance around the distant sun. The image zoomed on the Earth-Moon-rings system.

"For the last five hundred Earth years, there has been less and less activity on the modulated radio, gravitonic, and neutrino spectrums from the post-humans' polar and equatorial habitation rings," said Asteague/Che. "For the last century, none at all. On the Earth itself, only residual traces—possibly due to robotic activity."

"Does the small group of original humans still exist?" asked Ri Po, the small Callistan.

"We don't know," said Asteague/Che. The integrator passed his hand across the allboard and an image of Earth filled the window.

Mahnmut felt his breathing stop. Two-thirds of the planet was in sun-light. Blue seas and a few traces of brown continents were visible under moving masses of white clouds. Mahnmut had never seen Earth before, and the intensity of color was almost overwhelming.

"Is this a real-time image?" asked Koros III.

"Yes. The Five Moons Consortium has constructed a small optical deep-space telescope just outside the bow-shock front of the Jovian mag-netodisk. Ri Po was involved in the project."

"I apologize for its lack of resolution," said the Callistan. "It has been over a Jovian century since we've resorted to visible light astronomy. And this project was rushed."

"Are there signs of the originals?" asked Orphu of Io.

The descendents of your Shakespeare, Orphu said on tightbeam to Mahnmut.

"Unknown," said Asteague/Che. "The greatest resolution is just under two kilometers and we've seen no sign of original-human life or artifacts, other than previously mapped ruins. There is some neutrino fax activity, but it may be automated or residual. In truth, the humans are of no concern to us right now. The post-humans are."

My Shakespeare? You mean our Shakespeare! Mahnmut tightbeamed to the big Ionian.

Sorry, Mahnmut. As much as I love the sonnets—and even your Bard's plays—my own concentration has been on Proust.

Proust! That aesthete! You're joking!

Not at all. There came a rumble on the subsonic spectrum of the tight-band which Mahnmut interpreted as the Ionian's laughter.

The integrator brought up images of some of the millions of orbital habitations moving in their stately ring-dance around Earth. Many were white, others silver. As brilliant as they looked in the heavy light so close to the sun, they also looked strangely cold. And empty.

"No shuttles. No evidence of ring-to-Earth neutrino faxing. And the convoy-bridge of heavy materials being accelerated between the rings and Mars—observed as recently as twenty Jovian years ago, two hun-dred forty-some Earth/pH ring years ago—is gone."

"You think the post-humans are gone?" asked Koros III. "Died off somehow? Or migrated?"

"We know there was a sea change in their energy use, chronoclastic, quantum, and gravitational," said the integrator. The unit was taller and a bit more humanoid than Mahnmut, sheathed in bright yellow surface-shield materials. His voice was soft, calm, carefully modulated. "Our in-terest now turns to Mars."

The image of the fourth planet filled the window.

Mahnmut's interest in Mars was marginal at best, and his images of it were from the Lost Age. This world looked nothing like the photos and holos from that era.

Instead of a rust-red world, this recent image of Mars revealed a blue sea covering most of the northern hemisphere, the Valles Marineris river valley showing a ribbon of blue many kilometers wide connecting to that ocean. Much of the southern hemisphere remained reddish-brown, but there were also large splotches of green. The Tharsis volcanoes still ran southwest to northeast in dark procession—one with a visible smoke plume—but Olympus Mons now rose within twenty kilometers or so of a huge bay arcing in from the northern ocean. White clouds clumped and grouped across the sunlit half of the image and bright lights glowed somewhere near Hellas Basin beyond the dark edge of the terminator. Mahnmut could see a hurricane spiraling north of the Chryse Planitia coastline.

"They terraformed it," Mahnmut said aloud. "The posts terraformed Mars."

"How long ago?" asked Orphu of Io. None of the Galileans had any special interest in Mars—in any of the Inner Worlds, for that matter (except for their literature)—so this could have happened any time in the twenty-five hundred terrestrial years since the break between moravecs and humanity.

"In the last two hundred years," said Asteague/Che. "Perhaps in the last century and a half."

"Impossible." Koros III's statement was flat and final. "Mars could never be terraformed in so short a time."

"Yes, impossible," agreed Asteague/Che. "But it was."

"So the posts migrated there," said Orphu of Io.

Little Ri Po answered. "We think not. Resolution on our observation of Mars has been a bit better than that of Earth. For instance, along the coastlines . . ."

The window showed an area along a twisting peninsula north of where the broad Valles Marineris rivers—more of a long inland sea, actually—emptied into a bay, flowed through an isthmus, and then opened into the northern ocean. The image zoomed. All along the coast where the land came down to the sea—sometimes showing red-desert hills, elsewhere green and heavily forested plains—tiny black specks followed the shoreline. The image zoomed a final time.

"Are those . . . sculptures?" asked Mahnmut.

"Stone heads, we think," said Ri Po. The image shifted and the shadow of one of the blurry images suggested a brow, a nose, a bold chin.

"This is ridiculous," said Koros III. "There would have to be millions of these Easter Island heads to border the entire northern ocean."

"We count four million, two hundred three thousand, five hundred and nine," said Asteague/Che. "But the construction is incomplete. Note this photograph taken some months ago during Mars's closest approach."

A myriad of tiny, blurry forms pulled what might be a great stone head on rollers. The stone face was looking skyward, its shadow-eyes staring straight into the space telescope. The tiny figures appeared to be attached to the heads by mutliple cables, pulling them along, Mahnmut thought, like Egyptian slaves hauling a pyramid block.

"Human workers?" said Orphu. "Or robots?"

"We think neither," said Ri Po. "The size is wrong. And you notice the coloring of the figures on the spectral analysis bands."

"Green?" said Mahnmut. He liked literary puzzles, not real-life ones. "Green robots?"

"Or a species of small green humanoids not previously encountered," Asteague/Che said seriously.

Orphus of Io rumbled subsonic laughter. "LGM," he said aloud.

[?] sent Mahnmut.

Little Green Men, Orphu of Io sent on the common band and rumbled again.

"Why were we called here?" Mahnmut asked Asteague/Che. "What does this terraforming have to do with us?"

The integrator returned the window to transparency. The bands of Jupiter and plains of Europan ice in the evening light looked dull and muted after all the vibrant inner-system blues and whites. "We're sending a team to Mars to investigate this and report back," said Asteague/Che. "You've been chosen. You can say 'no' now."

The four remained silent on all communications spectra.

"I said 'report back,' " continued the prime integrator, "but not necessarily 'come back.' We have no sure way of returning you to the Jovian system. Please signal if you would like to be replaced on this mission."

All four remained silent.

"All right," said the Europan integrator. "You'll download the specifics of the expedition in a few minutes, but let me cover the high points. We will use Mahnmut's submersible for the actual surveillance on the planet. Ri Po and Orphu will map from orbit while Mahnmut and Koros III go to the surface. We're especially interested in activity on and around Mons Olympos, the largest volcano. Quantum-shift activity there has been massive and inexplicable. Mahnmut will deliver Koros III to the coastline, and our Ganymedan friend will carry out reconnaissance."

Mahnmut knew from his records and readings that Lost Age humans had signaled pending interruption by clearing their throats. He made a throat-clearing noise. "You have to excuse my stupidity, but how do we get *The Dark Lady*—my submersible—to Mars?"

"That's not a stupid question," said the integrator. "Orphu of Io?"

The giant armored horseshoe crab shifted on its repellors so that various black lenses looked at Mahnmut. "It's been centuries since we've sent anything in-system. And anything delivered the old-fashioned way would take half a Jovian year. We've decided to use the scissors."

Ri Po shifted in his slab niche. "I thought the scissors were going to be used only for interstellar exploration."

"The Five Moons Consortium has decided that this takes precedence," said Orphu of Io.

"I presume there will be some sort of spacecraft," said Koros III. "Or are you going to fling us one after the other, naked, like so many chickens fired from a trebuchet?"

Orphu's subsonic rumble shook the slab. He obviously liked Koros' image.

Mahnmut had to access the common net. A *trebuchet* was a Lost Age human siege engine from their Level Two civilizations—pre-steam— mechanical but much more powerful than a mere catapult, able to launch huge boulders more than a mile.

"A spacecraft exists," said Asteague/Che. "It has been designed to reach Mars in a few days and configured to hold Mahnmut's submersible. The spacecraft has an atmospheric entry package for Mahnmut's subermisible—*The Dark Lady*."

"Reach Mars in a few days," repeated Ri Po. "What are the delta-v factors leaving Io's flux tube?"

"Just under three thousand gravities," said the integrator. "*Earth* g's."

Mahnmut, who had never experienced a gravity-load greater than Europa's less than one-seventh Earth-g, tried to imagine 21,000 such g's. He couldn't.

"During acceleration, the ship, including *The Dark Lady*, will be packed with gel," said Orphu of Io. "We'll be as comfy as circuit chips in a gelatin mold." It was obvious that Orphu had been involved in planning the spacecraft and Ri Po in observing the two worlds. Koros III had probably had advance warning about his command role in such an expedition. It seemed to Mahnmut that only he had been left out of the preparation for this mission, probably because his role—driving *The Dark Lady* through the Martian seas—was so unimportant. Perhaps, he thought, *I should opt out of this expedition after all.*

Proust? he tightbeamed the big Ionian.

Too bad we aren't going to Earth, my friend. We could visit Stratford-on-Avon. Buy a souvenir mug.

It was an old joke between them, but in the present context, it seemed funny again. Mahnmut tightbeamed a decent simulacrum of Orphu's heavy laughter and the big construct rumbled so heavily in return that all four of the others could hear it through the thick air.

Ri Po was not laughing. He was obviously computing. "Such a scissors' fling would give us an initial velocity of almost two-tenths light speed, and even after drastic magnetic scoop deceleration in-system, we'll have an approach velocity of about one-thousandth light speed—more than 300 kilometers per second. We'll get to Mars quickly enough, even while it's on the far side of the sun as it is now. But has anyone given any thought as to how we might slow down once we get there?"

"Yes," said Orphu of Io, his rumbling abating. "We've given that some thought."

Even after thirty Jovian years of existence, Mahnmut had no one to say good-bye to on Europa. His exploration partner, Urtzweil, had been destroyed in a closing lead near Pwyll Crater eighteen J-years earlier, and Mahnmut had grown close to no other conscious entity since then.

Sixteen hours after the conference, Conamara Chaos Central ordered dedicated orbital tugs to lift *The Dark Lady* out of an open lead and boost it into orbit, where hard-vac moravecs, supervised by Orphu of Io, tucked the submersible into the waiting Marscraft and let ancient interlunar induction haulers truck the stack downhill to Io. Mahnmut and the other three expedition moravecs had briefly discussed naming the spacecraft, but imagination failed them, the impulse faded, and from that point on they referred to it only as "the ship."

Like most spacecraft constructed by moravecs in the thousands of years since spacefaring began, the ship was something less than elegant, at least by classical standards. It was one hundred and fifteen meters long and was comprised primarily of buckycarbon girders, with wrinkled radiation-shield fabric wrapped around module niches, semiautonomous sniffer probes, scores of antennae, sensors, and cables. This ship was notably different from Jovian-system machines primarily because of its gleaming magnetic dipole core and its sporty out-rider deflectors. Packed away in its lumpy snout were four fusion en-gine bells and the five horns of the Matloff/Fennelly scoop. A ten-meter-wide pimple on the stern held the folded boron sail. Neither scoop nor sail would be needed until the deceleration part of the jour-ney and the fusion engines had nothing to do with the acceleration phase of the mission.

Mahnmut stayed inside *The Dark Lady*—now packed with gel—while Koros III and Ri Po rode sixty meters away in the forward control module they'd come to call the bridge. The plan was for Ri Po to han-dle all navigation chores during their brief mad-mouse ride in, while Koros III served as titular commander of the expedition. The plan also called for the Ganymedan to transfer to Mahnmut's submersible shortly before *The Dark Lady*—emptied of its gel—was to be dropped into the Martian atmosphere. Once in the oceans of Mars, Mahnmut was to serve as a taxi driver—delivering Koros III to whatever landing point the commanding Ganymedan chose for his land-based spying. Koros had been downloaded various specifics of the mission that would not concern Mahnmut.

Orphu of Io had installed himself in his crèche on the outer shell of the ship behind the ten solenoid toruses and in front of the sail-cable struts, and was connected to the bridge and the submersible by every sort of voice, data, and comm link imaginable. Most of his nontechnical conversation was with Mahnmut.

I'm still most interested in your theory of the dramatic construct of the son-nets, my friend. I hope we live long enough for you to analyze more of the cycle.

But Proust! responded Mahnmut. *Why Proust when you can spend all of your existence studying Shakespeare?*

Proust was perhaps the ultimate explorer of time, memory, and perception, replied Orphu.

Mahnmut made a static sound.

The scarred Ionian sent his rumble through the audio line. "I look forward to convincing you that both can be enjoyed and learned from, Mahnmut, my friend."

Koros III's message came over the common line—*Everyone might want to raise bandwidth on the visual lines. We're approaching Io's plasma torus.*

Mahnmut opened all visual feeds as requested. He preferred to watch external events through Orphu of Io's lenses, but at the moment the more interesting views were from the forward ship cameras, and not necessarily in the visible-light spectra.

They were accelerating toward the great red-and-yellow-blotched face of Io, coming at the moon from below the plane of the ecliptic and making ready to pass over its northern pole just before flying into the Io–Jupiter flux tube.

During the short trip in from Europa, Orphu and Ri Po had downloaded pertinent information about this region of Jupiter space. A creature of Europa, Mahnmut had always focused primarily on sonar and some visual-light perception within the black oceans there, but now he perceived the Jovian magnetosphere as the loud, crowded place it was. Looking ahead on the decametric radio bandwidths, he could see Io's Jupiter-thick plasma torus and, at right angles to the torus, Io's flux tube running like wide horns to Jupiter's north and south poles. Far beyond Jupiter and its moons, beyond the magnetopause, Mahnmut could sense the bow shock turbulence crashing like great white waves on a hidden reef, could hear the upstream Langmuir waves singing in the magnetic darkness past that reef, and could pick out the ion acoustic waves crackling after their long voyage uphill from the sun. The sun itself was little more than a very bright star from Jupiter space.

Now, as the ship swept up and over Io and into the flux tube, Mahnmut could hear the Whistler-mode chorus and hiss that the little moon made as it plowed through its own plasma torus, eating its own tail, as it were. He could see the deep bands of equatorial emissions and had to tone down the decametric and kilometric radio roar coming from the flux tube itself. All of Galilean space was a furnace of hard radiation and electromagnetic activity—Mahnmut had spent his whole existence with its background roar in his virtual ears—but passing from torus to flux tube so close to Jupiter sent violent cascades of tortured electrons hissing around their ship like banshees screaming to be let in a beleaguered house. It was a new experience and Mahnmut found it a bit unnerving.

Then they were in the flux tube and Koros III shouted "Hang on!" before sound channels were drowned out by the hurricane roar.

The Io plasma torus was a giant doughnut of charged particles stirred up within the trail of sulfur dioxide, hydrogen sulfide, and other gases left behind—and then accumulated again—by Orphu's violent home moon. As Io sped in its fast 1.77-day orbit around Jupiter, slicing through the gas giant's magnetic field and plowing into its own plasma torus, it created a huge electrical current between Jupiter and itself, a double-horned cylinder of incredibly concentrated magnetic surges called the Io flux tube. The tube connected to Jupiter's north and south magnetic poles and created wild auroras there, while the horns of the flux tube itself carried a constant current of some five megaamperes and constantly produced more than two trillion watts of energy.

The Five Moons Consortium had decided some decades ago that two trillion watts of energy would be a terrible thing to waste.

Mahnmut watched as Io's north pole flicked beneath them. Ejecta from various sulfur volcanoes—especially from Prometheus far south near the moon's equator—was being spewed 140 kilometers high and higher above the pockmarked surface, as if the violent moon was shooting at them, trying to make them turn back before they reached the point of no return.

Too late. They were already there.

On the common forward video, Ri Po's superimposed navigation brackets showed their proper insertion into the flux tube and projected alignment with the scissors. Jupiter rushed at them, rapidly filling the view ahead like a multi-striped wall.

The physical blades of the scissors—that dual-armed, rotating, magnetic wave accelerator set within the natural particle accelerator of Io's flux tube—were 8,000 kilometers long, only a fragment of the flux tube's length of more than half a million curving kilometers connecting the north pole of Io to the north pole of Jupiter.

But the scissors could move. As Orphu of Io had explained to Mahnmut, "Angular momentum can be a many-splendored thing, my little friend."

The ship nestling Mahnmut's beloved submersible had approached Io and the flux tube—even after full acceleration from the ion-tugs—at a velocity of only some 24 kilometers per second, less than 86,000 kilometers per hour. At that speed, it would take more than four hours just to traverse the flux tube distance between Io's north pole and Jupiter's, e-years to reach Mars. But they had no intention of continuing on at that creeping pace.

The ship entered the crackling, roaring, twitching field of the flux tube, found the vertex of the scissors, aligned itself with the upper blade, and then used the tube's own accelerator properties to hurl the spacecraft-solenoid through the five-kilometer-wide field coils of the superconducting dipole accelerator. As soon as the ship entered the first gate like some clumsy croquet ball passing through the first of several thousand wickets, the blade of the accelerator-scissors began snapping open with a differential angular velocity nearing—and theoretically even surpassing—light speed. They were riding a rippling bullwhip one second and then flicked from the tip of it the next, using as much of that two trillion watts of energy as the scissors-accelerator could grab.

The ship—and everything in it—went from zero-g to almost 3,000-g's within two-point-six seconds.

Jupiter zipped toward, past, and under them in an eyeblink. Mahnmut slowed all his monitors down so that he could appreciate their departure.

"Wheeehaw!" cried Orphu from the outer hull.

The ship and submersible strained, creaked, groaned, and whinnied from the g-force, but it was all made of tough stuff—*The Dark Lady* itself had been built to withstand several million kilograms per square centimeter of pressure in Europa's deep seas—and so were these moravecs.

"Holy shit," said Mahnmut, meaning to send the comment just to Orphu of Io, but managing to broadcast to all three of his colleagues.

"Indeed," responded Ri Po.

Jupiter's broiling polar lights—the brilliant auroral oval surrounding the gas giant's north pole, accompanied by Io's blazing footprint where the flux tube met atmosphere—flashed beneath them and disappeared astern.

Ganymede, which had been a million kilometers away across the system a few seconds before, zoomed toward them, flicked past, and was lost to sight behind them.

"Uruk Sulcus," said Koros III on the common band and for a moment Mahnmut thought the command-moravec was choking or cursing before he noted the slightly sentimental tone to his usually cool voice and realized that Koros must have been referring to some region on Ganymede itself—a half-glimpsed grooved and dirty snowball flashing past—that must be home to the Ganymedan.

The tiny moon Himalia, which none of the crew had visited—nor cared to—whipped by like a firefly with its hair on fire.

"We've passed through the bow shock front," reported Ri Po in his flat Callistan accent. "Out of the local pond for the first time, at least for this moravec."

Mahnmut glanced at his screens. Ri Po's readout reported that they were fifty-three Jupiter diameters out now and still accelerating. Mahnmut had to check unused memory banks and see that Jupiter had a diameter of almost 142,000 kilometers before he got a sense of their speed. The ship was arcing above the plane of the ecliptic, but Mahnmut vaguely remembered that the plan was for the sun's gravity to hook them back down toward Mars, which was on the far side of the sun at the moment. At any rate, navigation wasn't his concern. His job would begin when they landed in the ocean of Mars, and sailing there seemed simple enough—rich sunlight, warm temperatures, shallow depths with no pressure to speak of, stars to navigate by at night, geo-positioning satellites that they'd drop into orbit so they could navigate during the day, almost no radiation compared to the surface on Europa. No kraken! No ice. *No ice!* It all seemed too simple.

Of course, if the post-humans were hostile, there was a good chance that the moravecs would not survive the trip to Mars or the atmospheric entry, and even they did, there was a high probability that they could never return to their homes in Jupiter space, but there was nothing Mahnmut could do about any of that now. His thoughts began to turn back to Sonnet 127.

"Everyone all right?" asked Koros III.

Everyone reported in that they were fine. It took more than a few thousand gravities sitting on their respective chests to get this crew down. Morale was high.

Ri Po began reporting some other navigational and spacefaring facts, but Mahnmut wasn't really paying attention. He was already caught up in the gravity field of Sonnet 127, the first of the "Dark Lady" sonnets.

8

Ardis

Daeman slept well and dreamt of women.

He found it slightly amusing, if not odd, that he dreamt of women only when he was not sleeping with one. It was as if he required warm female flesh next to him every night, and his subconscious supplied them when his daily efforts failed. As he awoke, late, in his comfortable room at Ardis Hall, the dream fled in fragments and tatters, but enough remained—along with usual morning erection—to bring back a vague memory of Ada's body, or someone very much like Ada—warm, white-skinned, perfumed, with full buttocks and round breasts and solid thighs. Daeman looked forward to the weekend's coming conquest and had little doubt this lovely morning that he would succeed.

Later, showered, shaved, dressed impeccably in what he considered rural casual—white-and-blue-striped cotton trousers, wool serge vest, pastel jacket, white silk shirt and ruby cravat stone, carrying his favorite wood walking cane and wearing black leather shoes a slight bit more sturdy than his usual formal slipper-pumps—he breakfasted in the sun-lit conservatory and learned, to his satisfaction, that Hannah and that Harman person had left early that morning. "Preparing for the evening's pour" was Ada's cryptic explanation and Daeman did not have suffi-cient interest to ask for clarification. He was just glad the man was gone.

Ada did not bring up conversational absurdities such as books or spaceships, but spent the late morning with him, serving as guide, re-acquainting him with Ardis Hall's many wings and gabled corridors, its elaborate wine cellars and secret passages and ancient attics. He re-membered a similar tour on his first visit there and the feckless girl-Ada leading him up a rickety ladder to the rooftop jinker platform and Dae-man, alert as ever to such revelations, had half glimpsed a young man's heaven up her hoisted skirt as she climbed above him: he perfectly remembered the milky thighs and dark, stippled shadows there.

This morning they climbed the same ladder to the same jinker platform, but this time Ada gestured him ahead, only smiling at his gentlemanly protests that she go first, the smile suggesting some vixen memory of the event he had thought had gone unnoticed by her at the time.

Ardis Hall was a tall manor and the jinker platform, its mahogany planks still gleaming, thrust out between gables to an overhang sixty feet above the gravel drive where voynix stood like rusted upright scarabs. Daeman stayed back from the unrailed edge, but Ada ignored the exposure and walked right to the brink, gazing wistfully at the long lawn and distant line of forest.

"Wouldn't you give anything to have a working jinker?" she said. "Even if just for a few days?"

"No. Why would I?"

Ada gestured with her long-fingered hands. "Even with just a child's jinker you could fly over the forest and river, over those hills to the west, fly on for days and days away from here, away from any faxport."

"Why would anyone want to do that?"

Ada looked at him for a moment. "You're not curious? About what's out there?"

Daeman tapped at his vest as if brushing away crumbs. "Don't be absurd, my dear. There's nothing of interest out there . . . pure wilderness . . . no people. Why, everyone I know lives within a few miles of a faxport. Besides, there are *Tyrannosaurus rex*es out there."

"A tyrannosaurus? In our forest?" said Ada. "Nonsense. We've never seen one here. Who told you that, cousin?"

"You did, my dear. The last time I visited, half a Twenty ago."

Ada shook her head. "I must have been teasing you."

Daeman thought about this, about his years of anxiety over the thought of ever visiting Ardis again, about his tyrannosaurus nightmares over the years, and could only scowl.

Ada seemed to read his thoughts and smiled slightly. "Did you ever wonder, Cousin Daeman, why the posts decided to keep our population at one million? Why not one million and one? Or nine hundred thousand, nine hundred ninety-nine? Why one million?"

Daeman blinked at this, trying to see the connection in her thoughts between talk of a Lost Age child's jinker and dinosaurs and the human population that had been the same . . . well . . . forever. And he didn't like her reminding both of them that they were cousins, since old superstitions sometimes inhibited sexual relations between family members. "I find that such idle speculations lead to indigestion, even on such a beautiful day, my dear," he said. "Shall we return to a more felicitous topic?"

"Of course," said Ada, blessing him with the sweetest of smiles. "Why don't we go down and find some of the other guests before lunch and our trip to the pour site?"

This time she went first down the ladder.

Luncheon was served outside on the northern patio by floating servitors and Daeman chatted amiably with some of the young people—it seemed that several more guests had faxed in for the evening's "pour"—whatever that was to be—and after the meal, many of the guests found couches in the house or comfortable lounge chairs on the shaded lawn in which to recline while draping their turin cloths over their eyes. The usual time under turin was an hour, so Daeman strolled near the edge of the trees, keeping an eye out for butterflies as he walked.

Ada joined him near the bottom of the hill. "You do not use the turin, Cousin Daeman?"

"I do not," he said, hearing that he had sounded more prissy than he had intended. "I've accustomed myself to the things after almost a decade, but I don't indulge. You also abstain, Ada, my dear?"

"Not always," said the young woman. She was twirling a peach-colored parasol as she strolled, and the soft light gave her pale complexion a beautiful glow. "I check in on the events now and again, but I seem to be too busy to become as addicted as so many are these days."

"Turins do seem to be ubiquitous."

Ada paused in the shade of a giant elm with broad, low branches. She lowered and closed the parasol. "Have you tried it?"

"Oh, yes. It was all the rage halfway between my Twenties. I spent some weeks enjoying the . . . excess of it all." He could not completely strain out the tone of distaste at the memory. "Since then, no."

"Do you object to the violence, cousin?"

Daeman made a neutral gesture. "I object to its . . . vicariousness."

Ada laughed softly. "Precisely Harman's reason for never indulging. You two have something in common."

The thought of this was so unlikely that Daeman's only response was to flick away dead leaves on the ground with the point of his walking stick.

Ada looked up at the sun rather than calling up a time function on her palm. "They will be rousing themselves soon. 'One hour under the cloth equals eight hours of turgid experience.' "

"Ah," said Daeman, wondering if her use of the cliché had been in the form of a double entendre. Her expression, always pleasant but bordering on the mischievous, gave no clue. "This pour thing—will it last long?"

"It's scheduled to go most of the night."

Daeman blinked in surprise. "Surely we're not bivouacking down at the river or wherever this event is to be staged?" He wondered if sleeping out under the stars and rings would improve his chances of spending the night with this young woman.

"There will be provisions for those who want to stay all night at the pour site," said Ada. "Hannah promises that this will be quite spectacular. But most of us will come back up to the manor sometime after midnight."

"Will there be wine and other drinks at the . . . ah . . . pour?" asked Daeman.

"Most assuredly."

It was Daeman's turn to smile. Let the others stay for this spectacle, he would keep pouring Ada drinks through the evening, follow up on her "turgid" line of suggestive conversation, accompany her home (with luck and proper planning, just the two of them in a small carriole), pour the full force of his not-inconsiderable powers of attention upon her—and, with only an added bit of additional luck, this night he would not have to dream of women.

By late afternoon, the twenty or so guests at the manor—some babbling about the day's turin-experienced events, going on and on about Menelaus being shot by a poisoned arrow or somesuch nonsense—were gathered together by helpful servitors and everyone departed for the "pour site" in a caravan of droshkies and carrioles. Voynix pulled the vehicles while other voynix trotted alongside as security, although—Daeman thought—if there were no tyrannosauruses in the woods, he failed to see a reason for security.

He had maneuvered to be in the lead carriole with their hostess, and Ada pointed out interesting trees, glens, and streams as they rumbled and hummed two or more miles down the dirt path toward the river. Daeman took up more room on their side of the red leather bench than he had to even given his pleasant plumpness, and was rewarded with the feel of Ada's thigh alongside his for the duration of the voyage.

Their destination, he saw as they came out on the limestone ridge above the river valley, was not the river, exactly, but a tributary to the main channel, a literal backwater some hundred yards across, where erosion and flooding had created a wide shelf of sand—a sort of beach—

on which a tall, rickety structure of logs, branches, ladders, troughs, ramps, and stairways had been constructed. It looked like a crude gallows to Daeman, although he had never seen an actual gallows, of course. Torches rose from the shallow tributary and the rickety contraption itself stood half on sand and half over water. A hundred yards out, blocking this channel from the actual river was a narrow island—overgrown with cycads and horsehair ferns—from which birds and small flying reptiles exploded into flight with a maximum of cries and frenzied flapping. Daeman wondered idly if there were butterflies on the isle.

On a grassy area above the beach, colorful silken tents, lounge chairs, and long tables of food had been set up. Servitors floated to and fro, sometimes bobbing above the heads of the arriving guests.

Walking behind Ada from the carriole, Daeman recognized some of the workers on the strange scaffolding: Hannah at the apex, tying on more structural elements, a red bandana tied around her head; the demented man, Harman, shirtless, sweating, showing bizarrely tanned skin, was stoking a contained fire twenty feet below Hannah; other young people, presumably friends of Hannah's and Ada's, shuttled back and forth up the wooden ramps and ladders, carrying heavy loads of sand and extra branches for construction and round stones. A raging fire burned in the clay core of the structure and sparks rose into the early evening sky. All of the workers' actions appeared purposeful, even though Daeman could see no possible purpose to the tall stack of sticks and troughs and clay and sand and flame.

A servitor floated by and offered him a drink. Daeman accepted and went off in search of a lounge chair in the shade.

"This is the cupola," Hannah explained to the assembled guests later that evening. "We've been working on it for about a week, floating materials down the river in canoes. Cutting and bending branches to fit."

It was after a fine dinner. Sunlight still illuminated the high hills on the near side of the river, but the valley itself was in the shadows and both rings were glowing bright in the darkening sky. Sparks leaped and floated toward the rings and the puff of bellows and roar of furnace were very loud. Daeman took another drink, his eight or tenth of the evening, and lifted a second one for Ada, who shook her head and turned her attention back to Hannah.

"We've woven wood into a basket shape and coated the center of the furnace—the well—with refractory clay. We made this by shovel, mixing dry sand, bentonite, and some water. Then we rolled the claylike goop into balls, wrapped them in wet ferns and leaves to keep them from drying out, and lined the furnace well with the stuff. That's what keeps the whole wooden cupola structure from catching fire."

Daeman had no idea what the woman was going on about. Why build a big, gawky structure of wood and then set a fire at its center if you don't want the thing to burn down? This place was an asylum.

"Mostly," continued Hannah, "we've spent the last few days feeding the fire while putting out all the little fires the cupola furnace started. That's why we built this thing near the river."

"Wonderful," muttered Daeman and went in search of another drink while Hannah and her friends—even the insufferable Harman—droned on, using nonsensical terms such as "coke bed," "wind belt," "tuyere" (which Hannah was explaining meant some little air entrance on their clay-lined furnace, near which the young woman named Emme kept working the wheezing bellows) and "melting zone" and "molding sand" and "taphole" and "slag hole." It all sounded barbarous and vaguely obscene to Daeman.

"And now it's time to see if it works," announced Hannah, her voice revealing both exhaustion and exaltation.

Suddenly the guests had to stand back on the sandy river's edge, Daeman retreating to the grassy sward near the tables, as all the young people—and that damnable Harman—leaped into a frenzy of action. Sparks flew higher. Hannah ran to the top of the so-called cupola while Harman peered into the clay-furnace-contained flames below and shouted for this and that. Emme worked the bellows until she fell over, and was relieved by the thin man named Loes. Daeman half listened to Ada breathlessly explaining even more details to huddled friends. He caught phrases like "blast pipe" and "blast gate" and "chilled slag" (even though the flames were raging hotter and higher than every before) and "blast pressure." Daeman moved another fifteen or twenty feet further back.

"Tapping temp of twenty-three hundred degrees!" Harman shouted up to Hannah. The thin woman wiped sweat from her brow, made some adjustment to the cupola far above, and nodded. Daeman stirred his drink and wondered how long it would be before he could get Ada alone in a carriole on the way back to Ardis Hall.

Suddenly there was a commotion that made Daeman look up from his drink, sure that he would see the whole structure in flames, Hannah and Harman burning like straw figures. Not quite. While Hannah *was* using a blanket to swat out flames on the ladder below the top of the cupola—waving away helpful servitors and even a voynix that had come in close to protect the humans from harm—Harman and two others had finished poking inside the fiery furnace and had just opened a "taphole," allowing what looked to be yellow lava to flow down wooden troughs to the beach.

Some of the guests surged forward, but Hannah's shouts and the radiating heat from the flow of liquid metal forced them back.

The crudely carved and lined troughs smoked but did not burst into flame as the yellow-red metal flowed sluggishly from the cupola structure, past the ladders, spilling the last foot or two into a cross-shaped mold set in the sand.

Hannah rushed down a ladder and helped Harman seal off the taphole. They both peered through a peephole into the furnace, did something to— Ada was explaining to a guest—the "slag hole" (different from the taphole, Daeman vaguely noticed) and then the young woman and the older man—soon to be a dead older man, Daeman thought cruelly—leaped from the cupola structure onto the sand and rushed over to look at the mold.

More guests surged down the beach. Daeman wandered down, setting his drink on a passing servitor's tray.

The air was very cool down here by the river, but the heat from the red-glowing mold in the sand struck Daeman's face like a fiery fist.

The molten stuff was congealing into a red and gray cross-shaped mass.

"What is it?" Daeman asked loudly. "Some sort of religious symbol?"

"No," said Hannah. She took off her bandana and wiped her sweaty, soot-streaked face. She was smiling like a crazy person. "It's the first bronze cast in . . . what, Harman? A thousand years?"

"Probably three times that long," the older man said quietly.

The guests muttered and applauded.

Daeman laughed. "What good is it?" he asked.

Harman looked up at him. "Of what good is a newborn baby?" said the sweating, bare-chested man.

"Precisely my point," said Daeman. "Loud, demanding, smelly . . . useless."

The others ignored him as Ada gave Hannah, Harman, and the other workers hugs, just as if they'd actually done something of worth. Guests milled. Harman and Hannah climbed ladders and started fussing, peering through peepholes and poking into the furnace with metal bars as if there was to be more of this lava production. Evidently, thought Daeman, this pyrotechnics show was to continue into the night.

Suddenly needing to urinate, Daeman wandered up past the tables, considered the tent-covered rest room pavilion, and decided—in the spirit of all this pagan nonsense—to respond to this call of nature al fresco. He climbed above the grassy shelf toward the dark line of trees, following a monarch butterfly that had fluttered past him. There was nothing unusual at seeing a monarch, but it was late in the day and season for it to be out and flying. He walked past the last voynix and moved under the high branches of elms and cycads.

Somebody, possibly Ada, shouted something from the river's edge a hundred feet away, but Daeman had already unbuttoned his trousers and did not want to act the cad. Instead of turning back to respond, he moved another twenty feet or so into the concealing darkness of the forest. This would just take a minute.

"Ahhh," he said, still watching the butterfly's orange wings ten feet above him as the patter of his urine fell on a dark tree trunk.

The huge allosaurus, thirty feet long from snout to tail, pounded out of the darkness at twenty miles per hour, ducking under branches as it lunged.

Daeman had time to scream but chose to tuck himself back into his trousers rather than turn and run while thus exposed. For all his lechery, Daeman was a modest man. He raised his heavy wooden walking stick to fight off the beast.

The allosaurus took the cane and arm both, ripping the arm free at the shoulder. Daeman screamed again and pirouetted in a fountain of his own blood.

The allosaurus knocked him down and ripped his other arm off—tossing it into the air and catching it like a morsel—and then proceeded to hold Daeman's armless but still thrashing torso down with one massive clawed foot until ready to lower its terrible head again. Casually, almost playfully, the monster bit Daeman in half, swallowing his head and upper torso whole. Ribs and spinal column crunched and disappeared into the thing's maw. Then the allosaurus gobbled the man's legs and lower body, flinging pieces of flesh around like a dog with a rat.

The fax buzz started then, even as two voynix rushed up and killed the dinosaur.

"Oh, my God," cried Ada, stopping at the edge of the trees as the voynix finished their bloody rendering.

"What a mess," said Harman. He waved the other guests back. "Didn't you warn him to stay inside the voynix perimeter down here? Didn't you tell him about the dinosaurs?"

"He asked about tyrannosauruses," Ada said, her hand still over her mouth. "I told him there weren't any around here."

"Well, that's true enough," said Harman.

Behind them, the crucible continued to roar and shoot sparks into the darkening sky.

Ilium and Olympos

Aphrodite has turned me into a spy, and I know the punishment we mortals have always dealt out to spies. I can only imagine what the gods will do to me. On second thought, I'd rather not.

This morning, the day after I became a secret agent for the Goddess of Love, Athena quantum teleports herself down from Olympos and morphs into a Trojan, the spearman Laodocus. Obeying Zeus's command that the warriors of Ilium should be made to break the current truce, she seeks out the archer Pandarus, son of Lycaon.

Using the cloaking Hades Helmet and private teleportation medallion that my Muse gave me, I QT after Athena, then morph into a Trojan captain named Echepolus, and follow the disguised goddess.

Why did I choose Echepolus? Why is this minor captain's name familiar to me? I realize then that Echepolus has only hours to live; that if Athena is successful in using Laodocus to break the peace, this Trojan—at least according to Homer—is going to get an Argive spear through his skull.

Well, Mr. Echepolus can have his body and identity back before that happens.

In Homer's *Iliad,* this breaking of the truce occurred just after Aphrodite had spirited Paris away from his one-on-one battle with Menelaus, but here in the reality of *this* Trojan War, that non-confrontation between Menelaus and Paris had happened years ago. This truce is a more mundane thing—some of King Priam's representatives meeting with some of the Achaeans' heralds, both sides working out some abtruse agreement about time off from the fighting for festivals or funerals or somesuch. If you ask me, one of the reasons this siege has dragged out for almost a decade is all this time off from the fighting; the Greeks and Trojans have as many religious celebrations as our Twenty-first Century Hindus had and as many secular holidays as an American postal worker. One wonders how they ever manage to kill each other amidst all this feasting and sacrificing to the gods and ten-day-funeral celebrations.

What fascinates me now, so soon after I vowed to rebel against the gods' will (only to find myself much more of a pawn to their will than ever before), is the question of how quickly and how sharply real events in this war can swerve from the details of Homer's tale. Disparities in the past—the sequence of the Gathering of the Armies, for instance, or the timing of Paris's aborted battle with Menelaus—have all been minor discrepancies, easily explained by Homer's need to include certain past events in the short span of the poem set in the tenth year of the war. But what if events *really* take a different course? What if I were to walk up to—say—Agamemnon this morning and stick this spear (poor doomed Echepolus' spear, to be sure, but still a working spear) through the king's heart? The gods can do many things, but they can't return dead mortals to life. (Or dead gods either, as oxymoronic as that sounds.)

Who are you, Hockenberry, to thwart Fate and defy the will of the gods? queries a craven, professorial little pissant voice that I listened to and followed most of my real life.

I am me, Thomas Hockenberry comes the reply from the contemporary me, as fragmented as he is, *and right now I'm fed up with these power-addled thugs who call themselves gods.*

Now, in my role as spy rather than scholic, I stand close enough to hear the dialogue between Athena—morphed as Laodocus—and that buffoon (but fine archer) Pandarus. Speaking as one Trojan warrior to another, Athena/Laodocus appeals to the idiot's vanity, tells him that Prince Paris will shower him with gifts if he kills Menelaus, and even compares him to the ultimate archer—Apollo—if he has the skill to bring off this shot.

Pandarus falls for the ruse hook, line, and sinker—"Athena fired the fool's heart within him" was the way one fine translator described this moment—and has some of his pals hide him from view with their shields while he prepares his long bow and chooses the perfect arrow for this assassination. For centuries, scholics—*Iliad* scholars—have argued the issue of whether or not the Greeks and Trojans used poison on their arrows. Most scholics, myself included, argued the negative—such behavior simply did not seem to meet these heroes' high standards of honor in battle. We were wrong. They sometimes do use poison. And a lethal, fast-acting poison it is. This explains why so many of the wounds listed in the *Iliad* were so quickly fatal.

Pandarus lets fly. It's a brilliant shot. I track the arrow as it flies hundreds of yards, arcing and then hurtling directly toward Agamemnon's redheaded brother. The shaft will skewer Menelaus as he stands at the forefront of his fighters watching the heralds jabbering away in no-man's-land. That is, it will skewer him if no Greek-friendly god intervenes.

One does. With my enhanced vision, I see Athena abandon Laodocus' body and QT to Menelaus' side. The goddess is playing a double game here—tricking the Trojans into breaking the truce and then rushing to make sure that one of her favorites, Menelaus, is not actually killed. Cloaked head to toe, invisible to friend and foe but visible to this scholic, she slaps the arrow aside the way a mother flicks a fly from her sleeping son. (I think I stole that imagery, but it's been so long since I actually *read* the *Iliad*, in translation or the original, that I can't be sure.)

Still, despite her protective and deflective slap, the arrow hits home. Menelaus shouts in pain and goes down, the arrow protruding from his midsection, just above the groin. Has Athena failed?

Confusion ensues. Priam's heralds flee back behind the Trojan lines and the Achaean negotiators scurry back behind the protection of Greek shields. Agamemnon, who has been using the truce time to inspect his troops lined up row upon row (perhaps the inspection is timed to show his leadership this first morning after Achilles' mutiny), arrives to find his brother writhing on the ground, captains and lieutenants huddled around him.

I aim a short baton. Although the baton looks like the kind of swagger stick a minor Trojan commander might carry, this is not Captain Echepolus' property; it is mine, standard issue for us scholics. The baton is actually a taser and a shotgun microphone, picking out and amplifying sound from as much as two miles away, feeding the pickup to the hearplugs I wear whenever I'm on the plains of Ilium.

Agamemnon is giving his dying brother one hell of a eulogy. I see him cradle Menelaus' head and shoulders in his arms and hear him go on about the terrrible vengeance he—Agamemnon—will wreak on the Trojans for the murder of noble Menelaus, after which he laments about how the Achaeans will—despite Agamemnon's bloody vengeance—lose heart, give up the war, and take their black ships home after Menelaus dies. After all, what's the use of rescuing Helen if her cuckolded husband is dead? Holding his moaning brother, Agamemnon plays the prophet—"But the plowlands here in Priam will feed your flesh to the worms and rot your bones, O My Brother, as you lie dead before the unbreached walls of Troy, your mission failed." Cheery stuff. Just the kind of thing a dying man wants to hear.

"Wait, wait, wait," grunts Menelaus through gritted teeth. "Don't bury me so fast, big brother. The arrowhead's not lodged in a mortal spot. See? It penetrated my bronze war-belt and got me in the love handle I've been meaning to lose, not in the balls or belly."

"Ahh, yes," says Agamemnon, frowning at the wound where the arrow has only lightly penetrated. He almost, not quite, sounds disappointed. The whole eulogy is moot now and it sounded as if he'd worked on it for a while.

"But the arrow *is* poisoned," gasps Menelaus as if trying to cheer his brother up. Menelaus's red hair is matted with sweat and grass, his golden helmet having rolled away when he fell.

Standing, dropping his brother's shoulders and head so quickly that Menelaus would have crashed back to the ground if his captains had not caught him, Agamemnon shouts for Talthybius, his herald, and orders the man to find Machaon, Asclepius' son, Agamemnon's own doctor and a damned good one, too, since Machaon is supposed to have learned his craft from Chiron, the friendly centaur.

Now it looks like any battlefield from any age—a fallen man screaming and cursing and crying as the pain begins to flow through the initial shock of injury, friends on one knee gathered around, helpless, useless, then the medic and his assistants arriving, giving orders, pulling the barbed bronze head out of ripping flesh, sucking out poison, packing clean dressings on the wound even while Menelaus continues to scream like the proverbial stuck pig.

Agamemnon leaves his brother to Machaon's ministrations and goes off to rouse his men to combat, although the Achaeans—even without Achilles in their ranks today—seem hung over and angry and surly and in little need of a rousing to get them to fight.

Within twenty minutes of Pandarus's ill-conceived arrow shot, the truce is over and the Greeks attack Trojan lines along a two-mile stretch of dust and blood.

It's time for me to get out of Echepolus' body before the poor son of a bitch catches a spear in the forehead.

I don't remember much of my real life on Earth. I don't remember if I was married, if I had children, where I lived—except for murky images of a book-lined study where I read my books and prepared my lectures—nor all that much about the university I taught at in Indiana, except images of stone and brick buildings on a hill with a wonderful view to the east. One of the odd things about being a scholic is that fragments of non-scholic-essential memories do return after months and years, which may be one of the reasons the gods don't allow us to live that long. I am the oldest exception.

But I remember classes and my students' faces, my lectures, some discussions around an oval table. I remember a fresh-faced young woman asking, "But why did the Trojan War go on so long?" I also remember being tempted to point out to her that she had been raised in an era of fast food and fast wars—McDonald's and the Gulf War, Arby's and the war on terrorism—but that in ancient days, the Greeks and their foes would no more think of hurrying a war than of rushing through a fine meal.

Instead of insulting my students' attention spans, I explained to the class how these heroes had welcomed battle—how one of their words for combat was *charme*, which came from the same root as *charo*—"rejoice." I read to them a scene in which two warriors facing one another were described as *charmei gethosunoi*—"rejoicing in battle." I explained the Greek concept of *aristeia*—warrior-to-warrior or small-group combat in which an individual can show his valor—and how important it was to these ancients and how the larger battle would often pause so that the soldiers on each side could witness such examples of *aristeia*.

"So like, you mean, like," stammered one fresh-faced female student, her brain running in place, her stammer illustrating that irritating speech and thought defect that spread like a virus among young Americans during the end of the Twentieth Century, "like the war would have, like, been over a lot sooner if they hadn't kept, like, stopping for this ariste-whatchamacallit?"

"Precisely," I had said with a sigh, looking at the old Hamilton clock on the wall in the hope of deliverance.

But now, after more than nine years watching *aristeia* in action, I can say in certainty that these one-on-one combats so beloved by both Trojans and Argives *are* one of the reasons for this prolonged, endless, slow-as-molasses siege. And like even the most sophisticated Middle American traveling too long in France, one of my urges now was to get back to fast food—or, in this case, fast war. A little bombing, a little airborne invasion, bim, bang, thank you ma'am, home to Penelope.

But not this day.

Echepolus is the first Trojan captain to die in the Achaean attack.

Perhaps it is because the man is still groggy and disoriented after my borrowing of his body, but as his group of Trojan fighters closes with a Greek group led by Nestor's son Antilochus, a good friend of Achilles, poor Echepolus is slow to raise his long spear, so Antilochus thrusts first.

The bronze spearpoint hits Echepolus' horsehair helmet right at the ridge and drives down through his skull, popping one eye out and driving the man's brains out between his teeth. Echepolus goes down, as Homer likes to say, like a toppled tower.

Now begins a dynamic I've seen all too often, but which never ceases to fascinate me. The Greeks and Trojans fight for reasons of honor first, it is true, but booty comes in a close second. These men are professional warriors; killing is their work and plunder is their pay. A large part of both honor and plunder is the elaborate, beautifully tooled armor—shield, breastplate, greaves, war belt—of their fallen foes. Capturing an enemy's gear is the heroic Greek equivalent of a Sioux warrior's counting coup on an opponent, and much more lucrative. At the very least, a captain's protective gear is made of precious bronze, and—for the more important officers—it is often hammered out of gold and decorated with jewels.

And thus the fight begins for dead Captain Echepolus' gear.

An Achaean commander named Elephenor rushes in, grabs Echepolus' ankles, and begins dragging the gory corpse back through the melee of spears and swords and crashing shields. I've seen Elephenor around the Achaean camp over the years, watched him fight in lesser skirmishes, and I have to say that the man's name suits him—he's huge, with gigantic shoulders, powerful arms, heavy thighs—not the sharpest knife in Agamemnon's drawer of fighters, but a big, strong, brave and useful brawler. Thus Elephenor, Chalcodon's son, thirty-eight years old this past June, commander of the Abantes and Lord of Euboea, drags Echepolus' corpse behind the screen of thrusting Achaean attackers and begins stripping the body.

Then Agenor—a Trojan fighter, son of Antenor, father of Echeclus (both of whom I've seen on the streets of Ilium)—slips between the battling Achaeans and catches sight of Elephenor's exposed ribs as the big man bends low beneath the protection of his shield to finish stripping Echepolus' corpse. Agenor leaps forward and stabs his spear into Elephenor's side, splintering ribs and pulping the big man's heart into a shapeless mass. Elephenor vomits blood and collapses. More Trojan fighters surge forward, beating off the Achaean attack, as Agenor rips his spear free and begins to strip Elephenor of *his* war belt and sheaves and chestplate. Other Trojans drag Echepolus' near-nude body back toward Trojan lines.

The fighting begins to swirl around these fallen men. The Achaean called Ajax—Big Ajax, the so-called Telemonian Ajax from Salamis, not to be confused with Little Ajax, who commands the Locrisians—hacks his way forward, sheaths his sword, and uses his spear to cut down a very young Trojan named Simoisius, who has come forward to cover Agenor's retreat.

Just a week earlier, in the walled safety of Ilium's quiet parks, while morphed as the Trojan Sthenelus, I had drunk wine and swapped ribald stories with Simoisius. The sixteen-year-old boy—never wed, never even bedded by a woman—had told me about how his father, Anthemion, had named him after the Simois River, which runs right next to their modest home a mile from the walls of the city. Simoisius had not yet turned six when the black ships of the Achaeans had first appeared on the horizon and, until a few weeks ago, his father had refused to allow the sensitive boy to join the army outside Ilium's walls. Simoisius admitted to me that he was terrified of dying—not so much of death itself, he said, but of dying before he ever touched a woman's breast or felt what it was like to be in love.

Now Big Ajax lets out a cry and thrusts his spear forward—batting aside Simoisius' shield and striking the boy's chest above the right nipple, shattering his shoulder and running the bronze point through and out until it protrudes a foot beyond the boy's mangled back. Simoisius staggers to his knees and stares in astonishment—first at Ajax and then at the spear protruding from his chest. Big Ajax sets his sandaled foot on Simoisius' face and rips the spear free, allowing the boy's body to fall facefirst into the blood-dampened dust. Big Ajax pounds his chestplate and roars for his men to follow him.

A Trojan named Antiphus, standing not more than twenty-five feet away, hurls his spear at Big Ajax. The spear misses its target but strikes an Achaean named Leucus in the groin even as Leucus is busy helping Odysseus haul off the corpse of another Trojan captain. The spear passes through Leucus' groin and comes out his anus, the tip trailing curls of gray and red colon and intestine. Leucus falls on the Trojan captain's corpse but lives another terrible moment, writhing, grasping the spear and trying to pull it from his groin but only succeeding in spilling more of his bowels into his own lap. All the time he is tugging at the spear, Leucus is also screaming and tugging at his friend Odysseus' bloody arm.

Leucus dies at last, his eyes glazing over, one hand still tight around Antiphus' spear and the other still clinging to Odysseus' wrist. Odysseus breaks the dead man's grip and whirls around, dark eyes blazing under the rim of his bronze helmet, seeking out a target—any target. Odysseus hurls his spear and rushes after it. More Achaeans follow him into the gap he creates in the Trojan lines.

Odysseus' first spearshot kills Democoon, a bastard son of Ilium's King Priam. I was in the city nine years ago on the morning Democoon arrived to help defend Priam's Ilium. It was common knowledge that Priam had put the young man in charge of his famed racing stables in Abydos, a city northeast of Troy on the southern shore of the Hellespont, to keep him out of sight of Priam's wife and legitimate sons. The horses stabled in Abydos were the fastest and finest in the world, and it was said that Democoon considered it an honor to be named stablemaster at so young an age. Now that young Trojan is in the act of turning his head toward Odysseus' maddened war cry when the bronze spearpoint hits him in his left temple and passes through and out his right temple, knocking him off his feet and pinning his shattered skull to the side of an overturned chariot. Democoon literally never knew what hit him.

The Trojans are retreating all along the line now, falling back before the fury of Odysseus and Big Ajax, trying to haul their noble dead when possible, abandoning them when not.

Hector, Ilium's greatest fighter and most honest man, leaps off his command chariot and wades into the retreat, trying to bring his spear and sword to bear, urging the Trojans to hold fast, but the Achaean attack is too strong at this salient, and even Hector gives ground, all the while urging the men to discipline. The Trojans fight and hack and cast spears as they retreat.

Morphed as a minor Trojan spearman, I fall back faster than most, staying out of spear range, not afraid to be a coward. Earlier, I had cloaked myself from mortal view and started to move forward to where I could see Athena behind Achaean lines—soon joined by Hera, both goddesses invisible to men—but the fighting had erupted too quickly and escalated too fiercely, so I'd left the front lines after Echepolus fell, trusting to my enhanced vision and shotgun microphone to keep me in touch with events.

Suddenly everything freezes. The air thickens. Spears stop in midair, blood ceases to flow. Men seconds away from dying get a reprieve they will never know about as all sound ceases, all motion stops.

The gods are playing games with time again.

Apollo arrives first, his chariot QTing into existence not far from Hector. Then the war god Ares flicks into sight, talks to Athena and Hera an angry minute, and uses his own chariot to fly over the battle lines, landing near Apollo. Aphrodite joins them, glancing my way—to where I pretend to be frozen in place like the other mortals—for only an instant before smiling and talking to her two Trojan-loving allies, Ares and

Apollo. I watch her out of the corner of my eye as the goddess stands there, pointing and gesturing toward the battlefield like a big-breasted George Patton.

The gods are here to fight.

Apollo raises his hand, sound crashes in, time begins again like a tsunami of dust and motion, and the killing resumes in earnest.

10

Paris Crater

Ada, Harman, and Hannah waited the two days usually observed as a minimum decent interval after a firmary visit, and then faxed to Paris Crater to find Daeman. It was late and dark and chilly there and—they discovered as soon they stepped out from under the Guarded Lion fax-node roof—raining. Harman found them a covered barouche and a voynix pulled them northwest along a dried riverbed filled with white skulls, past miles of tumbledown buildings.

"I've never been to Paris Crater," said Hannah. The young woman, just two months shy of her First Twenty, did not like big cities. PC was one of the most populated faxnodes on Earth, with some 25,000 semi-permanent residents.

"It's one reason I faxed us to the Guarded Lion node rather than a port called Invalid Hotel that's closer to where Daeman lives on the rim," said Ada. "Everything about this town is ancient. It's worth taking one's time to look around."

Hannah nodded, but doubtfully. The row upon row of stone and steel buildings, most sheathed in shiny everplas, looked empty and dark and cheaply slick in the rain. Servitors and glow globes floated purposefully here and there down the dark streets, voynix stood silent and still on corners, but very few humans were visible. Then again, as Harman pointed out, it was after 10 P.M. Even a city as cosmopolitan as Paris Crater had to sleep.

"*That's* interesting," said Hannah, pointing to the structure rising a thousand feet above the city.

Harman nodded. "It's early Lost Age. Some say it's as old as Paris Crater, maybe even as old as the city that was here before the crater. It's a symbol of the city and the people who built it long ago."

"Interesting," Hannah said again. A thousand feet tall, the rough representation of a naked woman appeared to be made of some clear polymer. The head was sometimes obstructed by low clouds, then briefly visible, and Hannah could see that the face was featureless except for a gaping grin between red lips. Black coiled springs fifty feet long spiraled like curls from the spherical head. The legs were spread wide, feet hidden from view behind the dark buildings to the west, but the thighs bunched as thick and wide as Ardis Hall. The breasts were huge, globular, absurd, alternately filling and emptying with broiling, photoluminescent red liquid, levels now rising, now filling, now waterfalling down the insides of the belly and legs, then sometimes rising again all the way to the raised arms and smiling face. The light from the glowing belly and breasts and massive buttocks painted the tops of taller structures around the crater a ruby red.

"What's it called?" she asked.

"*La putain enormé,*" said Ada.

"What does it mean?"

"No one knows," said Harman. He instructed the voynix to turn left onto a rickety bridge and they clip-clopped onto what had once been an island when water flowed in the river of dry skulls, toward the ruins of a building that once must have been quite large. Now a low dome glowing with a purple light sat inside the tumbled walls like a strange egg in a nest of scattered stones.

"Wait here," Harman told the voynix and led the two women through the overgrown ruins and into the translucent dome.

A slab of white stone about four feet high sat in the center of the space. There were gutters at the base of the slab and drains in the stone floor. Behind and above the slab rose a crude statue of a naked man carved from the same white rock. The man held a bow and a notched arrow.

"This is marble," said Hannah, running her hand over the surface of the block. She knew stone. "What is this place?"

"A temple to Apollo," said Harman.

"I've heard of these new temples," said Ada, "but I've never seen one before. I thought it was rare—a few altars in the forest done as a gag, that sort of thing."

"There are temples like this all over Paris Crater and in the other big cities," said Harman. "Temples to Athena, Zeus, Ares . . . all the gods in the turin tale."

"The drains and gutters . . ." began Hannah.

"To drain the blood of the animals sacrificed," said Harman. "Mostly sheep and cattle."

Hannah stepped back from the slab and crossed her arms over her chest. "The people wouldn't . . . kill the animals?"

"No," said Harman. "They have the voynix do that. So far."

Ada stood at the open doorway. Rain dripped down the glowing portal, turning it into a purple-tinted waterfall. "What was this place . . . before? The ruins?"

"I'm pretty sure it was a Lost Age temple," said Harman.

"To Apollo?" Hannah's body was rigid, her arms folded tight against her body.

"I don't think so. In the rubble here are bits and pieces of statuary—not gods, not people, not voynix . . . not quite . . . demons, I think. An old word for them was 'gargoyle'—but I'm not sure what they signify."

"Let's get out of here," said Ada.

Across the river of skulls and west again toward the crater, the broad boulevards ended where the Lost Age buildings became crowned with newer, taller structures—some very new, probably less than a thousand years old—a rising latticework of black buckylace and rain-glistening bamboo-three. Hannah called up a function to find Daeman, and the rectangle of light floating above her left palm glowed now amber, now red, then green again as they took stairways and lifts from street level to mezzanine level, from mezzanine level to the hanging esplanade fifteen stories above the old rooftops, then up from esplanade level to the residential stacks. Hannah paused at the esplanade rail to look down, mesmerized as most first-time viewers are as they stare into the unblinking red eye miles and miles below in the bottomless black circle of the crater; Ada had to pull her away with a hand on Hannah's elbow and lead her to the next lift and stairway.

Surprisingly, it was a person, not a servitor, who answered the door at Daeman's domi. Ada introduced her group, and the woman, who looked to be in her mid-forties as all three and four Twenties did, identified herself as Marina, Daeman's mother. She led the way down warmly painted hallways and up interior staircases and through common rooms to the private areas on the crater-side of the domi complex.

"The servitor brought the message you were coming, of course," said Marina, pausing outside a beautifully carved mahogany door, "but I haven't told Daeman. He is still . . . perturbed . . . by the accident."

Harman said, "But he doesn't remember it?"

"Oh, no, of course not," said Marina. She was an attractive woman and Ada could see the resemblance to her son in her red hair and pleasantly stocky build. "But you know what they say about such things . . . the cells remember."

But they're not the same cells, thought Ada. She said nothing.

"Will it upset Daeman to see us?" asked Hannah. To Ada's ear, the young woman sounded more curious than concerned.

Marina made a graceful shrugging motion with her hand, as if to say "We shall see." She knocked on the door and opened it when Daeman's muffled voice bid them enter.

The room was large and draped with richly colored fabrics, floating silk tapestries, and lace curtains around Daeman's sleeping area, but the far wall was all glass opening onto a private porch. Lamps in the large room were set low, but the brightly lighted city's edge beyond the balcony curved away on both sides, and more constellations of lanterns, glow globes, and soft electric lights were visible half a mile away across the dark crater. Daeman was sitting in a nesting chair by the rain-streaked window, staring out as if pondering the lights. He blinked at the sight of Ada, Harman, and Hannah, but then waved them over to the circle of soft furniture. Marina excused herself and closed the door behind her as the three took their seats. The glass doors had been opened and the cool air coming through the screens smelled of rain and wet bamboo.

"We wanted to see you how you were doing," Ada said. "And I wanted to apologize in person for the accident . . . for not taking better care of my guest."

Daeman smiled and shrugged, but his hands were trembling slightly. He set them on his silk-robed knees. "All I remember is something large crashing through the trees—and the smell of carrion, I remember that—and then waking up in the firmary crèche-tank. The servitors here told me what happened, of course. It would be amusing if the idea weren't so . . . revolting."

Ada nodded, leaned closer, and took his hand. "I do apologize, Daeman *Uhr*. The allosauruses have come onto the estate only very rarely in recent decades and the voynix are always there to protect us . . . ."

Daeman frowned but did not remove his hand from hers. "Evidently they didn't do a very good job protecting me."

"That *is* strange," said Harman, crossing his legs and tapping the corrugated-paper arms of his chair. "Very strange. I can't remember the last time a voynix failed to protect a human in such a situation."

Daeman looked at the older man. "You're used to situations where recombinant animals eat people, Harman *Uhr*?"

"Not at all. I meant situations where human beings are in jeopardy."

"I apologize again," said Ada. "The security failure on the part of the voynix was inexplicable, but my own carelessness was inexcusable. I'm sorry that your weekend at Ardis Hall was ruined and that your sense of harmony was perturbed."

"Perturbed, yes . . . perhaps an inadequate word to describe being devoured by a six-ton carnivore," said Daeman, but he smiled slightly and bowed his head even more slightly to acknowledge his acceptance of the apology.

Harman leaned closed and clasped his hands, bobbing them up and down for emphasis as he spoke. "We had an unfinished item for discussion, Daeman *Uhr* . . ."

"The spaceship." Now Daeman's tone of irony had dripped into sarcasm.

Harman was not deterred. His clasped hands rose and fell with the syllables. "Yes. But not just a spaceship . . . that's the ultimate goal, of course . . . but any form of flying machine. Jinker. Sonie. Ultralight. Anything to allow us to explore between faxports . . ."

Daeman sat back, away from Harman's intensity, and folded his arms. "Why do you persist with this? Why do you bother me about this?"

Ada touched his arm. "Daeman, Hannah and I had both heard, from different people, that at a recent party in Ulanbat—about a month ago, I believe—you told some acquaintances of ours there that you'd once met someone who mentioned seeing a spaceship . . . and someone who spoke of flying between nodes . . ."

Daeman managed to look both blank and irritated for a moment, but then he laughed and shook his head. "The witch," he said.

"Witch?" said Hannah.

Daeman opened his hands in an echo of his mother's graceful shrugging gesture. "We called her that. I forget her real name. A crazy woman. Obviously in her last Twenty . . ." He shot a glance toward Harman. "People begin losing touch with reality in their later years."

Harman smiled and ignored the gibe. "You don't remember this woman's name?"

Daeman gestured again, less gracefully this time. "No."

"Where did you meet her?" asked Ada.

"The last Burning Man. A year and a half ago. I forget where it was held . . . somewhere cold. I just followed friends from Chom when they faxed there. Lost Age ceremonies never interested me very much, but there were many fascinating young women at this gathering."

"I was there!" Hannah said, her eyes bright. "About ten thousand people came."

Harman pulled a much-folded sheet of paper from a tunic pocket and began spreading it on the padded ottoman between them. "Do you remember which node?"

Hannah shook her head. "It was one of the half-forgotten nodes. One of the empty ones. The organizers sent the node code around the day before the ceremony began. No one lived there, I think. It was a rocky valley surrounded by snow. I remember that it was light all day, all night, for the five days of Burning Man. And cold. The servitors had set up a Planck field over the whole valley and heaters here and there in the valley itself, so it wasn't uncomfortable, but no one was allowed beyond the edges of the valley."

Harman looked at his faded and folded sheet of microvellum. The page was covered with squiggly lines, dots, and arcane runes like those found in books. He stabbed a finger down on a dot near the bottom. "Here. In what used to be Antarctica. A node called 'The Dry Valley.' "

Daeman looked at him blankly.

"This is a map I've been working on for fifty years," said Harman. "A two-dimensional representation of the Earth with all the known fax-nodes mapped on it, along with their codes. Antarctica was a Lost Age name for one of the seven continents. I have seven Antarctic faxnodes recorded, but only one of them—this dry valley that I've heard of but never visited—is free of snow and ice."

This obviously did nothing to enlighten Daeman. Even Ada and Hannah looked confused.

"It doesn't matter," said Harman. "But if the sun was out all day and all night, this dry valley is the probable faxport. During the polar summers, there are days when the sun doesn't set there."

"The sun doesn't set in June in Chom," Daeman said, obviously bored. "Is that near your dry valley?"

"No." Harman pointed to a dot near the top of the map. "I'm pretty sure that Chom is on this large peninsula up here, above the arctic circle. Near the north pole, not the south."

"North pole?" said Ada.

Daeman looked at the two women. "And I thought the witch at Burning Man was crazy."

"Do you remember anything else this woman, this witch, said?" asked Harman, obviously too excited to be insulted.

Daeman shook his head. He looked tired. "Just babble. We'd been drinking a lot. It was the night of the burning and we'd been awake for days and nights in that damned daylight—catching a few hours of nap in one of the big orange tents. It was the last night and there are usually orgies on the last night and I thought that perhaps she . . . but she was too old for my tastes."

"But she talked about a spaceship?" Harman was visibly trying to be patient.

Daeman shrugged again. "Someone there . . . a young man, about Hannah's age . . . was bemoaning the fact that we didn't have sonies to fly around in since the final fax, and this . . . witch . . . who had been very quiet but who was obviously also very drunk . . . said we did, that there were jinkers and sonies if you knew where to look for them. She said she used them all the time."

"And the spaceship?" prompted Harman.

"She said she'd seen one, is all," said Daeman, rubbing his temples as if they hurt. "Near a museum. I asked her what a museum was, but she didn't answer."

"Why did you call this older woman a witch?" asked Hannah.

"I didn't start it. Everyone called her that." Daeman sounded a bit defensive. "I think it's because she said she hadn't faxed in, but had walked, when it was obvious that she couldn't have . . . there were no other nodes or structures around the valley and the Planck field sealed it off."

"That's true," said Hannah. "That last Burning Man may have been in the most remote place I've ever faxed to. I'm sorry I didn't meet this woman there."

"I only remember her there two nights," said Daeman. "The first and the last. And she kept to herself except for this one crazy exchange."

"How did you know that she was old?" Ada asked softly.

"You mean other than her obvious insanity?"

"Yes."

Daeman sighed. "She *looked* old. As if she had been to the firmary too many times . . ." He paused then and frowned, obviously thinking about his own recent visit there. "She looked older than anyone I've ever seen. I think she actually had those grooves on her face."

"Wrinkles?" said Hannah. The girl sounded envious.

"But you don't remember her name?" said Harman.

Daeman shook his head. "Someone by the fire called her by name that night but I can't quite . . . I'd been drinking too, you know, and not sleeping."

Harman glanced at Ada, took a breath, and said, "Could it have been Savi?"

Daeman's head came up quickly. "Yes. I think it was. Savi . . . yes, that sounds right. Unusual." He saw Harman and Ada exchange meaningful glances again and said, "What? Is this significant? Do you two know her?"

"The Wandering Jew," said Ada. "Have you heard that legend?"

Daeman smiled tiredly. "About the woman who somehow missed the final fax fourteen hundred years ago and who's been condemned to wander the earth ever since? Of course. But I didn't know the woman in the legend had a name."

"Savi," said Harman. "Savi's her name."

Marina came in with two servitors carrying mugs of mulled wine and a tray of cheese and breads. The uncomfortable silence was broken by small talk while they ate and sipped.

"We'll fax there tonight," Harman said to Hannah and Ada. "To the dry valley. There might be some clue left."

Hannah held her steaming mug in both hands. "I don't see how. That Burning Man was, as Daeman said, more than eighteen months ago."

"When's the next one?" asked Ada. She never went to such dementia-era ceremonies.

It was Harman who answered. "One never knows. The Burning Man Cabal sets the time and notifies people only days before the event. Sometimes they're a few months apart. Sometimes a dozen years. The one in the dry valley was the last one. If you've been to any of the previous three, you're invited. I missed it because I was hiking in the Mediterranean Basin."

"I want to go with you to find this woman," said Daeman.

The others, including his mother, looked at him with surprise. "Do you feel up to it?" asked Ada.

He ignored the question and said, "You'll need me to identify the woman if you find her. This . . . Savi."

"All right," said Harman. "We appreciate your help."

"But we'll fax out in the morning," said Daeman. "Not tonight. I'm tired."

"Of course," said Ada. She looked at Hannah and Harman. "Shall we fax back to Ardis?"

"Nonsense," said Marina. "You'll be our guests tonight. We have comfortable guest domis on the upper level." She caught Ada's subtle glance in Daeman's direction. "My son has been very tired since the . . . accident. He may sleep ten hours or more. If you stay as our guests, you'll be ready to leave together after he wakes. After breakfast."

"Of course," Ada said again. There was a seven-hour difference between Paris Crater and Ardis—it was not yet dinnertime back at Ardis Hall—but like all fax travelers, they were used to adapting to local times.

"We'll show you to your rooms," said Marina, leading the way across the room with her twin servitors floating beside her.

The "rooms" were actually small domis, elaborate suites of their own, one flight up from Marina and Daeman's place and reached by a broad spiral staircase. Hannah expressed approval of her space but then went out to explore Paris Crater on her own. Harman said his good nights and disappeared into his domi. Ada locked the door behind her, inspected the interesting tapestries, enjoyed the view of the crater from the balcony—the rain had stopped and the moon and rings were visible between scattering clouds—and then went in and ordered a light dinner from the servitors. Afterward, she drew a bath and luxuriated in the hot, perfumed water for half an hour or more, feeling the ache of tension leave her muscles.

She had met Harman only twelve days earlier, but it seemed much longer ago. The man and his interests fascinated her. Ada had gone to a summer solstice party at a friend's estate near the ruins of Singapore, not because she liked parties—she tended to avoid both faxing and parties when she could help it, traveling almost solely to old friends' homes for small gatherings—but because her younger friend Hannah was going to be there and had urged her to attend. The solstice party had been fun, in its way, and many of the people interesting, since her friend there had just celebrated her fourth Twenty—Ada had always enjoyed the company of people older than herself—but then she had met Harman, coming across him as he was poking through the estate's library. The man was quiet, reticent even, but Ada had drawn him out, using some of the tactics her smarter friends had used on her to get her to talk more.

Ada did not know what to think about Harman's trick of learning how to read without a function—he had not confessed the ability until another meeting at another friend's house just six days before the gathering at Ardis Hall—but the more Ada thought about it, the more amazed she was. Ada had always considered herself to be well educated—she knew all the usual folk songs and legends, she had memorized the Eleven Families and all their members, she knew many of the faxnodes by heart—but Harman's breadth of both knowledge and curiosity left her breathless.

The map he had laid out in front of Daeman—so underappreciated even by curious, adventurous Hannah—continued to astound Ada. She had never even run across the concept of "map" before Harman had shown her the diagrams less than a week earlier. It was Harman who had explained to her that the world was a sphere. How many of Ada's friends knew that? How many of them had ever wondered about the *shape* of the world on which they lived? Of what use was that arcane bit of knowledge? The "world" was your home and the fax network you used to see your friends and their homes. Who ever thought about the shape of the physical structure that lay beneath and beside that faxnet? And why would they?

Ada knew even from that first weekend around Harman that the man's interest in the long-departed post-humans bordered on obsession. *No*, amended Ada, lying in the warm bathwater and moving bubbles up her breasts to her throat with her long, pale fingers, *it is an obsession with Harman. He can't stop thinking about the post-humans—where they are, why they left. To what purpose?*

Ada did not know the answer, of course, but she had come to share in Harman's passionate curiosity, approaching it as a game, an adventure. And he kept asking questions that would have made any of Ada's other friends simply laugh—*Why are there just a million of us humans? Why was that number chosen by the posts? Why never one more, one less? And why a hundred years assigned to each of us? Why do they save us even from our own folly so we can live a hundred years?*

The questions were so simple and so profound that they were embarrassing—it was like hearing an adult ask why we have belly buttons.

But Ada had joined in the quest—for a flying machine, perhaps a spaceship to fly up to the rings and talk to the post-humans in person, now for this final fax-era legend of the Wandering Jew—and every day that passed brought more excitement.

Like Daeman being eaten by an allosaurus.

Ada blushed, seeing her pale skin redden down to the line of water and bubbles. That had been terribly embarrassing. None of the other guests could ever remember anything similar happening. Why hadn't the voynix offered better protection?

What exactly are *the voynix?* Harman had asked her twelve days earlier in the treehouse complex near Singapore. *Where do they come from? Did the Lost Age humans build them? Are they a produce of the rubicon dementia? Did the posts create them? Or are they alien to this world and time and here for their own purposes?*

Ada remembered her uneasy laughter that evening as they sat on the vined terrace, champagne in hand, when he had asked such an absurd question in such serious tones. But she had not been able to answer it then—nor had her friends in the intervening days, although their laughter was more nervous even than her own had been—and now Ada, after a lifetime of seeing voynix every day, looked at them with a curiosity bordering on alarm. Hannah had begun to react the same way.

What are *you?* she had wondered just that evening as they had stepped out of their barouche in Paris Crater and left the voynix stand-ing there, apparently eyeless, its rusted carapace and leathery hood wet from the rain, its killing blades retracted but manipulator pads extended and curled, still holding the stays of their carriage.

Ada stepped out of the water, dried herself, slipped into a thin robe, and told the servitors to leave her. They exited via one of their osmotic wall membranes. Ada went out onto the balcony.

Harman's room and balcony adjoined hers on the right, but privacy on the porches was assured by a tightly latticed bamboo-fiber screen that extended three feet out beyond the porch railing. Ada walked to the par-tition, stood at her rail a moment—looking down at the red-eyed crater below—lifted her eyes to the clearing sky with its stars and moving rings, and then she flung her leg over the railing, feeling the smooth, wet bam-boo against the flesh of her inner thigh an instant before she stepped out, barefoot, feeling her way along the thin rim of the partition.

For a second she was connected to the porch only by the pressure of her toes and fingertips, feeling blindly around the partition on the other side to find the matching narrow ledge, feeling gravity pull her back into emptiness. *What would it feel like, to fall so far toward burning magma, to know that I would be dead after a few terrible and totally free minutes of falling?* She knew she would never know. If she let go now, if her bare toes and fingers slipped now, she would never remember the next seconds and minutes after she awoke in the firmary tanks. The post-humans did not grant humans memories of their own death.

Ada pressed her breasts against the edge of the partition, fought to find balance, and swung her left leg around, her bare foot finding the narrow bamboo seam running back to Harman's porch. She did not dare look up to see if Harman was out on his balcony or at the glass door; all her attention was focused keeping her toes from slipping, her fingers from sliding off the wet and slippery bamboo-three.

She reached the porch and stepped onto the edge of it, clinging to the railing so tightly that her arms were shaking. Feeling her strength ebbing in the post-adrenaline surge of weakness, she quickly swung her left leg up and over, feeling the robe fall open, scratching the underside of her leg on a seam in the railing.

Harman was sitting cross-legged on a white-cushioned chaise longue, watching her. His balcony was lighted by a single glass-shielded candle.

"You might have helped," she whispered, not knowing why she said it or why she was whispering. She saw that Harman was also wearing nothing but a thin silk guest robe, only loosely sashed.

He smiled and shook his head. "You were doing fine. But why not just come around and knock?"

Ada took a deep breath and, as in answer, loosened the belt of her robe and let it open. The air moving in from above the crater was cool, but with currents of warmer air embedded in the breeze as it caressed her lower belly.

Harman rose, crossed to her, looked her in the eyes, and closed her robe, tying it without pressing his fingers against her. "I am honored," he said, also whispering now. "But not yet, Ada. Not yet." He took her hand and led her to the chaise longue.

When both of them were lying back on it side by side, Ada blinking in surprise and blushing in something like humiliation—whether at the rejection or at her own brazenness she was not sure—Harman reached behind the chair and come out with two cream-colored turin scarves. He folded each so that the embroidered microcircuitry was properly positioned.

"I don't . . ." began Ada.

"I know. But just this once. I think that something important's about to happen. Let us share this."

She lay back on the soft cushion and let Harman adjust the turin across her eyes. She felt him lie back next to her, his right hand lying loosely across her left hand.

The images and sounds and sensations flowed in.

11

The Plains of Ilium

The gods have come down to play. More precisely, they have come down to kill.

The battle has been raging for some time now with the god Apollo lashing on the Trojans, with Athena spurring on the Argives, and other gods lounging in the shade of a tree on the nearest hill, sometimes laughing, Iris and their other servants pouring them wine. I've watched the Thracian chief Pirous, a bold Trojan ally, kill gray-eyed Diores with a rock. Diores, co-commander of the Epean contingent of the Greeks, went down with only a broken ankle after battled-maddened Pirous threw the rock, but most of Diores' comrades fell back, Pirous hacked his way through the few who had stayed to guard their fallen captain, and—helpless now, his ankle smashed—poor Diores had to lie there while Pirous rushed in, speared the Thracian in the belly with his long casting spear, and pulled the man's bowels out, hooking them on the barbed spearpoint and twisting more out while while Diores screamed.

This was the flavor of the last half-hour's battle and it was a relief when Pallas Athena raised her hand, received nodded permission from other watching gods, and stopped time and motion in their tracks.

Now with my enhanced vision—enhanced by the contact lenses from the gods—I can see Athena across the milling no-man's-land of lances, preparing Tydeus' son, Diomedes, as a killing machine. I mean this almost literally. Like the gods themselves, and like me, Diomedes the man will now be part machine, his eyes and skin and very blood enhanced by nanotechnologies from some future age far beyond my short life span. In frozen time, Athena sets contact lenses similar to mine in the Achaean's eyes, allowing him to see both the gods and, somehow, to slow time a bit when he concentrates in the thick of the action, thus—to the unenhanced onlooker's view—increasing his reaction time three-fold. Homer had written that Athena had "set the man ablaze," and now I understand the metaphor; using the nanotechnology embedded in her palm and forearm, Athena is busy turning the neglible, latent electro-magnetic field around Diomedes' body into a serious forcefield. In the infrared, Diomedes' body and arms and shield and helmet suddenly blazed "with tireless fire like the star that flames at harvest." I realize now, watching Diomedes glow in the thick amber of god-frozen time, that Homer must have been referring to Sirius, the Dog Star, rising as the brightest star in the Greek (and Trojan) sky in late summer. It is in the eastern sky this night.

As I watch, she also injects billions of nanotech molecular machines into Diomedes' thigh. As always with such a nano-invasion, the human body deals with it as an infection and Diomedes' temperature goes up at least five degrees. I can watch the invading army of molecular machines moving up his thigh to his heart, from his heart to his lungs and arms and legs again, the heat making his body glow even more brightly in my infrared vision.

All around me, battlefield death is held in abeyance these stretched minutes. Ten yards to my left, I see a chariot frozen in a bubble of dust and human sweat and equine saliva. The Trojan charioteer—a short, even-tempered man named Phegeus, son of Troy's foremost priest to the god Hephaestus and brother to stout Idaeus; in my morphed disguises, I had broken bread and drunk wine with Idaeus a dozen times in the past few years—is petrified in the act of leaning over the front of his chariot, the chariot rim in his left hand, a long throwing spear in his right. Ideaus stands next to his brother, frozen in the act of whipping on the motion-halted horses while clutching the rigid reins in his other hand. The chariot has been halted in the act of bearing down on Diomedes, all the human players here unaware that the goddess Athena has stopped everything while she plays dolls with her chosen champion, dressing Diomedes in forcefields and thru-view contact lenses and nano-augmenters like some pre-teen girl playing with her Barbie. (I remember a small girl playing with Barbie dolls, perhaps a sister from my own childhood. I don't believe I had a daughter of my own. I'm not sure, of course, because the memories returning over the past months are like shards of glass with clouded reflections in them.)

I am close enough to the chariot to see the exultation of combat chis-eled into Phegeus' tanned face, and the fear frozen into his unblinking brown eyes. If Homer reported all this correctly, Phegeus will be dead in less than a minute.

I see other gods flocking to the battle site now like carrion crows to slaughter. There is Ares, god of war, flicking into solidity on my side of the battle lines, stepping close to the time-halted chariot holding Idaeus and his doomed brother. Ares palms open his own forcefield behind the frozen chariot carrying the two brothers toward death.

Why does Ares care what happens with these two? True, Ares is no lover of the Greeks—he has obviously learned to hate them in this war and kills them through his instruments or his own agency when he can—but why this obvious concern about Phegeus or his brother Idaeus? Is it just a countermove to Athena's strategy of enabling Diomedes? This chess game with real human beings falling and screaming and dying has grown old to me, an obscenity. But the strategy still intrigues me.

Then I remember that the god of war is half-god-brother to Hephaestus, the god of fire, also born to Zeus's wife, Hera. Phegeus' and Idaeus' father, Dares, has performed long and faithful service to the fire god within Troy's walls.

This idiot war is more complicated and senseless than the Vietnam War I half remember from my youth.

Suddenly Aphrodite, my new spymaster and boss, QT's into existence thirty yards to my left. She's also here to help the Trojans and to enjoy the slaughter. But—

In the last slowed seconds before real-time resumes, I remember that if the actual fighting goes the way of the old poem, Aphrodite herself will be injured by Diomedes in the coming hour. *Why would she come down to the fray knowing that a mortal will wound her?*

The answer is the same that I've been reminded of so forcibly over the past nine years, but now the fact of it hits me with the force and flash of a nuclear explosion—*The gods don't know what will happen next!* None but Zeus, it seems, is allowed to peer ahead at Fate's checklist.

All of us scholics are aware of this—we are not allowed, by Zeus's prohibition, to discuss future events with the gods and they are forbidden to ask us about the future books of the *Iliad*. Our task is only to confirm after the fact that Homer's *Iliad* has been truthful to the events of the day we are tasked to observe and record. Many's the time that Nightenhelser and I, while watching the little green men haul their face-stones toward the shore as the sun sets behind the sea to the west, have commented on this paradox of the gods' own blindness to coming events.

I know that Aphrodite will be injured this day, but the goddess herself does not. How can I use this information? If I were to tell Aphrodite, Zeus would know—I don't know how he would know, but I know he would—and I would be atomized and Aphrodite punished in some lesser way. *How can I use the information that Aphrodite, the goddess giving me these gifts to spy with, will be—may be—injured by Diomedes this day?*

I don't have time to find the answer. Athena finishes her fussing with Diomedes and releases her grip on space and time.

Real light and terrible noise and violent motion resumes. Diomedes steps forth, body and face and shield blazing, the light evidently apparent even to the other mortals, visible to his fellow Achaeans and the opposing Trojans.

Idaeus completes the motion of lashing his horses forward. The chariot roars and rumbles toward the Greek line, directly at the startled Diomedes.

Phegeus hurls his spear at Diomedes. The spear misses by an inch, the spearpoint passing over the son of Tydeus' left shoulder.

Diomedes, skin flushed, forehead blazing with fever-sweat and battle heat, hurls his own spear. It flies true, catching Phegeus dead-center in the chest—"between the nipples," I think Homer had sung it in Greek—and Phegeus is flung backward off the chariot, striking the ground and cartwheeling several times, the spear breaking off and splintering as the corpse tumbles to a stop in the dust of the chariot he had been riding five seconds before. Death, when it comes, comes fast on the plains of Ilium.

Idaeus leaps off the chariot, rolls, and struggles to his feet, sword in hand, prepared to protect his brother's body.

Diomedes snatches up another spear and rushes forward again, obviously ready to spit Idaeus the way he has just slaughtered the young man's brother. The Trojan turns to flee—leaving his brother's body behind in the dust in his panic—but Diomedes throws strong and true, casting the long spear at the center of the running man's back.

Ares, the god of war, flies forward—*literally* flies forward, using the same type of levitation harness the gods have issued me—and pauses time again, protecting Idaeus from a flying spear now frozen not ten feet from the running man's back. Then Ares extends his forcefield around Idaeus, resuming time long enough for the energy field to deflect Diomedes' spear. Then Ares quantum teleports the terrified man off the battlefield completely, sending him somewhere safe. To the shocked and terrified Trojans, it is as if a blink of black night has snatched their comrade away.

So that Ares' brother Hephaestus, the fire god, will not have lost both his future priests, I think, but then lurch backward to safety as the battle resumes and more Greeks follow Diomedes into the breach created by the killing of Phegeus. The empty chariot bounces across the rocky plain, and is captured by cheering Achaeans.

Ares is back now, QTing into semisolidity, a tall godshape as he tries to rally the Trojans, shouting in a godvoice for them to regroup and fend off Diomedes. But the Trojans are split—some running in terror at the approach of blazing Diomedes, some turning in obedience to the war god's booming voice. Suddenly Athena levitates across the heads of Greeks and Trojans, seizes Ares' wrist, and whispers urgently to the furious god.

The two QT away.

I look to my left again and the goddess Aphrodite—invisible to the Greeks and Trojans struggling and cursing and dying around her—motions with her hand for me to follow them.

I pull down Death's Helmet and become invisible to all the gods except Aphrodite. Then I trigger the medallion around my neck and QT after Athena and Ares, following their passage through space-time as easily as I would follow footprints in wet sand.

It's easy being a god. If you have the right equipment.

They have not teleported far, only about ten miles, to a shaded place along the banks of the Scamander, the gods call it the Xanthus—the broad river that runs across the plains of Ilium. When I QT into solidity about fifteen paces from them, Ares' head snaps around and he stares right at me. For an instant I know that the Hades Helmet has failed, they see me, and I am dead.

"What is it?" asks Athena.

"I thought I . . . felt something. A stir. A quantum stir."

The goddess turns her gray eyes in my direction. "There's nothing there. I can see in all the phase-shift spectra."

"I can as well," snaps Ares and turns his gaze away from me. I let out a shaky breath as silently as I can; the Hades Helmet still cloaks me. The god of war begins pacing up and down the river's edge. "Zeus is everywhere these days."

Athena walks beside him. "Yes, Father is angry at us all."

"Then why do you provoke him?"

The goddess stops. "Provoke him how? By defending my Achaeans from slaughter?"

"By preparing Diomedes to *do* slaughter," says Ares. I notice for the first time the reddish tint to the tall, perfectly muscled god's curly hair. "This is a dangerous thing you do, Pallas Athena."

The goddess laughs softly. "We've been intervening in this battle for nine years. It's the Game, for God's sake. It's what we *do*. I know that you plan to intervene on your beloved Ilium's behalf this very day, slaughtering my Argives like sheep. Is this not dangerous—this active participation by the god of war?"

"Not as dangerous as arming one side or the other with nanotech. Not as dangerous as retrofitting them with phase-shift fields. What are you thinking, Athena? You're trying to turn these mortals into us—into gods."

Athena laughs again but puts on a serious expression when she notices that her laughter only makes Ares more angry. "Brother, my augmentation of Diomedes is short-lived, you know that. I want only for him to survive this encounter. Aphrodite, your darling sister, has already urged on the Trojan archer Pandarus to wound one of my favorites— Menelaus—and even as we speak, she's whispering in the archer's ear— *Kill Diomedes*."

Ares shrugs. I know that Aphrodite is his ally and his instigator. Like a pouting little boy—an eight-foot-tall pouting little boy with a pulsing energy field—he finds a smooth stone and skips it across the water. "What does it matter if Diomedes dies today or next year? He's mortal. He'll die."

Now Athena laughs without embarrassment. "Of *course* he will die, my dear brother. And *of course* a single mortal's life or death is of no consequence to us . . . to me. But we must play the *Game*. I'll not let that bitch-whore Aphrodite change the will of the Fates."

"Who among us knows the will of the Fates?" snaps Ares, still pouting, his arms folded across his powerful chest.

"Father does."

"Zeus *says* he does," says the god of war with a sneer.

"Are you doubting our lord and master?" Athena's tone is almost, not quite, light and teasing.

Ares looks around quickly, and for a second I fear I've given myself away by making a noise where I stand on a flat boulder, afraid to leave footprints in the sand. But the war god's gaze moves on.

"I show no disrespect to our Father," Ares says at last, his voice reminding me of Richard Nixon's when he was speaking into the hidden Oval Office microphone he knew was there. Putting his lies on the record. "My allegiance and loyalty and love all go to Zeus, Pallas Athena."

"Which our Father must certainly note and reciprocate," responds Athena, no longer hiding the sarcasm in her voice.

Suddenly Ares' head snaps up. "God damn you," he shouts. "You just brought me here to get me away from the battlefield while your cursed Achaeans kill more of my Trojans."

"Of course." Athena launches the two syllables as a taunt, and for a second I think I'm going to witness something I've not seen in my nine years here—a direct battle between two gods.

Instead, Ares kicks sand in a final show of petulance and QT's away. Athena laughs, kneels by the Scamander, and splashes cold water on her face. "Fool," she whispers—to herself, I presume, but I take it as a statement directed at me protected here only by the Hades Helmet's distortion field; "Fool" seems to me an accurate judgment of my folly.

Athena QT's back to the battlefield. After a minute devoted to trembling at my own foolishness, I phase-shift and follow.

The Greeks and Trojans are still killing each other. Big news.

I seek out the only other scholic visible on the field. To the unaided eye, Nightenhelser is just another slovenly Trojan foot-soldier hanging back from the worst of the fighting, but I can see the telltale green glow the gods have marked us scholics with even when we're morphed, so I take off the Hades Helmet, morph into the form of Phalces—a Trojan who will be killed by Antilochus by and by—and I walk over to join Nightenhelser where he stands on a low ridge looking down on the carnage.

"Good morning, Scholic Hockenberry," he says when I approach. We're speaking in English. No other Trojan is near enough to hear us over the clash of bronze and the rumble of chariots and both of these motley coalitions are used to odd tribal languages and dialects.

"Good morning, Scholic Nightenhelser."

"Where have you been the last half hour or so?"

"Taking a break," I say. It happens. Sometimes the carnage gets to be too much even for us scholics and we QT away to Troy for a quiet hour or so—or for a large flagon of wine. "Did I miss much?"

Nightenhelser shrugs. "Diomedes came charging in about twenty minutes ago and was struck by an arrow. Right on schedule."

"Pandarus' arrow," I say, nodding. Pandarus is the same Trojan archer who wounded Menelaus earlier.

"I saw Aphrodite inciting Pandarus," says Nightenhelser. The big man has his hands in the pockets of his rough cape. Trojan capes had no pockets, of course, so Nightenhelser had sewn these in.

This was news. Homer had not sung of Aphrodite urging Pandarus to shoot Diomedes, only of Athena's earlier prompting of the archer to wound Menelaus so the war would resume. Poor Pandarus is literally a fool of the gods this day—his last day.

"Flesh wound for Diomedes?" I say.

"Shoulder. Sthenelus was there and pulled it out. Evidently this arrow wasn't poisoned. Athena QT'd into the fray a minute ago, took her pet Diomedes aside, and *'put energy into his limbs, his feet, and his fighting hands.'* " Nightenhelser was quoting some translation of Homer that I'm not familiar with.

"More nanotech," I say. "Has Diomedes found the archer and killed him yet?"

"About five minutes ago."

"Did Pandarus give that endless speech before Diomedes killed him?" I ask. In my favorite translation, Pandarus bemoans his fate for forty lines, has a long dialogue with a Trojan captain named Aeneas— yes, *the* Aeneas—and the two go charging at Diomedes in a chariot, flinging spears at the wounded Achaean.

"No," says Nightenhelser. "Pandarus just said 'Fuck me' when the arrow missed its mark. Then he leaped on the chariot with Aeneas, tosssed a spear that went right through Diomedes' shield and breast-plate—but missed flesh—and said, 'Shit,' in the second before Diomedes' spear caught him right between the eyes. Another case, I pre-sume, of Homer's poetic license in all the speech-making."

"And Aeneas?" That encounter is crucial to history as well as the *Iliad*. I can't believe I missed it.

"Aphrodite saved him just a minute ago," confirms Nightenhelser. Aeneas is the mortal son of the goddess of love and she watches over him carefully. "Diomedes smashed Aeneas' hipbone to bits with a boul-der, just as in the poem, but Aphrodite protected her wounded boy with a forcefield and is carrying him off the field now. It really pissed Diomedes off."

I shield my eyes with my hand. "Where is Diomedes now?" But I see the Greek warrior before Nightenhelser can point him out, about a hun-dred yards away, in the center of a melee, far behind Trojan lines. There is a mist of blood in the air around shining Diomedes and a heap of corpses on each side of the slashing, hacking, stabbing Achaean. The augmented Diomedes appears to be hacking his way through waves of human flesh to catch up to the slowly retreating Aphrodite. "Jesus," I say softly.

"Yeah," says the other scholic. "In the last few minutes he's killed Astynous and Hypiron, Abas and Polyidus, Xanthus and Thoon, Echem-mon and Chromius . . . all the captain Pairs."

"Why in twos?" I ask, thinking aloud.

Nightenhelser looks at me as if I'm a slow student in one of his freshman classes. "They were in *chariots*, Hockenberry. Two men per chariot. Diomedes killed them all as the chariots came at him."

"Ah," I say, embarrassed now. My attention isn't on the murdered Trojan captains but on Aphrodite. The goddess has just paused in her retreat from the Trojan lines, still carrying the wounded Aeneas, and is now strutting to and fro, clearly visible to the milling and frightened Trojans fleeing Diomedes' attack. Aphrodite is forcing the Trojan fighters back toward the fray with stabs of electricity and shimmering forcefield shoves.

Diomedes sees the goddess and goes berserk, hacking his way through a final protective line of Trojans to confront the goddess herself. He does not speak but readies his long spear. Aphrodite raises a forcefield almost casually, still carrying the wounded Aeneas, obviously not worried by a mere mortal's attack.

She has forgotten Athena's modifications of Diomedes.

Diomedes leaps forward, the goddess's forcefield crackles and gives way, the Achaean lunges with his long spear and the shaft and barb of it tear through Aphrodite's personal forcefield, silken robes, and divine flesh. The razor-sharp spearpoint slashes the goddess's wrist so that red muscle and white bone show. Golden ichor—rather than red blood—sprays into the air.

Aphrodite stares at the wound for a second and then screams—an inhuman scream, something huge and amplified, a female roar out of a bank of amplifiers at a rock concert from hell.

She reels, stil screaming, and drops Aeneas.

Rather than press home his successful attack on Aphrodite, Diomedes unsheaths his sword and prepares to decapitate the unconscious Aeneas.

Phoebus Apollo, lord of the silver bow, QT's into solidity between the berserk Diomedes and the fallen Trojan and holds the Achaean at bay with a pulsing hemisphere of plasma forcefield. Blinded by bloodlust, Diomedes hacks away at the forcefield, his own energy field crashing red against Apollo's defensive yellow shield. Aphrodite is still staring at her mangled wrist, and it looks as if she may swoon and lie there helpless in front of the still-raging Diomedes. The goddess seems unable to concentrate enough to QT while in such pain.

Suddenly her brother Ares arrives in a blazing flying chariot, shoving aside Trojans and Greeks alike as he widens the ship's plasma footprint to land by his sister. Aphrodite is blubbering and wailing in pain, trying to explain that Diomedes has gone mad. "*He'd* fight Father Zeus!" screams the goddess, collapsing in the war god's arms.

"Can you fly this?" demands Ares.

"No!" Aphrodite does swoon now. She falls into Ares' arms, still cradling the injured left hand and wrist in her bloody—or ichorish—right hand. It is strangely disturbing to watch. Gods and goddesses don't bleed. At least not in my nine years here.

The goddess Iris, Zeus's personal messenger, flicks onto the battlefield between the chariot and Apollo's forcefield where the god still protects the fallen Aeneas. The Trojans have backed away now, eyes bugging, and Diomedes is being held at bay by the overlapped energy fields. The Achaean is radiating heat and fury in the infrared, looking all the world like a warrior made out of pulsing lava.

"Take her to her mother," commands Ares, laying the unconscious Aphrodite on the floor of the chariot. Iris lifts the energy-craft skyward and phase-shifts it out of sight.

"Amazing," says Nightenhelser.

"Fan-fucking-tastic," I say. It is the first time in my more than nine years here that I have seen a Greek or Trojan successfully attack a god. I turn to see Nightenhelser staring at me in shock. I forget sometimes that the scholic is from a previous decade. "Well, it is," I say defensively.

I want to follow Aphrodite to Olympos and see what happens between her and Zeus. Homer had written about it, of course, but there already has been enough disparity between the poem and real events here today to pique my interest.

I begin edging away from Nightenhelser—who is watching events so raptly that he does not notice my departure—and ready myself to don the Hades Helmet and twist the personal QT medallion's controls. But something is happening on the battlefield.

Diomedes lets out a war cry almost as loud as Aphrodite's still-echoing scream of pain, and then the augmented Achaean charges Aeneas and Apollo again. This time, Diomedes' nano-strengthened body and phase-shifted sword hack through Apollo's outer layers of energy shield.

The god stands motionless as Diomedes hacks and cuts his way through the shimmering forcefield like a man shoveling invisible snow.

Then Apollo's voice rings out with amplification that must be audible two or three miles away. "*Think*, Diomedes! Back off! Enough of this mortal insanity—warring with the gods. We're not of the same breed, human. We never were. We never will be." Apollo grows in size from his imposing eight feet of stature to become a giant more than twenty feet tall.

Diomedes halts his attack and backs away, although it is impossible to tell whether it is out of temporary fear or sheer exhaustion.

Apollo bends down and opaques the forcefields around him and the fallen Aeneas. When the black fog disappear a minute later, the god is gone but Aeneas is still lying there, wounded, hip shattered, bleeding. The Trojan fighters rush to form a circle around their fallen and abandoned leader before Diomedes slaughters him.

It is not Aeneas. I know that Apollo has left a tensile hologram behind and carried the real wounded prince to the heights of Pergamus—Ilium's citadel—where the goddesses Leto and Artemis, Ares' sister, will use their nanotech god-medicine to save Aeneas' life and mend his wounds in minutes.

I'm ready to flick away to Olympos when suddenly Apollo QT's back to the battlefield, shielded from mortal view. Ares, still rallying Trojans behind his defensive shield, looks up when the other god arrives.

"Ares, destroyer of men, you stormer of ramparts, are you going to let that piece of dogshit insult you like that?" Invisible to the Achaeans, Apollo is pointing at the panting and recovering Diomedes.

"Insult me? How has he insulted me?"

"You idiot," thunders Apollo in ultrasonic frequencies audible only to the gods and scholics and the dogs in Troy, who set up a fearsome howling in response. "That . . . that *mortal* . . . has just assaulted the goddess of love, your sister, slashing the tendons of her immortal wrist. Diomedes even charged *me*, one of the most powerful of the gods. Athena has made him into something superhuman to make Ares, war god, reeking of blood, into a laughingstock!"

Ares' head swivels back toward the panting Diomedes, who has been ignoring the god since his attempt to cut through the forcefields failed.

"He makes fun of *me!?*" screams Ares in a shout everyone from here to Olympos can hear. I've noted over the years that Ares is rather stupid for a god. He's proving it today. "He dares make jest of *me!!??*"

"Kill him," cries Apollo, still speaking in the ultrasonic. "Cut out his heart and eat it." And the god of the silver bow QT's away.

Ares is going crazy. I decide I can't leave yet. I desperately want to QT to Olympos and see how badly injured Aphrodite is, but this is just too interesting to miss.

First, the war god morphs into the runner Acamas, prince of Thrace, and runs to and from among the milling Trojans, urging them back into the battle to push the Greeks out of the salient they have created following Diomedes into the Trojan lines. Then Ares morphs into the form of Sarpedon and taunts Hector—the hero is holding back from the fight with rare reticence. Shamed by what he thinks are Sarpedon's accusations, Hector rejoins his men. When Ares sees that Hector is rallying the main body of Trojan fighters, the god becomes himself and joins the circle of fighters holding the Greeks away from the hologram of unconscious Aeneas.

I confess I've never seen fighting this fierce during my nine years here. If Homer taught us anything, it is that the human being is a frail vessel, a fleshly flagon of blood and loose guts just waiting to be spilled.

They're spilling now.

The Achaeans don't wait for Ares to get his second wind, but rush in with chariot and spear behind the wild leadership of Diomedes and Odysseus. Horses scream. Chariots splinter and tumble. Horsemen drive their steeds into a wall of spearpoints and gleaming shields. Diomedes flames to the front again, calling his men forward even while he kills every Trojan who comes within his reach.

Apollo flicks back to the battlefield in a swirl of purple mist and releases the healed Aeneas—the real Aeneas—into the fray. The young man has been healed and more—he flows with light the way modified Diomedes did when Athena had finished with him. The Trojans, already rallying behind Hector, let out a massed yell at the sight of their resurrected prince and launch their counterattack.

Now it is Aeneas and Diomedes leading the fighting on opposite sides of the line, killing enemy captains by the bucketful, while Apollo and Ares urge more Trojans into the fray. I watch as Aeneas slaughters the carefree Achaean twins, Orsilochus and Crethon.

Now Menelaus, recovered from his own wound, shoves past Odysseus and rushes toward Aeneas. I hear Ares laugh. The war god would love it if Agamemnon's brother, Helen's real husband, the man who started this war by mislaying his wife, was cut down dead this day. Aeneas and Meneleus come within arm's reach of each other, the other fighters backing away in respect for *aristeia*, the two warriors' spears thrusting and feinting, thrusting and feinting.

Suddenly Nestor's brother, Antilochus, good friend to the all-but-forgotten Achilles, leaps forward to stand shoulder to shoulder with Menelaus, obviously afraid the Greek cause will die with their captain if he does not intervene.

Confronted with two legendary killers rather than one, Aeneas backs away.

Two hundred yards east of this confrontation, Hector has waded into the Achaean line with such ferocity that even Diomedes falls back with his men. With his augmented vision, Diomedes must see Ares—invisible to the others—fighting at Hector's side.

I still want to leave, to check on Aphrodite, but I can't tear myself away right now. I can see Nightenhelser madly taking notes on his recorder ansible. This makes me laugh, since the thousands of noble Trojans and Argives battling here are all as preliterate as two-year-olds. If they found Nightenhelser's scribblings, even in Greek, they would mean nothing to these men.

All the gods are getting into the act now.

Hera and Athena blink back into existence, Zeus's wife visibly urging Athena into the fight. Athena does not resist. Hebe, the goddess of youth and servant to the older gods, flashes down in a flying chariot, Hera takes control, and Athena also leaps aboard, dropping her robe while buckling on her breastplate. Athena's battle shirt gleams. She lifts a crackling energy shield of bright yellow and pulsing red, and her sword sends bolts of lightning to the Earth.

"Look!" It's Nightenhelser shouting to me above the fray. There's real lightning coming from the north, a towering bank of dark stratocumulus rising forty thousand feet or higher into the hot afternoon sky. The cloud suddenly shapes itself into the form and visage of Zeus.

"LEAP TO IT THEN, WIFE AND DAUGHTER," roars the thunder from that storm. "ATHENA, SEE IF YOU'RE THE WAR GOD'S MATCH. BRING HIM DOWN IF YOU CAN!"

Black clouds roil low over the battlefield while rain and lightning strike down at Trojan and Argive alike.

Hera brings the chariot low over the heads of the Greeks, then lower still, scattering Trojans like leather-and-bronze tenpins.

Athena leaps down into a real chariot next to exhausted, blood-encrusted Diomedes and his faithful driver, Sthenelus. "Are you done for this day, mortal?" she screams at Diomedes, the last word dripping sarcasm. "Are you half the size of your father to stop when your opponents hold the field so?" She gestures to where Hector and Ares are sweeping the Greeks back before their charge.

"Goddess," Diomedes gasps, "the immortal Ares protects Hector and . . ."

"DO I NOT PROTECT YOU?" roars Athena, fifteen feet tall and growing, looming over the fading glow of Diomedes.

"Yes, Goddess, but . . ."

"Diomedes, joy of my heart, cut down that Trojan and the god who protects him!"

Diomedes looks startled, even horrified. "We mortals may not kill a god . . ."

"Where is that written?" booms Athena and leans over Diomedes, injecting him with something new, pouring energy from her personal god-field to his. The goddess grabs the hapless Sthenelus and throws him thirty feet from the chariot. Athena takes the reins of Diomedes' chariot and whips the horses forward, straight toward Hector and Ares and the entire Trojan army.

Diomedes readies his spear as if he fully plans to kill a god—to slay Ares.

And Aphrodite wants to use me to kill Athena herself, I think, heart pounding with the terror and excitement of the moment. Things may soon be going quite differently than Homer predicted here on the plains of Troy.

12

Above the Asteroid Belt

The ship began decelerating almost as soon as it left the Jovian magnetosphere, so their great ballistic arc above the plane of the ecliptic to Mars on the far side of the sun would take several standard days rather than hours. This was good for Mahnmut and Orphu of Io since they had a lot to discuss.

Soon after their departure, Ri Po and Korus III in the forward control module announced that they were deploying the boron sail. Mahnmut watched through ship's sensors as the circular sail was unfolded and trailed seven kilometers behind them on eight bucky cables, then deployed to its full radius of five kilometers. It looked like a black circle cut out of the starfield to Mahnmut as he watched the stern video feed.

Orphu of Io left his hull-crèche and scuttled down the main cable, along the solenoid torus, and then out along the support cables like a horseshoe-crab Quasimodo, testing everything, tugging everything, scooting on reaction jets above the sail surface to check for cracks or seams or imperfections. He found nothing wrong and shuttled back to the ship with a strange and imperious zero-gravity grace.

Koros III ordered the modified Matloff/Fennelly magnetic scoop fired up and Mahnmut felt and recorded the ship's energies changing as the device on the prow of their ship generated a scoop field radius of 1,400 kilometers, shoveling in loose ions and concentrating on gathering up the solar wind.

How long is this going to take to decelerate us enough to be able to stop at Mars? asked Mahnmut on the common line, thinking that Orphu would answer.

It was the imperious Koros III who responded. *As ship velocity decreases and the effective area of the scoop increases, always keeping sail temper-*

ature from exceeding its melting point of two thousand degrees Kelvin, ship mass will equal 4×10 to the sixth power, and therefore deceleration from our current velocity of 0.1992 c to 0.001 c—the inelastic collision point—will require 23.6 standard years.

Twenty-three-point-six standard years! cried Mahnmut over the common line. That was more discussion time than he had bargained for.

That would slow us only to a still-sizable velocity of 300 kilometers per second, said Koros III. One thousandth light speed is nothing to sneeze at where we're going in-system.

Sounds like it's going to be a hard landing on Mars, said Mahnmut.

Orphu made a rumbling, sneezing sound on the line.

The Callistan navigator came online. We're not going to depend only upon the ion boron-sail deceleration, Mahnmut. The actual trip will take a little under eleven standard days. And our velocity upon entering Mars orbit will be less than six kilometers per second.

That's better, said Mahnmut. He was in the control cradle of The Dark Lady, but all his familiar sensors and controls were dark. It was strange to be picking up all data other than his own life support from the larger ship's sensors. What makes the difference?

The solar wind, said Orphu through the hull-crèche hardline. It averages about 300 km/sec out here and has an ion density of 10 to the sixth protons/m to the third power. We started with a half tank of Jovian hydrogen and a quarter tank of deuterium, and we're going to strip more hydrogen and deuterium from the solar wind with the Matloff/Fennelly scoop and fire the four fusion engines on the bow just after passing the sun. That's where the real deceleration is going to kick in.

I can't wait, said Mahnmut.

Me too, said Orphu of Io. He made the rumbling, sneezing sound again. Mahnmut thought that the huge moravec had either no sense of irony or a wickedly sharp one.

Mahnmut read À la recherche du temps perdu—Proust's In Search of Lost Time—while the ship passed some 140,000,000 kilometers above the Asteroid Belt.

Orphu had downloaded the French language in all of its classic intricacies along with the novel and biographical information on Proust, but Mahnmut ended up reading the book in five English translations because English was the lost language he had concentrated his own studies in over the past e-century and a half and he felt more comfortable judging literature in it. Orphu had chuckled at this and reminded the smaller moravec that comparing Proust to Mahnmut's beloved Shakespeare was a mistake, that they were as different in substance as the rocky, terraformed in-system world they were headed for and their own familiar Jovian moons, but Mahnmut read it again in English anyway.

When he was finished—knowing that it had been a cursory multiple reading, but eager to start the dialogue—he contacted Orphu on tight-beam since the Ionian moravec was out of his crèche, checking the boron-sail cables again, lashed firmly to lifelines this time because of the increasing deceleration.

I don't know, said Mahnmut. *I just don't see it. It all seems like the over-wrought musings of an aesthete to me.*

Aesthete? Orphu swiveled one of his communication stalks to lock in the tightbeam while his manipulators and flagella were busy spot-welding a cable connector. To Mahnmut, watching on rear video, the white welding-arc looked like a star against the black sail behind the awkward mass of Orphu. *Mahnmut, are you talking about Proust or his Marcel-narrator?*

Is there a difference? Even as he sent the sarcastic query, Mahnmut knew he was being unfair. He had sent Orphu hundreds—perhaps thousands—of e-mails over the last dozen e-years, explaining the difference between the Poet named "Will" in the sonnets and the historical artist named Shakespeare. He suspected the Proust, however dense and impenetrable, to be just as complex when it came to identity of author and characters.

Orphu of Io ignored that question and sent back—*Admit that you loved Proust's comic vision. He is, above almost all else, a comic writer.*

Was there a comic vision? I saw little comedy in the work. Mahnmut was serious about this. It was not that the human sense of humor was alien to Mahnmut or moravecs; even the earliest spacefaring, self-evolving, only dimly sentient robots created and dispatched by the human race before the rubicon pandemic had been programmed to understand humor. Communication with human beings—real, two-way communication—had been impossible without humor. It was as human as anger or logic or jealousy or pride—all elements he had noticed and noted in Proust's endless novel. But Proust and his protagonists as comic writers, comic characters? Mahnmut failed to see it, and if Orphu were right, it was a major oversight. It had been Mahnmut who spent decades on finding the word-play humor and satire in the Bard's plays, Mahnmut who had ferreted out even the tiniest ironies in Shakespeare's sonnets.

Listen, said Orphu as he scuttled back along one of the taut bucky-lines to the ship, reaction jets pulsing. *Read this part of "Swann in Love" again. This is where Swann, in thrall to the faithless and fickle Odette, is using all his skill as an emotional blackmailer to keep her from going to the theater without him. Listen to the humor here, my friend.* He downloaded text.

"I swear to you," he told her, shortly before she was to leave for the theatre, "that, in asking you not to go, I should hope, were I a selfish man, for nothing so much as that you should refuse, for I have a thousand other things to do this evening, and I shall feel trapped myself, and rather annoyed, if, after all, you tell me you're not going. But my occupations, my pleasures are not everything; I must think of you also. A day may come when, seeing me irrevocably sundered from you, you will be entitled to reproach me for not having warned you at the decisive hour in which I felt that I was about to pass judgment on you, one of those stern judgments which love cannot long resist. You see, your *Nuit de Cléopâtre* (what a title!) has no bearing on the point. What I must know is whether you are indeed one of those creatures in the lowest grade of mentality and even of charm, one of those contemptible creatures who are incapable of forgoing a pleasure. And if you are such, how could anyone love you, for you are not even a person, a clearly defined entity, imperfect but at least perfectible. You are a formless water that will trickle down any slope that offers itself, a fish devoid of memory, incapable of thought, which all its life long in its aquarium will continue to dash itself a hundred times a day against the glass wall, always mistaking it for water. Do you realize that your answer will have the effect—I won't say of making me cease loving you immediately, of course, but of making you less attractive in my eyes when I realise that you are not a person, that you are beneath everything in the world and incapable of raising yourself one inch higher? Obviously, I should have preferred to ask you as a matter of little or no importance to give up your *Nuit de Cléopâtre* (since you compel me to sully my lips with so abject a name) in the hope that you would go to it none the less. But, having decided to make such an issue of it, to draw such drastic consequences from your reply, I confessed it more honourable to give you due warning."

Meanwhile, Odette had shown signs of increasing emotion and uncertainty. Although the meaning of his tirade was beyond her, she grasped that it was to be included in the category of "harangues" and scenes of reproach or supplication, which her familiarity with the ways of men enabled her, without paying any heed to the words that were uttered, to conclude that they would not make unless they were in love, and that since they were in love, it was unnecessary to obey them, as they would only be more in love later on. And so she would have heard Swann out with the utmost tranquility had she not noticed that it was growing late, and that if he went on talking much longer she would "never," as she told him with a fond smile, obstinate but slightly abashed, "get there in time for the Overture."

Mahnmut laughed out loud in the tight confines of *The Dark Lady*'s pressurized control room. He saw it now. The humor was brilliant. He had read that passage the first time focusing on the human emotion of jealousy and the obvious effort of the Swann character to manipulate the behavior of the woman named Odette. Now it was . . . clear.

Thanks, he said to Orphu as the six-meter horseshoe-crab-shaped moravec settled into his hull-crèche. *I think I hear the humor coming through now. I appreciate it. Everything is different than Shakespeare's tone and language and structure, but something is—the same.*

Obsession with the puzzle of what it means to be human, suggested Orphu. *Your Shakespeare looks at all the facets of humanity through reaction to events, finding the deep-internal through characters defined as actions. Proust's characters delve deep into memory to see the same facets. Perhaps your Bard is more like Koros III, leading this outward expedition. My sweet Proust is more like you, wrapped in the coccoon of* The Dark Lady *and diving deep, seeking the geography of reefs and the hard bottom and other living things and the whole world through echo-location.*

Mahnmut thought about this for several rich nanoseconds. *I don't see how your Proust solved this puzzle—or rather, how he* tried *to solve it other than through immersion in memory.*

Not just in memory, Mahnmut my friend, but in time.

Tens of meters away, shielded by his near-invulnerable and impenetrable double-hull of his submersible and that of of the ship carrying it, Mahnmut felt as if the Ionian had reached out and touched him in some personal—some profound—manner.

Time is separate from memory, muttered Mahnmut on their private line, speaking now mostly to himself, *but is memory ever separate from time?*

Precisely! boomed Orphu. *Precisely. Proust's protagaonists—primarily the "I" or "Marcel" narrator, but also our poor Swann—have three chances to sniff*

out and put together the thick puzzle of life. Their three approaches fail but some-
how the story itself succeeds, despite its narrator's and even author's failures!

Mahnmut thought about this for a time in silence. He switched his vision from external camera to external camera, looking away at the complexities of the ship itself and its frightening circular sail "downward" toward the rocks, toward the Belt. He willed the image to full magnification and there it was.

A solitary asteroid was tumbling against black. There was no danger of impact. Not only was their ship now 150,000,000 kilometers above the plane of the ecliptic and passing the Belt at blinding speed, but this asteroid—he queried Ri Po's astrogation banks and identified the rock as Gaspra—was tumbling away from them. Still, it was a sizable mini-world—the overlay data said that Gaspra sized out at 20×16×11 kilometers—and the magnification, equal to a pass at about 16,000 kilometers—showed an irregular, sharpened-potato mass with a complicated pattern of cratering. More interestingly, there were obvious artificial elements in the image—straight lines gouged in the rock, gleams of light in dark craters, clear patterns of light sources on the asteroid's flattened "nose."

Rockvecs, Orphu said softly. He was obviously looking at the same video source. *There are a few million scattered around the Belt.*

Are they as hostile as everyone says? As soon as he sent his question, Mahnmut was afraid it would type him as anxious.

I don't know. My guess is that they are—they chose to evolve in a much more competitive culture than we created. Word is that they fear and loathe post-humans and flatly hate us outlying moravecs. Koros III might know if the legends of their ferocity are true.

Koros? Why would he know?

Not many moravecs know it, but he led an expedition to the rocks about sixty e-years ago for Asteague/Che and the Five Moons Consortium. Nine moravecs went with him. Only three others returned.

Mahnmut pondered this for a minute. He wished he knew more about weapons; if the rockvecs wanted to kill them now, did they possess an energy weapon or hyperkinetic missile that could catch this ship? It seemed unlikely—not at their current velocity of more than 0.193 light speed. Mahnmut said to Orphu, *What are the three ways Proust's characters tried to solve the puzzle of life—and failed?*

The big deep-space moravec cleared his virtual throat. *First, they followed their noses down the scent-trail to nobility, title, birthright, and the landed gentry,* said Orphu. *Marcel, the narrator, tries this route for two thousand pages or so. At least he believes that in the more important aristocracy lies nobility of character. But it all comes up empty.*

Just snobbery, says Mahnmut.

Never just *snobbery, my friend,* sends Orphu, his booming voice growing more animated over their private line. *Proust saw snobbery as the glue
that holds society—any society, in any age—together. He studies it on all levels throughout the book. He never tires of its manifestations.*

I did, Mahnmut said quietly, hoping that his honesty wouldn't offend
his friend.

Orphu's rumble, vibrating in the subsonic even on the line, assured
Mahnmut that he hadn't.

*What was the second path he tried to follow to the answer of the puzzle of
life?* asked Mahnmut.

Love, said Orphu.

Love? repeated Mahnmut. There had been plenty of it in the more
than 3,000 pages of *In Search of Lost Time,* but it had all seemed so—
hopeless.

Love, boomed Orphu. *Sentimental love and physical lust.*

*You mean the sentimental love that Marcel—and Swann, I guess—felt for
their family, Marcel's grandmother?*

*No, Mahnmut—the sentimental attraction to familiar things, to memory it-
self, and to the people who fall into the realm of familiar things.*

Mahnmut glanced at the tumbling asteroid called Gaspra. According
to Ri Po's databar, it took Gaspra about seven standard hours to revolve
completely around his axis. Mahnmut wondered if such a place could
ever be a source of familiarity, of sentimental attraction, to him, to any
sentient being. *Well, the dark seas of Europa are.*

Pardon?

Mahnmut felt his organic layers prickle when he realized he had spoken aloud on the private line. *Nothing. Why didn't love lead to the answer
to the puzzle of life?*

*Because Proust knew—and his characters discover—that neither love nor
its more noble cousin, friendship, ever survive the entropy blades of jealousy,
boredom, familiarity, and egotism,* said Orphu, and for the first time in their
direct communication, Mahnmut fancied that he heard a tone of sadness
in the big moravec's voice.

Never?

Never, said Orphu and rumbled a deep sigh. *Remember the last lines of
"Swann in Love"?—"To think that I wasted years of my life, that I hoped to die,
that I had my greatest love affair with a woman who didn't appeal to me, who
wasn't even my type!"*

I noted that, said Mahnmut, *but I didn't know at the time if it was supposed to be terribly funny or horribly bitter or unspeakably sad. Which was it?*

All three, my friend, sent Orphu of Io. *All three.*

What was Proust's characters' third path to the puzzle of life? asked Mahnmut. He increased the O_2 input to his chamber to clear away the cobweb-tendrils of sadness that were threatening to gather in his heart.

Let's save that for another time, said Orphu, perhaps sensing his interlocutor's mood. *Koros III is going to increase the scoop radius and it might be fun to watch the fireworks on the X-ray spectra.*

They passed Mars's orbit and there was nothing to see; Mars, of course, was on the opposite side of the sun. They passed Earth's orbit a day later and there was nothing to see; Earth was far around the curve of its orbit on the plane of the ecliptic far below. Mercury was the only planet clearly visible on the monitors as they flashed above it, but by then the roar and blaze of the sun itself filled all their viewing screens.

As they passed over the sun at a perihelion of only 97,000,000 kilometers—radiator filaments trailing heat—the boron sail was collapsed, reeled in, and folded into its aft dome. Orphu helped the remote handlers with the job and Mahnmut watched on the ship's screens as his friend shuttled to and fro, his surface scars and pitting quite visible in the blazing sunlight.

Two hours before they were scheduled to fire the fusion engines, Koros III surprised Mahnmut by inviting everyone to gather at the control-room module near the magnetic scoop horns.

There were no internal corridors in the ship. The plan had been for Koros to transfer to *The Dark Lady* via cables and grabholds once the ship was finished decelerating and in Martian orbit. Mahnmut was dubious about making the trip across the hull now to the control room.

Why should we physically gather to talk? he asked Orphu on their private line. *And you can't fit in the control-room module anyway.*

I can hover outside, view all of you through the port, connect hardlines to the control module for a secure communication.

Why is that better than conferencing on the allcall?

I don't know, said Orphu, *but we fire the engines in one hundred fourteen minutes, so why don't I shuttle around to the ship's hold and pick you up?*

That's what they did. Mahnmut had no problem with vacuum and hard radiation, of course, but the thought of disconnecting from the ship and somehow being left behind had rattled him. Orphu met him at the cargo bay and Mahnmut had an unforgettable glimpse of *The Dark Lady,* starkly illuminated by the sun's blinding rays, tucked in the spacecraft's hold like a salt shark in a kraken's belly.

Orphu used his manipulators to place Mahnmut in a sheltered niche in the Ionian's carapace and clipped onto guidelines for the reaction-jet trip around the dark belly of the ship, up its girdered and torused ribs, and forward along the upper hull. Mahnmut glanced at the spherical fusion engines, clipped onto the prow like design afterthoughts, and checked the time—one hour and four minutes until ignition.

Mahnmut studied the ultrastealth material enclosing the ship proper—dead-black and porous baffle-wrap that made the ship, minus its fusion engines, boron sail, and other expendables, theoretically invisible to sight, radar, deep radar, gravitonic reflection, infrared, UV and neutrino probes. *But what difference does that make if we go in on four pillars of fusion flame for two days?*

The control room had an airlock. Mahnmut helped Orphu connect his shielded hardline, and then he cycled through the lock and resumed breathing air the old-fashioned way.

"This ship is carrying weapons," said Koros III without preamble; he spoke the words through the air. His multifaceted eyes and black humanoid shell reflected the red halogen lights.

The third moravec in the small, pressurized control room—the tiny Callistan, Ri Po—situated himself at the third point of the moravec triangle.

Are you hearing this? subvocalized Mahnmut on his private line to Orphu. The huge Ionian was visible outside the forward windows.

Oh yes.

"Why are you telling us now?" Mahnmut asked Koros III.

"I thought you and the Ionian had a right to know. Your existences are at stake here."

Mahnmut looked at the navigator. "You knew about the weapons?"

"I knew about the defense weaponry built into the ship," replied Ri Po. "I didn't know until now that there would be weapons brought to the surface. But it was a logical assumption."

"To the surface," repeated Mahnmut. "There are weapons in *The Dark Lady's* hold." It was not really a question.

Koros III nodded in that age-old humanoid signal of confirmation.

"What kind?" demanded Mahnmut.

"I am not at liberty to say," the tall Gaynmedan said stiffly.

"Well, perhaps I'm not at liberty to transport weapons in my submersible," snapped Mahnmut.

"You have no choice in the matter," said Koros III. His voice sounded more sad than imperious.

Mahnmut seethed.

He's right, said Orphu and Mahnmut realized that the Ionian had spoken on the common line. *None of us have any choice at this point. We have to go ahead.*

"Then why tell us?" Mahnmut demanded again.

It was Ri Po who responded. "We've been monitoring Mars since we came over the sun. From this distance, our instruments confirm the quantum activity detected from Jovian space—but the intensity is several magnitudes greater than we estimated. This world is a threat to the entire solar system."

How so? asked Orphu. *The post-humans experimented quantum shifting for centuries in their orbital cities around Earth.*

Koros III shook his head in that quaint humanlike way, although "quaint" was not a word that came to Mahnmut's mind when he stared at the tall, shiny-black figure with his gleaming fly's eyes. "Nothing to this extent," said their mission leader. "The amount of quantum phase-shifting occurring on Mars right now amounts to a hole torn in the fabric of space-time. It's not stable. It's not a sane exercise of quantum technology."

Does it have something to do with the voynix? asked Orphu. All most Jovian moravecs knew of the fabled voynix was that the planet Earth had radiated unprecedented quantum phase-shift activity when the creatures had first been mentioned in monitored post-human neutrino communications more than two thousand e-years earlier.

We don't know if the voynix are involved, or, indeed, if they are still on Earth, Koros sent on the common band. "I'll repeat that I felt it ethically imperative to inform all of you that there are weapons aboard this ship and aboard the submersible on which Mahnmut will be transporting me. The decisions to use these weapons will not be yours. The responsibility lies solely with me when I am aboard this ship, and with Ri Po for ship defense when Mahnmut and I have dropped to the planet's surface. The decision to use deadly force on Mars itself will be mine alone."

"The ship's weapons are not offensive then? Not to be used against targets on Mars?" asked Mahnmut.

"No," said Ri Po. "The shipboard weapons are defensive only."

But the weapons aboard The Dark Lady *include weapons of mass destruction?* asked Orphu of Io.

Koros III paused, obviously weighing his orders against the crew's right to know. Finally, he said, "Yes."

Mahnmut tried to decide what these weapons of mass destruction might be. Fission bombs? Fusion weapons? Neutrino emitters? Plasma explosives? Antimatter devices? Planet-busting black-hole bombs? He had no idea. His centuries of existence gave him no experience with weapons outside those nonlethal nets, prods, and galvanizers needed to ward off kraken or capture Europan sea life.

"Koros," he asked softly, "did you bring weapons on your mission to the rocks some decades ago?"

"No," said the Ganymedan. "There was no need. However warlike and ferocious the asteroid moravecs have become in their recent evolution, they posed no threat to the existence of all sentient beings in the solar system." Koros III projected the time; they had forty-one minutes until the fusion engines fired. *Any other questions?*

Orphu had one. *Why are we wrapped in ultrastealth if we're approaching Mars behind four fusion trails that will light us up like a supernova, visible day and night for sols to anything with eyes on the Martian surface? Wait . . . you're trying to get a response. Trying to make them attack us.*

"Yes," said Koros. "It was the easiest way to assess their intentions. The fusion engines will shut off while we are still eighteen million kilometers from Mars. If they have not attempted to intercept us by then, we will jettison the engines, the solenoid toruses, and all other external devices, and enter Martian orbit with passive countermeasures hiding our location. Currently we do not know if the post-humans—or whatever entities have terraformed Mars and are currently residing there—have a technical or post-technical civilization."

Mahnmut considered this. They would be jettisoning every form of propulsion that could get them home.

I would say that massive quantum phase-shift activity is a sign of something pretty technological, said Orphu.

"Perhaps," said Ri Po. "But there are idiot savants in the universe."

With that cryptic statement, the meeting ended, atmosphere was drained out of the control room, and Orphu hauled Mahnmut back to his submersible in the ship's hold.

The four engines fired on cue. For the next two days, Mahnmut was pinned to his high-g couch as the ship decelerated down onto the plane of the ecliptic toward Mars at more than 400-g's. The hold around *The Dark Lady* was again filled with high-g gel, but his living compartment wasn't, and the weight and lack of mobility grew tiring to Mahnmut. He couldn't imagine the stress on Orphu out in his hull-cradle. Mars and all forward images were obscured by the four-sun glare of the engines, but Mahnmut passed the time by checking on video of the hull, the stars astern, and by rereading parts of *À la recherche du temps perdu* and finding connections and disparities with his beloved Shakespearean sonnets.

Mahnmut's and Orphu's love of lost-age human languages and literature was not all that unusual. More than two thousand e-years earlier, the first moravecs to be sent out to Jovian space to explore the moons and to contact the sentients known to be in the atmosphere of Jupiter were programmed by the first post-humans with elaborate full-sensory tapes of human history, human culture, and the human arts. The rubicon had already occurred, of course, and before that the Great Retreat, but there had still been some hope of saving the memory and records of the human past even if the last 9,114 old-style humans on Earth could not be saved by the final fax. In the centuries since contact had been lost with Earth, human art and human literature and human history had become the hobbies of thousands of the hardvac and moon-based moravecs. Mahnmut's former partner, Urtzweil—who had been destroyed in an icefall under the European ice crater of Tyre Macula eighteen J-years before—had been passionate about the King James Bible. A copy of that bible still sat in the cubby under Mahnmut's stowed work table, next to the gel-insulated lava lamp Urtzweil had given his partner as a gift.

Watching the filter-dimmed flare of the forward fusion engines on his video monitor, Mahnmut tried to connect his image of the historical Marcel Proust—a man who took to his bed for the last three years of his life, in his famous cork-lined room, surrounded by his always-arriving galley proofs, old manuscripts, and bottles of addictive potions, visited only by the occasional male prostitute and workers putting in one of the first opera-delivering telephones in Paris—with the Marcel-narrator of the exhausting work of perception that was *In Search of Lost Time.* Mahnmut's memories were prodigious—he could call up the street maps of Paris in 1921, could download every photograph or drawing or painting ever done of Proust, could look at the Vermeer that caused Proust's character to faint, could cross-check every character in the books with every real human being Proust had known—but none of this helped that much in Mahnmut's understanding of the work. Human art, Mahnmut knew, simply transcended human beings.

Four secret paths to the truth of the puzzle of life, Orphu had said. The first—Proust's characters' obsession with nobility, with aristocracy, with the upper echelons of society—was obviously a dead end. Mahnmut did not have to wade through 3,000 pages of dinner parties the way Proust's protagonist had in order to realize this.

The second, the idea of love as the key to life's puzzle, this fascinated Mahnmut. Certainly Proust—like Shakespeare but in a completely different way—had attempted to explore all facets of human love—heterosexual, homosexual, bisexual, familial, collegial, interpersonal—as well as love of places and things and of life itself. And Mahnmut had to agree with Orphu's analysis that Proust had rejected love as a true line to deeper understanding.

The third path for Marcel had been art—art and music—but while that had led Marcel to beauty, it had not led to truth.

What is the fourth path? And if that failed for Proust's heroes, what was the true path under and behind the pages, unknown to the characters but perhaps glimpsed by Proust himself?

All Mahnmut had to do to find out was open the line to Orphu. Lost in their own thoughts, perhaps, the two friends had communicated very little during this last day of deceleration. *He'll tell me later,* thought Mahnmut. *And perhaps by then I'll see it myself . . . and see if it connects to Shakespeare's analysis of what lies beyond love.* Certainly the Bard had all but rejected sentimental and romantic and physical love by the end of the sonnets.

The fusion engines stopped firing. The release from high-g and hull-transmitted noise and vibration was almost terrifying.

Immediately the spherical fuel-engine spheres were jettisoned, small rockets carrying them away from the ship's trajectory.

Releasing sail and solenoid came Orphu's voice on the common line. Mahnmut watched on various hull video feeds as these components were ejected into space.

Mahnmut went back to the forward video. Mars was clearly visible now, only eighteen million kilometers ahead and below them. Ri Po provided trajectory overlays on the image. Their approach looked perfect. Small internal ion-thrusters were continuing to slow the ship and preparing to inject it into a polar orbit.

No records of radar or other sensor tracking during our descent, said Koros III. *No attempt at interception.*

Mahnmut thought that the Ganymedan had great dignity but also a propensity for stating the obvious.

We're getting data through our passive sensors, said Ri Po.

Mahnmut checked the readouts. If they had been approaching— say—Europa, the displays would have shown radio, gravitonic, microwave, and a host of other technology-related emissions coming from the moravec-inhabited moon. Mars showed nothing. But the terraformed world was certainly inhabited. Already the bow-mounted telescope was able to pick up images of the white houses on Mons Olympos, the straight and curved slashes of roads, the stone heads lining the shore of the Northern Sea, and even some glimpses of individual movement and activity, but no radio traffic, no microwave relays, none of the electromagnetic signature of a technological civilization. Mahn-mut remembered the phrase that Ri Po had used—idiot savants?

Prepare to enter Mars orbit in sixteen hours, announced Koros. *We will observe from orbit for another twenty-four hours. Mahnmut, prepare your sub-mersible for de-orbit burn thirty hours from now.*

Yes, said Mahnmut over the common line, stifling the urge to add a "sir."

Mars seemed quiet enough for most of the twenty-four hours they were in polar orbit around it.

There were artificial things in Stickney Crater on Phobos—mining ma-chinery, what was left of a magnetic accelerator, broken habitation domes and robotic rovers—but they were cold and dusty and pockmarked and more than three millennia old. Whoever had terraformed Mars in the past century had nothing to do with the ancient artifacts on the inner moon.

Mahnmut had seen images of Mars when it was the Red Planet—al-though he always thought it more orange than red—but it was reddish-orange no longer. Coming in over the north pole, the telescopic view resolving things down to a meter in length, what was left of the polar ice cap—just a squiggle of water-ice now, all the CO_2 having long since been sublimed away in the terraforming—a white island in the blue northern sea. Spirals of clouds moved across the ocean that covered more than half of the northern hemisphere. The highlands were still orangish and most of the land masses were brown, but the startling green of forests and fields were visible without using the telescope.

No one and nothing challenged the ship: no radio calls, no search or acquisition radar, no tightbeam or laser or modulated neutrino queries. As the tense minutes moved into long hours of silence, the four moravecs watched the views and prepared for the descent of *The Dark Lady.*

There was obviously life on Mars—human or post-human life, from the looks of it, along with at least one other species: the stone-head movers, possibly human, but short and green in the telescope photos. White-sailed ships moved along the northern coastline and up the water-filled canyons of Valles Marineris, but not many ships. A few more sails were visible on the cratered sea that had been Hellas Basin. There were obvious signs of habitation on Olympus Mons—and at least one high-tech people-mover stairway or escalator along the flanks of that volcano—and photographs of half a dozen flying machines near the summit caldera of Olympus, and a few glimpses of a few other white houses and terraced gardens on the high slopes of the Tharsis volca-noes—Ascraesus Mons, Pavonis Mons, and Arsia Mons—but no signs whatsoever of an extensive planetary civilization. Koros III announced over the common line that he estimated no more than three thousand of the pale human-looking people lived on the four volcanoes, with perhaps twenty thousand of the green workers congregated in tent cities along the shorelines.

Most of Mars was empty. Terraformed but empty.

Hardly a danger to all sentient life-forms in the solar system, then, is it? asked Orphu of Io.

It was Ri Po who responded. *Look at the planet through quantum mapping.*

"My God," Mahnmut said aloud to his empty enviro-crèche. Mars was a blinding red blaze of quantum-shift activity, with flow lines converging on the major volcano, Olympus Mons.

Could the few flying vehicles be causing this quantum havoc? asked Orphu. *They don't register on the electromagnetic spectrum and they certainly aren't chemically propelled.*

No, said Koros III. *While the few flying machines move in and out of the quantum flux, they are not generating it. Or at least not the primary source.*

Mahnmut looked at the bizarre quantum map overlay another minute before venturing a suggestion he'd been thinking about for days. *Would it make sense to contact them via radio or another medium? Or just land openly on Olympus Mons. To come as friends rather than spies?*

We have considered this course of action, said Koros. *But the quantum activity is so intense that we find it imperative to gather more information before revealing ourselves.*

Gather information and get these weapons of mass destruction as close to that volcano as possible, Mahnmut thought with some bitterness. He had never wanted to be a soldier. Moravecs were not designed to fight and the thought of killing sentient beings warred with programming as old as his species.

Nonetheless, Mahnmut prepared *The Dark Lady* for descent. He put the submersible on internal power and separated all life support umbilicals from the ship, remaining connected only through the comm cables that would be severed when they moved out of the hold. The submersible had been wrapped in ultrastealth and a reaction-pak of thrusters now girdled the bow and stern of the sub, but these would be controlled by Koros III during the entry phase, then jettisoned. The final add-on was the blister-circle of parachutes that would slow their fall after re-entry. These would also be controlled and jettisoned by Koros III. Only after they reached the ocean would Mahnmut guide his own submersible.

Preparing to come down to the submersible, called Koros III from the control deck.

Permission to board granted, replied Mahnmut, although their titular commander had not asked for permission. He was not Europan and did not know the protocols. Mahnmut saw the warning that the ship's bay doors were opening, exposing *The Dark Lady* to space again so that Koros could make the transfer by guide cable.

Mahnmut flicked on the video feed from the hull where Orphu nestled. The Ionian noticed the attention. *Good-bye for a while, my friend,* said Orphu. *We'll meet again.*

I hope so, said Mahnmut. He opened the submersible's lower airlock and prepared to blow the last comm cables.

Wait, said Ri Po. *Coming around the limb of the planet.*

Control-room video showed Koros III dogging the airlock hatch he had just opened and returning to the instruments. Mahnmut removed his finger from the button arming the commline pyrotechnics.

Something was coming around the edge of Mars. Currently it was just a radar blip. The forward telescope gimbaled to acquire it.

It must have launched from Olympos when we were out of line of sight, said Orphu.

Hailing it now, said Ri Po.

Mahnmut monitored the frequencies as their ship began calling. The blip did not answer.

Do you see this? said Koros III.

Mahnmut did. The object was less than two meters long—an open chariot sans horses and surrounded by a gleaming forcefield. There were two humanoids in the open vehicle, a man and a woman, the female apparently steering it and the taller male just standing there, staring straight ahead as if he could see the stealth-wrapped ship some eight thousand kilometers away. The woman was tall and regal and blonde; the man had short gray hair and a white beard.

Orphu rumbled his laugh on the common line. *It looks like pictures of God,* he said. *I don't know who his girlfriend is.*

As if hearing this insult, the gray-bearded man raised his arm.

The video input flared and died the same instant Mahnmut was thrown against the restraints of his high-g couch. He felt the ship shudder twice, terribly, and then begin tumbling wildly, centrifugal forces throwing Mahnmut hard to the right, then up, then to the left.

Is everyone all right? he screamed on the all-line. *Can you hear me?*

For several tumbling seconds the only response was silence and line-noise, then Orphu's calm voice came through the snarl of static. *I can hear you, my friend.*

Are you all right? Is the ship all right? Did we fire on them?

I'm damaged and blinded, said Orphu as the static hissed and crackled. *But I saw what happened before the blast blinded me. We didn't fire on them. But the ship is—half gone, Mahnmut.*

Half gone? Mahnmut repeated stupidly. *What—*

Some sort of energy lance. The control room—Koros and Ri Po—gone. Vaporized. All the bow gone. The upper hull is slagged. The ship is tumbling about twice per second and beginning to break up. My own carapace has been breached. My reaction jets are gone. Most of my manipulators are gone. I'm losing power and shell integrity. Get the submersible away from the ship—hurry!

I don't know how! called Mahnmut. *Koros had the control package. I don't know . . .*

Suddenly the ship lurched again and the comm and video lines were severed completely. Mahnmut could hear a violent hissing through the hull and realized that it was the ship boiling away around him. He switched on the submersible's own cameras and saw only plasma glow everywhere.

The Dark Lady began tumbling and twisting more wildly, although whether with the dying ship or by itself, Mahnmut could not tell. He activated more cameras, the submersible's underwater thrusters, and the damage control system. Half the systems were out or slow to respond.

Orphu? No response. Mahnmut activated the omni-directional masers, attempting a tightbeam lock. *Orphu?*

No response. The tumbling intensified. *The Dark Lady's* hold, pressurized for Koros's arrival, suddenly lost all of its atmosphere, spinning the submersible more wildly.

I'm coming for you, Orphu, called Mahnmut. He blew the inner airlock door and slapped his restraint straps off. Behind him somewhere, either in the ship tearing itself apart or in *The Dark Lady* herself, something exploded and slammed Mahnmut violently against the control panel and then down into darkness.

13

The Dry Valley

In the morning, after a good breakfast prepared by Daeman's mother's servitors at her Paris Crater apartments, Ada and Harman and Hannah and Daeman faxed to the site of the last Burning Man.

The faxnode was lighted, of course, but outside the circular pavilion, it was deep night and the wind howl was audible even through the semipermeable forcefield. Harman turned to Daeman. "This was the code I had—twenty-one eighty-six—does it seem right to you?"

"It's a *faxnode pavilion*," whined the younger man. "They all look alike. Plus, it's *dark* outside. And it's empty here now. How am I supposed to tell if it's the same as some place I visited eighteen months ago, in daylight, with a mob of other people?"

"The code sounds sort of right," said Hannah. "I was following other people, but I remember that the Burning Man node had a high number, not one I'd ever faxed to before."

"And you were what?" sneered Daeman. "Seventeen at the time?"

"A little older," said Hannah. Her voice was cool. Where Daeman was mostly pale flab, Hannah showed tanned muscle. As if recognizing that disparity—even though Daeman had never heard of two human beings physically fighting outside the turin-cloth drama—he took a step backward.

Ada ignored the prickly conversation and walked to the edge of the pavilion, putting her slim fingers against the forcefield. It rippled and bent but did not give way. "This is *solid*," she said. "We can't get out."

"Nonsense," said Harman. He joined her and the two pushed and prodded, leaned their weight against the elastic but ultimately unyielding energy shield. It wasn't semipermeable after all—or at least not to physical objects like human beings.

"I've never heard of this," said Hannah, joining them to put her shoulder against the invisible wall. "What sense does it make to have a forcefield in a fax pavilion?"

"We're trapped!" said Daeman, eyes rolling. "Like rats."

"Moron," said Hannah. The two did not appear to be getting along well today. "You can always fax out. The portal's right there behind you and *it's* still working."

As if to prove Hannah's point, two spherical, general-use servitors came through the shimmering faxportal and floated toward the humans.

"This field is keeping us in," Ada said to the servitors.

"Yes, Ada *Uhr*," said one of the machines. "We regret the delay in getting here to help you. This faxnode is . . . rarely used."

"So what?" said Harman, crossing his arms and scowling at the lead servitor. The other sphere had moved off to float near one of the supply cubbies in the pavilion's white column. "Since when are faxnodes sealed off?" continued Harman.

"My apologies again, Harman *Uhr*," said the servitor in the almost-male voice used by all general-purpose servitors everywhere. "The climate outside is inhospitable in the extreme at this time of year. Were you to venture out without thermskins, your chances of survival would be low."

The second servitor extracted four thermskins from the cubby and floated past the four humans, offering the less-than-paper-thin molecular suits to each person in turn.

Daeman held the suit in two hands and looked puzzled. "Is this a joke?"

"No," said Harman. "I've worn one before."

"So have I," said Hannah.

Daeman unfurled the thermskin. It was like holding smoke. "This won't fit on over my clothes."

"It's not supposed to," said Harman. "It has to go next to the skin. There's a hood on it as well, but you'll be able to see and hear through it."

"Can we wear our regular clothes over it?" asked Ada. There was a hint of concern in her voice. After her useless exhibitionism the night before, she was not feeling very adventurous. At least not when it came to nudity.

The first servitor answered. "Except for footwear, it is not advisable to wear other layers, Ada *Uhr*. For the thermskin to be effective, it must be fully osmotic. Other clothes reduce its efficiency."

"You have to be kidding," said Daeman.

"We could always fax back home and get our coldest weather clothing," said Harman. "Although I'm not sure that it would be up to the conditions outside here." He glanced at the shimmering forcefield wall. The howling wind was still quite audible and frightening beyond it.

"No," said the second servitor, "standard jackets and coats and capes would not be adequate here in the Dry Valley. We can facture more modest extreme-weather clothing and return with it within the next thirty minutes if you prefer."

"Hell with it," said Ada. "I want to see what's out there." She walked to the center of the pavilion, behind the faxportal itself, and began disrobing in plain view. Hannah took five steps and joined her, peeling off her tunic and silken balloon trousers.

Daeman goggled a moment. Harman walked over to the younger man, touched his arm, and led him to the far side of the circle, where he began undressing as well. Yet even as he disrobed, Daeman glanced over his shoulder several times at the women—Ada's skin glowing rich and full in the light from the overhead halogens; Hannah lean and strong and brown. Hannah glanced up from tugging the thermskin up her legs and scowled at Daeman. He looked away quickly.

When the four stood in the center of the pavilion again, wearing only their shoes or boots over the thermskins, Ada laughed. "These things are more revealing than if we were naked," she said.

Daeman shuffled with embarrassment at the truth of the statement, but Harman smiled through his mask. The thermskin was more paint than clothing.

"Why are we different colors?" asked Daeman. Ada was bright yellow, Hannah orange, Harman a brilliant blue, Daeman green.

"To identify each other easily," answered the servitor as if the question had been directed to it.

Ada laughed again—that free, easy, unselfconscious laugh that made both of the men glance at her. "Sorry," she said. "It's just that . . . it's pretty obvious, even from a distance, which of us is which."

Harman walked to the forcefield and set his blue hand against it. "Can we pass now?" he asked the servitors.

The machines did not answer, but the force shield wavered slightly, Harman's hand passed through it, and then his blue body appeared to be moving through a silver waterfall as he stepped through.

The servitors followed the four into the windy darkness.

"We don't need your escort," Harman said to the machines. Daeman noticed that the other man's voice was lost in the wind, but he could hear clearly through the thermskin cowl. There was some sort of transmission device and earphones in the molecular suit.

"I apologize, Harman *Uhr,*" said the first servitor, "but you do. For the light. " Both servitors were illuminating the rough ground with multiple flashlight beams from their shells.

Harman shook his head. "I've used these thermskins before, in the high mountains and far north. They have light-enhancement devices in the cowl lenses." He touched his temple, feeling around for a second. "There. I can see perfectly well now. The stars are brilliant."

"Oh, my," said Ada as her night vision switched on. Rather than the small circles of light afforded by the servitors' flashbeams, the entire Dry Valley was now visible, each rock and boulder glowing brightly. When she looked up, the blazing stars took her breath away. When she turned her head, the lighted faxnode pavilion was a glowing, roaring furnace of light. Their thermskins glowed in color.

"This is so . . . wonderful," said Hannah. She walked twenty paces away from the group, jumping from rock to rock. They were at the bottom of a wide, rocky valley, with gradual cliffs on either side. Above them, snowfields glowed bright blue-white in the starlight, but the valley itself was all but free from snow. Clouds moved in front of the stars like phosphorescent sheep. The wind howled around them, buffeting them even when they stood still.

"I'm cold," said Daeman. The pudgy young man was shifting from foot to foot. He had worn only walking slippers.

"You may return to the pavilion and leave us," Harman said to the servitors.

"With all due respect, Harman *Uhr,* our person-protection programming does not allow us to leave you here alone to run the risk of injury or getting lost in the Dry Valley," said one of the servitors. "But we shall retreat a hundred yards, if that is your preference."

"That's our preference," said Harman. "And turn off those damned lights. They're too bright in our night-vision lenses."

Both servitors complied, floating back toward the faxnode pavilion. Hannah led them across the valley. There were no trees, no grass, no signs of life whatsoever, outside of the four human beings glowing in bright color.

"What are we hunting for?" asked Hannah, stepping over what might have been a small stream in summer—if, indeed, summer ever came to this place.

"Is this the site of the Burning Man?" asked Harman.

Daeman and Hannah both looked around. Finally Daeman spoke. "It could be. But there were—you know—tents and pavilions and rest rooms and flowdomes and the forcefield over the valley and big heaters and the Burning Man and daylight and . . . it was different then. Not so *cold*." He hopped gingerly from foot to foot.

"Hannah?" said Daeman.

"I'm not sure. That place was also rocky and desolate, but . . . Daeman's right, it looked different with the thousands of people and sunlight. I don't know."

Ada took the lead. "Let's fan out and hunt for some sign that the Burning Man was held here . . . campfires, rock cairns . . . something. Although I don't think we'll find your Wandering Jew person here tonight, Harman."

"Shhh," said Harman, glancing over his blue shoulder at the distant servitors, then realizing that they were broadcasting their conversation anyway. "All right," he said with a sigh, "let's spread out, say a couple of hundred feet apart, and look for anything that . . ."

He stopped as a large, only vaguely humanoid shape appeared from a side canyon. The creature picked its way across the rocks with a familiar awkward grace. When it got within thirty feet, Harman said, "Go back. We don't need a voynix here."

One of the servitors answered, its voice in their ears even though the sphere itself floated far behind them. "We must insist, my gentlemen and ladies. This is the most remote and hostile of all known faxnodes. We cannot risk the small chance that something here could harm you."

"Are there dinosaurs?" asked Daeman, his voice on edge.

Ada laughed again and opened her arms and hands to the dark and howling cold. "I doubt it, Daeman. They'd have to be some tough recombinant winter breed I've never heard of."

"Anything's possible," Hannah said, pointing to a large rock near the entrance to another side canyon about fifty yards to their right. "That could be an allosaurus right there, just waiting for us."

Daeman took a step back and almost tripped over a rock.

"There aren't any dinosaurs here," said Harman. "I don't think there's *any* living thing here. It's too damned cold. If you doubt me, lift your cowls for a second."

The others did. The molecular earphones rang with their exclamations.

"You stay back unless called," Harman directed the voynix. The creature moved back thirty paces.

They walked up the valley—northwest according to their palm direction finders. The stars shook from the force of the wind and occasionally all four of them would have to huddle in the shelter of a large boulder to keep from getting blown over. When the gale lessened in intensity, they spread out again.

"There's something here," came Ada's voice.

The others hurried to join the yellow form a hundred feet to their south. Ada was looking down at what at first appeared to be just another rock, but as Daeman got closer, he saw the brittle hair or fur, the odd flipper appendages, and the black holes or eyes. The thing appeared to be carved from weathered wood.

"It's a seal," said Harman.

"What's that?" asked Hannah, kneeling to touch the still figure.

"An aquatic mammal. I've seen them near coastlines . . . away from faxnodes." He also knelt and touched the animal's corpse. "This thing's dried out . . . mummified is the word. It may have been here for centuries. Millennia."

"So we're near a coast," said Ada.

"Not necessarily," said Harman, standing and looking around.

"Hey," said Daeman, "I remember that big boulder. The beer pavilion was pitched just below it." He made his way slowly to the boulder near the cliff wall.

"Are you sure?" asked Ada when they'd caught up. There was only the rock slab rising toward the coldly burning stars and hurrying clouds. Everyone looked on the ground for signs of the tent or campfires or carriole tracks, but there was nothing.

"It was a year and a half ago," said Harman. "The servitors probably cleaned up well and . . ."

"Oh, my God," interrupted Hannah.

They all turned quickly. The orange-suited young woman was looking skyward. They lifted their heads, even as they each noticed the play of colored light on the rocks around them.

The night sky was alive with curtains of shimmering, dancing light—bars of blues and yellows and dancing reds.

"What is it?" whispered Ada.

"I don't know," Harman responded, also whispering. The light continued to writhe across the uncloudy portions of the sky. Harman lifted off his thermskin cowl. "My God, it's almost as brilliant without the night-vision. I think I saw something like this once decades ago when I was . . ."

"Servitors," interrupted Daeman, "what is this light?"

"A form of atmospheric phenomenon associated with charged particles from the sun interacting with Earth's electromagnetic field," came the voice from the distant machine. "We no longer have the particulars of the scientific explanation, but it goes under different names, including . . ."

"All right," said Harman. "That's enough . . . hey." He had pulled on his cowl again and was looking at the rock slab in front of them.

There were complex scratchings on the rock. They did not look as if they had been made by the wind or other natural causes.

"What is it?" asked Ada. "It doesn't look like the symbols in the books."

"No," agreed Harman.

"Something from the Burning Man?" said Hannah.

"I don't remember scratches on the rock near the beer tent," said Daeman. "But maybe the servitors scratched up the surface moving some of the stuff out after the celebration."

"Perhaps," said Harman.

"Should we keep hunting around here?" asked Ada. "Try to find some sign that this woman you're after was here? Or even that the Burning Man was here? Maybe there are some ashes left."

"In this wind?" laughed Daeman. "After a year and a half?"

"A pit," said Ada. "A campfire. We could . . ."

"No," said Harman. "We're not going to find anything here. Let's fax somewhere warm and get some lunch."

Ada turned her yellow head to look at Harman, but she said nothing.

The two servitors had floated toward them and the voynix loomed just behind them.

"We're going," Harman told the closer servitor. "You can use your flashlight beams to illuminate our way back to the fax pavilion."

It was just after midday in Ulanbat and the usual hundred or so guests were milling at Tobi's ongoing Second Twenty party on the seventy-ninth floor of the Circles to Heaven. The hanging gardens rustled and sighed from the breeze blowing off the red desert. Daeman was greeted by a host of young men and women who had not noticed his absence over the past few days, but he followed Harman, Hannah, and Ada as they found hot finger food at the long banquet table and had cold wine poured by a servitor. Harman led them away from the crowd to a stone table near the low wall at the edge of the circle. Eight hundred feet below, camel caravans driven by servitors and followed by voynix padded in on the hard-packed Gobi Highway.

"What is it?" said Ada as they sat in the garden shade and ate. "I know something happened back there."

Harman started to speak, paused, and waited for a servitor to float past. "Do you ever wonder," he asked, "if that utility servitor is the same one you just saw somewhere else? They all look alike."

"That's absurd," said Daeman. Between bites on a chicken leg, he was licking his fingers and sipping his chilled wine.

"Perhaps," said Harman.

"What did you see back there in the dark?" asked Hannah. "Those scratches on the rock?"

"They were numbers," said Harman.

Daeman laughed. "No they *weren't*. I know numbers. We all know numbers. Those weren't numbers."

"They were numbers written out in words."

"It didn't look like the jiggles in books," said Ada. "Words."

"No," said Harman. "I think was the kind of writing people used to do by hand. The words were all loopy and connected and worn down some by the wind—I suspect that they were written there way back at the last Burning Man—but I could read them."

"Words," laughed Daeman. "A minute ago you said they were numbers."

"What did they say?" asked Hannah.

Harman looked around him again. "Eight-eight-four-nine," he said softly.

Ada shook her head. "It sounds like a faxnode code, but it's way too high. I've never heard of a code that started with two eights."

"There aren't any," said Daeman.

Harman shrugged. "Maybe. But when we're done here, I'm going to try it out at the core node here."

Ada looked out at the distant horizon. The rings were visible above them, two milky strings crossing in a pale blue sky. "Is that why you kept the four thermskins rather than throwing them in the disposal bin as the servitors told us to do?"

"I didn't know you noticed that I did," said Harman. He grinned and drank wine. "I tried to do it on the sly. I guess I'm not very good at secrets. At least the servitors had already faxed away."

As if on cue, a servitor floated over to replenish their drinks. The little spherical machine floated beyond the wall—eight hundred feet above the red-yellow ground—as its dainty, white-gloved hands poured wine into their glasses.

If Harman hadn't insisted they change into their thermskins and wear them under their clothes before faxing, they might have died.

"Good God," cried Daeman, "where are we? What's going on?"

There was no faxnode pavilion. Code 8849 had brought them straight into darkness and chaos. Wind howled. There was ice underfoot. The four crashed into sharp things with every step they took in the screaming blackness. Even the faxportal had disappeared behind them.

"Ada!" called Harman. "The light!" Their hoods provided night vision, but none of them had their hoods up at the moment and there seemed to be no ambient light to magnify in this absolute blackness.

"I'm trying to get it on . . . there!" The small flashlight she'd borrowed from Tobi poured a thin beam into the night, illuminating an open door rimmed with frost, icicles three feet long, frozen waves of ice under foot. Ada swung the light and three thermskinned faces stared back at her, surprise clearly visible on each face.

"There's no pavilion," Harman said aloud.

"Every faxnode has a pavilion," said Daeman. "There can't be a portal without a node pavilion. Right?"

"Not in the old days," said Harman. "There were thousands of private nodes."

"What's he talking about?" shouted Daeman. "Let's get *out* of here!"

Ada had swung the light back into the space they'd faxed into. There was no portal. They were in a small room with shelves and counters and walls, all covered with ice. Unlike all fax pavilions, there was no faxnode code-plate pedestal in the center of the room. And that meant there was no way out, no way back. A million flakes of ice danced in the flashlight beam. Beyond the walls, the wind howled.

"Daeman, what you said earlier seems to be true now," said Harman.

"What? What did I say earlier?"

"That we're trapped. Trapped like rats."

Daeman blinked and the flashlight beam moved on to the frosted walls. The wind howled more loudly.

"It sounds like the wind in the Dry Valley," said Hannah. "But there were no buildings there. Were there?"

"I don't think so," said Harman. "But I suspect we're still in Antarctica."

"*Where?*" said Daeman, his teeth chattering. "What's ant . . . antattica?"

"The cold place we were at this morning," said Ada. She stepped through the doorway, leaving the others in darkness for a moment. They scrambled to catch up and huddled behind her like goslings. "There's a hallway here," said Ada. "Watch your step. The floor is under a foot of ice and snow."

The frozen hallway led to a frozen kitchen, the frozen kitchen opened onto a frozen living room with overturned couches drifted with snow. Ada ran her flashlight beam across a wall of windows triple-glazed with ice.

"I think I know where we are," whispered Harman.

"Never mind that," said Hannah. "How do we get *out*?"

"Wait," said Ada, lowering the flashlight beam to the icy floor so that everyone's faces were illuminated by the bounce light from below. "I want to know where you think we are."

"According to the story I've heard, the woman I'm hunting for—the Wandering Jew—had a home, a domi, on Mount Erberus, a volcano in Antarctica."

"In the Dry Valley?" asked Daeman. The young man kept glancing over his shoulders at the darkness behind him. "God, I'm *freezing*."

Hannah moved so quickly over the ice toward Daeman that he staggered back and almost slipped. "Silly, you have to put your thermskin hood on," she said. "We all do. We're going to get frostbite if we don't. Plus, we're losing a lot of body heat through our scalp right now." She pulled the green cowl of the thermskin free of his shirt and tugged the hood into place over his head.

Everyone hurried to follow suit.

"That's better," said Harman. "I can see now. And hear better as well—the suit earphones damp out the wind howl."

"You were saying before that this woman had a place on a volcano—near the Dry Valley? Close enough for us to walk to the fax pavilion there?"

Harman gestured helplessly. "I don't know. I'd wondered if that's how she had shown up at the Burning Man—just walked there—but I don't know the geography. It might be one mile or a thousand miles from here."

Daeman looked at the black, iced windows where the wind flexed the shatterproof panes. "I'm not going out there," he said flatly. "Not for any reason."

"For once I agree with Daeman," said Hannah.

"I don't understand any of this," said Ada. "You said that this woman lived here long ago—lifetimes ago—centuries and centuries. How could she . . ."

"I don't know," said Harman. He borrowed the flashlight from Ada and started walking down the next hallway. He was stopped by what looked to be white bars. While the others watched, he went back into the drifted living room, picked up the heaviest piece of furniture he could pry free of the ice—a heavy table, the legs snapping off as he tugged it free—and walked back to smash the icicles one after the other, battering a path down the snow-filled hallway.

"Where are you going?" called Daeman. "What good is it going to do to go down there. No one's been there for a million years. We're just going to freeze when . . ."

Harman kicked open a door at the end of the hallway. Light poured out. So did heat. The other three moved as quickly as they could across the treacherous surface to join him.

Much like the room they had faxed into, this space was windowless and about twenty feet square. But unlike the other room, this one was warm, lighted, and free of snow or ice. And unlike the other room, this one was almost filled with an oval metal machine about fifteen feet long. The thing was floating silently three feet off the concrete floor, and a forcefield shimmered like a glass canopy over its top surface. On that surface were six indentations with a soft black material lining them; each indentation was the length of a human body with two short grips or controllers near where the hands would be.

"It looks like someone was expecting two more of us," whispered Hannah.

"What *is* it?" said Daeman.

"I think it's a sonie . . . also called an AFV," said Harman, his own voice hushed.

"*What?*" said Daeman. "What do those words mean?"

"I don't know," said Harman. "But people in the lost ages used to fly around in them." He touched the forcefield; it parted like quicksilver under his fingers, flowed around his hand, swallowed his wrist.

"Careful!" said Ada, but Harman had already lowered himself first onto his knees and then onto his stomach, then prone and settling into the black material. His head and back rose just slightly above the curved upper surface of the machine.

"It's fine," he said. "Comfortable. And warm."

That settled it for the others. Ada was the first to crawl onto the craft, stretching out on her stomach and grasping the two handlgrips. "Are these controls of some sort?"

"I have no idea," said Harman as Hannah and Daeman crawled onto the disk and settled into the outer impressions, leaving the two rear-center depressions empty.

"You don't know how to fly the thing?" asked Ada, a bit more shrilly this time. "From the books? From your reading?"

Harman just shook his head.

"Then what are we *doing* on it?" said Ada.

"Experimenting." Harman twisted the top off his right handgrip. There was a single red button there. He pressed it.

The wall ahead of them disappeared as if it had been blown out into the antarctic night. Cold wind and flying snow swept around them in a blinding implosion, as if the air in the room had been sucked out and the storm pulled back in in its place.

Harman opened his mouth to say "Hang on!" but before he could speak, the sonie leaped out of the room at an impossible velocity, pressing the bottoms of their boots back against metal and making them each cling wildly to the handgrips.

The forcefield bubble over their heads kept them alive as the sonie, the AFV, the *thing*, flew out from the white volcano with its ice-crusted and shattered buildings clinging to its seaward side. The night-vision lenses in their thermskin hoods showed them the fir forest along the coast gone back to ice and death, the abandoned and drifted-over robotic equipment along the curve of a bay, and then the white sea—the frozen sea.

The sonie leveled off about a thousand feet above that frozen sea and hurtled out away from land.

Harman released one of the handgrips long enough to activate the direction finder on his palm. "Northeast," he said to the others over their suit comms.

No one replied. Everyone was clinging and shaking too fiercely to comment on the direction the machine was headed while taking them to their deaths.

What Harman did not say aloud was that if the old maps he had studied were accurate, there was nothing out this direction for thousands of miles. Nothing.

Ten minutes of flight and the sonie began losing altitude. They had passed beyond the ice and now were flying over black water scattered with icebergs.

"What's happening?" said Ada. She hated the quaver in her own voice. "Is this thing out of energy . . . fuel . . . whatever it uses?"

"I don't know," said Harman.

The sonie leveled off a mere hundred feet above the water. "Look," called Hannah. She raised a hand from its grip to point ahead of them.

Suddenly the back of something huge, alive, barnacled with age, flesh corrugated-tough, broke the cold sea, its mammal heat radiating like throbbing blood in their night-vision-enhanced sight. A spout of water shot high toward them and Harman smelled fish on the fresh air that the forcefield allowed through.

"What . . ." began Daeman.

"I think it's called . . . a whale, I think that's how to pronounce it . . . but I thought it was extinct millennia ago," said Harman.

"Maybe the post-humans brought it back," Ada said over their suit intercoms.

"Maybe."

They hurtled farther out to sea, always east-northeast, and after a few more minutes of the sonie holding its altitude, the four passengers began relaxing a bit, adapting, as humans have done since time immemorial, to a strange new situation. Harman had rolled on his side and was looking up at the brilliant stars becoming visible between scattered clouds when Ada startled him by shouting, "Look! Ahead!"

A large iceberg had become visible over the dark horizon and the sonie was hurtling straight toward it. The machine had flown over or past other icebergs, but none this broad—it stretched sideways for miles like a gleaming blue-white wall in their night vision—and none this tall—it was apparent that the top of the monstrous thing was higher than their current altitude.

"What can we do?" asked Ada.

Harman shook his head. He had no idea how fast the sonie was going—none of them had ever traveled faster than a voynix-pulled droshky—but it was fast enough, he knew, that the impact would destroy them.

"Do you have other controls on your handgrip?" asked Hannah. Her voice was strangely calm.

"No," said Harman.

"We could jump," said Daeman from behind and to the left of Harman. The sonie tilted a bit as Daeman got to his knees and elbows, his head just within the forcefield bubble.

"No," said Harman, putting the force of command in the syllable. "You wouldn't last thirty seconds in that sea, even if you survived the fall . . . which you wouldn't. Get down."

Daeman dropped to his belly again.

The sonie did not slow or change course. The face of the iceberg—Harman guessed that the thing was at least two miles across—rushed at them and grew taller. Harman estimated that it rose at least three hundred feet above the water. They would strike it two-thirds of the way down its cold face.

"There's nothing we can do?" said Ada, making it more a statement than a question.

Harman pulled his hood off and looked at her. The cold air was not so bad within their forcefield cockpit. "I don't think so," he said. "I'm sorry." He reached across with his right hand to take her left hand. She swept her thermskin hood off to show him her eyes. She and Harman interlaced fingers for a few seconds.

A few hundred yards before fiery collision, the sonie slowed again and gained altitude. It whisked over the top edge of the iceberg with ten feet to spare and banked to the right until it was flying south above the icy surface. It slowed more, hovered, and settled onto the surface, snow hissing under its heated underside.

Harman and the others lay where they were for a silent moment, hanging on to the handgrips, not sharing their thoughts.

The forcefield bubble disappeared and suddenly the terrible cold and wind burned at Harman's face. He pulled his hood down in a hurry, glancing at Ada as she did the same.

"We should get off this thing before it decides to take us somewhere else," Hannah said softly on the comm.

They scrambled off. The wind shoved them off balance, relented, shoved at them again. Spindrift pelted their outer clothing and hoods.

"What now?" whispered Ada.

As if in answer, a double row of red infrared beacons winked on, outlining a ten-foot-wide path from the sonie for a hundred yards to . . . nothing.

They walked together, holding each other upright in the wind. If the beacon lights had not burned so brightly in their night vision, they would have turned their backs to the wind and been lost in seconds—lost until they stepped off the edge of the iceberg somewhere to their right.

The path ended in a hole in the iceberg's surface. Steps had been hacked out of the ice and disappeared toward another red glow far below.

"Shall we?" said Hannah.

"What choice do we have?" asked Daeman.

The steps were slippery under their street boots, but some sort of climbing rope had been attached to the right wall with metal spikes and loops, and the four clung to the line while descending. Harman had counted forty steps when the stairway ended in a wall of ice. No, the steps continued to their right and down—fifty steps this time—then left and down again for fifty more, the whole descent illuminated by spaced infrared cold-flares set into the ice.

At the bottom of the steps, a corridor led deep into the iceberg, the way illuminated now by green and blue cold-flares as well as red. At places they came to junctions, but one choice was always dark, the other illuminated. Once they climbed along a slowly ascending corridor; another time they descended for a hundred feet or more. The bends and junctions and choices became too labyrinthine to keep track.

"Someone's expecting us," whispered Hannah.

"I'm counting on it," said Ada.

They emerged into a broad hall, perhaps a hundred feet across at the widest, the ice ceiling thirty feet above, various other entrances dotting the walls and connected by ice stairways, the floor graded to different levels. Heaters on pedestrals glowed orange and there were a variety of light sources spiked into the walls, floors, and ceilings. On one of the low platforms lay what looked to be furry animal hides, cushions, and a low table with bowls of food and pitchers and goblets of drink. The four gathered around the table but looked dubiously at its contents.

"It's all right," said a woman's voice behind them. "It's not poisoned."

She had emerged from a high ice door near the platform and now she descended a zigzag of stairs toward them. Harman had time to notice the woman's hair—gray-white, an almost unheard-of choice except for a few eccentrics—and her face: lined with wrinkles just as Daeman had said. This woman was old in a way none of them—except for Daeman at the last Burning Man—had ever seen, and the effect unsettled even Harman with his ninety and nine years.

Other than the obvious age, the woman was attractive enough. Her stride was strong and she wore a commonplace blue tunic top, cord trousers, and solid boots, the one dash of eccentricity being the red wool cape over her shoulders. The cape's cut was complicated, never quite resolving itself into simple folds. As she stepped onto the platform a few feet from them, Harman noticed the dark metal object in her right hand.

As if noticing the device for the first time herself, she raised it toward them. "Do any of you know what this is?"

"No," said Daeman, Ada, and Hannah in a soft chorus.

"Yes," said Harman. "It's some sort of Lost Age weapon."

The other three looked at him. They had seen weapons in the turin-cloth drama—swords, spears, shields, bows and arrows—but nothing so machinelike as this blunt black thing.

"Correct," said the woman. "This is called a gun and it only does one thing—it kills."

Daeman took a step toward the old woman. "Are you going to kill us? Did you bring us all this way to kill us?"

The old woman smiled and set the weapon on the table, next to a bowl of oranges. "Hello, Daeman," she said. "It's nice to see you again, although I'm not sure you'd remember me from our last meeting. You were in a pretty advanced state of inebriation."

"I remember you, Savi," said Daeman, his tone cool.

"And all of you," continued the old woman, "Hannah, Ada, Harman . . . welcome. You were very persistent in following clues, Harman." She sat on the furs, gestured, and one after the other, the four sat around the low table with her. Savi picked up an orange, offered it, and began peeling it with a sharp fingernail when the others declined.

"We haven't met," said Harman. "How do you know my name . . . our names?"

"You've left quite a wake behind you—what is your people's honorific these days? Harman *Uhr*."

"Wake?"

"Hiking far from faxnodes so the voynix have to follow you. Learning to read. Seeking out the few remaining libraries in the world . . . including Ada *Uhr*'s." She nodded in Ada's direction and the young woman nodded in return.

"How do you know that voynix followed me anywhere?" asked Harman.

"The voynix monitor anyone unusual," said Savi. She separated the orange into segments, put two segments on four linen cloths, and offered them around. All four accepted them this time. "I monitor *you*," she finished, looking at Harman.

"Why?" Harman looked at the slices and set the cloth down on the table. "Why spy on me? And how?"

"Two different questions, my young friend."

Harman had to smile at this. No one who knew him had called him young in a very long time. "Then answer the first," he said. "Why spy on me?"

Savi finished the second slice of orange and licked her fingers. Harman noticed Ada studying the older woman with fascination, looking at her wrinkled fingers and age-mottled hands. If Savi noticed the inspection, she ignored it. "Harman . . . may I drop the *Uhr*?" She did not wait for an answer, but went on, "Harman, right now you are the only human being on Earth, out of a population of more than three hundred thousand souls . . . the only human being other than *me* . . . who can read a written language. Or who wants to."

"But . . ." began Harman.

"Three hundred thousand people?" interrupted Hannah. "There are a million of us. There have *always* been a million of us."

Savi smiled but shook her head. "My dear, who told you that there a million living human beings on the Earth today?"

"Why . . . no one . . . I mean, everyone knows . . ."

"Precisely," said Savi. "Everyone knows. But there is no mechanism to count the population."

"But when someone ascends to the rings . . ." continued Hannah, showing her confusion.

"Another child is allowed to be born," finished Savi. "Yes. So I have noticed during the last millennium or so. But there is no population of a million of you. Far fewer."

"Why would the posts lie to us?" asked Daeman.

Savi raised one eyebrow. "The posts. Ah, yes . . . the posts. Have you spoken to a post-human recently, Daeman *Uhr*?"

Daeman must have considered that question rhetorical; he did not answer.

"I have spoken to post-humans," Savi said quietly.

This carried the others into silence. They waited silently. Such an idea was—at least to Harman and Ada—literally breathtaking.

"But that was a long time ago," the old woman said, speaking so softly that the other leaned closer to hear. "A *long*, long time ago. Before the final fax." Her eyes, a startling gray-blue a second before, now looked clouded, distracted.

Harman shook his head. "I was the one who heard the story about you—the Wandering Jew, the last of your Lost Age—but I don't understand. How can you live beyond your Fifth Twenty?"

Ada blinked at Harman's rudeness, but Savi did not seem to mind. "First of all, this hundred-year life span is a relatively recent addition to humankind, my dears. It is something the posts came up with only after the final fax. Only after they botched everything—our future, the Earth's future—in that disastrous final fax. Only centuries after my nine thousand one hundred and thirteen post-rubicon fellow humans were faxed into the neutrino stream—never to be returned, *although the posts promised them they would be*—only after that . . . genocide . . . did your precious post-humans rebuild the core population of your ancestors and come up with this idea of one hundred years and a theoretical herd population of a million people . . ."

Savi stopped and took a breath. She was obviously agitated. She took another breath and gestured to the pitchers on the table. "I have tea here, if you are interested. Or a very strong wine. I am going to take some wine." She did so, pouring with slightly shaking hands. She gestured to their goblets. Daeman shook his head. Hannah and Ada took tea. Harman accepted a goblet of red wine.

"Harman," she began again, more composed now, "you asked two questions before I digressed from my answer. First, why have I noticed you. Second, how have I survived for so long.

"The answer to your first question is that I am interested in what the voynix are interested in and alarmed by, and they are interested in and alarmed by your behavior over the past decades . . ."

"But why would the voynix notice or care about me . . . " began Harman.

Savi held up one finger. "To your second question, I can say that I stay alive over these past centuries by sleeping much of the time and by hiding when I am awake. When I move, it is either by sonie—you enjoyed a ride in one today—or through walking, hiking between the faxnode pavilions."

"I don't understand," said Ada. "How can you hike between faxnodes?"

Savi stood. The others stood with her. "I understand it's been a busy day for you, my young friends, but much lies ahead if you choose to follow me. If not, the sonie will return you to the nearest faxnode pavilion . . . in what used to be Africa, I believe. It is your choice." She looked at Daeman. "Each of you must choose."

Hannah drank the last of her tea and set the goblet down. "And what are you going to show us if we follow you, Savi *Uhr*?"

"Many things, my child. But first of all, I will show you how to fly and to visit places you've never heard of . . . places you've never dreamt of."

The four looked at each other. Harman and Ada nodded to each other, agreeing that they would follow the woman. Hannah said, "Yes, count me in."

Daeman seemed to be pondering the choice for a silent moment. Then he said, "I'll go. But before I go, I want some of that strong wine after all."

Savi filled his goblet.

Low Mars Orbit

Mahnmut reset his systems and did a quick damage assessment. Nothing disabling to either his organic or cybernetic components. The explosion had caused rapid depressurization of three forward ballast tanks, but twelve remained intact. He checked internal clocks; he had been unconscious for less than thirty seconds before reset and he was still connected virtually to his submersible across the usual bandwidths. *The Dark Lady* was reporting wild tumbling, some minor hull breach, monitoring-system overloads, hull temperatures above boiling, and a score of other complaints, but there was nothing that demanded Mahnmut's immediate attention. He rebooted video connections, but all he could see was the red-hot glowing interior of the spacecraft's hold, the open bay doors, and—through those doors—tumbling starfields.

Orphu?

There was no response on the common band or on any of the tight-beam or maser channels. Not even static.

The airlock was still open. Mahnmut grabbed a personal reaction pack and coils of unbreakable microfilament rope and pulled himself out the airlock doors, fighting the vector forces of the tumbling by grabbing handholds he knew from decades of deep-sea work. On his own hull, he checked that the sub's payload-bay doors were fully opened, estimated how much room he would need, and then grabbed some of Koros's carefully folded machines at random and jetted them out of his sub, out of the disintegrating spacecraft, tumbling away through the blobs of molten ship metal and glowing plasma. Mahnmut didn't know if he was jettisoning the weapons of mass destruction that Koros had been planning to bring to the surface—*on my ship!* thought Mahnmut with the same outrage he'd felt earlier—or if he was jettisoning gear that he would need for survival if he ever reached Mars. At that moment, he didn't care. He needed the space.

Tying the rope off to brackets on *The Dark Lady*'s hull, Mahnmut jetted out into space, taking care not to collide with the shattered ship-bay doors.

Once outside and a safe hundred meters from the tumbling ship, he rotated to get his first view of the damage.

It was worse than he'd thought. As Orphu had described, the entire bow of the spacecraft was gone—the control room and everything ten meters aft of where the control room had been. Sheared off as if it had never existed. Only a glowing and dissipating cloud of plasma around the bow showed where Koros III and Ri Po had been.

The rest of the ship's fuselage had cracked and fragmented. Mahnmut could only guess the catastrophic results if the fusion engines, hydrogen tanks, Matloff/Fennelly scoop, and other propulsion devices had not been jettisoned long before this attack. The secondary explosions would certainly have vaporized Orphu and him.

Orphu? Mahnmut was using radio now as well as tightbeam, but the reflector antennae had been slagged off the hull for the maser relay. There was no response.

Trying to avoid the flying shrapnel, blobs of glowing metal, and the worst of the expanding plasma cloud while keeping slack in the line so that the tumbling wouldn't fling him around the dying ship, Mahnmut used the reaction thrusters to come up and over the hull of the ship. The tumbling was so fierce now—stars, Mars, stars, Mars—that Mahnmut had to shut down his eyes and use the pack's radar feed to find his way around the hull.

Orphu was still in his cradle. For a second, Mahnmut was joyous— the radar signature showed his friend intact and in place—but then he activated his eyes and saw the carnage.

The blast that had sheared off the bow had also scorched and fractured the upper hull of the ship all the way back to Orphu's position and—as the Ionian had reported—had cracked and blackened his heavy carapace for a third of his length. Orphu's forward manipulators were gone. His forward comm antennae were missing. His eyes were gone. Cracks ran the last three meters of Orphu's upper shell.

"Orphu!" called Mahnmut on direct tightbeam.

Nothing.

Using every meg of his computational abilities, Mahnmut gauged the vectors involved and jetted over to the upper hull, all ten jets firing in microbursts to adjust his dangerous trajectory, until he was within a meter of the hull. He pulled the k-tool from the pack's belt and fired a piton into the hull, then looped his line around it, making sure to keep it from getting tangled. He would have to pull free in a minute.

Pulling the line tight, swinging like a pendulum arm, Mahnmut arced aft to Orphu's cradle—although scorched crater seemed a better description of the indentation in the hull now.

Hanging on to Orphu's carapace, his short legs swinging wildly above him, Mahnmut slapped a hardline stick-on against his friend's body just aft of where his eyes had been. "Orphu?"

"Mahnmut?" Orphu's voice was cracked but strong. Mostly, it was surprised. "Where are you? How are you reaching me? All my comm is down."

Mahnmut felt the kind of joy that only a few of Shakespeare's characters ever achieved. "I'm in contact with you. Hardline. I'm going to get you out of here."

"That's idiotic!" boomed the Ionian's voice. "I'm useless. I don't . . ."

"Shut up," explained Mahnmut. "I have a line. I need to tie you on. Where . . ."

"There's a tie-on bracket about two meters aft of my sensor bundle," said Orphu.

"No, there isn't." Mahnmut hated the idea of firing a piton into Orphu's body, but he would if he had to.

"Well . . ." began Orphu and stopped for a terrible few seconds of silence as the extent of his own injuries obviously sank in. "Aft then. Farthest from the blast. Just above the thruster cluster."

Mahnmut didn't tell his friend that the external thrusters were also gone. He kicked back, found the tie-on, and tied the microfilament line with an unbreakable knot. If there was one thing that moravec Mahnmut had in common with the human sailors who had preceded him on Earth's seas for millennia, it was knowing how to tie a good knot.

"Hang on," said Mahnmut over the hardline. "I'm going to pull you out. Don't worry if we lose contact. There are a lot of vector forces right now."

"This is insane!" cried Orphu his voice still scratchy on the hardline. "There's no room in *The Dark Lady* and I can't do you any good if you get me there. I don't have anything left to hang on with."

"Quiet," said Mahnmut, his voice calm. He added, "My friend."

Mahnmut triggered all the reaction-pack jets, tugging loose the piton line as he did so.

The jets got Orphu up and out of his hull cradle. The tumbling of the ship did the rest, swinging both moravecs a hundred meters out and away from the ship.

Delta-v computations clouding his vision field, Mars and stars still exchanging places every two seconds, Mahnmut let the line go taut and then he fired the thrusters—using up energy at a fearsome rate—matching tumble velocities and reeling himself up the long line to *The Dark Lady.*

Orphu's mass was considerable, its pull made the worse by the tumbling, but the line was unbreakable and so was Mahnmut's will at the moment. He ratcheted them closer to the open bay of the waiting submersible.

The spacecraft began breaking up from the stresses, pieces of the stern snapping off and flying past Mahnmut where he clung to Orphu's carapace, two tons of metal missing the smaller moravec's head by less than five meters. Mahnmut pulled them in.

It was no use. The ship was coming apart around *The Dark Lady,* explosions further rending the hull as trace reaction gases and internal pressurized chambers gave way. Mahnmut would never get to the sub before it was torn apart.

"All right," muttered Mahnmut. "The mountain has to come to Mohammed."

"What?" cried Orphu, sounding alarmed for the first time.

Mahnmut had forgotten the hardline was still operative. "Nothing. Hang on."

"How can I hang on, my friend? My manipulators and hands are all gone. You hang on to *me.*"

"Right," said Mahnmut and fired every thruster he had, using up the pack's energy supplies so quickly that he had to go to emergency reserve.

It worked. *The Dark Lady* emerged from the dark ship's bay only seconds before the belly of the spacecraft began to come apart.

Mahnmut thrusted further away, seeing blobs of molten metal splatter on Orphu's poor battered carapace. "I'm sorry," whispered Mahnmut as he used the last of his fuel to tug the tumbling submersible farther from the dying spaceship.

"Sorry for what?" asked Orphu.

"Never mind," panted Mahnmut. "Tell you later."

He tugged, shoved, thrust, and generally moravec-hauled the huge Ionian into the almost-empty payload bay. It was better in the darkness of the bay—the wildly spinning stars/planet/stars/planet no longer gave Mahnmut vertigo. He crammed his friend into the main payload niche and activated the adjustable clamps.

Orphu was secure now. It was probable that all three of them—*The Dark Lady* and the two moravecs—were doomed, but at least they'd end their existence together. Mahnmut attached the sub's comm leads to the hardline port.

"You're safe for now," gasped Mahnmut, feeling the organic parts of his body nearing overload. "I'm going to cut my hardline comm now."

"What . . ." began Orphu but Mahnmut had cut the portable line and pulled himself hand over hand to the payload bay airlock. It still cycled.

With the last of his strength, he pulled himself up the vacuum-filled internal corridor to the enviro-niche, dogged the hatch, but did not pressurize the chamber, connecting to life-support lead instead. O_2 flowed. Comm hissed static. The ship's systems reported ongoing but survivable damage.

"Still there?" said Mahnmut.

"Where are you?"

"In my control room."

"What's the status, Mahnmut?"

"The ship's essentially spun itself to bits. The sub's more or less intact, including the stealth wrapping and the thrusters fore and aft, but I don't have any idea how to control them."

"Control them?" Then it obviously dawned on Orphu. "You're still going to try to enter Mars' atmosphere?"

"What choice do we have?"

There was a full second or two of silence while Orphu thought about that. Finally, he said, "I agree. Do you think you can fly this thing into the atmosphere?"

"No chance in hell," said Mahnmut, sounding almost cheerful. "I'm going to download what control software Koros put in and let you fly us in."

There came that rumbling-sneezing noise over the hardline, although Mahnmut found it very hard to believe that his friend was laughing at this particular moment. "You *have* to be joking. I'm blind—not just eyes and cameras missing, but my whole optical network burned out. I'm a mess. Essentially, I'm a bit of a brain in a broken basket. Tell me you're joking."

Mahnmut downloaded the programming the sub's banks had on the external add-on thrusters, parachutes—the whole cryptic smash. He activated all the sub's hull cameras but had to look away. The tumbling was as terrible and vertigo-producing as before. Mars filled the view now—polar cap, blue sea, polar cap, blue sea, bit of black space, polar cap—and watching it made Mahnmut sick. "There," he said as the download ended. "I'll be your eyes. I'll give you whatever navigational data the sub can crib from the reaction software. You get us stabilized and fly us in."

This time there was no mistaking the rumbling laughter. "Sure, why not," said Orphu. "Hell, the fall alone will kill us."

The rings of thrusters on *The Dark Lady* began to fire on Orphu's command.

15

The Plains of Ilium

Diomedes, literally driven into battle by war-geared, cloud-cloaked, horse-handling Athena, rushes to attack Ares.

I've never seen anything like this. First Aphrodite is wounded by the enhanced Argive, Tydeus' son, and now the war god himself has been called to single combat with Diomedes. *Aristeia* with a god. Incredible.

Ares, in his usual fashion, had promised Zeus and Athena only this morning that he would help the Greeks and now, spurred on by the taunts of Apollo and his own treacherous nature, he has begun attacking the Argives without quarter. Minutes ago, the god of war slaughtered Periphas—Ochesius' son, the best fighter the Aetolian contingent of the Greeks had to offer—and is in the act of stripping Periphas naked when he looks up to see the chariot driven by Athena bearing down on him. The goddess herself is hidden now by a stealth cloak of darkness. Ares must know that *some* god or goddess is driving the chariot, but he does not take time to try to see through the stealth cloud; he is too eager to kill Diomedes.

The god strikes first, casting his spear with the accuracy only a god can command. The spear flies up and over the edge of the chariot, straight at Diomedes' heart, but Athena reaches out from her cloud of darkness and slaps it aside. For an instant, all Ares can do is stare with incredulity as his god-wrought spear goes flying off to embed its tungsten-alloy tip in rocky soil.

Now, as the chariot clatters by, it is Diomedes' turn; he leans far out and lunges with his own energy-enhanced bronze spear. Pallas Athena's shared sheath of Planck field allows the human weapon to penetrate first the war god's forcefield, then the war god's ornate belt, then the war god's divine bowels.

Ares' scream of pain, when it comes, makes Aphrodite's earlier world-shaking howl seem a whisper. I remember that Homer described this noise as "a shriek, roaring, thundering loud as nine, ten thousand combat soldiers . . . when massive armies clash." That, it turns out, is an understatement. For the second time this bloody day, both armies freeze in the grim business of their slaughter out of mortal fear at such divine noise. Even noble Hector, intent now on nothing more noble than hacking his way through Argive flesh to murder the retreating Odysseus, halts his assault and turns his head toward the patch of bloody ground where Ares has been wounded.

Diomedes jumps from his Athena-driven chariot to finish the job on Ares, but the war god, still writhing in divine pain, is shifting, growing, changing, losing human form. The air around Diomedes and the other milling Greeks and Trojans fighting over Periphas' now-forgotten corpse is suddenly filled with dirt, debris, bits of cloth and leather, as Ares abandons his god-human shape and becomes . . . something else. Where the tall god Ares had stood a minute before, now rises a twisting, cyclone of black plasma-energy, its static electricity discharging in random lightning bolts which strike Argive and Trojan alike.

Diomedes halts his attack and cringes back, his bloodlust temporarily blunted by the cyclone's fury.

Then Ares is gone, QTing away with his bowels held in only by his own ichor-bloodied hands, and the battlefield remains almost as frozen as if the gods have stopped time again. But no—the birds still fly, dust still settles, the air still moves. This motionlessness now is awe; nothing more, nothing less.

"Have you ever seen anything like that, Hockenberry?" Nightenhelser's voice startles me. I'd forgotten he was there.

"No," I say. We stand in silence a moment until the mortal battle begins anew, until Athena's cloaked form disappears from Diomedes' charging chariot, and then I begin to walk away from the other scholic. "I'm going to morph and see how the royal family on the walls of Ilium is taking this," I tell Nightenhelser before disappearing from his sight.

I morph all right, but it is only a ruse to cover my real disappearance. Hidden by dust and confusion in the Trojan ranks, I lift Death's Helmet over my head and, activating the medallion, QT after the wounded Ares, following his quantum trail through twisted space to Olympos.

I emerge from quantum shift not on the grassy swards of Olympos nor in the Hall of the Gods, but in some vast space that looks more like the control room of a late Twentieth Century medical clinic than any structure or interior space I've seen on Olympos. There are clusters of gods and other creatures visible in the sterile-looking space, and for half a minute after phase-shifting I hold my breath—yet again—heart pounding as I wait to see if these gods and their minions are able to detect my presence.

Evidently not.

Ares is on some sort of medical examination table with three humanoid but not-quite-human entities or constructs hovering around him and offering care. The creatures may be robots—although sleeker and more organic-looking and *alien* in appearance than any robots dreamt of in my day—and I see that one has started an IV drip while another is passing a glowing ultraviolet ray over Ares' torn belly.

The god of war is still holding his guts in with his bloodied hands. Ares looks pained and frightened and angry. He looks, in other words, human.

Along the long white wall, giant vats rise twenty feet or more and are filled with a bubbling violet fluid, various umbilicals and filaments, and . . . gods: tall, tanned, perfect human forms in various stages of what could be either reconstruction or decomposition. I see open organ cavities, white bone, striated red flesh, the sickening flash of bare skull. I don't recognize the other god-forms, but in the next-to-closest tank floats Aphrodite, naked, eyes closed, hair floating, body perfect except for her perfect wrist and hand almost severed from her perfect arm. A roiling cluster of green worms is spiraling around the ligaments and tendons and bones there, either devouring or suturing or both. I look away.

Zeus enters the long room and sweeps across the space between medical monitors with no dials, past robots wrapped in what looks to be synthetic flesh, between gods who bow their heads and stand back to honor him. For an instant, the great god's head swivels my way, the startling eyes under gray brows look directly into me, and I know I have been discovered.

I wait for the Zeus-boom and lightning blast. None comes. Zeus turns away—is he smiling?—and stops in front of Ares, who still sits hunched on the examination table between hovering machines and flesh-tending robotic things.

Zeus stands in front of the wounded god with his arms crossed, toga draped, head lowered, all trimmed gray beard and untrimmed gray brows, his bare chest radiating bronze light and strength, his expression fierce—more irritated school principal than concerned father, I would say.

Ares speaks first. "Father Zeus, doesn't it infuriate you to see such human violence, such bloody work? We're the everlasting, immortal gods, but god *damn*, we suffer injuries and insults—thanks to our own divine arguments and conflicting wills—every time we show these stinking mortals a bit of kindness. And it's bad enough we have to fight these nano-crazed mortal sons of bitches, Lord Zeus, but we also have to fight *you*."

Ares takes a breath, grimaces in pain, and waits. Zeus says nothing, but continues to glower as if pondering the war god's words.

"And *Athena*," gasps the injured god. "You've let that girl go too far, O Son of Kronos. Ever since you gave birth to her from your own head—that child of *chaos* and destruction—you've always let her have her way, never blocked her reckless will. And now she's turned the mortal Diomedes into one of her weapons, spurred him on to ravage against us gods."

Ares is excited and furious now. Spittle flies. I can still see the blue-gray coils of his intestines in what appears to be golden blood.

"First she incited that . . . that . . . *mortal* to lunge at Aphrodite, stabbing her wrist, spilling her divine blood. The Healer's attendants tell me that she'll be in the vat for a full day, recovering. Then Athena spurs on Diomedes to charge me—*me, the god of war*—and his nano-augmented body was fast enough that he would have had me in the vats myself for days or weeks, perhaps even to need resurrection, if I hadn't been faster still. If he had taken my heart on his spear point, I'd still be writhing among the human corpses down there, feeling more pain than I do, trying to soldier on but being beaten down by mere mortal bronze, weak as some breathless ghost from our old Earth days and . . ."

"ENOUGH!!" bellows Zeus and not only stops Ares' diatribe, but freezes every god and robot in the place. "I'll hear no more whining prattle from you, Ares, you lying, two-faced, treacherous sparrowfart, you miserable excuse for a man, much less for a god."

Ares blinks at this, opens his mouth, but—wisely, I think—does not choose to interrupt.

"Listen to you whining and wimpering here from your little cut," sneers Zeus, unfolding his mighty arms and holding one giant hand out as if preparing to will the war god out of existence with a command. "You—I hate you most of all the maggots chosen to become gods when it came time for our Change, you miserable hypocrite. You coward-hearted lover of death and grim battles and the bloody grist-mill of war. You have your mother's meanness, Ares, *and* her rage—I confess that I can barely keep Hera in her place, especially when she decides on some little pet project close to her heart, such as slaughtering the Achaeans to a man."

Ares doubles over as if Zeus's words are hurting him, but I suspect the cause of pain is really the hovering spherical robot-thing stitching the lining of his abdomen shut with what looks to be an industrial-strength portable sewing machine.

Zeus ignores the ministrations of the medics and paces back and forth, coming within two yards of me before turning and walking back to stand in front of the hunched and grimacing Ares.

"I hope it's your mother's promptings, Hera's urgings, that have made you suffer like this, *O God of War* . . ." I can hear the godly sarcasm in Zeus's voice. "I'd just as soon have you die . . ."

Ares looks up in real shock and terror now.

Zeus laughs at the war god's expression. "You didn't know that we can die? Die beyond vat reconstruction or recom resurrection? We can, my son, we can."

Ares looks down in confusion. The machine is almost finished tucking the divine bowels back in and stitching up the last of the muscle and flesh.

"Healer!" booms Zeus and something tall and very not-human emerges from behind the bubbling vats. The thing is more centipede than machine, with multiple arms, each with multiple joints, and fly-like red eyes set fifteen feet high on its segmented body. Straps and devices and odd organic bits hang from harnesses strung around the Healer's giant bug-body.

"You are still my son," Zeus says to the grimacing war god. The Lord of Thunder's voice is softer now. "You are my son as I am Kronos's son. To me your mother bore you."

Ares reaches up his bloodied hand as if to grasp Zeus's forearm, but the older god ignores the gesture. "But trust me, Ares. If you had sprung from the seed of another god and still grown into such a shit-eating disappointment, believe me when I say that I'd long since have dropped you into that deep, dark pit below where the Titans writhe to this day."

Zeus waves the Healer forward and then turns and strides out of the hall.

I step back—so do the other gods in attendance—as the giant Healer lifts Ares in five of its arms, carries him to the empty tank, attaches various fibers and tentacles and umbilicals, and drops him into the bubbling violet liquid. As soon as his face is under the surface, Ares closes his eyes and the green worms flock out of apertures in the glass and go to work on the war god's ravaged gut.

I decide it's time to leave.

I am learning the rhythm of quantum teleportation with this medallion device. Clearly picture the place you want to go, and the device QT's you there. I clearly picture my college campus in Indiana in the last years of the Twentieth Century. The device does nothing. Sighing once, I picture the scholic dormitory at the base of Olympos.

The medallion phase-shifts me there at once. I blink into existence—although not visibility because of the Hades Helmet—just outside the red steps in front of the green doors of the red-stone barracks building.

It's been a damned long day and all I want to do is find my bunk, get out of all this gear, and take a nap. Let Nightenhelser report to the Muse.

As if my thought had summoned her, I see the Muse flick into existence just two yards from me and swing aside the barracks' doors. I'm amazed. The Muse has never come to the barracks before; we always ride the crystal elevator to her.

Secure in whatever Hades-technology conceals me, I follow her into the common room.

"Hockenberry!" she yells in her powerful goddess voice.

A younger scholic named Blix, some Homer scholar from the Twenty-second Century who has been assigned the night shift at Ilium, comes from his first-floor room, knuckling his eyes and looking stunned.

"Where is Hockenberry?" demands my Muse.

Blix shakes his head, his mouth sagging open. He sleeps in boxer shorts and a stained undershirt.

"Hockenberry!" demands the impatient Muse. "Nightenhelser says that he went to Ilium, but he's not there. He hasn't reported to me. Have you seen any of the day-shift scholics come through here?"

"No, Goddess," says poor Blix, bowing his head in some sort of approximation of deference.

"Go back to bed," the Muse says disgustedly. She strides outside, looks downhill toward the shore where the green men strain hauling their stone heads from the quarry, and then she QT's away with a soft clap of inrushing air.

I could follow her trail through phase-shift space, but . . . why? She obviously wants the helmet and the medallion back. With Aphrodite in the vat, I'm a loose cannon to her—it is my bet that besides Aphrodite, only the Muse knows that I've been outfitted as a spy with these gadgets.

And perhaps even the Muse does not know how Aphrodite plans to use me—

To spy on Athena and then to kill her.

Why? Even if Zeus's harsh words to his son, Ares, are true—that gods can die the True Death—is it possible for a mere mortal to do them in? Diomedes had done his best this day to kill two gods.

And did manage to put two of the gods out of action, floating in vats with green worms working on them.

I shake my head. Suddenly I'm very tired and very confused. My effort to defy the gods, only twenty-fours old now, has all but ended. Aphrodite will have me terminated by this time tomorrow.

Where to go?

I can't hide from the gods for very long, and if it becomes obvious that I'm trying, Aphrodite will have my guts for garters that much sooner. As soon as the Goddess of Love is back in action tomorrow, she'll see me—find me.

I can QT back to the battlefield below Ilium and allow myself to be found by the Muse. It may be my best chance. Even if she appropriates my gear, she will probably allow me to live until Aphrodite is devatted. What do I have to lose?

One day. Aphrodite will be in the vat for one day, and none of the other gods can see me or find me until she's back. *One day.*

Effectively, I have one day left to live.

With that in mind, I finally decide where I am going.

16

South Polar Sea

The four travelers decided to eat after all.

Savi disappeared into one of her lighted tunnels for a few minutes and returned with warmer dishes—chicken, heated rice, curried peppers, and strips of grilled lamb. The four had munched on their food in Ulanbat hours earlier, but now they ate with enthusiasm.

"If you're weary," said Savi, "you can sleep here tonight before we head off. There are comfortable sleeping areas in some of the nearby rooms."

Each said he or she was not that tired—it was only late afternoon Paris Crater time. Daeman looked around, swallowed some of the grilled lamb he was chewing, and said, "Why do you live in a . . ." He turned to Harman. "What did you call it?"

"An iceberg," said Harman.

Daeman nodded and chewed and turned back to Savi. "Why do you live in an iceberg?"

The woman smiled. "This particular home of mine might be the result of . . . let's say . . . an old woman's nostalgia." When she saw Harman looking at her intently, she added, "I was on a sort of sabbatical in a 'berg much like this when the final fax went on without me fourteen of your allotted life spans ago."

"I thought that everyone was stored during the final fax," said Ada. She wiped her fingers on a beautiful tan linen napkin. "All the millions of old-style humans."

Savi shook her head. "Not millions, my dear. There were just a few more than nine thousand of us when the posts carried out their final fax. As far as I can tell, none of those people—many of them my friends— were reconstituted after the Hiatus. All of us survivors of the pandemic were Jews, you know, because of our resistance to the rubicon virus."

"What are Jews?" asked Hannah. "Or what *were* Jews?"

"Mostly a theoretical race construct," said Savi. "A semidistinct genetic group brought about by cultural and religious isolation over several thousand years." She paused and looked at her four guests. Only Harman's expression suggested that he might have the slightest clue to what she was talking about.

"It doesn't really matter," Savi said softly. "But it's why you heard of me referred to as 'the Wandering Jew,' Harman. I became a myth. A legend. The phrase 'Wandering Jew' survived after the meaning was lost." She smiled again, but with no visible humor.

"How did you miss the final fax?" asked Harman. "Why did the post-humans leave you behind?"

"I don't know. I've asked myself that question for centuries. Perhaps so that I could serve as . . . witness."

"Witness?" said Ada. "To what?"

"There were many strange changes in heaven and Earth in the centuries before and after the final fax, my dear. Perhaps the posts felt that someone—even if just one old-style human being—should bear witness to all these changes."

"Many changes?" said Hannah. "I don't really understand."

"No, my dear, you wouldn't, would you? You and your parents and your parents' parents' parents have known a world that does not seem to change at all, except for some of the individuals—and there only at a steady pace of a century per person. No, the changes I'm talking about were not all visible, to be sure. But this is not the Earth that the original old-styles or the early posts once knew."

"What's the difference?" asked Daeman, his tone showing everyone how little the answer might interest him.

Savi trained her clear gray-blue eyes on him. "For one thing—a small thing to be sure, certainly small when compared to all the others, but important to me, nonetheless—there are no other Jews."

She showed them the way to private toilet areas and suggested that they remove their thermskins for the voyage.

"Won't we need them?" asked Daeman.

"It'll be cold getting to the sonie," said Savi. "But we'll manage. And you won't need them after that."

Ada changed out of her thermskin and was back in the main room on the couch, looking at the ice walls and thinking about all this, when Savi came out of a different side chamber. The older woman was wearing thicker trousers than before, stronger and higher boots, a lined cape, and a cap pulled low, her hair pulled back in a gray ponytail. She was carrying a faded khaki backpack that looked heavy. Ada had never seen a woman dress quite like this and was fascinated by the old woman's style. She realized that she was fascinated by Savi in general.

Harman was also fascinated, it seemed, but with the weapon still visible in Savi's belt. "You're still considering shooting one of us?" he asked.

"No," said Savi. "At least not right now. But there are other things that may need shooting from time to time."

The walk up and out of the interior and across the surface to the sonie *was* cold—the wind was still howling and the snow was still pelting—but the machine was warm under its bubble forcefield. Savi took the front spot that Harman had occupied during the flight out and Ada settled into her place on the right, noticing that when Savi passed her hand over the black cowl under the handgrip, a holographic control panel appeared.

"Where did *that* come from?" asked Harman from his spot to the left of the old woman. One occupant indentation was still empty between Daeman and Hannah.

"It wouldn't have been a good idea for you to try to fly the sonie on your way here," said Savi. She checked to make sure that everyone was settled in and secure in their prone positions; then she tweaked the handgrip, the machine hummed deeply, and they rose vertically seven or eight hundred feet above the ice, did a full inverted loop—the forcefield kept them pressed in their places but it *felt* as if there was nothing but air standing between them and a terrible death falling to the blue ice and black sea so far below—and then the machine righted itself, banked left, and climbed steeply toward the stars.

When the machine was flying northwest at high speed and serious altitude, Harman said, "Can this take us there?" He gestured with his left hand, his fingers pressing into the elastic forcefield above him.

"Where?" said Savi, still concentrating on the holographic displays in front of her. She raised her eyes. "The p-ring?"

Harman was almost on his back, staring up at the polar ring moving north to south above them—the tens of thousands of individual components burning startlingly bright in the clear, thin air at this altitude. "Yes," he said.

Savi shook her head. "This is a sonie, not a spacecraft. The p-ring is *high*. Why would you want to go up there?"

Harman ignored the question. "Do you know where we could find a spacecraft?"

The old woman smiled again. Watching Savi carefully, Ada was noticing the variety of the woman's expressions—the smiles with real warmth, those with none, and this kind, that suggested something actively cold or ironic.

"Perhaps," she said, but her tone warned against further questioning.

Hannah asked, "Did you actually meet post-humans?"

"Yes," said Savi, raising her voice slightly to be heard above the sonie's hum as they hurtled northward. "I actually met some."

"What were they like?" Hannah's voice was slightly wistful.

"First off, they were all women," said Savi.

Harman blinked at this. "They were?"

"Yes. A lot of us suspected that only a few posts ever came down to earth, but that they used different forms. All female. Perhaps there were no male post-humans. Perhaps they didn't retain gender as they controlled their own evolution. Who knows?"

"Did they have names?" asked Daeman.

Savi nodded. "The one I knew best . . . well, the one I saw the most . . . was named Moira."

"What were they like?" Hannah asked again. "Their personalities? Their looks?"

"They preferred floating to walking," Savi said cryptically. "They liked to throw parties for us old-styles. They tended to speak in delphic riddles."

There was silence for a minute except for the wind rushing over the polycarbon hull and the forcefield bubble. Finally Ada said, "Did they come down from their rings much?"

Savi shook her head again. "Not much. Very rarely toward the end, in the last years before the final fax. But it was rumored that they had some installations in the Mediterranean Basin."

"Mediterranean Basin?" said Harman.

Savi smiled and Ada thought it was one of her amused smiles.

"A thousand years before the final fax, the posts drained a sizable sea south of Europe—dammed it up between a rock called Gibraltar and the tip of North Africa—and made it out of bounds for old-styles. A lot of it was turned to farmland—so the posts told us—but I did some trespassing there before being discovered and tossed out, and I found that there were . . . well, cities might be the best description, if something solid state can be called a city."

"Solid state?" said Hannah.

"Never mind, child."

Harman was prone again, on his elbows. He shook his head. "I've never heard of this Mediterranean Basin. Or Gibraltar. Or . . . what was it? North Africa."

"I know you've discovered a few maps, Harman, and learned how to read them . . . after a fashion," said Savi. "But they were poor maps. And old. The few books that the post-humans allowed to survive to this postliterate age were vague . . . harmless."

Harman frowned again. They flew north in silence.

The sonie carried them out of the polar night into afternoon light, away from the dark ocean, and across land at a height they could only guess at and at a speed they could only dream of. The p-ring faded as the sky grew blue and the e-ring became visible to the north.

They crossed land hidden by tall white clouds, then saw high, snow-covered peaks and glacial valleys far below. Savi swooped the sonie lower, east of the peaks, and they flew a few thousand feet above rain forest and green savannahs, still moving so quickly that more peaks appeared like dots above the horizon and then grew into mountains in mere minutes.

"Is this South America?" asked Harman.

"It used to be," said Savi.

"What does that mean?"

"It means that the continents have changed quite a bit since any of the maps you've seen were drawn," said the old woman. "And they had quite a few more names since then as well. Did the maps you saw show this landmass connected to the one called North America?"

"Yes."

"No more." She touched the holographic symbols, twisted the handgrip, and the sonie flew lower. Ada rose up on her elbows, hair against the force-field bubble, and looked around. Silently, except for the rush of air over their force bubble, the sonie flew just above treetop height—cycads, giant ferns, ancient, leafless trees flicked past. To the west rose the foothills along the line of high peaks. Farther east, rolling grasslands were dotted with more of these primitive trees. Large animals lumbered like mobile boulders near the rivers and lakes. Grazing animals with improbable snouts were streaked with white, brown, tan, red. Ada could identify none of them

Suddenly a herd of these grazing animals stampeded past a hundred feet beneath the sonie, all panicked, fleeing for their lives. After them loped half a dozen birdlike creatures—massive, eight feet tall or taller, Ada guessed, with wild feather plumage flying back from the largest beaks and the ugliest faces Ada had ever seen. The grazing animals were running fast—thirty or forty miles per hour Ada guessed in the seconds before the sonie carried them out of sight—but the birds were moving faster, perhaps sixty miles per hour, four times as fast as any droshky or carriole that Ada or the other three had ever ridden in.

"What . . ." began Hannah.

"Terror Birds," said Savi. "*Phorushacos*. After the rubicon, the ARNists had a wild few centuries of such play. It's sort of fitting, since the real Terror Birds wandered these plains and hills about two million years ago, but that kind of recombinant crap—like your dinosaurs up north—plays havoc with the ecology. The posts promised to clean it all up during the final fax Hiatus, but they didn't."

"What's an ARNist?" asked Ada. The animals—red-beaked Terror Birds and prey alike—were out of sight behind them. Larger herds with larger animals were visible now to the west, being stalked by tigerish-looking things. The sonie swung higher and turned toward the foothills.

Savi sighed as if weary. "RNA artists. Recombinant freelancers. Social rebels and merry pranksters with sequencers and bootleg regen tanks." She looked over at Ada, then at Harman, then back at Daeman and Hannah. "Never mind, children," she said.

They flew another fifteen minutes above steaming forests and then turned west into a mountain range. Clouds moved around and between the mountain peaks below them and snow whipped around the sonie, but somehow the forcefield kept the elements at bay.

Savi touched a glowing image; the sonie slowed, circled, and turned west toward the late-afternoon sun. They were very high.

"Oh my," said Harman.

Ahead of them, two sharp peaks rose on either side of a narrow saddle covered by grassy terraces and truly ancient ruins, stone walls with no roofs. A bridge—also from the Lost Age but obviously not as ancient as the stone ruins—ran from one of the sharp-toothed peaks to the other above the ruins. There was no road beyond the suspension bridge—the roadway ended in a wall of rock at both ends—and the foundations were sunk into rock between the ruins below.

The sonie circled.

"A suspension bridge," whispered Harman. "I've read about them."

Ada was good at estimating the size of things, and she guessed that the main span of this bridge was almost a mile in length, although the roadbed had broken away in a score of places, showing rusted rebar and empty air. She guessed the two towers—each showing ancient orange paint, but sporting mostly rust—to be more than 700 feet tall, the top of each tower rising higher than the mountains at either end. The double-towers were green with what looked to be ivy from a distance, but as the sonie circled closer, Ada could see that the "growth" was artificial—green bubbles and stairways and globs of flexible glasslike material, wrapping around the towers, strung along the heavy suspension cables, even trailing down the support cables and hanging free above the ruined roadway. Clouds moved down from the high peaks and mixed with the fog rising from the deep canyons below the ruins on the hilltop, curling and writhing around the south tower and obscuring the roadway and hanging cables there.

"Does this place have a name?" asked Ada.

"The Golden Gate at Machu Picchu," said Savi as she touched the controls to bring them closer.

"What does that mean?" asked Daeman.

"I have no idea," said Savi.

The sonie circled the northern tower—dull orange and scabrous rust-red in the bright sunlight here beyond the clouds—and floated slowly, carefully, to the top of the tower, touching down without a sound.

The forcefield died away. Savi nodded and everyone crawled out, stretched, looked around. The air was cold and very thin.

Daeman wandered over to the rusted edge of the tower top, leaning out to look. Growing up with Paris Crater as his home base, he had no fear of heights.

"I wouldn't fall if I were you," said Savi. "There's no firmary rescue here. You die away from the faxnodes, you stay dead."

Daeman lurched backward, almost falling in his haste to get back from the edge. "What are you talking about?"

"Just what I said," said Savi, hoisting her pack to her right shoulder. "There's no fax to the firmary here. Try to stay alive until you get back."

Ada looked skyward to where both rings were visible through the high, thin air. "I thought the post-humans could fax us from anywhere if we . . . got into trouble."

"To the rings," said Savi, her voice flat. "Where the firmary heals you. To where you ascend after your Fifth Twenty to join the post-humans."

"Yes," Ada said weakly.

Savi shook her head. "It's not the posts who fax you away when something bad happens, rebuilding you. All that's myth. Or to be less polite—bullshit."

Harman opened his mouth to speak but it was Daeman who spoke first. "I was just there," he said, anger in his voice. "In the firmary. In the rings."

"In the firmary, yes," said Savi. "But not healed by post-humans. If they're up there, they don't care a whit about you. And I don't think they're up there anymore."

The four stood on the rusted tower summit more than five hundred feet above the ruined roadway, eight hundred feet above the grassy saddle and stone ruins. Wind from the higher peaks buffeted them and blew their hair.

"After our last Twenty, we go up to join the posts . . ." began Hannah, her voice small.

Savi laughed and led the way toward an irregular glass globule blobbing up over the west end of the ancient tower top.

There were rooms and anterooms and stairways descending and frozen escalators and smaller rooms off the main chambers. Ada thought it strange that the sky and the orange towers and the hanging cables and glimpses of the jungle and roadway below were not tinted green through the material, nor was the sunlight streaming in turned green— the green glass somehow passed colors accurately.

Savi led them down and around from one green module to the next, from one side of the bifurcated tower to another through thin tubes that should have been swinging in the strong breeze, but weren't. Some of the chambers extended thirty or forty feet out beyond the tower, and Ada had no clue how the green globule was attached to the concrete and steel.

Some of the rooms were empty. Others had—artifacts. A series of animal skeletons stood silhouetted against the mountain skyline in one room. In another, what appeared to be replicas of machines lined display counters and hung from wires. In yet another, plexiglas cubes held fetuses of a hundred creatures, none of them human but some disturbingly close to human. In another room, faded holograms of starfields and ringfields moved over and through the observers.

"What is this place?" asked Harman.

"A sort of museum," said Savi. "I think most of the important displays are missing."

"Created by whom?" asked Hannah.

Savi shrugged. "Not by the posts, I think. I don't know. But I'm pretty sure that the bridge—or the original of this bridge, it may be a replica— once stood above water near a Lost Age city on what was then the west coast of the continent north of here. Have you heard of such a thing, Harman?"

"No."

"Perhaps I dreamt it," said Savi with a rueful laugh. "My memory plays tricks on me after all these centuries of sleep."

"You mentioned sleeping through the centuries once before," Daeman said, his tone sounding brusque to Ada. "What are you talking about?"

Savi had led them down a long spiral staircase in the green-glass tube strung between the suspension cables, and now she gestured to a line of what appeared to be crystal coffins. "A form of cryosleep," she said. "Only not cold—which is silly, because that's what 'cryo' meant originally. Some of these cocoons still work, still freeze molecular motion. Not through cold, but through some microtechnology that draws power from the bridge."

"From the bridge?" said Ada.

"The whole thing is a solar power receiver," said Savi. "Or at least the green parts are."

Ada looked at the dusty crystal coffins and tried to imagine going to sleep in one and waiting . . . what? Years before waking? Decades? Centuries? She shuddered.

Savi was looking at her and Ada blushed. But Savi smiled. One of her sincerely amused smiles, Ada thought.

They climbed to a long green glass cylinder hanging from a frayed and rusted support cable that was thicker than Harman was tall. Ada found herself treading softly, trying to lift her weight by sheer will, afraid that their combined weight would bring the cylinder down, the cable, the whole bridge. Again she caught Savi watching her. This time Ada did not blush but frowned back, tired of the old woman's scrutiny.

All four of them stopped a minute, alarmed. It appeared that they had walked into a meeting hall filled with people—people standing along the edges of the room, men and women in weird garb, people sitting at desks and standing at control panels, people who did not move or turn their gazes in the direction of the newcomers.

"They're not real," said Daeman, walking to the nearest man—dressed in a dusty blue suit with some sort of fabric at his throat—and touching the figure's face.

The five walked from figure to figure, staring at the men and women dressed in odd clothes, people with strangely patterned hair and unusual personal adornment—tattoos, strange jewelry, dyed hair and skin.

"I read that once servitors came in the shape of human beings . . ." began Harman.

"No," said Savi. "These aren't robots. Only mannequins."

"What?" said Daeman.

Savi explained the word.

"Do you know who they're supposed to be?" asked Hannah. "Or why they're here?"

"No," said Savi. She stood back while the others explored.

At the end of the chamber, set in a glass alcove as if in pride of place, the figure of a man was posed in an ornate wood and leather-slung chair. Even seen sitting, it was obvious that this figure was shorter than most of the other male mannequins in the hall, and dressed in some sort of tan tunic that looked like a short, belted dress made out of rough cotton or wool. The figure's feet were shod with sandals. The short man could have been comic, but his features—short, curly gray hair, hawk nose, and fierce gray eyes staring out boldly from under heavy brows—were so powerful that Ada found herself approaching the mannequin warily. The man's forearms were shaped with such muscle and so many scars, the stubby fingers were curled easily but with much strength on the wooden arms of the camp chair—everything about the carved form gave an impression of such coiled strength—of will as well as body—that Ada stopped six feet away from it. The man was visibly older than humans chose to look in this age—somewhere between Harman's Second Twenty and Savi's old age. The man's tunic hung low enough that Ada could see the graying hair on his broad, bronzed chest.

Daeman hurried forward. "I know this man," he said, pointing. "I've seen him before."

"From the turin drama," said Hannah.

"Yes, yes," said Daeman, snapping his fingers in an attempt to remember. "His name is . . ."

"Odysseus," said the man in the chair. He stood and took a step toward the startled Daeman. "Odysseus, son of Laertes."

17

Mars

"She's stabilizing," said Mahnmut over the hardline to Orphu. "Roll rate down to about one revolution every six seconds. Pitch and yaw are approaching zero."

"I'm going to try to flatten out the roll," said Orphu. "Tell me when you have the polar cap in the reticule."

"Okay, no—it's drifting. Damn. What a mess." Mahmut was trying to line up the slash on the video feed with the white blur of the Martian polar cap through a blizzard of tumbling debris and still-glowing plasma.

"Yes," said Orphu from the hold, "I am a mess."

"I wasn't talking about you."

"I know. But I'm still a mess. I'd give half my Proust library if I had just one of my six eyes back."

"We'll get you hooked up to some visual feed," said Mahnmut. "Hell. We're tumbling again."

"Let it tumble until right before we enter the atmosphere," said Orphu. "Save our thruster fuel and energy. And—no—we're not going to get this vision thing fixed. I did a damage check after you plugged me in here, and it's not just the eyes and cameras that are missing. I was looking toward the bow when the ship was slagged, and the flash burned out every channel down to the organic level. My internal optic nerves are ash."

"I'm sorry," said Mahnmut. He felt sick and it wasn't just from the tumbling. After a minute, he said, "We're running fairly low on everything consumable here—water, air, reaction-pack fuel. Are you sure you want to stay inside this debris field?"

"It's our best chance," said Orphu. "On radar, we're just another chunk of the destroyed spaceship."

"*Radar?*" said Mahnmut. "Did you see what attacked us? A god-damned *chariot*. You think a chariot has radar?"

Orphu rumbled a laugh. "Do you think a *chariot* can launch an energy lance like the one that vaporized a third of the ship, including Koros and Ri Po? And yes, Mahnmut, I *saw* the chariot—it was the last thing I'll ever see. But I don't believe for a second that it was actually a chariot with an oversized human male and female riding in open vacuum. Uh-uh. Too cute . . . too cute by half."

Mahnmut had nothing to say to that. He wished Orphu had damped all the roll—the sub was also pitching and yawing again—but everything else in the debris field was tumbling, so it made sense that they should be too.

"Want to talk about Shakespeare's sonnets?" asked Orphu of Io.

"Are you shitting me?" The moravecs loved the ancient human colloquial phrases, the more scatological the better.

"Yes," said Orphu. "I am most definitely shitting you, my friend."

"Wait a minute, wait a minute," said Mahnmut. "The debris is beginning to glow. So are we. Picking up ionization." He was pleased that his voice stayed calm. Ahead of them, larger bits of the destroyed spacecraft were glowing a dull red. The bow of *The Dark Lady* was also beginning to glow. *The Dark Lady*'s external sensors started reporting hull temperature rising. They were entering Mars's atmosphere.

"Time to straighten us out," said Orphu, getting the relayed data down in the submersible's hull, doing what he could with the partial Koros III control download as he fired the sub's strap-on thrusters and realigned her gyros. "Roll gone?"

"Not quite."

"We can't wait. I'm going to turn this pile of scrap iron around before we burn up."

"This 'pile of scrap iron' is called *The Dark Lady* and she may save our lives," Mahnmut said coldly.

"Right, right," said Orphu. "Tell me when the hash mark on the aft video monitor is centered on the limb of Mars above the pole. I'll begin flattening the tumble then. God, what I'd give for one of my eyes back. Sorry, last time I'll say that."

Mahnmut watched the monitor. Because of the widening debris cloud, the only reliable fixes he'd been able to make for Orphu over the past thirty minutes or so came from Mars itself. Even the two little moons were invisible. Now the thrusters thumped hollowly and the damaged sub pivoted slowly, the bow camera losing its view of Mars and showing glowing plasma, white-hot melted metal, and a million shining shards that had once been their spacecraft and traveling companions.

The orange-red-brown-green bulk of Mars filled the aft camera and the hash mark Orphu had directed Mahnmut to draw in the monitor drifted up, up, crossing the cloud-dappled coastline, showing blue sea, then white . . .

"Polar cap," reported Mahnmut. "There's the upper limb."

"Okay," said Orphu. All the thrusters hammered. "See the pole now on the aft camera?"

"No."

"Any recognizable stars?"

"No. Just more hull ionization."

"Close enough for government work," said the Ionian. "I'm going to use the ring of thrusters on the stern as braking rockets now."

"Koros III was going to use the big reaction pack on the bow to slow us for re-entry, then jettison it before we hit the atmosphere," said Mahnmut. The stern glow was a deeper red now.

"I'm keeping those heavier thrusters on while we enter the atmosphere," said Orphu.

"Why?"

"You'll see."

"Isn't it possible that if we keep those thrusters attached, they'll explode when they heat up during reentry?"

"It's possible," grunted the Ionian.

"We're pretty battered," said Mahnmut. "Any chance we'll break up as stuff burns away from the hull?"

"Sure, there's a chance," said Orphu. He fired the heavy-ion thrusters.

Mahnmut was pressed into his acceleration couch for thirty seconds and then released as the noise and vibration ceased. He heard the heavy thump as the attitude-control ring was ejected into space.

A fireball flicked past the bow camera, although the bow camera was now showing the view behind them as they entered the atmosphere stern first. "We're definitely hitting atmosphere," said Mahmut, noticing that his voice wasn't quite as calm as before. He'd never been in a real planetary atmosphere before and the idea of all those close-packed molecules added queasiness on top of his nausea. "The jettisoned thruster-pack just turned white-hot and burst into flame. I can see the stern beginning to glow. So is the main reaction pack on the bow, but not as badly. Most of the heat and shock wave seems to be around our stern. Wow—we're falling behind some of the debris field, but it's all burning up ahead of us. It's like we're in the middle of a huge meteor storm."

"Good," said Orphu. "Hang on."

What had been the moravec spacecraft hit the thickened Martian atmosphere very much as Mahmut had described to Orphu—as a meteor storm with the larger fragments massing several metric tons and stretching tens of meters across. A hundred fireballs arced through the pale-blue Martian sky and a rattle of deep sonic booms shattered the silence of the northern hemisphere. The fireballs crossed the northern polar cap like a flight of fiery birds and continued south across the Tethys Sea, leaving long plasma vapor trails as they passed. It looked eerily as if the fragments were flying rather than falling.

For hundreds of millions of years, Mars had boasted a negligible atmosphere, of some 8 millibars, mostly carbon dioxide, as opposed to Earth's thick 1,014 millibars of pressure at sea level. In less than a century, through a process that none of the moravecs understood, the world had been terraformed to a very breathable 840 millibars.

The fireballs streaked across the northern kilometer in rough formation, leaving sonic-boom footprints in their wake. Some of the smaller pieces—large enough to survive the fiery atmospheric entry but small enough to be deflected by the thick air—began splashing down some eight hundred kilometers south of the pole. If one were looking from space, it would appear that some deity was firing a string of oversized machine-gun bullets—tracer rounds—into Mars' northern ocean.

The Dark Lady was one of those tracer rounds. The stealth material around the stern and two-thirds of the hull burned off and joined the plasma trail streaming behind the hurtling submersible. External antennae and sensors burned away. Then the hull began to char and chip and flake.

"Ah . . . " said Mahmut from his acceleration couch, "shouldn't we think about popping the parachutes?" He knew enough of Koros's landing plan to know that the buckycarbon-fiber 'chutes were supposed to deploy at around 15,000 meters, lowering them gently to the ocean's surface. Mahmut's last glimpse of the ocean before the stern optics had burned away convinced him that they were lower than 15,000 meters and coming down very fast.

"Not yet," grunted Orphu. The Ionian had no acceleration couches in the hold and it sounded as if the deceleration gravities were affecting him. "Use your radar to get our altitude."

"Radar's gone," said Mahmut.

"Will your sonar work?"

"I'll try." Amazingly, it did work, showing a return of solid—well, liquid water—surface coming at them at a distance of 8,200 meters—8,000 meters—7,800 meters. Mahmut relayed the information to Orphu and added, "Shall we pop the parachutes now?"

"The rest of the debris isn't deploying parachutes."

"So?"

"So do you really want to drift down under a canopy, showing up on all their sensors?"

"*Whose* sensors?" snapped Mahnmut, but he understood Orphu's point. Still . . . "Five thousand meters," he said. "Velocity three thousand two hundred klicks per hour. Do we really want to hit the water at this speed?"

"Not really," said Orphu. "Even if we survive the impact, we'd be buried under hundreds of meters of silt. Didn't you say that this northern ocean is only a few hundred meters deep?"

"Yes."

"I'm going to rotate your ship now," said Orphu.

"*What?*" But then Mahnmut heard the heavy thruster pack firing—just some of its jets—and the gyros whirred, although the noise was more a grinding than a whirring.

The Dark Lady began a painful tumble, bringing its bow around from the back. Wind and friction tore at the hull, ripping away the last of the mid-ship sensors and breaching a dozen compartments. Mahnmut switched off screaming alarms.

Bow forward now, one of the last working video pickups showed splashes in the ocean—if one can call steam and plasma impact plumes 2,000 meters high "splashes"—and Mahnmut guessed it would be their turn in seconds. He described the impacts to Orphu and said, "Parachutes? Please?"

"No," said Orphu and fired the main thrusters that should have been jettisoned in orbit.

The deceleration forces threw Mahnmut forward in his straps and made him wish for the acceleration gel they'd used in the Io Flux Tube slingshot maneuver. More columns of steam rose around the hurtling submersible like Corinthian columns flicking past and the ocean filled the viewscreen. The thrusters roared and swiveled, slowing their velocity. Mahnmut saw the pack ring jettison and fly off behind them the instant the firing stopped. They were only a thousand meters above the ocean and the surface looked as hard as Europan surface ice to Mahnmut's eye.

"Para . . ." began Mahnmut, pleading now and not ashamed of it.

The two huge parachutes deployed. Mahnmut's vision went red, then black.

They hit the Tethys Sea.

"Orphu? Orphu?" Mahnmut was in darkness and silence, trying to get his data feeds back on line. His enviro-niche was intact, O_2 still flowing. That was amazing. His internal clocks said that three minutes had passed since impact. Their velocity was zero. "Orphu?"

"Arugghh," came a noise over the hardline. "Every time I get to sleep, you wake me."

"How are you?"

"*Where* am I might be the better question," rumbled Orphu. "I ripped free of the niche. I'm not even sure if I'm still in *The Dark Lady*. If I am, the hull is breached here—I'm in water. Salt water. Wait, maybe I just pissed myself."

"You're still attached by hardline," said Mahnmut, ignoring the Ionian's last comment. "You're probably still in the hold. I'm getting some sonar data. We're in bottom silt, but just under a few meters of the stuff, about eighty meters beneath the surface."

"I wonder how many pieces I'm in," mused Orphu.

"Stay there," said Mahnmut. "I'm going to unclip from the hardline and come below to get you. Don't move."

Orphu rumbled his laugh. "How can I move, old friend? All my manipulators and flagella have gone to that big moravec heaven in the sky. I'm a crab without claws. And I'm not too sure about my shell. Mahnmut . . . wait!"

"What?" Mahnmut had unstrapped himself and was removing umbilicals and virtual-control cables.

"If . . . somehow . . . you could get to me, assuming the internal corridor isn't smashed flat and the hull doors aren't completely buckled or welded shut by the entry heat . . . what are you going to do with me?"

"See if you're all right," said Mahnmut, pulling the optical leads free. It was all darkness on the monitors anyway.

"*Think*, old friend," said Orphu. "You drag me out of here—if I don't come apart in your hands—what next? I won't fit in your internal access corridors. Even if you hauled me around the outside of the sub, I can't fit into your enviro-niche and I sure as hell can't cling to the hull. Do you walk across the ocean bottom for a thousand klicks or so, carrying me as you go?"

Mahnmut hesitated.

"I'm still functioning," continued Orphu. "Or at least still communicating. I even have O_2 flowing through the umbilical and some electrical energy coming in. I must be in the hold, even if it's flooded. Why don't you get *The Dark Lady* working and drive us somewhere more comfortable before we try to get together again?"

Mahnmut went on external air and took several deep breaths. "You're right," he said at last. "Let's see what's what."

The Dark Lady was dying.

Mahnmut had worked in this submersible, through its various iterations and evolutions, for more than an Earth century, and he knew it was tough. Properly prepared, it could take many metric tons per square centimeter of pressure and the stresses of the 3,000-g flux-tube acceleration in stride, but the tough little sub was only as strong as its weakest part, and the energy stresses of the attack in Mars orbit had exceeded those weakest-part tolerances.

Her hull had stress fractures and unmendable flash burns. At the moment, they were buried bow-down with most of the sub in more than three meters of silt and harder seabed with only a few meters of the stern free of the mud, the hull and frame were warped, the hold-bay doors were warped shut and unreachable, and ten of the eighteen ballast tanks had been breached. The internal gangway between Mahnmut's control room and the hold was flooded and partially collapsed. Outside, two-thirds of the stealth material had burned away, carrying all of the external sensors with it. Three of the four sonar arrays were out of action and the fourth could only ping forward. Only one of the four primary propulsion jets was operable and the maneuvering pulsers were a scrambled mess.

Of greater concern to Mahnmut was the damage to the ship's energy systems: the primary reactor had been damaged by energy surge during the attack and was operating at 8 percent efficiency; the storage cells were on reserve power. This was enough to keep a minimum of life support running, but the nutrient converter was gone for good and they had only a few days' worth of fresh water.

Finally, the O_2 converter was offline. Fuel cells weren't producing air. Long before they ran out of water or food, Mahnmut and Orphu would be out of oxygen. Mahnmut had internal air supplies, but only enough for an e-day or two without replenishing. All Mahnmut could hope was that since Orphu worked in space for months at a time, a little thing like no oxygen wouldn't harm him now. He decided to ask the Ionian about it later.

More damage reports came in over the sub's surviving AI systems. Given an e-month or more in a Conamara Chaos ice dock with a score of service moravecs working on her, *The Dark Lady* could be saved. Otherwise, her days—whether measured in Martian sols, Earth days, or Europan weeks—were numbered.

Keeping in touch with the mostly silent Orphu on the hardline— afraid his friend would cease to exist without warning—Mahnmut gave the most positive report he could and launched a periscope buoy. The buoy was deployed from the section of the stern still above the silt line and it still worked.

The buoy itself was smaller than Mahnmut's hand, but it packed a wide array of imaging and data sensors. Information started flowing in.

"Good news," said Mahnmut.

"The Five Moons Consortium launched a rescue mission," rumbled Orphu.

"Not quite that good." Rather than download the nonvisual data, Mahnmut summarized it to keep his friend listening and talking. "The buoy works. Better than that, the communication and positioning sats Koros III and Ri Po seeded in orbit are still up there. I wonder why the . . . persons who attacked us . . . didn't sweep them out of space."

"We were attacked by an Old Testament God and his girlfriend," said Orphu. "They might not deign to notice comsats."

"I think they looked more Greek than Old Testament," said Mahnmut. "Do you want to hear the data I'm getting?"

"Sure."

"The MPS puts us in the southern reaches of the Chryse Planitia region of the northern ocean, only about three hundred and forty kilometers from the Xanthe Terra coast. We're lucky. This part of the Acidalia and Chryse sea is like a huge bay. If our trajectory had been a few hundred klicks to the west, we would have impacted on the Tempe Terra hills. Same distance to the east, Arabia Terra. A few more seconds of flight time south over Xanthe Terra highlands . . ."

"We'd be particles in the upper atmosphere," said Orphu.

"Right," said Mahnmut. "But if we get *The Dark Lady* unstuck, we can sail her right into the Valles Marineris delta if we have to."

"You and Koros were supposed to land in the other hemisphere," said Orphu. "North of Olympus Mons. Your mission was to do recon and deliver this device in the hold to Olympos. Don't tell me the sub is in good enough shape to carry us up and around the Tempe Terra peninsula . . ."

"No," admitted Mahnmut. In truth, it would be an amazing stroke of luck if *The Dark Lady* held together and kept functioning long enough to get them to the nearest land, but he wasn't going to tell the Ionian that.

"Any other good news?" asked Orphu.

"Well, it's a pretty day on the surface. All liquid water as far as the buoy could see. Moderate swells of less than a meter. Blue sky. Temperature in the high twenties . . ."

"Are they looking for us?"

"Pardon me?" said Mahnmut.

"Are the . . . people . . . that slagged us looking for us?"

"Yes," said Mahnmut. "Passive radar showed several of those flying machines . . ."

"Chariots."

". . . several of those flying machines crisscrossing above the sea in the several thousand square kilometers of the debris impact footprint."

"Looking for us," said Orphu.

"No register of radar or neutrino search," said Mahnmut. "No energy search spectra at all . . ."

"Can they find us, Mahnmut?" Orphu's voice was flat.

Mahnmut hesitated. He didn't want to lie to his friend. "Possibly," he said. "Almost certainly if they were using moravec technology, but they don't seem to be. They're just . . . *looking*. Perhaps just with eyes and magnetometers."

"They found us in orbit easily enough. Targeted us."

"Yes." There was no question that the chariot or its occupants had some sort of target acquisition device that had worked well at 8,000 klicks of distance.

"Did you reel in the buoy?"

"Yes," said Mahnmut. There were several seconds of silence except for the creak of the damaged hull, the hiss of ventilation, and the thump and hum of various pumps working in vain to clear the flooded sections. "We have several things going for us," Mahnmut said at last. "First, there are tons and tons of metal debris from the spacecraft in this footprint, and it's a long footprint. The first impacts weren't that far south of the polar cap.

"Second, we've settled in bow first, and the only section of the sub above the silt line, the stern, still has some tatters of loose stealthwrap on it. Third, we're powered down to the point that we have almost no energy signature at all. Fourth . . ."

"Yes?" said Orphu.

Mahnmut was thinking of the dying power supply, the dwindling reserves of air and water, and the doubtful propulsion system. "Fourth," he said, "they still don't know why we're here."

Orphu rumbled softly. "I don't think we do either, old friend." After a minute of no communication, Orphu said, "Well, you're right. If they don't find us in the next few hours, we may have a chance. Or is there any other bad news?"

Mahnmut hesitated. "We have a slight problem with our air supply," he said at last.

"How serious a problem?"

"We're not producing any."

"Well, that *is* a problem," said the Ionian. "How much in reserve?"

"About eighty hours. For two of us, that is. Certainly twice that, probably more, if it's just for me."

Orphu rumbled slightly over the intercom. "Just for you? Are you planning on stepping on my air hose, old friend? My organic parts need air too, you know."

For a second Mahnmut couldn't speak. "I thought . . . you're a hard-vac moravec . . . I mean . . ."

"You're thinking that I spend long months in space without topping off from the Io tender," sighed Orphu. "I produce my own oxygen from the internal fuel cells, using the the photovoltaics on my shell to power them."

Mahnmut felt his pulse slow. Their chances of survival had just gone up if Orphu did not need ship's air.

"*But* my shell photovoltaics are blasted to hell," Orphu said softly, "and the fuel cells haven't been producing O_2 since the attack. I'm surviving on the ship's supply. I'm sorry, Mahnmut."

"Look," Mahnmut said quickly, strongly. "I was planning to keep the air running to both of us anyway. It's not a problem. I did the numbers— we have about eighty hours at our present consumption rate. And I can lower that. This whole control room and enviro-niche of mine is flooded. I'll pour it back in and parcel it out. Eighty hours easy, and then we'll come up for air. Their search should be over by then."

"Are you sure you can get *The Dark Lady* out of the mud?" asked Orphu.

"Absolutely positive," lied Mahnmut, voice firm.

"I vote we lie doggo in the seabed for . . . say . . . three sols, three Martian days, seventy-three hours or so, to see if their chariot search is really called off. Or twelve hours after our last radar contact with them. Whichever comes first. Will that give us enough time to get out of the mud and to the surface, plus leave some oxygen and energy to spare?"

Mahnmut looked at his virtual wall of red alarm and non-function lights. "Seventy-three hours should be plenty of extra time," he said. "But if they go away sooner than that, we should get to the surface and head for the coast. The *Lady* can do about twenty knots on the surface with the reactor at this level, so it'll take the better part of the day and a half to get to land anyway, especially if we're picky about where to put in."

"We'll just have to avoid being picky," said Orphu. "All right, it looks like the only thing we have to worry about for the next couple of days is boredom. Shall we play poker? Did you bring the virtual cards?"

"Yes," said Mahnmut, brightening.

"You wouldn't rob a blind moravec, would you?" said Orphu.

Mahnmut stopped in the process of downloading the green baize card table.

"I'm *kidding*, for Christ's sake," said Orphu. "My visual nodes are gone, but I still have memory and parts of my brain left. Let's play chess."

Three sols was 73.8 hours and Mahnmut did not want to stay in the seabed that long. The reactor was losing power faster than he'd estimated—the pumps were draining more energy than he'd planned on—and all the life support was flirting with failure.

During their first sleep period, Mahnmut went on internal power, took pry bars and cutting equipment, and descended the narrow crawlways and corridors to the hold. The interior spaces were flooded, the vertical gangway without power and pitch black. Mahnmut activated his shoulder lamps and swam lower. The water here was much warmer than Europa's sea. Beams and girders had crumpled, blocking the last ten meters of the approach. Mahnmut cut them away with the torch. He had to check on Orphu's condition.

Two meters from the airlock to the hold, Mahnmut was stopped cold. The impact had buckled the aft bulkhead, pressing it almost flat against the forward bulkhead. The already narrow corridor had been squashed into a space less than ten centimeters across. Mahnmut could see the hatchway to the hold—closed, dogged, and twisted—but he couldn't reach it. He would have to cut his way through one or both of the thick pressure bulkheads and then probably use the torch to cut through the hatch itself. It would be a six- or seven-hour job and there was a basic problem—the torch ran on oxygen, just as he and Orphu did. Whatever he gave the torch came out of their air supply.

For several minutes, Mahnmut floated head-down in the darkness, silt floating in front of his lenses in the twin beams from his shoulder lamps. He had to decide *now*. Once Orphu awoke and realized what he was doing, the Ionian would try to talk him out of it. And logic dictated that he be talked out of it. Even if he got through the bulkheads in six or seven hours, Orphu had been correct—Mahnmut wouldn't be able to move the huge moravec while they were still embedded in the seabed. Even first aid would be limited to the kits and system inputs that Mahnmut kept onboard for himself—they might not even work with the huge hardvac moravec. If Mahnmut could really get *The Dark Lady* free of the silt and to the surface, *that* would be the best time for Mahnmut to get to Orphu—even if he had to cut through the hull bay doors or outer hull. O_2 would be plentiful then. And he could remove Orphu if he had to, find a way to lash him to the upper hull, in the sunlight and air.

Mahnmut kicked his way around and swam upward in the tilted and torn corridor, letting himself through the airlock into his personal space again. He stowed the cutting equipment. *Later.*

He was no sooner in his acceleration couch again when Orphu's voice came over the comm. "You awake, Mahnmut?"

"Yes."

"Where are you?"

"At the controls. Where else would I be?"

"Yes," said Orphu, his deep voice sounding weary and old on the hardline. "But I was dreaming. I thought I felt a vibration. I thought you might be . . . I don't know."

"Go back to sleep," said Mahnmut. Moravecs slept, if only to dream. "I'll wake you for the buoy check in two hours."

Mahnmut would deploy the periscope buoy for a few seconds every twelve hours, quickly scan the skies and gentle seas, and reel it back in. Flying machines were still crisscrossing the skies day and night at the end of the first forty-nine hours, but further north, nearer the pole.

Mahnmut was fairly comfortable. His control room and connecting enviro-niche was undamaged, warm, and tilted only slightly bow-down. He could move about if he wished. Several of the other habitable chambers had been flooded—including the science lab and Urtzweil's former cubby—but although the pumps soon cleared these spaces, Mahnmut didn't bother flooding them with air. In fact, the first thing he had done after their initial conversation was to hook into his O_2 umbilical and drain his enviro-niche and control room. He told himself it was to save the oxygen, but he knew that part of the reason was that he felt guilty being so comfortable in his cozy niches when Orphu was in pain—existential pain at least—and floating in the flooded darkness of the hold. There was nothing Mahnmut could do about that yet—not with three-fourths of the damaged sub embedded in the ocean floor—but he went into the vacuum-filled science lab and cobbled together comm units and other things he'd need if he ever managed to free the Ionian.

And free myself, thought Mahnmut, although being separated from *The Dark Lady* did not seem like freedom to him. All deep-sea Europan cryobots had carried the kernel of agoraphobia in them—true terror of open spaces—and their evolved moravec descendents had inherited it. On the second day, after their eighth chess game, Orphu said, "*The Dark Lady* has some sort of escape device, doesn't it?"

Mahnmut had hoped that Orphu wouldn't know this fact. "Yes," he said at last.

"What kind?"

"A little life bubble," said Mahnmut, in a foul mood for having to talk about this. "Not much bigger than me. Mostly meant to survive deep pressures and get me to the surface."

"But it has a beacon, its own life support system, some sort of propulsion and navigation systems? Some water and food?"

"Yes," said Mahnmut, "what of it?" *You wouldn't fit in it and I can't tow you behind it.*

"Nothing," said Orphu.

"I hate the idea of leaving *The Dark Lady*," Mahnmut said truthfully. "And I don't have to think about it now. Not for days and days."

"All right," said Orphu.

"I'm serious."

"All *right*, Mahnmut. I was just curious."

If Orphu had rumbled amusement at him at that moment, Mahnmut might well have crawled into the survival bubble and cast off. He was furious at the Ionian for raising this topic. "Want to play another game of chess?" Mahnmut asked.

"Not in this lifetime," said Orphu.

At sixty-one hours after splashdown, there was only one chariot visible to radar, but it was circling just eight klicks above them and ten to the north. Mahnmut reeled in the periscope buoy as quickly as he could.

He sat listening to music over the intercom—Brahms—and, down in his flooded hold, Orphu presumably was doing the same.

Suddenly the Ionian asked, "Ever wonder why we're both humanists, Mahnmut?"

"What do you mean?"

"You know, humanists. All moravecs evolved into either us humanists with our odd interest in the old human race, or the more interactive types like Koros III. They're the ones who forge moravec societies, Five Moon Consortiums, political parties . . . whatever."

"I never noticed," said Mahnmut.

"You're kidding me."

Mahnmut stayed silent. He was beginning to realize that in almost a century and a half of existence, he had managed to stay ignorant of almost everything important. All he knew were the cold seas of Europa—which he would never see again—and this submersible, which was hours or days away from ceasing to exist as a functioning entity. That and Shakespeare's sonnets and plays.

Mahnmut barely resisted laughing on the hardline. *What could be more useless?*

As if reading his mind again, Orphu said, "What would the Bard say about this predicament?"

Mahnmut was scanning the energy data and the consumable readouts. They couldn't wait the seventy-three hours. They would have to try to break free in the next six hours or so. And even then, if they weren't able to pull themselves free right away, the reactor might cease functioning altogether, overload, and . . .

"Mahnmut?"

"I'm sorry. Dozing. What about the Bard?"

"He must have something to say about shipwrecks," said Orphu. "I seem to remember lots of shipwrecks in Shakespeare."

"Oh, yes," said Mahnmut. "Lots of shipwrecks. *Twelfth Night, The Tempest,* the list goes on and on. But I doubt if there's anything in the plays to help us in this situation."

"Tell me about some of the shipwrecks."

Mahnmut shook his head in the vacuum. He knew that Orphu was just trying to take his mind off current realities. "Tell me about your beloved Proust," he said. "Does the narrator Marcel ever say anything about being lost on Mars?"

"He does, actually," said Orphu with the slightest hint of a rumble.

"You're joking."

"I *never* joke about *À la recherche du temps perdu,*" said Orphu in a tone that almost, not quite, convinced Mahnmut that the Ionian was serious.

"All right, what does Proust say about surviving on Mars?" said Mahnmut. In five minutes he was going to deploy the periscope buoy again and bring them up even if the chariot was hovering ten meters overhead.

"In Volume Three of the French edition, Volume Five of the English translation I downloaded to you, Marcel says that if we suddenly found ourselves on Mars and grew a pair of wings and a new respiratory system, it would not take us out of ourselves," said Orphu. "Not as long as we have to use our same senses. Not as long as we're stuck in our same consciousnesses."

"You're kidding," said Mahnmut.

"I *never* kid about the character Marcel's perceptions in *À la recherche du temps perdu*," Orphu said again in a tone that told Mahnmut that he was kidding all right, but not about that particular odd Mars reference. "Didn't you *read* the editions I sent you at the beginning of the voyage in-system?"

"I did," said Mahnmut. "I really did. I just sort of skipped over the last couple of thousand pages."

"Well, that's not uncommon," said Orphu. "Listen, here's a passage that comes after the growing wings and new lungs on Mars bit. Do you want it in French or English?"

"English," Mahnmut said quickly. This close to a terrible death from suffocation, he didn't want the added torture of listening to French.

"*The only true voyage, the only Fountain of Youth,*" recited Orphu, "*would be found not in traveling to strange lands but in having different eyes, in seeing the universe with the eyes of another person, of a hundred others, and seeing the hundred universes each of them sees, which each of them is.*"

Mahnmut actually forgot about their imminent asphyxiation for a minute as he thought about this. "That's Marcel's fourth and final answer to the puzzle of life, isn't it, Orphu?"

The Ionian stayed quiet.

"I mean," continued Mahnmut, "you said that the first three failed for Marcel. He tried believing in snobbery. He tried believing in friendship and love. He tried believing in art. None of it worked as a transcendent theme. So this is the fourth. This . . ." He could not find the right word or phrase.

"Consciousness escaping the limits of consciousness," Orphu said quietly. "Imagination outstripping the bounds of imagination."

"Yes," breathed Mahnmut. "I see."

"You need to," said Orphu. "You're my eyes now. I need to see the universe through your eyes."

Mahnmut sat in the umbilical O_2 hiss silence for a minute. Then he said, "Let's try to take *The Dark Lady* up."

"Periscope buoy?"

"To hell with them if they're up there waiting. I'd rather die fighting than choke to death in the mud down here."

"All right," said Orphu. "You said 'try' to take the *Lady* up. Is there some doubt that you can get us out of the slime?"

"I have no fucking idea if we can break free of this stuff," said Mahnmut, flicking virtual switches with his mind, powering the reactor up into the red, arming the thrusters and pyros. "But we're going to give it a good try in . . . eighteen seconds. Hang on, my friend."

"Since my grapplers, manipulators, and flagella are gone," said Orphu, "I presume you mean that rhetorically."

"Hang on with your *teeth*," said Mahnmut. "Six seconds."

"I'm a moravec," said Orphu, sounding slightly indignant. "I don't have any teeth. What were you . . ."

Suddenly the comm line was drowned out by the firing of all the thrusters, the booming of bulkheads creaking and giving way, and a great moaning sound as *The Dark Lady* fought to break free of Mars' slimy grip.

18

Ilium

This city—Ilium, Troy, Priam's City, Pergamus—is most beautiful at night.

The walls, each more than a hundred feet high, are lit with torches, illuminated by braziers on the ramparts, and backlit by the hundreds of fires of the Trojan army camping on the plain below. Troy is a city of tall towers, and most of these are lighted late into the night, windows warm with light, courtyards glowing, terraces and balconies warmed by candles and firepits and more torches. The streets of Ilium are broad and carefully paved—I once tried to slide my knifeblade between the stones and couldn't—and most are lighted by open doorways, torches set into wall sconces, and by the cooking campfires of the thousands upon thousands of non-Trojan soldiers and their families living here now, allies to Ilium all.

Even the shadows in Ilium are alive. Young men and women of the lower classes make love in the dark alleys and on shadowy terraces. Well-fed dogs and eternally clever cats slip from shadow to shadow, narrow alley to courtyard, loping along the edges of the broad thoroughfares where fruit and vegetables, fish and meat have fallen from the day's market carts and are theirs for the eating, and then slink back to narrow alleys' gloom and darkness under the viaducts.

The residents of Ilium have no fear of starvation or deadly thirst. At the first alarm of the Achaeans' approach—many weeks before the dark ships arrived more than nine years ago—hundreds of cattle and thousands of sheep were herded into the city, emptying farm fields for 400 square miles around the city. More such cattle drives happen regularly, and most of the beef gets to the city despite the Greeks' half-hearted efforts to interdict. Vegetables and fruits flow easily into

Ilium, delivered by the same shrewd farmers and traders who sell food to the Achaeans.

Troy was built where it was so many centuries ago largely because of the huge aquifer under it—the city has four giant wells that always run fresh and deep—but to be on the safe side, Priam long ago ordered a tributary of the River Simois to the north of Ilium diverted and run through easily defended canals and underground viaducts into the city proper. The Greeks have more trouble finding fresh water than do the technically besieged residents of Ilium.

The population of Ilium—easily the greatest city on Earth at this time—has more than doubled since the war began. First into the city for protection came the farmers and goatherders and fishermen and other peripatetic former denizens of the plains of Ilium. Following them came the armies of the allies of Troy—not only the fighting men, but often their wives and children and elders and dogs and cattle.

These allies include different groups: the "Trojans" not from Troy itself—the Dardanians and others from smaller cities and outlying areas far beyond Ilium, including the Trojan-loyal fighters from under Mount Ida and from as far north as Lykia. Also present now are the Adresteians and other fighters from places many leagues east of Troy, as well as the Pelasgians from Larisa in the south.

From Europe have come the Thracians, Paionians, and Kikones. From the south shores of the Black Sea have come the Halizones—dwellers near the River Halys and related to the Chalybes metalworkers of ancient legend. One can hear campfire songs and curses in the city from the Paphlagoes and Enetoi, a people from farther north along the Black Sea who may be the great-great-ancestors of the future Venetians. From north-central Asia Minor have come the shaggy Mysians—Ennomos and Nastes are two Mysian men I've spent time with and who will, according to Homer, be cut down by Achilles in the river battle to come—a slaughter so terrible that not only will the Scamander run red for months, but the river will be dammed up by the corpses of all the men Achilles will massacre there, including the unclaimed bodies of Nastes and Ennomos.

Also here, recognizable by their wild hair, by their oddly shaped bronze gear, and by their smell, are the Phrygians, Maionians, Karians, and Lykians.

This city is full and wonderfully alive and raucous all but two or three of its twenty-four hours each day. This is the finest and grandest and most beautiful city in the world—in this era or my era or any era in the history of all humankind.

I am thinking this as I lie naked next to Helen of Troy in her bed, the linens smelling of sex and of us, the breeze cool through billowing curtains. Somewhere thunder rumbles as a storm approaches. Helen stirs and whispers my name—"Hock-en-bear-eeee . . ."

I came into the city in late afternoon after QTing down from the hospital of the gods on Olympos, knowing that the Muse was looking for me to kill me, and that if she did not find me today, Aphrodite would when the goddess got out of her healing tank.

I had thought to blend in with the soldiers watching the last of this long day's battles—somewhere out there in the late-afternoon sun and dust, Diomedes was still slaughtering Trojans—but when I saw Hector walking back to the city with only a few of his usual retinue, I morphed into one of the men I knew—Dolon, a spearman and trusted scout, soon to be killed by Odysseus and Diomedes—and followed Hector. The noble warrior came in through the Scaean Gates—Ilium's main gates, made of sturdy oak planks as tall as ten men the size of Ajax—and he was immediately besieged by the wives and daughters of Troy asking about their husbands and sons and brothers and lovers.

I watched Hector's tall red Trojan crest move through the mob of women, his head and shoulders swimming above the sea of beseeching faces, and saw him when he finally stopped to address the growing mob. "Pray to the gods, you women of Troy," was all he said before turning on his heel and marching toward Priam's palace. Some of his soldiers crossed tall spears and covered his retreat, holding back the wailing mass of Trojan women. I stayed with the last four of his guard and silently accompanied Hector into Priam's magnificent palace, built wide, as Homer said, and gleaming with porches and colonnades of polished marble.

We stepped back against the wall—evening shadows already creeping into the courtyards and sleeping chambers here—and stood guard as Hector met briefly with his mother.

"No wine, Mother," he said, waving away the cup she had ordered a servant to bring. "Not now. I'm too tired. The wine would sap what little strength and nerve I have left for the killing to come this evening. Also, I'm covered with blood and dirt and all the filth of battle—I'd be ashamed to lift a cup to Zeus with such dirty hands."

"My son," said Hector's mother, a woman I had seen act with warmth and a good heart over the years, "why have you left the fighting if not to pray to the gods?"

"It's you who have to pray," said Hector, his helmet next to him on the couch. The warrior was indeed filthy—face grimed with layers of dirt and blood turned to a reddish mud by his sweat—and he sat as only the deeply exhausted can sit, forearms on his knees, head bent, voice dulled. "Go to Athena's shrine, gather the most noble of Ilium's noblest women, and take the largest, most beautiful robe you can find in Priam's palace. Spread it across the knees of Athena's gold statue and promise to sacrifice twelve yearling heifers in her temple if only she will pity Troy. Ask the grim goddess to spare our city and our Trojan wives and help-less children from the terror of Diomedes."

"Has it come to that?" whispered Hector's mother, leaning closer and taking one of her son's bloody hands in hers. "Has it finally come to that?"

"Yes," said Hector and struggled to his feet and lifted his helmet and left the hall.

With the three other spearmen, I followed the exhausted hero as he walked six city blocks to the residence of Paris and Helen, a large com-pound with its cluster of regal terraces and residential towers and pri-vate courtyards.

Hector brushed past guards and servants, pounded up steps, and flung open the door to Paris and Helen's private quarters. I half ex-pected to see Paris in bed with his stolen consort—Homer had sung that the horny couple had gone straight to bed hours earlier when Paris had been whisked from his showdown with Menelaus—but instead, Paris looked up from fondling his armor and battle gear as Helen sat nearby, directing female servants in their embroidery.

"What the fuck are you doing?" Hector snarled at the smaller man. "Sitting here like a woman, like a mewling infant, playing with your armor while the real men of Ilium die by the hundred, while the enemy surges around the citadel and fills our ears with his foreign battle cries? Get up, you goddamn deserter. Get up before Troy is burned to cinders around your cowardly ass!"

Instead of leaping to his feet in indignation, the royal Paris just smiled. "Ah, Hector, I deserve your curses. Nothing you say is unjust."

"Then get off your butt and into that armor," Hector said brusquely, but the fury in his tone had suddenly died away, either robbed of force by fatigue or by Paris's calm refusal to defend himself.

"I will," said Paris, "but first hear me out. Let me tell you some-thing."

Hector remained silent, swaying slightly on his sandaled feet. He was carrying his crested helmet under his left arm and had an extra-long throwing spear, borrowed from the sergeant of our small guard, gripped in his right hand. Now Hector used the butt of that spear to steady himself.

"I'm not keeping to my chambers for so long just out of anger or outrage," said Paris, gesturing toward Helen and her servants as if they were part of the furniture. "But out of grief."

"Grief?" repeated Hector. He sounded contemptuous.

"Grief," Paris said again. "Grief at my own cowardice today—although it was the gods who carried me away from battle with Menelaus, not my own will—and grief at the fate of our city."

"That fate isn't written in stone," snapped Hector. "We can stop Diomedes and his battle-maddened minions. Put on your armor. Come back to the battle with me. There's another hour of daylight left. We can kill many Greeks in the bloody light of the setting sun and more in the cool twilight."

Paris smiled at this and stood. "You're right. Battle now strikes even me—the world's greatest lover, not its greatest fighter—as the better way. Fate and victory shift, you know, Hector—now this way, now that way—like a line of unarmored men under a hail of enemy arrows."

Hector put on his helmet and waited, silent, obviously not trusting Paris's promise to join the fighting.

"You go on," said Paris. "I have to don all this war gear. You go on, I'll catch you up."

Hector remained silent at this, still not willing to leave without Paris, but beautiful Helen—and she *was* beautiful—rose from her chair and crossed the marble floor to touch Hector's blood-streaked forearm. Her sandals made soft sounds on the cool marble.

"My dear friend," she said, her voice quavering with emotion, "my dear brother, dear to me—bitch that I am, vicious, scheming cunt that I am, a female horror to freeze the blood—oh, how I wish my mother had drowned me in the dark Ionian Sea the day I was born rather than be the cause of all this." She broke down, removed her hand from Hector, and began weeping.

The noble Hector blinked at this, raised his free hand as if to touch her hair, quickly drew back his hand, and cleared his throat in embarrassment. Like so many heroes, the great Hector was awkward with women other than his wife. Before he could speak, Helen went on—still weeping, hiccuping words between racking sobs.

"Or, Noble Hector, if the gods have truly ordained all these terrible years of bloodshed for me, I wish I had been the wife of a better man—a fighter rather than a lover, a man with a will to do more for his city than take his wife to bed in the long afternoon of his city's doom."

Paris took a half step toward Helen then, as if to slap her, but her proximity to the tall Hector held him back. We foot soldiers near the wall stared at nothing and pretended we had no ears.

Helen looked at Paris. Her eyes were red and brimming. She still spoke to Hector as if Paris—her kidnapper and putative second husband—was not in the room. "This . . . one . . . has earned the scalding scorn of real men. He has no steadiness of spirit, no grit. Not now, not . . . ever."

Paris blinked and a flush rose into his cheeks as if he had been slapped.

"But he'll reap the fruits of his cowardice, Hector," continued Helen, literally spitting out the words now, her saliva striking the marble floor. "I swear to you that he will reap the fruits of his weakness. By the gods, I swear this."

Paris stalked out of the room.

Helen turned to the standing, grime-streaked warrior. "But come to the couch and rest next to me, dear brother. You are the one hit hardest by all this fighting—and all for me, Hector, whore that I am." She sat on the cushioned couch and patted a place next to her. "The two of us are bound together in this fate, Hector. Zeus planted the seed of a million deaths, of the doom of our age, in each of our breasts. My dear Hector. We are mortals. We will both die. But you and I will live for a thousand generations in song . . ."

As if unwilling to hear more, Hector turned on his heel and left the room, donning his tall helmet so that it flashed in the low-slanting rays of the evening sun.

Looking one last time at Helen as she sat, head bowed, on the cushioned bench, noting her perfect pale arms and the softness of her breasts visible in her thin gown, I lifted my spear—the scout Dolon's spear—and followed Hector and his other three loyal spearmen.

This is important that I tell it like this. Helen stirs, whispers my name, but goes back to sleep. *My* name. She whispers, "Hock-en-bear-eeee," and it as if I have been speared through the heart.

And now, lying next to the most beautiful woman in the ancient world, perhaps the most beautiful woman in history—or at least the one woman who has caused the greatest number of men to die in her name—I remember more about my life. About my former life. About my *real* life.

I was married. My wife's name was Susan. We met as undergraduates at Boston College, married shortly after graduation. Susan was a high school counselor but rarely worked after we moved to Indiana where I began teaching classics at Indiana University in 1972. We had no children, but not for want of trying. Susan was alive when I grew ill from liver cancer and went into the hospital.

Why in God's name am I remembering this now? After nine years of almost no personal memories, why remember Susan now? Why be slashed and cursed by the jagged shards of my former life now?

I don't believe in God with a capital G and, despite their obvious solidity, I don't believe in the gods with their small g's. Not as real forces in the universe. But I believe in the bitch-goddess Irony. She crosses all time. She rules men and gods and God alike.

And She has a wicked sense of humor.

Like Romeo lying next to Juliet, I hear the thunder move toward us from the southwest, the sound echoing in the courtyard, the leading wind stirring the curtains on the terraces on both sides of the large bedroom. Helen stirs but does not wake. Not yet.

I close my eyes and pretend to sleep a few more minutes. My eyes feel gritty, as if I have sand under my eyelids. I'm getting too old to stay awake so long, especially after making love three times to the most beautiful and sensual woman in the world.

After leaving Helen and Paris, we followed Hector to his home. The hero who had almost never run from a fight in his life was running from the temptation Helen had offered—running home to his wife Andromache and their one-year-old son.

In all my nine years of observing and hanging around Ilium, I had never spoken to Hector's wife, but I knew her story. Everyone in Ilium knew her story.

Andromache was beautiful in her own right—no comparison to Helen or the goddesses, it was true, but beautiful in her own more human way—and she was royalty as well. She came from the Trojan area known as Cilicia in Thebes, and her father was the local king, Eetion, admired by most, respected by all. Their small palace was on the lower slopes of Mount Placos in a forest famous for its timber; the great Scaean Gates of Ilium were built from Cilician timber, as were the siege-engine towers sitting on their wheels behind Greek lines less than two miles away.

Achilles had killed her father, cutting Eetion down in combat when the swift-footed Achaean man-killer had led his men against the outlying Trojan cities shortly after the Greeks had landed. Andromache had seven brothers—none of them fighters, but sheepherders and tenders of oxen—and Achilles had killed them on that same day, finding them in the fields and chasing them down to their death in the rocky hills below the forest. Achilles' plan was obviously to leave no male vestige of the Cilician royal family alive. That night, Achilles had his men dress Eetion's body in war-bronze and he burned the corpse with respect, heaping a grave-mound above the old king's ashes. But Andromache's brothers' bodies lay untended in the fields and woods, food for wolves.

Rich with the plunder of a dozen cities, Achilles still demanded a literal king's ransom for Eetion's queen—Andromache's mother—and he had received it. Ilium was still rich then, and free to bargain with its invaders.

Andromache's mother had returned home to the halls of their empty palace in Cilicia and there—according to Andromache's frequent telling of her woeful tale—"Artemis, in a shower of arrows, shot her down."

Well, in a way.

Artemis, daughter of Zeus and Leto and sister of Apollo, is the goddess of the hunt—I saw her on Olympos only yesterday—but she is also the goddess presiding over childbirth. At one point in the *Iliad*, an infuriated Apollo flung shouts at his sister, in front of their father Zeus—"He lets you kill off mothers in their labor"—meaning that Artemis is responsible for dispensing *death* in childbirth as well as for serving as the divine midwife to mortal women.

Andromache's mother died nine months after being taken hostage by Achilles on the day Eetion, Andromache's father, was killed. Andromache's mother died in childbirth, attempting to bring her husband's killer's child into the world.

Tell me that the bitch-goddess Irony doesn't rule the world.

Andromache and their baby were not at home. Hector rushed from room to room in the house, the four of us spearmen holding back, watching the entrance but not interfering. The hero was obviously worried and showed more visible anxiety that I had ever seen him show on the battlefield. Back at the doorway, he stopped two servant women coming in.

"Where's Andromache? Has she gone to the Temple of Athena with the other noble wives? To my sister's house? To see my brother's wives?"

"Our mistress has gone to the wall, master," said the oldest of the servants. "All of the Trojan women have heard of the day's terrible fighting, of Diomedes' wrath and the turn of fortune against the sons of Ilium. You wife has gone to the huge gate-tower of Troy to see what she can see, to learn if her master and husband still lives. She ran like a madwoman, Master, with the nurse running along behind, carrying your child."

We could hardly keep up with Hector as he ran to the Scaean Gates, and I realized a block from the wall that I *shouldn't* stay with him. This event—the meeting of Hector and Andromache on the ramparts—was too important. Too many gods would be viewing it. The Muse might well be there, hunting for me.

Several hundred yards from the Gates, I dropped away from the loping spearmen and fell into a crowd on a side street. The shadows were deep now, the air cooling, but the topless towers of Ilium were still lighted by the red sun setting in the west.

I chose one of these towers and climbed its winding interior staircase while still morphed as the spearman Dolon.

The tower was built something like a minaret—although Islam was still millennia in the future—and I was the only one on the narrow, circular balcony when I stepped out onto it. The sun was in my eyes, but by polarizing my visual filters and magnifying the focus on my god-given contact lenses, I had a clear view of the reunion on the wall.

Andromache rushed down the rampart and flung herself at her husband, her feet twirling in the air as he lifted her and returned the hug. His polished helmet caught the rich evening light. Other soldiers and worried wives on the wall stepped away, giving their leader and his bride some privacy. Only Andromache's nurse, holding the one-year-old boy, stayed close to the couple.

I could have eavesdropped on their conversation with my shotgun-microphone baton, but I chose just to watch them, seeing their mouths move, studying their expressions. After her rush of relief at seeing her warrior-husband alive and unharmed, Andromache frowned and began speaking quickly, urgently. I remembered from Homer's tale the rough outline of what she was saying—a retelling of her own woes, her loneliness after Achilles' murder of her father and brothers. I could actually read her lips on some of the words as she said, "*You* are my father now, Hector, and my noble mother as well. You are a brother to me now, my love. And you are also my husband, young and warm and virile and alive! Take pity on me, my husband! Do not abandon me. Do not go back out onto the plains of Ilium and die there and have your body dragged behind an Achaean chariot until your flesh is flayed from your bones. Stay here! Fight *here*. Protect our city by fighting on the ramparts, *here*."

"I can't," said Hector, his helmet flashing as he slowly shook his head.

"You *can*," I saw Andromache say, her face contorted with love and fear. "You *must*. Draw your armies up close to where that fig tree stands . . . do you see it? This is where our beloved Ilium lies most open to their attack. Three times the Argives have tried that point, hoping to overrun our city, three times their best fighters led the way—both Ajaxes, the big and little, and Idomeneus, and terrible Diomedes. Perhaps a prophet showed them our weakness there. Fight *here*, my husband! Protect us *here*!"

"I can't."

"You *can*," cried Andromache, pulling away from his embrace. "But you *won't*!"

"Yes," I watched Hector say, "I won't."

"Do you know what will happen to *me*, Noble Hector, when you die your noble death and become food for the Achaean dogs?"

I saw Hector wince but stay quiet.

"I will be dragged off as some sweaty Greek commander's whore!" shouted Andromache, her voice so loud that I heard it half a block away. "Carried off to Argos as booty, as some slave for Big Ajax or Little Ajax or terrible Diomedes or some lesser captain to fuck at his whim!"

"Yes," said Hector, his gaze pained but steady. "But I'll be dead, with the earth over me to muffle your cries."

"Yes, oh, yes," cried Andromache, weeping and laughing at the same time now. "Noble Hector will be dead. And his son, whom all the citizens of Ilium call Astyanax—'Lord of the City'—will be a slave to the Achaean pigs, sold away from his slave-whore mother. *That* will be your noble legacy, oh Noble Hector!"

And Andromache called the nurse closer and grabbed the child, holding him up like a shield between herself and Hector.

Now I saw the pain on Hector's face, but he reached for the tiny boy, holding his arms out. "Come here, Scamandrius," said Hector, calling their son by his given name rather than by the nickname given him by the city's folk.

The boy flinched back and started to howl. I could hear his cries from my perch on the tower half a dozen rooftops away.

It was the helmet. Hector's helmet. Polished, shining bronze, streaked with blood and grime, reflecting the sunlight and the distorted parapet and the boy himself. The helmet with its flaming red horsehair crest and its monstrously shining metal guards curving around Hector's eyes and covering his nose.

The boy screamed and cowered against his mother's breast, afraid of his father.

At such a moment, one would expect Hector to be devastated—no final hug from his son?—but the warrior laughed, threw back his head and laughed again, heartily and long. After a minute, Andromache laughed as well.

Hector swept the battle helmet off his head and set it atop the wall, where it blazed in the light of the setting sun. Then Hector swept his son up as well, hugging him and tossing him and catching him until the boy shrieked not in terror but delight. Holding his son in the crook of his strong right arm, Hector hugged Andromache to him with his left arm.

Still grinning, Hector raised his face to the sky. "Zeus, hear me! All you immortals, hear me!"

All the guards and women on the wall had fallen silent. The streets hushed in an eerie calm. I could hear Hector's strong voice from blocks away.

"Grant this boy, my son, with whom I am well pleased, that he may be like me—first in glory among Trojans and men! Strong and brave like me, Hector, his father! And grant, oh gods, that Scamandrius, son of Hector, may rule all Ilium in power and glory some day and that all men shall say, 'He is a better man than his father!' This is my prayer, oh gods, and I ask no other boon from thee."

And with that, Hector handed the child back to Andromache, kissed both of them, and left the wall for the battlefield.

I admit that the hours right after Hector bid good-bye to his wife were a low point for me. It didn't help my mood to know that in the next year, Andromache would, indeed, be driven from the burning city to the land where she would be an expensive slave for other men. Nor did it help to know that the Achaean who will capture her—Pyrrhos, destined to become ancestor to the kings of the Eperiote tribe of the Molossians and to be given a hero's tomb at Delphi—would rip Hector's child, Scamandrius (called Astyanax, "Lord of the City," by the residents of Ilium), from his nurse's breast and will fling the child from the high walls to his bloody death. The same Pyrrhos will murder Hector's and Paris's father, King Priam, at the altar of Zeus in his own palace. The House of Priam will become all but extinct in one night. The thought is depressing.

This is not a defense for what I did next, but I offer it as a partial explanation.

I wandered the streets of Ilium until nightfall and after, feeling more alone and depressed than any time in my nine years as a scholic there. No longer morphed as Dolon, I was still dressed as a Trojan spearman—with the Hades Helmet ready for donning at a second's notice, the QT medallion at the ready for instant escape—and soon found myself back near Helen's compound. I confess that I had come here often over the years, stealing time between my scholic observations, coming secretly to the city and to this place just on the off chance of seeing her . . . of seeing Helen, the most beautiful and alluring woman in the world. How many times had I stood across the street from this multistory compound, staring up like a lovestruck boy and waiting until the lights were lit in the upper apartments and terraces, hoping against hope for just a glimpse of the woman?

Suddenly my moonstruck reverie was broken by a more chilling sight—a flying chariot trolling slowly above the streets and rooftops, cloaked to mortal eyes but quite visible to my enhanced vision. Leaning over the railing, scanning the streets, was my Muse. I had never seen the Muse fly so low above the city or plains of Ilium before. I knew she was looking for me.

I pulled up the Hades Helmet in an instant, hiding myself—I hoped—from gods and man. The technology must have worked. The Muse's chariot floated less than a hundred feet overhead and never slowed.

When the chariot had passed, circling over the central marketplace a dozen blocks to the east, I activated the studs on my levitation harness. All of the scholics are outfitted with these harnesses, but we use them only rarely. Often, after a day's confused fighting on the field, I had used the levitation harness to lift over the battlefield, to get a larger picture of the tactical situation, and then I would fly to Ilium—here to Helen's house, to be honest—for a few minutes of hopeful gazing before QTing back to Olympos and my barracks.

Not now. I lifted above the street, invisible as I flew above the spearmen standing guard at the main entrance to Paris's and Helen's compound, crossed the high wall, and landed on one of the balconies of the inner courtyard outside the couple's private apartments. Heart pounding, I entered the open doorway through blowing curtains. My sandals were almost silent on the stone floor. The compound's dogs would have detected me—the Hades Helmet was no disguiser of scent—but the dogs were all on the ground floor and in the outer courtyard, not up here where the royal couple lived.

Helen was in her bath. Three female servants attended her, their bare feet leaving moist tracks as they carried warm water up and down marble steps leading to the sunken tub. Gauzy curtains surrounded the bath itself, but since the brazier tripods and the hanging lamps were inside the bathing area, the flimsy curtain material provided no obstacle to sight. Still invisible, I stood just outside the softly stirring fabric and stared at Helen in her bath.

So these are the boobs that launched a thousand ships, I thought, and immediately cursed myself for being such a jerk.

Shall I describe her to you? Shall I explain why the heat of her beauty, her naked beauty, can move men across three thousand years and more of cold time?

I think not—and not out of discretion or decorum. Helen's beauty is beyond my poor powers of description. Having seen so many women's breasts, was there anything unique about Helen's soft, full breasts? Or something more perfect about the triangle of dark hair between her thighs? Or more exciting about her pale, muscled thighs? Or more amazing about her milky white buttocks and strong back and small shoulders?

Of course there was. But I'm not the man to tell you the difference. I was a minor scholar and—in my fantasies in my lost life—perhaps a novelist. It would take a poet beyond Homer, beyond Dante, even beyond Shakespeare to do justice to Helen's beauty.

I stepped out of the bathing room, into the coolness of an empty terrace outside her bedroom, and touched the thin bracelet that allowed me to morph into other forms. The control panel of the bracelet only glowed when I called on it, but it spoke to my thumb with symbols and images. On it were stored the morphing data for all the men I had recorded in the past nine years. Theoretically, I could have morphed into a woman, but I had never found reason to do so and I certainly didn't this night.

You have to understand something about morphing; it is not a reshaping of molecules and steel and flesh and bone into another shape. I don't have a clue how morphing works, although a short-lived Twenty-first Century scholic named Hayakawa tried to explain his theory to me five or six years ago. Hayakawa kept stressing the conservation of matter and energy—whatever that is—but I paid little attention to that part of his explanation.

Evidently, morphing works on the quantum level of things. What doesn't with these gods? Hayakawa asked me to imagine all the human beings here, including him and me, as standing probability waves. On the quantum level, he said, human beings—and everything else in the physical universe—exist from instant to instant as a sort of collapsing wavefront—molecules, memory, old scars, emotions, whiskers, beer breath, everything. These bracelets the gods gave us recorded probability waves and allowed us to interrupt and store the originals—and, for a short time, merge our own probability waves with the stored ones, take our own memories and will along into a new body when we morphed. Why this didn't violate Hayakawa's beloved conservation of mass and energy, I don't know . . . but he kept insisting it did not.

This usurpation of another's form and action is why we scholics almost always morphed into minor figures in the battle for Troy; literal spear carriers like the unnamed bodyguard whose form I had assumed after Dolon's. If we were to become Odysseus, say, or Hector or Achilles or Agamemnon, we would look the part but the behavior would be our own—far inferior to the heroic character of the real person—and every minute we inhabited his form, we would carry actual events further and further from this unfolding reality that so paralleled the *Iliad*.

I have no idea where the real person went when we morphed into him. Perhaps the probability wave of that person simply floated around on the quantum level, no longer collapsing into what we called reality until we were finished with his form and voice. Perhaps the probability wave was stored in the bracelet we carried or in some machine or god's microchip on Mons Olympos. I don't know and don't especially care. I once asked Hayakawa, shortly before he displeased the Muse and disappeared forever, if we could use the morphing bracelet to change into one of the gods. Hayakawa had laughed and said, "The gods protect their probability waves, Hockenberry. I wouldn't try to mess with them."

Now I triggered the bracelet and flicked through the hundreds of men I'd recorded there until I found the one I wanted. *Paris*. It's probable that the Muse would have ended my existence if she'd even known that I had scanned Paris for future morphing. Scholics don't interfere.

Where is Paris right now? Thumb over the activate icon, I tried to remember. The events of this afternoon and this evening—the confrontation between Hector and Paris and Helen, the meeting of Hector and his wife and son on the walls—all occurred near the end of Book Six of the *Iliad*. Didn't they?

I couldn't think. My chest ached with loneliness. My head was swimming, as if I'd been drinking all afternoon.

Yes, the end of Book Six. Hector leaves Andromache and Paris does catch up to him before Hector leaves the city—or just as Hector leaves the city. How had my favorite translation gone? *"Nor did Paris linger long in his vaulted halls."* Helen's new husband had buckled on his armor, as promised, and rushed out to join Hector and the two of them had strode through the Scaean Gates together, into more battle. I remember writing a paper for a scholarly convention in which I'd analyzed Homer's metaphor of Paris racing along like a stallion breaking free of its tether, hair streaming like a mane back over his shoulders, eager for battle, blah, blah, blah.

Where is Paris now? After dark? What have I missed while wandering the streets and staring at Helen's lights and Helen's tits?

That was in Book Seven, and I'd always thought that Book Seven of the *Iliad* was a confusing, cobbled-together mess. It ended that long day that had begun in Book Two with Paris killing the Achaean named Menesthius and Hector slashing Eioneus' throat. So much for husbandly hugs and fatherly embraces. Then there was more fighting and Hector had taken on Big Ajax in one-on-one combat and . . .

What? Nothing much. Ajax had been winning—he was the better fighter—but then the gods started quarreling about outcome again, there had been a lot of talk by the Greeks and Trojans, a lot of bluster blown back and forth, and a truce, and Hector and Ajax had swapped armor and acted like old pals, and then they all agreed to a truce while they gathered the dead for corpse fires, and . . .

Where the hell is Paris this night? Does he stay with Hector and the army to supervise the truce, speak at the funeral rituals? Or does he act more in character and come to Helen's bed?

"Who gives a shit," I said aloud and thumbed the activation icon on the bracelet and morphed into the form of Paris.

I was still invisible, decked out in Hades Helmet, levitation harness, everything.

I took off the helmet and everything else except the morphing bracelet and the small QT medallion hanging around my neck, hiding the gear behind a tripod in the corner of the balcony. Now I was only Paris in his war gear. I took off the armor and left it on the balcony as well, appearing now only as Paris in his soft tunic. If the Muse swooped down on me now, I had no defense except to QT away.

I walked back through the balcony curtains into the bathing area. Helen looked up in surprise as I parted the curtains.

"My lord?" she said, and I saw first the defiance in her eyes and then the downward-cast gaze of what might have been apology and self-subordination for her earlier harsh words. "Leave us," she snapped at the servants and the women left on wet feet.

Helen of Troy came slowly up the steps of the bath toward me, her hair dry except for the wet strands over her shoulder blades and breasts, her head still lowered but her eyes looking up at me now through her lashes. "What will you have of me, my husband?"

I had to try twice before my voice would work properly. Finally, in Paris's voice, I said, "Come to bed."

Golden Gate
at Machu Picchu

They walked from green globule to green globule on the Golden Gate, down unmoving escalators and across green-glass-enclosed walkways connecting the giant cables that supported the roadway so far below. Odysseus walked with them.

"Are you really the Odysseus from the turin drama?" asked Hannah.

"I've never seen the turin drama," said the man.

Ada noticed that the man who called himself Odysseus had not really confirmed or denied anything, just sidestepped the question.

"How did you get here?" asked Harman. "And where did you come *from?*"

"It is a complicated answer," said Odysseus. "I have been traveling for some time now, trying to find my way home. This is only a stop on the way, a place to rest, and I shall be leaving in a few weeks. I would prefer to tell some of my story later, if you don't mind. Perhaps when we dine this evening. Savi *Uhr* may be able to help me make sense of parts of my tale."

Ada thought that it was very strange to hear someone speak Common English as if it were not his native tongue; she had never heard an accent before. There were not even regional dialects in Ada's fax-based world, where everyone lived everywhere—and nowhere.

The six emerged on the top of the tower where Savi had landed the sonie earlier. They emerged just as the sun was touching the top of southernmost of the two sharp peaks that anchored the bridge. The wind from the west was strong and cold. They walked to the railing at the edge of the platform and looked down at the sloping, grassy saddle with its terraced ruins more than eight hundred feet below.

"The last time I came to the Golden Gate, three weeks ago," said Savi,

"Odysseus was in one of the cryotemporal sarcophagi where I usually sleep. His arrival—and what it means—is the reason I finally contacted you, why I left those directions on the rock in the Dry Valley."

Ada, Harman, Hannah, and Daeman stared at the old woman, obviously not understanding the terms or real meaning of her statement. Savi did not explain. The four waited for Odysseus to say something that would enlighten them.

"What is for dinner?" asked Odysseus.

"More of the same," said Savi.

The bearded man shook his head. "No." He pointed a broad, blunt finger at Harman, then again at Daeman. "You two. There is an hour of twilight left. A good time of day for hunting. Do you want to come with me?"

"No!" said Daeman.

"Yes," said Harman.

"I want to come," said Ada, surprised at the urgency in her own voice. "Please."

Odysseus stared at her a long moment. "Yes," he said at last.

"I should join you," said Savi. She sounded dubious.

"I know how to handle your machine," said Odysseus, nodding toward the sonie.

"I know, but . . ." Savi touched the black weapon in her belt.

"No need," said Odysseus. "It's just food I'm seeking, not a war. There will be no voynix down there."

Savi still hesitated.

Odysseus looked at Ada and Harman. "Wait here. I'll be back as soon as I get my spear and shield."

Harman laughed before he realized that the barrel-chested man in the pale tunic was not joking.

Odysseus did indeed know how to fly the sonie. They lifted off the tower top, circled the high saddle with its ruins throwing complicated shadows in the low sunlight, and swooped down a valley at high speed.

"I thought you meant you'd be hunting below the bridge," said Harman over the wind hiss.

Odysseus shook his head. Ada noticed that the man's silver hair fell down his neck like a curly mane. "Nothing there except jaguars and chipmunks and ghosts," said Odysseus. "We have to get out on the plains to find game. And there's one prey in particular that I have in mind."

They flew out of the canyon mouth and mountains at high speed and soared over high grasslands sprinkled with towering cycads and fern-topped trees. The sun was setting but still above the mountains, and everything on the plain threw long shadows. A herd appeared below— large grazing animals that Ada could not identify, brown hides with white-striped butts. The hundreds of creatures were antelopelike in form but each was three times an antelope's size, with long, strangely jointed legs, long flexible necks, and dangling snouts that looked like pink hoses. The sonie made no noise as it swooped over them and none of the grazing animals even looked up.

"What are they?" asked Harman.

"Edible," said Odysseus. He circled lower and landed the sonie behind some high fern shrubs some thirty yards downwind of the grazing herd. The sun was setting.

In addition to two absurdly long spears—each was almost as long as the sonie and the butts and shafts of the spears had protruded well beyond the forcefield bubble and stern of the flying machine—Odysseus had brought a round shield made of intricately worked bronze and layers of ox-hide, as well as a short sword in a scabbard and a knife tucked into the belt of his tunic. To Ada—who had gone under the turin cloth more frequently than she had admitted to Harman—this juxtaposition of a man from the fantastical turin drama of Troy with her world, or this wild version of her world, made her somewhat dizzy. She rose and started to follow Odysseus and Harman away from the landed sonie.

"No," snapped Odysseus. "You stay with the vehicle."

"The hell I will," said Ada.

Odysseus sighed and spoke to them in a whisper. "Both of you stand here, behind this bush. Don't move. If anything approaches, get in the sonie and activate the forcefield."

"I don't know how to do that," whispered Harman.

"I left the AI active," said Odysseus. "Just lie down in it and say 'forcefield on.' "

Carrying both spears, Odysseus went out onto the grassy plain, walking slowly and silently toward the grazing beasts. Ada could hear the floppy-nosed animals grunting and munching, could hear the grass being snapped off by their teeth, and could smell their strong scent. They did not run in alarm when the man approached, and when the animals on the edge of the herd finally looked up, Odysseus was within forty feet. He stopped, set down one spear and his shield, and hefted the other long spear.

The grazing animals had quit chewing and were watching the strange biped carefully now, but they did not seem alarmed.

Odysseus' powerful body coiled, arced, and released. The spear flew flat and straight, hitting the closest animal above the chest and almost passing through its long, thick neck. It whirled, made a strangled noise, and fell heavily.

The other grazers snorted, bleated, and ran hard—each animal zig-ging and zagging in a way Ada had never seen before, the grazers' oddly jointed legs allowing almost instant changes of direction—until the entire herd thundered out of sight down a draw a mile or so to the north.

Odysseus dropped to one knee next to the dead animal and pulled the short, curved knife from his belt. With a few quick strokes he opened the abdominal cavity, pulled out organs and entrails—tossing them onto the grass except for what looked to be the liver, which he set on a small plastic tarp he had laid out next to him—and then sliced the hide back from one haunch, cutting a thick slice of red meat free and setting it on the tarp as well. Then he cut the dead animal's throat, draining more blood onto the grass, and tugged his spear free, taking care not to break it. He carefully wiped the shaft and bronze point on the grass.

Still standing near the bush, Ada felt a wave of dizziness pass over her and decided to sit down on the grass rather than run the risk of faint-ing. Ada had never seen an animal killed by a human being, much less butchered and partially skinned so expertly. It was terribly . . . *efficient*. Ashamed of her reaction but not wanting to faint, she lowered her head toward her knees until black spots quit dancing around the circle of her vision.

Harman touched her back in concern, but when she waved him away, he began walking out toward the carcass.

"Stay there," called Odysseus.

Harman paused, confused. "They're gone. Do you need help carry-ing . . ."

Odysseus held up one palm to keep Harman where he was. "This isn't what I'm hunting for. This is . . . *Don't move.*"

Harman and Ada turned their faces to the west. Two white-and-black-and-red bipedal forms were approaching at very high speed, faster even than the grazers had fled. Ada felt her breath catch in her throat and saw Harman freeze.

The creatures ran toward the bloody grazer carcass and the kneeling Odysseus at more than sixty miles per hour, then skidded to a stop in a small cloud of dust. Ada saw that they were the birds they'd seen from the sonie—*Terror Birds*, Savi had called them—but what had been strangely amusing from high in the air, ostrichlike creatures strutting like awkward chicks—turned out to be, in truth, terrifying.

The two Terror Birds had stopped five paces from the carcass, their eyes on Odysseus now. Each bird was more than nine feet tall, with short white feathers on their muscular bodies, black feathers on their vestigial wings, and powerful legs as thick as Ada's torso. The birds' beaks had to be at least four feet long, wickedly curved, red around the mouth—as if dipped in blood—and controlled by powerful jaw muscles that bulged below the half-dozen long red feathers that protruded from the back of each Terror Bird's skull. Their eyes were a terrible, malevolent yellow ringed by blue circles and set under saurian brows. In addition to their rending predator beaks, the birds had powerful footclaws—each as long as Ada's forearm—and an even more wicked-looking claw at the bend of each vestigial wing.

Ada knew at once that this monster was no mere scavenger, but a terrible predator.

Odysseus rose, a long spear in his left hand and his bloodied spear in his right hand. The Terror Birds' heads snapped back in unison, yellow eyes blinked at yellow eyes, and the hunting pair moved apart like well-choreographed dancers, preparing to attack Odysseus from either side. Ada could *smell* the carrion reek of the monsters. She had no doubt that those powerful, naked legs could propel each Terror Bird twenty feet or more at its prey—Odysseus—in a single hop, claws extended and ripping as the one-ton monsters landed. It was also obvious that the pair worked perfectly as a killing team.

Odysseus did not wait for them to get into position or attack. With lethal grace he cast his first spear—flat and straight and hard—into the muscled breast of the Terror Bird on his left, then wheeled to face the second bird. The first bird let out a terrible screech that froze Ada's lungs, but it was matched a second later by a roar and howl from Odysseus as he sprang across the grazer carcass, tossed the second killing spear from his left hand to his right, and thrust the bronze point at the second Terror Bird's right eye.

The first bird staggered backward, clawing at the spear protruding from its chest, snapping off the thick oak shaft. The second bird dodged Odysseus' thrust by whipping its head back like a cobra's. Obviously taken by surprise by being attacked by this small featherless biped, the bird hopped twice—carrying it ten feet backward—and clawed at the parrying spear.

Odysseus had to whip the unwieldy spear back quickly after each thrust to keep from having it torn out of his hands. Still shouting, the man stepped backward and seemed to trip over the bloody grazer carcass, rolling on his side.

The uninjured Terror Bird saw its chance and took it, leaping six feet into the air and coming down on Odysseus with talons and killing claws extended.

Still rolling, Odysseus came to one knee in a single fluid movement and planted the butt of the spear in the ground an instant before the Terror Bird came down on it with the full weight of its body driving the bronze point home, up through its muscled chest, into its awful heart. Odysseus had to roll again to get out of its way as the huge creature crashed lifeless where he had been kneeling.

"Look out!" cried Harman and began running toward the fray.

The first Terror Bird—pouring blood from the spear wound and broken shaft still embedded in his chest—was rushing at Odysseus' back. The bird's head snapped forward on six feet of feathered-snake neck and the huge beak snapped where Odysseus' head would have to be if he retreated. But the warrior had thrown himself forward rather than back, rolling again, but with empty hands this time as the Terror Bird ran past him and then wheeled, twisting and turning almost as impossibly fast as had the oddly jointed grazers.

"Hey!" shouted Harman and threw a rock at the giant bird.

The Terror Bird's head snapped high, the yellow eyes blinked at the impertinence, and the huge predator kicked forward toward Harman, who skidded in the dirt, said "Shit!" in a high voice, and scrambled back the way he had come. Suddenly Harman realized that he couldn't outrun the monster, and he turned, legs apart, fists raised, ready to meet the Terror Bird's charge with his bare hands.

Ada looked around for a rock, a stick, a weapon of any sort. There was none in reach. She leaped to her feet.

Odysseus swept up his shield and—using the grazer's carcass as a springboard—jumped aboard the Terror Bird's back, pulling his short sword from its scabbard as he did so.

The bird kept running in Harman and Ada's direction, but now its neck was twisted around, head snapping, giant red beak clacking against Odysseus' circular shield. Every time the massive jaws struck, Odysseus was knocked backward, but his legs were tight around the bird's body six feet above the ground, and though he bent far back, like a trick horseback rider in the turin drama, he never fell off. Then, as the Terror Bird's head swiveled around, finding Harman with its yellow eyes, Odysseus leaned forward and pulled the sword low across the giant bird's white-feathered neck, severing the jugular.

He jumped off, landed on his feet, and ran to Harman's side as the Terror Bird crashed to the ground and lay still not ten feet in front of them. Blood spurted five feet in the air and then the red fountain diminished and disappeared as the huge heart stopped beating.

Panting, covered with grazer gore and Terror Bird blood and grass and mud, his bloody sword and shield still held high, Odysseus grinned through his beard and said, "I only wanted one for dinner, but we'll carve up the second one for leftovers."

Ada came up to Harman and touched his arm. He never looked around. His eyes were wide.

Odysseus walked to the nearest bird, cut off its huge head, and ran his skinning knife down the length of its chest, peeling flesh and skin and feathers back as easily as someone would help remove a thick coat. "I'll need more plastic bags," he said to Harman and Ada. "There are some in a storage locker near the aft end of the sonie. Just say 'Open locker' to the machine and it will open. But hurry."

Harman had turned to walk back to the sonie but paused. "Hurry? Why?"

Odysseus wiped blood from his beard with the back of his hand and grinned whitely at them. "These birds smell blood up to ten leagues away . . . and there are hundreds of hunting pairs of Terror Birds out here on the plains at twilight."

Harman turned and ran hard toward the sonie to get the bags.

Ada noticed that Savi and Daeman were both drunk before dinner began.

The meal was served in a glass room attached to the side of the south tower's higher support. Savi was heating pre-prepared meals in a regular microwave bubble, but Ada was fascinated—she had never seen a meal prepared exclusively by a human being before. The absence of servitors in the Golden Gate residence areas was even more noticeable during a meal.

Odysseus was outside on the bridge's broad support strut and had erected a clumsy stone-and-metal structure in which he was burning wood he'd brought back from the plains. It had begun to rain and Odysseus had to build the fire high to keep it burning. Flames lighted the rust and faded orange paint on the side of the tower.

Looking out through the translucent green wall, sipping from his glass of gin, Harman said, "Is that some sort of altar to his pagan gods?"

"Not quite," said Savi. "It's how he cooks his food." She carried bowls and plates to the round table where the others were waiting. "Call him inside, would you?" she said to Harman. "Our food is getting cold while he's cremating his, and there's a lightning storm coming over the mountains. It's not a great idea to be out on the bridge superstructure during a lightning storm."

When they were finally seated, Odysseus setting the wooden plates of steaming meat on a nearby counter so that no one would have to stare at the fire-blackened stuff, Savi passed around a pitcher of wine. She poured her own glass last and Ada overheard the old woman whisper, *"Baruch atah adonai, eloheno melech ha olam, borai pri hagafen."*

"What is that?" Ada asked softly. Everyone else was laughing at something Daeman had said and had not seemed to notice Savi's muttering. The only time Ada had every heard another language was in the turin drama; there the battling men spoke in gibberish, but somehow the turin translated every word so that anyone under the cloth understood the meaning without actually listening.

Savi shook her head, although whether to say that she did not know the meaning of the odd words, or that she was not disposed to tell them, Ada could not tell.

"I explored all the levels of the bridge and bubbles around the bridge," Hannah was saying excitedly. "The metal of the bridge itself is old and rusty but . . . amazing. And there are strange shapes of metal in some of the rooms below. Just freestanding, not part of any structure. Some are in the shape of men and women."

Savi barked a laugh. She was already refilling her glass with wine. No strange words accompanied this pouring.

"Those are statues," said Odysseus. "Sculptures. Have you never seen such things?"

Hannah shook her head slowly. Even though the girl had spent years learning how to heat and pour metal, Ada knew, the idea of making things in the shape of human beings or other living things was shocking. Ada also found it strange.

"They have no art," Savi said brusquely to Odysseus. "No sculpture, no painting, no crafts, no photography, no holography, not even genetic manipulation. No music, no dance, no ballet, no sports, and no singing. No theater, no architecture, no Kabuki, no No plays, no nothing. They're as creative as . . . newborn birds. No, I take that back . . . even birds know how to sing and build a nest. These latter day *eloi* are silent cuckoos, inhabiting other birds' nests without so much as a song for payment." Savi was beginning to slur her words slightly.

Odysseus looked at Hannah, Ada, Daeman, and Harman, and his expression was unreadable. Meanwhile, the four guests stared at Savi, wondering why her tone was so angry.

"But then," continued Savi, looking only Odysseus in the eye, "they have no literature, either. And neither do you."

Odysseus smiled at the woman. Ada recognized the smile from when the man was carving flesh out of the flank of the grazing animal. Odysseus had bathed before dinner, even his gray curly hair was freshly shampooed, but Ada still imagined his arms and hands and beard as they had been—streaked with blood, clotted with gore. It wasn't any of her business, but she thought it probably unwise for Savi to goad him so.

"The preliterate, meet the postliterate," continued Savi, opening her hand as if introducing Odysseus to the other four. Then she held up one finger. "Oh, I forgot our friend Harman here. He is the Balzac and the Shakespeare of the current litter of old-style humanity. He reads at about the level of a six-year-old from the Lost Age, don't you, Harman *Uhr*? Lips move when you sound out the words, eh?"

"Yes," said Harman, smiling slightly. "My lips do move when I read. I didn't know there was any other way to do it. And it took me more than four Twenties to reach that level of proficiency." To Ada, it appeared as if the ninety-nine-year-old knew he was being insulted, but did not care, showing only interest in what Savi would say next.

Ada cleared her throat. "What was that animal you . . . killed . . . today?" she asked Odysseus, her voice bright and brittle. "Not the Terror Birds, the other one?"

"I just think of it as the floppy-nosed grazer," said Odysseus. "Want to try some?" He reached back to the counter and lifted the platter of fire-darkened meat, holding it in front of Ada.

Wanting to be polite, Ada took the smallest cut on the platter, handling it gingerly with utensils.

"I'll also take some," said Harman. The platter went around. Hannah and Daeman scowled at the meat, sniffed it, smiled politely, but didn't take any. When the platter came to Savi, she passed it on to Odysseus without a word.

Ada nibbled the smallest bit she could slice. It was delicious—like steak, only stronger and richer. The wood smoke gave it a flavor different than any microwaved thing she had ever tasted. She cut a larger piece.

Odysseus was eating with just a short, sharp knife he had brought to the table with him, slicing thin strips and chewing them from the end of the knife. Ada tried not to stare.

"*Macrauchenia*," said Savi between forkfuls of her salad and microwaved rice.

Ada looked up, wondering if this was more of the woman's strange language ritual.

"Pardon me?" said Daemon.

"*Macrauchenia.* That's the name of the animal that our Greek friend killed and our two other friends are eating like there's no second course. They covered these South American plains a couple of million years ago but went extinct before humankind showed up in South America. They were brought back by the ARNists during the crazy years after the rubicon, before the post-humans put a stop to reintroducing extinct species helter skelter. Once they had the *Macrauchenia* back, though, some ARNist thought it would be clever to bring back *Phorusrhacos.*"

"For-us-what?" said Daemon.

"*Phorusrhacos.* The Terror Birds. The ARNist geniuses forgot that those birds were the primary predator in South America for millions of years. At least until the Smilodonts wandered down from North America when the water level fell and the land bridge between the continents emerged. Did you know that the Panamanian Isthmus is underwater again? The continents separate again?" She looked around, obviously intoxicated, belligerent, and secure in the knowledge that none of them had any idea what she was talking about.

Harman sipped his wine. "Do we want to know what a *Smilodont* is?"

Savi shrugged. "Just a big fucking cat with big fucking sabertooth teeth. They'd eat Terror Birds for lunch and pick their sabers with the leftover claws. The idiot ARNists did bring sabertooths back, but not here. India. Anyone here know where that is . . . was? Should be? The post-humans ripped it free of Asia and broke it into a goddamned archipelago."

The five looked at her.

"Thank you for reminding me," said Odysseus with his stilted accent, and stood and went to the counter. "Next course, Terror Bird." He carried the big platter back to the table. "I've been waiting to taste this delicacy for quite a while, but never had the time to hunt one until today. Who will join me?"

Everyone but Daemon and Savi volunteered to try a slice. They all poured more wine for themselves. Outside, the thunderstorm had arrived with a vengeance and flashes of lightning streaked around the bridge structure, illuminating the saddle and ruins far below as well as the clouds and jagged peaks on either side.

Ada, Harman, and Hannah each tried a bite of the pale meat and then drank copious water and wine. Odysseus bit off slice after slice from the point of his knife.

"It reminds me of . . . chicken," Ada said into the silence.

"Yes," said Hannah, "definitely chicken."

"Chicken with a strange, strong, bitter taste," said Harman.

"Vulture," said Odysseus. "It reminds me of vulture." He took another large bite, swallowed, and grinned. "If I cook Terror Bird again, I'll use lots of sauce."

Five of them ate their microwaved rice in silence while Odysseus enjoyed more helpings of his Terror Bird and *Macrauchenia*, washed down with huge draughts of wine. The conversational silence might have been uncomfortable if it had not been for the storm. The wind had come up, lightning was almost continuous—illuminating the softly lit dining bubble in blasts of white light—and the thunder would have drowned out most conversation anyway. The green dining bubble seemed to sway ever so slightly when the wind howled and the four guests glanced at each other with barely concealed anxiety.

"It's all right," said Savi, no longer sounding angry or all that intoxicated, as if her earlier harsh words had vented some of the pressure from her bitterness. "The pariglas does not conduct electricity and we're firmly attached—as long as the bridge stands, we won't fall." Savi sipped the last of her wine and smiled without humor. "Of course, the bridge is older than God's teeth, so I can't guarantee it will remain standing."

When the worst of the storm passed and Savi was offering coffee and chai heated in odd-looking glass containers, Hannah said, "You promised to tell us how you got here, Odysseus *Uhr*."

"You want me to sing to you of all my twists and turns, driven time and again off course, in the days since my comrades and I plundered the hallowed heights of Pergamus?" he replied, voice soft.

"Yes," said Hannah.

"I shall," said Odysseus. "But first, I think, Savi *Uhr* has some business to discuss with all of you."

They looked at the old woman and waited.

"I need your help," said Savi. "For centuries I've avoided exposure to your world—to the voynix and the other watchers who wish me ill—but Odysseus is here for a reason, and his ends serve my own. I ask if you would take him back—to one of your homes, where others can visit him—and allow him to meet and speak with your friends."

Ada, Harman, Daeman, and Hannah exchanged glances.

"Why doesn't he just fax wherever he wants?" asked Daeman.

Savi shook her head. "Odysseus can no more fax than I can."

"That's silly," said Daeman. "Anyone can fax."

Savi sighed and poured the last of the wine into her glass. "Boy," she said, "do you know what faxing *is*?"

Daemon laughed. "Of course. It's how you go from where you are to where you want to be."

"But how does it *work*?" asked Savi.

Daeman shook his head at the old woman's obtuseness. "What do you mean, 'How does it work?' It just works. Like servitors or running water. You use a fax portal to go from one place to another, one faxnode to the next."

Harman held up his hand. "I think what Savi *Uhr* means is how does the machinery work that allows us to fax, Daeman *Uhr*."

"I wondered that myself a few times," said Hannah. "I understand how to build a furnace hearth than can melt metal. But how does one build a fax portal that sends us from here to there without having to . . . go in between?"

Savi laughed. "It doesn't, gentle children. Your fax portals don't send you anywhere. They destroy you. Rip you atom from atom. They don't even send the atoms anywhere, just store them until they're needed by the next person faxing in. You don't *go* anywhere when you're faxed. You just die and allow another you to be built somewhere else."

Odysseus drank his wine and watched the receding storm, apparently not interested in Savi's explanations. The other four stared at her.

"Why," said Ada, "that's . . . that's . . ."

"Insane," said Daeman.

Savi smiled. "Yes."

Harman cleared his throat and set down his coffee cup. "If we are destroyed every time we fax, Savi *Uhr*, how is it that we remember everything when we . . . arrive . . . somewhere else?" He held up his right arm. "And this small scar. I received it seven years ago, when I was ninety-two. Normally, these little problems are cleared up when we go the firmary every Twenty, but . . ." He stopped as if seeing the answer himself.

"Yes," said Savi. "The machine-minds behind the faxportals remember your little imperfections, just as they do your memories and personality's cell structure, sending the information—not you, but the *information*—from faxnode to faxnode, updating you and fixing your aging cells every twenty years—what you call your firmary visits—but why do you think you disappear on your hundredth birthday, Harman *Uhr*. Why do they quit renewing you when you reach a hundred? And where will you go on your next birthday?"

Harman said nothing but Daeman said, "To the rings, you foolish woman. On the Fifth Twenty, we all ascend to the rings."

"To become post-humans," said Savi, barely avoiding a sneer. "To ascend into heaven and sit at the right hand of . . . someone."

"Yes," said Hannah, but she made it sound like a question.

"No," said Savi. "I don't know what happens to the memory patterns the logosphere keeps of you until you turn one hundred, but I know they don't send the data to the rings. It may be stored, but I suspect it's just destroyed. Scrambled."

For the second time this long day, Ada felt as if she might faint. Still, she was the first to find her voice. "Why can't you and Odysseus *Uhr* use the faxnodes, Savi *Uhr*? Or do you just choose not to?" *Choose not to be destroyed, to have the atoms of your body ripped apart like the bodies of the grazer and Terror Bird we were eating tonight.* Ada dipped her fingers in her water glass and touched her fingertips to her cheek.

"Odysseus can't fax because the logosphere has no record of him," Savi said softly. "His first attempt to fax would be his last."

"Logosphere?" repeated Harman.

Savi shook her head again. "That's a complicated topic. Too complicated for an old woman who's had too much to drink today."

"But you will explain it soon?" pressed Harman.

"I'll *show* you all tomorrow," said Savi. "Before we go our different ways again."

Ada caught Harman's eye. He could barely contain his excitement.

"But this logosphere . . . whatever it is," said Hannah, "has a record of you? For the faxnodes? So you *could* fax?"

Savi showed her unhappy smile. "Oh, yes. It remembers me from more than fourteen hundred years ago and when I faxed every day of my life. The logosphere is waiting for me like some invisible Terror Bird . . . it would recognize me instantly if I were to try one of your regular fax portals. But that would be my last attempt as well."

"I don't understand," said Hannah.

"Let's put all this technical double-talk aside for a while," said Savi. "Accept that neither Odysseus here, nor I, can use your precious fax portals. And if I visited your wonderful society by flying there, it would be my life."

"Why?" asked Harman. "There's no violence in our world. Other than the turin drama. And none of us believe that is real." He looked pointedly at Odysseus, but the gray-haired man did not respond in any way.

Savi sipped her wine. "Just believe me when I say that to show myself openly would be death. Also believe me that it is imperative that Odysseus be allowed to meet people, to speak to them, to be heard. If I were to fly you back, would one of you host him at your home for a few weeks? A month?"

"Three weeks," interrupted Odysseus, sounding brusque, as if hearing himself spoken about as if he weren't there had irritated him. "No more."

"All right," said Savi. "Three weeks. Will any of you offer three weeks of hospitality to this stranger in a strange land?"

"Wouldn't Odysseus be in danger in the same way you are?" asked Daeman.

"Odysseus *Uhr* can take care of himself," said Savi.

The four were silent a minute, trying to understand the request and the circumstances of the request. Finally Harman said, "I'd like to host Odysseus, but I also want to visit this place you said might have spacecraft, Savi *Uhr*. My goal is to get to the rings. And as you pointed out, I'm approaching my final Twenty—I don't have any time to waste. I'd rather spend the time finding this drained sea where you say the posthumans kept something that can fly to the e- and p-rings. Perhaps if you showed me how to pilot your sonie . . ."

Savi rubbed her brow as if her head hurt. "The Mediterranean Basin? You can't fly there, Harman *Uhr*."

"You mean it's forbidden?"

"No," said Savi. "I mean you *can't* fly there. The sonies and other flying machines won't work over the Basin." She paused and looked around the table. "But it's possible to hike or drive into the Basin. I've tried and failed to go there over centuries, but I can lead you there. *If* one of your friends agrees to host Odysseus for three weeks."

"I want to go with you and Harman," said Ada.

"So do I," said Daeman. "I want to see this Whatchamacallit Basin."

Harman looked at the younger man in surprise.

"To hell with it," said Daeman. "I'm no coward. I'll wager that I'm the only one here who's been eaten by an allosaurus."

"I'll drink to that," said Odysseus, and drained the last of his wine.

Savi looked at Hannah. "That leaves you, my dear."

"I'd be happy to host Odysseus," said the young woman. "But I don't fax that much or go to parties. I live with my mother and she doesn't host groups that often either."

"No, that won't work, I'm afraid," said Savi. "Odysseus only has three weeks and we need to start with a place that is well known and where many can stay for weeks on end. Actually, Ardis Hall would have been perfect." She looked at Ada.

"How do you know about Ardis Hall, Savi *Uhr*?" asked Ada. "For that matter, how do you know about Harman's reading or anything about the world, if you cannot walk among us or use the faxnodes?"

"I do watch," said the older woman. "I watch and wait and sometimes fly to places where I can mingle with you."

"The Burning Man," said Hannah.

"Yes, among other places," said Savi. She looked around the table and said, "You all look exhausted. Why don't I show you to your rooms so you can get a good night's sleep? We'll continue the conversation in the morning. Just leave the dishes, I'll clear them and wash them later."

The idea of picking up or washing dishes had never occurred to the guests. Once again, Ada looked around and felt the absence of servitors and voynix.

Ada wanted to protest this enforced bedtime—they'd not yet heard Odysseus tell his tale—but she looked at her friends—Hannah hollow-eyed with fatigue, Daeman drunk and barely able to keep his head up, Harman's face showing his age—and felt the exhaustion working at her as well. It had been one hell of a day. It was time to sleep.

Odysseus stayed at the table as Savi led the other four from the dining room, down hallways lighted only by the diminishing lightning, up a glass-covered escalator that wound around the Golden Gate tower, and down a long corridor to a series of bubble-rooms at the highest point on the north tower. These sleeping rooms were not physically attached to the tower top, only to the glass corridor that had bridge steel as its south wall, and the sleeping cubbies themselves protruded precariously into space, like clusters of green grapes.

Savi was offering them all separate sleep-bubbles, and gestured Hannah into the first room along the corridor. The young woman hesitated at the entrance to the small space. Inside the sleeping cubbie, even the floor was transparent, so that Hannah took one step forward and then hopped quickly backward into the relative solidity of the carpeted access hall.

"It's perfectly safe," said Savi.

"All right," said Hannah and tried again. The bed was set against the far wall and there was a privately partitioned toilet and sink space near the corridor wall, ensuring privacy from the viewpoint of the other sleep bubbles, but elsewhere the curving walls and floor were so clear that you could look down eight hundred feet to the lightning-illuminated stones and hillside directly below.

Hannah walked gingerly across the clear floor and settled gratefully onto the solid shape of the bed. The other three laughed and applauded. "If I have to go to the toilet in the night, I may not have the nerve to cross that floor again," said Hannah.

"You'll get used to it, Hannah *Uhr*," said Savi. "You may close and open the door by voice command and it is keyed to your voice only."

"Door, close," said Hannah.

The door irised closed. Savi dropped them off one at a time in their cubbies—first Daeman, who staggered to his bed with no apparent fear of the empty space under his feet, then Harman, who wished them both good night before ordering his door closed, then Ada.

"Sleep well, my dear," said Savi. "The sunrises here are rather beautiful and I hope you enjoy the view in the morning. I shall see you at breakfast."

There were fresh silk sleeping clothes set out on her bed. Ada went into the toilet area, took a quick hot shower, dried her hair, left her clothes on the counter next to the sink, dressed in the silk sleeping gown, and returned to the bed. Once under the covers, she turned her face to the wall and looked out at the mountain peaks and cloud tops. The thunderstorm had passed on to the east now, the lightning illuminated the receding clouds from within, and now the nearby peaks and grassy saddle were illuminated by moonlight. Ada looked down at the roadway and stone ruins so far below. What had Oysseus said about that place? That it was inhabited only by jaguars, chipmunks, and ghosts? Looking at the ancient pale-gray stones in the moonlight, Ada almost believed in the ghosts.

There came a soft tapping at her door.

Ada slipped from the bed and tiptoed across the cold floor, setting her fingertips against the irised metal. "Who is it?"

"Harman."

Ada's heart thudded in her chest. She had been hoping, silently wishing, that Harman would join her tonight. "Door open," she whispered, stepping back, noting in the wall's reflection how milky her arms and thin gown looked in the moonlight.

Harman stepped just inside and paused as Ada whispered the door closed again. Harman was wearing only blue silk sleep garb. She waited for him to embrace her, to lift her in his arms and carry her to the soft bed against the clear, curved wall. What would it be like, she wondered, to make love as if one were floating above these clouds, these mountains?

"I needed to talk to you," Harman said softly.

Ada nodded.

"I think it's important that Odysseus be in the right place the next few weeks," he said. "And I don't think that Hannah's mother's cubbie is the right place."

Feeling foolish, Ada folded her arms across her breasts. She imagined that she could feel the cold night air of the high mountains through the glass under her feet. "You don't know what Odysseus wants to do or why," she whispered.

"No, but if he's really Odysseus, it may be *very* important. And Savi's right . . . Ardis Hall is the perfect place for him to meet people."

Ada felt anger coil in her. Who was this man to tell her what to do? "If you think it's so important that he be hosted somewhere," she said, "why don't you invite him to *your* home as *your* guest?"

"I don't have a home," said Harman.

Ada blinked at this, trying to understand. She couldn't. *Everyone* had a home.

"I've been traveling for many years," said Harman. "I own only what I carry, except for the books I've collected, which I store in an empty cubby in Paris Crater."

Ada opened her mouth to speak but could think of nothing to stay. Harman took a step closer, so close that Ada could smell the male and soap scent of him. He had also showered before coming to her room. *Will we make love after this conversation?* thought Ada, feeling her anger slip away as quickly as it came.

"I need to go to the Mediterranean Basin with Savi," said Harman. "I've been hunting for a way to get to the e- and p-rings for more than sixty years, Ada. To be so close . . . well, I have to go."

Ada felt the anger flare again. "But I want to *go with you*. I want to see this Basin . . . find a spaceship, go to the rings. It's why I've helped you the last few weeks."

"I know," whispered Harman. He touched her arm. "And I want you to go with me. But this thing with Odysseus may be important."

"I know, but . . ."

"And Hannah just doesn't know that many people. Or have the space to host visitors."

"I know, but . . ."

"And Ardis Hall *would* be perfect," whispered Harman. He released his soft hold on Ada's arm but still held her in the grip of his gaze. Ada was aware of the stars beyond the clear, curved ceiling above them.

"I know Ardis Hall would be perfect," said Ada. She felt sad and torn between imperatives and people. "But we don't even know what this Odysseus wants . . . or who he really is."

"True," whispered Harman. "But the best way to find out would be for you to host him while I hunt for a spaceship in the Mediterranean Basin. I promise you that if I find one that can get us to the rings, I'll come get you before I go there."

Ada hesitated before speaking again. Her face was raised slightly toward Harman's, and she had the feeling that if they did not speak, he would kiss her.

Suddenly lightning flashed and thunder from the receding storm shook the green-glass structure. "All right," Ada whispered. "I'll host Odysseus and have Hannah as my helper at Ardis Hall for three weeks. But *only* if you promise to take me to the rings if you find a way to get there."

"I promise," said Harman. He did kiss her then, but only on the cheek, and only the way her father might have, Ada thought, if she had ever known her father.

Harman turned as if leaving, but before Ada could command the door to iris open, he turned back toward her. "What do you think of Odysseus?" he asked.

"What do you mean? You mean, do I think he's really Odysseus?" Ada was confused by the question.

"No. I mean what do you *think* of him? Are you interested in the man?"

"Interested in his story, you mean?" said Ada. "He's intriguing. But I'll have to hear what he says before I decide whether he's telling the truth about things."

"No, I . . ." Harman stopped and rubbed his chin. He seemed embarrassed. "I mean, do you find him *interesting*? Are you attracted to him?"

Ada had to laugh. Somewhere to the east, the receding thunder echoed the sound. "You idiot," she said at last and, waiting no longer, walked to Harman, put her arms around him, and kissed him on the lips.

Harman responded passively for a few seconds and then embraced her and kissed her back. Through the thin silk that separated them, Ada could feel his excitement rise. Moonlight flowed over the skin of their faces and arms like spilled white milk. Suddenly a powerful gust of wind struck the bridge and the bubble of the sleeping cubbie swayed underfoot.

Harman lifted Ada and carried her to the bed.

20

The Tethys Sea on Mars

"I think it's Falstaff that made me fall out of love with the Bard."

"What's that?" said Mahnmut over the hardline. He was preoccupied, driving the dying submersible toward the still-out-of-sight coastline at a weakening eight knots, trying to keep the ship-functions on line, watching the skies for enemy chariots through the periscope buoy, and generally brooding about the improbability of their continued survival. Orphu had been silent down there in *The Dark Lady*'s hold for more than two hours. Now this. "What was that about Falstaff?" said Mahnmut.

"I was just saying that it was Falstaff that drove me away from Shakespeare and toward Proust," said Orphu.

"I would have thought that you'd love Falstaff," said Mahnmut. "He's so funny."

"I *did* love Falstaff," said Orphu. "Hell, I identified with Falstaff. I wanted to *be* Falstaff. For a while, I thought I *looked* like Falstaff."

Mahnmut tried to imagine this. He couldn't. He returned his attention to ship's functions and perusing the periscope. "What made you change your mind?" he asked.

"Do you remember the scene in *Henry IV, Part 1* where Falstaff finds the body of Henry Percy—Hotspur—on the battlefield?"

"Yes," said Mahnmut. The periscope and radar showed the skies clear of chariots. He had been forced to shut down the failing reactor during the night and battery reserves were down to 4 percent, giving them only six knots now, and the power was still dropping. Mahnmut knew that he'd have to take *The Dark Lady* up to the surface again soon: every time they surfaced he brought in Martian air for his own survival, storing it in his enviro-crèche and breathing it until it got foul, funneling all the ship-produced air down to Orphu. The submersible had never been designed to open itself to Europan "atmosphere," and he'd had to override a dozen safety protocols to let the Martian air in.

"Falstaff stabs Hotspur's corpse in the thigh just to make sure he's dead," said Orphu. "Then carries Hotspur's body on his back, trying to take credit for killing him."

"Right," said Mahnmut. The MPS said that they were within thirty kilometers of the coast, but there was no sign of it in the periscope, and he didn't want to direct the radar toward land. He prepared to blow the ballast tanks and surface again, but had the dive planes ready for an emergency dive if anything showed on the radar. *"The better part of valor is discretion, in which better part I have saved my life,"* he quoted. "All the Shakespearean commentary I read—Bloom, Goddard, Bradley, Morgann, Hazlitt, and even Emerson—says that Falstaff may be one of the greatest characters Shakespeare ever created."

"Yes," said Orphu and stayed silent a minute while the submersible shook and rumbled to the ballast tanks being blown. When the ship was silent again except for the ocean rushing over the hull, he said, "But I find Falstaff despicable."

"Despicable?" The sub broke the surface. It was just after dawn and the sun—so much larger than the point-star sun Mahnmut had grown up with on Europa—was just breaking free of the horizon. He opened the vents and breathed in fresh salt air.

"Wherein cunning but in craft? Wherein crafty but in villainy? Wherein villainous but in all things," said Orphu.

"But Prince Hal was joking when he said that." Mahnmut decided to run on the surface. It was far more dangerous—radar had picked up a flying chariot every hour or two while they were submerged—but they could make eight knots on the surface, and stretch out their dwindling power reserves.

"Was he?" said Orphu. "He rejects the old blowhard in *Henry IV, Part 2*."

"And Falstaff dies from it," said Mahnmut, breathing in the clean air and thinking of Orphu down in the black and flooded hold, connected to life only by the O_2 line and the intercom. The first time they had surfaced, Mahnmut had realized it would be impossible to get the big Ionian out of the hold until they reached land. *"The King has killed his heart,"* he said, quoting Hostess Quickly.

"I've decided he deserved to be rejected," said Orphu. "When he was ordered to recruit soldiers for the war with Percy, Falstaff took bribes to let the good ones off and recruited only losers. Men he called 'food for powder.' "

Feeling *The Dark Lady* surging ahead faster through the low waves, Mahnmut kept monitoring the sonar, radar, and periscope. "Everyone says that Falstaff is a much more interesting character than Hal," he said. "Funny, realistic, antimilitary, witty—Hazlitt wrote that *'The bliss of freedom gained in humour is the essence of Falstaff.'* "

"Yes," said Orphu. "But what kind of freedom is it? The freedom to mock everything? The freedom to be a thief and a coward?"

"Sir John *was* a knight," said Mahnmut. Suddenly his attention focused on what Orphu was saying—Orphu the cynic and humorous commentator on the folly of moravec existence. "You sound more like Koros III," he said.

This made Orphu rumble. "I'll never be a warrior."

"Was Koros a warrior? Do you think he killed moravecs during his mission to the Belt?" Mahnmut was curious.

"We'll never know what happened in the Belt," said Orphu, "and I doubt that Koros had any more eagerness to fight than do the rest of us peacable moravecs. But he was trained to leadership and duty—things that Falstaff mocked even in his beloved Prince Hal."

"And you're thinking that we've been called to duty here," said Mahnmut. There was a haze to the south.

"Something like that."

"And you think you might need to be more Hotspur than Falstaff?"

Orphu of Io rumbled again. "It may be too late for that. *I wasted time, and now doth time waste me.*"

"That's not Falstaff."

"Richard the Second," came the voice from the hold.

"You think you're too old for what lies ahead?" asked Mahnmut, wondering himself what might lie ahead.

"Well, I feel a little old, sans eyes, sans legs, sans hands, sans teeth, and sans shell," said the Ionian.

"You never had teeth," said Mahnmut. Koros's mission had been to carry out reconnaissance near the big volcano, Olympos, and to deliver the Device in the cargo bay as close to the summit of Olympos as possible. But *The Dark Lady* was close to death and Orphu might also be dying. Even if Orphu survived, he would not be able to see or move or take care of himself if they managed to reach land. How could Mahnmut possibly deliver the Device across more than three thousand kilometers of landmass while keeping himself and his friend from being detected and destroyed by the chariot people?

Worry about that when you get the Lady *to land and Orphu out of the hold,* he thought. *One thing at a time.* The blue sky was empty of threat, but he felt terribly exposed as the submersible continued to wallow southward through the waves. To Orphu, he said, "Does your friend Proust have any advice?"

Orphu cleared his throat with a rumble:

> *Old age hath yet his honour and his toil;*
> *Death closes all: but something ere the end,*
> *Some work of noble note, may yet be done . . .*
> *'Tis not too late to seek a newer world . . .*
> *Tho' much is taken, much abides; and tho'*
> *We are not now that strength which in old days*
> *Moved earth and heaven; that which we are, we are;*
> *One equal temper of heroic hearts,*
> *Made weak in time and fate, but strong in will*
> *To strive, to seek, and not to yield.*

"You can't convince me that's Proust," said Mahnmut. The haze to the south was resolving itself.

"No," said Orphu. "That's Tennyson's *Ulysses.*"

"Who's Ulysses?"

"Odysseus."

"Who's Odysseus?"

There was a shocked silence. Finally, Orphu said, "Ah, my friend, this gap in your otherwise excellent education calls out for repair. We may well need to know as much as we can about . . ."

"Wait," said Mahnmut. And a minute later, "Wait!"

"What is it?"

"Land," said Mahnmut. "I can see land."

"Anything else? Any details?"

"I'm changing magnification," said Mahnmut.

Orphu waited, but finally said, "And?"

"The stone faces," said Mahnmut. "I see the stone faces—on the cliff tops mostly—stretching as far to the east as I can see."

"Just to the east? None to the west?"

"No. The line of faces ends almost where we'd reach land. I can see movement there. Hundreds of people—or things—moving along the cliffs and beach."

"We'd better dive," said Orphu. "Wait for dark before we make landfall. Find an ocean cave or something where you can bring the *Lady* in unseen, where . . ."

"Too late," said Mahnmut. "The ship doesn't have more than forty minutes of life support and propulsion left in her. Besides, the shapes—the people—have given up their work moving the stone faces west. They're coming down to the beach by the hundreds. They've seen us."

21

Ilium

I *could* tell you what it's like to make love to Helen of Troy. But I won't. And not just because it would be totally ungentlemanly of me to do so. The details are just not part of my story here. But I can say truthfully that if the vengeful Muse or maddened Aphrodite had found me a moment after Helen and I ended our first bout of lovemaking, say, a minute after we rolled apart on the sweat-moistened sheets to catch our breath and feel the cool breeze coming in ahead of the storm, and if the Muse and the goddess had crashed in and killed me then—I can tell you without fear of contradiction that the short second life of Thomas Hockenberry would have been a happy one. And at least it would have ended on a high note.

A minute after that instant of perfection, the woman was holding a dagger to my belly.

"Who are you?" demanded Helen.

"I'm your . . ." I began and stopped. Something in Helen's eyes made me abort my lie about being Paris before I could vocalize it.

"If you say you are my new husband, I will have to sink this blade into your bowels," she said evenly. "If you are a god, that shouldn't matter. But if you aren't . . ."

"I'm not," I managed. The point of the knife was close enough to draw blood from the skin above my belly. *Where did this knife come from?* Had it been in the cushions while we were making love?

"If you aren't a god, how have you taken Paris's shape?"

I realized that this was Helen of Troy—the mortal daughter of Zeus— a woman who lived in a universe where gods and goddesses had sex with mortals all the time; a world where shapechangers, divine and otherwise, walked among mere humans; a world where the concept of cause and effect had completely different meanings. I said, "The gods gave me the ability to mor . . . to change appearances."

"Who are you?" she asked. "*What* are you?" She did not seem angry, nor even especially shocked. Her voice was calm, her beautiful features undistorted by fear or fury. But the blade was steady against my belly. The woman wanted an answer.

"My name is Thomas Hockenberry," I said. "I'm a scholic." I knew that none of this would make sense. My name sounded strange even to me, hard-edged in the smoother tones of their ancient language.

"Tho-mas Hock-en-bear-reeee," she mouthed. "It sounds Persian."

"No," I said. "Dutch and German and Irish, actually."

I saw Helen frown and knew I was not only *not* making sense to her with these words, but was sounding actively deranged.

"Put on a robe," she said. "We will talk on the terrace."

Helen's large bedroom had terraces on both sides, one looking down into the courtyard, the other looking out south and east over the city. My levitation harness and other gear—except for the QT medallion and morphing bracelet I had worn to bed—were hidden behind the curtain on the courtyard terrace. Helen led me to the outside terrace. We each wore thin robes. Helen kept her short, sharp knife in her hand as we stood at the railing in the reflected light from the city and from the occasional storm flash.

"Are you a god?" she asked.

I almost answered "yes"—it would be the easiest way to talk her out of putting that blade in my belly—but had the sudden, inexplicable, overwhelming urge to tell the truth for a change. "No," I said. "I'm not a god."

She nodded. "I knew you were not a god. I would have gutted you like a fish if you had lied to me about that." She smiled grimly. "You don't make love like a god."

Well, I thought, but there was nothing else to say to that.

"How is it," she asked, "that you can take the shape and form of Paris?"

"The gods have given me the ability to do so," I said.

"Why?" The tip of the dagger blade was only inches from my bare skin through the robe.

I shrugged, but then realizing that shrugs weren't used by the ancients, I said, "They lent me this ability for their own purposes. I serve them. I watch the battle and report to them. It helps that I can take the shape of . . . other men."

Helen did not seem surprised by this. "Where is my Trojan lover? What have you done to the real Paris?"

"He's well," I said. "When I abandon this likeness, he will return to what he was doing when I morphed . . . when I took his shape."

"Where will he be?" asked Helen.

I thought this was a slightly strange question. "Wherever he would have been if I hadn't borrowed his form," I said at last. "I think he'd just left the city to join Hector for tomorrow's fighting." Actually, when I morph out of Paris's form, Paris will be exactly where he would have been if he'd continued on during the time I had his identity—sleeping in a tent, perhaps, or in the midst of battle, or shagging one of the slave girls in Hector's war camp. But this was too difficult to explain to Helen. I didn't think she'd appreciate a discourse on probability wave functions and quantum-temporal simultaneity. I couldn't explain why it was that neither Paris nor those around him wouldn't necessarily notice his absence, or how it was that events might reconnect to the *Iliad* as if I hadn't interrupted the probability wave-collapse of that temporal line. Quantum continuity might be sewn up as soon as I canceled the morph function.

Shit, I *didn't* understand any of this.

"Leave his form," commanded Helen. "Show me your true shape."

"My Lady, if I . . ." I began to protest, but her hand moved quickly, the blade cut through silk and skin, and I felt the blood flow on my abdomen.

Showing her that my right hand was going to move very, very slowly, I opened the glowing functions and touched the icon on the morphing bracelet.

I was Thomas Hockenberry again—shorter, thinner, gawkier, with my slightly myopic gaze and thinning hair.

Helen blinked once and swung the dagger up fast—faster than I thought any person could move. I heard the ripping and tearing. But it wasn't my stomach muscles she had sliced open, only the tie of the robe and the silken material itself.

"Don't move," she whispered. Helen of Troy flung my robe open, using her free hand to slide it off my shoulders.

I stood naked and pale in front of this formidable woman. If a dictionary ever needed a perfect definition of "pathetic," a photograph of this moment would suffice.

"You may put the robe back on," she said after a minute.

I tugged it back up. The sash was torn, so I held it together with my hand. She seemed to be thinking. For several minutes we stood there on the terrace in silence. Even as late as it was, the towers of Ilium glowed from torchlight. Watchfires flickered along the ramparts on the distant walls. Farther to the south, beyond the Scaean Gate, the corpse fires burned. To the southwest, lightning flashed in the towering storm clouds. There were no stars visible and the air smelled of the rain coming from the direction of Mount Ida.

"How did you know I was not Paris?" I asked at last.

Helen blinked out of her reverie and gave a small smile. "A woman may forget the color of her lover's eyes, the tone of his voice, even the details of his smile or form, but she cannot forget how her husband fucks."

It was my turn to blink in surprise and not just at Helen's vulgar speech. Homer had literally sung the praises of Paris's appearance—comparing him to a "stallion full-fed at the manger" when describing Paris's rush to join Hector outside the city this very night, *sure in his racing stride . . . his head flung back, his mane streaming over his shoulders, sure and sleek in his glory.* Paris was, in the teenagers' parlance of my previous life, a hunk. And while I had been in Helen's bed, I had owned Paris's streaming hair, his sun-bronzed body, his washboard belly, his oiled muscles, his . . .

"Your penis is larger," said Helen.

I blinked again. Twice this time. She had not used the word "penis," of course—Latin was not yet a real language—and the Greek word she had chosen was slang closer to "cock." But that made no sense. When we were making love, I'd had Paris's penis . . .

"No, that wasn't how I knew you were not my lover," said Helen. She seemed to be reading my mind. "That is just my observation."

"Then how . . ."

"Yes," said Helen. "It was *how* you you bedded me, Hock-en-bear-eeee."

I had nothing to say to this, and could not have spoken clearly if I'd had anything to say.

Helen smiled again. "Paris first had me not in Sparta, where he won me, nor in Ilium, where he brought me, but on the little island of Kranae on the way here."

There was no island that I knew of named Kranae, and the word merely meant "rocky" in ancient Greek, so I took it to mean that Paris had interrupted their voyage to put into some small, rocky, unnamed island to have his way with Helen without the watching presence of the ship's crew. Which would mean that Paris was . . . impatient. *So were you, Hockenberry* came the voice of something not totally unlike my conscience. Too late for a conscience.

"He's had me—and I've had him—hundreds of times since then," Helen said softly, "but never like tonight. Never like tonight."

I was adither with confusion and smug with pride. Was this good? Was this a compliment? No, wait . . . that's absurd. Homer sings of Paris as nearly godlike in his physical beauty and charm, a great lover, irresistible to women and goddesses alike, which must mean that Helen only meant —

"You," she said, interrupting my confused thoughts, "*you* were . . . *earnest.*"

Earnest. I clutched the robe tighter and looked toward the coming storm to hide my embarrassment. Earnest.

"Sincere," she said. "Very sincere."

If she didn't shut up soon and quit hunting for synonyms for "pathetic," I thought I might wrestle the dagger away from her and cut my own throat with it.

"Did the gods send you here to me?" she asked.

I considered lying again. Certainly not even this strong-willed woman would gut someone on an errand from the gods. But again I chose not to lie. Helen of Troy seemed almost telepathic in her ability to read me. And telling the truth for a change felt good.

"No," I said. "No one sent me."

"You came here just because you wanted to bed me?"

Well, at least she hadn't used the f-word again. "Yes," I said. "I mean, no."

She looked at me. Somewhere in the city, a man laughed loudly, then a woman did the same. Ilium never slept.

"I mean—I was lonely," I said. "I've been here for the whole war by myself, with no one to talk to, no one to touch . . ."

"You touched me enough," said Helen.

I couldn't tell from her tone if it was sarcasm or an accusation. "Yes," I said.

"Are you married, Hock-en-bear-eeee?"

"Yes. No." I shook my head again. I must sound like a total idiot to Helen. "I believe I was married," I said, "but if I was, my wife is dead."

"You *believe* you were married?"

"The gods brought me to Mount Olympos across time and space," I said, knowing she would not understand but not caring. "I *believe* I died in my other life, and they somehow brought me back. But they did not return all my memory to me. Images come and go from my real life, my former life . . . like dreams."

"I understand," said Helen. I realized from her tone that somehow, amazingly, she did understand.

"Is there a particular god or goddess you serve, Hock-en-bear-eee?"

"I report to one of the muses," I said, "but I learned just yesterday that Aphrodite controls my fate."

Helen looked up in surprise. "And so has she controlled mine," she said softly. "Just yesterday, when the goddess saved Paris from Menelaus' fury and brought him back here to our bed, Aphrodite ordered me to go to him. When I protested, she flew into a rage and threatened to make me the butt of hard, withering hate—her words—of both Trojans and Achaeans."

"The goddess of love," I said softly.

"The goddess of lust," said Helen. "And I know much about lust, Hock-en-bear-eeee."

Again I didn't know what to say.

"My mother was named Leda, called the daughter of Night," she said in conversational tones, "and Zeus camed to her and fucked her while he was in the shape of a swan—a huge, horny swan. There was a mural in my home showing my two older brothers and an altar to Zeus and me as an egg, waiting to be hatched."

I couldn't help it—I barked a laugh. Then my stomach muscles clenched, waiting for the dagger's blade to rip through it.

Instead, Helen smiled broadly. "Yes," she said. "I know about abductions and being a pawn of the gods, Hock-en-bear-eeee."

"Yes," I said. "When Paris came to Sparta . . ."

"No," interrupted Helen. "When I was eleven, Hock-en-bear-eeee, I was carried off—abducted from the temple of Artemis Orthia—by Theseus, uniter of the Attica communities into the city of Athens. Theseus made me pregnant—I bore him a girl child, Iphigenia, whom I could not look upon with love and handed over to Clytaemnestra, to raise with her husband, Agamemnon, as their own. I was rescued from this marriage by my brothers and returned to Sparta. Theseus then went off with Hercules in his war against the Amazons, where he took time to invade hell, marry an Amazon warrior, and explore the Labryinth of the minotaur in Crete."

My head was spinning. Every one of these Greeks and Trojans and gods had a story and had to tell it at a drop of a hat. But what did this have to do with . . .

"I know about lust, Hock-en-bear-eeee," said Helen. "The great king Menelaus claimed me as his bride even though such men love virgins, love their bloodlines more than life, even though I was soiled goods in a man's world that loves its virgins so. And then Paris—spurred on by Aphrodite—came to abduct me again, to take me to Troy to be his . . . prize."

Helen stopped the recitation and seemed to be studying me. I could think of nothing to say. There was a bottomless depth of bitterness beneath her cool, ironic words. No, not bitterness I realized, looking into her eyes—sadness. A terrible, tired sadness.

"Hock-en-bear-eeee," continued Helen. "Do you think I am the most beautiful woman in the world? Did you come here to abduct me?"

"No, I did not come here to abduct you. I have nowhere to take you. My own days are numbered by the wrath of the gods—I have betrayed my Muse and her boss, Aphrodite, and when Aphrodite heals from the wounds Diomedes inflicted on her yesterday, she will wipe me off the face of the earth as sure as we're standing here."

"Yes?" said Helen.

"Yes."

"Come to bed . . . Hock-en-bear-eeee."

I wake in the gray hour before dawn, having slept only a few hours after our last two bouts of lovemaking, but feeling perfectly rested. My back is to Helen, but somehow I know that she is also lying awake on this large bed with its elaborately carved posts.

"Hock-en-bear-eeee?"

"Yes?"

"How do you serve Aphrodite and the other gods?"

I think about this a minute and then roll over. The most beautiful woman in the world is lying there in the dim light, propping herself up on one elbow, her long, dark hair, mussed by our lovemaking, flowing around her naked shoulder and arm, with her eyes, pupils wide and dark, intent on mine.

"How do you mean?" I ask, although I know.

"Why did the gods bring you across time and space, as you say, to serve them? What do you know that they need?"

I close my eyes for a moment. How can I possibly explain to her? It will be madness if I answer honestly. But—as I admitted earlier—I'm terribly tired of lying. "I know something about the war going on," I say. "I know some of the events that will happen . . . *might* happen."

"You serve an oracle?"

"No."

"You are a prophet, then? A priest to whom one of the gods has given such vision?"

"No."

"Then I don't understand," says Helen.

I shift on my side and sit up, moving cushions to be more comfortable. It is still dark but a bird begins to sing in the courtyard. "In the place whence I came," I whisper, "there is a song, a poem, about this war. It's called the *Iliad*. So far, the events of the actual war resemble those sung about in this song."

"You speak as if this siege and this war were already an old tale in the land you came from," says Helen. "As if all this has already occurred."

Don't admit this to her. It would be folly. "Yes," I say. "That is the truth."

"You are one of the Fates," she says.

"No. I'm just a man."

Helen smiles with wicked amusement. She touches the valley between her breasts where I had climaxed just a few hours earlier. "I *know* that, Hock-en-bear-eeee."

I blush, rub my cheeks, and feel the stubble there. No shaving in the scholics barracks for me this morning. *Why bother? You only have hours to live.*

"Will you answer my questions about the future?" she asks, her voice terribly soft.

It would be madness to do so. "I don't really know your future," I say disingenuously. "Only the details of this song, and there have been many discrepancies between it and the actual events . . ."

"Will you answer my questions about the future?" She sets her hand on my chest.

"Yes," I say.

"Is Ilium doomed?" Helen's voice is steady, calm, soft.

"Yes."

"Will it be taken by strength or stealth?"

For God's sake, you can't tell her that, I think. "By stealth," I say.

Helen actually smiles. "Odysseus," she murmurs.

I say nothing. I tell myself that perhaps if I give no details, these revelations will not affect events.

"Will Paris be killed before Troy falls?" she asks.

"Yes."

"By Achilles' hand?"

No details! clamors my conscience. "No," I say. *Fuck it.*

"And the noble Hector?"

"Death," I say, feeling like some vicious hanging judge.

"By Achilles' hand?"

"Yes."

"And Achilles? Will he go home from this war alive?"

"No." *His fate is sealed as soon as he slays Hector, and he has known this all along . . . knew it from a prophecy he has carried with him like a cancer for* years. *Long life or glory? Homer said that it was . . . is . . . will be, the decision he must make. But, the prophecy goes, if he chooses long life, he will be known only as a man, not as the demigod he will become if he kills Hector in combat. But he has a choice. The future is not sealed!*

"And King Priam?"

"Death," I say, my whisper hoarse. *Slaughtered in his own palace, in his private temple to Zeus. Hacked to bloody bits like a heifer being sacrificed to the gods.*

"And Hector's little boy, Scamandrius, whom the people call Astyanax?"

"Death," I say. I close my eyes against the image of Pyrrhos flinging the screaming infant down from the wall.

"And Andromache," Helen whispers. "Hector's wife?"

"A slave," I say. If Helen keeps up this litany of questions, I'm pretty sure I'll go crazy. It was all right from a distance—from a scholic's disinterested observer's stance. But now I'm talking about people I have known and met and . . . slept with. It strikes me that Helen has not asked about her own fate. Perhaps she never will.

"And will I die with Ilium?" she asks, her voice still calm.

I take a breath. "No."

"But Menelaus will find me?"

"Yes." I feel like one of those black Crazy-8 tell-your-fortune toys that were popular when I was a kid. Why hadn't I answered her like that black ball would have? That would be more like the Oracle at Delphi— *The future is cloudy.* Or *Ask again.* Am I showing off for this woman?

It's too late now.

"Menelaus finds me but does not kill me? I survive his anger?"

"Yes." *I remember Odysseus' telling of this in the* Odyssey—*Menelaus finding Helen hiding in Deiphobos' quarters in the great royal palace, near the shrine of the Palladion, and of the cuckolded husband throwing himself upon her, sword drawn, fulling intending to kill this beautiful woman. Helen will uncover her breasts to her husband, as if inviting the blow, as if willing it—and then Menelaus will drop his sword and kiss her. It's not clear whether Deiphobos, one of the sons of Priam, is killed by Menelaus before this or after he . . .*

"But he takes me back to Sparta?" whispers Helen. "Paris dead, Hector dead, all the great warriors of Ilium dead or put to the sword, all the great women of Troy dead or dragged off to slavery, the city itself burned, its wall breached, its towers dragged down and broken up, the earth salted so that nothing will ever grow here again . . . but I live and am taken back to Sparta by Menelaus?"

"Something like that," I say, hearing how lame it sounds.

Helen rolls out of bed, stands, and walks naked to the courtyard terrace. For a minute I forget my role as Cassandra and just gaze in something like awe at her dark hair tumbling down her back, at her perfect buttocks, and at her strong legs. She stands naked at the railing, not turning back my way as she says, "And what about you, Hock-en-bear-eeee? Have the Fates told you your own destiny through this song of theirs?"

"No," I confess. "I'm not important enough to be included in the poem. But I'm pretty sure I will die today."

She turns. I expect Helen to be weeping after all I've told her—if she believes me—but she's smiling slightly. "Only 'pretty sure'?"

"Yes."

"You will die because of Aphrodite's wrath?"

"Yes."

"I've felt that wrath, Hock-en-bear-eeee. If she takes a whim to kill you, she will."

Well, that's encouraging. I say nothing for a while. There is a drone from the open terrace doorways on the city side. "What's that?" I ask.

"The Trojan women are still entreating Athena for mercy and divine protection, chanting and sacrificing at her temple, as Hector ordered," says Helen. She turns away from me again and stares down into the interior courtyard as if trying to find that solitary singing bird.

Too late for Athena's mercy, I think. Then, without thinking about it, I say, "Aphrodite wants me to kill Athena. She's given me the Hades Helmet and other tools so I can do just that."

Helen's head snaps around and even in the dim light I can see the expression of shock on her face, the pallor. It's as if she has finally reacted to all my terrible oracle news. Naked, she comes back and sits on the edge of the bed where I am propped up on one elbow.

"Did you say *kill* Athena?" she whispers, voice lower than at any time since we began speaking.

I nod.

"Can the gods be killed then?" asks Helen, her voice so soft I can barely hear it from a foot away.

"I think they can," I say. "Only yesterday, I heard Zeus tell Ares that gods could die." Then I tell her about Aphrodite and Ares, their wounds, the strange place where they are healing. I explain how Aphrodite will emerge from that vat today sometime—how it's possible she already has, since Olympos is on the same day-night schedule as Ilium and it's already "tomorrow" there as well.

"You're able to travel to Olympos?" she whispers. Helen appears to be lost in thought. Her expression has slowly melted from shock to . . . what? "Travel back and forth from Ilium to Olympos whenever *you* please?" she asks.

I hesitate here. I know I've told too much already. *What if this Helen is merely my Muse in morphed form?* I know she isn't. Don't ask me how I know. And to hell with it if she is.

"Yes," I say, also whispering now, although the household is not coming awake yet. "I can go to Olympos when I want and stay there unseen by the gods." Except for the single bird deluded to think it's almost dawn, the city and the palace are eerily silent. There are guards at the front entrance, I know, but I cannot hear their shuffle of their sandals or the scrape of their spear butts on stone. The streets of Ilium, never totally silent, seem hushed now. Even the women's chanting from the Temple of Athena has ceased.

"Did Aphrodite give you the means to kill Athena, Hockenberry? Some weapon of the gods?"

"No." I don't tell her about the Hades Helmet of Death or the QT medallion or my taser baton. None of these things could kill a goddess.

Suddenly that short dagger is in her hand again, inches from my skin. *Where does she keep that thing? How does she make it appear that way?* We both have our little secrets, I guess.

The dagger moves closer. "If I kill you now," whispers Helen, "will it change the song of Ilium you know? Change the future . . . *this* future?"

This isn't the time to be honest, Tommy boy, warns the sane part of my brain. But I speak the truth anyway. "I don't know," I say. "I don't see how it can. If it's my . . . fate . . . to die today, I suppose it doesn't matter whether it's by your hand or Aphrodite's. Anyway, I'm not an actor in this drama, only an observer."

Helen nods but still appears distracted, as if her question about my death were of little consequence either way. She lifts the dagger until its point is almost touching the firm white flesh under her chin.

"If I take my own life right now, will it change the song?" she asks.

"I don't see how it will save Ilium or change the outcome of the war," I answer. This isn't completely true. Helen is a central figure in Homer's *Iliad* and I have no idea whether the Greeks would stay to finish the fight if she kills herself. What would they be fighting for with Helen dead? *Glory, honor, plunder.* But then again, with Helen removed as the prize for Agamemnon and Menelaus, and Achilles still sulking in his tent, would mere plunder be enough to keep the tens and tens of thousands of other Achaeans in the fight? They've been plundering islands and Trojan coastal cities for almost a decade now. Perhaps they've had enough and are looking for an excuse. Isn't that why Menelaus accepted the one-on-one combat with Paris to decide it all, before Aphrodite whisked Paris away? *Back to this bed, Helen and Paris having sex in this bed mere hours ago.* Perhaps Helen's suicide *would* end the war.

She lowers the dagger. "I've thought of this self-murder for ten years, Hock-en-bear-eeee. But I have too much lust to live and too little fondness for death, even though I deserve to die."

"You don't deserve to die," I say.

She smiles. "Does Hector deserve to die? Does his baby? Does lordly Priam, the most generous of fathers to me? Do all those people you hear awakening out there in the city deserve to die? Do even the warriors—Achilles and all the rest who have already gone down to cold Hades—deserve to die because of one fickle woman who chose passion and vanity and abduction over fidelity? And what about all the thousands of Trojan women who have served their gods and husbands well, but who will be torn from their homes and children and be sold into slavery because of me? Do they deserve such a fate, Hock-en-bear-eeee, just because I choose to live?"

"You don't deserve to die," I say stubbornly. The scent of her is still on my skin, my fingers, and in my hair.

"All right," says Helen and slides the dagger under the mattress. "Then will you help me live and stay free? Will you help stop this war? Or at least change its outcome?"

"What do you mean?" I'm suddenly wary. I have no interest in trying to help the Trojans win this battle. And I couldn't do it if I tried. Too many forces are in play here, not to mention the gods. "Helen," I say, "I was serious about not having any time left. Aphrodite will be free of her recovery vat today, and while I might hide for a while from the other gods, she has a way she can find me when she wants to. Even if she doesn't kill me right away for disobeying her, I won't be free to act in the short time I have left as a scholic."

Helen slides the sheet off my lower body. The light is coming up now and I can see her better than any time since I watched her in her bath the night before. She swings her leg up and straddles me, one hand flat on my chest while her other hand goes lower, finding, encouraging.

"Listen to me," she says, looking down over her breasts at me. "If you are going to change our fates, you must find the fulcrum."

I take this as an invitation and try to move into her.

"No, not yet," she whispers. "Listen to me, Hock-en-bear-eeee. If you're going to change our fates, *you must find the fulcrum*. And I don't mean what you're doing now."

It's difficult, but I pause long enough to listen.

An hour and a half later the city is coming alive and I am walking the streets, fully garbed in my usual scholic's gear and morphed as a Thracian spearman. The sun has risen and the city is coming fully alive, with crowded streets, opening market stalls, driven animals, running children, and swaggering warriors breaking their fast before going out to kill.

Near the marketplace, I find Nightenhelser—morphed as a Dardanian watchman but visible as Nightenhelser through my lenses—eating breakfast in an outdoor restaurant we've both frequented. He looks up and recognizes me.

I don't flee or use the Hades Helmet to disappear. I join him at the table under a low tree and order bread, dried fish, and fruit for breakfast.

"Our Muse was hunting for you at the barracks before dawn this morning," says the portly Nightenhelser. "And again near the walls here this morning. She was asking after you by name. She seems eager to locate you."

"Are you worried about being seen with me?" I ask. "Want me to move on?"

Nightenhelser shrugs. "All of us scholics are on borrowed time anyway. What does it matter? *Tempus edax rerum.*"

I've been thinking in ancient Greek for so long that it takes me a second to translate the Latin. *Time is a devourer.* Perhaps so, but I want more of it. I break the fresh, hot bread and eat, marveling at the glorious taste of it and of the sweet breakfast wine. Everything looks, smells, and tastes crisper, cleaner, newer and more wonderful this morning. Perhaps it was the night's rain. Perhaps it was something else.

"You smell suspiciously perfumed this morning," says Nightenhelser.

At first my only response is a blush—can the other scholic smell the night's revelries on me?—but then I realize what he's talking about. Helen had insisted I bathe with her before leaving. The old female slave who had directed the carrying of the hot water to the bath, I'd learned, was Aithra, Pittheus' daughter, wife of King Aigeus and mother of the famous Theseus—ruler of Athens and the man who had abducted Helen when she was eleven. I remembered the name Aithra from my graduate-school days, but my instructor, Dr. Fertig, a fine Homerian scholar, had

insisted that the name had been drawn at random from the epic stock—
"Aithra, daughter of Pittheus" must have sounded good to Homer or
some poetic predecessor who needed a name for a mere slave, said Dr.
Fertig, and that the noble Theseus' mother couldn't possibly be Helen's
servant in Troy. Well . . . *wrong*, Dr. Fertig. Just half an hour ago, lounging in the sunken marble tub with a naked Helen, she mentioned that
the old slave-woman Aithra was, indeed, Theseus' mum . . . that Helen's
brothers Castor and Polydeukes, when they rescued her from Theseus'
captivity, had carried off the old lady as punishment, and Paris had
brought her along to Troy with Helen.

"Thinking about something, Hockenberry?" asked Nightenhelser.

I blushed again. Right then I had been thinking about Helen's soft
breasts visible through the bubbles in the bath. I ate some fish and said,
"I wasn't on the field yesterday evening. Anything interesting happen?"

"Nothing much. Just Hector's big duel with Ajax. Just the showdown
we've been waiting for since the Achaean ships first touched their bows
to shore down there. Just *all* of Book Seven."

"Oh, that," I said. Book Seven was an exciting duel between Hector and
the Achaean giant, but nothing *happened*. Neither man hurt the other even
though Ajax was obviously the better fighter, and when evening made it
too dark to fight, Ajax and Hector called a truce, exchanged gifts of armor
and weapons, and both sides went back to burn their dead. I hadn't missed
anything crucial; nothing to give up one minute with Helen.

"There was something odd," said Nightenhelser.

I ate bread and waited.

"You know that Hector was supposed to come out of the city with his
brother, Paris, and both were supposed to lead the Trojans back into battle. Homer says that Paris kills Menesthius at the beginning of the fight."

"Yes?"

"And later, do you remember when King Priam's counselor, Antenor,
advises his fellow Trojans to give back Helen and all the treasures looted
from Argos—give them back and let the Achaeans go away in peace?"

"That's while Ajax and Hector are pals after they fail to kill each
other, exchanging gifts on the field, right?" I say.

"Yes."

"Well what about it?"

Nightenhelser sets his goblet down. "Well, it was Paris who was supposed to answer Antenor and urge his fellow Trojans to refuse to surrender Helen but offers to give up the treasures in exchange for peace."

"So?" I say, realizing where this is going. My stomach suddenly feels
queasy.

"Well, Paris wasn't there last night—not to come out of the Scaean Gates with Hector, not to kill Menesthius, and not even to offer the peace proposal at dusk."

I nod and chew. "So?"

"So that's one of the largest discrepancies we've seen, isn't it, Hockenberry?"

I have to shrug again. "I don't know. Book Seven has the Achaeans building their defensive wall and trench near the shore, but you and I know that those defenses have been there since the first month after they arrived. Homer messes up the chronology sometimes."

Nightenhelser looks at me. "Perhaps. But the absence of Paris to refute Antenor's suggestion about giving up Helen was strange. Finally, King Priam spoke for his son—saying that he was sure that Paris would never surrender the woman, but that he might give up the treasure. But without Paris being there in person, a lot of the Trojans in the crowd were mumbling their agreement. It's the closest thing to peace breaking out that I've seen in all the years I've been here, Hockenberry."

My skin feels cold. My self-indulgence with Helen last night, my long impersonation of Paris, has already changed something important in the flow of things. If the Muse had known the details of the *Iliad*—which she didn't—she would have known at once that I had taken Paris's place in bed with Helen.

"Did you report the discrepancy to the Muse?" I ask softly. Nightenhelser would have gone off shift when darkness fell. Since I was missing, he was the only scholic on duty last evening. It was his duty to report such oddities.

Nightenhelser chews the last of his bread slowly. "No," he says at last, "I didn't dictate that to the word stone."

I let out a breath. "Thank you," I say.

"We'd better go," says the other scholic. The restaurant is filling up with Trojan men and their wives waiting for a seat. As I drop coins on the table, Nightenhelser grips my forearm. "Do you know what you're doing, Hockenberry?"

I look him in the eye. My voice is firm when I respond. "Absolutely not."

Once on the street, I go the opposite direction from Nightenhelser. Stepping into an empty alley, I pull up the cowl of the Hades Helmet and touch the QT medallion.

It is sunrise on the summit of Mount Olympos. The white buildings and green lawns reflect the rich but lesser light here. I've always wondered why the sun seems smaller on and around Olympos than in the skies above Ilium.

I had envisioned the chariot stand near the Muse's building, and that's where I have arrived. I hold my breath as a chariot spirals down from the morning sky and lands not twenty feet from me, but Apollo steps out and strides away without noticing me. The Hades Helmet still works.

I step onto the chariot and touch the bronze plate near the front. I had watched the Muse carefully as she flew us across the caldera lake the other day. A glowing, transparent keyplate comes into existence inches above the brass. I touch the icons there in the sequence I'd watched the Muse use.

The chariot wobbles, rises, wobbles again, and steadies itself as I move the glowing, virtual energy controller next to the readouts. I twist it left and the chariot banks left fifty feet above the summit grass. I touch the forward-arrow icon and the chariot leaps ahead, flying south over the blue lake. To any god watching, it should look like an empty chariot flying itself, but no god is visible to watch.

Across the lake, I gain a bit of altitude and try to find the right building. *There—just beyond the Great Hall of the Gods.*

Some goddess—I do not recognize her—cries out from the front steps of the huge building and points toward my seemingly empty chariot, but it's too late—I've identified the building I want: huge, white, with an open doorway.

I'm getting the knack of the chariot controls now and I dive within twenty feet of the ground and accelerate toward the building. I have to lift the left side of the chariot almost perpendicular to the ground—I do not fall, there is some artificial gravity in the machine—as I zip between the giant columns at forty or fifty miles per hour.

Inside, the space is as I remember it: the giant vats filled with bubbling, violet liquid, green worms roiling around the unconscious, floating, healing gods. The Healer—the giant centipede-thing with metallic arms and red eyes—is on the opposite side of Aphrodite's reconstruction vat, preparing to remove her from it, I presume; his red eyes look my way and his many arms quiver as the chariot rushes into the quiet space, but he is not between me and my target and I accelerate forward before he or anything else can stop me.

It is only at the last second that I decide to jump rather than to stay with the chariot. It must be the memory of Helen, the night with Helen— the renewed pleasure of life in those hours with Helen.

The Hades Helmet still shielding me, I leap from the speading chariot, land hard, feel something bruise if not break in my right shoulder, and then I tumble to a stop on the floor as the chariot flies directly into the reconstruction vat, smashing plastic and steel, throwing violet liquid a hundred feet into the air of the giant room. Something—either part of the chariot or a huge shard of vat glass—slices the giant centipede Healer in two.

Aphrodite's body rolls out onto the floor in a wave of violet liquid and a coiling mass of writhing green worms. The other vats—including the one holding Ares in his nest of worms—rock but do not break or tumble.

Claxons, alarms, and sirens go off, deafening me.

I try to rise, but my head, left leg and right shoulder ache terribly and I sink back to the floor. I crawl to one side of the room, trying to stay out of the violet goo. I'm afraid of what the chemicals will do to me, but more afraid that the outline of my body will be visible in the flood if I can't get away from it. Black spots dance in my vision and I realize I'm going to pass out. Gods and floating robot-machines are rushing into the great healing chamber.

In the seconds before I lose consciousness, I see mighty Zeus stride in, his cloak billowing, his brow furrowed.

Whatever's going to happen next will have to happen without me. I set my forehead against the cool floor, close my eyes, and let the blackness wash over me.

The Coast of
Chryse Planitia

"I killed my friend, Orphu of Io," Mahnmut told William Shakespeare.

The two were walking in neighborhoods along the bank of the Thames. Mahnmut knew that it was the late summer of 1592 A.D., although he did not know how he knew. The river was busy with barges, wherries, and low-masted rivercraft. Beyond the Tudor buildings and ramshackle tenements on the north bank rose a profusion of London's steeples and a few contorted towers. A hot haze hung over the river and behind the slums on either side.

"I should have saved Orphu, but I could not," said Mahnmut. He had to walk quickly to keep up with the playwright.

Shakespeare was a compact man, in his late twenties, soft-spoken and dressed in a more dignified manner than Mahnmut would have expected from an actor and playwright. The young man's face was a sharp oval, showing a hairline already receding, sideburns, and a wisp of a beard and thin mustache—as if Shakespeare were tentatively experimenting with a more permanent beard. His hair was brown, his eyes a grayish-green, and he wore a black doublet from which the wide, soft collars of a white shirt were visible, white drawstrings hanging down. There was a small gold hoop in the writer's left ear.

Mahnmut wanted to ask Shakespeare a thousand questions—what was he writing now? what was life like in this city that would soon be overwhelmed by the plague? what is the hidden structure of the sonnets?—but all he could talk about was Orphu.

"I tried to save him," explained Mahnmut. "The *Dark Lady*'s reactor shut down and then the batteries went dead less than five kilometers from the coast. I was trying to find an inlet in one of the many caves along the cliffs—someplace we could hide the sub."

"*The Dark Lady?*" asked Shakespeare. "This is the name of your ship?"

"Yes."

"Pray continue."

"Orphu and I were talking about the stone faces," said Mahnmut. "It was night—we were approaching the coast at night, under cover of darkness, but I was using the night-vision scope and was describing the faces to him. He was still alive. The ship was providing just enough O_2 for him."

"O_2?"

"Air," explained Mahnmut. "As I say, I was describing the great stone heads to him—"

"Great stone heads? Statues?"

"Stone monoliths each about twenty meters tall," said Mahnmut.

"Did you recognize the statue's visage? Was he someone of your acquaintance, or perhaps a famous king or conqueror?"

"It was too far away for me to see details of the faces," said Mahnmut.

They had come to a wide, multiarched bridge covered with three-story buildings. A passageway about four meters wide ran right through the structures, like a road through a tunnel, and at the moment pedestrians in motley were dodging a mass of sheep being driven north into the city. All along that walkway, human heads—some dried and mummified, some almost skulls except for tufts of hair or bits of rotted flesh, others so shockingly fresh that there was still a blush to the cheeks or lips—had been mounted on posts.

"What is all this?" asked Mahnmut. His organic parts felt queasy.

"London Bridge," said Shakespeare. "Tell me what happened to your friend."

Tired of looking up at the playwright, Mahnmut scampered up onto a stone wall that served as a railing. He could see a forbidding tower in the east, and he assumed it was *the* Tower from *Richard III*. Knowing that he was either dreaming or dying from lack of air himself, Mahnmut did not want this dream to end before he asked Shakespeare a question or two. "Have you begun writing your sonnets yet, Master Shakespeare?"

The playwright smiled and looked out at the reeking Thames, then turned to gaze at the stinking city. Raw sewage was everywhere, as were the carcasses of dead horses and cattle rotting in the mudflats, while a wild effluvium of bloody chicken parts flowed out from open gutters and swirled in stagnant backwaters. Mahnmut had all but shut off his olfactory input. He didn't know how this human with his full-time nose could stand it.

"How do you know about my experiment with the sonnet?" asked Shakespeare.

Mahnmut approximated a human shrug. "A guess. So you've begun them?"

"I've considered playing with the form," admitted the playwright.

"And who is the Young Man in the sonnets?" asked Mahnmut, hardly able to breathe at the thought of unraveling this ancient mystery. "Is it Henry Wriothesley, the Earl of Southampton?"

Shakespeare blinked in surprise and looked carefully at the moravec. "You seem to follow close on my heels in such things, tiny Caliban."

Mahnmut nodded. "So Wriothesley is the Youth in the sonnets?"

"His lordship will have seen nineteen years this October and the down on his upper lip, it is said, has turned to sedge," said the playwright. "Hardly a youth."

"William Herbert then," suggested Mahnmut. "He's only twelve years old and he'll become the third Earl of Pembroke nine years from now."

"You know the dates of future succession and accession?" Shakespeare said with a tone of irony. "Does Master Caliban sail time's sea as well as this ocean of Mars he speaks of?"

Mahnmut was too excited about solving this mystery to respond to that. "You'll dedicate the large *Folio* of 1623 to William Herbert and his brother, and when your sonnets are printed, you'll dedicate them to 'Mr. W.H.'"

Shakespeare stared at the moravec as if he were a fever dream. Mahnmut wanted to say *No, you're the dream of a dying brain, Master Shakespeare. Not I.* Aloud, he said, "I just think it's interesting that you have a young man or a boy as a lover."

Mahnmut was surprised by the poet's reaction. Shakespeare turned, drew a dagger from his belt, and held it under the moravec's head-unit. "Do you have an eye, Little Caliban, that I may bury my blade in it?"

Careful not to lower his permiflesh deeper onto the point of the blade, Mahnmut shook his head very slightly and said, "I apologize. I am a stranger to your town, to your country, and to the manners here."

"See those closest three heads on posts on the bridge?," asked Shakespeare.

Mahnmut shifted his vision without moving his head. "Yes."

"This time last week, they were strangers to our manners," hissed the poet.

"I get the point," said Mahnmut. "No pun intended, sir."

Shakespeare slid the dagger back in its leather scabbard. Mahnmut remembered that the man was an actor, given to flourishes and exaggerations, although the dagger had been no stage prop. Nor had Shakespeare's response been a denial to Mahnmut's question.

Both looked back out at the river. The sun hung impossibly large and orange and low in the river haze to the west. Shakespeare's voice was soft when he spoke. "If I pen these sonnets, Caliban, I will do so to explore my own failures, weaknesses, compromises, self-conceits, and sad ambiguities in the way that one probes a bloody socket for the missing tooth after a barroom brawl. How did you kill your friend, this Orphu of Io?"

Mahnmut had to take a second to catch up to the question. "I couldn't get *The Dark Lady* to the cave inlet I had seen along the coast," he said. "I tried and failed. The sub's reactor died suddenly, the power went out. The *Lady* went aground in less than four fathoms of water, three kilometers or so from the cave. I tried blowing all the ballast tanks to bring her on her side—so I could free the bay doors to get to my friend—but she was already stuck fast."

Mahnmut looked at the poet. Shakespeare seemed to be paying attention. The buildings on the bridge behind him were red with the Thames sunset. "I went outside and went on internal O_2 and dived for hours," continued Mahnmut. "I used pry bars and the last of the acetylene and my manipulator fingers, but I couldn't open the bay doors, couldn't clear the debris in the flooded accessway to the hold. Orphu was on commline for a while, but then I lost him as the internal systems failed. He never sounded worried, never frightened, just tired . . . very tired. Right up to when the comm failed. It was dark. I must have lost consciousness. Perhaps I'm at the bottom of the Martian ocean right now, dead with Orphu, or dying, dreaming this conversation as the last cells of my organic brain shut down."

"Thy bosom is endeared with all hearts," said Shakespeare, his voice a monotone. "Which you by lacking have supposed dead, and there reigns love, and all love's loving parts, and all the friends which you thought buried."

Mahnmut regained consciousness to find himself on the beach, in low morning Martian daylight, and surrounded by dozens of little green men. They were bent over him, staring with small black eyes set into their green, transparent faces, and they backed a step or two away when Mahnmut sat up with a slight whir of his servos.

They *were* little. Mahnmut was just over a meter tall. These . . . persons . . . were shorter than that. They were humanoid in form, more so than Mahnmut, but not really human in appearance. They were bipedal, with arms and legs, but had no ears, no noses, and no mouths. They wore no clothes and had only three fingers on each hand, rather like cartoon characters Mahnmut had seen in the Lost Age media archives. They were sexless, Mahnmut noted, and their flesh—if flesh it was—was transparent, like soft plastic, revealing insides without organs or veins, bodies filled with floating green globules and clumps, particles and blobs, all flowing and bubbling in a way not that different from the insides of Mahnmut's beloved lava lamp, now abandoned with the sunken submersible.

More little green men were coming down a trail set into the cliff face. Mahnmut could see the last of the erected stone faces a kilometer or so to the east. Another was visible, horizontal on a long wooden pallet set on rollers far above them near the edge of the cliff, bound about by ropes. The details of the faces were not discernible.

To hell with the heads. Mahnmut whirled and searched the sea and beach. Tepid waves rolled in with the regularity of a metronome. *Where's The Dark Lady?*

There she was—two hundred meters out, part of the upper hull and command superstructure clearly visible. Her fathometer and sonar had died before she had, and Mahnmut had committed perhaps the most ancient and most grievous of sea captain's offenses—running his ship aground. He had been on internal O_2 while working wildly to free the hold doors on the sandy, muddy seabottom, but he realized that he must have passed out, been washed ashore here during the night.

Orphu! How long had he been unconscious, dreaming of Shakespeare? Mahnmut's internal chronometer said that it had been a bit less than four hours.

He still might be alive in there. He started walking toward the water, intending to walk the bottom all the way out to the stranded submersible.

A dozen little green men moved between Mahnmut and the water, blocking his way. Then twenty. Then fifty. A hundred more surrounded him on the beach.

Mahnmut had never lifted his hand or manipulator in anger, but he was ready to fight now, to punch and slash and kick his way through this mob if he had to. But he would try to talk to them first. "Get out of my way," he said, voice on full amplification and sounding loud in the Martian air. "Please."

The black eyes in green faces stared at him. But they had neither ears to hear him with nor mouths to speak with.

Mahnmut laughed sadly and started to push his way through them, knowing that however much stronger he might be, they could overcome him by sheer numbers—sit on him while they tore him apart. The thought of such violence, his or theirs, made his organic insides clutch with horror.

One of the little green men held his hand up as if to say "stop." Mahnmut paused. All the green heads turned to the right and looked up the beach. The mob parted magically as a little green man who looked exactly like the other little green men approached, stopped in front of Mahnmut, and extended both hands as if cupping an invisible bowl or praying.

Mahnmut did not understand. Nor did he want to take time to parley through sign language even if he could. Orphu might still be alive.

He started to brush past the little man, but a score of others closed ranks behind this emissary, blocking Mahnmut's way. He would either have to fight *now* or pay attention to the gesturing green figure.

Mahnmut let out a sigh not much different than a moan and paused, holding his hands out in mimicry of the little green man's gesture.

The emissary shook his head, touched Mahnmut's left arm—both organic and moraveccian sensors told him that the green fingers were cool—and lowered Mahnmut's left arm, then gripped the right. The little green man pulled Mahnmut's hand closer, closer, until the moravec's fingers and palm were flat against the cool, transparent flesh.

The little green man pulled harder, pushing himself forward and pulling Mahnmut's hand hard enough that the moravec's palm dented the flat chest, pressed the flesh inward, then . . . penetrated.

Mahnmut would have drawn his hand back in shock at this, but the little green man did not relent with his grip or with his strong pull. Mahnmut could *see* his dark hand entering the fluid of the little green man's chest, could *feel* the transparent flesh closing tight around his forearm in a vacuum seal.

All of the little green men raised their hands to their chests.

Mahnmut's splayed fingers encountered something hard, almost spherical. He could see a green blob about the size of a human heart centered in the man's chest. His palm felt it pulse.

The little green man pulled again and Mahnmut understood. He closed his organic fingers around the organ.

WHAT
DO
YOU
NEED?

Shocked, Mahnmut almost jerked his hand free. He forced himself to leave his fingers where they were, wrapped around the little man's green heart-blob. Mahnmut had *felt* the question flow up to his brain in pulses, throbs, vibrations. Not in words, certainly not in English or French or Russian or Chinese or Primary or any language Mahnmut had ever used. He did not know how to respond in kind, so he spoke. "I need to save my friend, who is trapped in the ship out there."

A hundred and fifty green heads turned in unison to look at the submersible. Three hundred black eyes gazed a few seconds and then turned their gaze back on Mahnmut.

TELL

US

WITH

YOUR

THOUGHTS

WHERE

HE

IS

Mahnmut closed his eyes and formed an image of Orphu in the blocked hold, an image of the bay doors, an image of the interior corridor. The vibration-response throbbed back up his arm:

WAIT

Mahnmut's hand was suddenly free and he pulled it from the little green man's tight flesh with an audible squishing sound. The little green man collapsed onto the sand then, rolling on his side and lying motionless; the green blobs in his body ceased to flow, his black eyes clouded white and stared blindly, and his fingers twitched once and were still. The hundred and forty-something of the others turned away and went efficiently about the task of saving Orphu.

Mahnmut collapsed onto the sand next to what was clearly the emissary's lifeless corpse. *Mother of God,* thought the moravec. *It kills them to communicate.*

More little green men kept coming down the steep path from the cliff. Two hundred. Three hundred. Six hundred. Mahnmut quit trying to count and—ignoring the dead emissary's request for him to wait—he waded and then paddled through the slight surf to the grounded submersible. Mahnmut went down through the conning tower airlock into his dry enviro-crèche, checking to see if any of the batteries had come back online. They hadn't. He cycled through the internal airlock into the flooded corridor to the hold and swam down to the collapsed hull there. No way through to Orphu that way. Returning to the control room, he tried the hardline comm again. Silence. Salvaging his hardback edition of the sonnets, safe in a waterproof wrapper, Mahnmut stuffed other gear into a backpack—the remote comm he'd devised for Orphu if he could get him out, the ship's log disks, hardcopy maps, a flare pistol, power cells—and clambered up to the top of the conning tower.

The little green men had brought great coils of their black cable down from the stone head they had been hauling along the cliff. They also brought scores of the rollers that the huge pallet had been moving on. They worked with an unbelievable efficiency—some swimming out to the submersible and attaching lines both above and under the waterline, others sinking metal rods from the rollers deep into the sand while pounding others into the rocky cliff face, still rigging pulleys and running the cable from the shore to the sub and back to the shore.

The sub was heavy—especially heavy with its water-damped reactor, flooded hold and corridors—and Mahnmut had trouble imagining these tiny green men actually moving the thing.

But they did.

Within twenty minutes, there were hundreds of cables running to the sub and then ashore and many little green men on each cable. They understood it was a rescue mission; the first thing they did was pull hard enough from the shore—the cables stretching like a black web back to the beach to the east—to tip the sub on its right side.

Mahnmut's instict was to go help pull on the cables, but he knew that would be useless. Instead, he waited on the hull of *The Dark Lady*—shifting as the submersible shifted—and as soon as the bay doors were clear of the mud, he dove into the shallow water with a cell-bowered pry bar, his shoulder lamps on full bright.

The hull-bay doors had been twisted and partially melted by entry into the atmosphere, and Mahnmut was unable to open them more than a few centimeters before they jammed completely. Wanting to weep with frustration, pounding the hull with impotent fury, he suddenly had the sense that he was not alone and he swung around in the silt-filled seawater.

Half a dozen little green men stood on the bottom of the sea nearby, watching him. They did not seem to need to breathe.

Not wanting to "communicate" with them again at the price of killing one of them, Mahnmut pointed to the pried-up section of door, pointed to the surface, made a gesture of rolling cable and wrapping it around the torn flange of metal, and pantomimed pulling.

All six of the little green men nodded and kicked for the surface three meters above them.

A minute later sixty of them returned, some pulling cable, others with the black rods that slid out of the rollers they used to pull the stone heads. Again they worked with improbable efficiency, some working as a team to twist back a few centimeters of the doors at the opposite end of the hold bay, others running cable through as if threading a needle. Within a few minutes, they had dozens of strands of the strong cable running beneath the jammed bay doors. They kicked to the surface again, gesturing Mahnmut to follow.

Again he breathed air, felt sunlight on his polymer and skin, and stood on *The Dark Lady*'s hull as hundreds of the little green men rigged the cables through a system of cliff-side pulleys and pulled. And pulled again.

The submersible creaked, the hull groaned, silt surrounded them, and *The Dark Lady* rolled another thirty degrees to starboard and twisted around until the belly of the ship was in the air and the stern was pointed toward the beach. The alloy bay doors bent but did not open.

Mahnmut attacked the doors with his powered pry bar again. The tortued and twisted metal would not relent. His acetylene torch was out of O_2 and energy.

The little green men gently pulled him away from his fruitless labors. Mahnmut pulled free and stumbled across the slippery hull toward the hold again, intent on prying at the warped and jammed doors until his own energy cells died, but then he saw that the LGM weren't finished with their efforts.

They knotted and spliced cable, turning the fifty stands into one. Then they ran the lengthened cable up the cliff face and through a series of oversized pulleys connected to a latticework of support rods they had somehow driven into the stone. Finally, they ran the cable to the huge stone head and wrapped the ends around the figure's neck a dozen times before tying it off.

Five of the little green men came over and pushed Mahnmut into the water, pulling him away from the sub.

Mahnmut could not believe what he was seeing. He had assumed that the great stone faces were sacred to the little green men, their positioning and raising along the coast a religious or psychological imperative calling for all of their time, energy, and devotion, the stone heads their only priority. Evidently he was wrong.

Hundreds of the green figures wrestled the head around on its pallet, got behind it, shoved, and pushed it off the cliff.

The stone head—its face to the cliff now—fell sixty meters, striking rocks at the base of the cliff and shattering into a dozen pieces, but the cable whirred on pulleys, rods popped out of stone, and the tied-off ends ripped the hold-bay doors off and threw them twenty meters into the air before dragging the torn metal up the cliff and back down again.

Hundreds of little green men swam for the sub, but Mahnmut reached it first, flicking on his searchlights again.

There were the three objects he'd left in the hold, including the large Device they were supposed to deliver to Mons Olympus. And tucked into the crèche, battered and torn and silent, was Orphu of Io.

Mahnmut used the last power in his pry bar to rip free the arresting flanges and tie-downs. Orphu's great bulk sagged free, sloshing in sea-water. But the bay was opened skyward now, the sub on its back, and there was no way that Mahnmut could ever get the Ionian out of the partially flooded pit the storage bay had become.

A dozen more little green men jumped into the space with Mahnmut, found grasping points on Orphu's pitted and cracked carapace, and forced green arms and legs under the hard-vac moravec's ungainly shape. Together, they found leverage and lifted. Working silently, never slipping or dropping him, they lifted Orphu out, gently wrapped more cables around him, slid him across the curve of *The Dark Lady*'s hull, lowered him to the water, set buoyant rollers under him, lashed them together into a raft, and gently propelled the Ionian's body to the beach.

The little green men—at least a thousand strong on the beach now—stood back and gave Mahnmut room as he worked to find out if Orphu was dead or alive. The Ionian lay inert on the red-sand beach like some storm-battered, oversized trilobite washed ashore in one of Earth's dim prehistoric ages.

Checking the skies for flying chariots that Mahnmut was sure were overdue, he emptied his backpack and waterproof bags of the gear he'd salvaged from *The Dark Lady*. First, he laid out five of the small but heavy power cells, connected them in series, and ran the cable to one of Orphu's surviving input connectors. There was no response from the big Ionian, but the virtual indicator showed that the energy was flowing somewhere. Next, Mahnmut crawled up the curve of Orphu's carapace—marveling at seeing the physical damage clearly for the first time here in the strong morning light—and screwed the radio receiver into the hardline socket. He tested the connection—receiving a carrier wave hum—and activated his own microphone.

"Orphu?"

No response.

"Orphu?"

Silence. The scores of little green men looked on impassively.

"Orphu?"

Mahnmut spent five minutes at the task, calling once every twenty seconds, using all comm frequencies and rechecking the receiver's connections. The comm unit was receiving his transmission. It was Orphu who was not responding.

"Orphu?"

There wasn't silence, exactly. From his external pickups, Mahnmut could hear more ambient noise than he'd ever encountered in his life: the lap of waves against the sand, the hiss of wind against the cliff behind him, the soft stir of the little green men shifting position from time to time, and the thousand nuances of vibrations in such a thick planetary atmosphere. It was just the commline and Orphu that were dead.

"Orphu?" Mahnmut checked his chronometer. He had been at it for more than thirty minutes. Reluctantly, in slow motion, he slid down off his friend's carapace, walked fifteen paces down the beach, and sat in the wet sand where the water rolled in. The little green men made way for him and then surrounded him again at a respectful distance. Mahnmut looked at them—at the wall of tiny green bodies, expressionless faces, and unblinking black eyes.

"Don't you all have work to do?" he asked, his voice sounding strange and choked to his own auditory inputs. Perhaps it was the acoustics of the Martian atmosphere.

The LGM did not move. The stone head was smashed into rubble of at the base of the cliff, but the little green men ignored it. A score of cables still ran out to the submersible where it lay inert in the low, rolling surf.

Mahnmut felt a sudden and immeasurably deep wave of loss and homesickness roll over him. He'd had three close relationships in his three Jovian decades—more than three hundred Martian years—of existence. First, *The Dark Lady*, which had been only a semi-sentient machine, but for which he'd been designed and in which he fit perfectly; the *Lady* was dead. Second, his exploration partner, Urtzweil, killed 18 J-years ago, half of Mahnmut's lifetime ago. Now Orphu.

Now here he was hundreds of millions of kilometers from home, alone, unfit, untrained, and unprepared for this mission they'd sent him on. How was he supposed to get the 5,000 or so kilometers to Olympus Mons to plant the Device? And what if he did? Koros III may have known what to do there, what this mission was really about, but lowly Mahnmut, late of *The Dark Lady,* didn't have a fucking clue.

Quit feeling sorry for yourself, idiot, he thought. Mahnmut glanced at the LGM. It surely must be an illusion that they seemed downcast, even sad. They hadn't mourned the death of one of their own, how could they show that emotion at the end of a moravec, a sentient machine they'd never imagined?

Mahnmut knew that he would have to communicate with the little green men again, but he hated the thought of reaching into one of the creatures' chests, of killing it through communication. No, he wouldn't do that until he had to.

He stood, returned to Orphu's corpse, and began disconnecting the power cells.

"Hey," said Orphu on the commband, "I'm still eating."

Mahnmut was so startled he actually jumped backward in the sand. "Jesus, you're alive."

"As much as any of us moravecs are 'alive.' "

"God *damn* you," said Mahnmut, feeling like laughing and crying, but mostly like hitting the big, battered horseshoe crab. "Why didn't you answer me when I called? And called? And called?"

"What do you mean?" said Orphu. "I was in hibernation. Have been ever since the air and energy ran out on *The Lady.* You expect me to chat with you while I'm in hibernation?"

"What is this hibernation shit?" said Mahnmut, pacing around Orphu. "I never heard of moravecs going into hibernation."

"You Europan vecs don't have it?" asked Orphu.

"Obviously not."

"Well, what can I say? Working alone in Io's radiation torus, or anywhere in Jovian space, we hardvac moravecs sometimes run into situations where we just have to shut down everything for a while until someone can get to us to repair and recharge us. It happens. Not often, but it happens."

"How long could you have stayed in this . . . hibernation?" asked Mahnmut, his anger shifting into something like giddiness.

"Not long," said Orphu. "About five hundred hours."

Mahnmut extended fingers through his manipulator pads, picked up a rock, and bounced it off Orphu's shell.

"Did you hear something?" asked the Ionian.

Mahnmut sighed, sat in the sand near the end of Orphu that used to house his eyes, and began describing their current situation.

Orphu convinced Mahnmut that he'd have to communicate with the LGM through a translator again. The Ionian hated the idea of causing the death of one of the little green men as much as Mahnmut did—especially since the LGM had rescued him—but he argued that the mission depended on them communicating and communicating fast. Mahnmut had tried talking again, had tried sign language, had tried drawings in the sand—showing maps of the coast where they were and the volcano they had to get to—had even tried the idiot's version of speaking a foreign language: shouting. The LGM all stared calmly but did not respond. Finally it was a little green man who took the initiative, stepping forward, seizing Mahnmut's hand, and pulling it to his chest.

"Shall I?" Mahnmut asked Orphu over the commline.

"You have to."

Mahnmut winced as his hand was pulled through the yielding flesh, as his fingers encircled and then gripped what could only be a beating green heart in the warm, syrupy fluid of the little man's body.

HOW
CAN
WE
HELP
YOU?

Mahnmut had a hundred questions he wanted to ask, but Orphu helped him put first things first.

"The sub," said Orphu. "We have to get it out of sight before a chariot flies over."

Through a combination of language and images, Mahnmut conveyed the thought of moving the submersible a kilometer or so to the west, of pulling it into the ocean-cave in the cliff that jutted out to sea at the headland.

YES

Scores of the little green men began work even while Mahnmut stood there, his hand deep in the translator's chest. They began sinking rods into the sand, running more cables to *The Dark Lady,* and rigging pulleys. The translator waited with Mahnmut's hand around his heart.

"I want to ask him about the stone heads," said Mahmut over the commline. "Ask him who they are, why they're doing this."

"Not until we try to find a way to get to Olympus," insisted Orphu.

Mahmut sighed and communicated the request for help in getting to the large volcano. He transmitted images of Olympus Mons as he'd seen it from orbit and asked if there was anyway the LGM could help them travel either overland over the Tempe Terra highlands or east along the Tethys coast for more than four thousand kilometers, then south along the Alba Patera coast to Olympus Mons.

THAT
IS
NOT
POSSIBLE

"What does he mean?" asked Orphu when Mahnmut relayed the response. "Does he mean it's not possible to help us, or to travel east that way?"

Mahnmut had felt something like relief when the LGM translator had all but pronounced their mission over, but now he forwarded Orphu's request for clarification.

NOT
POSSIBLE
FOR
YOU
TO
TRAVEL
EAST
SECRETLY
BECAUSE
THE
DWELLERS
ON
OLYMPOS
WOULD
SEE
YOU
AND

KILL
YOU

"Ask him if there's another way," said Orphu. "Maybe we could go overland along the Kasei Valles."

NO
YOU
WILL
GO
TO
THE
NOCTIS
LABYRINTH
BY
FELUCCA

"What's a felucca?" asked Orphu when Mahnmut relayed the answer. "It sounds like an Italian dessert."

"It's a two-masted, lateen-rigged sailing ship," said Mahnmut, whose training for the black underseas of Europa had included everything available in download about sailing the liquid seas of Earth. "Used to ply the Mediterranean millennia ago."

"Ask them when we can leave," sent Orphu.

"When can we leave?" asked Mahmut, feeling the question as a vibration through his fingers and a tickling in his mind.

THE
STONE
BARGE
ARRIVES
IN
THE
MORNING.
THE
FELUCCA
WILL
BE
WITH
IT.
YOU

CAN
LEAVE
ON
IT.

"We'll need some other things salvaged from our submersible," said Mahnmut. He sent the images of the Device and the two other pieces of cargo in the hold, visualized it being brought ashore and transported to the sea cave. Then he sent the image of LGM rolling Orphu to the same cave.

As if in response, dozens of the little green men began to wade and paddle back out to the ship. Others walked closer to Orphu and began arranging the rollers into an Orphu-sized pallet.

"I don't think I can hold this man's heart any longer," Mahnmut said to Orphu over the comm. "It's like grabbing a live electric wire."

"Let go then," said the Ionian.

"But . . ."

"Let go."

Mahnmut thanked the translator—thanked all of them—and released his grip. Just as with the first translator, this little green man fell to the sand, twitched, hissed, dried out, and died.

"Oh, God," whispered Mahnmut. He leaned back against Orphu's shell. The little green men were already lifting the Ionian's bulk, sliding rollers under him.

"What are they doing?"

Mahnmut described the translator's body and the work all around him—their preparation to transport Orphu and the Device and other objects already being hauled in from the ship, the cables being attached to the sub, the hundreds of LGM pulling at the cables from the shore, already dragging *The Dark Lady* west toward the ocean cave where it would be safe from airborne eyes.

"I'll go with you to the cave," Mahnmut said dully. The translator's body was like a dry, shriveled brown husk on the red sand. All of the interior organs had dried up and the fluid had flowed out of it, making the mud under it run like red blood. The other little green men ignored the translator's corpse and were already beginning to roll Orphu along the sand toward the west.

"No," said Orphu. "You know what you have to do."

"I already described the faces to you when I saw them from the sea."

"That was at night, through the periscope buoy," said Orphu. "We need to look at one or two of them in the daylight."

"The one at the base of the cliff is in pieces," said Mahnmut, feeling like whining. "The next one is a full kilometer to the east. Way up on the cliffs."

"You go ahead," said Orphu. "I'll stay in touch on comm while they trundle me off to the cave. You'll be able to see how they handle *The Lady* during most of your walk."

Mahnmut grudgingly complied, walking east, away from the crowd of LGM pulling his dead sub along the coast and rolling Orphu toward the cool shadow of the sea cave.

The fallen head was in too many pieces to make out its features. Mahnmut struggled up the steep trail that the little green men had descended with such apparent effortlessness. The path was narrow and frighteningly steep and wet-sandstone-slick.

At the top, Mahnmut paused a second to recharge his cells and to look around. The Tethys Sea stretched out as far as he could see to the north. To the south, inland, red stone gave way to low red hills and—several klicks further south—Mahnmut could make out the green of forests of shrubs on the foothills. There was some grass along the path he followed east along the edge of the cliff.

Mahnmut paused to look at the pad and prepared hole for the face the little green men had sacrificed in shoving off the cliff to pry open the hold-bay doors. It had been prepared carefully and Mahnmut could see how the stem at the base of the great stone heads' necks slid down into the hole in the stone and then locked in place. These little green men were craftsmen and skilled stone workers.

Mahnmut walked east. He could see the next head along the eastern horizon. The moravec was not designed for walking—his role was mostly to sit in an exploration submersible, sometimes to swim—and when he grew tired of being a biped, he altered the workings of his joints and spine and padded along like a dog for a while.

When he reached the next stone head he paused by its broad base, seeing how the stone at the neck had been filled in with something like cement. He looked east at the path the rollers and thousands of LGM had created along the cliff top, and west to where the green mob had pulled the sub and pushed Orphu almost to the headland cave.

"There yet?" came Orphu's voice.

"Yes. Leaning against the thing."

"How about the face?"

"This is a bad angle from beneath," said Mahnmut. "Mostly lips and chin and nostrils."

"Get out on the beach again. These faces are meant to be seen from the sea for some reason."

"But . . ." began Mahnmut, looking down at the steep cliff dropping at least a hundred meters away to the sand. There was a faint path on the greasy rock, just as at the other site. "If I break my neck getting down there," he sent, "it's your damned fault."

"Understood," said Orphu. "I can feel the vibration as they move me along here, but I have no idea how close we are to the cave. Can you see?"

Mahnmut magnified his vision as he looked to the west. "Just a couple of hundred meters from the overhang," he said. "I'm going to climb down now. Are you sure you want me to check the next head as well? It's another kilometer east and the heads looked all the same from orbit."

"I think we should check it," said Orphu.

"Sayeth the 'vec with no legs," muttered Mahnmut. He began the long, steep descent to the beach.

He stood as far away as he could, backing up until the low waves lapped at his legs. The face was distinct but not familiar. Saying nothing, lost in his own thoughts, he walked another kilometer east along the water's edge. The next face was identical to the first: proud, imperious, commanding, its visage staring fiercely out to sea, the sculpted stone showing an old man's face, mostly bald on top but with long hair flowing back on either side of the wrinkled face, small eyes under hard, downward slashes of eyebrows, wrinkles at the corner, high cheekbones gouged into stone, a small but firm chin, thin lips curving into a frown, and the same severe countenance.

"It's an old man," Mahnmut said on the comm. "Definitely an elderly human male, but I don't recognize him from the history databanks."

There was only static for a few seconds. "Fascinating," said Orphu. "Why would an old man from Earth deserve thousands of these stone heads all along the Martian coastline?"

"I have no idea," said Mahnmut.

"Is he one of the chariot people?" asked Orphu. "Does he look like a god?"

"Not a Greek god," said Mahnmut. "More than anything else, he looks like a powerful but dyspeptic old man. Can I come back now? Before one of the toga-wearing graybeards in a chariot does come flying along and sees me standing out here gawking like a tourist?"

"Yes," said Orphu. "I think you should come back."

Texas Redwood Forest

Odysseus didn't tell the story of his travels that morning during breakfast in the green bubble atop the Golden Gate at Machu Picchu. No one remembered to ask him. Ada thought that everyone seemed preoccupied, and she soon realized why.

Ada was preoccupied because she'd slept little, but spent the most wonderful night of her life with Harman. Ada'd "had sex" before—what woman her age had not?—but she realized that she'd never *made love* before. Harman had been exquisitely tender yet eagerly insistent, attentive to her needs and responses but not controlled by them, sensitive but forceful. They slept a little—coiled together on the narrow bed by the curving glass window—but woke often, their bodies renewing the lovemaking before their minds were fully engaged. When the sun rose over the spire to the east of Machu Picchu, Ada felt like a different person—no, that wasn't right, she realized, she felt like a *larger,* fuller, more connected person.

Ada thought that Hannah was also acting strangely that morning— flushed, hyperalert, attentive to every comment the man who called himself Odysseus made, glancing at Ada occasionally and then looking away, almost blushing. *My God,* Ada realized just as breakfast was ending and they were ready to leave, to fly north together to Ardis Hall, *Hannah slept with Odysseus.*

For a minute, Ada couldn't believe it, for never during their friendship had Hannah had ever commented on being with men or on sexual matters, but then she caught the glances Hannah was giving the bearded man, and the physical signs—the young woman sitting across from Odysseus but her body still reacting to every move the man made, hands nervous, leaning forward—and Ada realized it had been a busy night in the domis atop the Golden Gate.

Daemon and Savi were visibly the odd people out. The young man was in no better a mood than he'd been in the night before, barking questions about the Mediterranean Basin, eager to get going on his adventure with Harman and Savi, but obviously nervous about it. Savi seemed withdrawn, almost sorrowful, and in a hurry to leave.

Harman was quiet and—Ada thought—obviously still focused on Ada, although not obvious about it to the others. She caught his glance once or twice and something warm moved in her chest when he smiled at her. Once he put his hand on the outside of her leg under the table and patted twice.

"So what's the plan?" Daeman asked as they were finishing their breakfast of hot croissants—Ada had watched in amazement as Savi had baked the bread earlier—and butter and berries and fresh-squeezed fruit juice and rich coffee.

"The plan is to fly Odysseus, Hannah, and Ada to Ardis Hall—we're running late if we're to get them there before dark—and then for you, Harman, and me to go on to the Mediterranean Basin," said Savi. "Are you still game for that expedition, Daeman *Uhr*?"

"I'm still game." Daeman did not sound game to Ada; he sounded tired or hung over or both.

"Then let's get our gear in bags and our asses in gear and go," said the ancient woman.

They flew out on the same sonie they'd flown in on, even though Hannah told Ada that there were other flying machines hangared in one of the rooms attached to the south tower of the bridge. The little sonie had a surprising number of compartments at the rear for Savi's backpack and their other gear, but it was Odysseus who carried the most baggage—including a short sword in a scabbard, his shield, changes of raiment, and the two javelins he had used to hunt the Terror Birds. Savi lay in the front center depression, handling the glowing virtual controls, with Ada on her left and Harman on her right. Daeman, Odysseus, and Hannah filled the three concavities behind them, and Ada glanced back once to find her friend looking longingly at the bearded man.

They flew east over high mountains and then dropped lower and turned due north again, passing over thick jungle and a wide brown river that Savi said was called the Amazon. The jungle itself was solid rain forest canopy broken here and there only by a few blue glass pyramids whose apexes were a thousand feet high, parting low-moving rain clouds. Savi did not tell them what the pyramids might be and the others seemed too tired or preoccupied with their own thoughts to ask.

A half hour after the last of the pyramids had disappeared behind them, Savi banked the sonie hard left and they flew west by northwest across high mountains again. The air was so high and thin here that the forcefield bubble popped up even at their apparent low altitude of five hundred feet or so above the terrain, and the air in the bubble pressurized again to a higher oxygen content.

"Aren't we going out of our way?" asked Harman after the long silence.

Savi nodded. "I had to give a wide berth to the Zorin Monoliths that run along the coastal shelf of what used to be Peru, Ecuador, and Colombia," she said. "Some of them are still armed and automated."

"What are the Zorin Monoliths?" asked Hannah.

"Nothing we have to worry about today," said Savi.

"How fast are we traveling?" asked Ada.

"Slowly," said Savi. She glanced at the virtual display surrounding her wrists and hands. "About three hundred miles per hour right now."

Ada tried to imagine that speed. She couldn't. She'd never traveled in anything faster than voynix-pulled droshky before their first trip in this sonie, and she had no idea how fast a droshky went. Probably not three hundred miles per hour, she thought. Certainly the mountains and ridges below were flicking past much faster than the familiar countryside had in the droshky or carriole ride between the fax portal and Ardis Hall.

They flew on another hour. At one point Hannah said, "I'm getting a sore neck craning to look over the edge of the sonie and the bubble's too low to let me sit up. I wish . . ." She screamed. Ada, Daeman, and Harman let out similar yells.

Savi had moved her hand through the virtual control panel and the solid sonie under them had simply disappeared. In the brief seconds before Ada closed her eyes tight, she looked around at the perfect illusion of the six humans, their luggage, and Odysseus' spears flying along in midair, unsupported by anything other than empty air.

"Warn us if you're going to do something like that again," Harman said shakily to Savi.

The old woman muttered something.

Ada spent a full minute or two touching the cold metal of the cowl ahead of her, feeling the soft leatherlike solidity of the contour couch beneath her legs and belly and chest, before daring to open her eyes again. *I'm not falling, I'm not falling, I'm not falling,* she told herself. *Yes, you ARE falling,* her eyes and inner ear told her. She closed her eyes again, opening them just as they came out of the highlands and followed a peninsula running northwest from the mainland.

"I thought you might want to see this," Savi said to Harman, as if the rest of them wouldn't know what they were talking about.

Ahead of them, the ocean sliced through the isthmus, open water visible for a gap of at least a hundred miles. Savi gained altitude and turned them north across open seas.

"The maps I've seen show old the isthmus connecting North and South America above sea level the whole way," said Harman, straining up out of his couch to look behind them.

"The maps you've seen are useless," said Savi. Her fingers moved and the sonie accelerated and gained more altitude.

It was past midday when another coastline came into sight. Savi dropped the sonie lower and they were soon flicking over swamps which quickly gave way to mile after mile of redwoods and sequoia — Savi named the trees—the tallest towering two or three hundred feet into the humid air.

"Anyone want to stretch their legs on solid ground while we stop for lunch?" asked Savi. "Or have some privacy in case nature is calling?"

Four of the five passengers loudly voted aye. Odysseus smiled slightly. He had been dozing.

They had lunch in a clearing on a small rise, surrounded by cathedral giants. The e- and p-rings moved palely through the bit of blue sky visible overhead.

"Are there dinosaurs around here?" Daeman asked, peering into the shadows beneath the trees.

"No," said Savi. "They tend to prefer the middle and northern parts of the continent."

Daeman relaxed against a fallen log and nibbled at his fruit, sliced beef, and bread, but sat straight up when Odysseus said, "Perhaps Savi *Uhr* is actually saying that there are more ferocious predators around here that keep the recombinant dinosaurs away."

Savi frowned at Odysseus and shook her head, as if sighing over an incorrigible child. Daeman looked into the midday shadows under the trees again and moved closer to the sonie to finish his meal.

Hannah, rarely taking her gaze off Odysseus, did take time to pull her turin cloth from a pocket and set it over her eyes. She reclined for several minutes while the others ate silently in the shadowed heat and stillness. Finally Hannah sat up, removed the microcircuit-embroidered cloth, and said, "Odysseus, would you like to see what's happening with you and your comrades in the war for the walled city?"

"No," said the Greek. He tore off a strip of cold Terror Bird leftover with his white teeth and chewed slowly, then drank from the wineskin he'd brought with him.

"Zeus is angry and has tilted the balance toward the Trojans, led by Hector," continued Hannah, ignoring Odysseus' reticence. "They've driven the Greeks back through their defenses—the moat and the stakes—and they're fighting around the black ships. It looks like your side is going to lose. All of the great kings—including you—have turned and run. Only Nestor stayed to fight."

Odysseus grunted. "That garrulous old man. He stayed because his horse had been shot out from under him."

Hannah glanced at Ada and grinned. It was obvious that Hannah's goal had been to draw Odysseus into conversation and equally obvious that she thought she'd won. Ada still didn't believe that this all-too-real man—sun-bronzed, wrinkled, scarred, so different than the firmary-renewed males of their experience—was the same person as the Odysseus of the turin drama. Like most intelligent people she knew, Ada believed that the turin cloth provided a virtual entertainment, probably written and recorded during the Lost Age.

"Do you remember that fight by the black ships?" prompted Hannah.

Odysseus grunted again. "I remember the feast the night before that miserable dog's-ass day. Thirty ships arrived from the isle of Lemnos bringing wine—a thousand measures full, enough wine to drown the Trojan armies with, if we hadn't had a better use for it. Euneus, Jason's son, sent it as a gift for the Atrides—Agamemnon and Menelaus." He squinted at Hannah and the others. "Now Jason's voyage, *there's* a story worth hearing."

Everyone except Savi looked blankly at the barrel-chested man in his belted tunic.

"Jason and his Argonauts," repeated Odysseus, looking from face to face. "Surely you've heard *that* tale."

Savi broke the embarrassed silence. "They haven't heard any tales, son of Laertes. Our so-called old-style humans here are without past, without myth, without stories of any sort—except for the turin cloth. They're as perfectly postliterate as you and your comrades were pre-literate."

"We didn't need scratches on bark or parchment or mud to make us men to be reckoned with," growled Odysseus. "Writing had been tried in some age before ours and had been abandoned as a useless thing."

"Indeed," Savi said dryly. " 'Does an illiterate's tool stand any less erect?' I think Horace said that."

Odysseus glared.

"Will you tell us about this Jason and his . . . his what?" asked Hannah, blushing in a way that convinced Ada that her friend had indeed slept with Odysseus the night before.

"Ar-go-nauts," Odysseus said slowly, emphasizing each syllable as if speaking to a child. "And no, I won't."

Ada found her gaze wandering to Harman and her mind wandering to memories of the long night before. She wanted to walk off with Harman and talk to him in private about what they'd shared, or—failing that—just to close her eyes in the humid heat of the sun-dappled glade and nap, perhaps to dream about their lovemaking. *Or better yet,* thought Ada, peering at Harman through lowered lashes, *we could just steal off into the forest dim and make love again, rather than just dream about it.*

But Harman didn't seem to notice her glances and obviously had his lover's telepathy-receiver turned off. Ada's beloved appeared to be amused and interested by Odysseus' comments. "Will you tell us a story about your turin cloth war?" he asked the bearded man.

"It was called the Trojan War and fuck your turin rag," said Odysseus, but he'd been drinking steadily from his wineskin and appeared to have mellowed. "But I can tell you a story that your precious diaper cloth doesn't know."

"Yes, please," said Hannah, shifting closer to the warrior.

"The Lord deliver us from storytellers," muttered Savi. She rose, packed away her lunch package in the boot of the sonie, and walked into the forest.

Daeman watched her go with visible anxiety. "Do you really think there are worse predators here than dinosaurs?" he asked no one in particular.

"Savi can take care of herself," said Harman. "She has that gun-weapon."

"But if something were to eat her," said Daeman, still staring into the forest, "who would fly the sonie?"

"Hush," said Hannah. She touched Odysseus' wrist with her long tan fingers. "Tell us the story that the turin cloth doesn't know. Please."

Odysseus frowned, but Ada and Harman were nodding in agreement with Hannah's request, so he flicked crumbs out of his beard and began.

"This experience wasn't and won't be shown in your turin-rag tale. The events I will share with you now happened after the death of Hector and Paris but before the wooden horse."

"Paris dies?" interrupted Daeman.

"Hector dies?" asked Hannah.

"Wooden horse?" said Ada.

Odysseus closed his eyes, combed fingers through his short beard, and said, "May I continue without interruption?"

Everyone except the absent Savi nodded.

"The events I will describe to you now happened after the death of Hector and Paris, but before the wooden horse. It was true in those days that, among its most potent treasures, the city of Ilium possessed a divine image that had fallen from heaven—you would call it a meteorite—but a stone cast and formed by Zeus himself generations before our war as a sign of the Father of the Gods' approval of the founding of the city itself. This metallic-stone figure was called a Palladion, because it was in the form of Pallas . . . not, I should explain, Pallas Athena, as we call our goddess, but Pallas, Athena's companion in her youth. This other Pallas—the word itself can be accented to have a feminine or masculine meaning in our language, but here it is close to the Latin word *virago*, which means 'strong virgin'—had been killed in a sham fight with Athena. And it was Ilios, sometimes called Ilus, father of Laomedon, who in turn would be father to Priam, Tithonus, Lampus, Clytius, and Hicetaon, who had found the star-stone in front of his tent one morning and who recognized it for what it was.

"This ancient Palladion, long a secret source of Ilium's wealth and power, was three cubits in height, carried a spear in its right hand and a distaff and spindle in its left, and was associated with the goddess of death and fate. Ilios and the other ancestors of the current defenders of Troy had ordered made many replicas of the Palladion, in many different sizes, and hid and guarded these false statues as surely as they did the real one, since everyone knew that the continued survival of Ilium itself depended on their possession of the Palladion. It was the gods themselves who revealed this fact to me in dreams in those last weeks of the siege of Ilium, and so I told Diomedes of my plan to go into the city and locate the true Palladion so that he and I could return to the city, steal it, and seal Troy's doom.

"First, I disguised myself in rags as a beggar and had my own servant whip me with a lash, thus disfiguring myself with stripes and welts. The citizens of Ilium, you see, were notoriously weak-stomached when it came to disciplining their servants—they tended to spoil slaves more often than punish them, and no Trojan servant serving a good family would be allowed to go abroad sporting torn clothes and flogging stripes—so I reasoned that rags and stench and, most important, the bloody whip-marks would make the citizens turn away in embarrassment upon seeing me—a perfect disguise for a spy, don't you think?

"I chose myself for this task because I was the stealthiest and craftiest of all the Achaeans, and also, because I had been within the walls of Troy before, more then ten years earlier, sent there to lead a delegation tasked with peacefully negotiating the release of Helen before our black ships arrived in force and a war began. Obviously, those negotiations failed—all of us true Argives had hoped they'd fail, since we were spoiling for a fight and hungry for plunder—but I well remembered the layout of the city within those great walls and gates.

"In my dream, the gods—most likely Athena, since she favored our cause more than any of the others—had revealed to me that the Palladion and its many replicas were secreted somewhere in Priam's royal palace, but did not tell me where in the palace it might be hidden, nor how I could tell the real Palladion from its many pretenders.

"I waited until the deepest hours of the night, when the rampart fires are at their lowest and the human senses are at their weakest, and then I used grapple and rope to go over the towering walls, killing a guard as I did so and hiding his body under fodder stacked high within the walls for the Thracian cavalry. Ilium was large—the largest city in the world—and it took me a while to navigate its streets and alleys to Priam's palace. I was challenged twice by armed sentinels in the streets, but I grunted and made strangled sounds while gesturing meaninglessly with my whip-bloodied arms, and they judged me an idiot slave, well and truly whipped for his idiocy, and they let me pass.

"Priam's palace was large—it had fifty bedrooms, one for each of Priam's fifty sons—and it was well guarded by the most elite of Trojan's elite troops, with alert guards at all the doors and outside each street-level window, with still more guards within the courtyards and on the palace walls—no sleepy sentinels would idly wave me on here, no matter how late the hour or how bloody my stripes or how idiotic my grunts—so I made my way south a few blocks to Helen's home, which was also well guarded, but less so after I knifed my second Trojan of the night and hid his body as best I could.

"After Paris's death in an archery duel, Helen had been given in marriage to another of Priam's sons, Deiphobos, whom the people of Ilium called 'the router of the enemy' but whom we Achaeans referred to on the field as 'oxen-buttocks,' but her new husband was not at home this night and Helen slept alone. I woke her.

"I don't believe I would have killed Helen if she had cried for help— I had known her for many years, you know, both in my role as guest in Menelaus' noble house and, before that, as one of Helen's first suitors when she became eligible for marriage, although this was just a formality, since I was happily married to Penelope even then. It was I who had counseled that Tyndareos should take an oath of the suitors to acquiesce to Helen's choice, thus avoiding much bloodshed from the losers' bad manners. I think Helen always appreciated that advice.

"Helen did not cry out for help that night I awakened her from her troubled sleep in her home in Ilium. She recognized me right away and hugged me and asked after the health of her true husband, Menelaus, and of her daughter so far away. I told her that all were well—although I did not tell her that at this point in the war, Menelaus had been seriously wounded twice on the battlefield and moderately wounded half a dozen times, including his recent arrow in the hip, and was in a surly mood. Instead, I expressed to her how much her husband and daughter and their family in Sparta missed her and wished her home and well.

"Helen laughed then. 'My lord and husband Menelaus wishes me dead, and you know it, Odysseus,' she said. 'And I am sure that he will do the deed himself when the great walls and Scaean Gate of Ilium fall away soon, as Cassandra has prophesied.'

"I did not know this particular oracle—Delphi and Pallas Athena are the only seers of the future who have my ear—but I could not argue with her; it seemed probable that Menelaus would indeed slit her throat after all the bitter years of her disloyalty in the arms and beds of his enemies. But I did not tell Helen this. Instead, I told her that I would intercede with Menelaus, son of Atreus, convincing him to spare her life, if Helen would not betray me this night, but would help me find a way into Priam's palace and instruct me on how to choose the true Palladion.

" 'I would not betray thee anyway, Odysseus, son of Laertes, true and crafty counselor,' said Helen. And she told me how to pierce the palace defenses and how to know the real Palladion when I saw it amongst its imitators.

"But it was almost dawn. Too late to complete my mission that night. So I went out and down the streets and up and over and down the wall through the gaps I had left by killing the watchmen, and I slept late the next day, and bathed, and ate and drank, and had Machaon, the son of Asclepius and the finest healer in the army's pay, dress my flog wounds and apply a healing salve.

"The next night, knowing that I would need an ally since I could not fight and carry the heavy Palladion stone at the same time, I enlisted Diomedes in my plan. Together in the deepest hour of the night, the son of Tydeus and I went up and over the wall—killing this sentinel with a well-placed arrow. Then we moved quickly down the streets and alleys—no dumb show as flogged slaves this night, but, rather, efficiently and silently killing any who challenged us—and made our way into Priam's palace via a hidden sewer drain that Helen had told me how to find.

"Diomedes, a proud man like so many of those thick-skulled heroes from Argos, did not like wading through a sewer for any purpose, not even to ensure the downfall of Ilium. He grumbled and bitched and pissed and moaned and was in a truly foul mood by the time we added insult to injury by having to climb up through a hole in one of the ten-man crappers in the privies of the palace basement, where Priam's treasure vaults were located in the midst of his elite guard's barracks.

"We were stealthy, but our stench preceded us and we had to kill the first twenty guards we encountered in those corridors; the twenty-first showed us how to open the treasure-vault doors without tripping alarms or deadfalls, and then Diomedes cut that man's throat as well.

"In addition to tons of gold, mountains of precious stones, deep pools of pearls, stacks of inlayed fabrics, chests of diamonds, and much of the rest of the wealth of the fabled East in those vaults, there were forty or so statues of the Palladion arrayed in niches. They were alike in everything except size.

" 'Helen said to take only the smallest,' I said to Diomedes, and I did so, wrapping the Palladion in a red cape I had taken from the last guard we'd killed. We had the downfall of Ilium in our hands. All we had to do now was escape.

"This is the point when Diomedes decided that he wanted to loot Priam's vaults then, that night, at once, immediately. The lure of all that plunder was too much for the greedy, brainless bastard. Diomedes would have traded ten years of our blood and toil for a few hundred pounds of gold.

"I . . . dissuaded him. I will not describe the fight we had when I set the red-wrapped Palladion on the floor and drew my sword to stop the son of Tydeus, king of Argos, from ruining our mission through his greed. The fight was over quickly, won by stealth. All right, if you insist, I'll tell you—no noble combat here. No glorious *aristeia* here. I suggested that we remove our reeking tunics before fighting, and while the great lummox was disrobing, I threw a ten-weight lump of gold at the great ox and knocked him cold.

"In the end, I ended up fleeing Priam's palace with the heavy Palladion in the crook of one arm and the heavier, naked Diomedes slung over my shoulder.

"I couldn't carry him over the wall like that, so I was ready, willing, and on the verge of leaving him by the cesspool of sewage where the great drain let out near where the river ran under Ilium's walls, but Diomedes regained consciousness right then and agreed to leave the city with me. We departed quietly. Very quietly. He did not speak to me again that day, nor again that week, nor after the fall and plunder of Ilium, nor during our preparations to sail for home.

"Nor have I spoken to Diomedes since that day.

"I should add that it was shortly after that, after I bore away the Palladion to our Argives' camp where we hid it well, sure now that Troy was in its final hours, that we began work on the gigantic wooden horse. The horse had three purposes—first, as a ruse, of course, to carry me and a carefully chosen band of my staunchest fighters into the city; second, as a means to have the Trojans themselves remove the great stone lintel over the Scaean Gate in order to let the votive offering pass into their city, since prophecy said that these two things had to come to pass before Ilium would fall—the loss of the Palladion and the destruction of the Scaean lintel; and third, and finally, we crafted the great horse as a gift to Athena to make up for the loss of her Palladion, since she was also known as Hippia, 'horse goddess,' since it was she who had bridled and tamed Pegasus for Bellerophontes and she who took such pleasure in riding and exercising her own horses at every opportunity.

"And this, my friends, is my short tale of the theft of the Palladion and the downfall of Ilium. I hope the telling pleased you. Are there any questions?"

Ada caught Harman's eye. *This was his* short *tale?* she thought, and saw her lover catch her thought like a blown kiss.

"Yes, I have a question," said Daeman.

Odysseus nodded.

"Why do you call it Troy some of the time and Ilium the rest of the time?" asked the pudgy young man.

Odysseus shook his head slightly, rose, took his scabbard and short sword from the sonie, and walked off into the forest.

24

Ilium, Indiana, and
Olympos

Zeus is angry. I've seen Zeus angry before, but this time he is very, very, very angry.

When the Father of the Gods sweeps into the ruins of the healing chamber on Olympos, surveys the damage, stares at Aphrodite's body lying pale amidst a nest of writhing green worms on the wet floor, and then turns to look in my direction, I am sure that Zeus *sees* me—that he looks right through whatever cloaking device powers the Hades Helmet and *sees* me. But although he stares directly at me for several seconds and blinks those glacially cold gray eyes of his as if coming to some decision—he looks away again, and I, Thomas Hockenberry, formerly of Indiana University and, more recently, of Helen of Troy's bed, am allowed to continue living.

My right arm and left leg are badly bruised, but nothing is broken, and—still cloaked by the Hades Helmet from the sight of the scores of gods rushing into the healing room—I escape the building and QT to the only place I can think of, other than Helen's bedroom, where I can rest and recuperate—the scholics' barracks at the foot of Olympos.

Out of old habit, I go to my own cubicle, my own bare bed, but I keep the Hades Helmet cowl pulled up and activated as I flop on it and doze fitfully. It has been one hell of a long day and night and morning. The Invisible Man sleeps.

I awake to the sound of screams and thunderclaps on the floor below. By the time I rush out to the hallway, the scholic named Blix runs by—almost runs into me actually, since I'm invisible to him—and explains breathlessly to another scholic named Campbell, "The Muse is here and she's killing everybody!"

It's true. I cower in the corner of a stairway as the Muse—our Muse, the one Aphrodite had called Melete—strikes down the few fleeing scholics left alive in the blazing barracks. The goddess is using bolts of pure energy from her hands—corny, clichéd, but horribly effective on mere human flesh. Blix is doomed, but there's nothing I can think of to do for him or the others.

Nightenhelser. The stolid scholic has been my one real friend the last years. Panting, I run to his room in the barracks. The marble is scarred, the wood is ablaze, the window glass has melted, but there's no charred corpse here as there are littering the hallways and lounges. None of those burned bodies had looked large enough to be the burly Nightenhelser. Suddenly there come final screams from the third floor, then silence except for the increasing roar of flames. I look out a window and see the Muse flit by in her chariot, holographic horses in full stride. Near panic, choking audibly on the smoke—if the Muse was still in the barracks she would hear me now—I force myself to visualize Ilium and the restaurant where I'd last seen Nightenhelser. Then I grasp and twist the QT medallion, and escape.

He's not at the restaurant where I'd seen him early that morning. I flick to the battlefield; he's not in his usual spot on the ridge above the Trojan lines. I take just enough time to notice that Hector and Paris are leading the Trojan troops in a successful attack against the fleeing Argives, and then I QT to a shady place behind Greek lines, near their moat and line of stakes, where I've bumped into Nightenhelser in the past.

He's there, disguised as Dolops, son of Clytius, who has some days left before being killed by Hector if Homer is right. Not bothering to morph into into any shape other than gawky Hockenberry, I pull off the Hades Helmet cowl and run to the other scholic.

"Hockenberry, what . . ." Nightenhelser is shocked by my unprofessional behavior and by the reaction of other Achaeans nearby. Drawing attention to oneself is the last thing a scholic wants. Except, perhaps, to be burned to cinders by a vengeful Muse. I have no idea why our Muse is wiping out all the scholics this day, but my guess is that I've somehow caused this slaughter of the innocents.

"We have to get out of here," I say, shouting over the din of rushing reinforcements, neighing horses, and rumbling chariots. It looks from this dusty vantage point that the entire center of the Greek lines has given way.

"What are you talking about? This is an important day. Hector and Paris are . . ."

"Fuck Hector and Paris," I say in English.

The Muse has QT'd into solidity high above the Trojan lines where

Nightenhelser and I often station ourselves, another muse driving her flying chariot as she leans over the side and scans the troops with her enhanced vision. Morphing will not save us mortal scholics this day.

As if to demonstrate this, the Muse named Melete—"my" Muse—raises her palms and fires a coherent beam of energy earthward, striking a Trojan foot soldier named Dius, who should be alive to be bossed around in Book 24 according to Homer, but who dies this day in a flash of flame and a whirlwind of smoke and heat. Other Trojans flinch away, some fleeing back toward the city, not understanding this goddess's wrath on a day of victory ordained by Zeus, but Hector and Paris are a quarter of a mile to the southeast, leading their charge, and don't even look back.

"That wasn't Dius," gasped Nightenhelser. "It was Houston."

"I know," I say, returning my enhanced vision to normal scope. Houston was the youngest and newest of the scholics. I'd barely spoken to him. He was probably on the Trojan lines today because I'd gone missing.

The Muse's chariot banks sharply and flies directly toward us. I don't think the bitch-Muse has seen us yet—we're standing amidst hundreds of milling men and horses—but she will in a few seconds.

What do I do? I can pull the Hades Helmet on and run like a coward again, leaving Nightenhelser to die just as I failed Blix and the others. There's no way this single cowl can hide us both from the goddess's divine vision. *Or we can run—toward the black ships.* We won't get twenty yards.

The chariot drops lower and cloaks itself so that it's hidden from the view of the surging Greeks and Trojans below. With our nano-altered vision, Nightenhelser and I can still see it coming on.

"What the hell?" cries Nightenhelser, almost dropping his recording wand as I embrace him, throwing both arms and one leg around him like a skinny foot soldier trying to rape this burly bear of a man.

Arm around the big scholic's neck, I grab the QT medallion and twist.

I have no idea if this will work. It shouldn't. The medallion is obviously designed to transport just the person wearing it. But my clothes come with me when I QT, and more than once I've carried something else from place to place through Planck space, so perhaps the quantum field established for teleportation includes things my body is in touch with or that my arms surround.

What the hell indeed. It's worth a try.

We pop into existence in darkness, tumble down a hill, and roll apart. I look around wildly, trying to determine where we are. I hadn't had

time to visualize a destination properly—I'd simply willed myself elsewhere and quantum-teleported us both . . . somewhere.

Where?

There's moonlight, so it's just light enough for me to see Nightenhelser staring at me in alarm, as if I might jump him again at any second.
Ignoring that, I look at the sky—stars, sliver of moon, Milky Way—and
then at the land: tall trees, a grassy hillside, a river running by.

We're definitely on the Earth—the ancient Earth of Ilium at least—
but it doesn't feel like the Peloponnese or Asia Minor.

"Where are we?" asks Nightenhelser, getting to his feet and brushing
himself off. "What's going on? Why is it night?"

The opposite side of the ancient world, I think. I say, "I think we're in Indiana."

"*Indiana?*" Nightenhelser takes another step away from me.

"The Indiana of 1200-plus B.C.," I say. "Give or take a century or so."
I've hurt my arm and leg again rolling down the hill.

"How'd we get here?" Nightenhelser has always been a mellow sort,
mildly grumpy in his rambling, rumbling, ursine way, but never really
angry about anything. He sounds angry now.

"I QT'd us."

"What the hell are you talking about, Hockenberry? We were
nowhere near the QT portal."

I ignore him and sit on a small rock, rubbing my arm. There aren't many
hills in Indiana, even in my other life there, but there were hilly, wooded,
rocky areas around Bloomington, where Susan and I lived. I believe that,
in my panic, I visualized . . . well, *home.* I wish to hell the QT medallion had
moved us through time as well as space and plunked us down into late
Twentieth Century Indiana, but something about the pure darkness of the
night sky and the purely clean smell of the air here tells me otherwise.

Who's here in 1200 B.C.? Indians. It would be ironic if the QT medallion
had whisked us away from imminent death by our Muse's hand—literally—only to bring us to the New World where we'll be scalped by Indians. *Most of the tribes didn't scalp their victims before the white men arrived,*
drones on the pedantic part of my professor's brain. *Although I seem to
remember reading somewhere that sometimes they took ears as proof of their kill.*

Well, that makes me feel better. You can always trust a murderer to
have a good prose style, so the saying goes, and a professor to come up
with something depressing when you're already depressed.

"Hockenberry?" demands Nightenhelser, sitting on a nearby
footstool-sized rock—not too close to me, I notice—and rubbing his own
elbows and knees.

"I'm thinking, I'm thinking," I say in my best Jack Benny voice.

"Well, when you're finished thinking," says Nightenhelser, "maybe you could tell me why the Muse just killed young Houston."

This sobers me, but I'm not sure how to respond. "There are things going on with the gods," I say at last. "Plots. Intrigues. Pacts."

"Tell me about it," says Nightenhelser, meaning it both in irony and as a serious request.

I raise both hands, palms up. "Aphrodite was trying to use me to assassinate Athena."

Nightenhelser stares. He manages—barely—not to drop his jaw.

"I know what you're thinking," I say. "Why me? Why use Hockenberry? Why give him the power to QT by himself and the Hades Helmet to hide under? And I agree—it doesn't make any sense."

"I wasn't thinking that," says Nightenhelser. A meteorite slices across the star-filled sky above us. Somewhere in the forest beyond the hill, an owl makes its not-quite-hooting noise. "I was just wondering what your first name was."

It's my turn to stare. "Why?"

"Because the gods discouraged use of first names and we were afraid of getting to know each other well because scholics were always being . . . disappeared and replaced by the gods," says the big man, bearlike even in shadow-darkness. "So I want to know your first name."

"Thomas," I say after a second. "Tom. Yours?"

"Keith," says the man I've known slightly for four years. He stands up and looks at the dark woods. "Well, what now, Tom?"

Insects, frogs, and other night critters are making noise in those black woods. Unless they're really Indians sneaking up on us.

"Do you know how to . . . I mean, have you camped a lot . . . I mean . . ." I begin.

"You mean, will I die if you leave me here alone?" asks Nightenhelser . . . Keith.

"Yeah."

"I don't know. Probably. But I suspect my chances are a hell of a lot better here than back on the plains of Ilium. At least while the Muse is on the warpath . . ."

I guess that Keith is fixated on Indians right now as well.

"Plus I have all my little scholic tech-toys and gear. I can make fire, use the levitation harness to fly if I have to, morph into an Indian if necessary, even use the weapon taser. So I guess you should QT back to wherever you have to go and do whatever you have to do," says Nightenhelser. "Fill me in later on the details . . . if there is a later."

I nod and stand. It seems strange . . . wrong . . . to leave the other scholic here alone, but I don't see any choice.

"Can you find your way back?" he asks. "*Here,* I mean. To fetch me."

"I think so."

"Think so? *Think* so?" Nightenhelser rubs his hand through his wild hair. "I hope you weren't the chairman of your department, Hockenberry."

I guess the era of first names is over.

There's no place in the universe that I'd less rather be than Olympos. When I arrive, the inhabitants of this mountaintop are gathered in the Great Hall of the Gods. Making sure that the cowl of the Hades Helmet is pulled on tight and that I throw no shadow, I slip into the huge Parthenon-style building.

In my nine-plus years as scholic, I've never seen so many gods in one place. On one side of the long hologram pool sits Zeus, high on his golden throne, larger than I have ever seen him. As I've mentioned, the gods are usually eight or nine feet tall except when they take mortal form, and Zeus usually towers over them by three or four feet, a divine adult to their cosmic children. But today Zeus is twenty-five feet tall or taller, each of his muscled forearms as long as my torso. I fleetingly wonder what this does to that conservation of mass and energy the other scholic tried to teach me about years ago, but that's not important now. Staying back against the wall, away from the milling gods, and not making any noise or movement or sneeze that will betray me to all these refined superhero senses—*that's* important.

I thought that I knew all the gods and goddesses by name, but there are scores here that I don't recognize. Those that I do know, the gods and goddesses who have been most involved in the fighting at Troy, stand out in the crowd like movie stars at a meeting of minor politicians, but even the least of these gods is taller, stronger, handsomer, and more perfect than any human movie star I remember from my other life. Nearest Zeus, opposite him across the hologram pool—which divides the room like a long moat now—I can see Pallas Athena, the war god Ares (obviously out of his healing tank, which was not damaged when I destroyed Aphrodite's), Zeus's younger brothers—the sea god Poseidon (who rarely comes to Olympos), and Hades, ruler of the dead. Zeus's son, Hermes, stands near the pool, and the guide and giant killer is as lean and beautiful as statues I've seen of him. Another son of Zeus, Dionysus, the god of ecstatic release, is talking to Hera and—contrary to his public image—he has no goblet of wine in his hand. For a god of ecstatic release, Dionysus looks pale, feeble, and dour—like a man in only the third week of a twelve-step program. Beyond them, looking older than time, is Nereus, the true sea god, the Old Man of the Sea. His fingers and toes are webbed and there are gills visible below his armpits.

The Fates and the Furies are here in force, milling by accident or design between the gods and the goddesses. These are gods—of sorts—yet sometimes they have regulatory power over the other gods. They are not as human in appearance as the regular gods and goddesses, and I confess I know almost nothing about them except that they don't live on Olympos, but on one of the three volcanoes far to the southeast, near where the muses reside.

My Muse, Melete, is here, standing with her sisters, Meneme and Aoide. The more "modern" muses are also in the crowd—the real Kalliope, Polymnia, Ourania, Erato, Kleis, Euterpe, Melpomene, Terpsichore, and Tahleia. Just beyond the muses are the A-list goddesses. Aphrodite is not among them—that is the first thing I notice. If she were, I would be as visible to her as these divinities are to me. But her mother, Dione, is in attendance, speaking to Hera and Hermes and looking very serious indeed. Near that group are Demeter—the goddess of crops—and her daughter Persephone, Hades' wife. Behind them I can see Pasithea, one of the Graces. Farther back, as befits their lesser place, are the Nereids, nude to the waist, lovely, and treacherous-looking.

The meta-goddess called Night stands alone. Her gown and veil are of a purple so dark as to be black, and even the other gods and goddesses give her a wide berth. I know nothing about Night, except rumors that even Zeus is afraid of her, and I've never seen her on Olympos before.

I feel like a gawking movie fan in the crowd outside the Academy Awards, trying to separate the superstars from the lesser gods. Hebe there, for instance, standing near the males—she is the goddess of youth, Zeus and Hera's child, but only a servant to the gods—and there, red hair like flames, is Hephaestus, the great artificer, talking to his wife, Charis, who is only one of the Graces. Pecking order among gods and goddesses I realize, not for the first time, is complicated stuff.

Suddenly the goddess Iris, Zeus's messenger, flies forward—yes, flies—and claps her hands. "The Father will speak," she says, her voice as clear and crisp as a flute solo.

Immediately the scores of soft conversations cease and the great, echoing hall goes silent.

Zeus stands. His gold throne and the gold steps leading up to it exude a glow that bathes him in divine light.

"Hear me, all you gods, and goddesses, too," says Zeus, his voice soft but so strong that I feel the vibration of it off the high marble walls. "Some god or goddess this day has tried to hurt Aphrodite, now healing in our hall of healing, and—while she will live—it was a close thing and she will need many more days to heal again. *Some god or goddess tried to kill an immortal this day—tried to kill one of us who is not fated for death.*"

The muttering and shocked conversation start as a buzz and rise to a roar in the huge room.

"**SILENCE!!**" roars Zeus, and this time his voice is so loud that it knocks me down and slides me across the marble floor like a tumbleweed in a tornado. Luckily, I hit none of the gods or goddesses in my slide, and the noise I make is drowned out by the echoes of Zeus's shout.

"Hear me now, oh gods and goddesses," he continues, his voice amplified as if from the ultimate public address system. "Let no beautiful goddess, nor no god either, attempt to defy my strict decree. You will submit to my will—**NOW!**"

This time I am ready for the hurricane force of his voice and I cling to a column until the energy of it has passed.

"Listen to me," says Zeus, almost whispering now, the sense of his power even more terrible for the soft tone. "Any god who violates my decree by helping the Trojans or Achaeans the way I have seen this month, back that god or goddess comes to Olympos, whipped on by my lightning and scourged by my thunder, eternally disgraced, banned henceforth from Olympos. Defy me, and find what it is like to be cast down to the murk of Tartarus half a universe away in space and time, in the deepest gulf that yawns beneath our quantum selves."

As he speaks, the long hologram pit boils and bubbles, turns pitch-black, and then becomes something other than a hologram; the rectangular pit—looking like a dozen Olympic-sized swimming pools laid end to end, now broiling and filled with bubbling black oil—suddenly lets loose with a roar of its own, and becomes a hole opening on someplace dark and fiery and terribly deep. The stench of sulfur roils up and the gods and goddesses near the edge back away.

"Behold Tartarus," cries Zeus, "the lowest depths of the House of Hades, a place as far below hell as Hades' home is beneath the earth itself. Do you remember—you senior gods and goddesses amongst us—when you followed me into that ten-year war with the Titans who ruled before us? Do you remember that I cast Kronos and Rhea—my own parents—beyond these iron gates and brazen thresholds—aye, and Iapetus, too, for all his god-power?"

The hall is silent except for the muted roars and bellows and screams coming up from the open Tartarus Pit. I have no doubt whatsoever that this is a hole to hell, not a hologram, falling away not thirty feet from where I cower.

"IF I CAST MY PARENTS DOWN INTO THIS PIT OF PITS FOR ALL ETERNITY," roars Zeus, "DO YOU DOUBT THAT I WILL THROW YOUR SCREAMING SOUL THERE IN A SECOND?"

The gods and goddesses do not answer, except to take several paces farther back from that foul void.

Zeus smiles terribly. "Come, try me, immortals, so that all can learn."

A huge golden cable falls from the roof of the hall, straddling the hole to hell. Gods and goddesses scurry to get out of the way of its fall. It stikes marble with a resounding crash. The rope is thicker than a ship's hawser and seems to be spun of thousands of inch-thick strands of true gold. It must weigh many tons.

Zeus strides down his golden stairs and lifts the cable, holding it easily in his giant hands. "Grasp your end," he says almost cheerfully.

The gods and goddesses look at each other and do not move.

"GRASP YOUR END!"

Hundreds of immortals and their immortal servants rush to comply, scrambling for a handhold on the long cable like kids at a picnic tug-of-war. In a minute there is Zeus alone on his side of the Tartarus Pit, casually holding the cable, and the countless mob of gods and goddesses on the other side, powerful god-hands gripped tight on gold.

"Drag me down," says Zeus. "Drag me down from sky to earth to Hades and deeper, to Tartarus' stinking depths. Drag me down, I say."

Not a single god moves a bronzed muscle.

"DRAG ME DOWN, I COMMAND THEE!" Zeus grasps the golden cable and begins to haul on it. Gods' sandals slip and squeak and scuff on marble. Several hundred gods and goddesses all in a row are pulled closer to the pit, some stumbling, some going to their knees.

"PULL, GODDAMN YOU!" howls Zeus. "PULL OR BE DRAGGED INTO STINKING TARTARUS UNTIL TIME ITSELF ROTS AWAY FROM THE BONES OF THE UNIVERSE!"

Zeus tugs again and twenty yards of gold cable coils behind him. The conga line of gods and goddesses and graces and furies and nereids and nymphs and you-name-it on the other side—everyone pulling except purple-gowned Night—slides and screeches closer to the pit. Athena is the first on the cable and is only thirty feet from the edge when she screams, "Pull, you gods! Pull the old bastard in!!"

Ares and Apollo and Hermes and Poseidon and the rest of the most powerful gods put their backs into it. They quit sliding. The cable pulls tighter, fraying and creaking from the tension. The goddesses scream and pull in unison, Hera—Zeus's wife—pulling even harder than the others. The gold cable stretches and groans.

Zeus laughs. He is holding them all at check with only one hand on the rope. Now he grabs the cable with his other hand and pulls again.

The gods scream like children on a roller coaster. Athena and those near her on the cable go sliding across the marble as if it were ice, closer and closer to the raging Tartarus Pit, even as dozens of lesser immortals surrender and throw themselves away from the cable. But Athena will not release her grip. The gray-eyed goddess is pulled relentlessly to the edge of the steaming trapdoor to hell. It looks as if the whole line of straining, sweating, cursing immortals is going in.

Zeus laughs and drops the cable. Score upon score of gods and goddesses fly backward and land unceremoniously on their immortal asses.

"You gods and goddesses, children, brothers, sisters, sons, daughters, cousins, and servants—you cannot drag me down," says Zeus. He walks back to his throne and sits. "Not even if you pulled your arms from their sockets, if you pulled yourselves to death, could you budge me if I do not choose to move. I am Zeus, the highest, mightiest of kings."

He raises one huge finger. "But . . . if I choose to drag you up in earnest, I'd hoist you off this Olympos, dangle you in black space above Tartarus, tie on the earth and sea as well, hook the end around the horn of this hill called Olympos, and leave you dangling there in darkness until the sun grows cold."

If I hadn't just seen what I have seen, I'd think the old bastard was bluffing. Now I know better.

Athena gets to her feet, not more than a yard from the edge of the Tartarus Pit, and says, "Our Father, son of Kronos, who art in the highest throne of heaven, we know your power, Lord. Who can stand against you? Not us . . ."

All the immortals seem to be holding their breath. Athena's temper is legendary, her diplomacy skills frequently lacking—if she says the wrong thing now . . .

"Even so," says Zeus's gray-eyed daughter, "we pity these mortals, my doomed Argive spearmen, acting out their little roles on their little stage, dying their terrible deaths, drowning in their own blood at the end of their little lives."

She takes another two steps, so that the tips of her sandals are hanging over the edge of the black pit. Somewhere thousands of feet below her in the lightning-lashed Tartarus darkness, something large bellows in pain and fear. "Yes, Zeus," continues Athena, "we will keep clear of the war as you command. But grant us—at the very least—permission to offer our mortal favorites tactics that may save them, so that they all won't fall beneath the lightning of your immortal wrath."

Zeus looks at his daughter a long moment and I for one can't read his eyes. Fury? Humor? Impatience?

"Tritogeneia—third-born child—dear daughter," says Zeus, "your courage has always given me a headache. But do not lose heart, for nothing of the lesson I showed you here today flows from anger, but only seeks to show all gathered here the consequences of their disobedience."

And having spoken, Zeus steps down from his throne and his personal chariot flies in between the giant pillars, his pair of bronze-hooved horses—real, I see, not holograms—landing near him, their golden manes streaming behind them. Strapping on his golden armor and lifting his whip from its stand, Zeus climbs aboard his battle car, cracks the lash, and I watch the matched team and chariot roll across marble and then take to the air, circling the hall once a hundred feet above the gods' and goddesses' heads before flying out between the pillars and disappearing in a crack of quantum thunder.

Slowly the gods and goddesses and lesser sorts file out of the hall, murmuring and plotting among themselves, none—I'm sure—planning to obey their lord and king.

And me—I just sit here for a while—invisible and glad to be so. My jaw is hanging slack and I am breathing shallowly, like a whipped dog on a hot day. It feels like I'm drooling slightly.

Sometimes, up here on Olympos, it's hard to believe completely in cause and effect and the scientific method.

25

Texas Redwood Forest

Daeman was all alone now, just him and the sonie in the forest clearing, and he didn't like it.

After Savi left, Odysseus had told his endless, pointless story and walked into the woods at the end of it. Hannah had waited a minute and then gone after the old man. (Daeman had known immediately that morning that Hannah and the bearded man had slept together the night before—his sex radar was seldom wrong.) A few minutes later, Ada and the other old man, Harman, had said they were going for a short walk and then disappeared under the trees in the opposite direction. (Daeman knew that they'd had sex the night before as well. Evidently he and the old witch, Savi, were the only ones not having any fun.)

So now Daeman was alone in the forest glade, leaning against the hull of the landed sonie and listening to leaves stirring and branches breaking in the dark woods and not liking it one bit. If an allosaurus appeared, he was ready to leap into the sonie—but what then? He didn't even know how to access the holographic controls, much less how to activate the forcefield bubble or fly away. He'd be an hors d'oeuvre on a plate for the dino.

Daeman considered shouting into the woods, calling for Savi or any of the others to return, but immediately thought better of it. Were dinosaurs and other predators attracted to noise? He wasn't going to experiment to find out. Meanwhile, he was acutely uncomfortable—not just from the anxiety, but from the need to go to the toilet. The others may have scampered off into the forest with the tissues Savi had provided, but Daeman was a civilized human being; he'd never gone to the toilet without . . . well . . . a toilet, and he wasn't going to start now. Of course he didn't know how many hours it would be until they got to

Ardis Hall, and Savi was talking as if she wasn't even going to stop there, just drop off Hannah, Ada, and the preposterous impostor calling himself Odysseus, and then head on to the Mediterranean Basin or wherever it was. Daeman knew he couldn't wait *that* long.

He realized that he was discouraged more than frightened. Everyone had seemed surprised yesterday when he volunteered to go with the old woman and Harman on their preposterous expedition, but no one had guessed his real reason for choosing that alternative. First of all, he was afraid of the dinosaurs around Ardis Hall. He wasn't going back there. Second, all that talk of faxing being a sort of destruction and rebuilding of people had made him extremely nervous. Well, who wouldn't be, so shortly after waking up in the firmary and knowing that your real body had been destroyed? Daeman had faxed almost every day of his life, but the thought of stepping into a faxportal now, knowing that it was going to break down his muscles, bones, brain, and memory, and then just build a copy somewhere else—if the old woman was telling the truth— well, that idea bothered the hell out of him.

So he'd opted for traveling on the sonie for a few more days, facing neither Ardis dinosaurs nor fax destruction of his atoms or molecules or whatever.

Now he just wanted a toilet and a servitor or his mother to make him supper. Perhaps he would demand that the old woman drop him off at Paris Crater after Ardis. It wasn't that far away, was it? Even though he'd got a glimpse of Harman's scribbles—his "map"—Daeman had no concept of the world's geography. Everything was as precisely as far away as everything else—a faxportal step.

The old woman stepped out of the forest, saw Daeman alone, leaning against the floating sonie, and said, "Where is everyone?"

"That's what I was wondering. First the barbarian left. Then Hannah went after him. Then Ada and Harman walked off *that* way . . ." He gestured toward the tall trees on the opposite side of the glade.

"Why don't you use your palm?" said Savi, and smiled as if something she'd said amused her.

"I already tried," said Daeman. "On your ice-thingee. At the bridge. Here. It doesn't work." He raised his left palm, thought of the finder function, and showed her the blank rectangle of white floating there.

"That's just the immediate locator function," said Savi. "Just an arrow-guide once you're close to something, like inside a library hunting for a volume but in the wrong aisle. Use farnet or proxnet."

Daeman stared at her. From his first glimpse of the old woman, he had doubted her sanity.

"Ah, that's right," said Savi, still smiling that unamused smile. "You've all forgotten the functions. Generation after generation."

"What are you talking about?" said Daeman. "The old functions like reading don't work anymore. They went away when the post-humans left." He pointed to the rings crossing in the patch of blue sky above.

"Nonsense," said Savi. She walked over, leaned against the sonie next to him, and gripped his left arm, turning it palm toward her. "Think three red circles with blue squares in the center of each."

"What?"

"You heard me." She continued to hold his wrist.

Idiocy, thought Daeman, but he visualized three red circles with blue squares floating in the center of each.

Instead of the small rectangle of white-yellow light that the finder function generated, a large blue oval of light now floated six inches above his palm.

"Whoa!" cried Daeman, pulling his wrist from her grasp and flicking his hand wildly as if a huge insect had just landed in it. The blue oval flickered with it.

"Relax," said Savi. "It's blank. Just visualize someone."

"Who?" Daeman actively did not like this sensation—his body doing something he did not know it could do.

"Anyone. Someone close to you."

Daeman closed his eyes and visualized his mother's face. When he opened his eyes again, the blue oval was busy with diagrams. Street grids, a river, words that he could not read—an aerial view of the black circle that could only be the crater in the heart of Paris Crater. The image zoomed and suddenly he was in a stylized structure, fifth floor, back domi near the crater—not his home. Two stylized human figures, cartoon characters but with real, human faces, were in bed, the female above the male, moving . . .

Daeman closed his hand into a fist, shutting off the oval.

"Sorry," said Savi. "I forgot that no one's using trace inhibitors these days. Your girlfriend?"

"My mother," said Daeman, tasting bile. It had been Goman's domicomplex across the crater—he knew the layout of the rooms from when he was a boy, playing in the inner rooms while his mother consorted with the tall, dark-skinned man with the wine-smooth voice. Daeman didn't like Goman, and hadn't known his mother was still seeing him. According to what Harman had said earlier, it was already night in Paris Crater.

"Let's try to see where Hannah and Ada and the others are," said

Savi. She chuckled. "Although they may wish they'd activated farnet inhibitors as well."

Daeman didn't want to uncurl his fist.

"Recycle it," said Savi.

"How?"

"How do you get rid of your arrow-finder?"

"I just think 'off,' " said Daeman, mentally adding, "*stupid*."

"Do it."

Daeman thought, the blue oval winked off.

"You activate proxnet by thinking one yellow circle with a green triangle in it," said Savi. She looked at her own palm and a bright yellow
rectangle appeared above it.

Daeman did the same.

"Think of Hannah," said Savi.

He did so. Both of their palms showed a continent—North America,
but Daeman could not identify it—then a zoom to the south-central section, zoom north of the coastline, zoom to a complex series of unreadable
words and topographic maps, zoom below stylized trees to a stylized female form with Hannah's head on the cartoon body, walking alone—no,
not alone, Daeman realized, for there was a question mark walking next
to her.

Savi chuckled again. "Proxnet doesn't know how to process
Odysseus."

"I don't see Odysseus," said Daeman.

Savi reached into his yellow holographic cube and touched the question mark. She pointed to two red figures at the edge of the cloud. "That's
us," she said. "Ada and Harman must be off the grid to the north."

"How do we know it's Hannah?" asked Daeman, although he'd
glimpsed the top of her head

"Think 'close-up,' " said Savi. She showed him her palm cloud,
which had zoomed lower, leveled out, and was watching the stylized
Hannah with the real Hannah's face walk between stylized trees, along
a stylized stream.

He thought "close-up" and marveled at the clarity of the image. He
could see the tree shadows on her features. She was speaking animat-
edly to the symbol—Savi had called it a question mark—floating next to
her. Daeman was glad that he hadn't found Hannah in the middle of sex.

Savi must have visualized Ada and Harman, for her yellow palm
cloud shifted and showed two figures walking on topographic symbols
somewhere north of the stationary red dots that she'd said were Savi
and Daeman.

"Everybody's alive, nobody eaten by dinosaurs," said Savi. "But I wish to hell they'd get back so we could leave. It's getting late. If this were the old days, I'd just call them on their palms and tell them to get their butts back here."

"You can use this to communicate?" said Daeman, holding up his bare palm.

"Of course."

"Why don't we know that?" His voice came out sounding almost angry.

Savi shrugged. "You don't know much of anything anymore, you so-called old-style humans."

"What do you mean, 'so-called old-style'?" demanded Daeman. He was angry now.

"Do you really think the lost-age humans, the old-styles, had all this genetically tweaked nano-machinery in their cells and bodies?" asked Savi.

"Yes," said Daeman, although he realized that he knew absolutely nothing about the Lost Age old-styles, and cared less.

Savi said nothing for a minute. She looked tired to Daeman's eye, but perhaps all ancient, pre-firmary humans looked this bad—he didn't know.

"We should go fetch them," she said at last. " I'll take Hannah and Odysseus, you get Ada and Harman. Set your palm on proxnet, activate your finder the usual way, and that'll lead you to them. Tell them that the bus is leaving."

Daeman had no idea what "bus" meant, but that wasn't important. "Are there other functions?" he asked before she could walk off.

"Hundreds," said Savi.

"Show me one," challenged Daeman. He didn't believe her—not hundreds—but even one or two more would make him popular at parties, of interest to young women.

Savi sighed and leaned back against the sonie. A wind had come up and stirred the sequoia branches far above them. "I can show you the function that finally drove the post-humans off the Earth," she said softly. "The allnet."

Daeman closed his fist again and pulled his hand away. "Not if it's dangerous."

"It's not," said Savi. "Not to us. Here, I'll go first." She lowered his arm, pulled his fingers open, and touched his palm in a way he found almost exciting. Then she set her own left palm next to his.

"Visualize four blue rectangles above three red circles above four green triangles," she said softly.

Daeman frowned—that was difficult, the shapes skittered right at the edge of his ability to hold the image—but he managed at last, his eyes closed.

"Open your eyes," said Savi.

He did so, wildly grabbing the sonie for support with both hands a second later.

There was no palm cloud. No unreadable maps or cartoon figures.

Instead, everything within his sight had been transformed. The nearby trees he had been ignoring except to borrow their shade were now towering complexities—transparent, layer upon layer of pulsing, living tissue, dead bark, vesicules, veins, dead inner material showing structural vectors and rings with columns of flowing data, the moving green and red of life—needles, xylem, phloem, water, sugar, energy, sunlight. He knew that if he could read the flowing data, he would understand exactly the hydrology of the living miracle that was that tree, know exactly how many foot-pounds of pressure it was taking to osmotically raise all that water from the roots—Daeman could look down and *see* the roots under the soil, see the energy exchange of water from the soil into those roots and the long voyage, hundreds of feet, from roots to the vertical tubules raising that water—hundreds of feet vertically! Like a giant sucking from a straw!—and then the lateral motion of the water, molecules of water in pipelines only molecules wide, out along branches fifty, sixty, seventy feet wide, narrowing, narrowing, life and nutrients in that water, energy from the sun . . .

Daeman looked up and saw sunlight for the discrete rain of energy it was—sunlight striking pine needles and being absorbed, sunlight striking the humus beneath his feet and warming the bacteria there. He could count the busy bacteria! The world around him was a torrent of information, a tidal wave of data, a million micro-ecologies interacting all at once, energy to energy. Even death was part of the complex dance of water, light, energy, life, recycling, growth, sex, and hunger flowing all around him.

Daeman could see a dead mouse almost buried in the humus on the opposite side of the glade, little more than hair and bones now, but still a beacon of red-light energy as the bacteria feasted and the fly eggs incubated into maggots in the afternoon sunlight and the slow unraveling of complex protein molecules continued on the molecular level, and . . .

Gasping, almost gagging, Daeman whirled away, trying to shut off this vision, but everywhere was the complexity—the tagged and streaming ebb and flow of energy being passed, nutrients being absorbed, cells being fed, molecules dancing in the transparent trees, and breathing soil and sky ablaze with its rain and surge of sunlight and radio messages from the stars.

Daeman clasped his hands over his eyes, but too late; he'd looked at Savi—the old woman, but also a galaxy of life. Life nested in the flashing neurons of her brain behind that grinning skull and firing like lightning on the string of shocks along her retinal nerve and in the billions upon billions of living forms in her gut, busy and indifferent all, and— trying to look away, Daeman made the mistake of looking down at himself, into himself, past himself at his connection to the air and ground and sky . . .

"Off!" said Savi; Daeman's mind echoed the command.

The brilliant midday sunlight bouncing off the trees and needle-strewn soil suddenly seemed as dark as midnight to Daeman. His legs ceased to work. Gasping, Daeman slid along the edge of the sonie and collapsed on the ground, rolling onto his stomach, arms extended, palms pushed flat, face pressed against pine needles.

Savi crouched next to him and patted his shoulder. "It'll go away in a minute," she said softly. "You rest here. I'll go find the others."

Ada had been hesitant to go when Harman suggested they take a walk —she was afraid that Savi would be angry or alarmed at everyone's absence when she returned to the glade—but Hannah had already run off in search of Odysseus, and Ada didn't want to stay there by the sonie alone with Daeman. Besides, she didn't know if she'd have another chance to speak in private with her new lover before she returned to Ardis and he went flying off to the Mediterwhatsis Basin with Savi.

They walked up a hill, then followed a stream down the other side. The forest was alive with birdsong, but they saw no animals larger than a squirrel. Harman seemed preoccupied, lost in thought, and the only time he touched Ada was when he extended his hand to help her across the stream just above a ten-foot waterfall. She wondered if their night together had been a mistake, a miscalculation on her part, but when they stopped to rest at the base of the waterfall, she saw his eyes focus on her, saw the affection and tenderness in his gaze, and was glad they'd become lovers.

"Ada," he said, "do you know your father?"

She had to blink at this. The question was not quite shocking—people knew they had fathers, of course, theoretically—but such a thing was rarely asked. "Do you mean know who he was?" she asked.

Harman shook his head. "I mean *know* him. Have you met him?"

"No," she said. "My mother told me his name at one point, but I believe he . . . reached his Fifth Twenty some years ago." She had almost said *Ascended to the rings,* the most common euphemism for passing on bodily into the heaven of the post-humans. Her heart pounded when she wondered why Harman was asking her this odd question. Did he think there was a chance that *he* had been her father? It happened, of course. Young women made love with older men who could be their anonymous sperm-fathers—there was no taboo on incest, since there was no chance that a child could be born from such a union, and there were no brothers or sisters since every woman could reproduce only once—but it was strangely disturbing to think about it.

"I didn't know who my father was," said Harman. "Savi said that at one point in time—even after the Lost Age—fathers were almost as important to children as mothers are now."

"That's hard to imagine," said Ada, still confused. What was he trying to tell her? That he was too old for her? That was nonsense.

"If I'm ever a father," said Harman, "I want the child to know me. I want to be with the child as he or she grows up . . . just as a mother would."

Ada was too shocked to speak.

He began walking again and she followed him in under the trees. It was cooler in the shade, but the air was thicker there. The waterfall made a soft noise behind them. Suddenly Ada looked around, alarmed.

"Did you hear something?" asked Harman, stopping next to her.

"No. It's just . . . something's wrong."

"No servitors," said Harman. "No voynix."

That was it, realized Ada. They were alone. For the last two days, the absence of omnipresent servitors and voynix had been like a missing background noise, but it was more apparent now that they were alone, just the two of them.

Suddenly, for no apparent reason, she shivered. "Can you find the way back to the sonie?"

Harman nodded. "I've been making notes on the terrain and watching the sun." He pointed with the branch he was using as a walking stick. "The glade is just over that hill."

Ada smiled, but she wasn't totally convinced. She checked her palm-finder, but it was as blank as it had been since they'd left the Antarctic domi. She'd been in the woods before—usually on her Ardis estate—but never without a servitor floating nearby to show the way home or without a voynix for protection. But this was just background tension to the central anxiety about Harman's odd question and comment.

"Why are you talking about fathers?" she asked.

He looked at her as they strolled farther down the hill, deeper into the sequoia forest. The shade was almost gloomy here, although shafts of light slanted down here and there through the cathedral hush. "Something Savi said to me this morning," he said. "Something about me being old enough to be your grandfather. About me going after this quest to find the firmary—and getting involved with you—as a sort of denial of my Final Twenty."

Ada's first response was anger, followed immediately by a stab of jealousy. The anger was at Savi's stupid remark—it was none of the old woman's business who Ada slept with or how old he was; the jealousy came from the fact that Harman had left their bed that morning at sunrise to go down and talk to Savi. Ada had simply kissed him good-bye when he'd slipped out of bed, soniced and dressed that morning, feeling some disappointment that her new lover did not want to spend another hour with her before they all had to rise for breakfast, but respecting his choice, imagining that he was just an early riser from old habit.

But what was so important that he had to leave her at dawn to go talk to Savi? Wasn't he planning to spend the next several days with Savi in his stupid quest for a spaceship? In fact, realized Ada, Savi was taking *her* place in that quest.

She studied Harman's face—so much younger looking than Odysseus' shocking crow's feet and gray hair—and saw that he hadn't noticed her flash of anger and jealousy. Harman was still preoccupied, obviously mulling over his own thoughts, and Ada wondered if his attention and sensitivity to her the last few days—culminating in their wonderful lovemaking last night—were aberrations, just part of a prelude to sex, and not his usual demeanor. She didn't think so, but she didn't know. Was all this closeness she'd been feeling with Harman an illusion, something she'd generated out of her infatuation with him?

"Do you know how you choose to get pregnant?" asked Harman, still poking the ground distractedly with his walking stick.

Ada stopped in shock. That question was . . . astounding.

Harman stopped and looked at her as if he had said nothing unusual. "I mean, do you know how the mechanism works?" he said, still seemingly oblivious to how inappropriate his question was. Men and women simply did not discuss such things.

"If you're going to lecture me on the birds and the bees," Ada said stiffly, "it's a bit late."

Harman laughed easily. Over the past couple of weeks, that laugh had enchanted Ada. Now it irritated the hell out of her.

"I don't mean the sex, my dear," he said. Ada noticed that it was the first time he'd used an endearment with her, but she was in no mood to appreciate it. "I mean when you receive permission to get pregnant, perhaps decades from now—and choose the sperm donor."

Ada was blushing and the fact that she couldn't stop blushing made her angry. She blushed more deeply. "I don't know what you're talking about."

She did, of course. It was men who weren't supposed to know or discuss such things. Most women decided to apply for pregnancy around their Third Twenty. Usually the waiting period was one to two years before permission was granted—relayed from the post-humans through servitors. At that point, the woman would cease sexual intercourse, take the prescribed pregnancy uninhibitor, and decide which of her former mates would be the sperm-father of her child. Pregnancy ensued within days and the rest was as ancient as . . . well, humankind.

"I'm talking about the mechanism by which you decide which stored sperm-packet is chosen by your body," continued Harman. "The real old-style human females didn't have that choice . . ."

"Nonsense," snapped Ada. "We *are* the old-styles. It's always been this way."

Harman shook his head slowly, almost sadly. "No," he said. "Even in Savi's day, just fourteen hundred years ago, pregnancy was more of a slapdash thing. She says that this sperm-storage and selection mechanism was something the posts built into us—into women—based on some borrowed genetic structure from moths."

"Moths!" said Ada, no longer simply shocked but truly, deeply angry now. This was as absurd as it was demeaning. "What the hell are you talking about, Harman *Uhr*?"

His head snapped up and he seemed to notice her reaction for the first time, as if her retreat to the formal honorific had been a slap in the face bringing him back to reality.

"It's true," he said. "I'm sorry if I upset you, but Savi says that the posts genetically structured this ability to choose father-sperm years after intercourse from the genes of a moth species named . . ."

"Enough!" shouted Ada. Her hands were balled into fists. She'd never struck anyone in her life, or wanted to, but at this moment she was close to swinging at Harman. "Savi says this, Savi says that. I've had enough of that old bitch. I don't even believe she *is* that old . . . or wise. She's just crazy. I'm going back to the sonie." She walked off into the woods.

"Ada!" called Harman.

She ignored him, walking uphill, slipping on needles and wet humus.

"Ada!"

She strode on, ready to leave him behind.

"Ada, that's the wrong direction."

Hannah had caught up with Odysseus a few hundred yards from the glade. He whirled and put his hand on the hilt of his sword when he heard her crashing through the brush, but relaxed when he saw who it was.

"What do you want, girl?"

"I want to see your sword," said Hannah, brushing her dark hair back from her face.

Odysseus laughed. "Why not?" He unclipped the leather sheath from his belt and handed over the weapon. "Be careful with the edges, girl. I could shave with this blade, if I ever chose to shave."

Hannah drew the short sword and hefted it tentatively.

"Savi tells me that you work with metals," said Odysseus. He bent to a stream, cupped his hand, sipped. "She says that you may be the only person, male or female, in all this brave new world, who knows how to forge bronze."

Hannah shrugged. "My mother remembered old tales about forging metal. She played with fire and open hearths when she was younger. I continue the experiments." She swung the sword overhand, chopping down.

"You've seen us fight in your turin cloth," said Odysseus.

Hannah nodded. "So?"

"You're using the sword properly, girl. Hacking rather than stabbing. This tool is made for severing limbs and spilling guts, nothing more refined."

Hannah grimaced and handed the weapon back. "Is this the sword you used on the plains of Ilium?" she asked softly. "And in your adventure to steal the Pallodian?"

"No." He lifted the blade vertically until some of the light spilling down between the high branches danced on its surface. "This particular sword was a gift to me, from . . . a female . . . during my travels."

Hannah waited for more explanation, but instead of telling another story, Odysseus said, "Would you like to see what makes this sword different?"

Hannah nodded.

Odysseus used his thumb to tap at the hilt guard twice, and suddenly the sword seemed to shimmer slightly. Hannah leaned closer. Yes, there was a subtle but persistent hum coming from the blade. She lifted one hand toward the metal but Odysseus' hand shot out quickly, grabbing her wrist.

"If you touched it now, girl, you'd lose all your fingers."

"Why?" She didn't struggle to pull her wrist away, and after a few seconds Odysseus released it.

"It's vibrating," said Odysseus, holding the sword blade flat just below eye level. Hannah noticed again that she was exactly the same height as Odysseus. The night before, she had heard him in the green bubble hall on the bridge after the others had turned in, joined him for a walk, returned to his domi to talk for hours, and had gone to sleep on the floor next to his cot. Hannah knew that Ada thought they'd become lovers; she didn't mind and couldn't think of a reason to disabuse her friend of the notion.

"It's almost as if it's singing," said Hannah, turning slightly better to hear the high-pitched hum.

Odysseus laughed loudly at this, although Hannah didn't know why. "Don't worry," he said. "It wasn't tossed to me by some Lady of the Lake, although that's not too far from the truth of it." He laughed again.

Hannah looked at the bearded man. She had no clue as to what he was talking about. She wondered if he did. "Why does it vibrate?" she asked.

"Stand back," said the barrel-chested man.

Most of the sequoia around them were six to ten feet thick, some thicker, but a smaller pine—perhaps a ponderosa or Douglas fir—was growing in a sunny patch a few yards to their left. The tree was probably thirty or forty years old, about fifty feet tall, with a trunk perhaps eighteen inches thick.

Odysseus planted his feet, gripped the sword in one hand, and swung idly at the trunk in an effortless backhand stroke.

The blade moved so smoothly through its arc that it appeared that he'd missed completely. There was no noise of impact. A few seconds later, the tall pine tree shivered, shifted, and fell noisily to the ground.

Odysseus thumbed the hilt again and the faint vibration hum ceased.

Hannah stepped closer to inspect the chest-high stump and the fallen tree. The trunk sections looked as if they had been surgically separated, not sawed. She laid her palm on the top of the severed stump. There was no sap, no shavings. The wood was so smooth it felt as if it had been sealed in plastic, cauterized somehow. She turned back to Odysseus.

"That must have come in handy during the siege of Troy," she said.

"You weren't listening, girl," said Odysseus. He slipped the weapon back in its sheath and strung it to his broad belt. "This was a gift some years after I'd left the war and begun my travels. If I'd had this at Ilium . . ." Odysseus grinned horribly. "There wouldn't be a Trojan, god, or goddess left with a head on his or her shoulders, girl. I promise you that."

Hannah found herself grinning back at the old man. They weren't lovers—not yet—but Hannah was planning to stay at Ardis Hall while Odysseus was visiting there, and who knew what might happen?

"There you are," said Savi, striding down the slope toward them. She closed her fist and what looked like a palm finder-field blinked out.

"Time to go on?" asked Odysseus, speaking to Savi but glancing toward Hannah as if they were old conspirators.

"Time to go on," said Savi.

26

Between Eos Chasma and Coprates Chasma in East-Central Valles Marineris

Three weeks into the voyage west up the river—inland sea, really—of Valles Marineris, and Mahnmut was close to losing his moravec mind.

Their felucca, crewed by forty little green men, was just one of many ships plying their way east or west in the flooded rift valley or north-south up or down the estuary opening onto the Chryse Planitia Sea of the Northern Tethys Ocean. In addition to a score of other LGM-crewed feluccas, they had passed at least three 100-meter-long barges each day, each hauling four great, uncarved stones for heads, all headed east from the cliff quarry on the south side of Noctis Labryinthus at the west end of Valles Marineris, still some 2,800 kilometers ahead of Mahnmut's west-bound felucca.

Orphu of Io had been rolled aboard and secured on the lower mid-deck, hidden from aerial view by a raised tarp, tied down next to the major pieces of cargo and other items recovered from *The Dark Lady*. Even the thought of his submersible—left behind in the shallow sea cavern along the Chryse Planitia coastline some 1,500 kilometers behind them—depressed Mahnmut.

Until this voyage, Mahnmut hadn't known that he was capable of depression—capable of feeling such a terrible emotional malaise and sense of hopelessness that could leave him with almost no will and even less ambition—but the violent separation from his sub had shown him just how low he could feel. Orphu—blinded, crippled, hauled aboard like so much useless ballast—seemed in good spirits, although Mahnmut was learning how carefully and rarely his friend showed his true feelings.

The felucca had arrived, as promised, early that next Martian morning after their arrival on the coast, and while the LGM were man-hauling poor Orphu aboard, Mahnmut had gone down into the flooded sub several times, pulling out all the removable power units, solar cells, communication equipment, log disks, and all the navigation gear that he could haul.

"You swam naked out to the wreck and stuffed your pockets with biscuits before swimming back, eh?" Orphu had said that morning after Mahnmut told him about the salvage efforts.

"What?" Mahnmut wondered if the battered Ionian had finally lost his mind.

"Little continuity error in Defoe's *Robinson Crusoe*," rumbled Orphu. "I always enjoy continuity errors."

"I never read it," Mahnmut said. He was in no mood for banter. Leaving *The Dark Lady* behind was tearing him apart.

They discussed his reaction during the first three weeks of their voyage, since they had little to do aboard the felucca except discuss things. The short-range radio receiver transmitter that Mahnmut had grafted onto Orphu's commline jack worked well.

"You're suffering from agoraphobia as much as from depression," said Orphu.

"How so?"

"You were designed, programmed, and trained to be part of the sub, hidden under Europan ice, surrounded by darkness and crushing depths, comfortable in your tight spaces," said the Ionian. "Even your short forays on the ice surface of Europa didn't prepare you for these vast vistas, distant horizons, and blue skies."

"The sky's not blue right now," was all that Mahnmut said in response. It was early morning, and, like most mornings, Valles Marineris was filled with low clouds and thick fog. The LGM had furled the felucca's sails and were moving ahead by oars alone—thirty of the little green men rowed, fifteen on a side, seemingly indefatigable—whenever the wind didn't move the two-masted, lateen-rigged sailing ship. Lanterns glowed on the bow, forward mast, both sides, and stern, and the felucca was barely moving. This section of the Valles Marineris was more than 120 kilometers wide and the section they would soon be entering would be 200 kilometers across—an inland sea rather than river, where, even on clear days, the high cliffs of the north or south banks of the waterway would be invisible in the distance—but there was enough LGM ship traffic along these channels to justify such caution in the fog.

Mahnmut realized that Orphu was right—that agoraphobia was part of his problem, since he felt the depression most acutely on the clear days where the views were unlimited—but he also knew that it was more complicated than being separated from the secure crèche and sensory jacks of his ship. Mahnmut was—had always been—a sea captain, and he knew from his own history programming and later reading that nothing hurt captains more than the loss of their ships. On top of that, he'd been tasked with an important mission—delivering Koros III to the oceanward base of Olympus Mons—and he had failed miserably. Koros III was dead, as was Ri-Po, the moravec who should be waiting in orbit to receive, interpret, and relay Koros's important reconnaissance data.

To whom? How? When? Mahnmut didn't have a clue.

They talked about that as well during their weeks of quiet voyaging. It was even quieter at night, since the LGM went into hibernations as soon as the sun set, securing the felucca with a complicated sea anchor— Mahnmut had done echo soundings and determined that the water under them was more than six kilometers deep—and not stirring again until sunlight touched their green, transparent skin the next morning. It seemed obvious that the LGM gained energy solely through sunlight, even from the diffused light through morning fog. Certainly Mahnmut had never seen any of the little green men eat or secrete anything. He could ask them, but even though Orphu hypothesized that the individual LGM did not really "die" after communication—that the little green men were an aggregate consciousness rather than an assembly of real individuals—Mahnmut did not trust the hypothesis enough to reach into another little green person's chest, grip what could be his heart, and ask questions that might be deferred until another day.

But Mahnmut had no reservations about asking Orphu questions.

"Why did they send us?" he asked on their tenth day. "We don't understand the mission and aren't suited to carry it out even if we did know what we're supposed to do. It was madness to send us here this ignorant."

"Moravec administrators are used to compartmentalizing duties and assigning specialties," said Orphu. "You were the best they could find to drive Koros III to the volcano. I was the best moravec they could get to service the spacecraft. They never considered the possibility that you and I would be the team left to do the work of the other two."

"Why not?" said Mahnmut. "They must have known that the mission would be dangerous."

Orphu rumbled softly, "Probably they thought that if was all or nothing—that we'd all die if worse came to worst."

"We almost did," muttered Mahnmut. "We probably will."

"Describe the day," said Orphu. "Has the fog lifted yet?"

The days and the scenery and the nights were beautiful. Mahnmut's knowledge of breathable-atmosphere worlds came exclusively from his data bank records of Earth, and this terraformed Mars was an interesting variation.

The skies varied from a bright light blue at midday to a pink-red sky at sunset that sometimes shifted hues toward a pure gold light that infused everything with radiance. The sun itself looked significantly smaller than the sun seen from Earth in old video-records, but it was immensely larger and brighter and warmer than any sun known by Galilean moravecs in the last two thousand e-years. The breeze was soft and smelled of salt sea and—sometimes, shockingly—of vegetation.

"Do you ever wonder why they gave us that sense?" Orphu had asked when Mahnmut described the vegetation scent as they entered the broad Valles Marineris Estuary from the Tethys.

"What's that?" said Mahnmut.

"Smell."

The Europan moravec had to think about that. He'd always taken his sense of smell for granted, although it was useless underwater or on the surface of Europa, and all but useless in *The Dark Lady*'s environmental crèche—in other words, everywhere he'd existed. "I could smell toxic fumes in the sub or in the pressurized cubbies of Conamara Chaos Central," he said at last, knowing that this wasn't a satisfactory answer. Moravecs had better built-in alarms for such dangers.

Orphu rumbled softly. "I might have smelled the sulfur when I was on Io's surface, but who would want to?"

"You can smell things?" said Mahnmut. "That doesn't make much sense for a hardvac moravec."

"Indeed," said Orphu. "Nor does the fact that I spend . . . spent . . . a majority of my time viewing things on the human's visible-light spectrum, but I did whenever possible."

Mahnmut thought about this as well. It was true; he did the same, even though he could easily see deep into the infrared and UV reaches of the spectrum. Orphu's vision, Mahnmut knew, incorporated visualizations of radio frequencies and magnetic field lines, neither common to old-style humans, which made a lot more sense for a moravec working in the hard radiation fields of Galilean space. So why did the Ionian choose the limited human "visible" wavelengths most frequently?

"I think it's because our designers and all the subsequent generations of moravecs secretly wanted to be human," said Orphu, answering Mahnmut's unstated question with no accompanying rumble of irony or amusement. "The Pinocchio Effect, as it were."

Mahnmut didn't agree with that, but he felt too depressed to argue the point.

"What do you smell now?" asked Orphu.

"Rotting vegetation," said Mahnmut as the felucca took the far southern channel into the broad estuary. "It smells like Shakespeare's Thames at low tide."

On the first week of sailing upriver, to keep from going mad from the inactivity, Mahnmut disassembled and inspected—as best he could—the three other pieces of recovered cargo, Orphu being the fourth.

The smallest artifact, a smooth ovoid not much larger than Mahnmut's compact torso, was the Device—the single most important element in the late Koros III's mission. All Mahnmut and Orphu knew about the Device was that the Ganymedan was supposed to deliver it to Olympus Mons, and, under proper circumstances not shared with Mahnmut or Orphu, activate it.

Mahnmut probed the Device with sonar and removed a tiny part of its reflective transalloy shell. Its function was not revealed. The actual machine, if machine it was, was macromolecular—essentially a single nano-squared machined molecule with a chewy central core of tremendous energy contained only by the macromolecule's internal fields. The only "device-device" that Mahnmut could find associated with the shell was a current-generated zipper initiator. Thirty-two volts applied to just the right place on the shell would . . . do something . . . to the macromolecule inside.

"It could be a bomb," said Mahnmut as he carefully replaced the square centimeter of metal shell.

"Quite a bomb," muttered Orphu. "If the em-molecule is mostly a binding eggshell, we're talking a planet-buster here. The yolk would be on us."

Pretending he hadn't heard the pun in order to preserve their friendship and to keep from having to throw Orphu over the railing, Mahnmut had looked out at the passing canyon walls—they were still sailing within three kilometers of the high southern cliffs bordering the broad inland sea that day—and imagined all that red-rocked, terraced and striated beauty gone. He thought of the periscoping mangroves that grew in the Martian lower estuary marshlands, the natural topiary-gorse visible on the valley cliffs' higher walls, even the fragile blue sky with ripples of high cirrus above the rock—and tried to imagine it all destroyed by one quantum explosion huge enough to rip a world apart. It hardly seemed right.

"Can you think of anything else it could be other than a bomb?" he asked Orphu.

"Not offhand," said the Ionian. "But something containing that much pent-up implosive quantum energy represents technology way beyond my understanding. I'd suggest you treat the Device gently, put some cushions under it or something, but since it's already survived the chariot people's attack and atmospheric entry that fried me and killed your ship, it can't be too delicate. Give it a kick in the ass and move on. What's the next piece of cargo?"

The next piece of cargo was just a bit larger than the Device, but much more understandable. "It's some sort of squirt communicator," said Mahnmut. "It's all folded in on itself, but I can see that if I activate it, it'll unfurl onto its own tripod, aim a large dish toward the sky, and fire a serious burst of . . . something. Encoded energy in tightband or k-maser or perhaps even modulated gravity."

"Why would Koros have needed that?" asked Orphu. "The comsats are still in orbit and the spaceship could have relayed any sort of tightbeam or radio back to Galilean space. Hell, even your sub could have contacted home."

"Maybe this wasn't meant to broadcoast to Jupiter space," suggested Mahnmut.

"Where then?"

Mahnmut had no suggestions.

"How was Koros going to code the message?" asked the Ionian.

"There are virtual jackports," said Mahnmut after inspecting the compact machinery carefully under its nanocarbon skin. "We could download everything we've seen and learned, encrypt it, and activate it. Unless it needs an activation code or something. Want me to jack in and check?"

"No," said Orphu. "Not yet."

"I'll close it then."

"What does this communicator use for a squirt power source?" asked Orphu before Mahnmut could close up the device.

Mahnmut wasn't familiar with the technology, but he described the magnetic container and forcefield schematics.

"My, my," said Orphu. "That's Chevkovian *felschenmass*. Artificial antimatter of the kind the Consortium used to fuel the first interstellar probe. There's enough energy there to keep us alive and kicking for another several earth centuries if there were a way for us to tap into it."

Mahnmut had felt his organic heart skip a beat. "Could we have used it to replace the fusion reactor on the *Lady*?"

Orphu was quiet for several long seconds. "No, I don't think so," he said at last. "Too much energy released too fast and too hard to tame. It's possible that you and I could tap into its trickle field, but I don't think we could have powered up *The Dark Lady* with it even if the sub could have been repaired. And you said you couldn't do the repairs alone, right?"

"It would have taken the Conamara Chaos ice docks," said Mahnmut, feeling a strange combination of regret and relief at the news that this wasn't a fix for the poor *Lady*. As much as the death of his ship depressed him, the thought of turning back and sailing the 2,000-plus kilometers back to it was even more depressing.

The last piece of cargo was the largest, the heaviest, and the hardest for Mahnmut to figure out.

The container was a bamboo-three cube a meter and a half tall by two meters wide, wrapped in clear transpolymer. A brief inspection showed Mahnmut that the cube was filled with hundreds of square meters of micro-thin polyethylene stealth-composite with high-performance solarcell-strips embedded in the fabric, 24 interconnected, partially nested, articulated conical titanium segments, four pressurized canisters containing what his sensors said was helium, an oxygen-nitrogen mix, and methanol, 8 atmospheric pulse thrusters with jack-in controllers, and, finally, 12 fifteen-meter folded buckycarbon cables attached to the four sides of the bamboo-three box the thing came in.

"I give up," said Mahnmut after several minutes of pondering and poking and refolding. "What the hell is it?"

"A balloon," said Orphu.

Mahnmut shook his moravec head. There were both living and moravec balloon creatures in the atmosphere of Jupiter, more swimming in the soup of Saturn, but what would Koros III have wanted with an artificial balloon on Mars?

Orphu transmitted the answer even as Mahnmut heard it in his own mind. "Koros's mission was to get to the top of Olympus Mons, to the locus of the quantum disturbance, and this way he wouldn't have to climb the volcano. What are the dimensions of this . . . balloon?"

Mahnmut told the Ionian.

"Inflated with helium here at null-null, Martian sea level, that would give a diameter of just over sixty meters and a height of about thirty-five meters, which should easily lift the gondola, you, the Device, and the squirt radio to the fringes of space . . . or the top of Olympus," said Orphu.

"Gondola?" said Mahnmut, still trying to absorb this concept.

"The box it came in. That's obviously what Koros III planned to ride in. Does it have a transpolymer hood—some sort of pressurizable cover?"

"Yes."

"There you have it."

"But Olympus Mons has an escalator going up its south side," Mahnmut said stupidly.

"Koros and the moravecs who planned this mission didn't know that," said Orphu.

Mahnmut looked away from the balloon for a minute to think. The southern cliffs of Valles Marineris were just a thin red line against the blue-green horizon as the felucca moved deeper into the center channels of the estuarial river. "The gondola is too small to carry you," he said.

"Well, naturally . . ." began Orphu.

"I'll build a bigger gondola," interrupted Mahnmut.

"Do you really think we'll be ascending to the summit of Olympus Mons?" Orphu said softly.

"I don't know," said Mahnmut, "but I do know that we'll still be more than two thousand kilometers from the volcano when . . . if . . . we ever reach the western end of Valles Marineris in this little ship. I didn't have any idea how we were going to get through the jumble of Noctis Labyrinthus and over the Tharsis Plateau to Olympus, but this . . . balloon . . . might work. Maybe."

"We could start now," said Orphu. "It would be faster than this . . . what did you call it?"

"Felucca," said Mahnmut, glancing up at the rigging and sails sharp against the pink and blue sky. Several of the little green men were swinging effortlessly from line to line in the rigging. "And no, I don't think we should try the balloon until we have to. It uses chameleon-stealth fabric, even on the gondola, but I'm not convinced that the flying-chariot people couldn't track it. We'll launch it when we reach Noctis Labyrinthus. That'll be a long and difficult enough aerial journey as it is, since three of the tallest volcanoes on Mars will be between us and Olympus."

Orphu rumbled close to the subsonic. "*Around the World in Eighty Days,* eh?"

"Not around the world," said Mahnmut. "Counting this boat trip, we have to travel just a little more than one-fourth the way around it."

Mahnmut tried to pass the time and shake himself out of his low mood by reading Shakespeare's sonnets from the physical book he'd salvaged from *The Dark Lady.* It didn't work. Whereas during the past few years he'd disappeared into analysis, ferreting out hidden structures, word-connections, and dramatic content, the sonnets seemed like sad things now. Sad and rather nasty.

Mahnmut the moravec could care less what "Will" the "poet" in the sonnets did to the "Young Man" or expected done in return—Mahnmut had neither penis nor anus and longed for neither—but the copious flattery and flagrant bullying of the thick-witted but wealthy "youth" by the older poet was oppressive to Mahnmut now, bordering on the perverse. He skipped to the "Dark Lady" sonnets, but these were even more cynical and perverse. Mahnmut agreed with the analysis that the poet's interest in this woman was centered precisely on her promiscuity—this woman of the dark hair, dark eyes, dun breasts, and dark nipples was, if the poet was to be trusted, not a whore, but certainly something of a slut.

Mahnmut had long since downloaded Freud's 1910 essay, "A Special Type of Choice of Object Made by Men," in which the lost-age witch doctor had documented cases of human males who could be sexually aroused only by women well known to be promiscuous. Shakespeare had no hesitation of describing a woman's vagina as *the bay where all men ride* and sneeringly punning—*O cunning love*—about his Dark Lady's easy promiscuity, and Mahnmut had spent happy years finding deeper levels and dramatic structures behind these vulgarities, but this day— the sun close to setting straight down the great inland sea, the cliffs glowing rose-red to the north—he could see the sonnets only as dirty linen, a raunchy poet's private confessions.

"Reading your sonnets?" asked Orphu.

Mahnmut closed the book. "How'd you know? Have you taken up telepathy now that you've lost your eyes?"

"Not yet," rumbled the Ionian. Orphu's great crab shell was lashed to the deck ten meters from where Mahnmut sat near the bow. "Some of your silences are more literary than others, is all."

Mahnmut stood and turned toward the sunset. The little green men were hustling in the rigging and along the sea-anchor hawser, readying the ship for their sleep. "Why'd they program some of us to have a predisposition for human books?" he asked. "What possible use is that to a moravec now that the human race may be extinct?"

"I've wondered that myself," said Orphu. "Koros III and Ri Po were free from our affliction, but you must have known others who were obsessed with human literature."

"My old partner, Urtzweil, read and re-read the King James version of the Bible," said Mahnmut. "He studied it for decades."

"Yes," said Orphu. "And me and my Proust." He hummed a few bars of "Me and My Shadow." "Do you know what all these works we gravitate toward have in common, Mahnmut?"

Mahnmut thought about it for a moment. "No," he said at last.

"They're inexhaustible," said Orphu.

"Inexhaustible?"

"Incapable of being used up. If we were human, these particular plays and novels and poems would be like houses that always opened onto new rooms, hidden stairways, undiscovered attics . . . that sort of thing."

"Uh-huh," said Mahnmut, not buying into this metaphor.

"You don't sound happy with the Bard today," said Orphu.

"I think his inexhaustibility has exhausted me," admitted Mahnmut.

"What's happening on deck? A lot of activity?"

Mahnmut turned away from the sunset. Three-fourths of the ship's complement of LGM were silently scurrying and tying down and clambering and letting out the sea anchor and securing. There were only three or four minutes of usable sunlight left before they went into hibernation—lying down, curling up, and shutting down for the night.

"Did you feel the vibrations in the deck?" Mahnmut asked his friend. Except for smell, it was the last sense left to Orphu.

"No, I just knew it was that time of day," said the Ionian. "Why don't you help them?"

"Pardon me?"

"Help them," repeated Orphu. "You're an able-bodied seaman. Or at least you know a hawser from a hacksaw. Give them a hand—or your nearest moravec equivalent."

"I'd just get in the way." He looked at the quick work and perfect precision of the little green men. They scuttled out along the rigging and up the masts like videos he'd seen of monkeys. "We don't have telepathy," added Mahnmut, "but I'm pretty sure they do. They don't need my help."

"Nonsense," said Orphu. "Make yourself useful. I'm going back to reading about Monsieur Swann and his faithless girlfriend."

Mahnmut hesitated a moment, but then slipped the irreplaceable book of sonnets into his backpack, trotted to the mid-deck, and joined in the lashing down of the lowered lateen sail. At first the LGM paused in their synchronized work and just stared at him—black-button anthracite eyes staring from their clear, featureless green faces—but then they made room and Mahnmut, glancing at the setting sun and breathing in the clean Martian air, set to work with a will.

Over the next few weeks, Mahnmut's mood changed from depression to satisfaction to something like the moravec equivalent of joy. He worked every day with the LGM, keeping up his conversation with Orphu even as he sewed sails, spliced rigging, swabbed decks, pulled on the anchor, and took his turn at the tiller. The felucca was making about forty kilometers progress a day, which seemed like very little until one took into account that they were moving upstream, sailing with irregular winds, rowing much of the time, and stopping completely during the night. Since the Valles Marineris was about 4,000 kilometers long—almost the width of the Lost Age nation called the United States—Mahnmut was resigned to making the transit in about a hundred Martian days. Beyond the west edge of the inland sea, he kept reminding himself and Orphu reminded him when he forgot, was more than 1,800 kilometers of Tharsis Plateau.

Mahnmut was in no hurry. The pleasures of the sailing ship—she had no name as far as the moravec could tell, and he wasn't about to kill a little green man to ask—were simple and real, the scenery was astounding, the sun was warm in the day and the air deliciously cool at night, and the desperate urgency of their mission was fading under the reassuring cycle of routine.

Near the end of the sixth week on the water, Mahnmut was working on the forward of the felucca's two masts when a chariot appeared less than a kilometer dead ahead of the ship, flying low—only thirty meters or so higher than the ship's sails—allowing Mahnmut no time to scurry for cover. He was alone at the intersection of the two segments of mast—a felucca's sails are triangular, its two masts segmented, the upper section slanted rakishly back—and no little green men were in the rigging. Mahnmut was completely exposed to the gaze of anyone or anything flying the chariot.

It passed over traveling several hundred kilometers per hour, and so low that Mahnmut could see that the two horses pulling the chariot were holograms. A man in a tan tunic was the only occupant, standing tall and holding the virtual reins. The figure was golden-skinned, powerfully handsome, with long blond hair streaming behind him. He did not deign to look downward.

Mahnmut used the opportunity to study the vehicle and its occupant with every visual filter, frequency, and wavelength he had at his disposal, tightbeaming the data to Orphu in case the chariot god had seen him and decided to blast Mahnmut off the mast with a wave of his hand. The horses, reins, and wheels were holographic, but the chariot was real enough—composed of titanium and gold. Mahnmut couldn't detect any rocket, ion-pulse, or jet wake, but the chariot was putting out energy all across the EM spectrum—enough to drown out Mahnmut's radio narrative to Orphu if they hadn't been on tightbeam. More ominously, the flying machine was trailing four-dimensional streamers of quantum flux. Part of the thing's energy profile was captured in a forcefield that Mahnmut could clearly see in the infrared—a shield of energy forward of the hurtling aircraft to protect it from the wind of its own passage and a broader defensive bubble all around. Mahnmut was glad he hadn't thrown a rock at the chariot or shot at it—if he'd had a rock or energy weapon, which he did not. That forcefield, Orphu calculated, would keep the driver safe from anything short of a low-yield nuclear explosion.

"What's making it fly?" asked Orphu as the chariot receded in the east. "Mars doesn't have enough of a magnetic field to propel any EM flying machine."

"I think it's the quantum flux," said Mahnmut from his perch on the mast. It was a windy day and the felucca was rocking from side to side as it tacked back and forth and the whitecaps batted at it from the south.

Orphu made an impolite sound. "Directed quantum distortion can rip time and space apart—people and planets, too—but I don't see how it can fly a chariot."

Mahnmut shrugged despite the fact that his friend, invisible under the tarp rigged on the mid-deck, couldn't see him. "Well, it didn't have propellers," he said. "I'll download you the data, but it looked to me like the awkward thing was surfing on a curl of quantum distortion."

"Peculiar," said Orphu. "But even a thousand such flying machines couldn't explain the locus of quantum distortion Ri Po recorded on Olympus Mons."

"No," agreed Mahnmut. "At least this . . . god . . . didn't see us."

There was a pause in the conversation and Mahnmut listened to the crash of the felucca's bow against the waves and the flap of the lateen-rigged canvas as the big sails filled with wind again. There was a soft wind-strum through the rigging up where Mahnmut was, and he enjoyed the sound of it. He also enjoyed the less-than-gentle pitch and roll of the ship as it tacked, even while he compensated for it easily as he clung to the mast with one hand, his other hand on a taut line. They were deep into the widest section of the flooded rift valley now, in an area called Melas Chasma, with the huge, radiating sub-sea of Candor Chasma opening up to the north and the seabed more than eight kilometers beneath them, but there were cliffs belonging to huge islands—some several hundred kilometers long and thirty or forty kilometers across—visible on the horizon to the south.

"Perhaps he saw you and just radioed back to Olympus for reinforcements," suggested Orphu.

Mahnmut sent the radio static equivalent of a sigh. "Always the optimist," he said.

"Realist," amended Orphu. But the tone of the next broadcast was serious. "You know, Mahnmut, that you'll have to talk to the little green men again soon. We have too many questions that need answering."

"I know," said Mahnmut. The thought made him vaguely ill in a way that the pitching and rolling of the felucca never could.

"Perhaps we should inflate and launch the balloon sooner rather than later," Orphu suggested again. Mahnmut had spent several days cobbling together a wider, broader gondola from the bamboo-three of the first one and some borrowed planks from one of the felucca's less essential bulkheads. The LGM had not seemed to mind his borrowing their boards.

"I still don't think we should launch yet," said Mahnmut. "We're not even sure about the prevailing winds this month, and the pulse-thrusters won't give us much steering once the balloon gets up into the Martian jetstream. We'd better get as close to Olympus as we can before we risk the balloon."

"I agree," said Orphu after a silence, "but it is time we talked to the LGM again. I have a theory that it's not telepathy that they're using—either when they communicate with you or pass information among themselves."

"No?" said Mahnmut, looking down at a dozen of the little green men as they came up from the oardecks and began working efficiently on the forward rigging. "I can't imagine what else it could be. They certainly don't have mouths or ears, and they're not transmitting data on any radio, tightbeam, maser, or light frequency."

"I think the information is in the particles in their bodies," said Orphu. "Nanopackets of encoded information. That's why they insist you use your hand to grasp that internal organ—it's a sort of telegraph-central—and your hand, as opposed to, say, your general manipulators, is organic. Living molecular machines can pass into your bloodstream via osmosis and travel to your organic brain, where the same nanobytes help translate."

"Then how do they communicate among themselves?" asked Mahnmut, dubious. He'd liked the telepathy theory.

"The same way," said Orphu. "Touch. Their skins are semipermeable, probably with data passing to and fro with every casual contact."

"I don't know," said Mahnmut. "Remember how this crew seemed to know everything about us when the felucca arrived? Where we were going? I had the feeling that our presence had been broadcast telepathically all along the little green man psychic network."

"Yes, it appeared that way to me as well," said Orphu, "but besides the fact that neither human nor moravec science has ever established even a theoretical framework for telepathy, Occam's razor would dictate that the felucca crew learned of us through simple physical contact with the LGM at our landing site—or from others who had been there."

"Nanopackets of data in the bloodstream, eh?" said Mahnmut, allowing the skepticism to be audible in his tone. "But one of these individuals still has to die if I'm going to ask more questions."

"Regrettably," said Orphu, not bringing up his earlier arguments that individual LGM probably had no more autonomous personality than did human skin cells.

Several of the little men were clambering on the forward mast near Mahnmut now, tying off lines and sliding down the lateen sail with the ease of acrobats. They nodded their green heads amicably as they passed on their way up or down.

"I think I'll wait until later to ask them," said Mahnmut. "There's a huge brown-red cloud on the southern horizon right now, and they'll need all hands to get the ship ready for the coming storm."

27

The Plains of Ilium

The Trojans are massacring the Greeks. My students in my other life would have said that they're "decimating" the Greeks, using that term for total destruction so loved by late Twentieth and early Twenty-first Century lazy journalists and illiterate TV anchorpersons, but since "to decimate" was a precise term—the Romans killing every tenth man in a village in response to uprisings—and that would only result in 10 percent casualties, it's fair to say that they're doing much worse than decimating the Greeks.

The Trojans are *massacring* the Greeks.

After Zeus's ultimatum to the other gods, he QT's to Earth in his golden chariot and lands on the slopes of Mount Ida, the tallest mountain within easy god-view of Ilium, and assumes his oversized throne on the mountaintop there, gazing down and out at the high walls of the city and the hundreds of Achaean warships on the beach and at anchor offshore. The other gods are too intimidated to come down to play after Zeus's demonstration of raw power, so the Father of the Gods holds out his golden scales and weighs the fates of death for the men below—one weight molded in the form of a Trojan horseman, the other an Argive spearman armored in bronze.

Zeus raises high the sacred scales, holding the beam mid-haft, and down goes the Achaeans' day of doom while the fortunes of Troy go lifting skyward. Zeus smiles at this, and I'm close enough to see that the old bastard had his thumb on the scales.

The Trojans come broiling out of their city gates like hornets out of a disturbed hive. The sky is low, gray, seething with dark energy, and Zeus's thunderbolts strike the battlefield frequently—and always among the Argives and long-haired Achaeans. Clearly seeing the signs of the displeasure of the King of the Gods, the Greeks still surge forward to fight—what else can they do?—and the plains of Ilium echo to the crash of shields pounded hide to hide, the scrape of pike, the rumble of chariots, and the screams of dying men and horses.

It goes badly for the Achaeans from the start. Lightning strikes among them, frying men like bronze-clad chickens on a rotisserie. Hector charges forward like a force of nature, and the quiet man I admired on the walls of Ilium with his wife and child is gone, replaced by a bloodied berserker cutting men down like stalks of grass and screaming to his followers for more blood, more carnage. His followers obey, the entire Trojan army and allies shouting as if from a single throat and surging forward en masse, rolling over the retreating Achaeans like a bronze-and-leather tsunami.

Paris—whom I dismissed as a fop in my description of his meeting with Hector only the day before and then proceeded to cuckold—rides near Hector and also comes on like some demon-possessed killing machine. Paris's killing expertise is archery, and on this day his long arrows never seem to miss. Achaeans and Argives drop with Paris's long-shaft arrows in their throats, hearts, genitals, and eyes. Every shot is a hit.

Hector slashes his way through every pocket of Greek resistance, hacking necks like daisy stems, offering no quarter and hearing no pleas for mercy in the deafness of his killing frenzy. When Achaeans manage to rally against the Trojan onslaught in a brave clump of resistance here or there, a bolt of blue energy from the roiling clouds explodes among them like a cosmic grenade and the thunder that follows mixes with the cries of dying men.

Ideomeneus and the great king Agamemnon cut and run. Then Big and Little Ajax, campaigners of a thousand battles, lose heart and flee the field. Odysseus, the "long-enduring," can't endure this slaughter and decides that the greater part of valor must reside in the safety of his ships back on the beach. He runs damned fast for a short-legged man. The only man who doesn't turn and flee is old Nestor, and that's only because Helen's husband has put an arrow through the skull of Nestor's lead horse, tangling the other steeds in their panic. Nestor cuts the traces clear with his sword, obviously with every intent of vacating the battlefield as fast as he can, but Hector's chariot surges forward, the men around Nestor fall dead with Paris's arrows protruding from their chests and necks, and the horses flee even faster than the departed Greek heroes, leaving old Nestor standing in his horseless chariot with Hector fast approaching.

When Odysseus sprints by, not even giving the old man a glance,

Nestor cries, "Where are you going in such a hurry, son of Laertes, O cool tactician . . ." but his sarcasm is wasted. Odysseus disappears in the dust cloud of panicked retreat without slowing for his old friend.

Diomedes, always more afraid of being called a coward than he is of pain or death, drives his chariot back into the fray, obviously intent on rescuing Nestor and driving back Hector. He swoops Nestor up like a wrinkled bag of laundry and the old charioteer seizes the reins in both hands, driving Diomedes' chariot not *away* from the charging Hector, but *toward* him. Diomedes gets close enough to cast his spear at Hector, but the heavy shaft kills Hector's driver, Eniopeus, son of Thebaeus, and for a moment, as the driver's corpse flies backward into the surprised foot soldiers and Hector's horses rear out of control, everything changes.

I've read that there is a moment like this in many battles, where everything hangs in the balance. As Hector fights to regain control of his horses and the Trojans with him pause in confusion, the Greeks see a possible reversal of fortune and rush into the gap, loping after old Nestor and Diomedes. For an instant the Achaeans have the initiative again, shouting their defiance and hacking down the men leading the Trojan assault.

Then Zeus intervenes again. Thunder booms. Lightning splits the earth and horses disappear in a flash of light and the stink of sulfur and burning hooves. Achaean chariots near Diomedes and Nestor explode in a tumble of horseflesh and flying bodies. Bronze melts and leather shields burst into flame. It's obvious even to the thick-skulled Diomedes that Zeus is not pleased with him this day.

Nestor tries to drag the rearing horses around but they have the metaphorical bit in their very real mouths and can't be managed. Their chariot—all alone now since the other Achaeans have turned tail and fled—bounces toward ten thousand angry Trojans.

"Quick, Diomedes, grab the reins and help me swing these stallions around!" cries Nestor. "To fight more today is to die today!"

Diomedes grabs the reins from the old man but does not turn the chariot. "Old Soldier, if I run today, Hector will brag to his troops— 'Diomedes ran for his ships, and I drove him back!' "

Nestor grabs Diomedes by his muscled throat. "What are you, six years old? Turn the fucking chariot, you asshole, or Hector will be wearing both our guts for garters before it's teatime in Troy!"

Or some words to that effect. I am a hundred yards across the battlefield when this occurs, and the shotgun mike on my baton might not be working correctly. Also, since I am morphed into the shape of a Trojan foot soldier, I'm running with the rest, watching all this over my shoulder as Paris's arrows fall around us and among us.

Diomedes wrestles with his dilemma for two or three seconds and then wrestles the horses instead, turning their heads, driving the chariot back toward the black ships and safety.

"Hah!" screams Hector over the din. He has a new driver—Archeptolemus, Iphitus' handsome son—and is coming on again with the renewed vigor of a man truly enjoying his work. "Hah! Diomedes—made you run! You coward! You girly girl! You glittering little puppet! You quavering sparrowfart!"

Diomedes turns again in the chariot, glowering with fury and embarrassment, but Nestor has the reins now and the horses themselves have figured out which way safety lies. The chariot rolls over boulders, ruts, and fleeing Greek foot soldiers in the horses' wild gallop toward the beach and safety, and the only way Diomedes can fight Hector now is by leaping off the chariot and fighting the thousands of Trojans on foot. He chooses not to do this.

"If you want to change our fates, you must find the fulcrum," Helen had said that morning.

She'd asked me then about my knowledge of the *Iliad*—although she thought of it as my oracle-sense of the future—and pressed me to find the fulcrum of events, the single point in the ten-year war on which everything pivoted. Fate's hinge, as it were.

I'd hemmed and hawed that morning, distracting her and myself with a final bout of lovemaking, but I'd thought about that question in the crazy hours since.

If you want to change our fates, you must find the fulcrum.

I'd bet my tenure as a Homerian scholar that the fulcrum of this particular tragic tale was fast approaching—the embassy to Achilles.

So far, events continue—more or less—to follow the poem, even with Aphrodite and Ares sidelined by wounds. Zeus has laid down the law and intervened on the side of the Trojans. I have no intention of QTing back to Olympos unless I have to, but I can guess that Homer's narrative is being played out there as well—Queen Hera fretting that her Argives are getting pummeled and trying to persuade Poseidon to intervene on their behalf, but the "god who rocks the earth" being shocked by the suggestion—he has no desire to battle Zeus. Then, when the Greeks are really routed later today, Athena will strip naked, then dress in her best battle armor and glistening breastplate—well, I confess that it might be worth QTing to Olympos for *that*—but is stopped cold by Zeus's messenger, Iris. Zeus's message will be succinct—

"If you and Hera come to oppose me by clash of arms, my gray-eyed girl, I'll maim your racers from beneath their yokes, hurl both you goddesses down from your chariot, smash your car, and rend both of you so terribly with my lightning bolts that you'll be in the healing vats ten slow wheeling years before the green worms can stitch you together again."

Athena will stay on Olympos. The Greeks, after a few hours of successful counterattack, will suffer heavier losses and fall back behind their own fortifications—a trench dug ten years ago shortly after landing, a thousand sharpened stakes, all the defenses recently deepened and built back up at Agamemnon's order—but even behind their own wall, the panicked Achaeans will lose hope and vote to sail for home.

Agamemnon will try to rally them by throwing a great feast for his commanders—even as Hector and his thousands organize for the final charge that they know will end in the burning of the Achaeans' black ships and the settling of this war for once and all—and at the Greek king's feast, Nestor will argue that their only hope lies in Agamemnon making up with Achilles.

Agamemnon will agree to pay Achilles a king's ransom—*more* than a king's ransom—seven fire tripods, ten bars of gold, twenty burnished cauldrons, a dozen stallions, seven beautiful woman, and I can't remember what else—a partridge in a pear tree, perhaps. Most important, the bribe will include Briseus' daughter Briseis—the slave wench who was at the center of this whole argument. To wrap this gift in a red ribbon, Agamemnon will also swear that he's never bedded Briseis. As a final incentive, he also throws in seven citadels, Greek kingdoms—Cardamyle, Enope, Hire, Anthea, Pherae, Aepea, and Pedasus. Of course, Agamemnon doesn't own or rule these citadels—he's giving away his neighbors' lands—but I suppose it's the thought that counts.

The one thing Agamemnon will not offer Achilles is his apology. The son of Atreus is still too proud to bow. "Let him bow down to me!" he'll shout at Nestor, Odysseus, Diomedes and the other captains in a few hours. "I am the greater king, I am the elder born, and, I claim, the greater man."

Odysseus and the other will see a way out despite Agamemnon's arrogance. They realize that if they bring the message of Briseis' return and all these other marvelous gifts—and just happen to leave out the "I'm the greater man" bit—there's a chance that Achilles might rejoin the fight. At least this embassy to Achilles offers a ray of hope.

But here the complicated part begins—here the fulcrum may yet be found.

As a scholar, I know in my soul that the embassy to Achilles is the heart and pivot of the *Iliad*. Achilles' decisions upon hearing the embassy's entreaties will determine the flow of all future events—the death of Hector, the subsequent death of Achilles, the fall of Ilium.

But here's the tricky part. Homer chooses his language *very* carefully—perhaps more carefully than any other storyteller in history. He tells us that Nestor will name five men for the embassy to Achilles—Phoenix, Big Ajax, Odysseus, Odios, and Eurybates. The last two are mere heralds, decorations for the sake of protocol, and will not walk to Achilles' tent with the real ambassadors nor take part in the discussion there.

The problem here is that Phoenix is an odd choice—he hasn't appeared in the story before, he's more of a Myrmidon tutor and retainer to Achilles than a commander, and it makes little sense that he would be sent to persuade his master. To top that off, when the ambassadors are walking along the ocean's edge—"where the battle line of breakers crash and drag"—on their way to Achilles' tent, the verb form that Homer uses is a dual form—a Greek verb set between singular and plural always relating to *two people*—in this case, Ajax and Odysseus. Homer uses seven other words that, in the Greek of his day—this day—relate to *two* men, not three.

Where's Phoenix during this walk from Agamemnon's camp to Achilles' part of the encampment? Is he somehow already in Achilles' tent waiting for the embassy? That makes little sense.

A lot of scholars, before and during my time on earth, argued that Phoenix was a clumsy addition to the tale, a character added centuries later, which explains the dual verb form, but this theory ignores the fact that Phoenix will give the longest and most complex argument of the three ambassadors. His speech is so wonderfully digressive and complicated that it reeks of Homer.

It's as if the blind poet himself had been confused about whether there were two or three emissaries to Achilles and what, exactly, Phoenix's role was in the conversation that would decide all the players' fates.

I have a few hours to think about this.

If you want to change our fates, you must find the fulcrum.

But that's hours in my future. It's still mid-afternoon here, and the Trojans are pausing on the Ilium-side of the Achaeans' moat while the

Greeks mill around like ants behind their wall of rocks and sharpened stakes. Still morphed as a sweaty Achaean spearman, I manage to get close to Agamemnon as the king first berates his men and then pleas for Zeus's aid in their darkest hour.

"Shame on all of you!" shouts the son of Atreus at his bedraggled army. Only a hundredth of the men can hear him, of course, ancient acoustics being what they are, but Agamemnon has a powerful voice and those in the back pass the message on to others.

"Shame! Disgrace! You dress like splendid warriors, but it's pure sham! You vowed to burn this city and you gorged yourself on cattle—bought at my expense!—and drank to the full those brimming bowls of wine—bought and shipped here at my expense!—and now look at you! Beaten rabble! You bragged that each of you could stand up to a hundred Trojans—two hundred!—and now you're no match for one mortal man—Hector.

"Any minute Hector will be here with his hordes, gutting our ships with blazing fire, and this vaunted army of . . . *heroes* . . ."—Agamemnon all but spits the word—"will be fleeing home to wife and kids . . . *at my expense!*"

Agamemnon gives up on the army and lifts his hands to the southern sky, toward Mount Ida, from where the storms and thunder and lightning bolts have come. "Father Zeus, how can you tear away my glory so? How have I offended thee? Not once—I swear, not a single time!—have I passed a shrine of yours, not even on our ocean voyage here, but did I stop and burn the fat and thighs of oxen to *your* glory. Our prayer was simple—to raze Ilium's walls to its roots, kill its heroes, rape its women, enslave its people. Is that too much to ask?

"Father, fulfill this prayer for me: let my men escape with their lives—at least that. Don't let Hector and these Trojans beat us like rented mules!"

I've heard Agamemnon give more eloquent speeches—hell, *all* of the speeches I've heard from him have been more eloquent than this, and I understand Homer's need to rewrite all this—but at that second a miracle occurs. Or at least the Achaeans take it as a miracle.

Out of nowhere, an eagle appears, flying from the south, a huge eagle, carrying a fawn in its talons.

The mob who had been surging toward their ships and safety on the seas and who paused only briefly for Agamemnon's speech freeze in place and point at the sight of this.

The eagle soars, circles, dips lower, and drops the still-kicking fawn a hundred feet to a sandy bump right at the base of the stone altar the Achaeans had raised to Zeus upon their landing so many years ago.

That does it. After fifteen seconds of stunned silence, a roar goes up from the men—men beaten into cowardice ten minutes earlier, but a fighting mob now, hearts and hands strengthened by this clear sign of forgiveness and approval from Zeus—and without further ado, fifty thousand Achaeans and Argives and all the rest surge back into formation behind their captains, horses are re-tethered to chariots, chariots are driven out across the earth-bridges still spanning the defensive trenches, and the battle is on again.

It becomes the hour of the archer.

Although Diomedes leads the counterattack, followed closely by the Atrides, Agamemnon and Menelaus, followed in turn by Big Ajax and Little Ajax, and although these heroes take their toll on the Trojans in spearcasts and shortsword clashes, the fighting now is centered around the Achaean archer Teucer, bastard son of Telamon and half-brother to Big Ajax.

Teucer has always been considered a master-archer, and I've seen him shoot dozens of Trojans over the years, but this is his day in the limelight. He and Ajax get into a rhythm whereby Teucer crouches under the wall of his half-brother's shield—Big Ajax uses a giant rectangular shield that military historians say wasn't even in use during the time of the Trojan War—and when Ajax lifts the shield, Teucer fires from beneath it into the Trojan ranks some sixty yards away. On this day he can't seem to miss his mark.

First he kills Orsilochus, putting a barbed arrow in the short man's heart. Then he kills Ophelestes, putting a point through the captain's right eye when the Trojan peeks above his rawhide shield. Then Daetor and Chromius fall mortally wounded from two fast, perfectly placed shots. Each time Teucer fires, the Trojans unleash their own arrows and spears in a vain attempt to kill the archer, but Big Ajax crouches over both of them and his massive shield deflects every missile.

The Trojan volleys pause, Ajax lifts his shield, and Teucer shoots Lycophontes, prince of his distant city, but just wounds the man. As Lycophontes' captains rush to his aid, Teucer puts a second arrow into the fallen man's liver.

Polymaeon's son, Amopaon, falls next, Teucer's shaft through his throat. Blood fountains five feet high and the powerful Amopaon tries to rise, but the arrow has pinned him to the ground, and he bleeds out in less than a minute, his body kicking and spasming ever more weakly. The Achaeans cheer. I know . . . knew . . . Amopaon. The Trojan used to eat in the little open restaurant where Nightenhelser and I liked to meet, and we'd spoken many a time of trivial things. He told me once that his father, Polymaeon, had known Odysseus in friendlier times, and once, when traveling to Ithaca and joining the friendly Greeks on a hunt, Polymaeon had killed a wild boar that had deeply gored Odysseus' leg and would have killed him if Polymaeon's spearcast had missed its mark. Amopaon told me that Odysseus bears the scar to this day.

Ajax crouches, holding his massive metal shield over him and his half-brother like a roof, and Trojan arrows rattle against it. Ajax rises, lifts the shield, and Teucer kills Melanippus—eighty yards away—with a shot that enters the man's groin and protrudes from his anus as the Trojan falls. His comrades step away and grimace as Melanippus writhes on the ground and dies. The Achaeans cheer again.

Agamemnon swings down off his chariot and shouts encouragement at Teucer, promising the archer second choice of tripods or purebred teams of horses—if Zeus and Athena ever allow him to plunder the treasure troves of Troy, he says—and then promises Teucer a beautiful Trojan woman to bed as well, perhaps Hector's wife, Andromache.

Teucer is angered by Agamemnon's offer. "Son of Atreus, do you think I'll try any harder than I already am, spurred on by your talk of plunder? I'm firing as fast and accurately as I can. Eight arrows—eight kills."

"Shoot at Hector!" cries Agamemnon.

"I *have* been shooting at Hector," screams Teucer, his face red. "All this time—Hector's been my target. I just can't hit the son of a bitch!"

Agamemnon falls silent.

As if responding to the challenge, Hector suddenly urges his chariot to the front of the Trojan ranks, trying to rally his men who've lost heart because of the archer's slaughter.

Ajax doesn't bother to lift his shield this time, because Teucer stands, goes to full draw, takes careful aim at Hector, and lets fly.

The shaft misses Hector's heart by a hand's breadth, striking Gorgythion as that son of Priam steps behind Hector's chariot. The big man stops, looks surprised, stares down at the protruding shaft and feathers as if he is the butt of some barracks joke, but then Gorgythion's head appears to become too heavy for his massive neck and falls limp to his shoulder as the weight of his helmet pulls it down; then Gorgythion falls dead in the blood-muddied sand.

"Damn!" says Teucer and fires again. Hector is the closest of all the Trojans now, turned full-torso toward Teucer.

This arrow catches Archeptolemus, Hector's driver, full in the chest. The horses—war-trained as they are—rear and leap ahead as Archeptolemus' blood geysers onto their flanks, and the young man pitches backward and off and into the dust.

"Cebriones!" cries Hector, grabbing the reins and calling to his brother—another bastard son of profligate Priam—to be his driver. Cebriones leaps up onto the chariot just as Hector jumps down. Enraged, beside himself with fury and grief at the death of his faithful Archeptolemus, Hector runs into no-man's-land—a clear target for Teucer—and grabs the largest, sharpest rock he can lift in one hand.

Hector seems to have forgotten all the finesse of warfare he's bragged about so many times and has reverted to caveman tactics, lifting the rock and cocking his left arm far back, looking like nothing so much—I think—as Sandy Koufax preparing to unleash a pitch. I haven't noticed until today that Hector is ambidextrous.

Teucer sees his chance, grabs another arrow from his quiver, and draws full back, aiming at Hector's heart, sure he can get off a shot, perhaps two, before Hector throws.

He's wrong. Hector pitches hard, fast, flat, and accurately.

The rock hits Teucer in the collarbone, just beside the throat, an instant before the archer releases the arrow. Bones crack. Tendons rip. Teucer's hand goes limp, the bowstring snaps, and the arrow buries itself in the ground between the archer's sandaled feet.

Hector rushes forward, scattering Achaeans like chaff, and the Trojan archers fire arrow after arrow at the fallen Teucer, but Big Ajax doesn't abandon his brother; he covers him with his wall of a shield while other Achaeans fight off the Trojan infantry. At Ajax's call—bellow, really—Mecisteus and Alastor rush forward and carry the moaning, semiconscious Achaean archer back across the trench-bridge to relative safety in the shadow of the hollow ships.

But Teucer's fifteen minutes of fame are up.

Things get worse for the Greeks very fast after this. Hector sees his survival as another sign of Zeus's love and approval and leads his men in charge after charge against the dispirited, retreating Achaeans.

Agamemnon, Menelaus, and the other lords who'd led their men into joyous combat just hours before are truly beaten now. The Achaeans are too routed at first even to man their defenses along the trench and stakes and makeshift wall, and the only thing that stops the Trojans from burning the ships right now is the setting sun and the sudden fall of darkness.

While the Achaeans mill about in confusion, some of the men already readying their ships for departure, others sitting shell-shocked and vacant-eyed, Hector does his *Henry V* thing, roaming tirelessly up and down the Trojan ranks, urging his men on to more carnage come the dawn, sending men back to the city to herd cattle out for slaughter and sacrifice and feasting, ordering in rations of honeyed wine, calling up the wagons of fresh-baked bread that the ravenous Trojans attack as if it were Agamemnon himself, and giving the command to set hundreds of watchfires just beyond the Achaean defenses, so the fearful Greeks will get no sleep this night. I don my Hades Helmet and walk invisible among the Trojans.

"Tomorrow," cries Hector to his cheering men, "I'll gut Diomedes like a flopping fish in front of his men if he doesn't choose to flee tonight. I'll break his spine with the tip of my spear and we'll nail the braggart's head above the Scaean Gates!"

The Trojans roar. The watchfires send sparks flying up toward the hard-burning stars. Invisible to gods and men, I recross the trench bridge, wind my way through the sharpened stakes, and walk again amongst the dispirited Greeks.

For me, it's time for truth or consequences. Agamemnon's already called the meeting of his captains and they're arguing courses of immediate action—flee or send an embassy to Achilles?

There's no turning back now. I morph into the form of Phoenix, Achilles' faithful Myrmidon tutor and friend, and walk across the cooling sand to join the council.

If you're going to change our fates, you must find the fulcrum.

The Mediterranean Basin

Savi followed the Atlantic Breach across the ocean, sometimes flying lower than the surface, hopping and dipping the sonie every few miles to avoid the connecting current cones that crisscrossed the Breach like transparent pipes in a long green hallway.

Lying prone to the left of Savi—seeing Harman lying in his spot to her right—Daeman was aware of the older man's grim expression and of the empty passenger slots behind them. Daeman was thinking about the last twenty-four hours.

Harman and Ada had seemed at odds when they'd flown away from the big-tree place. At first that had pleased Daeman. He didn't know what the falling-out had been about, of course, but it had been obvious that both were agitated after their walk in the woods—Ada looking cool and distant but inwardly seething, Harman visibly confused. But after the hours of flying to Ardis and the events there—and Daeman's decision to continue with this nonsense quest—the tension between Harman and Ada seemed like just another thing to worry about.

It had been late afternoon when they'd arrived at Ardis. The estate and grounds looked different from the air, at least to Daeman, although the layout of the hills and forest and meadows and river were just as he remembered. Whenever he thought of their picnic down to the river—to Hannah's silly metal-pouring exhibition—he thought of the attacking dinosaur and his heart began to pound.

"This area used to be called Ohio in the last part of the Lost Age," said Savi as they circled and then flew lower. "I think."

"I thought it was called North America," said Harman.

"That, too," said the old woman. "They had a surplus of names for places."

They landed about a quarter of a mile from Ardis Hall, in a pasture north of a line of screening trees. Daeman still had to use the toilet, but he was damned if he'd walk all that way to the estate if there was any chance of dinosaurs being in the area.

"It's safe," Ada said brusquely when she saw him hesitate, the only one still lying on the sonie. "The voynix patrol a perimeter within two or three miles of the hall."

"How far from the house was Hannah's hot-metal picnic?" asked Daeman.

"Three and a half miles," said Hannah. The young woman was standing near Odysseus behind the sonie.

Ada turned to Savi. "Are you sure you won't come up to the house?"

"I can't," said the old woman. She extended her hand and after a second, Ada took it. Daeman had never seen women shake hands before. "I'll wait here for Harman and Daeman to return," said Savi.

Ada looked at Harman. "You're coming up to Ardis for a minute, aren't you?"

"Just to say good-bye." The two held their intense gaze.

"Can we just *go*?" said Daeman, hearing the whine in his own voice. He didn't care. He had to *go*.

Everyone except Savi had started walking toward the distant house then, through the field of waist-high grass, past the occasional head of cattle—Daeman gave each of the cows a wide berth, since he wasn't comfortable around large animals—when suddenly a lone voynix stepped out of the treeline ahead of them.

"It's about time," said Daeman. "This walking is ridiculous." He gestured to the iron-and-leather form. "You! Go back to the hall and bring back two large carrioles to transport us there!"

Incredibly, the voynix ignored Daeman and kept walking toward the five humans—or to be more precise, toward Odysseus.

The old bearded man pushed Hannah away from him as the eyeless voynix slowly approached.

"It's just curious," said Ada, although her voice lacked conviction. "It's probably never . . ."

The voynix was five feet from Odysseus when the man swept his sword from his belt, activated the humming blade with his thumb, and swung the sword with both hands, slicing down and across the voynix's presumably impenetrable chest shell and left arm. For a second, the voynix just stood there, apparently as shocked at Odysseus' behavior as the four humans were, but then the top half of the creature's body slid, tilted, and fell to the ground, arms spasming. The lower half of the voynix's torso and its legs continued standing for several more seconds before tumbling over into the grass.

For a minute there was no sound except for the wind in the tall grass. Then Harman shouted, "Why in the hell did you do that?" Blue fluid, as thick as blood, was everywhere.

Odysseus pointed at the voynix's right arm, still attached to the lower torso. As he wiped his sword on the grass, he said, "It had its killing blades extended."

It was true. As the four gathered around the fallen voynix, each could see the blades—used for defending humans against such threats as dinosaurs—extended where the manipulator pads usually were.

"I don't understand," said Ada.

"It didn't recognize you," said Hannah, taking another step away from the bearded man. "Maybe it thought you were a threat to us."

"No," said Odysseus, sliding his short sword back into its scabbard.

Daeman was staring with appalled fascination at the cross section of the voynix—soft white organs, a profusion of blue tubules, clusters of what looked to be pink grapes, certainly not the clockwork mechanism and gears he'd always imagined to be the interior of a service voynix. The speed of the violence and now the white gore visible had almost made Daeman lose control of his anxious bowels.

"Come on," he'd said, and started walking quickly toward Ardis Hall. The others had mistaken this for leadership and followed.

It was after Daeman had used the toilet, taken time to shower, shaved, ordered the nearest Ardis servitor to fetch him clean new clothes, and then wandered into the kitchen hunting for something to eat that he realized that it was insane to go any further with Harman and the crazy old woman. To what purpose?

Ardis Hall, despite Ada's absence—or perhaps because of it—had filled with friends faxed in to visit and party. The servitors kept them happy with food and drink. Young people—including several beautiful young women Daeman knew from other parties, other places, from his happy life before Harman and all this nonsense—were playing lawnball-and-hoop games on the broad, sloping lawn. The evening was lovely, shadows long on the grass, laughter in the air like the sound of chimes, and dinner being prepared by servitors at the long table under the giant elm tree.

Daeman realized that he could stay here and have a proper meal and a good night's sleep, or—better yet—summon a voynix for the short carriole ride to the fax portal and sleep in his own bed in Paris Crater this night after a late dinner prepared by his mother. Daeman missed his mother; he'd been completely out of touch with her for more than two days. He looked at the voynix in the curved driveway at the side of the large house and felt a pang of anxiety—Odysseus' destruction of that voynix had been unwarranted and insane. One didn't damage or destroy vonixes, any more than one would set fire to a droshky or trash one's own domi. It didn't make any sense, and it was another reason he should get away from these people at once.

As he came out onto the drive, he saw Harman and Ada speaking softly but urgently to one side. Farther down the hilly lawn, he could see Hannah introducing Odysseus to several curious guests. The voynix were staying far away from the bearded man, but Daeman had no idea whether that was by coincidence or design. Did voynix communicate with one another? And if so, how? Daeman had never heard one utter a sound.

He gestured to a voynix to bring a carriole around just as Ada and Harman's conversation came to an end—Ada stalking into the house, Harman turning on his heel and heading back across the drive toward the fields and the waiting sonie. Harman walked up to Daeman and the older man's expression was so grim that Daeman took a half-step back.

"Are you coming with us?"

"I . . . ah . . . no," stammered Daeman. The voynix trotted up with the single-wheeled carriole behind it, upholstery gleaming in the evening light, gyroscopes humming.

Harman turned without saying another word and walked off into the field behind the house.

Daeman climbed into the conveyance, said "Fax portal" to the voynix, and sat back as the carriole hummed around the driveway, white shells crunching under the wheel. One of the young women on the lawn—Oelleo, he thought her name was—cried a good-bye to him. The carriole rolled down toward the road with the silent voynix trotting between its stays.

"Stop," said Daeman. The voynix halted in its tracks, still holding the cart shafts. The internal gyro hummed softly to itself.

Daeman looked back behind Ardis Hall but Harman was already out of sight through the trees. For no reason in particular, he tried to remember where he had met Oelleo—at a party in Bellinbad two summers ago? At Verna's Fourth Twenty in Chom only a few months before? At one of his own sleepover parties in Paris Crater?

He couldn't remember. Had he slept with Oelleo? He had an image of the girl naked, but that could have been from one of the swimming parties or one of the living art displays that had been in vogue last winter. He couldn't remember if he'd gone to bed with the woman. There were so many.

Daeman tried to remember Tobi's Second Twenty celebration in Ulanbat only three days ago. It was a blur—a smear of laughter and sex and drink blending into all the other parties near all the other faxnodes. But when he tried to remember the Dry Valley in . . . what was it called? Antarctica? . . . or the iceberg, or the Golden Gate Bridge above Machu Picchu, or even the stupid redwood forest . . . everything was clear, distinct, sharp.

Daeman climbed down from the carriole and began walking toward the fields. *This is crazy,* he thought. *Crazy, crazy, crazy.* Halfway to the treeline, he broke into a lumbering, clumsy run.

He was out of breath and sweating heavily by the time he reached the far side of the field. The sonie was gone, only a depression in the high grass near a stone wall where it had been.

"God *damn* it," said Daeman, looking up at the evening sky, empty except for the turning equatorial-ring and polar-ring. "Damn it." He sat down heavily on the moss-slick stone wall. The sun was setting behind him. For some reason, he felt like crying.

The sonie came in low over the trees to the north, swooped, and hovered ten feet off the ground.

"I thought you might change your mind," called down Savi. "Want a ride?"

Daeman stood.

They had flown east into darkness, climbing high enough that the stars and the orbital rings illuminated the tops of clouds already glowing from lightning rippling like visible peristalsis through milky interiors. They stopped near the coast that night and slept in a strange treehouse made up of separate little domi-houses connected by platforms and winding staircases. The place had plumbing, but no servitors or voynix, and there were no other people or dwellings nearby.

"Do you have many places like this where you stay?" Harman asked Savi.

"Yes," said the old woman. "Away from your three hundred faxnodes, most of the Earth is empty, you know. At least empty of people. I have favorite places here and there."

They were sitting outside on a sort of dining platform halfway up the tall tree. Below them, fireflies winked on and off in a grassy glade that held an array of huge, ancient, rusted machines that had been mostly reclaimed by the grass and ferns and hillside. Ringlight fell down between the leaves and painted the high grass a soft white. The storms they'd flown over had not reached this far east yet, and the night was warm and clear. Although there were no servitors here, there were freezers with food, and Savi had supervised the cooking of noodles, meat, and fish. Daeman was almost getting used to this odd idea of fixing the food one ate.

Suddenly Harman asked Savi, "Do you know why the post-humans left the Earth and haven't come back?"

Daeman remembered the strange data-vision he'd suffered in the redwood clearing earlier that day. Just the memory made him a bit nauseated.

"Yes," said Savi, "I think I do."

"Are you going to tell us?" asked Harman.

"Not right now," said the old woman. She rose and walked up the winding stairs to a lighted domi ten meters higher up the trunk.

Harman and Daeman looked at each other in the soft light, but they had nothing to say to each other and eventually went off to their own domis to sleep.

They followed the Breach across the Atlantic at high speed, swooped south before reaching land, and paralleled something that Savi called the Hands of Hercules.

"Amazing," said Harman, rising almost to his knees to look to their left as they flew south.

Daeman had to agree. Between a big, slab-sided mountain on the north—which Savi called Gibraltar—and a lower mountain some nine miles to the south, the ocean simply stopped, held out of the deep basin stretching away to the east by a series of huge golden human hands rising from the seabed. Each hand was over five hundred feet tall and the splayed fingers held back the wall of the Atlantic from the dry Mediterranean Basin dropping like a deepening valley into clouds and fogs to the east.

"Why the hands?" asked Daeman as they reached land on the south side of the fog-shrouded Basin and turned east again. "Why didn't the post-humans just use forcefields to hold back the sea, the way they did in the Breach?"

The old woman shook her head. "The Hands of Hercules were here before I was born and the posts never told us why they did it that way. I've always suspected it was just a whim on their part."

"A whim," repeated Harman. It seemed to trouble him.

"Are you sure we can't just fly straight across the Basin?" asked Daeman.

"I'm sure," said Savi. "The sonie would drop out of the sky like a stone."

Through the late afternoon they flew across swamps, lakes, fern forests, and broad rivers above a land that Savi called the Northern Sahara. Soon the swamps dwindled and died and the land became drier, rockier. Herds of huge striped beasts—not dinosaurs, but as large as dinosaurs—moved by the hundreds across grasslands and rocky uplands.

"What are those?" asked Daeman.

Savi shook her head. "I have no idea."

"If Odysseus were here, he'd probably want to kill one and have it for dinner," said Harman.

Savi grunted.

It was late afternoon again when they lost altitude, circled a strange, walled city set on highlands only twenty-five miles from the Mediterranean Basin, and landed on a rocky plain just west of the city.

"What is this place?" asked Daeman. He'd never seen walls or buildings so old, and even from a distance it was unsettling.

"It's called Jerusalem," said Savi.

"I thought we were going down into the Basin to look for spaceships," said Harman.

The old woman got out of the sonie and stretched. She looked very tired, but then, Daeman though, she *had* been driving the sonie for two straight days. "We are," she said. "We'll get transport here. And there's something I want you to see at sunset."

This sounded ominous to Daeman, but he followed her and Harman across the rocky plain, over rubble of what once might have been suburbs or newer sections of the old walled city but which now was a rising plain paved with stones pounded and ground fine as pebbles. She led them up to and though a gate in the wall, keeping up a mostly meaningless narration as they walked. The air was dry and cooling, the low sunlight rich on the ancient buildings.

"This was called the Jaffa Gate," she said, as if that might mean something to them. "This is David Street, and it used to separate the Christian Quarter from the Armenian Quarter."

Harman glanced at Daeman. It was obvious to Daeman that even the learned old man, so proud of his useless ability to read, had never heard the words "Christian" or "Armenian." But Savi was babbling on, pointing out something called the Church of the Holy Sepulchre in the tumbled ruins to their left, and neither man interrupted her with a question until Daeman asked, "Aren't there any voynix or servitors here?"

"Not now," said Savi. "But when my friends Pinchas and Petra were here in the last minutes before the final fax fourteen hundred years ago, there were tens of thousands of voynix suddenly active near the Western Wall. I have no idea why." She stopped walking and looked at each of them. "You understand, don't you, that the voynix popped out of the temporalclastic cloud two centuries before the final fax, but they were immobile—rust and iron statues—not the obedient servants you have now? That's important to remember."

"All right," said Harman, but his voice carried a hint of being patronizing. She was babbling. "But you said you were in an iceberg down near Antarctica when the final fax came," continued Harman. "How do you know where your friends were and what the voynix were doing?"

"Farnet, proxnet, and allnet records," said the old woman. She turned and led them further east down the steet.

Harman glanced at Daeman again, as if to share his concern about her nonsense-talk, but Daeman felt a rush of something—pride? superiority?—as he realized that he knew exactly what she meant when she talked about farnet and proxnet. He looked at his own palm and keyed the finder function, but the glow was blank. What would happen, he wondered, if he visualized the four blue rectangles above three red circles above four green triangles to summon the full-data function the way she'd taught him in the forest glen yesterday?

Savi stopped and spoke as if she'd read his mind. "You don't want to invoke the allnet function here, Daeman. You wouldn't be virtually immersed in energy-microclimate interactions like you were in the forest . . . not here in Jerusalem. You'd be dealing with five thousand years of pain, terror, and virulent anti-Semitism."

"Anti-Semitism?" repeated Harman.

"Hatred of Jews," said Savi.

Harman and Daeman looked at each other with quizzical expressions. The idea made no sense.

Daeman was beginning to be sorry that he'd changed his mind and come along. He was hungry. The sun was setting behind them. He didn't know where he was going to sleep this night, but he suspected that it would be uncomfortable.

"Come," said Savi and led them another block, through stone doorways, down a narrow alley, and out into a space dominated by a tall, blank wall.

"Is this what we came to see?" said Daeman, disappointed. It was a dead end—a courtyard bound around by lower walls, stone buildings, and this one big wall with some sort of round metallic structure just visible atop it. There was no way to get up there from here.

"Patience," said Savi. She squinted at the disappearing sun. "And today's Tisha b'Av, just as it was on the day of the final fax."

Looking as if he was tired of repeating nonsense syllables, Harman said, "Tisha b'Av?"

"The Ninth of Av," said Savi. "A day of lamentation. Both the First and Second Temples were destroyed on Tisha b'Av, and I think the voynix built this blasphemous Third Temple on the Ninth of Av on the day of the final fax." She pointed to the black metal half-dome beyond the wall.

Suddenly there was a rumble so deep that Daeman's bones and teeth rattled. Both he and Harman took a frightened step back, the air filled with ozone and static so thick that the hair on Daeman's head rose and rippled like tall grass in a high wind, and—with an explosive crash faster and louder than a lightning strike—a solid shaft of pure blue, blindingly brilliant light some sixty feet across shot up from the metal half-dome, pierced the evening sky, and disappeared arrow-straight into space, barely missing the orbital e-ring in its eternal rotation to the east.

Candor Chasma

For eight Martian days and eight Martian nights, the dust storm raised waves ten meters high, howled through the rigging, and pounded the little felucca northward toward the leeward shore and death for all hands, including the two moravecs.

The little green men aboard were competent sailors, but they ceased to function at night and now were inert much of the day when the dust clouds overhead blotted out the sun. To Mahnmut, when the LGM found their dark corners beneath decks and curled up in niches to keep from rolling around, it was like sailing in a ship of the dead, like Bram Stoker's *Dracula*, where the ship arrives crewed only by corpses.

The felucca's sails were made of a tough, lightweight polymer rather than canvas, but the ferocity of the wind out of the southeast and the particles and pebbles being blasted at them tore the sheets to shreds. The deck was no longer a safe place to be, and, during a brief interval of sunlight, twenty LGM helped Mahnmut cut a hole in the mid-deck and lower Orphu to the deck below, where Mahnmut constructed a wood and tarp shelter for the Ionian and tucked him away from the pelting wind. Mahnmut himself sensed the airborne grit getting into his seams and works when he spent too much time helping the LGM abovedecks, so he hunkered down on the lower deck near Orphu when he could, making sure his friend was roped and bolted into place as the felucca pitched forty degrees to each side and the water—now mixed with the blowing red sand and as red as blood—forced its way through every crack. A dozen of the forty little green men aboard manned handpumps every hour they were conscious, pumping out the bilge and lower decks, and Mahnmut worked alone on a pump through the long nights.

They had used the wind to good advantage before the sails, rigging, and sea anchor were all damaged, working hard, tacking hard, sailing into the wind, waves crashing over the bow, to get deeper into the central inland sea, obviously all worried about the kilometer-high cliffs behind them to the north, and covering hundreds of kilometers in the first two days of the storm. They were somewhere now between Coprates Chasma and the islands of Melas Chasma, with the huge flooded-canyon complex of Candor Chasma ahead somewhere on their starboard side.

Then the storms grew worse, the skies grew darker, the LGM tucked and tied themselves into secure places belowdecks while they shut down in the sandstorm gloom, and both the bow and stern sea anchors—two elaborate curves of polycanvas dragging on cable trailing hundreds of meters beneath the ship—gave way on the same day. Mahnmut knew from earlier sightings that there were kilometer-high cliffs to their north, and—somewhere—the broad opening to the flooded canyons of Candor Chasma—but the electrostatic charge in the dust storm was defeating his GPS receiver, and it had been two days since he'd had a decent star or sunsight. The cliffs and their doom might be a half hour away for all he knew.

"Is there a chance we might sink?" asked Orphu that afternoon of the fourth day.

"The odds are good," said Mahnmut. He didn't want to lie to his friend, so he tried to couch the phrase as ambiguously as he could.

"Can you swim in this storm?" asked Orphu. He'd understood that the "good" odds in that sentence was bad news for the both of them.

"Not really," said Mahnmut. "But I can swim *under* the waves."

"I'll sink like the proverbial rock," said Orphu with a soft rumble. "How deep did you say Valles Marineris was here?"

"I didn't say," said Mahnmut.

"Well, say now."

"About seven kilometers deep," said Mahnmut, who had echo-sounded it just an hour earlier.

"Would you crush at that depth?" asked Orphu.

"No. I've worked at much deeper pressures. I'm designed for it."

"Would I crush?"

"I . . . don't know," said Mahnmut. In truth, he did not, but he knew that Orphu's moravec line had been designed for the zero pressure of space and for the occasional forays into the upper reaches of a gas giant or the sulfur pits of Io—not for the punishing pressures of a saline sea seven thousand meters deep. Most likely, his friend would be crushed to the size of a crumpled can or simply implode long before he reached three kilometers of depth.

"Is there any chance of putting ashore?" asked Orphu.

"I don't think so," said Mahnmut. "The cliffs I saw were enormous, sheer, with giant boulders at their base. Waves must be crashing fifty or a hundred meters high there now."

"An interesting image," said Orphu. "Is there any chance of the LGM bringing us to safe harbor?"

Mahnmut looked around at the gloomy space on the lower decks. The LGM were tucked away and lashed to the decks like so many chlorophyll dolls, green arms and legs flopping with the wild pitching and rolling of the ship. "I don't know," he said, and let his tone convey his skepticism.

"Then you'll just have to get us through this," said Orphu.

Mahnmut did his damnedest to save them. On the fifth day, with the sky a bloody darkness and the wind howling through the tattered sails, the LGM stowed like cordwood below, and the double-wheel on the rear deck tied to hold the rudder straight, Mahnmut lowered what was left of the sails and brought out the cord and huge needles he'd seen the LGM use to mend the polycanvas; only now he was sewing while the ship was lurching to and fro, fifteen-meter waves striking it side-on, slewing the felucca around, waves washing over the mid-deck.

He rigged a smaller, makeshift sea anchor first, deploying it from the bow anchor cable to bring the bow into the wind again, trying to beat away from the unseen but ever-present lee shore behind them. He'd started work mending the triangular mainsail when the rudder cables belowdeck snapped. The felucca staggered, shipped several huge waves of red water, tore away its weatherhelm, and then slewed around and ran before the wind again, tall waves crashing over the rear deck. Only the crude sea anchor had kept them from capsizing when the rudder went. Mahnmut went to the bow, and there—as the red clouds parted for just a moment and as the felucca rose to the top of the next wind-driven wave—he could see the high cliffs of the north side of Valles Marineris visible through the spume and gloom. The ship would be on the rocks in less than an hour if the steering wasn't fixed and fixed soon.

Mahnmut rigged a rope and went down over the stern to make sure that the rudder was still physically attached—it was, but swinging free on its massive gimbal—and then he climbed the wet rope through crashing waves, crossed the mid-deck, slid down stairways to the second deck, found the emergency steering center there—just a platform with pulleys where the LGM could steer the ship by physically pulling on the tiller ropes if the steering mechanism was damaged above, found the two large cables there slack, scrambled down another ladder to the darkness of the third deck, flicked on his chest and shoulder lamps to illuminate his way, exchanged his manipulatives for cutting edges, and hacked through the deck to where he guessed the tiller ropes had parted. The moravec had no idea if this was the way the ancient Earth feluccas had been rigged—he guessed not—but this large Martian felucca was steered by a double-wheel on the high stern deck, which turned two massive hemp ropes that parted ways, ran along each side of the ship through a system of pulleys, and then came together again to run through this long wooden shaft to the physical tiller that turned the rudder. During the weeks of voyage, he'd wandered the ship, learning the rigging and the layout of the various cable systems. If one or both of the great cables had simply parted—unthreaded by the stress of the storm— he might be able to splice them, but he had to be able to reach them. If they'd snapped farther back toward the tiller where he couldn't reach them, everyone aboard the ship was doomed. Would he jump at the last moment, try to swim beneath the crashing surf past the high cliffs, searching for a calm harbor somewhere along the thousand kilometers of shoreline of Candor Chasma from which to drag himself from the sea? One thing was certain—he couldn't bring Orphu of Io with him. Breaking through into the tiller rope shaft, he switched his beams to bright and looked fore and aft. He couldn't see the cables.

"Everything going all right?" asked Orphu.

Mahnmut jumped at the sound of the radio voice in his ears. "Yes," he said. "Doing a little rudder repairs." *There they were!* The twin cables had snapped, the aft segements were about six meters away in the narrow guide box, the forward segments just visible ten meters forward. He ran back and forth, smashing through the hardwood planking and pulling each section of thigh-thick cable out of its box and dragging them toward the center using every erg of energy in his system.

"You sure everything's all right?" asked Orphu.

He retracted his cutting edges and extended all his manipulatives, setting his fine motor control to *Extra Fine*. He began splicing the strands of thick hemp so rapidly that his metallic fingers became a blur in the shafts of his halogen lights cutting through the third-deck darkness. Water sloshed back and forth past him and over him as the ship rolled backward up each terrible wave and then slid down the wave's rear side, slewing into the trough. Then Mahnmut would brace himself for the next wave crashing into the stern again with the sound and impact of a cannon being fired. And he knew that every wave meant the ship was that much closer to the waiting rocks and cliffs.

"Everything's good," said Mahnmut, fingers flying, weaving strands, using the low-wattage lasers at his wrist to spotweld the metallic fibers that ran through the ragged hemp. "I'm busy right now."

"I'll check back in a few minutes," suggested Orphu.

"Yes," said Mahnmut, thinking, *If I can't regain the steerage, we'll be on the rocks in thirty minutes or so. I'll tell him fifteen minutes before the fact.* "Yes," answered Mahnmut, "do that. Check back in a few minutes."

She wasn't *The Dark Lady*—the crude felucca had no name—but she was sailable and steerable again. Up on the rear deck, his legs and feet braced against the pitch and roll, the storm-lashed cliffs clearly visible less than a kilometer dead ahead, the tatters of canvas he'd sewn into crude sails raised on both masts, Mahnmut grabbed the wheel. The tiller cable held and the rudder responded. He wrestled the ship around into the wind and called Orphu to inform him of the situation. He told the Ionian the truth—they probably had less than fifteen minutes before the ship would be dashed on those rocks, but he was sailing this pig of a ship for all she was worth.

"Well, I appreciate your honesty," said Orphu. "Is there anything that I can do to help?"

Mahnmut, leaning all his weight on the large wheel, turning the ship up the coming wave so as not to capsize her, said, "Any suggestions would be appreciated."

The dust cloud showed no signs of lifting nor the wind of abating. Lines hummed, torn polycanvas flapped, and the bow disappeared in a wall of white foam that struck Mahnmut twenty meters back. Orphu said, "Yet again? What do you here? Shall we give o'er and drown? Have you a mind to sink?"

It took Mahnmut a few seconds to place this. Riding over the next wave in near zero-g, looking back over his shoulder and seeing the thousand-meter cliffs closer, the moravec brought up *The Tempest* in his secondary memory and cried, "A pox o'your throat, you bawling, blasphemous incharitable dog!"

"Work you, then."

"Hang, cur, hang, you whoreson insolent noisemaker," said Mahnmut, shouting over the wind and crash of wave even though the radio comm needed no shouts to carry. "We are less afraid to be drowned than thou art."

"I'll warrant him for drowning," rumbled Orphu, "though the ship were no stronger than a nutshell and as leaky as an unstanched wench . . . Mahnmut? What exactly *is* an 'unstanched wench'?"

"A menstruating woman," said Mahnmut, fighting the wheel to port now, leaning into it. Tons of water washed across him. He could no longer see the cliffs over his shoulder because of the swirling red mist and higher waves, but he could *feel* the rocks behind him.

"Oh," said Orphu. "How embarrassing. Where was I?"

"Lay her a-hold," prompted Mahnmut.

"Lay her a-hold, a-hold! Set her two courses, two courses! Off to sea again! Lay her off!"

"All lost!" recited Mahnmut. "To prayers, to prayers! All lost! . . . Wait a minute!"

"I don't remember 'Wait a minute!' " said Orphu.

"No, *wait a minute.* There's a break in the cliffs ahead—an opening in the coastline."

"Big enough to sail into?" asked Orphu.

"If it's the opening to Candor Chasma," said Mahnmut, "it's a body of water bigger than Conamara Chaos on Europa!"

"I don't remember how large Conamara Chaos was," admitted Orphu.

"Larger than all three of the North American Great Lakes with Hudson Bay thrown in," said Mahnmut. "Candor Chasma is essentially another huge inland sea opening to the north . . . there should be thousands of square kilometers in which to maneuver. No lee shore!"

"Is that good?" asked Orphu, obviously unwilling to get his hopes up.

"It's a chance for survival," said Mahnmut, pulling on lines to fill what was left of the mainsail with wind. He waited until they'd crested the next wave and swung the wheel, turning the heavy ship ponderously to starboard, swinging the bow toward that ever-widening gap in the coastal cliffs. "It's a chance for survival," he said again.

It ended on the afternoon of the eighth day. One hour the dust clouds were still low and scudding, the wind was still raging, and the seas within the great Candor Chasma basin remained white and wild; the next hour, after a final bloody rain, the skies were blue, the seas grew placid, and the little green men stirred from their niches and came up on deck like children rising from a restful nap.

Mahnmut was spent. Even with a recharge trickle from the portable solar cells and occasional jolts from their draining energy cubes, he was worn out organically, mentally, cybernetically, and emotionally.

The LGM seemed to marvel at what remained of the mended sails, at the spliced tiller cables, and at other repairs Mahnmut had carried out in the past three days. Then they got to work crewing the bilge pumps, hosing down the blood-red decks, mending more canvas, caulking the warped hull and bulkhead planks, repairing splintered masts, untangling lines, and sailing the ship. Mahnmut went to the mid-deck and supervised the lifting of Orphu from the soggy lower deck, helped secure his friend to the deck and rig the sun-tarp over him, and then Mahnmut found a warm, sunny place on the mid-deck, out of the way, with a wooden wall behind him and a coil of rope in front ameliorating the agoraphobia a bit, and there he allowed himself to float into a half-stupor. When he shut down his eyes, he could still see the high waves approaching, feel the pitching deck beneath, and hear the howl of wind, despite the calm seas around them now. He peeked. The ship was sailing south again, tacking into the mild southwestern wind, heading back toward the broad opening where Candor Chasma opened into the Valles Marineris at the place called Meles Chasma. Mahnmut shut down his vision again and allowed himself to doze off.

Something touched Mahnmut's shoulder and he started awake. One by one, the forty LGM were filing past him, each green figure touching him on the shoulder as it passed. He reported this to Orphu, using the subvocal channel.

"Perhaps they're expressing their gratitude for your saving them," said the Ionian. "I know I would if I had arms or legs left to pat you with."

Mahnmut said nothing, but he could hardly believe that this was the reason for the contact. He hadn't seen any emotions from the LGM—not even when their translators had withered and died after communicating with him—and he found it hard to believe they were all grateful, even though the LGM were good enough sailors to realize that the ship would have sunk had it not been for Mahnmut's intervention.

"Or maybe they just think you're lucky and they're trying to get some of it to rub off," added Orphu.

Before Mahnmut could express his opinion of this idea, the last of the LGM in line had reached him, but instead of patting the moravec's carbonfiber shoulder and moving on, the little green man went to his knees, lifted Mahnmut's right hand, and set it against his chest.

"Oh, no," Mahnmut groaned to Orphu. "They want to do the communication thing again."

"That's good," said the Ionian. "We have questions to ask."

"The answers aren't worth the death of another of these little green men," said Mahnmut. He was pulling his hand back as hard as the black-eyed LGM was tugging it toward his green chest.

"It might well be worth it," said Orphu. "Even if the LGM unit does undergo anything similar to our idea of death, which I doubt. Besides, it's his initiative. Let him make contact."

Mahnmut quit struggling and let the LGM pull his hand against its chest—*into* its chest.

Once again there was the shocking, sickening feeling of his fingers sliding through flesh and being immersed in the warm, thick saline solution, of his hand contacting and then encircling that pulsing organ the size of a human heart.

"Try holding it a bit less tightly this time," suggested Orphu. "If the communication is truly through molecular packets of organic nanobytes, less surface area of contact might cut down the volume of their thoughts."

Mahnmut nodded, realized that Orphu could not see his nod, but then focused only on the strange vibration from his hand through his arm to his mind as the little green man began the conversation.

WE GIVE YOU
GRATITUDE FOR
SAVING
OUR SHIP.

"You're welcome," Mahnmut said aloud, focusing his thoughts through spoken language at the same time he shared the exchange with Orphu on the tightbeam band. "Who *are* you?" he asked. "What do you call yourselves?"

ZEKS.

The word meant nothing to Mahnmut. He felt the LGM's communication organ pulse in his hand and had the wild urge to release it, to rip his fist from this doomed person's chest—but that would help neither of them now. *Do you know this word—'Zeks'?* Mahnmut asked Orphu.

Just a minute, sent Orphu. *Accessing third-tier memory. Here it is—from* A Day in the Life of Ivan Denisovich. *It was a slang term related to the Russian word "sharashka"—"a special scientific or technical institute staffed with prisoners"—the prisoners of these Soviet labor camps were called zeks.*

Well, sent Mahnmut, *I don't think these chlorophyll-based Martian LGM are prisoners of some short-lived Earth regime from more than two thousand years ago.* The entire exchange with Orphu had taken less than two seconds. To the little green man, he said, "Would you tell us where you're from?"

This time the answer was not in words but images—green fields, a blue sky, a sun much larger than the one in Mars's sky, a distant range of mountains hazy in the thick air. "Earth?" said Mahnmut, shocked.

NOT THE STAR IN THE NIGHT SKY HERE

was the LGM's response.

A DIFFERENT EARTH.

Mahnmut pondered this but did not know how to phrase a clarifying question other than his clumsy "Which Earth, then?"

The little green man answered only with the same images of green fields, distant mountains, an Earthlike view of the sun. Mahnmut could feel this LGM's energy fading, the heartlike organ pulsing with less vitality. *I'm killing him,* he thought in panic.

Ask about the stone faces came Orphu on the commline.

"Who is the man represented in the stone faces?" Mahnmut asked dully.

THE MAGUS.
HE OF THE BOOKS.
LORD OF THE SON OF SYCORAX, WHO BROUGHT US HERE.
THE MAGUS IS MASTER EVEN OF SETEBOS, OUR LORD'S MOTHER'S GOD.

Magus! sent Mahnmut to Orphu.

It means magician, sorcerer—as in the Three Magi . . .

Goddammit, Mahnmut sent fiercely, angrily—he was wasting this dying green person's time. The heart-organ pulsed more weakly with every second that passed. *I know what "magus" means, but I don't believe in magic and neither do you, Orphu.*

But it appears that our LGM do, responded Orphu. *Ask about the dwellers on Olympus.*

"Who are the chariot people on Olympus?" Mahnmut asked dutifully, feeling that he was asking all the wrong questions. But he could think of none better to pose.

MERE GODS,

responded the little green man through bursts of nanobyte images decohering to words.

HELD IN THRALL HERE
BY A BITTER HEART THAT BIDES ITS TIME AND BITES.

"Who is . . ." began Mahnmut but too late—the little green man had suddenly toppled backward, the moravec's hand holding nothing but a desiccated wrapper instead of a pulsing heart now. The LGM began to wither and contract as soon as his body hit the deck. Clear fluid ran across the boards as the little person's anthracite eyes sank into its collapsing green face, then brown face as the skin changed color and wrinkled inward and ceased to be the shape of a man. Other LGM came closer and carried the shriveled brown skin-envelope away.

Mahnmut began shivering uncontrollably.

"We have to find another communicator and finish this conversation," said Orphu.

"Not now," said Mahnmut between shudders.

" 'A bitter heart that bides its time and bites,' " quoted Orphu. "You must have recognized that."

Mahnmut shook his head dully, remembered his friend's blindness, and said, "No."

"But you're the Shakespeare scholar!"

"That's not from Shakespeare," said Mahnmut.

"No," agreed Orphu. "Browning. 'Caliban upon Setebos.' "

"I've never heard of it," said Mahnmut. He managed to get to his feet—two feet—and stagger to the rail. The water curling back alongside the felucca now was more blue than red. Mahnmut knew that if he were human, he'd be vomiting over the side now.

"Caliban!" Orphu all but shouted over the tightbeam line. " 'A bitter heart that bides its time and bites.' The deformed creature, part sea-beast, part man, had a mother who was a witch—Sycorax—and her god was Setebos."

Mahnmut remembered the dying LGM using those words, but he couldn't concentrate on their meaning now. The entire conversation had been like stringing bloody beads on a sinew of living tissue.

"Could the LGM have heard us reciting from *The Tempest* three days ago when you first regained control of the felucca?" asked Orphu.

"Heard us?" echoed Mahnmut. "They don't have ears."

"Then it's us, not them, echoing to this strange new reality," rumbled the Ionian, but with a rumble more ominous than his usual laughter.

"What are you talking about?" asked Mahnmut. Red cliffs had become visible to the west. They rose seven or eight hundred meters above the water of the widening delta of Candor Chasma.

"We seem to be in some mad dream," said Orphu. "But the logic here is consistent . . . in its own mad way."

"What are you *talking* about?" repeated Mahnmut. He was in no mood for more games.

"We know the identity of the stone face now," said Orphu.

"We do?"

"Yes. The magus. He of the books. Lord of the son of Sycorax."

Mahnmut's mind wouldn't work to connect these obvious dots. His system was still filled with the alien surge of nanobytes, a peaceful but dying clarity that was alien to Mahnmut but welcome . . . very welcome. "Who?" he said to Orphu, not caring if his friend thought him dull.

"Prospero," said Orphu.

Achaean Compound,
Coast of Ilium

So far this evening's gone just as Homer said it would.

The Trojans have built their hundreds of watchfires just beyond the Achaean trench—the Greeks' last line of defense down here on the beach—but the Achaeans, beaten so soundly through the long day and evening into night, have forgone even cooking fires in their milling confusion. I've morphed into the form of Old Phoenix and joined the gathering near Agamemnon's tent where the weeping son of Atreus—weeping! This king of Greek kings weeping!—is urging his commanders to take their men and flee.

I've seen Agamemnon use this strategy before—pretending to want to run away so as to rally his men to defiance—but this time, it's obvious, the older king is in earnest. Agamemnon, hair wild, armor bloody, muddy cheeks rivuleted with tears, wants his men to flee for their lives.

It's Diomedes who challenges Agamemnon, all but calling their king a coward and promising, with Sthenelus alone if all the others flee, to "fight on alone until we see the fixed fate of Ilium." The other Achaeans shout support for this bluster, and then it is Old Nestor, citing his years as his passport to speak, who suggests that everyone calm down, have something to eat, post sentries, send men to watch the trench and ramparts, and talk this over before stampeding for the ships, the sea, and home.

And this, just as Homer described, is what they do.

Then the seven chiefs of the guard, led off by Nestor's middle-aged son, Thrasymedes, each take their hundred fighters out to set up new defensive positions between trench and rampart and to light their dinner fires. The handful of Greek fires—joined soon by Agamemnon's feast fire—seems pitiful set against the hundreds of Trojan watchfires just beyond the trench, their sparks leaping high toward the lowering thunderclouds.

Here at Agamemnon's council feast, attended by all the assembled Achaean lords and commanders, the dialogue continues just as Homer reported it. Nestor speaks first, praising Agamemnon's courage and sagacity but telling him, essentially, that he really screwed the pooch when he chose to steal the slave girl Briseis from Achilles.

"You're not lying there, old man," is Agamemnon's honest response. "I was insane. Insane *and* blind to offend Achilles so."

The great king pauses, but no one of the dozens of chiefs hunkered around the central cooking fire rises to argue with him.

"Mad blind I was," continues Agamemnon, "and not even I would deny it. Zeus loves that young man so that Achilles is worth an entire battalion . . . no, an entire army!"

Still no one argues the point.

"And since I *was* made mad and blind by my own rage, I'll set things right now by paying a king's ransom to bring him back to Achaean ranks."

Here the assembled chieftains, Odysseus included, make grumbling sounds of agreement around their mouthfuls of beef and chicken.

"Here before you all assembled, I will count off my gifts in their splendor to purchase young Achilles' love," cries Agamemnon. "Seven tripods untouched by flame, ten talents' weight of gold, twenty servant-shined and new-burnished cauldrons, twelve great stallions, fleet of foot, who've won races and prizes for me . . ."

And blah and blah and blah. Just as Homer wrote. Just as I predicted to you earlier. And, also as I predicted, Agamemnon vows to return Briseis, unbedded, as well as twenty Trojan women—if and after the walls of Ilium fall, of course—and, as a sort of pièce de résistance, the pick of Agamemnon's own three daughters, Chrysothemis, Laodike, and Iphianassa—and as an inveterate scholic, I note the continuity error here with earlier and later tales, especially the absence of Elektra and the possible confusion of Iphigeneia's name, but that's not important right now—and then, for dessert, Agamemnon throws in the "seven citadels," strongly settled.

And, just as Homer has reported, Agamemnon offers these things in lieu of an apology. "All this, I will offer him if he will end his wrath," cries the son of Atreus to his listening commanders. Thunder rumbles and lightning flickers overhead as if Zeus is impatient. "But let Achilles submit to me! Only Hades, the god of death, is as pitiless and relentless as this upstart. Let Achilles yield place and bow to me! I am the elder-born and the kinglier king. I am—I claim—the greater man!"

Well, so much for apologies.

It's raining now. A steady drizzle laced with Zeus's lightning and drunken cries from the Trojan lines less than a hundred yards away drift across the rain-filled ditch and muddy ramparts. I want the embassy to Achilles to be chosen so I can walk up the beach with Odysseus and Ajax and get on with it. This is the most important night of my life—at least of this second life as a scholic—and I keep rehearsing what I will say to Achilles.

If you will change all of our fates, you must find the fulcrum.

I think I've found it. Or at least *a* fulcrum. Certainly nothing will be the same for the Greeks and gods and Trojans—or for me—if I do what I plan to do this night. When old Phoenix speaks at this embassy to Achilles, it will be not only to end Achilles' wrath but to unite his cause with Hector's—to turn both Greeks and Trojans against the gods themselves.

Nestor suddenly cries out, "Son of Atreus, generous marshal and lord of men, our Agamemnon—no man, not even our Prince of Men, Peleus' son, Achilles, could spurn such gifts. Come, we'll send a small embassy of carefully chosen men to carry these offers and our love to Achilles' tent this night. Quick, whomever my eye lights on, let these take the duty!"

Robed in old Phoenix's flesh, I step to the edge of the circle near Big Ajax, making myself visible to Nestor.

"First of all," cries Nestor, "let Ajax the Great take up this task. And with Big Ajax, let our tactful and brilliant king, Odysseus, add his counsel. For heralds—I choose Odius and Eurybates to escort our embassy. Water for all their hands now! And a moment of prayerful silence while we all beseech Zeus in our own manner—that the great god will show us mercy and let Achilles smile on our entreaty!"

I stand in shock while the ablutions are administered and the commanders bow their heads in silent prayer.

Nestor ends the silence by urging on the embassy—the embassy of four, not five!—by shouting at the leaving men, "Try hard now! Bring him around and make him pity us, our invincible, pitiless Achilles!"

And the two ambassadors and the two heralds leave our circle of firelight and walk away up the beach.

I wasn't chosen! Phoenix wasn't chosen! He hasn't even been mentioned! Homer was wrong! The events of this Ilium have just wildly diverged from the events of the *Iliad*, and suddenly I'm as blind to future events as Helen and the other players here, as blind as the gods above, as blind as Homer himself, damn his missing eyes!

Stumbling on my old, skinny legs—on useless *Phoenix'* old, skinny legs—I shove my way through the circle of Greek chieftains and run along the crashing water's edge to try to catch up to Big Ajax and Odysseus.

I catch up to the two halfway down the dark beach to Achilles' compound. Ajax and Odysseus are alone, speaking softly as they walk along the wet sand. They stop when I come up to them.

"What is it, Phoenix, son of Amyntor?" asks Big Ajax. "I was surprised to see you at the king's feast, since word is that you've stayed close to your Myrmidon healers in recent months. Has Agamemnon sent you after us with some final admonition?"

Gasping as if I'm actually as old as Phoenix, I say, "Greetings, noble Ajax and royal Odysseus—in truth, Lord Agamemnon has sent me to join you in your embassy to Achilles."

Big Ajax looks perplexed at this but Odysseus looks downright suspicious. "Why would Agamemnon choose you for this duty, honorable elder? Why would you even be in Agamemnon's camp this dangerous night when the Trojans bay across our ditch like hungry dogs?"

I have no answer for the second question, so I try to bluff my way through the first. "Nestor suggested that I join you to help gain Achilles' ear, and Agamemnon thought it a wise suggestion."

"Come then," says Ajax the Greater. "Join us, Phoenix."

"But do not speak unless I tell you to," says Odysseus, still squinting at me as if I were the impostor I truly am. "Nestor and Agamemnon may have seen some reason for you to visit Achilles' tent, but there can be no reason for you to speak."

"But . . ." I begin. I have no argument. If I'm not allowed to speak, after Odysseus but before Ajax as Homer had it, I lose all leverage, lose the fulcrum, I fail. If I'm not allowed to speak, the events of this night will diverge from the *Iliad*. But, I realize, they already have diverged. Phoenix should have been chosen by Nestor, his presence in the embassy seconded by Agamemnon. *What's going on here?*

"If you join us in Achilles' tent, Old Phoenix," warns Odysseus, "you must wait in the foyer with the heralds, Odius and Eurybates, and enter or speak only on my command. These are my conditions."

"But . . ." I begin again and see the uselessness of any protest. If Odysseus becomes more suspicious and marches me back to Agamemnon's camp, my ruse will be up, and with it, my entire plan to turn the mortals against the gods. "Yes, Odysseus," I say, nodding like the old horseman and tutor Phoenix was. "As you command."

Odysseus and Big Ajax walk along the crashing sea and I follow.

I've talked about Achilles' tent and you might picture some sort of backyard camping tent, but the son of Peleus lives in a canvas compound that's closer in size to the main tent of a traveling circus I recall from my childhood . . . recall from what I *am beginning to remember* from my childhood. Thomas Hockenberry had a life, it seems, and after almost a decade here, some of the memories are leaking back into my mind.

This night, the hundreds of tents and campfires around Achilles' main tent paint as chaotic a scene as the rest of the mile-long Achaean encampment, with some of Achilles' loyal Myrmidons packing his black ships for departure, others looking to the ramparts to defend their area of beach should the Trojans win through before dawn, and still others gathering around campfires much as Agamemnon's commanders had been.

Odius and Eurybates have announced our arrival to the captains of the guard, and Achilles' personal guards snap to attention and allow us into the inner compound. We leave the beach and climb the low dune to the rise where Achilles' main tent is situated. I follow the two Achaeans in—Big Ajax ducking his head to go through the lower inner entrance, Odysseus, almost a foot shorter than his comrade, entering without having to duck his head. Odysseus turns and gestures me to a place in the foyer near the entrance. I can see and hear what is happening within, but I won't be part of it if I stay here.

Achilles, just as Homer described, is playing his lyre and singing an epic song of ancient heroes not so different than the *Iliad* itself. The lyre, I know, was a spoil of war, won when Achilles conquered Thebe and murdered Andromache's father, Eetion. Hector's wife had grown up listening to this same silver lyre being played in the hearth of her royal home there. Now Patroclus, Achilles' dearest friend, sits across from him, waiting for Achilles to finish his part of the song so that Patroclus can sing the remaining lines.

Achilles quits plucking the instrument and stands in surprise as Ajax and Odysseus enter. Patroclus scrambles to his feet as well.

"Welcome!" cries Achilles. He gestures to Patroclus. "Look, dear friends have come—I must be needed badly to bring them here—and my dearest friends in all the Achaean ranks, even in my anger I acknowledge this."

He leads the two emissaries to low couches and throws rich purple carpets across the cushioned frames. To Patroclus, Achilles says, "Come, son of Menoetius, a bigger wine bowl. Here . . . put it here. We'll mix stronger wine. A cup for each of my noble guests—since these men who have come under my roof are those I love the best."

I watch the unfolding of these surprisingly gracious rituals of heroic hospitality. Patroclus sets a heavy chopping block next to the fire and lays out the chines of a sheep and a goat, next to the fat-marbled back cut of a pig. Automedan, friend and charioteer of both Achilles and Patroclus, holds the slabs of meat while Achilles cuts off prize strips, salts each, and sets them on spits. Patroclus builds up the fire for a minute and then scatters the embers and sets the spits across the hottest part of the fire, salting each strip again.

I realize that I'm famished. If I am called in to speak now—if all of our fates depended on it—I couldn't do it because my mouth is watering so.

As if hearing my stomach rumbling, Achilles looks out into the foyer and almost freezes with surprise. "Phoenix! Honored mentor, noble horseman! I thought you ill in your tent these weeks last. Come in, come in!"

With that the young hero comes into the foyer, embraces me, and leads me into the firelit center of his home, the air smelling now of roasting mutton and pork. Odysseus shoots daggers from his eyes, silently warning me to keep silent during the discussions.

"Be seated, beloved Phoenix," says Achilles, this old man's former student. But he sets me on red cushions, not purple, and farther from the fire than is either Odysseus or Ajax. Achilles is loyal to his old friends, but he understands protocol.

Patroclus brings in wicker baskets of fresh-baked bread and Achilles rakes the meat from their spits and sets the steaming portions out on wooden platters. "Let us sacrifice to the gods, dear friends," Achilles says, nodding to Patroclus, who tosses the firstlings—the strips of meat chosen as offerings—into the flames.

"Now, eat," commands Achilles, and all of us set into the bread and wine and meat with a will.

Even while I'm chewing and enjoying the food, my mind is racing: How do I get to make the speech I have to make to change the fates of everyone here, of the gods themselves? It seemed so simple an hour earlier, but Odysseus hasn't bought my statement that Agamemnon sent me along as an emissary. In the poem, Odysseus speaks soon—relaying Agamemnon's offer to Achilles—then Achilles replies in what I've suggested to my students is the most powerful and beautiful speech in the *Iliad*, then Phoenix gives his long, three-part monologue—part personal history, part the parable of the "Prayers," and part allegory of Achilles' situation in the myth of Meleagros—a *paradeigma* where a mythical hero waits too long to accept offered gifts and to fight for his friends. All in all, Phoenix's speech is by far the most interesting entreaty from the three ambassadors sent to persuade Achilles. And, according to the *Iliad*, it is Phoenix's argument that persuades the angry Achilles to back away from his vow to sail away the next morning. By the time Ajax speaks, after me, Achilles will agree to stay around the next day to see what the Trojans do and, if necessary, to protect his own ships from the enemy.

My plan is to repeat parts of Phoenix' long speech from memory, then veer away to insert my own suggestions. But I see Odysseus frowning at me from across the tent and know that I'm not going to get the chance.

And what if I do? I've considered the fact that the gods will be monitoring this assembly—it's one of the key elements of the *Iliad*, after all, although perhaps only Zeus knows that in advance. But even without advance knowledge, some of the gods and goddesses must be watching this meeting in their video pools and on their image-tabula. Zeus has ordered them not to intervene this day, and most are complying with his ultimatum, but that must make their curiosity about the embassy to Achilles even greater. If Achilles agrees to Agamemnon's bribe price and the power of Odysseus' persuasion this night, then Hector's offensive and perhaps even the will of Zeus himself will be thwarted. Achilles is a one-man army.

So if I suborn him to heresy this night as I've planned, if I try to rally Achilles to war against the gods, won't Zeus intervene at once, blasting this tent and all its occupants? And even if Zeus holds back his wrath, I can imagine Athena or Hera or Apollo or one of the other interested parties swooping down to destroy this . . . "Phoenix" . . . for suggesting a course of action so inimical to their ends. I've imagined these things, of course, but trusted the QT medallion and the Hades Helmet to save me.

But so what if I save myself by fleeing again, but these heroes end up killed or dissuaded by the wrath of the gods? The whole plan will have been for nothing and my existence revealed to all the gods. The Hades Helmet and QT medallion won't help me then—they'll track me to the ends of the earth, to prehistorical Indiana if need be. And that, as they say, will be that.

Perhaps Odysseus has done me a service by not letting me speak.

Then why am I here?

When we've all feasted well, empty platters pushed aside and only crusts of bread remaining in the baskets, and are ready for our third cup of wine, I see Ajax nod ever so slightly to Odysseus.

The great strategist takes the hint and lifts his cup in a toast to Achilles.

"Your health, Achilles!"

We all drink and the young hero bows his blond head in acknowledgment.

"I see that we lack nothing for this feast," continues Odysseus, his voice surprisingly low and soft, almost mellifluous. Of all the great Achaean captains, this bearded man is the softest spoken and the most devious. "We lack nothing either in Agamemnon's camp nor here in the house of the son of Peleus. But it's not the bounteous feast that's on our minds this stormy night—no, it's a terrible disaster, bred and willed by the gods, that we're looking on and fearing tonight."

Odysseus goes on, slowly, smoothly, never rushing, rarely reaching for rhetorical effect. He describes the rout of the afternoon, the Trojans' victory, the Achaeans' panic and will to flee, and Zeus's complicity.

"These brazen Trojans and their boasting allies have pitched their tents within a stone's throw of our ships, Achilles," continues Odysseus, speaking as if Achilles has not already heard all of this from Patroclus, Automedan, and his other friends. Or simply watched it from the hill outside his tent.

"Nothing can stop them now," continues Odysseus. "That's their boast, and thousands of their watchfires back that boast with threat tonight. They plan to bring those flames to our ships at first light, then hurl themselves at our blackened hulls, slaughtering the survivors. And Zeus, son of Kronos, sends them signs of encouragement, firebolts crashing on our left wing, all the while Hector rages on furiously, drunk on his strength. He fears nothing, Achilles, neither man nor god. Hector is like a rabid, frenzied dog this day, and the demons of *katelepsis* have him in their grip."

Odysseus pauses. Achilles says nothing. His face shows nothing. His friend Patroclus is watching Achilles' face all this time, but the hero does not even glance his way. Achilles would make one hell of a poker player.

"Hector is eager for the dawn," Odysseus continues, voice even softer now, "since, at first light, he threatens to shear the horns from our ship sterns, light those ships with consuming fire, and—with all our comrades trapped against the burning hulls, rout and kill and cut down us Achaeans to the man. A nightmare, Achilles—I fear it with all my heart—I fear the gods will give Hector the means to carry out these threats and our destiny will be to die here on the plains of Ilium, far from the horse-pasturing hills of Argos."

Achilles says nothing when Odysseus pauses again. The dying embers crack. Somewhere several tents away, someone is playing a slow dirge on a lyre. From the opposite direction comes the drunken laugh of a soldier who obviously thinks himself doomed.

"Up with you then, Achilles," says Odysseus, voice rising at last. "Now, rise with us *now,* eleventh hour though it be, if you *want* to rescue the doomed sons of the Achaeans from Trojan slaughter."

And now Odysseus is asking Achilles to put aside his wrath and describes Agamemnon's offer, using the same words Agamemnon had chosen to list his unfired tripods and dozen racehorses and so on, and so forth. I think he lingers a bit too long on the description of unbedded Briseis and the Trojan maidens waiting to be ravished and Agamemnon's three beautiful daughters, but he ends with a passionate peroration, reminding Achilles of his own father's advice, Peleus' admonition to value friendship over quarrels.

"But if the son of Atreus is too much hated in your heart for you to accept these gifts," finishes Odysseus, "at least take pity on all the rest of us Achaeans. Join our fight and save us now and we will honor you like a god. Also, remember that if your wrath keeps you from fighting—if your disdain sends you home over the wine-dark sea before this war with Troy is finished—you'll never know if you could have killed Hector. This is your chance for that *aristeia,* Achilles, since Hector's murderous frenzy will bring him to close combat tomorrow after all these years of his aloofness behind the high walls of Ilium. Stay and fight with us, noble Achilles, and now, for the first time, you can meet Hector head-on in combat."

I have to admit, Odysseus' speech has been one hell of a performance. I might be persuaded, if I were the young demigod lounging on the cushions six feet from me in the tent. We all sit silently until Achilles sets down his cup of wine and answers.

"Noble son of Laertes, seed of Zeus, resourceful tactician, dear Odysseus—I have to tell you frankly and honestly how I feel and how all this will end, so you won't keep crowding me, one embassy after another, coaxing and murmuring one after the other like a line of cooing doves.

"As much as I detest the doorways of Death, Hades' dark gates, so do I detest a man who says one thing with his mouth but hides another in his heart."

I blink at that. Is this a deep dig at Odysseus, "resourceful tactician," known by all Achaeans as someone who will bend the truth when it serves his purposes? Perhaps, but Odysseus does not react in any way, so I keep Phoenix's expression neutral.

"I'll say this clearly," continues Achilles. "Will Agamemnon win me back, persuade me with all these . . . *gifts*?" The hero all but spits this last word. "No. Not for all the world. Nor could all the armies and captains of the Achaeans convince me to return, since their gratitude is too little and too late . . . Where was the gratitude of the Achaeans during my years upon years of warring against their enemies, battle after battle, year after year in harness, fighting every day with no end in sight?

"Twelve cities I've stormed from my ships; eleven I've claimed by wetting the fertile loam of Ilium's lands with Trojan blood. And from all these cities I dragged heaps of plunder, mountains of loot, great, crying herds of beautiful women, and always I gave the best of the lot to Agamemnon—that *son of Atreus,* safe in his racing black ships or skulking far behind the lines. And he would take it all . . . all and more.

"Oh, yes . . . sometimes he'd hand out scraps to you and the other commanders, but always he kept the lion's share for himself. To all of you, whose loyalty he needs to prop up his regime, he *gives*—only from me does he *take*—including the slave girl who would have been my bride. Well, fuck it and fuck him and fuck her, my dear comrades. *Let* Agamemnon bed Briseis . . . to the hilt, if the old man is up to it."

With his grievances aired anew, Achilles goes on to question why his Myrmidons and the Achaeans and the Argives should even be fighting this war. "For Helen with her loose and lustrous hair?" he asks contemptuously, saying that Menelaus and his brother Agamemnon are not the only men here with missing wives, reminding Odysseus of his own wife, Penelope, left alone these ten long years.

And I think of Helen sitting up in bed just these few nights ago, her loose and lustrous hair hanging over her shoulders, her pale breasts white in the starlight.

It's hard to pay attention to Achilles, even though this speech is as wonderful and surprising as Homer reported. In this short talk, Achilles undermines the very heroic code that makes him a superhero, the code of conduct that makes him a god in the eyes of his men and equals.

Achilles says that he has no ambition to battle glorious Hector—neither will to kill him nor will to die by his hand.

Achilles says that he is taking his men and sailing at dawn, leaving the Achaeans to their fates—leaving them to Hector's mercy when the Trojan and his hordes cross the ditch and rampart tomorrow.

Achilles says that Agamemnon is a dog armored in shamelessness and that he wouldn't marry one of the old king's daughters even if she somehow ended up with Aphrodite's looks and Athena's crafts.

Then Achilles says something truly amazing—he confesses that his mother, the goddess Thetis, told him that two fates would bear him on to his day of death: one where he stays here, lays siege to Troy, kills Hector, but then dies himself within a few days. In that direction, his mother told him, lies eternal glory in the memories of men and gods alike. His other fate lies in flight—sailing home, losing his pride and glory, but living a long, happy life. The fates are his to choose, his mother told him years ago.

And, Achilles tells us now, he chooses life. Here this . . . this . . . hero, this mass of muscle and testosterone, this living-legend demigod . . . he chooses life over glory. It's enough to make Odysseus squint in disbelief and Ajax gape.

"So Odysseus, Ajax, brothers both," he says, "go back to the great commanders of Achaea. Report my answer. Let *them* figure out how to save the hollow ships and save the men who will be pressed back to these very ships' burning hulls at this time tomorrow. As for silent Phoenix, here . . ."

I jump three inches off the red cushion when he turns toward me. I've been so lost in preparing what I have to say and the moral implications of it that I've forgotten that we're in a discussion here.

"Phoenix," says Achilles, smiling indulgently, "while Odysseus and Ajax here must report back to their *master,* you are free to spend the night here with Patroclus and me, and voyage home with us come the dawn. But only if Phoenix wishes . . . I would never force any man to go."

This is my chance to speak. Ignoring Odysseus' scowl, I look around, stand awkwardly, clear my throat to begin Phoenix' long speech. How does it start? All those years of teaching and studying it, of learning the nuance of every Greek word, and now my mind is a blank.

Ajax stands. "While that old fool tries to decide whether to run away with you or not, Achilles, I'll tell you that you're as much of a fool as old Phoenix!"

Achilles, the man-killer who will brook no insult to his person, the hero who will let all of his Achaean friends be murdered rather than suffer indignities over a slave girl from Agamemnon, merely smiles and cocks an eyebrow at Ajax's direct insult.

"Giving up glory and twenty beautiful women for one woman you can't even have . . . bah!" cries Ajax and turns away. "Come, Odysseus, this golden boy has never drunk from the teat of human friendship. Let's leave him to his wrath and deliver our dark message to the waiting

Achaeans. Tomorrow's sunrise is coming fast enough, and I for one need some sleep before the fight. If I'm going to die tomorrow, I don't want to die sleepy."

Odysseus nods, stands, nods again in the direction of Achilles, and follows Big Ajax out of the tent.

I'm still standing with my mouth agape, ready to deliver Phoenix's long, three-part speech—that clever speech!—with my own clever amendments and hidden agendas.

Patroclus and Achilles stand, stretch, and exchange glances. Obviously they've been expecting this embassy and both men knew Achilles' shocking answer in advance.

"Phoenix, old father, loved by the gods," Achilles says warmly, "I don't know what really brought you here this stormy night, but well I remember when I was a lad and you'd lift me and carry me off to bed after lessons. Stay here this night, Phoenix. Patroclus and Automedon will prepare a soft bed for you. In the morning, we'll sail for home and you can come . . . or not."

He gestures and goes into his sleeping quarters in the back of the tent and I stand here like the fool I am, speechless in every sense, stunned at this wild veering away from the plotline of the *Iliad*.

Achilles has to be persuaded to stay, even if he doesn't join in the fighting, so the *Iliad* works itself out this way—the Trojans winning again and the Greeks in full retreat with all of their great commanders wounded—Odysseus, Agamemnon, Menelaus, Diomedes, all of them—then, feeling sympathy for his friends while knowing that Achilles will never join the fight, Patroclus will put on Achilles' golden armor and rout the Trojans back until, in single combat with Hector, Patroclus is killed, his body violated and desecrated. *That* will bring Achilles out of his tent, filled with killing wrath, thus sealing the fate of Hector and Ilium and Andromache and Helen and all the rest of us.

He's really leaving? I can't quite grasp this. Not only didn't I find the fulcrum and change things, now the entire *Iliad* has run off the rails. More than nine years I've been a scholic here, watching and observing and reporting to the muse and never once has there been a deep rift between the events in this war and Homer's reporting in the poem. Now . . . *this*. If Achilles leaves, which he shows every indication of doing come the dawn, the Achaeans will be defeated, their ships burned, Ilium saved, and Hector, not Achilles, will be the great hero of the epic. It seems unlikely that Odysseus' *Odyssey* will ever happen . . . and certainly not the way it's sung now. Everything has changed. *Just because the real Phoenix wasn't here to give his real speech? Or have the gods been tamper-*

ing with this fulcrum before I had a chance to? I'll never know. My chance to persuade Achilles and Odysseus in council, my clever plan, is lost forever.

"Come, old Phoenix," Patroclus says, taking my arm as if I'm a child, leading me to a side room in the great tent where my cushions and coverlets are laid out. "It's time to go to bed. Tomorrow's another day."

Jerusalem

"What is it?" asked Harman. He and Daeman were standing in the shadow of the Western Wall in Jerusalem, just a few steps behind Savi, and all three were staring up at the solid beam of blue light that stabbed vertically into the darkening sky.

"I think it's my friends," said the old woman. "All nine thousand one hundred and thirteen of my friends—all the old-styles that were swept up in the final fax."

Daeman looked at Harman and realized that they were both doubtful about Savi's mental condition.

"Your friends?" said Daeman. "That's a blue light."

Savi tore her gaze away from the beam—it was illuminating the top of the ancient buildings and walls around them now, bathing everything in blue glow as the daylight faded further—and she looked at them with what might have been a rueful smile. "Yes. That beam of blue light. My friends." She gestured for them to follow and began leading them away from the courtyard, away from the wall back the way they came, away from the base of the shaft of blue light.

"The posts told us that the final fax was a way of storing us while they cleaned up the world," continued Savi, her voice soft but still echoing in the narrow alleyways here. "The plan was, they explained, to reduce our codes—we were all fax codes to the post-humans, even then, my friends—reduce our codes and put us in a continuous neutrino loop for ten thousand years while they tidied up the planet."

"What does that mean?" said Harman. "Tidy up the planet?"

They walked under a long archway and Daeman could just barely see Savi's face as she smiled again. "Things got messy toward the end of the Lost Age," she said. "Messier after the rubicon. Then came the Demented Times. Freelance ARNists were bringing back dinosaurs and Terror Birds and long-extinct botanic forms, screwing up the planet's ecology even as the biosphere and datasphere were beginning to merge into the self-aware noosphere—the logosphere. The post-humans had already fled to their rings by then—the Earth's sentient noosphere didn't trust them any longer—and for good reason, the posts were experimenting with quantum teleportation, opening portals onto places they didn't understand, opening doors they shouldn't have opened."

Harman stopped as they came out onto a broader street. "Would you make sense, Savi? We don't understand two-thirds of what you're talking about."

"How could you?" asked Savi, looking at Harman with an expression of either pain or severe displeasure. "How could you understand anything? No history. No technology. No books."

"We have books," said Harman, his voice defensive.

Savi laughed.

"What does all this talk of dinosaurs and noospheres have to do with the blue beam?" asked Daeman.

Savi sat on a low wall. The breeze had come up and it whistled through broken tiles on the rooftops. The air was cooling quickly. "They needed to get us out of the way while they cleaned things up," repeated Savi. "A torus of neutrinos, they said. No mass. No muss. No fuss. Ten thousand years for them to tidy up the earth. Less than a blink of an eye for us old-styles. So they said."

"But they left you behind," said Harman.

"Yes."

"By accident?"

"I doubt it," said the old woman. "Very little the posts did was by accident. Perhaps they had some purpose for me. Perhaps they were punishing me for digging into histories better left buried. That's what I was, you know—an historian. Cultural historian." She laughed again for no reason that Daeman could fathom.

"So neutrinos are blue?" asked Daeman. He was determined to get a straight answer.

She laughed again. "I very much doubt it. I don't think neutrinos have any color . . . or charm. But that blue beam appears every *Tisha b'Av*, every Ninth of Av, and something tells me that the rest of the old-style humans—all my friends—are stored and coded in that blue beam. I don't think that machine is generating the beam. I think the Earth passes through the neutrino beam every year at this point on its orbit, and that machine merely makes the beam visible."

"But it hasn't been ten thousand years," said Harman. "Only fourteen hundred, you say, since the final fax."

Savi nods tiredly. "And things haven't been tidied up much since the final fax, have they, my young friends?" She stands, lifts her backpack, and starts down the narrow street before suddenly freezing.

"A voynix!" says Daeman. "Now we won't have to walk back to the sonie. We'll have it fetch a carriole and . . ."

The voynix, an iron-and-leather silhouette in the western archway ahead of them, suddenly retracted its manipulatives and clicked cutting blades into place. Then it charged directly at them, running along the side of the building on all fours like a frenzied spider.

Savi had been wildly rummaging in her pack since Daeman had pointed, and now she brought out the black plastic-and-metal device—a gun, she'd called it—and aimed it at the charging voynix.

Daeman was too shocked to move. He was the closest to the scuttling voynix, still eight feet up the wall and loping on all fours, but the creature seemed focused on Savi and was hurtling right past Daeman. Suddenly the evening air was torn by a noise—RRRIIIIPPPPPPPPPPP—as if wooden paddles were being dragged against stone slats, and the wall flew apart in a spray of masonry chips, the voynix was thrown backward and down onto the cobblestones, and Savi stepped forward, aimed, and fired again.

Scores of fingertip-sized holes appeared in the voynix's carapace and metallic hood. Its right arm flew up as if it was going to throw something at them, but then more flechettes struck it and the arm became unhinged, tore off, flew backward. The voynix struggled to its feet, one cutting blade still whirring.

Savi shot it again, almost severing it at the waist. Its blue, milky internal fluid spattered the walls and paving stones. What remained of the voynix fell, twitched, and lay still.

Harman and Daeman cautiously moved closer, trying not to step in the blue fluid or on pieces of the creature. This was the second voynix they'd seen destroyed in two days.

"Come on," said Savi, pulling an empty crystal flechette clip from her gun and slapping in a replacement. "If there are more around, we're in serious trouble. We have to get to the sonie. And quickly."

Savi led them down a narrow street, turned into a narrower alley, then turned again into something smaller than an alley—a crack between stone buildings. They emerged into a wide, dusty courtyard, went under a stone arch, and came into a smaller courtyard.

"Hurry," whispered Savi. She led them up an outside staircase, across a rooftop terrace duned with dust, and then up a rotted wooden ladder past shuttered windows to a higher rooftop.

"What are we doing?" whispered Harman as the three came out into the cool night air atop the building. "Don't we have to get back to the sonie?"

"I'll call it to us," said Savi. She went to one knee by the low rooftop wall and activated her proxnet function, shielding the glow above her palm. Harman crouched next to her.

Daeman remained standing. The air up here was cool after the heat of the cobblestoned streets and narrow alleys and the view was interesting from this point on the hill. To their right stabbed the blue beam, bathing all the domes and rooftops and streets in its pale light. It was dark now and stars were visible across the sky. The city had no lights burning, but ancient domes and spires and some arches gleamed to the blue light. Savi had told them that the walled compound on the hill where the beam burned was called Haram esh-Sharif, or Temple Mount, and the two domed structures at the base of the beam machine were the Dome of the Rock and the Al-Aksa Mosque.

"*Itbah al-Yahud!*" came a sudden, shrill, amplified cry from the streets behind them. The cry was repeated from the warren of narrow streets to their west, between them and the sonie.

"*Itbah al-Yahud!*"

Savi looked up from her palm display.

"What is *that*?" asked Harman in a shrill whisper. "Voynix don't speak."

"No," said Savi. "It's coming from the ancient, automated muezzin call-to-prayer speakers on all the mosques."

"*Itbah al-Yahud!*" came the tremulous but urgent voice echoing from all over the dark city. "*Al-jihad!*" cried the amplified voice. "*Itbah al-Yahud!*"

"Damn!" said Savi, looking at her palm display. "No wonder it isn't responding to the remote."

"What?" Daeman and Harman both stepped closer, crouching to see the rectangular display floating inches above her palm. The view was of the front of the sonie where they had landed it. The fields of rocks and walled city glowed greenly in the camera's low-light vision. Closer, looming over the lens, scores of voynix were milling around the sonie, throwing their bodies onto the machine, battering it with boulders and stacking huge rocks on top of it.

"They defeated the forcefield and broke something," whispered Savi. "The sonie's not coming to us."

"*Allahu akbar!*" cried the echoing, amplified, trembling voices from all points of the low-roofed city. "*Itbah al-Yahud! Itbah al-Yahud!*"

The three walked to the edge of the rooftop. For a second, Daeman thought that the buildings and cobblestoned streets and walled court-yards were trembling, crumbling, dissolving in the reflected blue light, but then he realized that things were crawling across the stone and domes and walls and rooftops. Thousands of things—like an invasion of roaches scrambling wildly toward the blue light. But then Daeman real-ized how far away the shimmering, crawling buildings were, computed the scale, and realized that it wasn't roaches or spiders scrambling and scrabbling toward them, but voynix.

"*Itbah al-Yahud!*" screamed the metallic voice from everywhere. The syllables echoed back from the Mount without losing their demented urgency.

"What does that *mean?*" asked Daeman.

Savi was watching the blue-lighted voynix scrabbling closer over rooftops and through the maze of narrow, winding streets. The wave of huge insectoid shapes was less than two city blocks away now, close enough that they could all hear the scratch and tear of cutting blade and sharp manipulators on stone and tile. Savi turned slowly. Her face looked older than ever in the pulsing blue light.

"*Itbah al-Yahud,*" she repeated softly. "*Kill the Jew.*"

Achilles' Tent

I have to kill Patroclus.

That realization comes to me like a whisper in the night as I lie here in the Myrmidon encampment, in Achilles' tent, wrapped in the shell of Phoenix' old body.

I have to kill Patroclus.

I've never killed anyone. Jesus Christ, I protested the Vietnam War as a college student, couldn't put the family dog to sleep—had to have my wife take her to the vet—and considered myself a pacifist for most of my academic life. I've never *hit* another man, for Christ's sake.

I *have* to kill Patroclus.

It's the only way. I trusted that rhetoric would do it—old Phoenix's revised rhetoric—that rhetoric would persuade the man-killer Achilles into meeting with Hector, into ending this war, into burying the hatchet.

Yeah, right in my forehead.

Achilles' decision to leave—to return to a long life of pleasure but little glory—is deeply shocking to this scholic, to any student of the *Iliad*, but it makes sense. Honor is still more important than life to Achilles, but after Agamemnon's insults, he sees no honor in killing Hector and then being killed in turn. Odysseus—that ultimate rhetorician—was eloquent in his explanation and evocation of how the living Achaeans and countless generations after would honor Achilles' memory, but it's not *their* honor that Achilles cares about. Only *his* sense of honor counts here, and there will be no honor now for him in killing Agamemnon's enemies and dying for Agamemnon's and Menelaus' objectives. Only Achilles' honor counts, and he'd rather sail for home in a few hours and live the life of a lesser mortal, forsaking his chance to be part of this band of brothers twenty centuries before Prince Hal and Agincourt, than compromise any more honor here on the bloody plains of Ilium.

I see that now. Why didn't I see it before? If Odysseus could not convince Achilles to fight—Odysseus of the crafty ways and silver tongue—why did I think I'd succeed? I was a fool. Homer made me a fool, but I was still a fool.

I have to kill Patroclus.

Not long after Odysseus and Big Ajax left, just after the torches and tripod fires were extinguished in the main room of Achilles' tent, I heard slave girls being escorted in for the pleasure of Achilles and Patroclus. I'd never seen either of these slave girls, but I knew their names—Homer leaves no one nameless in the *Iliad*. Achilles' girl (I couldn't have used that word while teaching at Indiana University in my other life or the Political Correctness Police would have had my job, but here it doesn't seem appropriate to call these giggling sex toys "women") was named Diomede, Phorbas' daughter from the isle of Lesbos—although she was no lesbian. Patroclus' main squeeze was named Iphis. I almost laughed out loud as I caught a glimpse of them through the folds in the tent door—Achilles, who is tall and blond and statuesque and chiseled with muscle, preferred the tiny, stocky, brunette and large-breasted Diomede; Patroclus, who is much shorter than Achilles and dark-haired, had opted for the tall, blonde, thin, small-busted Iphis. For half an hour or so, I could hear the women's laughter, the men's rough conversation, and then the moans and cries from all four in Achilles' sleeping chamber. Obviously the hero and his pal had no qualms about having sex in the same room with each other, even commenting on it while it was occurring, which makes me think more of Bloomington, Indiana, male Realtors or lodge brothers having a weekend in the big city than it does of the noble warriors of this heroic age. *Barbaric.*

Then the girls left—giggling again—and there was silence except for muttered exchanges between the guards outside the tent and the crackle of brazier flames keeping those guards warm. That and monstrous snoring from Achilles' sleeping chamber. I hadn't heard Patroclus leave, so either he or the golden hero sounded like he had a deviated septum.

Now I lie here and consider my options. No, first I morph out of Phoenix's old form—damn the consequences!—and lie here as Thomas Hockenberry and consider my options.

I have my hand on the QT medallion. I can jump to Helen's sleeping chambers again—I know for a fact that Paris is out beyond the trench here, miles from the city, waiting for dawn to join Hector in the final slaughter of Greeks and the burning of the Achaean ships. Helen might be happy to see me. Or she might have no further use or amusement from the night-visitor named Hockenberry—how strange that someone here other than another scholic knows my name!—and she might call her guards. No problem with that; I can always QT away in an instant.

To what destination?

I can give up this mad plan to change the course of the *Iliad*, abandon my goal—formed on the night that Agamemnon and Achilles first quarreled—of defying the immortal gods, QT to Olympos, apologize to the Muse and to Aphrodite when they decant her, ask Zeus for a personal audience, and beg for a pardon.

Uh-huh. What are the odds that they'd forgive and forget, Hockenbush? You stole the Hades Helmet, the QT medallion, and all your scholic gear and used them for your own purposes. You fled from the Muse. Worst of all, you hijacked a flying chariot and tried to kill *Aphrodite in her healing tank.*

My best hope after apologizing would be that Zeus or Aphrodite or the Muse would kill me quickly, rather than turn me inside out or cast me down into the murky pit of Tartarus, where I'd probably be eaten alive by Kronos and the other barbarous Titans banished there by Zeus.

No, I've buttered my bread and now I have to lie in it. Or however that phrase goes. In for a penny, in for a pound. No guts, no glory. Better safe than sorry. But while I'm struggling for a cliché, any cliché, a profound realization settles over me in a profoundly unprofessorial but absolutely convincing phrasing—

If I don't think of something soon, I am well and truly fucked.

I can go reason with Odysseus.

Odysseus is the sane one here, the civilized man, the wise tactician. Odysseus may be the answer tonight. I'll have a better chance convincing Odysseus that an end to this war with the Trojans and common cause against the all-too-human gods is an option. To tell you the truth, I always enjoyed teaching the *Odyssey* to my students more than the *Iliad*; Fitzgerald's sensibilities in the *Odyssey* are so much more humane than the rough bellicosity of Mandelbaum's and Lattimore's and Fagles's and even Pope's *Iliad*. I was mistaken to think that I could find the fulcrum of events by coming here with the embassy to Achilles. No, Achilles isn't the man to approach this night—what's left of this night—but Odysseus, son of Laertes, a man who might understand a scholar's pleas and the compelling logic of peace.

I actually rise and touch the QT medallion, ready to go find Odysseus and make my plea. There's only one little problem that keeps me from

QTing in search of Odysseus: if Homer was telling the truth, I know what's happening elsewhere while I've been lying in this tent and brooding. Agamemnon and Menelaus can't sleep for their own brooding on the course of events, and some time around now, or perhaps in the last hour or so, the older and more royal brother calls for Nestor and asks for ideas that might stave off the massacre that seems so imminent. Nestor recommends a war counsel with Diomedes, Odysseus, Little Ajax, and some of the other Achaean captains. Once these leaders are gathered, Nestor suggests that the boldest among them should sneak behind Trojan lines and divine Hector's intentions—will the Trojans and their allies try to burn the ships in a few hours' time? Or is it possible that Hector has had enough blood and victory for now, and will lead his hordes back into the city to celebrate before opening further hostilities?

Diomedes and Odysseus are chosen to go find out, and since the two have come to this counsel from sleep, without their own weapons, they're given gear by the guards, including a bull's-hide helmet for Diomedes and a famous Mycaenaean boar's-tusk helmet for Odysseus. With the skin of a lion that Diomedes has thrown across his shoulders and Odysseus' black-leather helmet studded around with white teeth, the two warriors are terrifying to look upon.

Should I QT to that conference and observe it?

There's no reason. Diomedes and Odysseus may already have left on their commando raid. Or Homer might have been lying or mistaken about this action, just as he was with Phoenix's speech. Besides, it won't help with my problem right now. I'm not a scholic anymore, just a man trying to find away to survive and end this war—or at least turn it against the gods.

Although there's another part of tonight's action elsewhere that comes to mind and chills my blood. When Diomedes and Odysseus venture out, they discover Dolon—the spearman whose body I borrowed just two nights ago when I followed Hector into his meeting with Helen and Paris—who's been sent behind Achaean lines to spy for Hector. Dolon's carrying a reflex bow and wearing a cap made of weasel skin and he's sneaking carefully through the field of newly fallen dead in the dark, hunting for a way across the trench and past the Greek guards on the line, but sharp-eyed Odysseus sees him coming in the darkness and he and Diomedes lie among the corpses, surprise Dolon, and disarm him.

The Trojan begs for his life. Odysseus will tell him—if he hasn't already—that "Death is the last thing you have to worry about"—and then calmly, quietly pumps the young spearman for specific information about the disposition of Hector's Trojans and their allies.

Dolon tells all—the location of the Carians and Paeonians and Leleges and Cauconians, the sleeping areas of the crack Pelesgians and the stolid, faithful Lycians and the cock-strutting Mysians, the whereabouts of the camp of the famed Phrygian horsemen and the Maeonian charioteers—he tells everything and begs for his life. He even suggests that they tie him up and keep him prisoner until they see for themselves that his information is correct.

Odysseus will smile, or perhaps he already has, and will pat the shaking, terrified Dolon on the shoulder—I remember the muscled balance of Dolon's body from when I was morphed as the boy—and then the son of Laertes and Diomedes will strip the young man's cap and bow and wolf pelt—Odysseus softly telling the terrified boy that they're disarming him before bringing him to camp as a prisoner—and then Diomedes will hack Dolon's head off with one savage blow of his sword. Dolon's head will still be shrieking for mercy as it bounces across the sand.

And Odysseus will hold up the boy's spear and bow and weasel cap and wolf-pelt, and will offer them to Pallas Athena, crying—"Rejoice in these, Goddess. They're yours! Now guide us to the Thracian camp so that we can kill more men and steal their horses! Those spoils, too, will be yours."

Barbarians. I'm among barbarians. Even the gods here are barbarians. One thing is sure—I won't be going to talk to Odysseus tonight.

But why does Patroclus have to die?

Because I was right the first time—Achilles *is* the key, the fulcrum through which I can shift the fates of everyone, gods and men alike.

I don't think that Achilles will leave in a few hours when Dawn stretches forth her rosy fingertips. Uh-uh. I think Achilles will stay and observe, just as he does in Homer's tale, taking pleasure in further misfortune for the Greeks. "I think now that the Achaeans will come crawl at my knees," Achilles will say after the next bad day, when all the great captains—Agamemnon, Menelaus, Diomedes, and Odysseus—are hurt. And this is *after* last night's embassy to Achilles, where they've *already* groveled to get him back. Achilles will take pleasure in the defeat of his fellow Argives and Achaeans, and it's only Hector's murder of his friend Patroclus, snoring now in the next room, that will bring the man-killer back to the battlefield.

So Patroclus has to die to turn the direction of events now.

I stand and take inventory of the things I'm wearing and carrying. A short sword, yes, to blend in with the troops, but I've never used the damned thing and know it doesn't even have an edge. The Muse gave it to me as a prop, not a weapon. For real defense these past nine years, I've been equipped with the lightweight layer of impact armor—enough to stop a sword thrust or errant spear or arrow, we were told in the scholics barracks, although I have never had to test it—and the 50,000-volt taser tucked into the end of the shotgun mike baton we all carry. That weapon was designed only to stun an aggressor long enough for us to escape to a QT portal. Other hardware includes the lenses that enhance my vision, filters that boost my hearing, the stolen, cowl-like Hades Helmet furled around my shoulders, the QT medallion on its chain around my neck, and the morphing bracelet on my wrist.

Suddenly a plan—or at least part of a plan—begins to form in my tired mind.

I act before I can lose my nerve. Pulling up the Hades Helmet, disappearing from mortal and divine sight, feeling like Frodo or Bilbo or the gollum slipping on the ring that binds them all, I tiptoe from the sleeping annex where they laid out Phoenix's cushion to Achilles' bedchamber.

Achilles and Patroclus are sleeping together naked, the slave girls long gone, Patroclus' arm flung across the man-killer's shoulders.

This sight in the dim light stops me in my tracks. *Achilles is gay? That means that stupid gay- and lesbian-obsessed junior professor in the department was right—his ranting papers correct—all that politically correct babble true!*

I shake this out of my head. It means nothing except that I'm three thousand years away from Twenty-first Century Indiana and that I don't know *what* I'm seeing. These two men have just fornicated with slave girls for two hours and fell asleep where they lay. And besides, who cares about the secret love life of Achilles?

I trigger the morphing band and bring up the scan I'd made two days earlier in the hall of the gods on Olympos. I don't know if this will work—the other scholics used to laugh at the idea.

Probability waves shift through quantum layers I can't perceive. The air seems to quiver, stand still, then quiver again. I slip the soft Hades Helmet off my head and become visible.

Visible as Pallas Athena, Tritogenia, Third Born of the Gods, Daughter of Zeus, defender of the Achaeans. Nine feet tall, radiating my own divine light, I step closer to the bed as both Achilles and Patroclus awake with a start.

I can feel the instability in every atom in this morphed form. The morphing bracelet was *not* designed for us to take the form of gods, but although my shape hums like a hardstruck harp, I use the short time this quantum substitution will give me. I work to ignore the sensation not only of suddenly having breasts and a vagina—I've never morphed into the form of a woman before—but also ignore the sensation of being a goddess.

The form is unstable. I know in my heart that I haven't assumed the powers of Athena, just borrowed her quantum shell for these few seconds. Feeling as if there's going to be some nuclear reaction, a morphing meltdown, if I don't shed the quantum waveform of Athena quickly, I speak fast.

"Achilles! Wake! On your feet!"

"Goddess!" cries the fleet-footed man-killer, rolling from the cushions to the floor. "What brings you here in the middle of the night, Child of Zeus?"

Rubbing his eyes, Patroclus also struggles to his feet. Both men are naked, their bodies more sculpted and beautiful than the finest Greek statues, their uncircumcised penises dangling against their muscled and tanned thighs.

"BE QUIET!" I bellow. Athena's voice comes out amplified, superhuman. I know that I'm waking the others in Achilles' tent and probably alarming the guards outside. I have less than a minute. As if to prove my point, Athena's golden arm quivers, shifts to Professor Thomas Hockenberry's pale and hairy forearm, and then morphs back to Athena's. I see that Achilles' eyes are downcast and that he hasn't noticed. Patroclus stares wide-eyed, confused.

"Goddess, if I have offended you . . ." begins Achilles, raising his eyes but keeping his head bowed.

"SILENCE!!" I bellow. "CAN AN ANT CRAWLING IN THE DIRT OFFEND A MAN? CAN THE LOWEST AND UGLIEST FISH IN THE SEA OFFEND THE SAILOR WHOSE THOUGHTS ARE ON OTHER THINGS?"

"An ant?" repeats Achilles, his handsome, sculpted face showing a rebuked child's confusion.

"YOU'RE ALL LESS THAN ANTS TO THE GODS," I roar, taking a step closer so that Athena's radiance flickers over them like radioactive light. "YOU'VE AMUSED US WITH YOUR DEATHS, ACHILLES . . . SON OF PELEUS AND IDIOT CHILD OF THETIS."

"Idiot child," repeats Achilles, red rising to his high cheekbones. "Goddess, how have I . . ."

"SILENCE, COWARD!" I've amplified Athena's voice until they could hear this insult in Agamemnon's camp almost a mile down the beach. "WE CARE NOTHING FOR YOU. NOTHING FOR ANY OF YOU. YOUR DEATHS AMUSE US . . . BUT YOUR COWARDICE DOES NOT, *SWIFT-RUNNING ACHILLES!*" I sneer these last few words, turning the poet's honorific into a demeaning insult.

Achilles balls his fists and takes a half step forward, as if approaching a foe. "Goddess, Pallas Athena, Defender of Achaeans, I have always offered you the finest sacrifices . . ."

"A COWARD'S SACRIFICE MEANS NOTHING TO US ON OLYMPOS," I roar. I feel the probability wave that is the real goddess Athena approaching critical collapse. I have only seconds in this half-morphed form.

"WE'LL TAKE AND BURN OUR OWN SACRIFICE FROM THIS MOMENT ON," I say and Athena's arm extends toward Patroclus, the baton hidden under my forearm, my finger on the activator. "IF YOU WANT YOUR BOYFRIEND'S CORPSE, FIGHT YOUR WAY TO THE HALLS OF OLYMPOS TO GET IT, COWARD ACHILLES!"

I taser Patroclus in the center of his tanned, hairless chest, the near-invisible electrodes and invisible wires carrying 50,000 volts into him.

Patroclus seizes his chest as if struck by a lightning bolt, cries out, twitches and writhes as if in the throes of an epileptic fit, pisses himself, and collapses.

Before Achilles can react—the swift-footed warrior stands there naked with his hands balled into fists and his eyes bugging out, too shocked to move—I have Athena take two steps forward, grab the collapsed and apparently dead Patroclus by his hair, and drag him roughly across the floor.

Achilles unfreezes, snarls, and pulls his sword from its scabbard on the chair.

Still dragging the limp Patroclus by his hair, Athena's form quivering out of quantum morph stability now and as static-lashed as a bad TV picture, I touch the medallion at my throat and quantum teleport Patroclus and me the hell out of Achilles' tent.

Jerusalem and
the Mediterranean Basin

Savi led Daeman and Harman off the roof, down the ladders and steps, and into one of the narrow alleys. The starlight and blue glow from the neutrino beam on the Temple Mount gave just enough illumination for them not to crash into walls or fall into wells as they ran, although shadows were a solid black in the doorways and empty windows. Daeman soon fell behind, gasping. He'd never run, even as a child. It was an absurd thing to do.

Closer now, less than a short block away in the maze of flat-topped buildings and labrynthine alleys, came the scrabbling of the hundreds of hurrying voynix.

Itbah al-Yahud! rasped the voice from those loudspeakers Savi had called muezzin.

Savi led them across a cobblestoned street, down another dark, narrow alley, across a small clearing strewn with glowing human bones, and into an interior courtyard that was even darker than the alley. The pad-thump and manipulator-scratch of voynix running at high speed along walls was closer now.

Itbah al-Yahud! The amplified cry seemed more urgent.

Only Savi here is a Jew, whatever that is, thought Daeman, his lungs burning, staggering to keep up. *If Harman and I let her go on by herself, the voynix will leave us alone, probably even help us get home. There's no reason we should share her fate.*

Harman was running hard behind the old woman as she crossed the courtyard and ducked through a low arch into the ruins of an ancient building. *Or I can take care of myself,* thought Daeman. *Harman can stay with her if he wants.*

Daeman slid to a stop on the dusty cobblestones. Harman paused in the black rectangle of a doorway and waved him on. Daeman looked over his shoulder toward the sounds behind them—like claws or hollow bones rattling against stone—and, in the light of the blue beam, saw the first of a dozen voynix running in the street they had just crossed.

Daeman felt his heart lurch—he wasn't used to the emotion of fear and found the thought of doing anything alone right now as the most terrifying option—and then he ran into the dark doorway behind Harman and the old woman.

Savi led the way down a series of increasingly narrow staircases, each flight of steps older and more worn than the one above. Four flights down, she tugged a flashlight from her backpack and flicked it on as the last of the reflected light disappeared from the dim blue glow above. The narrow beam illuminated a wall at the bottom of the narrowest flight of steps and Daeman's heart lurched again. Then he saw what looked like a flap of dirty burlap hung over a hole he was sure was too small to allow him through.

"Hurry," whispered Savi. She pulled the gunny sack material aside and slipped through the hole. Daeman heard echoes as if from a well. Harman quickly followed the old woman into the blackness.

Daeman heard scrabblings from the ruined house above, but no voynix footsteps sounded on the stairs. Not yet at least.

He leaned into the little hole, squeezed his narrow shoulders through, found that he was hanging over a bottomless black circle less than four feet across, and then his flailing hands found iron rungs in the wall opposite and he grunted as he pulled his torso and hips through the opening, scraping skin against ancient plaster until his legs were free and dangling. Then his feet found purchase on the rusty metal rungs and he began clambering down toward the muted sounds of Savi and Harman descending below him.

Cold air flowed up past his face. Daeman's fingers and feet shifted uncertainly downward from cold rung to cold rung, he heard whispers below, and suddenly there were no rungs under his feet and he dropped four or five feet onto a brick floor.

Harman's hands steadied him. He could see the circle of Savi's flashlight illuminating a round tunnel made of ancient stones or bricks.

"This way," she whispered and began running again, bent over to avoid the low ceiling. Harman and Daeman scrambled along behind, trying to avoid the irregular bricks in the curved floor by watching the circle of her flashlight rather than their own feet.

They came to a junction of tunnels. Savi checked her glowing palm function and they followed the left passage.

"I don't hear the voynix behind us," said Harman. He'd spoken softly, but his voice still echoed from the curved brick. The tallest of the three, Harman had to bend the most to walk.

"They're above us," said Savi. "Following us on the streets."

"Are they using proxnet?" asked Daeman.

"Yes." She paused at another junction, chose the center of three smaller passages. They all had to bend low here.

Harman looked at Daeman again, obviously curious about the proxnet comment, but not asking any questions now.

"They're following *you*, you know," said Savi, pausing to look first at Daeman and then at Harman. The harsh flashlight beam made her face look even older and more skull-like.

"Not you?" said Daeman, surprised.

She shook her head. "I don't register on any nets. The voynix don't even know I'm here. It's you two who are showing up out of bounds on their farnet and proxnet scans. I think the nearest faxportal is Mantua. They know you didn't walk this far."

"Where are we going now?" whispered Harman. "The sonie?"

Savi shook her head again. Her gray hair was wet with sweat or condensation and plastered to her skull. "These tunnels don't go beyond the old city. And the voynix have rendered the sonie inoperable by now. I'm headed for the crawler."

"Crawler?" said Daeman, but rather than explain, Savi turned away and began leading them through the tunnels again.

A hundred paces further and the round brick tunnel became a narrow corridor, thirty paces beyond that and the corridor became stairs, and then a wall stopped them.

Daeman felt his heart trying to pound through his chest wall. "What do we do?" he said. "What do we do? What do we do?" He spun away from the light, listening hard in the darkness for voynix sounds.

"Climb."

Daeman turned back to see Savi being lifted into another vertical well—this one narrower than the one they had descended—and then the light was gone as the flashlight bobbed above them.

Harman jumped up for the lowest rung, missed, cursed softly, jumped again, caught it, and pulled himself up. Daeman could barely see the outline of the older man's arm as he reached down. "Come on, Daeman. Hurry. The voynix are probably already up there, waiting for us."

"Then why are we climbing up there?"

"Come on." Harman seized Daeman's forearm in the darkness and pulled him up.

The voynix broke through the wall of the building just as the three humans were scrambling onto the crawler.

The huge machine took up much of the space in the central area of
what Savi said had once been a large church. When they came up the
stairs from the cellar, Savi's flashlight flicking this way and that, Daeman had paused on the steps, not sure of what he was seeing. The
crawler filled the space like some giant spider, its six wheels—each at
least twelve feet tall—linked by hinged spidery struts, its passenger
sphere glowing milkily in the center of the struts like a white egg at the
center of a web.

The battering against the church doors and walls began even before
Savi began climbing the thin, metallic access ladder hanging from the
struts. "Hurry," she said, no longer whispering.

Third in line—again—Daeman thought that the old woman was the
master of the unnecessary imperative. A boarded window sixty feet up a
wall exploded inward and five voynix scrabbled in, their bladed manipulators hacking into stone like ice hammers. The eyeless, rust-red domes
above their carapaces turned ponderously downward and fixed on the
crawler and the three people trying to get to its passenger sphere. Stones
burst from the far wall and half a dozen other voynix came in on two legs.

Savi touched a faded red circle on the underside of the sphere,
tapped digits into a small yellow energy diskey that appeared, and a section of the glass globe slid open with an audible rasp. She crawled up
and in, Harman followed, and Daeman got his legs in just as the first of
the voynix hurtled across the dusty stones toward him.

The slice in the sphere slid closed. There were six cracked-leather
contour seats in the center of the sphere, and he and Harman threw
themselves into side seats as Savi ran her hand over a flat metal wedge
protruding above the front seat. A softly glowing projection control
panel—much more complicated than the one on the sonie—pulsed into
life around her. She touched a virtual red dial, ran a bright yellow circle
along a green slide, and slipped her hand into a form-fitting controller.

"What if it doesn't start?" asked Harman, whom Daeman now nom-
inated for master of the poorly timed rhetorical question. A score of
voynix pulled themselves up and over the high black mesh wheels and
jumped like giant grasshoppers onto the top of the glass sphere. Daeman
flinched and ducked low.

"If it doesn't start, we die," said Savi. She twitched the virtual controller to the right.

There was no engine roar or gyro hum, just a soft buzz so low as to be almost subsonic. But searchlights stabbed out in front of the crawler and a dozen other virtual displays flicked into life.

The half-dozen voynix atop the passenger sphere had been pounding and clawing on the glass, but suddenly they slid away and fell to the ground twenty feet below. They weren't injured or damaged—each voynix leapt to its feet and jumped for the sphere again—but each then fell away again, unable to gain purchase on the surface they'd been clinging to only a few seconds earlier.

"It's a micron-thick forcefield," muttered Savi, her attention on the glowing designs and icons appearing all over the virtual panel. "Frictionless. It was designed to keep snow or rain from accumulating on the canopy, but it appears to shed voynix as well."

Daeman turned to watch a score of voynix scrambling up the huge wheels, battering at the metal mesh, pulling at the struts and braces. "We should go," he said.

"Yes." Savi pushed the virtual controller forward and the crawler crashed through the ancient church wall, fell a dozen feet before the wildly articulated wheels found purchase on the wall and ground, and then accelerated forward. The lane was slightly narrower than the crawler, but this didn't slow the machine a bit. Walls several thousand years old collapsed on either side until the crawler lurched out onto David Street and Savi turned it left, toward the west, away from the blue beam still stabbing skyward behind them.

Countless voynix scrabbled in pursuit while dozens more threw themselves in front of the speeding crawler and leapt for the passenger sphere. Still accelerating, the crawler ran over those in the street that failed to dodge and left the rest of the pack behind. Half a dozen persistent voynix still clung to the struts and were hacking away at the metal, clawing at the spinning wheels.

"Can they do damage?" asked Harman.

"I don't know," said Savi. "We're approaching the Sho'or Yafa—the Jaffa Gate. Let's see if we can get rid of them."

She swerved the still-accelerating crawler into walls on the left and then on the right side of David Street, finally smashing through an arch lower than the crawler. Vibration and falling masonry shook the clinging voynix off, but Daeman turned to see most of them rising out of the rubble and joining the pack giving chase. Then the crawler was through the gate, out of the old city, and picking up speed down the graveled hill where they'd left the sonie, but the only sign of their flying machine was a heap of rocks thirty feet high surrounded by forty or fifty more voynix. Immediately the creatures left the mound and rushed to cut off the crawler. Savi ran over some, dodged others, and found an ancient highway running west from the city.

"Tough machine," said Harman.

"They built tough machines toward the end of the Lost Age," said Savi. "With nano-maintenance, it should last damned near forever." She'd pulled her thermskin night-vision lenses from her pack and was driving with the crawler's headlights off now. Daeman found the effect of hurtling along in the dark unsettling as he heard the big wheels crunching over rusted artifacts on the road—probably ancient abandoned vehicles. Then he realized that they were hurtling over a bridge and then rumbling through a cut between hills. He couldn't see the pursuing voynix now in the dark—only the receding blue blade of light leaping straight up from the dark hill of Jerusalem—but he knew the voynix were still back there, still coming on.

Savi told them that it was about thirty miles to the coastline of the former Mediterranean Sea. They made the distance in less than ten minutes.

"Look at this," said Savi, slowing the crawler. She removed her night-vision glasses and flicked on the headlights, fog lights, and searchlights.

A mass of five or six hundred voynix had made a wedge near where the land suddenly tilted down into the dry Mediterranean Basin.

"Do we turn?" asked Harman.

Savi shook her head and accelerated the crawler forward. Later, Daeman thought that the sound of the machine hitting so many voynix at such high speed had been somewhat like a hailstorm he had heard on a metal roof in Ulanbat many years ago. But this was very large hail.

The crawler reached the former shoreline, Savi cried "Hang on," and the machine was airborne for ten seconds as it jumped the drop between shore and former sea. Then the six huge wheels hit the ground, the struts absorbed most of the shock and stabilized them, and they drove straight ahead down into the Basin, headlights and searchlights still stabbing white cones out of the darkness.

Daeman looked back and saw the surviving voynix, silhouetted by the distant blue beam, lining the shoreline behind them. "They won't follow?" he asked.

"Into the Basin?" said Savi. "Never." She slowed the crawler to a more reasonable speed, but before she slipped on her glasses and shut off the lights, Daeman saw that they were following a smooth red-clay road through verdant fields of crops. There were black metal crosses rising above the level of the wheat and corn and sunflowers and flax out there in the dark, and, impaled on each cross, was what looked to be a pale, writhing, naked human body.

The Coast of
Ilium, Indiana

Achilles raged, roared, and tore at the tent wall where the goddess Athena had disappeared, dragging the body of Patroclus. Then the man-killer went mad.

His guards rushed in. Still naked, Achilles lifted the first man and threw him at the head of the second guard. The third guard heard a roar and found himself also flying through the air, tearing through the canvas wall of the tent. The fourth threw down his spear and ran to wake the Myrmidons to let them know that their lord and captain had been possessed by a demon spirit.

Achilles gathered up his breechcloth, his tunic, his breastplate, his shield, his polished bronze greaves, his sandals, and his spear, wrapped them in a sheet, and, taking up his sword, cut his way through three canvas walls of tent. Outside, he shoved over the large tripod left burning in the center of his camp and ran past the darkened tents—toward the dark sea and away from all the encampments of men, toward his mother, the goddess Thetis.

The waves crashed in to shore, only the whites of each curl visible in the darkness here away from the fires. Achilles paced back and forth on the wet sand. He was still naked, his armor and his weapons scattered on the beach. While he paced, he pulled at his long hair and moaned aloud, occasionally crying out his mother's name in anguish.

And Thetis, daughter of the sea god Nereus, the Old Man of the Sea, answered Achilles' call, appearing from the salt-green depths, rising up from the rolling surf like a mist, but then solidifying into the tall form of the noble goddess. Achilles ran to her like an injured child and fell to one knee in the wet sand. Thetis cradled his head against her wet breast while he sobbed.

"My child—why the weeping? What sorrow has hurt your heart?"

Achilles groaned. "You know, you must know, Mother—don't make me tell it all again."

"I was with my father in the salt-green depths," murmured Thetis, stroking Achilles' golden hair. "Since mortals and gods were both sleeping so late, I did not see what transpired. Share it all, my son."

And Achilles did, sobbing with grief, choking with anger. He told of the appearance of Pallas Athena, of her insults and taunts. He described the apparent murder of his friend Patroclus.

"She took away his body, Mother!" cried Achilles. He was beyond comfort. "She took away his body so that I can't even perform the proper funeral rites for him!"

Thetis patted his shoulder and burst into tears herself. "Oh my son, my sorrow! Your birth was bitterness. All I bore was doom. Why did I raise you up, if it is Zeus's will to throw you down?"

Achilles raised his tear-streaked face. "So it *is* Zeus's will? It *was* Pallas Athena who just killed Patroclus—not some false image of the goddess?"

"It was Zeus's will," wept his mother. "And although I did not see it, I know it was Goddess Athena herself who taunted you and killed your friend this night. Oh, the pity that you were doomed not only to a short life, Achilles, my son, but to one so filled with heartbreak."

Achilles pulled away and stood. "Why did the immortal gods insult me so, Mother? Why would Athena, who has championed the Argive cause—and especially my own—for so many years, abandon me now?"

"The gods are fickle," said Thetis, water still running from her long hair down to her breasts. "Perhaps you've noticed."

Achilles paced back and forth in front of her, repeatedly balling his hands into fists and unballing them into splayed fingers as he stabbed at the air. "It makes no sense! To bring me so far—to help me in my conquests so frequently—only for Athena and her divine father to insult me so now."

"They are ashamed of you, Achilles."

The man-killer stopped in his tracks and turned a pale, frozen face her way. He looked as if he had been slapped hard. "Ashamed of me? *Ashamed* of fleet-footed Achilles, son of Peleus and the goddess Thetis? Ashamed of the grandson of Aeacus?"

"Yes," said his mother. "Zeus and the lesser gods, including Athena, have always had contempt for mortal men, even you heroes. From their vantage point on Olympos you are all less than insects, your lives are nasty, brutish, and short, and your very existences are justified only because you amuse them by your deaths. So by sulking in your tent while the fate of the war is sealed, you've irritated the Third Born daughter of Zeus and lord god Father Zeus himself."

"They *killed* Patroclus!" roared Achilles, stepping back from the goddess, his bare feet leaving footprints in the wet sand. Footprints that were washed away on the next roll of the surf.

"They think you are too much of a coward to avenge his death," said Thetis. "They leave his corpse for the crows and vultures on the heights of Olympos."

Achilles moaned and fell to his knees. He pulled great fistfuls of wet sand from the beach and smashed them to his bare chest. "Mother, why are you telling me this now? If you knew of the gods' contempt for me, why haven't you told me before? Always you taught me to serve and revere Zeus. To obey the goddess Athena."

"I always hoped the other gods would grant mercy on our mortal children," said Thetis. "But lord Zeus's cold heart and Athena's warrior ways have won the day. The race of men is of no interest to them any longer. Not even for sport. Nor are we few immortals who argue your case safe from Zeus's wrath."

Achilles stood and took three steps closer to his mother. "Mother, you're an immortal. Zeus cannot harm thee."

Thetis laughed without humor. "The Father can kill anything and anyone he wishes, my son. Even an immortal. Worse than that, he can banish us to the murk of Tartarus, throw us down into that hellish pit the way he did his own father, Kronos, and his weeping mother, Rhea."

"So you're in danger," Achilles said numbly. He teetered like a man who has drunk too much or like a sailor on the pitching deck of a small ship at sea in storm.

"I am doomed," said Thetis. "And so are you, my child, unless you do the one thing that no mortal—not even the brazen Herakles—has attempted before."

"What, Mother?" Achilles' face in the starlight was undergoing disturbing transformations as his emotions ran from despair to fury to something beyond fury.

"Bring down the gods," whispered Thetis. The words were barely audible above the crashing surf. Achilles stepped even closer, his head bent as if not believing. "Bring down the gods," she whispered again. "Storm Olympos. Kill Athena. Depose Zeus."

Achilles staggered back. "Can this be possible?"

"Not if you act alone," said Thetis. White waves curled around her feet. "But if you bring your warring Argives and Achaeans with you . . ."

"Agamemnon and his brother rule the Achaeans and the Argives and their allies this night," interrupted Achilles. He looked back at the fires burning along the miles of beach and then turned his head to look at the far more numerous Trojan watch fires burning just beyond the defensive trench. "And the Argives and the Achaeans are on the verge of rout this night, Mother. The black ships may burn by sunrise."

"*May* burn," said Thetis. "This day's victories to the Trojans are simply another sign of Zeus's whim. But the Argives and Achaeans will follow *you* to victory even against the gods, Achilles. Just this night, Agamemnon said to Odysseus and Nestor and the others gathered in his camp at midnight that *he* was the better man—wiser and stronger and more bold than Achilles. Show him otherwise, my son. Show *all* of them otherwise."

Achilles turned his back on her. He was looking toward distant Ilium where torches burned bright on the high walls. "I cannot fight the gods and the Trojans at the same time."

Thetis touched his shoulder until he turned. "You're right, my child, Achilles, swift-runner. You must end this senseless war with Troy, begun over Menelaus' bitch of a wife. Who cares where mortal Helen sleeps or if the Atridae—Menelaus and his arrogant brother Agamemnon—are cuckolded or not? End the war. Make peace with Hector. He too has reason to hate the gods this night."

Achilles looked quizzically at Thetis but she did not explain. He looked back at the torches and the distant city. "Would that I could see Olympos tonight so that I could kill Athena, throw down Zeus, and reclaim Patroclus' body for his rites." His voice was soft but terrible in its mad resolve.

"I will send a man to show you the way," said Thetis.

He wheeled on her again. "When?"

"Tomorrow, after you have spoken with Hector, made common bond with the fighting Trojans, and taken kingship of the Argives and Achaeans from posturing Agamemnon."

Achilles blinked at the breathtaking audacity of this. "How shall I find Hector without him killing me or me killing him?"

"I will send you a man to show you the way for that as well," said Thetis. She stepped back. The predawn surf crashed against the backs of her legs.

"Mother, stay! I . . ."

"I go to Father Zeus's halls to find my fate now," whispered his mother, voice all but lost in the sibilant surf. "I will argue your case a final time, my son, but I fear failure and banishment will be my lot. Be bold, Achilles! Be brave! Your fate has been set but not sealed. You still have the choice of death and glory or long life, but also life and glory . . . and such glory, Achilles! No mortal man ever dreamt of such glory! Avenge Patroclus."

"Mother . . ."

"The gods can die, my child. The . . . gods . . . can . . . *die.*" Her form wavered, shifted, became a mist, and disappeared.

Achilles stood staring out to sea for long minutes, stood staring until the cold light of Dawn began creeping from the east, and then he turned, donned his clothing and his sandals and his armor and his greaves, hefted his great shield, slid his sword into its sheath on his sword belt, took up his spear, and began walking toward Agamemnon's camp.

After this performance, I collapse. All through the dialogue, my morphing bracelet was beeping in my ear with its AI voice—"Ten minutes of power left before shutdown. Six minutes of power left before . . ." and so forth.

The morphing gear is almost out of charge and I have no idea how to recharge it. I have just under three minutes of morphing time left, but I'll need that to visit Hector's family.

You can't kidnap a child, comes the ever smaller voice that is all that's left of my conscience. *I have to,* comes the only response I have.

I have to.

I'm in this now. I've thought it through. Patroclus was the secret to Achilles. Scamandrius and Andromache—Hector's son and wife—are the secret to turning Hector. The only way.

In for a penny, in for a pound.

Earlier, when I'd QT'd into existence on the sunny-afternoon hill of what I still hoped to be Indiana, the unconscious Patroclus in my arms, there had been no sign of Nightenhelser. I dropped Patroclus quickly into the grass—I'm not homophobic, but dragging a naked man makes me feel odd—and I'd called toward the river and forest for Keith Nightenhelser, but no response. Perhaps the ancient Native Americans had scalped him by now, or adopted him into their tribe. Or perhaps he was just across the river and into the woods, gathering nuts and berries.

Patroclus groaned and stirred.

What are the ethics of leaving a groggy, naked man as a stranger in a strange land like this? Would a bear kill him? Not likely. It was more likely that Patroclus would find and kill poor Nightenhelser, although the Greek was naked and unarmed and Keith was still decked out in impact armor, taser baton, and prop sword. Yes, I'd put my money on

Patroclus. What are the ethics of leaving a pissed-off Patroclus in the same berry-gathering acre of land where I'd left a peace-loving academic?

I didn't have time to worry about it. I'd checked the morphing bracelet's power—found it waning—and QT'd back to the coast of Ilium. I'd learned a little about becoming a goddess from the Athena experience and Thetis wouldn't require as much energy to morph into as had Zeus's daughter. With a bit of luck, I thought, the morphing gear would work long enough to allow me my scene with Achilles and leave a bit left over for Hector's family.

And it did. And I do have a bit left over. I can morph a final time.

Hector's family. What have I become?

A man on the run, I think, as I pull the Hades Helmet over my head and walk along the sand. A desperate man.

Will the QT medallion run out of power soon as well? Does the taser hold another charge if I need it in Ilium?

I'll find out soon. Wouldn't it be ironic if I succeeded in turning both Achilles and Hector to my cause but then didn't have the quantum teleportation power to get them or me to Olympos?

I'll worry about that later. I'll worry about all this crap later.

Right now I have a 4 A.M. appointment with Hector's wife and baby boy.

35

12,000 Meters
Above the Tharsis Plateau

"What does Proust have to say about balloons?"

"Not much," said Orphu of Io. "He wasn't big on traveling in general. What does Shakespeare say about balloons?"

Mahnmut let that go. "I wish you could see this."

"I wish I could see it, too," said Orphu. "Describe everything to me."

Mahnmut looked up. "We're high enough here that the sky overhead is almost black, fading to dark blue, then to a lighter blue by the horizon, which is definitely curved. I can see the band of haze of atmosphere in both directions. Beneath us, it's still cloudy—the early morning light makes the clouds glow gold and pink. Behind us, the cloud cover is broken and I can see the blue water and red cliffs of Valles Marineris stretching back to the eastern horizon. To the west, the direction we're traveling, the clouds cover most of the Tharsis Plateau—they seem to be hugging the ground along the rising terrain—but the three closer volcanoes are poking up through the gold clouds. Arsia Mons is furthest to the left, then Pavonis Mons, then Ascraeus Mons farther over to the right, to the north. They're all a bright white, snow and ice, gleaming in the morning light."

"Can you see Olympus yet?" asked Orphu.

"Oh, yes. Even though it's the farthest away, Olympus Mons is the tallest thing in sight, rising over the western curve of the planet. It's between Pavonis and Ascraeus, but obviously further away. It's also white with ice and snowfields, but the summit is free of snow and red in the sunrise."

"Can you see Noctis Labyrinthus where we left the zeks?"

Mahnmut leaned over the edge of the gondola he'd built and looked below and behind them. "No, still cloud cover there. But when we were rising toward the overcast, I could see all of the quarry, the docks, and the whole tumble of Noctis. Beyond the seaport and quarry there, the jumble of canyons and cliff-collapses runs hundreds of kilometers west and scores of klicks north and south."

It had been raining the last days of their felucca voyage, raining when they put into the crowded docks at the LGM quarry site in Noctis Labyrinthus, and raining harder when Mahnmut had finally assembled the jury-rigged gondola, inflated the balloon from its own tanks, and set out above what could only be called a city of the little green men. One of the LGM—or zeks, as they called themselves—had obviously offered his heart for communication, but Mahnmut had shaken his head no. Perhaps they didn't die as individuals, as Orphu argued, but the sensation of *using up* another little green man was more than Mahnmut could handle. Instead, the gathered zeks had immediately understood what Mahnmut was doing with his homemade gondola, and they'd moved quickly to help connect tether cables, spread the fabric of the single-chamber, high-pressure balloon while it slowly inflated, and secure ground cables against the wind, all the while working as efficiently as a highly trained ground crew.

"What does the balloon look like?" asked Orphu. The deep-space moravec was tethered in the center of the enlarged gondola, strapped down by many meters of line and set into a frame Mahnmut had hammered together. Nearby, shielded and secured, were the transmitter and the smaller Device.

"It's like a giant pumpkin above us," said Mahnmut.

Orphu rumbled over the tightbeam. "Have you ever *seen* a pumpkin in real life?"

"Of course not, but we've both seen images. The balloon's an orange ovoid, wider than it is tall, about sixty-five meters across and about fifty meters tall. It has vertical ridges like a pumpkin . . . and it's orange."

"I thought it was sheathed in stealth material," said Orphu, sounding surprised.

"It is. Orange stealth material. I guess our moravec designers didn't consider the fact that the people we'd be sneaking up on might have eyes as well as radar."

This time Orphu's rumble sounded like deep thunder. "Typical," said the Ionaian. "Typical."

"Our cluster of buckycarbon cables is rigged from the bottom of the balloon," said Mahnmut. "Our gondola's hanging about forty meters beneath the fabric."

"Securely, I hope," said Orphu.

"As secure as I could make it, although maybe I forgot to tie a couple of knots."

Orphu rumbled again and went silent. Mahnmut watched the view for a while.

When Orphu made contact again, it was night. The stars burned coldly, but Mahnmut was still aware of more atmospheric twinkle than he'd ever seen in his life. The moon Phobos was hurtling low across the sky and Deimos had just risen. The clouds and volcanoes reflected the starlight. To the north, the ocean glimmered.

"Are we there yet?" asked Orphu.

"Not quite. Another day, day and a half."

"Is the wind still blowing us in the right direction?"

"More or less."

"Define 'less,' old friend."

"We're heading north-northwest. We may miss Olympus Mons by a shade."

"That takes a certain skill," said Orphu. "To miss a volcano the size of France."

"It's a *balloon*, " said Mahnmut. "I'm sure that Koros III planned to launch it from near the base of the volcano, not from twelve hundred kilometers away."

"Wait," said Orphu. "I seem to remember a little detail about the Tethys Sea being just north of Olympus."

Mahnmut sighed. "That's why I built this new gondola in the shape of an open boat."

"You never mentioned that while you were building it."

"It didn't seem relevant then."

They floated along in silence for a while. They were approaching the Tharsis volcanoes, and Mahnmut thought they might pass the northernmost, Ascraeus, by midday tomorrow. If the wind kept shifting, they'd miss the slopes completely, passing ten or twenty kilometers to the north of it. Mahnmut didn't even have to change his vision into light-enhancement mode to marvel at the beauty of the moons' light and the starlight on the icy upper regions of all four volcanoes.

"I've been thinking about this Prospero–Caliban thing," Orphu said suddenly, making Mahnmut jump slightly. He'd been lost in thought.

"Yes?"

"I presume you're thinking along the same lines that I've been—that these statues of Prospero and the LGM's knowledge of *The Tempest* are the result of some human or post-human dictator's interest in Shakespeare."

"We don't even know for sure that the stone heads are supposed to be Prospero," said Mahnmut.

"Of course not. But the LGM suggested they were, and I don't think the zeks ever lied to us. Perhaps they *can't* lie—not when communicating with you through molecular nanodata packages the way they were."

Mahnmut said nothing, but that had been his impression as well.

"Somehow," continued Orphu, "those thousands of stone heads circling the north ocean . . ."

"And the flooded Hellas Basin in the south," said Mahnmut, remembering the orbital images.

"Yeah. Somehow, those thousands of stone heads have something to do with Shakespeare's characters."

Mahnmut nodded at this, knowing that blind Orphu would take his silence as a nod.

"What if the dictator is actually Prospero?" said Orphu. "And not a human or post-human at all?"

"I don't understand." Mahnmut was confused. He checked the flow of oxygen from the tanks stowed near the Device. Both he and Orphu were securely jacked in and getting full flow. "What do you mean, what if the dictator was actually Prospero? You mean some post-human was playing the role of the old magician and forgot they were role-playing?"

"No," said Orphu. "I mean—*what if it's Prospero?*"

Mahnmut felt a stab of alarm. Orphu had been battered and blinded, zapped by huge quantities of ionizing radiation, and buffeted in the spaceship's fall into the northern sea. Perhaps his reason was going.

"No, I'm not crazy," said Orphu, sounding disgusted. "Listen to what I'm saying."

"Prospero is a literary character," Mahnmut said slowly. "A fictional construct. We know about him only because of the memory banks about human culture and history that were sent along with the early moravecs two e-millennia ago."

"Yes," said Orphu. "Prospero is a fictional construct and the Greek gods are myths. And that their presence here is just because they're humans or post-humans in disguise. *But what if they aren't?* What if they're really Prospero . . . really Greek gods?"

Mahnmut felt true alarm now. He had looked straight on at the terror of continuing on this mission alone should Orphu die, but he'd never considered the worse alternative of having a blinded, crippled, *insane*

Orphu of Io as a companion on this last stage of the mission. Could he bring himself to leave Orphu behind when they landed?

"How could the gods—or whatever these people in togas and flying chariots are—not be myths or post-humans lost in role playing?" asked Mahnmut. "Are you suggesting they're . . . space aliens? Ancient Martians who somehow weren't noticed during the Lost Age exploration of this planet? What?"

"I'm saying *what if the Greek gods are Greek gods*," Orphu said softly. "What if Prospero is Prospero? Caliban Caliban? Should we meet him, which I hope we don't."

"Uh-huh," said Mahnmut. "Interesting theory."

"God damn it, don't patronize me," snapped Orphu. "Do you know anything about quantum teleportation?"

"Just the theory behind it," said Mahnmut. "And the fact that this world is riddled with active quantum activity."

"Holes," said Orphu.

"What?"

"They're like wormholes. When quantum shift events are maintained like this, even for a few nanoseconds, you get a standing-wormhole singularity effect. You know what a singularity is, right?"

"Yes," said Mahnmut, irritated now at the way his friend was talking to him. "I know the definitions of wormholes, singularities, black holes, and quantum teleportation—and I know how all those conditions, except the last one, warp spacetime. But what the hell does that have to do with gods in togas and flying chariots? These are post-humans we're dealing with on Mars. Possibly crazy post-humans, self-evolved beyond sanity, but post-humans."

"You may be right," said Orphu. "But let's look at another alternative."

"Which is what? That fictional characters have suddenly come to life?"

"Do you know why moravec engineers gave up on developing quantum teleportation as a way to travel to the stars?" said Orphu.

"It's not stable," said Mahnmut. "There's evidence of some accident on Earth fifteen hundred or so years ago. The humans or post-humans were fooling around with quantum wormholes and it didn't work and backfired on them somehow."

"A lot of moravec observers think that it backfired precisely because it *did* work," said Orphu.

"I don't understand."

"Quantum teleportation is an old technology," said the Ionian. "The old-style humans were experimenting with it way back in the Twentieth or Twenty-first Century, before the posts even evolved themselves out of the human species. Before everything went to shit on earth."

"So?"

"So the essence of quantum teleportation was that you couldn't send large objects—nothing much bigger than a photon, and not even that, really. Just the complete *quantum state* of that photon."

"What's the difference between the complete quantum state of something or somebody and that thing or person?" asked Mahnmut.

"Nothing," said Orphu. "That's the sweet part. Quantum teleport a photon or a Percheron stallion, and you get a complete duplicate of the thing on the other end. So complete a duplicate that, to all intents and purposes, it *is* the photon."

"Or Percheron," said Manhmut. He'd always enjoyed looking at images of horses. As far as the moravecs knew, real horses had been extinct on Earth for millennia.

"But even if you teleport a photon from one place to another," continued Orphu, "the rules of quantum physics demand that the particle teleported can bring no information with it. Not even information about its own quantum state."

"Sort of useless then, isn't it?" said Mahnmut. Phobos had finished its fast hurtle across the Martian night sky and set behind the distant curve of the world. Deimos moved at a more stately pace.

"That's what the humans back in the Twentieth or Twenty-first Century thought," said Orphu. "But then the post-humans began playing with quantum teleportation. First on Earth, and then in their orbital cities or whatever those objects in near Earth orbit are."

"And they had more success?" said Mahnmut. "But we know that something went wrong about fourteen hundred years ago, right about the time the Earth was showing all that quantum activity."

"Something went wrong," agreed Orphu. "But it wasn't a failure of the quantum teleportation. The post-humans—or their thinking machines—developed a line of quantum transport based on entangled particles."

"Spooky action at a distance," said Mahnmut. He'd never been very interested in nuclear physics or astrophysics or particle physics—hell, in physics of any form—but he'd always enjoyed Einstein's damning phrase attacking quantum mechanics. Einstein had owned a wicked tongue when it came to shooting down colleagues or theories he didn't like.

"Yes," said Orphu. The Ionian obviously didn't enjoy getting interrupted. "Well, spooky action at a distance works on a quantum level, and the post-humans began sending larger and larger objects through quantum portals."

"Percheron stallions?" said Mahnmut. He didn't especially like being lectured at.

"No record of that, but the horses on Earth seem to have gone somewhere, so why not? Look, Mahnmut, I'm very serious here—I've been thinking about this since we left Jupiter space. Can I finish without the sarcasm?"

Mahnmut metaphorically blinked. Orphu did not sound so insane any longer, but he did sound serious . . . and hurt. "All right," said Mahnmut. "I apologize. Go ahead."

"We know that the post-humans accelerated their quantum research—fooling around, really—about the time we moravecs abandoned it, about fourteen hundred Earth years ago. They were punching holes in space-time left and right."

"Excuse me," said Mahnmut, interrupting as softly as he could. "I thought only black holes or wormholes or naked singularities could do that."

"And quantum tunnels left activated," said Orphu.

"But I thought quantum teleportation was instantaneous," said Mahnmut. He was trying hard to understand now. "That it *had* to be instantaneous."

"It does. With entanglement pairs, particles, or complex structures, shifting the quantum state of one member of the quantum twin-set instantly changes the quantum state of its partner."

"Then how can there be tunnels activated if the . . . tunneling . . . is instantaneous?" said Mahnmut.

"Trust me on this," said Orphu. "When you're teleporting something large, say a small slice of cheese, just the amount of random quantum data being transmitted shoots the shit out of space-time."

"How much raw quantum data would be in, say, a three-gram slice of cheese?"

"10^{24} bits," answered Orphu without hesitation.

"And how much in a human being?"

"Not counting the person's memory, but just his or her atoms," said Orphu, "10^{28} kilobytes of data."

"Well, that's just four more zeros than a slice of cheese," said Mahnmut.

"Mother of Mercy," whined Orphu. "We're talking *orders of magnitude here*. Which means . . ."

"I know what it means," said Mahnmut. "I was just being silly again. Go on."

"So about fourteen hundred years ago on Earth, the post-humans—

it had to be the post-humans, since our probes at the time were sure that there were just a thousand or so old-style humans left, like almost-extinct-species animals being kept around in a zoo—the post-humans began quantum teleporting people and machines and other objects."

"Where?" said Mahnmut. "I mean where did they send them? Mars? Other star systems?"

"No, you need a receiver as well as a transmitter with quantum tele-portation," said the Ionian. "They just sent them from somewhere on the Earth to somewhere else on the Earth—or in their orbital cities—but they had a big surprise when the objects materialized."

"Does this has something to do with a fly?" asked Mahnmut. His secret vice was old movies from the Twentieth Century to the end of the Lost Age.

"A fly?" said Orphu. "No. Why?"

"Never mind. What was the big surprise they got when they tele-ported these things?"

"First, that the quantum teleportation worked," said Orphu. "But more important, that when the person or animal or thing came through, it carried information with it. Information about its own quantum state. Information about everything it shouldn't have information about. Including memory for the human beings."

"I thought you said that the rules of quantum mechanics forbid that."

"They do," said Orphu.

"Magic again?" asked Mahnmut, feeling the tug of alarm at the direction Orphu was headed. "Are we talking Prospero and Greek gods here?"

"Yes, but not in the way you sarcastically mean," said Orphu of Io. "Our scientists at the time thought that the post-humans were actually exchanging tangled pairs with identical objects . . . or persons . . . in another universe."

"Another universe," Mahnmut repeated dully. "As in parallel universes?"

"Not quite," said Orphu. "Not like the old idea of an infinite or near-infinite number of parallel universes. Just a few—a very finite number—of quantum phase-shifted universes co-existing with or near our own."

Mahnmut had no idea what his friend was talking about, but he said nothing.

"Not only co-existing quantum universes," continued the deep-space moravec, "but *created* universes."

"Created?" repeated Mahnmut. "As in God?"

"No," said Orphu. "As in through acts of genius, *by* geniuses."

"I don't understand."

Deimos had set. The Martian volcanoes were visible now in starlight, masses of clouds creeping up their long slopes like pale-gray amoebae. Mahnmut checked his internal chronometer. One hour until Martian sunrise. He was cold.

"You know what human researchers found when they were studying the human mind millennia ago," said Orphu. "Back before the post-humans were even a factor. Our own moravec minds are built the same way, although we use artificial as well as organic brain matter."

Mahnmut tried to remember. "The human scientists were using quantum computers way back in the Twenty-first Century," he said. "To analyze biochemical cascades in human synapses. They discovered that the human mind—not the brain, but the *mind*—wasn't like a computer, it wasn't like a chemical memory machine, but was exactly like . . ."

"A quantum-state standing wavefront," said Orphu. "Human consciousness exists primarily as a quantum state waveform, just like the rest of the universe."

"And you're saying that consciousness itself created these other universes?" Mahnmut followed the logic, if it could be called that, but he was shocked by the absurd implications.

"Not just consciousness," said Orphu. "Exceptional types of consciousness that are like naked singularities in that they can bend space-time, affect the organization of space-time, and collapse probability waves into discrete alternatives. I'm talking Shakespeare here. Proust. *Homer*."

"But that's so . . . so . . . so . . ." stammered Mahnmut.

"Solipsistic?"

"Stupid," said Mahnmut.

They floated along in silence for several minutes. Mahnmut assumed that he might have hurt his friend's feelings, but that wasn't important right now. After a while, he said over the tightbeam, "So are you expecting to find the ghosts of the real Greek gods when we get to Olympus Mons?"

"Not ghosts," said Orphu. "But you saw the quantum readings. Whoever these people are on Olympus, they've punched quantum holes all around this world, all centered on or near Olympus. They're going *somewhere*. Coming from *somewhere else*. The quantum reality of this area is so unstable it may actually implode, and take a chunk of our solar system with it."

"Do you think that's what the Device is built to do?" asked Mahnmut. "Implode the quantum fields here before they reach some critical mass?"

"I don't know," said Orphu. "Perhaps."

"And do you think that's what screwed up the Earth and sent the post-humans to their orbital cities fourteen hundred years ago there? Some quantum failure?"

"No," said Orphu. "I think that whatever happened on Earth was a result of quantum teleportation *success*, not failure."

"What do you mean?" For a brief second, Mahnmut was not sure he wanted to hear the answer.

"I think they punched quantum tunnels into one or more of these alternate realities," said Orphu. "And they let something in."

They floated along in silence until sunrise.

The sun touched the top of the balloon first, painting the orange fabric in unreal light and causing each buckycable to gleam. Then it reached the three Tharsis volcanoes, glinting on ice, moving goldly down the east side of each of the three volcanoes like so much slow magma. Then the sun bathed the breaking clouds in pink and gold and illuminated the Valles Marineris Inland Sea all the way to the eastern horizon like a lapis crack in the world. Olympus Mons caught the sunlight a minute later and Mahnmut watched as the great peak seemed to rise above the western horizon like some advancing galleon with sails of gold and red.

Then the sun glinted on something closer and higher.

"Orphu!" sent Mahnmut. "We have company."

"One of the chariots?"

"Still too far away to tell. Even with vision magnification, it's lost in the sunrise glare."

"Anything we can do if it is the chariot people? Have you found any weapons without telling me?"

"All we have to throw at them is harsh language," said Mahnmut, still watching the gleaming speck. It was moving very fast and would be on them soon. "Unless you want me to trigger the Device."

"It might be a bit early for that," said Orphu.

"It seems odd that Koros III came on this mission without weapons."

"We don't know what he would have brought along from the command pod," said Orphu. "But that reminds me of something I've been thinking about."

"What's that?"

"You remember we were discussing Koros's secret mission to the asteroid belt a few years ago."

"Yes?" The sun was still blazing from the advancing aircraft, but Mahnmut could see that it was a chariot now, its holographic horses in full gallop.

"What if it wasn't a spy mission?" said Orphu.

"What do you mean?"

"I mean, the rock moravecs have one thing we five-moons types never bothered to evolve."

"Aggression?" said Mahnmut. "Bellicosity?"

"Exactly. What if Koros III was sent not as a spy, but as a . . ."

"Excuse me," interrupted Mahnmut. "But our guest is here. One large humanoid in a chariot."

Sonic booms crashed around Mahnmut, rippling the fabric of the huge balloon above. The chariot continued to decelerate. It circled the balloon once from a distance of a hundred meters.

"The same man who greeted us in orbit?" asked Orphu. His voice was perfectly calm. Mahnmut looked at the helpless shell lashed to the deck, without so much as an eye to watch what was going on.

"No," he said. "That Greek god had a gray beard. This one is younger and clean shaven. He looks to be about three meters tall." Mahnmut held up his hand, palm outward in the ancient sign for greeting, showing no weapon. "I think he . . ."

The chariot wheeled closer. The man at the reins held out his right hand, fist closed, and swept the fist from right to left.

The balloon exploded above them, helium venting as the fabric flamed. Mahnmut grabbed the wooden railing of the gondola to keep from being thrown out as the twisting mass of flaming fabric, bucky-carbon cable, and boat-shaped gondola plunged toward the Tharsis Plateau thirteen kilometers below. The little moravec was in negative-g, feet above his head, connected to the gondola only by his fierce grip on the railing as the platform began to tumble in freefall.

The chariot with its ghostlike horses flew right at and through the flaming balloon fabric above. The man—god—reached out and grabbed the black buckycable in one huge fist. Impossibly, absurdly, instead of ripping his arm out of its socket, the gondola jerked to a stop as the man held several tons in one hand. He whipped the horses with the reins, using his other hand.

Trailing the pitching gondola and its contents forty meters below and behind it, the chariot turned and flew west toward Olympus Mons.

The Mediterranean Basin

Savi drove another hour or so down the red-clay road, steering the crawler deeper into the fields and folds of the Mediterranean Basin. It was dark and raining hard now, with lightning flashing and thunder vibrating the glass-sphere of the passenger shell. Daeman pointed out the crosses with their humanoid shapes in one of the bright flashes. "What are those? People?"

"Not people," said Savi. *"Calabani."*

Before she could explain, Daeman said, "We have to stop."

Savi did so, turning on the headlights and overhead lights and removing her night-vision glasses. "What's wrong?" Evidently she could see the distress on Daeman's face.

"I'm starving," he said.

"I have two food bars in my pack . . ."

"I'm dying of thirst," he said.

"I have a water bottle in the pack. And we can crack the shell and get some fresh, cold rainwater . . ."

"I have to go to the toilet," said Daeman. "Bad."

"Ah, well," said Savi. "The crawler has a lot of nice amenities, but no onboard toilet. We could probably all use a rest stop." She touched two virtual buttons and the forcefield quit keeping rain off the glass and the slice in the side of the bubble slid open. The air was fresh and smelled of wet fields and crops.

"Outside?" said Daeman, not trying to hide his horror. "In the open?"

"In the cornfield," said Savi. "More privacy there." She reached into her pack and took out a roll of tissues, handing Daeman some.

He stared at the tissues with shock.

"I can use a rest stop," said Harman, accepting some of the flimsy tissues from her. "Come on, Daeman. Men to the right of the crawler. Ladies to the left." He stepped out through the slice and clambered down the strut ladder. Daeman followed, still holding the tissues like a talisman, and the old woman clambered down behind him with more grace than he'd shown.

"I'll have to go to the right as well," said Savi. "Different row of corn, perhaps, but not too far away."

"Why?" began Daeman, but then saw the black gun in her hand. "Oh."

She tucked the weapon in her belt and the three walked off the road, across a low ditch, across a muddy stretch of field, and into the high corn. The rain was falling heavily now.

"We'll be soaked," Daeman said. "I didn't bring my self-drying clothes . . ."

Savi looked up at the sky as lightning ripped from cloud to cloud and the thunder echoed down the broad basin. "I have both your thermskins in the pack. We get back in the crawler, you can wear those while the other clothes dry."

"Anything else in that magical pack that you want to tell us about?" asked Harman.

Savi shook her head. "A few food bars. Flechette clips. A flashlight and some maps I drew myself. All of our thermskins. Water bottle. An extra sweater I carry around. That's about it."

As eager as Daeman was to get into the privacy of the cornfield, he paused at the edge of it to peer around. "Is it safe out here?" he asked.

Savi shrugged. "No voynix."

"What about those . . . what did you call them?"

"Calibani," said Savi. "Don't worry about them tonight."

He nodded and stepped into the first row of corn. The stalks rose two or three feet higher than his head. Rain pattered heavily on the broad leaves. He stepped back out. "It's really dark in there."

Harman had disappeared into the corn already and Savi was walking the other direction, but she stopped, turned, walked back, and handed Daeman the flashlight. "There's enough lightning for me to see."

Daeman shouldered his way through the high stalks for eight or ten rows, trying to get far enough away from the edge of the field to be completely invisible. Then he walked another eight or nine rows to be safe. He found a row perhaps a bit less muddy than the other rows, looked around, set the flashlight against a cornstalk so the beam cut upward only—reminding him of the blue beam in Jerusalem—and then he dropped his trousers, squatted, and dug a shallow hole with his hands. *What did Savi call this?* he thought. *Camping?*

When he was finished—a terrific relief, despite the barbarous circumstances—he did the best he could with the wet and soggy tissues in his hand, found it not enough, tossed the tissues into the muddy hole, and then felt the bulge in his tunic pocket. He pulled out the thirty inches of folded material that he always carried. His turin cloth. In the light reflecting from the flashlight-illuminated cornstalks above him, he studied the fine linen and the beautiful microcircuit-imprinted embroidery that brought the turin drama directly to one's brain. Watching the Trojans battle the Achaeans had been an occasional habit of his for years, but after meeting the real Odysseus—if the bearded old man *was* the real Odysseus, which didn't seem at all likely—Daeman didn't retain much interest in the turin drama. Odysseus had not only slept with one of the girls Daeman had planned to seduce, Hannah, but he'd gone home to Ardis Hall with Daeman's primary target of opportunity, Ada. Still, he held the beautiful linen cloth in his hand as if weighing it.

To hell with it. Daeman used it—taking an unexpected pleasure in vicariously treating the arrogant Odysseus this way—tossed it in the hole, kicked mud over the hole, hitched up his trousers and set his tunic straight, tried to wash his hands against the rain-slick cornstalks, and then picked up his flashlight and walked the two dozen or so rows out of the field.

But there was no end to the field. After thirty-five rows or so, he was sure he had gone the wrong direction. He spun around, trying to ascertain the correct direction—all he had to do was follow his muddy footprints back in the opposite direction—but the spinning had disoriented him so that he couldn't tell which direction he'd been heading. And the footprints were nowhere to be found. The lightning was more intense now, the rain coming down harder.

"Help!" shouted Daeman. He waited a second, heard no reply, and shouted again. "Help! I'm lost in here!" Thunder drowned out both of his cries.

He turned again, then again, decided that this had to be the right direction back, and began running through the high corn, bending stalks aside, battering at them with the small flashlight. He forgot to count the rows, but must have gone forty or fifty wet rows before stopping again.

"Help! I'm in here!" This time no thunder drowned his shouting, but there was still no reply, no noise except for the hard patter of rain on the cornstalks and the squelch of his soggy city shoes.

He began moving up a row, watching to both sides for light or movement, not thinking of how this movement would just get him further away from the other two. After several minutes he had to pause for breath.

"Help!" Lightning struck less than a mile away and the thunder moved across the tall corn like a shock wave. Daeman blinked away the afterimages of the flash and noticed that the corn seemed less thick up the row and to his right. It had to be the edge of the field.

He ran the last fifteen rows or so and burst into the opening.

It was not the edge of the field where he'd entered, but a clearing, perhaps twenty feet wide and thirty feet deep. In the center of the clearing, rising six or eight feet taller than the corn, was a large metal cross. Daeman ran the beam of the flashlight from the base of the cross up to the top of it.

The figure was not *on* the cross, but, rather, nestled *in* the hollowed-out metal form, its naked torso wedged into the upright column, its bare arms extended in the crossmembers. The flashlight beam jiggled in the downpour as Daeman stared.

It was not a man—at least like no man Daeman had ever seen. The man-thing was naked and slick, scaled and greenish—not fish-green, but with the green Daeman had always imagined as the color of corpses before the firmary ended such barbarities. The scales were small and numerous and gleamed in the flashlight. The thing was well-muscled, but the muscles were *wrong*—the arms too long, forearms too lanky, wrists too powerful, knuckles far too large, yellow claws instead of fingernails, thighs too powerful, feet three-toed and oddly splayed. It was a male—the penis and scrotum were obscenely visible and garishly pink beneath the washboard stomach and muscled abdomen, again somehow *wrong*, like a turtle or shark with almost-human genitalia—but the thick upper torso, snakelike neck, and hairless head were the least human aspects of the creature. Rain ran off the muscles and scales and banded ligaments, dripping across the rough black metal of the cross.

The eyes were sunken under brows at once apelike and fishlike and the face extruded out more snout or gill-like than nose. Under the snout, the thing's mouth hung slightly open and Daeman stared at the long yellow teeth—not human, not animal, more fishlike if fish were monsters—and a far-too-long blue-ish tongue that stirred even as Daeman watched. He flicked the flashlight beam higher and almost screamed again.

The man-thing's eyes had opened—oblong yellow cat's-eyes, without a cat's cool connection to humanity—with tiny black slits in the center. The thing . . . what had Savi called it? A *calibani?*—stirred in its cross-niche, the hands opened from fists to extended fingers, long claws catching the light, and the legs and torso shifted as if the creature were waking and stretching.

There were no restraints on it. There was nothing to keep it from leaping down at Daeman this instant.

Daeman tried to run, but found that he couldn't turn his back on the thing. It stirred again, its right hand and most of its arm coming free from the cross-niche. Its feet, Daeman now saw, also held yellow claws at the end of the webbed toes.

There was a crashing and roar behind Daeman—more *calibani*, already free from their crosses, he was sure—and Daeman whirled to meet their charge, raising the flashlight like a club and losing the light from it.

His feet slipped, or his legs weakened, and Daeman went to his knees in the mud in the clearing. He felt like crying, but didn't think he did in the few seconds before the crawler burst from the row of corn, looming like a monstrous spider over Daeman and the cornfield and the cross and the unmoving *calibani*. The crawler's eight headlights switched on, blinding him. He threw his forearm across his face, but, he realized later, more to hide his tears than to protect his eyes from the light.

Dressed in thermskins, the two men reclining on the cracked leather chairs and the old woman lying on the inner curve of the glass sphere, they ate their foodbars, passed around the water bottle, and watched the storm in silence for a while. Daeman had asked Savi to get away from the field and the cross and the creature, so she'd driven a mile or two up the red clay road before pulling to the side and shutting off everything but the crawler's forcefield and dim virtual panels.

"What was that thing?" Daeman said at last.

"One of the *calibani*," said Savi. She actually looked comfortable lying on the glass wall, backpack behind her head.

"I know what you called them," snapped Daeman. "What *are* they?"

Savi sighed. "If I start explaining one thing, then I have to explain the rest. There's a lot you *eloi* don't know—almost everything, actually."

"Why don't you start with explaining why you call us *eloi*," said Harman. His voice was hard.

"I guess it started as a form of insult," said Savi. Lightning flashed, illuminating the lines on her face, but the storm had moved on far enough that the thunder came late, from very far away. "Although to be fair, I called my own people that before calling yours the word."

"What does it mean?" demanded Harman.

"It's a term from a very old story in a very old book," said Savi. "About a man who travels through time to the far future and finds humankind evolved into two races—one gentle, lazy, purposeless, basking in the sun, the *eloi*, and the other ugly, monstrous, productive, technological, but hiding in caves and darkness, the *morlocks*. In the old book, the *morlocks* provided food, shelter, and clothing for the *eloi* until the gentle people had fattened up nicely. And then the *morlocks* ate them."

Lightning flashed across the fields again, but it was a pale, receding light. "Is that what our world is like?" asked Daeman. "Us as the *eloi* and the *calibani* and voynix as the *morlocks*? Do they eat us?"

"I wish it were that simple," said Savi. She laughed softly, but the noise held no humor.

"What are the *calibani*?" said Harman.

Instead of answering, the old woman said, "Daeman, show Harman one of your palm tricks."

Daeman hesitated. "Which one?" he said. "Proxnet or farnet?"

"We know where *we* are, darling," the old woman said sarcastically. "Show him farnet."

Daeman scowled, but did so. He told Harman to think of three blue squares in the center of three red circles and suddenly a blue oval was floating over both of their palms. "Think of someone," Daeman said, feeling strange. He'd never taught anyone anything before, if one didn't count sexual techniques. "Anyone," he added. "Just visualize them."

Harman looked dubious but concentrated. An aerial representation of Ardis filled Harman's oval, then a diagram of the layout of Ardis Hall. A stylized female figure was standing with a group of stylized men and women on the front porch of the manor.

"Ada," said Daeman. "You were thinking of Ada."

"Incredible," said Harman. He stared at the image for a moment. "I'm going to visualize Odysseus," he said.

The image shifted, changed magnitude, searched, but came up with nothing.

"Farnet doesn't have a lock on Odysseus, according to Savi," said Daeman. "But go back to Ada. Look where she is."

Harman frowned but focused. The stylized cartoon of Ada was in a field a hundred yards or so behind Ardis Hall. There were scores of other human figures represented seated in front and around a void. Ada joined the crowd.

Daeman looked at Harman's palm image. "I wonder what's going on there. If Odysseus is in that empty spot, it looks as if the old barbarian's addressing a crowd."

"And Ada's listening to him or watching him perform," said Harman. He looked away from the palm oval. "What does this have to do with my question, Savi? Who are the *calibani*? Why are the voynix trying to kill us? What's going on?"

"A few centuries before the final fax," she said, folding her hands together, "the post-humans got too clever by half. Their science was impressive. To all intents and purposes, they'd fled the Earth to their orbital rings during the terrible rubicon epidemic. But they were still masters of the earth. They thought they were masters of the universe.

"The posts had rigged the whole Earth with the limited form of energy-data transmission and retrieval that you call faxing, and now they were experimenting—playing really—with time travel, quantum teleportation, and other dangerous things. A lot of their playing around was predicated on ancient sciences from as far back as the Nineteenth Century—black-hole physics, wormhole theory, quantum mechanics—but what they relied on most was the Twentieth Century discovery that, at its heart, everything is information. Data. Consciousness. Matter. Energy. Everything is information."

"I don't understand," said Harman. He sounded angry.

"Daeman, you've shown Harman the farnet function. Why don't you show him the allnet?"

"Allnet?" repeated Daeman, alarm in his voice.

"You know, four blue triangles above three red circles above four green triangles."

"No!" said Daeman. He thought off his own palm function. The blue glow winked out.

Savi looked at Harman. "If you want to begin to understand why we're here tonight, why the post-humans left Earth forever, and why the *calibani* and voynix are around, visualize four blue triangles above three red circles above four green triangles. It gets easier with practice."

Harman looked suspiciously at Daeman, but then he closed his eyes and concentrated.

Daeman concentrated on *not* visualizing those shapes. He forced himself to remember Ada naked as a teenager, to remember the last time he had sex with a girl, to remember his mother scolding him . . .

"My *God!*" cried Harman.

Daeman looked at the other man. Harman had stood, stumbling out of his chair, and was whirling, moving his head in jerks, staring openmouthed at everything.

"What do you see?" Savi asked softly. "What do you hear?"

"God . . . God . . ." moaned Harman. "I see . . . Jesus Christ. Everything. Everything. Energy . . . the stars are singing . . . the corn in the fields is speaking, to each other, to the Earth. I see . . . the crawler's full of little microbes, repairing it, cooling it . . . I see . . . my God, my hand!" Harman was studying his hand with a look of total horror and revelation.

"Enough for the first time," said Savi. "Think the word 'off.' "

"Not . . . yet . . ." gasped Harman. He stumbled against the glass wall of the passenger sphere and clawed at it weakly as if trying to get out. "It's so . . . so beautiful . . . I can almost . . ."

"Think *off!*" roared Savi.

Harman blinked, fell against the wall, and turned a pale, staring face in their direction.

"What *was* that?" he said. "I saw . . . everything. Heard . . . *everything.*"

"And understood nothing," said Savi. "But neither do I when I'm on allnet. Perhaps even the post-humans didn't understand it all."

Harman staggered to his chair and collapsed into it. "But where did it come from?"

"Millennia ago," said Savi, "the real old-style humans had a crude information ecology they called the Internet. Eventually they decided to tame the Internet and created a thing called Oxygen—not the gas, but artificial intelligences floating in and over and above the Internet, directing it, connecting it, tagging it, leading humans through it when they went hunting for people or information."

"Proxnet?" said Daeman. His hands were shaking and he hadn't even accessed farnet or allnet tonight.

Savi nodded. "What led to proxnet. Eventually, Oxygen evolved into the noosphere, a logosphere, a planet-wide datasphere. But that wasn't enough for the post-humans. They connected this super-Internet noosphere with the biosphere, the living components of the Earth. Every plant and animal and erg of energy on the planet, which—when connected to the noosphere—created a complete and total information ecology touching everything on, above, and within the Earth, a sort of sentient omnisphere that lacked only self-awareness and identity. Then the post-humans foolishly gave it that self-awareness—not just designing an overriding artifical intelligence, but allowing it to evolve its own persona. This super-noosphere called itself Prospero. Does that name mean anything to either of you?"

Daeman shook his head and looked at Harman, but even though the older man knew how to read books, he also shook his head.

"It doesn't matter," said Savi. "Suddenly the post-humans had an . . . opponent . . . that they couldn't control. And it wasn't over yet. The post-humans were using self-evolving programs and projects of other sorts as well, allowing their quantum computers to pursue their own goals. As impossible as it is to believe, they achieved stable wormholes, they achieved time travel, and they transported people—old-style humans as guinea pigs, since they'd never risk their own immortal lives—through timespace gates via quantum teleportation."

"What does that have to do with the *calibani*?" persisted Harman, obviously still shaking the images from the allnet out of his head.

Savi smiled. "The Prospero noosphere entity either has an advanced set of irony or none at all. The sentient biosphere, he christened it Ariel—a sort of Earth spirit—and together, Ariel and Prospero created the *calibani*. They evolved a strain of humanity—not old-style, not post, not *eloi*—into that monster you saw on the cross tonight."

"Why?" asked Daeman. He barely choked the single syllable out.

Savi shrugged. "Enforcers. Prospero is a peaceful entity, or so it likes to think. But its *calibani* are monsters. Killers."

"Why?" This time it was Harman asking the question.

"To stop the voynix," said the old woman. "To chase the post-humans off the Earth before they could do more harm. To enforce whatever whim the Prospero and Ariel points of the noosphere trinity wish enforced."

Daeman tried to understand this. He failed. Finally he said, "Why was the thing on a cross?"

"It wasn't *on* the cross," said Savi. "It was *in* the cross. Recharging cradle."

Harman looked so pale that Daeman thought the other man might be ill. "Why did the posts create the voynix?"

"Oh, they didn't create the voynix," said Savi. "The voynix came from somewhere else, serving someone else, with their own agenda."

"I always thought they were machines," said Daeman. "Like the other servitors."

"No," said Savi.

Harman looked out into the night. The rain had stopped and the lightning and thunder had moved over the horizon. A few stars were appearing between cloud tatters. "The *calibani* keep the voynix out of the Basin here," he said.

"They're one of the things that keeps the voynix away," agreed Savi. She sounded pleased, her voice holding a teacher's tone, as if one of her students had turned out not to be a total moron.

"But why haven't the *calibani* killed us?" asked Harman.

"Our DNA," said Savi.

"Our what?" said Daeman.

"Never mind, my darlings. Suffice it to say that I borrowed a snippet of each of your hair and that, along with a lock of my own, has saved us all. I made a deal with Ariel, you see. Allow us to pass this once, and I promised to save the soul of the Earth."

"You've met the Ariel Earth-entity?" asked Harman.

"Well, not *met* him exactly," said Savi. "But I've chatted with him across the noosphere-biosphere interface. We made a deal."

Daeman knew then that the old woman was truly mad. He caught Harman's eye and saw the same conclusion there.

"It doesn't matter," said Savi. She plumped her pack like a pillow and lay back and closed her eyes. "Get some sleep, my young darlings. You need to be rested tomorrow. Tomorrow, with any luck, we fly up, up, up to the orbitside layer."

She was asleep and snoring before Harman and Daeman could exchange another worried glance.

Ilium and Olympos

As it turns out, I can't do it. I don't have the guts or balls or ruthlessness or—perhaps—courage. I can't kidnap Hector's child, even to save Ilium. Even to save the child himself. Even to save my own life.

It isn't dawn yet when I QT to Hector's huge home in Ilium. I was here just two evenings before when—morphed then as the now-decapitated spearman Dolon—I followed Hector home in search of his wife and son. Since I know the layout from that visit, I QT directly to the nursery, not far from Andromache's sleeping chamber. Hector's son, less than a year old, is in a wonderfully carved cradle with mosquito netting draped over it. Nearby sleeps the same nurse who was on the battlements of Troy with Andromache that evening when Hector accidentally frightened his son with the reflection in his polished war helmet. She's also fast asleep, reclining on a nearby couch, wearing a thin, diaphanous gown draped with all the complexity of an Aubrey Beardsley print. Even this sleeping gown is sashed under her breasts in the Greek and Trojan manner, showing how large and white the nurse's bosom is, visible in the reflected light from the guardsmen's fire tripods on the terrace beyond. I'd guessed earlier that she's a wet nurse for the baby. This is relevant, actually, because my plot hinges on being able to kidnap the baby *with* the nurse, leaving Andromache behind—after "Aphrodite" appears to her and tells her that the child is being kidnapped by the gods, as punishment for unnamed failings on the part of the Trojans, and that if Hector wants the child, he can damned well come to Olympos to get him, blah, blah, blah.

First I have to gather up the baby and then grab the nurse—I suspect that she might be stronger than me, and almost certainly more adept at fighting, so I'll taser her if I have to, although I don't want to—and then

QT the two of them to that rapidly populating hill in ancient Indiana, find Nightenhelser—I haven't decided what I'm going to do with Patroclus—and convince the scholic to watch over the infant and his nurse until I come back for them.

Will Nightenhelser be up to the task of riding herd on this Trojan nurse for the days, weeks, or months until all this is over? Given the matchup of a Twentieth Century male classics professor versus a Trojan wet nurse circa 1200 B.C., I'd put my money on the nurse. And give my opponents good odds. Well, that's Nightenhelser's problem. My job is to find leverage against Hector, a way to convince him that he *has* to fight the gods—just as Patroclus' "death" was my best shot to enroll Achilles into this suicidal crusade—and that leverage is sleeping in front of me right now.

Little Scamandrius, whom the people of Ilium lovingly call "Astyanax, Lord of the City," mewls slightly in his sleep and rubs tiny fists against his reddened cheeks. Even though invisible under the Hades Helmet, I freeze and watch the nurse. She sleeps on, although I know that an actual cry from the baby will almost certainly wake her.

I don't know why I pull off the cowl of the Hades Helmet, but I do, becoming visible to myself. There's no one else here except my two victims, and they'll be 10,000 miles away from here in a few seconds, unable to give my description to any Trojan police sketch artist.

I tiptoe closer and remove the mosquito netting from above the infant. A breeze blows in from the distant sea and flutters both the terrace curtains and the gauzier material around the crib. Without a sound, the baby opens his blue eyes and looks right at me. Then he smiles at me, his kidnapper, although I thought little pre-toddlers were afraid of strangers, much less of strangers in their bedroom in the middle of the night. But what do I know about kids? My wife and I never had any, and all the students I taught over the years were actually partially or poorly formed adults, all gangly and bumpy and hairy and socially awkward and goofy looking. I couldn't even have told you that babies less than a year old *could* smile.

But Scamandrius is smiling at me. In a second he's going to start making noise and I'll have to grab him, grab the nurse, QT us the hell out of here—can I QT two other people along with me? We'll find out in a second. Then I have to come back and use my last three minutes of morphing time to steal Aphrodite's form and give my ultimatum to Andromache.

Will Hector's wife be hysterical? Will she weep and scream? I doubt it. After all, in recent years she's seen Achilles kill her father and her seven brothers, she's watched her mother become Achilles' plunder and then die trying to give birth to her rapist's bastard, she's watched her home occupied and defiled, and still she's borne up—not only borne up, but bore a healthy son to her husband, Hector. And now she has to watch Hector go out to battle every day, knowing in her heart that her beloved's fate has already been sealed by the cruel will of the gods. No, this is no weak woman. Even morphed as Aphrodite, I'd better keep a keen eye on Andromache's sleeves to make sure she doesn't have any daggers with which to greet the goddess's news of the kidnapping.

I actually reach for the baby, my fingers with their dirty nails just inches away from his pink flesh, before drawing back.

I can't do it.

I can't *do* it.

Stunned by my own impotence even in the face of doom—everyone's doom, for even the Greeks will be punished through their victory—I stagger out of the nursery, not even bothering to pull the Hades Helmet back on.

I put my hand on the QT medallion, but pause. Where do I go? What-ever Achilles is doing, it doesn't really matter now. He can't conquer Olympos on his own, or even with the Achaean army if the Trojans are still at war with them. In fact, my little charade with the man-killer may have been for nothing—Hector and his hordes may beat the Achaeans this very morning while Achilles is still ripping his hair out and scream-ing in grief over Patroclus' apparent murder. Achilles doesn't give a damn about the Trojans right now. And when Hector and the mystery man Athena promised Achilles—to lead him to Hector, she said, to show him how to get to Olympos—don't come to him, will he know that my act was only an act? Probably. Then the real Athena will visit Achilles to see what's wrong and will protest her innocence to the fleet-footed man-killer, and perhaps—just perhaps—the *Iliad* will get back on track.

It doesn't matter.

This whole idiot plan is finished. So is Thomas Hockenberry, Ph.D. Past time, probably.

But where to go until the violent Muse or the reawakened Aphrodite finally find me? Go visit Nightenhelser and pissed-off Patroclus? See how long it takes the gods to track my quantum trail once they under-stand what I've done . . . tried to do?

No. That would just bring doom down on Nightenhelser. Let him stay there in 1200 B.C. Indiana and procreate with the lovely Indian maidens, perhaps start a university and teach classics—although most of the classical tales haven't happened yet—and good luck to him about

Patroclus, whom I have no urge to taser again just to drag back to Achilles' tent. "April fool!" I could have my three-minute-morph Athena say. "Here's your friend back, Achilles. No hard feelings?"

No, I'll leave them alone there in Indiana.

Where to go? Olympos? The thought of the Muse hunting for me there, of Zeus and his radar eyes returning, of Aphrodite awakening . . . well, not to Olympos. Not tonight.

I think of one place and visualize it and touch the QT medallion and twist it and go there before I can change my mind.

I'm visible and Helen sees me at once in the soft light of candles. She rises on one arm on her cushions and says, "Hock-en-bear-eeee?"

I stand in her bedchamber and say nothing. I don't know why I'm here. If she calls her guards or even comes toward me with that dagger, I feel too tired to fight, too tired even to flee on the QT. I don't even think to wonder why her bedchamber is illuminated by candles at four-thirty in the morning.

She comes toward me, but not with the dagger. I'd forgotten how beautiful Helen of Troy is—her svelte, soft figure in the transparent gown making Scamandrius' busty nurse look just lumpy and squat by comparison. "Hock-en-bear-eeee?" she says softly, with that sweet pronunciation of my name, so difficult to say in Ancient Greek. I almost weep as I realize that she's the only human being on Earth, except for Nightenhelser—who may be dead by now—who knows my name. "Are you hurt, Hock-en-bear-eeee?"

"Hurt?" I manage. "No. I'm not hurt."

Helen leads me into the bathing room adjoining her bedchamber. This is where I first saw her that night. Candles are lighted here as well, there is water in a basin, and I see my reflection—red-eyed, stubble-cheeked, exhausted. I realize that I haven't really slept for . . . how long? I can't remember. "Sit," says Helen, and I collapse onto the ledge of a marble bathtub. "Why have you come, Hock-en-bear-eeee?"

Stumbling with words, I say, "I tried to find the fulcrum," and go on to explain my useless charade with Achilles, the kidnap of Patroclus, my plan to turn the heroes of the war against the gods to save . . . everyone, everything.

"But you did not kill Patroclus?" says Helen, her dark eyes intense.

"No. I just took him . . . elsewhere."

"Using the gods' method of travel," says Helen.

"Yes."

"But you could not spirit away Astyanax, Hector's son, this way?"

I shake my head dumbly.

I see Helen thinking, her beautiful dark eyes lost in reverie. How can she believe my explanations? Who in the hell does she think I am? Why had she befriended me before—"befriended" being somewhat of a euphemism for that long night of passion—and what will she do with me now?

As if to answer that last question, Helen rises with a grim look in her eye and goes out of the bathing room. I hear her calling names in the hallway and know that the guards will be back with her in less than a minute, so I raise my hand to the heavy QT medallion.

I can't think of anywhere to go.

I have charge left in my taser baton, but I don't reach for it as Helen returns with several others. But not guards—serving girls. Slaves.

A minute later they are undressing me, stacking my filthy garments by the wall as other young women bring in tall pitchers of steaming hot water for the bath. I let them take the morphing bracelet off me, but I cling to the QT medallion. I shouldn't get it wet, but I don't want it out of my reach.

"You are going to bathe, Hock-en-bear-eeee," says Helen of Troy. She lifts a short, gleaming razor blade. "And then I am going to shave you myself. Here, drink this. It will restore your energy and spirits." She hands me a goblet with a thick liquid inside.

"What is it?" I ask.

"Nestor's favorite drink," laughs Helen. "Or it was when the old fool used to visit my husband, Menelaus. It restores."

I sniff it, knowing that I'm being boorish. "What's in it?"

"Wine, grated cheese, and barley," says Helen, lifting the goblet closer to my lips by moving my cupped hands upward. Her fingers look very white against my sun-darkened and dirty skin. "But I also add honey to sweeten it."

"So does Circe," I say, laughing stupidly.

"Who, Hock-en-bear-eeee?"

I shake my head. "Never mind. It's in the *Odyssey*. Doesn't matter. Ir-reli . . . irrele . . . irrelevant and immaterial." I drink. The liquid has the punch of a Missouri mule. I wonder idly if there any mules in Missouri circa 1200 B.C.

The young servant girls have stripped me naked, having me stand to pull off my tunic and underthings. I don't even think to be embarrassed. I'm too tired and the drink has given my brain a distinct buzz.

"Bathe, Hock-en-bear-eeee," says Helen and offers me her arm to hold as I step into the deep and steaming bath. "I will shave you in the bath."

The water's so hot that I cringe like a child, lowering myself carefully, hesitating to let the steaming water touch my scrotum. But I do—I'm too tired to fight gravity—and when I lean back against the slanted marble back of the tub, Helen's servants lathering my whisker-stubbled cheeks and neck, I don't even worry about Helen handling the razor's blade so close to my eyes and jugular. I trust her.

Feeling Nestor's drink giving me energy again, deciding that if Helen offers me her bed I'll definitely ask her to share it with me in this last hour or so before dawn, I close my eyes for just a moment. Just a few seconds.

When I awake it's mid-morning, at least, with heavy light coming through small windows high on the wall. I'm shaved and clean, even perfumed. I'm also lying on a cold, stone floor in an empty room, not in Helen's high bed. And I'm naked—completely naked, not even the QT medallion in sight. As real awareness flows into my brain like reluctant water into a leaky basin, I notice that I'm tied with multiple leather straps to iron rings in the wall and floor. Leather restraints run from my wrists—knotted together over my head—to the wall. Straps from my bound ankles, legs spread apart, run a few inches to two other iron rings in the floor.

This posture and situation would be embarrassing and alarming even if I were alone, but I'm not. Five women are standing over me, staring down at me. None of them look amused. I tug at the leather reins as I instinctively try to cover my genitals, but the straps are short and my hands don't even lower to the level of my shoulders. Nor do the straps on my ankles allow me to close my legs. I see now that all of the women are carrying daggers, although some of the blades seem long enough to be called swords.

I know the women. Besides Helen in the center, there is Hecuba, King Priam's queen, Hector's and Paris's gray-haired but attractive mother. Next to Hecuba is Laodice, the queen's daughter and the warrior Helicaon's wife. To the left of Helen is Theano, Cisseus' daughter, the Trojan horseman Antenor's wife, but—and possibly more relevant to my current situation—Ilium's primary priestess serving the goddess Athena. I can't imagine that Theano will be happy to hear that this mere mortal man has taken the form and used the voice of the goddess she's served her entire life. I look at Theano's grim expression and guess that she's already heard the news.

Finally there is Andromache, Hector's wife, the woman whose child I was going to kidnap and carry away to exile in Indiana. Her expression is the sternest of all the women's. She is tapping a long, razor-sharp dagger against her palm and she looks impatient.

Helen sits on a low couch near me. "Hock-en-bear-eeee, you need to tell us all the story you have told me. Who you are. Why you have been watching the war. What the gods are like and what you tried to do during the night."

"Will you release me first?" My tongue feels thick. She drugged me.

"No. Speak now. Tell only the truth. Theano has been given the gift from Athena of telling truth from lies, even from someone whose accent is as barbaric as yours. Speak now. Leave nothing out."

I hesitate. Perhaps my best bet here might be to keep my mouth shut.

Leano goes to one knee next to me. She's a lovely young woman with pale gray eyes, like her goddess. Her dagger blade is short, broad, double-edged, and very cold. I know the cold part because she's just laid the blade under my testicles, lifting them like an offering on a silver serving knife. The dagger's point draws blood in my sensitive perineum and my whole body tries to contract and rise away, even as I just succeed in not crying out.

"Tell everything, lie about nothing," whispers Athena's high priestess. "At your first lie, I will feed you your left stone. Your second lie, you eat the right one. Your third lie and I will be feeding my hounds whatever is left."

So, all right, I tell everything. Who I am. How the gods have revived me for scholic duty. My impressions of Olympos. My revolt against my Muse, my attack on Aphrodite and Ares, my plot to turn Achilles and Hector against the gods . . . everything. The point of her dagger never moves and the metal under me never warms.

"You took the form of the goddess Athena?" whispers Theano. "You have this in your power?"

"The tools I carry do," I say. "Or they did." I actually close my eyes and grit my teeth, waiting for the cut, slash, plop.

Helen speaks. "Tell Hecuba, Laodice, Theano, and Andromache about your view of the near future. Our fates."

"He is no seer granted such vision by the gods," says Hecuba. "He is not even civilized. Listen to his speech. Bar bar bar bar."

"He admits to coming from far away," says Helen. "He can't help being a barbarian. But listen to what he sees in our future, noble daughter of Dymas. Tell us, Hock-en-bear-eeee."

I lick my lips. Theano's eyes are the transparent, North Sea gray of a true believer, a Waffen SS man's eyes. Hecuba's eyes are dark and don't show as much intelligence as Helen's. Laodice's gaze is hooded; Andromache's bright and fierce and dangerously strong.

"What do you want to know?" I say. Anything I say will be about the fate of these people's lives and husbands and city and children.

"Everything that is true. Everything that you think you know," says Helen.

I hesitate only a second then, trying to pay no attention to Theano's feminist blade against my nether regions.

"This is not a vision of the future," I say, "but rather my memory of a tale that is told of your future, which is my past."

Knowing that what I just said can't make any sense to any of them, and wondering if it even came through my barbarous accent—accent? I don't think I speak this Greek with an accent—I tell them about the days and months to come.

I tell them that Ilium will fall, that blood will run in the streets, and that all their homes will be put to the torch. I tell Hecuba that her husband, Priam, will be murdered at the foot of Zeus's statue in their private temple. I tell Andromache that her husband, Hector, will be cut down by Achilles when no one from the city has the nerve to go out and fight alongside her love, and that Hector's body will be dragged around the city behind Achilles' chariot and then be dragged back to the Achaean camp to be pissed on by the soldiers and worried by the Greek dogs. Then I tell her that in just a few weeks, her son, Scamandrius, will be thrown down from the highest point on the city's wall, his brains dashed out on the rocks below. I tell Andromache that her pain will not be over then, because she will be condemned to live and to be dragged back to the Greek isles as a slave, how she will end her days serving meals to the men who killed Hector and burned her city and killed her son. That she will end her days listening to their jokes and sitting silently while the aging Achaean heroes tell stories about these glorious days of rape and plunder.

I describe to Laodice and Theano the rape of Cassandra, and the rape of thousands of the Trojan women and girls and how thousands more will choose the sword rather than such shame. I tell Theano of how Odysseus and Diomedes will steal the sacred Palladion stone from Athena's secret temple and then return in conquest to desecrate and destroy the temple itself. I tell the priestess with the blade at my balls how Athena does nothing—nothing—to stop this rape and plunder and desecration.

And I repeat to Helen the details of Paris's death and her own enslavement at the hands of her former husband, Menelaus.

And then, when I've told everything I know from the *Iliad* and explain again how I don't know that all of this *will* come to pass, but explain how so much from the poem *has* come to pass during my nine years of duty here, I stop. I could tell them about Odysseus' wanderings, or about Agamemnon's murder after his homecoming, or even about Virgil's *Aenead* with the ultimate triumph of Troy in the founding of Rome, but they wouldn't care about any of that.

When I finish my litany of doom, I fall silent. None of the five women are crying. None of the five shows any expression that wasn't on her face when I'd begun my descriptions of their fate.

Exhausted, depleted, I close my eyes and await my own fate.

They allow me to dress, although Helen has the servants bring me fresh undergarments and tunic. Helen holds up each tool—the QT medallion, the taser baton, the Hades Helmet, and the morphing bracelet—and asks if it is part of my "power borrowed from the gods." I consider lying—I especially want the Hades Helmet back—but in the end I tell the truth about each item. "Will it work for one of us if we try to use it?" asks Helen.

Here I hesitate, because I really don't know. Did the gods make the baton and morphing bracelet fingerprint-dependent to keep the weapon out of Greek and Trojan hands if we fell on the battlefield? Quite possibly. None of us scholics ever asked. The morphing device and the QT medallion, at least, will require some training, and I tell the women that. The Hades Helmet will almost certainly work for anyone, since it is a stolen artifact. Helen keeps all of the tools, leaving me only the impact armor that is woven into my cape and leather breastplate. She puts the priceless gifts from the gods in a small embroidered bag, the other women nod, and we leave.

We leave Helen's house—the five women and me—and walk through the mid-morning city streets to the Temple of Athena.

"What's going to happen?" I ask as we hurry through the crowded lanes and alleys, five grim-faced women in black robes not dissimilar from Twentieth Century Muslim burkas and one confused man. I keep looking above the rooftops, expecting the Muse to appear in her chariot at any moment.

"Silence," hisses Helen. "We'll speak when Theano casts silence around us so even the gods cannot hear."

Before we enter the temple, Theano produces a black robe and insists I pull it on. Now we all look like robed women entering the temple through a back door, moving down empty corridors, although one of the six women is wearing combat sandals.

I've never been in the temple, and my glimpse into the main hall through open doors is not disappointing. The space is huge, mostly dark, lighted by hanging braziers and votive candles. It smells and feels most like a Catholic church to me—the scent of incense in a cavernous space where even the echoes are hushed. But instead of a Catholic altar and statues of the Virgin Mary and Child, this space is dominated by a huge central statue to Athena—thirty feet tall, at least, carved of white stone but garishly painted with red lips, blushing cheeks, pink skin—the goddess's gray eyes look to be made of mother of pearl stone—and she is brandishing an elaborate shield of real gold, a breastplate of burnished copper inlaid with gold, a sash of lapis lazuli, and a forty-foot spear of real bronze. It's impressive and I pause at the open door, staring into the sanctuary. There, right there by Athena's sacred sandaled feet, will Ajax the Great trap and rape Cassandra, Priam's daughter.

Helen comes back, seizes my arm, and roughly pulls me along the corridor. I wonder if I'm the first man ever to see into the inner sanctuary of Athena's Temple in Ilium. Isn't the Palladion statue and the temple itself watched over by young virgins? I look up to see the priestess Theano glaring at me and I hurry to catch up. Theano's no virgin—she's fierce Antenor's wife and a piece of tempered work to be reckoned with.

I follow the women down a shadowed staircase to a broad basement, lit only with a few candles. Here Theano looks around, moves a tapestry aside, removes an oddly shaped key from a pocket in her robe, slides it into a seemingly solid wall, and the slab of wall pivots, opening onto a steeper staircase lighted with torches. Theano hurries us all through.

There is a corridor leading to four rooms in this basement under the basement, and I'm herded into the final room, a small place by temple standards—little more than twenty feet by twenty feet, furnished only by a central wooden table, four fire tripods barely glowing—one in each corner—and a single statue of Athena, cruder and smaller than all of the sculptures above. This Athena is less than four feet tall.

"This is the real Palladion, Hock-en-bear-eeee," whispers Helen, referring to the sacred sculpture carved from a stone which fell from heaven one day, thus showing Athena's blessing over the city of Ilium. When the Palladion is stolen, so the century-old story goes, Troy will fall.

Theano and Hecuba stare Helen into silence. My former lover—well, my former one-night stand—dumps the contents of her bag on the table and we all sit on the wooden stools, staring at the Hades Helmet, morphing bracelet, taser baton, and QT medallion. Only the medallion looks like it might be worth anything. The rest of the stuff I'd probably pass over at a garage sale.

Hecuba speaks to Helen. "Tell this . . . man . . . that we must see if his story can be true. If these toys of his have any power." Hector's and Paris's mother lifts the morphing bracelet.

I know she can't activate it, but I still say, "That has only minutes of power in it. Don't fool around with it."

The old woman shoots me a scathing glance. Laodice picks up the taser baton and turns it in her pale hands. "This is the weapon you used to stun Patroclus?" she asks. It is the first time she's spoken in my presence.

"Yes."

"How does it work?"

I tell her the three spots I have to tap and twist to activate the wand. I'm certain that the thing is designed to work only when I'm holding it. Certainly the gods wouldn't be so foolish as to leave the weapon usable for others if I lost it, even though the double tap and single twist are a safety mechanism of sorts. I start to explain to Laodice and the others that only I can use the gods' tools.

Laodice aims the taser at my chest and taps the shaft of the wand again.

Once, when I was hiking with Susan in Brown County, Indiana, we were crossing a hilltop meadow when lightning struck just ten paces from me, knocking me off my feet, blinding me, and leaving me semiconscious for several minutes. We used to joke about that—about the odds against it—but the memory of the jolt used to make my mouth go dry.

This blast is worse.

It feels as if someone has hit me in the chest with a hot poker. I fly off my stool, land numbly on the stone floor, and remember spasming like an epileptic—my arms and legs kicking wildly—before I lose consciousness.

When I come to, hurting, my ears buzzing, my head aching, the four women are ignoring me, looking into the corner at nothing.

Four women? I thought there were five. I sit up and shake my head, trying to get my vision back in focus. *Andromache's missing.* Perhaps she went for help, to find a healer. Maybe the women thought I was dead.

Suddenly Andromache flickers into visibility in the empty space where the others are looking. Hector's wife pulls the Hades Helmet cowl from her shoulders and holds it out.

"The Helmet of Death works, just as the old tales say," says Andromache. "Why would the gods give it to such as he?" She nods in my direction and drops the leather and metal cowl-helmet onto the table.

Theano holds up the QT medallion. "We can't make this work," she says. "Show us." It takes me a fuzzy moment to realize that the priestess is speaking to me.

"Why should I?" I say, getting to my feet and leaning on the table. "Why should I help any of you?"

Helen comes around the table and puts her hand on my forearm. I pull my arm away.

"Hock-en-bear-eeee," she purrs. "Don't you know that the gods have sent you to us?"

"What are you talking about?" I look around the room.

"No, the gods can't hear us in here," says Helen. "The walls of this room are lined with lead. The gods can neither see nor hear through solid lead. This has been known for centuries."

I squint around me. What the hell. Why not? Superman's X-ray vision never worked through lead either. But why would there be a god-proof room in Athena's temple?

Andromache steps closer. "Helen's friend, Hock-en-bear-eeee, we—the women of Troy and Helen—have plotted for years to end this war. But the men—Achilles, the Argives, our own Trojan husbands and fathers—have power over us. They answer only to the gods. Now the gods have heard our most secret prayers and sent you as our instrument. With your help and our planning, we will change the course of events here, saving not only our city, our lives and our children's lives, but also the destiny of mankind—freeing us from the rule of cruel and arbitrary deities."

I shake my head again and actually laugh. "There's a slight flaw in your logic, madame. Why would the gods send me as your instrument if your goal is to overthrow the gods? That makes no sense."

The five Trojan women stare at me for a moment. Then Helen says, "There are more gods than are dreamt of in your philosophy, Hock-en-bear-eeee."

I stare at her for a second, then decide it has to be a coincidence. Either that or I'm not hearing correctly. My chest still hurts and my muscles ache from the spasms the taser caused.

"Give me the tools," I say, testing.

The women slide to me the Hades Helmet, the taser baton, the morphing bracelet, and the QT medallion. I lift the baton as if to hold them all at bay. "What's your plan?" I ask.

"My husband never would have believed me if I'd reported to him that the goddess Aphrodite had appeared and taken Scamandrius and his nurse away to be held for ransom," says Andromache. "Hector has served these gods all his life. He's not the egomaniac that man-killer

Achilles is. Hector would have thought that anything the gods did was only a test of him. Unless Aphrodite or another god were to kill our son in front of witnesses, in front of Hector himself. In that case, his rage would know no bounds. Why didn't you kill my son?"

I have no words to answer that. So Andromache answers for me.

"You are a sentimental fool," she snaps. "You say that Scamandrius will be dashed to his death on the rocks if you do not change the plans of the gods."

"Yes."

"And yet you refused to kill the child who already is fated to die, even though your entire plan to end this war and win your own battle with the gods depended upon it. You are weak, Hock-en-bear-eeee."

"Yes," I say.

Hecuba beckons me to sit, but I remain standing, taser baton in hand. "What's your plan to end this war?" I ask. I'm almost afraid to ask. Would Andromache kill her own son to get her way? I look into her eyes and I'm even more afraid.

"We will tell you our plan," says old Queen Hecuba, "but first you must prove to us that these last two god-toys work." She gestures to the morphing bracelet and the medallion.

Watching them all carefully, I slip the bracelet on. The indicator tells me that there's less than three minutes of actual morph time remaining. I use its scanning functioning to look at Hecuba, then trigger the morphing function.

The real Hecuba disappears as I assume her quantum probability wave space. "Believe me now?" I say in Hecuba's voice. I raise my wrist—Hecuba's wrist—and show them the morphing bracelet. I bring the taser baton out from her gown. The four remaining women, including Helen, gasp and step back, as shocked as if I'd cut the old dowager down with a short sword. More shocked, probably—death by swords, they know all too well.

I drop out of morph and Hecuba flicks back into existence on her side of the room. She blinks, although I know she's had no sense of time passing, and the five women gabble together. I check the bracelet's virtual indicator. Two minutes twenty-eight seconds of morph time left.

I slip the QT medallion chain around my neck. At least this device doesn't seem to have any power limits. "You want me to QT out of here and then back to show you that this also works?" I ask.

Hecuba has recovered her composure. "No," she says. "All of our plans—yours *and* ours—will depend upon your ability to travel to Olympos undetected and to return. Can you take one of us there now?"

I hesitate again. "I can," I say at last, "but the Hades Helmet provides invisibility only for one. If I brought one of you to Olympos with me, you'd be seen."

"Then you must bring something back here that will prove that you have traveled to Olympos," says Hecuba.

I lift my hands, palms up. "What? Zeus's chamber pot?"

All five women step back again, as if I've shouted some obscenity. I remember that—for very good reason—blasphemy is not the casual sport it was in my time, at the end of the Twentieth Century. These gods are very real, and insulting them has consequences. I glance at the walls and hope the lead really shields us from Olympos's view—not because of the chamber pot quip, but because we seem to be planning deicide here.

"When I was with Aphrodite during the judgment of the gods," Helen says softly, "I noticed that the goddess brushed her lustrous hair with a beautiful comb, forged in silver, shaped by some god of craft. Go to her chambers on Olympos and bring it back."

I start to remind them of what I'd told them—that Aphrodite was currently floating in a healing vat—but then realized that it made no difference. Her comb wouldn't be in the vat with her.

"All right," I say, grasping the medallion and lifting on the Hades Helmet. "Don't wander away while I'm gone." I had the cowl in place before I triggered the medallion, so my voice must have come from emptiness in the second or two before I QT'd.

I don't know for sure where Aphrodite's private chambers are—she probably has one of those white temple-sized homes along the crater lake up here—but I do remember that the time she took me aside, almost seducing me—when she told me that I had to kill Athena—the Muse had brought me to Aphrodite in a chamber just off the Great Hall of the Gods. If it wasn't her private chambers, it seemed at least an apartment she kept in the great hall, a sort of Olympian pied-à-terre.

I flick into solidity in the Great Hall and hold my breath.

The many mezzanines are empty, the hall is mostly dark, and the giant holographic viewing pool shows only three-dimensional static. But several gods are here, including Zeus, whom I'd thought to be away, sitting on Mount Ida watching the carnage on the Ilium battlefied. The King of Gods is on his high golden throne. Nearby are several other male gods, including Apollo. They're all ten feet tall or taller. I'm forty feet away, and I'm invisible under the Hades Helmet, but I almost QT away I'm so afraid that they'll hear me breathing. But their attention is on something else.

In front of and below the throne, in the center of the gods' circle of attention, looking incongruous here to say the least, are what looks like a giant, pitted, cracked metallic crabshell the size of a Ford Expedition, a couple of futuristic-looking devices, and a small, shiny, vaguely humanoid robot. The robot is speaking—in English. The gods are listening, but they don't look happy.

Atlantis and Earth Orbit

"I don't understand why the post-humans called this place we're headed 'Atlantis,' " said Harman.

Savi, at the crawler controls, said, "I can't say that I ever understood the vast majority of the posts' actions."

Daeman looked up from munching slowly on his third of the only remaining food bar. "What's odd about the name 'Atlantis'?"

"On the Lost Age maps," said Harman, "the Atlantic Ocean is the big body of water west of here, beyond the Hands of Hercules. We're in the basin of what used to be the Mediterranean Sea. It's not in the Atlantic."

"It's not?" said Daeman.

"No."

"So?" said Daeman.

Harman shrugged and fell quiet, but Savi said, "It's possible the posts were being whimsical when they named their base here. But I seem to recall that a pre–Lost Age writer named Plato had talked about a city or kingdom called Atlantis in these regions, back when there was water here."

"Plato," mused Harman. "I've run across references to him in books I've read. And an odd drawing I saw once. A dog."

Savi nodded. "A lot of the meaning of Lost Age iconography has been lost forever."

"What's a dog?" asked Harman. He sipped from Savi's water bottle. The third of the food bar hadn't been enough to satisfy his hunger, but there was no more food in the crawler.

"A small mammal that used to be very common, kept as a pet," said Savi. "I don't know why the posts allowed them to go extinct. Perhaps the rubicon virus targeted dogs as well."

"Like horses?" said Daeman. He'd thought the huge, scary animals in the turin drama had been pure fantasy until recently.

"Smaller and hairier than horses," said Savi. "But equally extinct."

"Why would the posts bring back dinosaurs," Daeman asked with a real shudder, "and not those wonderful turin horses and these dog things?"

"As I said," repeated Savi, "much of the posts' behavior was hard to understand."

They had awakened shortly after dawn and driven north-northwest all day, rumbling down the red-clay road through fields rich with every sort of crop Daeman was familiar with and many he'd never seen. Twice they'd come to shallow rivers and once a deep, empty permcrete canal, all of which the crawler had crossed easily with its huge wheels and wildly articulated struts.

There were servitors in the fields, and the commonplace look of them reassured Daeman until he realized that many of these servitors were huge—some twelve or fifteen feet tall and half that broad, much larger than the machines he was used to—and as they drove deeper into the Basin, both the crops and servitors continued to look more alien.

The crawler was lumbering between tall green walls of what Savi said was sugarcane, the road not quite wide enough for the crawler and green stalks crunching under the six wheels, when Harman noticed the gray-green humanoid things slipping through the fields on either side. The forms moved so fluidly and quickly that they did not disturb the close-packed cane, flowing like ghost-corpses passing through the tall stalks.

"*Calibani*," said Savi. "I don't think they'll attack."

"I thought you said you fixed it so they wouldn't," said Daeman. "You know, that D-and-A stuff from the hair you stole from Harman and me."

Savi smiled. "Deals with Ariel are never certain. But I suspect that if the *calibani* were going to stop us, they would have done it last night."

"Won't the forcefield around the sphere hold them off?" asked Daeman.

The old woman shrugged. "*Calibani* are more clever than voynix. They might surprise us."

Daeman shuddered and watched the fields, catching only glimpses of the pale figures. The crawler moved out of the lane between the sugar-cane fields and climbed a low hill. The road ran on through broad fields of winter wheat, stalks no taller than fifteen or sixteen inches, entire fields rippling in the breeze from the west. The *calibani*, at least a dozen on each side of the road, came out of the canefields behind them and loped along through the wheat, keeping a distance of sixty yards or so. Out in the open, they ran on all fours.

"I don't like the looks of them," said Daeman.

"You'd probably like the looks of Caliban even less," said Savi.

"I thought these were *calibani*," said Daeman. The old woman never seemed to make sense for long.

Savi smiled, steering the crawler across and over a row of six pipes carrying something from west to east or east to west. "It's said that the *calibani* are cloned from the single Caliban, the third element of the Gaiaic Trinity, along with Ariel and Prospero."

"*It's said*," mocked Daeman. "Everything's gossip with you. Don't you know anything from firsthand knowledge? These old stories are absurd."

"Some are," agreed Savi. "And even though I've been alive 1,500 years or more, that doesn't mean I've been *around* all that time. So I have to report secondhand things I hear and read."

"What do you mean, you haven't been around all that time?" asked Harman. He sounded very interested.

Savi laughed, but not, Daeman thought, with much amusement in her voice. "I'm better nano-engineered for repair than you *eloi*," she said. "But nobody lives forever. Or for fourteen hundred years. Or even a thousand. I spend most of my time like Dracula, sleeping in the long-term cryo crèches in places like the Golden Gate Bridge. I pop out from time to time, try to see what's going on, try to find a way to get my friends out of the blue beam. Then back into the cold."

Harman leaned forward. "How many years have you been . . . awake?"

"Fewer than three hundred," said Savi. "And even that's enough to tire a body out. And a mind. And a spirit."

"Who's Dracula?" asked Daeman.

Savi, not answering, kept driving the crawler north by northwest.

She'd told them the site they were headed for was about three hundred miles from the shoreline where they'd entered the Basin from the land that had been called Israel—a word Daeman had never heard. But the phrase "three hundred miles" meant little to Harman and nothing at all to Daeman, since trips by voynix-pulled carriole or droshky were never longer than a mile or two. Anything farther than that, and Daeman would fax. Anyone would fax.

Still, they had covered half that distance by midday, but then the red-clay road ended, the terrain grew rough, and the crawler had to move much more slowly, sometimes detouring for miles before returning to its course. Savi kept that course by using a small instrument from her pack and checking distances on a hand-drawn, much-folded map.

"Why don't you use the palm finding-function?" Daeman asked.

"Farnet and allnet work here in the Basin," said Savi, "but proxnet doesn't, and the place we're heading is in no net databank. I'm using a map and an ancient thing called a compass. Works, though."

"How does it work?" asked Harman.

"Magic," said Savi.

That was answer enough for Daeman.

They continued to descend, the Basin topography falling away above and behind them, the orderly rows of crops replaced now by boulder fields, gulleys, and occasional stands of bamboo or high ferns. The *calibani* were no longer visible, but it began to rain shortly after they reached the rough areas, and the creatures might have been just beyond the curtains of falling water.

The crawler passed odd artifacts—the hulls of numerous ships made of wood and steel, a city of tumbled Ionian columns, ancient plastic objects gleaming in gray sediment, the bleached bones of numerous sea creatures, and several huge, rusted tanks that Savi called "submarines."

In the afternoon the rain lifted some and the three saw a high mesa appear to the northeast. It was high and broad and rolling rather than peaked, more mountain than mesa, green on top, ridged on the sides with steep, rilled cliffs.

"Is that where we're going?" asked Daeman.

"No," said Savi. "That's Cyprus. I lost my virginity there one thousand, four hundred and eight-two years ago next Tuesday."

Daeman exchanged covert glances with Harman. Both men had the good sense not to say anything.

By late afternoon the terrain became lower and marshier and fields of crops began appearing on either side of a rough, red-clay road again. Oddly formed servitors were working in the fields, but none looked up to watch the crawler trundle past. Most of the machines didn't appear to have eyes. Once their way was blocked by a river at least two hundred yards across. Savi sealed the slice-door, shutting off the fresh air they'd been enjoying, made sure the sphere forcefield was activated, and rolled the crawler down the bank. The water was deep—forty feet or more near the center of the channel—and even the crawler's searchlights had trouble cutting through the silt and gloom. The current was stronger than Daeman would have imagined for such a wide, deep river, and the crawler was buffeted around violently enough that Savi had to work the virtual controls and fight the machine back onto the proper course. Daeman guessed that a machine with smaller wheels, less flexible struts, or less motor power would have been carried away to the west.

When they emerged on the north shore, the machine throwing mud thirty feet behind them and water rushing off the spider-struts like a waterfall, Harman said, "I didn't know the crawler could be driven underwater."

"Neither did I," said Savi. She took a bearing north by northwest and drove on.

The first energy constructs appeared shortly after that and Harman was the first to notice them.

The first device was shimmering and shifting thirty yards to the left of the clay road, in an opening beyond a stand of bamboo. Savi stopped so they could get out and see, although Daeman was leery of getting away from the crawler even though they'd seen no *calibani* for several hours. But Harman wanted to see it and Daeman didn't want to stay in the sphere alone, so he ended up following the two down the strut ladder and across the field toward the glowing object. It felt strange to Daeman to be walking again after so many hours sitting.

The first energy construct was small—about twenty feet long by eight or ten high, yellow and orange with moving green veins, roughly spherical with pseudopods growing out of the top, bottom, and ends, the forms blobbing into shapes of their own, and then being reabsorbed by the central mass. The thing floated about four feet off the ground and Daeman would get no closer than twenty paces, even as Savi and Harman walked right up to it.

"What is it?" asked Harman, his head and shoulders disappearing for a minute behind the slowly flowing thing.

"We're in the suburbs of Atlantis," said Savi, "even though we're still sixty miles or so away. The posts built their ground stations out of this material."

"What material?" said Harman. He stretched his hand toward the yellow ovoid. "Can I touch it?"

"Some of the shapes shock. Some don't. None kill. Go ahead and try it. It won't melt your hand."

Harman set his fingers against the curve of the shiny shape. His hand disappeared inside. When he quickly pulled it out, molten blobs of yellow and orange dripped off his fingers and then flew back to the shape. "Cold," he said. "Very cold." He flexed his fingers and winced.

"It's essentially one large molecule," said Savi. "Although how that's possible, I don't know."

"What's a molecule?" called Daeman. He'd taken a few steps backward when Harman's hand disappeared, and had to raise his voice to be heard now. He also kept checking over his shoulder. Savi had the gun in her belt, but the bamboo forest was too close for Daeman's comfort. It was almost dark.

"Molecules are the little things that everything else is made of," said Savi. "You can't see them without special lenses."

"I can see that one easily enough," said Daeman. Sometimes, he thought, talking to Siri was like talking to a young child, although Daeman had never spent time around a young child.

The three walked back to the crawler. Rich evening sunlight prismed off the passenger sphere and made the high, articulated struts glow. The tops of stratocumulus far to their east, toward the hill called Cyprus, caught the golden light.

"Atlantis is made up mostly of this macro-molecular frozen energy," said the old woman. "It's part of the quantum screwing around that the posts were always up to. There is real material mixed in—something the Lost Age scientists called 'exotic matter'—but I don't know the ratio, or how it works. I just know that it makes their cities—stations—whatever they are, sort of shapeshifters, phasing in and out of our quantum reality."

"I don't understand," said Harman, freeing Daeman of the necessity of saying it.

"You'll see for yourself soon enough. We should be able to see the city when we get over that large rise on the horizon. And be there about the time it gets dark."

They climbed into the crawler and took their seats. But before Savi could shift the big machine into gear, Harman said, "You've been here before." He didn't pose it as a question.

"Yes."

"But you said before that you've never been to the orbital rings. Was that your reason for coming before?"

"Yes," said Savi. "I still think the answer to freeing my friends from the neutrino beam lies up there." She flicked her head toward the e- and p-rings bright in the twilight sky above.

"But you didn't succeed before," said Harman. "Why?"

Savi swiveled in her chair and looked at him. "I'll tell you why and how I failed, if you'll tell me why you really want to go up there. Why you've spent years trying to find a way up to the rings."

Harman returned her gaze for a minute and then looked away. "I'm curious," he said.

"No," said Savi. She waited.

He looked back at her and Daeman realized that the older man's face showed the most emotion Daeman had seen from him. "You're right," snapped Harman. "It's not some sort of idle curiosity. I want to find the firmary."

"So you can live longer," Savi said softly.

Harman balled his fists. "*Yes.* So I can live longer. So I can continue to exist beyond this fucking Final Twenty. Because I'm greedy for life. Because I want Ada to have my child and I want to be around to see it grow up, even though fathers don't do things like that. Because I'm a greedy bastard—greedy for life. Are you satisfied?"

"Yes," said Savi. She looked at Daeman. "And what are your reasons for coming on this trip, Daeman *Uhr*?"

Daeman shrugged. "I'd jump home in a second if there was a fax portal nearby."

"There isn't," said Savi. "Sorry."

He ignored the sarcasm and said, "Why did you bring us, old woman? You know the way here. You know how to find the crawler. Why bring us?"

"Fair question," she said. "The last time I came to Atlantis, I came on foot. From the north. It was a century and a half ago, and I brought two *eloi* with me—I'm sorry, that's an insulting term—I brought two young women with me. They *were* curious."

"What happened?" said Harman.

"They died."

"How?" asked Daeman. "The *calibani*?"

"No. The *calibani* killed and ate the man and woman who came with me the time before that, almost three centuries ago. I didn't know how to contact the Ariel biosphere then, nor about the DNA."

"Why do you always come in threes?" asked Harman. Daeman thought it an odd question. He was ready to ask for more details about all these dead traveling companions. Did she mean *permanently* dead? Or just firmary-repair dead?

Savi laughed. "You ask good questions, Harman *Uhr*. You'll see soon. You'll see why I've come with two others after that first solo visit of mine to Atlantis more than a millennium ago. And not just to Atlantis—but to some of their other stations. In the Himalayas. Easter Island. One actually at the south pole. *Those* were fun trips, since a sonie can't get within three hundred miles of any of them."

She'd lost Daeman. He wanted to hear more about the killing and eating.

"But you've never found a spaceship, a shuttle, to get you up there?" said Harman. "After all these tries?"

"There *are* no spaceships," said Savi. She activated the virtual controls, slammed the crawler in gear, and guided them north by northwest as the sunset spilled red across the entire western sky.

The city of the post-humans spread for miles across the dry seabed, with glowing energy towers rising and falling a thousand feet high. The crawler trundled between energy obelisks, floating spheres, red energy stairways going nowhere, blue ramps that appeared and disappeared, blue pyramids folding into themselves, a giant green torus that moved back and forth along pulsing yellow rods, and countless colored cubes and cones.

When Savi stopped and slid the door slice open, even Harman seemed hesitant to get out. Savi had made sure they were wearing their thermskins and now she pulled three osmosis masks from the crawler's tool locker.

It was almost dark now, the stars joining the rotating rings in the purple-black sky above them. The glow from the energy city illuminated seabed and farm fields for five miles in each direction. Savi led them to a red stairway and then up—the macromolecular steps holding their weight, although Daeman thought it felt like walking on giant sponges.

A hundred feet above the seabed floor, the staircase ended at a black platform made out of a dull, dark metal that reflected no light. In the center of the square platform were three ancient-looking wooden chairs with high backs and red seat cushions. The chairs were equidistantly spaced around a black hole in the black platform, about ten feet apart, facing outward.

"Sit," said Savi.

"Is this a joke?" said Daeman.

Savi shook her head and sat in the chair facing west. Harman took his seat. Daeman walked around the black platform again, returned to the single empty chair. "What happens next?" he asked. "We have to wait here for something?" He looked at the tall yellow tower thrusting up hundreds of feet nearby, the energy-material rearranging itself like a rectangular yellow cloud.

"Sit and you'll find out," said Savi.

Daeman took his seat gingerly. The back of the chair and the thick arms were elaborately carved. There was a white circle on the left arm of the chair and a red circle on the right arm. He touched neither.

"When I count to three," said Savi, "depress the white button. That's the one on your left if you're colorblind, Daeman."

"I'm *not* colorblind, goddammit."

"All right," said the old woman. "One, two . . ."

"Wait, wait!" said Daeman. "What's going to happen to me if I press the white circle?"

"Absolutely nothing," said Savi. "But we have to press it at the same time. I learned this when I came here alone. Ready? One, two, three."

They all pressed their white circles.

Daeman leaped out of his chair and ran to the edge of the black platform and then the red platform thirty paces beyond that before turning to look back. The blast of energy behind his chair had been deafening.

"Holy crap," he shouted, but the two still in their chairs could not hear him.

It was like lightning, he thought. A searing blast of jagged energy, just a yard or so across, emanating from the black hole in the middle of the chair-triangle and rising up into the dark sky. Rising higher, higher . . . then curving to the west like some impossible, white-hot thread, arching west until the end of it disappeared from sight above, but the thread visible and also moving, as if the lightning were connected to . . .

It *was* connected, Daeman realized with a flood of fear that almost made him void his bowels. Connected to the moving e-ring thousands of miles above. Connected to one of the stars, one of the moving lights, now crossing from west to east in that ring.

"Come back!" Savi was shouting above the crackle and roar of the lightning thread.

It took Daeman several minutes to come back—to walk to that empty wooden chair, shielding his eyes, his shadow and the chair's shadow thrown out fifty feet across the black and red rooftop by the blinding, crackling light. He could never explain later, even to himself, how or why he returned to that chair, or why he did what he did next.

"On the count of three, depress the red circle," shouted Savi. The old woman's gray hair was standing on end, whipping around her head like short snakes. She had to scream above the energy roar to be heard. "One, two . . ."

I absolutely can't do this was Daeman's litany to himself. *I absolutely won't do this.*

"Three!" shouted Savi. She pressed her red circle. Harman pressed his red circle.

No! thought Daeman. But pressed down hard on his red circle.

The three wooden chairs shot skyward, rotating around the crackling, shifting, chord of lighting, shooting upward so quickly that a sonic boom echoed across the seabed floor, shaking the crawler on its springs. A second later, less than a second later, the three chairs were out of sight overhead as the thread of pure white energy twisted and writhed and arched to follow the hurtling points of light on the equatorial orbital ring.

Olympos, Ilium and Olympos

The little robot fascinates me and I'm tempted to stay in the Great Hall of the Gods and find out what's going on, but I'm leery of getting closer because the gods might hear me in this vast, hushed space. The dialogue between the gods and the robot has shifted to ancient Greek now—at least the gods, including Zeus, are speaking in the common language I've grown used to here—but I'm far enough way that I can catch only fragments of it.

"... little automatons ... toys ... from the Great Inland Sea ... should be destroyed ..."

Rather than try to creep closer, I remember why I'm here—Aphrodite's comb—and the importance of my getting back to the Trojan women. The fate of hundreds of thousands of people below may depend on what I do next, so I tiptoe backward, away from the gods and the odd machines, and find my way down the long side corridor to the little suite of rooms where I first met the Goddess of Love just a few days ago. Can it just be a few days ago? Much has happened since then, to say the least.

There are voices—gods' voices—echoing from elsewhere in the Great Hall, and I slip into Aphrodite's pied-à-terre with my pulse pounding in my throat. The place is as I remember it from a few days ago—windowless, lighted by only a few tripod braziers, with only the couch and a few other pieces of furniture, including a softly glowing blue screen on the marble desk. I'd thought at the time that the screen was like a computer screen, and I cross to it now to look. It's true—the glowing blue rectangle is separate from the desktop, hovering an inch or two above the marble surface, and while there's no Microsoft Windows menu on it, a single white circle floats there as if inviting me to touch it and activate the screen.

I leave it alone.

Near the couch is where I remember some of Aphrodite's personal items on a small round table, although I'm only hoping that there's a comb among them. There's not. I see a silver brooch and some silver cylinders—divine lipsticks?—and an elaborately carved silver mirror lying facedown, but no comb.

Damn it. I have no idea where Aphrodite's home is among the estates scattered around on the broad green summit of Olympos, and I certainly can't ask one of the gods for directions. I'd gambled and lost on Helen's challenge to bring back the comb. But the important thing was to show them that I have the ability to travel to Olympos and back, and speed is of the essence. I have no idea how long the Trojan women will wait.

I grab the mirror without looking at it carefully, envision the basement room in Ilium's Temple of Athena, and twist the QT medallion.

There are seven women there when I flick into existence, not the five women I'd left in the basement room a few minutes before. All of the women take a step back when I arrive, but one of them shrieks wildly and throws her hands over her face. I still have time to see that face and I recognize it—this is Cassandra, King Priam's loveliest daughter.

"Did you bring us the comb, Hock-en-bear-eeee, as proof of your ability to travel to and from Olympos as do the gods?" asks Hecuba.

"I didn't have time to search for it," I say. "I brought this instead." I hand the mirror to the nearest woman, Laodice, Hecuba's daughter.

Helen says, "The carving on the silver handle and the back of the mirror is similar to what I remember of the goddess's comb, but . . ."

She stops speaking as Laodice gasps and almost drops the mirror. The mirror is picked up by the priestess, Theano, who looks into it, goes white, and hands it to Andromache. Hector's wife looks into and blushes. Cassandra grabs it from Andromache, lifts it, stares into it, and screams again.

Hecuba grabs the mirror away and frowns at Cassandra. I can tell immediately that there is no love lost between these two women, and I remember why—Cassandra, given the power of prophecy by Apollo, had urged King Priam to have Hecuba's baby, Paris, killed upon birth. From her childhood onward, Cassandra has foreseen the disaster resulting from Helen's capture and the ensuing war. But, according to tradition, Apollo's gift of prophecy to the girl was accompanied by the curse that no one would ever believe her.

Now Hecuba is staring into the mirror, mouth slack.

"What is it?" I ask. There must be something wrong with the mirror.

Helen takes the mirror from Hector's mother and hands it to me. "Do you see, Hock-en-bear-eeee?"

I look into the glass. My reflection is . . . odd. I'm me there, but also not me. My chin is stronger, my nose smaller, my eyes bolder, my cheekbones higher, my teeth whiter . . .

"Is this what you've all seen?" I ask. "This idealized reflection of yourself?"

"Yes," says Helen. "Aphrodite's looking glass shows only beauty. We have looked upon ourselves as goddesses."

I can't imagine that Helen could be any more beautiful than she already is, but I nod and touch the surface of the mirror. It's not glass. It feels soft, resilient, rather like an LCD screen on a laptop computer. Perhaps that's what it is and inside the carved backing might be powerful microchips and video morphing programs running algorithms of symmetry, idealized proportions, and other elements of perceived human beauty.

"Hock-en-bear-eeee," says Helen, "let me introduce two others we've brought here this morning to judge whether you speak the truth. This younger woman is Cassandra, daughter of Priam. This older woman is Herophile, 'beloved of Hera,' the oldest of the Sibyls and priestess of Apollo Smithneus. It was Herophile who interpreted Hecuba's dream lo those many years ago."

"What dream is that?" I ask.

Hecuba, who, it appears, will not look at Herophile or Cassandra, says, "When I was pregnant with my second child, Paris, I dreamed that I gave birth to a burning brand that spread its fire to all of Ilium, burning it to the ground. And that child became a rampaging Erinyes—a child of Kronos, some say, the daughter of Phorkys say others, the offspring of Hades and Persephone say still others—but, all acknowledge, most likely the daughter of deadly Night. This Erinyes of flame had no wings, but it resembled the Harpies. The smell of its breath was sulfurous. A poisonous slaver poured from its eyes. Its voice was like the lowing of terrified cattle. It bore in its belt a whip of brass-studded thongs. It carried a torch in one hand and a serpent in the other, and its home was in the Underworld, and it was born to avenge all and any slights against mothers. Its approach was heralded by all the dogs of Ilium barking as if in pain."

"Wow," I say. "That's quite a dream."

"I perceived the Erinyes to be the child later named Paris," says the old hag named Herophile. "Cassandra also saw this, and recommended that the baby boy be killed the moment he emerged from the womb."

The old priestess gave Hecuba a scalding look. "Our advice was ignored."

Helen literally steps between the women. "Everyone here, Hock-en-bear-eeee, has had visions of Troy being put to the torch. But we do not know which of our visions arise merely from anxiety for ourselves, our children, and our husbands, and which visions are gifts of true sight from the gods. So must we judge yours. Cassandra has questions for you."

I turn to look at the younger woman. She is blonde and anorectic, but somehow still stunningly beautiful. Cassandra's fingernails are bitten short and bloody, and her fingers are always twitching and intertwining. She can't stand still. Her eyes are as red-rimmed as her nails. Looking at her reminds me of photos I've seen of gorgeous movie starlets in rehab for coke addiction.

"I have not dreamt of you, weak-looking man," she says.

I ignore the insult and say nothing.

"But I ask you this," she continues. "I once dreamt of King Agamemnon and his queen Clytaemnestra as a great royal bull and cow. What does this dream say to you, O Prophet?"

"I'm no prophet," I say. "Your future is merely my past. But you see Agamemnon as a bull because he will be slaughtered like an ox upon his arrival home to Sparta."

"In his own palace?"

"No," I say. I feel like I'm in the crucible of oral exams at Hamilton College, my undergraduate alma mater. "Agamemnon will be killed in the house of Aigisthos."

"By whose hand? At whose will?" presses Cassandra.

"Clytaemnestra's."

"For what reason, O Non-prophet?"

"Her anger at Agamemnon's sacrifice of their daughter, Iphigeneia."

Cassandra continues to stare at me, but she nods slightly to the other women. "And what do you dream of me and my future, O Seer?" she asks sarcastically.

"You will be savagely raped in this very temple," I say.

None of the women appears to be breathing. I wonder if I've gone too far. Well, this witch wants the truth, I'll *give* her the truth."

Cassandra seems unfazed, even pleased. I realize that the young prophetess has been seeing this rape for most of her life. No one has listened to her warnings. It must be refreshing for her to hear someone else confirm her vision.

But her voice sounds anything but pleased when she speaks again. "*Who* will rape me in this temple?"

"Ajax."

"Little Ajax or Big Ajax?" asks the woman. Cassandra looks neurotic and anxious, but also very lovely in a vulnerable way.

"Little Ajax," I say. "Ajax of Locris."

"And what will I be doing upstairs in this temple, Little Man, when Big Ajax of Locris ravages me?"

"Trying to save or hide the Palladion," I answer. I nod toward the small statue just ten feet from me.

"And does Little Ajax go unpunished, O Man?"

"He'll drown on his way home," I say. "When his ship is wrecked on the Gyraean Rocks. Most scholars think this is a sign of Athena's wrath."

"Will she bring doom to Ajax of Locris out of anger at my rape or to avenge the desecration of her temple?" demands Cassandra.

"I don't know. Probably the latter."

"Who else will be in the temple upstairs when I am raped, O Man?"

I have to think a second here. "Odysseus," I say at last, my voice rising at the end like a student's hoping his answer is correct.

"Who else besides Odysseus, the son of Laertes, will be witness to my defilement that night?"

"Neoptolemus," I say at last.

"Achilles' son?" interrupts Theano with a sneer. "He's nine years old back in Argos."

"No," I say. "He's seventeen years old and a fierce warrior. They will call him here from Skyros after Achilles is killed, and Neoptolemus will be with Odysseus in the belly of the great wooden horse."

"Wooden horse?" says Andromache.

But I can see from the dilated pupils in Helen, Herophile, and Cassandra that these women have had visions of the horse.

"Does this Neoptolemus have another name?" asks Cassandra. She has the tone and intensity of a dedicated public prosecutor.

"He will be known to future generations as Pyrrhos," I say. I'm trying to remember minutiae from the BD scholia, from the Cyclic poets, from Proclus' *Cypria*, and from my Pindar. It's been a long time since I read Pindar. "Neoptolemus will not sail back to Achilles' old home on Skyros after the war," I say, "but will land in Molossia on the western side of the island, where later kings will call him Pyrrhos and say they are descended from him."

"Will he commit any other acts on the night the Greeks take Troy?" presses Cassandra.

I look at my jury of Trojan women—Priam's wife, Priam's daughter, Scamandrius' mother, Athena's priestess, a Sibyl with paranormal powers. Then this vision-accursed child-woman and Helen, wife of both Menelaus and Paris. On the whole, I would prefer OJ's jurors.

"Pyrrhos, known now as Neoptolemus, will slaughter King Priam that night in Zeus's temple," I say. "He will throw Scamandrius down from the walls and dash the baby's brains out on the rocks. He will personally drive Andromache to the slaveship. This I have told the others already."

"And will this night come soon?" presses Cassandra.

"Yes."

"In months and years or days and weeks?"

"Days and weeks," I say. I try to estimate how many days it will be before Achilles will kill Hector and Troy will fall if and when the *Iliad* time-table reasserts itself. Not many.

"Now tell us—tell me, O Man—what my fate will be after the rape of Ilium and Cassandra," snaps Cassandra.

Here I hesitate. My mouth goes dry. "Your fate?" I manage.

"My fate, O Man of the Future," hisses the beautiful blond. "Surely, ravaged or not, I'll not be left behind when Andromache is dragged off to slavery and noble Helen is claimed again by angry Menelaus. What is to become of Cassandra, O Man?"

I try to lick my lips. *Can she see her own fate?* I have no idea if Apollo's gift of prophecy goes beyond the fall of Troy. Someone, I think it was the poet-scholar Robert Graves, translated Cassandra's name as 'she who entangles men.' " But she's also someone who has been cursed by the gods always to tell the truth. I decide to do the same.

"Your beauty will result in Agamemnon claiming you as his concubine," I say, my voice barely audible. "He'll take you home with him, as his . . . concubine."

"Will I bear him children before we arrive?"

"I think so," I say, sounding preposterous even to myself. I keep getting my Homer mixed up with my Virgil, my Virgil mixed up with my Aeschylus, and all of the above mixed up with Euripides. Hell, even Shakespeare took a whack at this story. "Twin sons," I say after a pause. "Teledamus and . . . uh . . . Pelops."

"And when I arrive at Sparta, Agamemnon's home?" prompts Cassandra.

"Clytaemnestra will kill you with the same axe she murders Agamemnon with," I say, my voice more shrill than I meant it to be.

Cassandra smiles. It is not a pleasant smile. "Before or after she beheads Agamemnon?"

"After," I say. *Fuck it.* If she can take it, I can. I'm probably dead anyway. But I'll use the taser on as many of these bitches as I can before they drag me down. "Clytaemnestra has to chase you for a while," I say. "But she catches you. She cuts your head off as well. And then she kills your babies."

The seven women look at me for a long, silent moment, and their gazes are unreadable. I tell myself never to play poker with any of these dames. Then Cassandra says, "Yes, this man knows the future. Whether his vision and presence here are a gift to us from the gods, or a trick of the gods to uncover our treachery, I do not know. But we must trust him with our secret. The time before the end of Ilium is too short to do otherwise."

Helen nods. "Hock-en-bear-eeee, use your medallion to go to the camps of the Achaeans. Bring Achilles back to the foyer of the nursery in Hector's house at the time of the next changing of the Ilium guards."

I think. The guards on the wall change and the gongs ring at what would be 11:30 A.M. That's about an hour from now.

"What if Achilles doesn't want to come with me?" I ask.

The collective gaze the women pour on me now is four parts contempt combined with three parts pity.

I QT the hell out of there.

I shouldn't do it, it's foolish, and it's mostly because I'm afraid to face Achilles, but all through Cassandra's oral quiz, I'd found myself curious about the little robot back on Olympos. I'd seen odd things on Olympos before, of course—not counting the gods and goddesses, who are weird enough—odd things such as the giant insectoid Healer. But something about the little robot, if that's what it is, had struck me. It didn't seem part of either of the worlds I've been dividing my time between over the past nine years—neither of Olympos nor of Ilium. The little robot seemed more of my world. My old world. The real world. Don't ask me why. I've never seen a humanoid robot except in sci-fi movies.

Besides, I tell myself, I have an hour before having to present Achilles to Hector. I tug on the Hades Helmet and quantum teleport back to the Great Hall of the Gods.

The little robot and the other devices, including the big crab-thing, are gone, but Zeus is still here. And so are more of the gods. Including the war god, Ares, who was last seen healing in the tank next to Aphrodite.

Mother of Mercy, where's Aphrodite now? She can see me, even when I'm wearing this helmet. She ordered the Muse to give the helmet to me only because she could track me down any time she wants. Is she out of the tank already? *Jesus Christ.*

Ares is roaring at all the gods while Zeus sits on his throne. "Madness rules below!" cries the god of war. "I'm gone for a few days, and you let the war get out of hand. Kaos rules! Achilles has killed Agamemnon and taken command of the Achaean armies. Hector is in retreat when victory for the Trojans was royal Zeus's command."

Agamemnon dead? Achilles in command? Holy shit. We're not in the *Iliad* anymore, Toto.

"And what of the automata I brought to you, Lord Zeus? These . . . moravecs?" demands Apollo, his voice echoing in the huge hall. I see more gods and goddesses filling the mezzanines above. The swimming pool viewing screen cut into the floor is showing scenes of madness and murder on the Trojan battle lines and in the Argive camp now. But my focus is on the huge, powerfully built, white-bearded Zeus where he sits on his golden throne. His wrists are massive, like something sculpted out of Carrara marble by Rodin. I'm close enough to see the gray hairs on Zeus's bare chest.

"Calm down, Apollo, noble archer," rumbles the god of all gods. "I've ordered the moravec automata eliminated. Hera has destroyed them both by now."

Can this get worse? I wonder.

Right then, Aphrodite enters the hall between Achilles' mother, Thetis, and my Muse.

40

Equatorial Ring

Daeman screamed *all* the way up.

Savi and Harman could have been screaming as well—*should* have been screaming—but Daeman could hear only his own screams. As soon as their chairs took off vertically and then began to pitch over as they rotated around their axis of lightning—Daeman facedown 10,000 feet above the green Mediterranean Basin and screaming all the way—two great restrictions began to push in on him: one the pressure of acceleration, but the other a constant, all-over pressing-in that had to be some kind of a forcefield. It not only held him tight on the red cushions of his hurtling chair, but it pressed against his face, chest, into his mouth, into his lungs.

Daeman still screamed.

The three chairs continued to rotate counterclockwise around the thick bolt of white energy, and suddenly Daeman was facing up at the stars and rings. He continued to scream, knowing that the chair would continue rotating, that this time he would fall out, and that now the fall would be from tens of thousands of feet higher.

He didn't fall, but he screamed down at the Earth as they flew higher. Their trajectory seemed almost flat now, almost parallel to the surface of the planet so far below. It was night over Central Asia, but towering cumulus stretching hundreds of miles was lighted from within, quick flickers of lightning illuminating the red landmass glimpsed between the pearly cloud cover. Daeman didn't know it was central Asia. The chairs rotated around again, showing him the stars and rings and a quite visible thin layer of atmosphere—*below* them now!—and the sun seemed to rise again in the west, prisming across that meniscus of atmosphere in bright red and yellow streamers.

They were out of 99 percent of the atmosphere now, but Daeman didn't know that. The forcefield fed him air, kept him from being torn apart by g-forces, and allowed a pocket of air into which he could scream. He was getting hoarse by the time he realized that they were approaching the e-ring.

The ring wasn't what he'd always imagined, but he was too busy clutching the arms of his chair and screaming to notice this. Daeman had always visualized the posts' e- and p-rings as being made up of thousands of glowing glass castles through which one could see the post-humans partying and doing whatever post-humans do. It wasn't that way at all.

Most of the glowing objects they were rising toward so quickly, the wiggling, writhing thread of lightning still pitching up and away from them as they rode it higher, were complex structures of struts and cables and long glass tubes, more like antennae than orbital houses. At the end of some these structures were glowing globes of energy, each with pulsing black spheres at their center. Other structures supported giant mirrors—each stretching miles across, Daeman realized through his screaming—which were reflecting or beaming blue or yellow or dull-white shafts of energy to still other mirrors. Gleaming rings and spheres, looking to be made of the same energy-matter and exotic materials as Atlantis, fired lasers and pulsed attitude thrusters in studied bursts that opened and spread in glowing cones of particles. None of the spheres or rings or structures looked like they could be homes for post-humans.

The Earth's horizon became noticeably curved, then curved further, like a bow being slowly bent. The sun set again in the west and the sky exploded with stars only slightly less bright than the glowing ring structures above. Far below Daeman—hundreds of miles, at least—he could see a range of snow-topped mountains glowing in the starlight and ring-light. Farther to the west, near the sharp-curved limb of the world, an ocean gleamed. Suddenly the rotation of the chairs slowed and Daeman craned his neck and looked up.

Set amidst the moving gantry-structures and mirrors moved a mountain with a glowing city wrapped around it.

Daeman paused in his screaming as the chairs tilted forward more wildly and the forcefield pressed him down into the cushions and straight-backed chair more fiercely, and in that second of pause he noticed that the torquing shaft of energy along which they were sliding ended in that glowing city on the giant slab of rock.

This city was not made of energy-stuff. It seemed to be made of glass, and each of the hundred thousand glass panes and facets was illuminated from within. It looked like a giant Japanese lantern to Daeman. Just as he realized that their twisting triangle of chairs was going to crash into one of the tallest circular spires on the near end of that orbiting mountain, his chair pitched completely over and the forcefield squeezed the breath out of him as they decelerated hard enough to make his vision go from red to black and back to red again.

They hadn't slowed enough. Daeman screamed a final time, his voice completely hoarse now, and then they slammed into the building that must have been a hundred stories tall.

There was no crash of breaking glass, no fatal sudden stop. The building wall warped and absorbed them and funneled them down a long glowing cone, as if they'd dived into yielding yellow rubber, and then the funnel spat them out into a room with six glowing white walls. The shaft of energy disappeared. The chairs flew different directions. The forcefields went off.

Daeman shouted a final time, slid across a hard floor, bounced off an even harder wall, then ricocheted to the ceiling and back to the floor. Then he saw only blackness.

He was falling.

Daeman jerked to consciousness as his body and brain told him he was tumbling, falling. From the chair? To the Earth? He opened his mouth to scream again but closed it as he realized that he was floating in midair with Savi holding one of his arms and Harman the other.

Floating? Falling! He writhed and wriggled, but Savi and Harman—who were also floating in the white room—tumbled in the air with him, still holding him by the arms.

"It's all right," said Savi. "We're in zero-g."

"In what?" gasped Daeman.

"Zero gravity. No weight. Here, put this on." She handed him one of the crawler's osmosis masks. Someone had already pulled his thermskin cowl over his face and the smartsuit had extended its gloves over his hands. Now Daeman struggled in confusion, but the old woman and the older man tugged the clear osmosis mask into place over his nose and mouth.

"It's meant as an emergency rebreather in case of fire or toxic gases," said Savi. "But it'll work in vacuum for a few hours."

"Vacuum?" repeated Daeman.

"The posts' city has lost gravity and a lot of its air," said Harman. "We've already been through the wall while you were unconscious. There's enough air to swim through, but not quite thick enough to breathe."

Enough air to swim through? Already been through the wall? thought Daeman through his headache. *They're both crazy now.* "How do you *lose* gravity?" he said aloud.

"I think they used forcefields to give them some gravity on this asteroid," said Savi. "This rock isn't big enough to generate much of its own, and the city inside shows some signs of being oriented toward the ground."

Daeman didn't ask what an asteroid was. He didn't particularly care. "Can we get back down?" he said, but immediately added, "I'm not sitting on one of those chairs again."

Savi's smile was visible through her osmosis mask. She'd taken off her outer clothing to let her thermskin work more efficiently—she was wearing a peach color—and the suit, no thicker than a coat of paint, showed how scrawny and bony the old woman really was. Harman was also wearing only his blue thermskin. Daeman looked down and realized they'd stripped him of his real clothes so that his green thermskin showed how pudgy he was. With the thermskin and osmosis mask in place, Daeman heard the others' voices through his cowl earpatches, and heard the slight echo of his own voice rasping in the built-in microphones.

"Those chairs aren't going anywhere for a while," said Savi. She nodded toward where bits of the broken chairs and the red cushions floated.

"I can't believe that the posts traveled regularly to the rings on those things," said Harman. The slight quaver in the older man's voice let Daeman know that he wasn't the only one who had hated that ride.

"Maybe they were all roller-coaster fans," said Savi.

"What's a . . ." began Daeman.

"Never mind," said the old woman. She lifted the backpack she'd had on her lap during the whole ride up and said, "Ready to go through the wall and meet the posts?"

Going through the wall wasn't hard at all. Passing through it felt to Daeman like pushing through some sort of yielding membrane, or perhaps like swimming through a warm waterfall.

Swimming. In air. Even after thirty minutes of doing it, it felt passing strange to Daeman. At first he flailed around with both arms and legs kicking almost at random, the antics moving him hardly at all and invariably sending him tumbling head over heels, but then he learned the trick of kicking off from one solid object to the next, even for distances of a hundred feet or more, using his legs to propel him and his cupped palms to make slight midcourse corrections.

All of the buildings seemed connected through their interiors, and what looked like bright internal lighting as they'd approached turned out to be an illusion. The windows glowed warmly, but it was the *windows* that were emitting the light. The vast interiors—the first space they entered after emerging from the white wall was three or four hundred feet across and at least a thousand feet high, with open terraces rising on three sides of the columnar space—were all dimly lighted by the orange glow from the distant wall windows, giving Daeman a sense of moving deep underwater. To add to that illusion of being underwater, various untended plants had grown forty and fifty feet high and were swaying to the slight breezes like tall stands of kelp.

Daeman could feel the thinness of the atmosphere as he tried to swim through what was left of the air. And while the thermskin covered all exposed skin and conserved all of his body heat, he could still sense the freezing cold beyond the molecular layer. He could see its effects as well, since the inner panels of glass were covered by a thin film of ice and occasional clusters of free-floating ice crystals caught the light like dust in shafts of cathedral light.

They came across the first bodies after only five minutes of kicking and swimming through the connected asteroid buildings.

The surface below had been covered with grass, terrestrial plants, trees, plants and flowers which Daeman had never seen on earth, but all of these had died except for the swaying kelp towers. While the surface had been parklike, open balconies on metal columns and dining and gathering areas festooned on walls and window surfaces showed how small the forcefield gravity must have been. The post-humans must have been able to push off from the "ground" and soar a hundred or more vertical feet before needing another open platform or aerial stepping-stone to push again. Many of these platforms still held hoarfrosted tables, overturned chairs, bulbous couches, and freestanding tapestries.

And bodies.

Savi kicked her way up to a terrace almost a hundred feet across. At one time it obviously stood beside and looked down on a thin waterfall tumbling from a balcony four or five hundred feet higher on the permcrete wall, but now the waterfall was frozen into a fragile latticework of ice and the eating area held only floating bodies.

Female bodies. All female, although the gray objects looked more like leathery mummies than anything either male or female.

There was little decomposition as such, but the effects of extreme cold and decreasing air pressure had freeze-dried the corpses over years or decades or centuries. When Daeman floated closer to the first cluster of bodies—all free-floating in the zero-g, but tangled in the mesh of what had once been some sort of decorative net between the dining area and the waterfall—he decided it had been centuries, not just decades, since these women had breathed and walked and flown in what Savi said had probably been one-tenth gravity and laughed and done whatever else post-humans had done before . . . before what? The women's eyes were still intact, although frozen and clouded white in the gray leathery faces, and Daeman looked into the milky stares of the half dozen or so of the bodies as if there might be some answer there. When none was forthcoming, he cleared his throat and said into his osmosis mask microphone, "What do you think killed them?"

"I was wondering the same thing," said Harman, floating near a separate cluster of bodies. The blue of his suit was almost shocking in the dim, funereal light and set against the gray skin of the corpses. "Sudden depressurization?"

"No," said Savi. Her face was only inches from the face of one of the dead women. "There's no hemorrhaging behind the eyes or signs of asphyxia or burst eardrums the way there would be if there had been a cataclysmic loss of atmosphere. And look at this."

The other two floated closer. Savi shoved three gloved fingers into a ragged hole in the corpse's leathery neck. The fingers disappeared to the knuckle. Disgusted, Daeman kick-floated backward, but not before noticing that the other corpses also had such ragged wounds on their necks, thighs, and rib cages.

"Scavengers?" said Harman.

"No, I don't think so," said Savi, floating from corpse to corpse, inspecting each wound. "Nor the effects of decomposition. I don't think there was much in the way of viable bacteria here even before the air began leaking out and the cold set in. Maybe post-humans didn't even have bacteria in their guts."

"How could that be?" asked Daeman.

Savi just shook her head. She floated to two bodies tangled in chairs on the next platform. These corpses showed wider wounds in the belly. Rags of loose, torn clothing floated in the thin, cold air. "Something chewed a hole into their bellies," whispered Savi.

"What?" Daeman heard how hollow his voice sounded on the thermskin comm.

"I think all these people—posts—died of wounds," said Savi. "Something chewed their throats and bellies and hearts out."

"What?" Daeman asked again.

Instead of answering, Savi removed the black gun from her pack and slapped it onto the stiktite patch on the thigh of her thermskin suit. She pointed down the open mall of the interior city to where it curved a half mile or so straight ahead. "Something's moving there," she said.

Without waiting to see if the two men would follow, Savi kicked off and floated in that direction.

41

Olympus Mons

After their capture, Mahnmut thought that his best shot would have been to trigger the Device—whatever it was—as soon as the blond god in the flying chariot had destroyed the balloon and begun hauling them back to Olympus Mons.

But he couldn't get to the Device. Or to the transmitter. Or to Orphu. It took everything Mahnmut had just to hang on to the railing of the gondola as they flew at almost Mach 1 toward the Martian volcano. If the Device, transmitter, and Orphu of Io hadn't been lashed down to the gondola platform with every meter of rope and wire Mahnmut had been able to scavenge, all three objects would have all dropped 12,000 meters and more to the high plateau between the northernmost of the Tharsis volcanoes—Ascraeus—and the Tethys Sea.

The god in the machine—still carrying these metric tons of dead weight and the added weight of the bunched cables in one hand—actually gained altitude as the chariot headed north, swung out to sea still gaining altitude, and came in toward Olympus Mons from the north. Even with his short legs dangling and his manipulators sunk deep into the gondola railing, Mahnmut had to admit it was one hell of a sight.

A near-solid mass of clouds covered most of the region between the Tharsis volcanoes and Olympus, with only the solid masses of the volcanoes rising from the cloud cover. The rising sun was small but very bright to the southeast, painting the ocean and the clouds a brilliant gold. The golden glare from the Tethys Sea was so bright that Mahnmut had to notch up his polarizing filters. Olympus itself, rising right at the edge of the Tethys ocean, was staggering in its immensity, an endless cone of icefields rising to an impossibly green summit with a series of blue lakes in its caldera.

The chariot dipped and Mahnmut could make out the 4,000-meter vertical cliffs at the very base of its northwestern quadrant, and although the cliffs were in shadow, he could also see tiny roads and structures in what looked to be a narrow strip of beach, although there were almost certainly two or three miles of coastline between the cliffs and the golden ocean. Farther north and farther out to sea, turned into an island by the terraforming, was the isle of Lycus Sulci, which resembled nothing so much as a lizard's head raised toward Olympus Mons.

Mahnmut described all of this to Orphu, subvocalizing on the tight-beam channel. The Ionian's only comment was, "Sounds pretty, but I wish we were taking this tour under our own steam."

Mahnmut remembered that he wasn't here for sightseeing when the godlike humanoid dipped the chariot toward the summit of the giant volcano. Three thousand meters above the upper snow slopes, they passed through a forcefield—Mahnmut's sensors registered the ozone shock and voltage differentials—and then leveled out for final approach to the green and grassy summit.

"I'm sorry I didn't see this guy in the chariot coming sooner and take some evasive action," Mahnmut said to Orphu in the last seconds before he had to shut down comm for landing.

"It's not your fault," said Orphu. "These deus ex machinas have a way of sneaking up on us literary types."

After landing, the god who'd captured them grabbed Mahnmut by the neck and carried him unceremoniously into the largest artificial space the little Moravec had ever seen. Other male gods went out to haul in Orphu, the Device, and the transmitter. Still more male gods came into the hall as Zeus listened to their chariot god describe their capture. Mahnmut was comfortable now thinking that these chariot people *thought* of themselves as gods, assuming now that their choice of Olympus Mons as a home was no coincidence. The holograms in niches of scores and scores more gods and goddesses reinforced his hypothesis. Then the über-god whom Mahnmut assumed to be Zeus began speaking and it was all Greek to the moravec. Mahnmut spoke a sentence or two in English. The gray-bearded gods and the younger ones frowned their incomprehension. Mahnmut cursed himself for never loading ancient or modern Greek into his language base. It hadn't seemed all that important at the time he'd first set out in *The Dark Lady* to explore the subsea oceans of Europa.

Mahnmut switched to French. Then German. Then Russian. Then Japanese. He was working his way through his modest database of human languages, framing the same sentence—"I came in peace and did not mean to trespass"—when the Zeus figure held up one massive hand to silence him. The gods spoke amongst themselves and didn't sound happy.

What's going on? tightbeamed Orphu. The Ionian's shell was five meters away, on the floor with the other two artifacts from the gondola. Their captors hadn't seemed to consider the possibility that there was a sentient person in that cracked and battered form, and they treated Orphu as another captured thing. Mahnmut had anticipated this. It's why he phrased his sentence "I came in peace . . ." rather than "we." Whatever the gods decided to do to him, Mahnmut, there was an outside chance that they would leave Orphu alone, although how the poor Ionian might be able to escape without eyes, ears, legs, or manipulators wasn't clear to Mahnmut.

The gods are talking, tightbeamed Mahnmut. *I don't understand them.*

Repeat a few of the words they're using.

Mahnmut did, sending them silently.

That's a variant on classical Greek, said Orphu. *It's in my database. I can understand them.*

Upload the database to me, sent Mahnmut.

On tightbeam? said Orphu. *It would take an hour. Do you have an hour?*

Mahnmut turned his head to watch the beautiful humanoid males barking syllables at each other. They seemed near a decision. *No,* he said.

Subvocalize what they say to me and I'll translate, we'll decide the proper answer, and I'll send back the phonemes for your response, said the Ionian.

In real time?

Do we have a choice? said Orphu.

Their captor was speaking to the bearded figure on the gold throne. Mahnmut sent on what he heard, got the translation within a fraction of a second, consulted with Orphu, and memorized the syllables of their response in Greek. It hardly seemed efficient to the little moravec.

". . . it is a clever little automaton and the other objects are worthless as plunder, my lord Zeus," said the two-and-a-half-meter-tall blond god.

"Lord of the silver bow, Apollo, do not dismiss such toys as worthless until we know whence they came and why. The balloon you destroyed was no toy."

"Nor am I a toy," said Mahnmut. "I came in peace and did not trespass intentionally."

The gods did a collective double take and murmured amongst themselves.

How tall are these gods? sent Orphu on the tightbeam.

Mahnmut described them quickly.

Not possible, said the Ionian. *The human skeletal structure begins to be inefficient at two meters of height, and three meters would be absurd. Lower leg bones would break.*

This is Martian gravity, Mahnmut reminded his friend. *It's the worst g-field I've ever experienced, but it's only about a third Earth-normal.*

So you think these gods are from Earth? asked Orphu. *It hardly seems likely unless . . .*

Excuse me, sent Mahnmut. *I'm getting busy here.*

Zeus chuckled and sat forward on his throne. "So the little toy person can speak the human language."

"I can," replied Mahnmut, getting the words from Orphu, although neither moravec knew the proper honorific for the god of all gods, the king of the gods, the lord of the universe. They'd decided not to try.

"The Healers can speak," snapped Apollo, still addressing Zeus. "They cannot think."

"I can speak and think," said Mahnmut.

"Indeed?" said Zeus. "Does the speaking and thinking little person have a name?"

"I am Mahnmut the moravec," Mahnmut said firmly. "Sailor of the frozen seas of Europa."

Zeus chuckled, but it was a deep enough rumble to vibrate Mahnmut's surface material. "Are you now? Who is your father, Mahnmut the moravec?"

It took Mahnmut and Orphu a full two seconds of back and forth tightbeaming to decide on the honest reply. "I have no father, Zeus."

"You are a toy then," said Zeus. When the god frowned, his great, white brows almost touched above his sharp nose.

"Not a toy," said Mahnmut. "Merely a person in a different form. As is my friend here, Orphu of Io, space moravec who works the Io Torus." He gestured toward the shell and all divine eyes turned on Orphu. It had been Orphu's insistence to reveal his nature. He said that he wanted to share whatever Mahnmut's fate would be.

"Another little person, but this one in the form of a broken crab?" said Zeus, not chuckling now.

"Yes," said Mahnmut. "May I know the names of our captors?"

Zeus hesitated, Apollo remonstrated, but in the end the king of the gods gave an ironic bow and opened his hand toward each god in turn.

"Your captor, as you know, is Apollo, my son. Next to him, doing much of the shouting before you joined our conversation, is Ares. The dark figure behind Ares is my brother Hades, another son of Kronos and

Rhea. To my right is my wife's son, Hephaestus. The royal god standing next to your crab-friend is my brother Poseidon, called here in honor of your arrival. Near Poseidon, with his collar of golden seaweed, is Nereus, also of the deep. Beyond noble Nereus is Hermes, guide and giant killer. There are many more gods . . . and goddesses, I see . . . coming into the Great Hall as we speak, but these seven gods and I shall be your jury."

"Jury?" said Mahnmut. "My friend Orphu of Io and I have committed no crime against you."

"On the contrary," said Zeus with a laugh. He switched to English. "You've come in from Jupiter space, little moravec, little robot, most probably with mischief in your heart. It was my daughter Athena and I who brought down your ship and I confess I thought you all destroyed. You're tough little abominations. But let this be the end of you today."

"You speak this creature's language?" Ares demanded of Zeus. "You know this barbarian tongue?"

"Your Father speaks all languages, God of War," snapped Zeus. "Be silent."

The massive hall and many mezzanines were filling up quickly with gods and goddesses.

"Have this little dog-man-machine and the legless crab taken away to a sealed room in this hall," said Zeus. "I will confer with Hera and others who have my ear, and we will decide shortly what to do with them. Take the other two objects to a nearby treasure room. We shall evaluate their worth by and by."

The gods named Apollo and Nereus approached Mahnmut. The little moravec debated fight and flight—he had a low-voltage laser on his wrist that might surprise the gods for a second or two, and he could run quickly on all fours for short distances, perhaps scurry out of this Great Hall and dive into the caldera lake to hide in its depths—but then Mahnmut glanced over at Orphu, already being lifted effortlessly by four unnamed gods, and he allowed himself to be lifted and carried out of the hall like a big metal doll.

According to Mahnmut's internal chronometer, they waited in the windowless storage room for thirty-six minutes before their executioner arrived. It was a big space, with walls of marble six feet thick and—Mahnmut's instruments told him—embedded forcefields that could withstand a low-yield nuclear explosion.

It's time to trigger the Device, tightbeamed Orphu. *Whatever it does, it's preferable to letting them destroy us without a fight.*

I'd trigger it if I could, said Mahnmut. *It didn't have a remote control. And I was too busy building our gondola to jury-rig one.*

Lost opportunities, sent Orphu with a rumble. *To hell with it. We gave it a good try.*

I'm not giving up yet, said Mahnmut. He paced back and forth, feeling around the edge of the metal door through which they'd come in. It was also sealed by forcefields. Perhaps if Orphu still had his arms, he could rip the door free. Perhaps.

What does Shakespeare say about the end of things like this? asked Orphu. *Did "Will the Poet" ever bid adieu to the Youth?*

Not really, said Mahnmut, feeling the walls with his organic fingers. *They parted on pretty sour terms. The relationship sort of petered out when they found they were having sex with the same woman.*

Was that a pun? asked Orphu, his voice severe.

Mahnmut was startled into motionless. *What?*

Never mind.

What does Proust say about all this? asked Mahnmut.

Longtemps, je me suis couche de bonne heure, recited Orphu of Io.

Mahnmut didn't like French—it always felt like a too-thick oil between his gears—but it was in his database and he could translate this. "A long time, I have laid me down to sleep at an early hour."

After two minutes twenty-nine seconds, Mahnmut said over the tightbeam, *The rest is silence.*

The door opened and a goddess two meters tall stepped into the room, closing and sealing the door behind her. She carried a silver ovoid in both hands, its small black ports aimed at both of them. Mahnmut instinctively knew that rushing her would do no good. He backed up until he could reach out and touch Orphu's shell, knowing full well that the Ionian couldn't feel the contact.

In English, the goddess said, "My name is Hera and I've come to put you foolish, foolish moravecs out of your misery once and for all. I've never liked your kind."

There was a flash and a jolt and an absolute blackness descended.

42

Olympos and Ilium

My impulse is to QT away from Olympos the second I see Thetis, Aphrodite, and my Muse enter the Great Hall, but I remember that Aphrodite must have the power she gave me of seeing and tracking perturbations in the quantum continuum. Any hasty quantum exit now may attract her attention. Besides, my business here is not quite finished.

Sliding sideways, putting tall gods and goddesses between me and the women entering, I tiptoe behind a broad column and then back out of the Great Hall. I can hear Ares' angry shouts, still demanding to know what's been happening on the Ilium battlefield in his absence, and then I hear Aphrodite say, "Lord Zeus, Father, still recovering from my terrible wounds as I am, I have asked to leave the healing vats and come here because it has been brought to my attention that there is a mortal man loose who has stolen a QT medallion and the Helmet of Death forged for invisibility by Lord Hades here himself. I fear that this mortal is doing great harm even as we speak."

The crowd of gods bursts into an uproar of shouted questions and babble.

So much for any advantage I might have had. Still shielded by the Helmet's field, I run down a long corridor, turn left at the first junction, swing right down another corridor. I have no idea where I'm headed, knowing that my only hope is to stumble onto Hera. Sliding to a stop in another junction, hearing the roar increase from the Great Hall, I close my eyes and pray—and not to these swinish gods. It's the first time I've prayed since I was nine years old and my mother had cancer.

I open my eyes and see Hera crossing a junction of corridors a hundred yards to my left.

My sandals make slapping noises that actually echo in the long marble halls. Tall golden tripods throw flame-light on the walls and ceilings. I don't care about making noise now—I have to catch up to her. More roars echo down the hallways from the agitated assembly in the Great Hall. I wonder for an instant how Aphrodite will hide her complicity in arming me and sending me out to spy on and kill Athena, but then realize that the Goddess of Love is a consummate liar. I'll be dead before I get a chance to tell anyone the truth of the matter. Aphrodite will be the hero who warned the other gods of my treachery.

Walking quickly, Hera suddenly stops and looks over her shoulder. I'd paused anyway and now I teeter on tiptoe, trying not to give away my position. Zeus's wife scowls, looks both ways, and slides her hand across a twenty-foot-high metal door. The metal hums, internal locks click open, and the door swings inward. I have to scurry to slide into the room before Hera gestures the door closed behind her. An even greater roar from the Great Hall covers the sound of my sandals on stone. Hera pulls a smooth gray weapon—rather like a seashell with deadly black apertures—from the folds of her robe.

The little robot and the crab-shell are the only other things in the room. The robot backs away from Hera, obviously expecting what is to come next, and sets an oddly human-looking hand on the huge, crack-shelled figure, and for the first time I realize that the other object must also be a robot. Whatever these machines are, they aren't part of Olympos—I'm convinced of that.

"My name is Hera," says the goddess, "and I've come to put you foolish, foolish moravecs out of your misery once and for all. I've never liked your kind."

I'd been pausing before she spoke. This is, after all, Hera, wife and sister to Zeus, queen of the gods and the most powerful of all of the goddesses with the possible exception of Athena. Perhaps it was the "your kind" part of "I've never liked your kind." I was born into the middle of the Twentieth Century, lived into the Twenty-first Century, and I've heard that sort of phrase before—too many times before.

Whatever the final reason, I aim my baton and taser the arrogant bitch.

I wasn't sure the 50,000 volts would work on a goddess, but it does. Hera spasms, starts to fall, and triggers the ovoid in her hands, blasting the glowing ceiling panels that illuminate the room. It goes absolutely dark.

I retract the taser electrode and thumb another charge ready, but it's pitch-black in the windowless room and I can't see a thing. I step forward and almost trip over Hera's body. She seems to be unconscious, but still twitching on the floor. Suddenly two beams of light shaft across the room. I pull the Hades Helmet cowl off and see myself in the twin beams.

"Get that light out of my eyes," I say to the little robot. The lights seem to be coming from his chest. The beams shift.

"Are you human?" asks the robot. It takes me a second to realize that he's spoken in English.

"Yes," I say. My own language sounds strange in my mouth. "What are you?"

"We're both moravecs," says the little form, moving closer, the twin beams shifting to Hera. Her eyelids are already fluttering. I stoop, pick up the gray weapon, and slide it into my tunic pocket.

"My name is Mahnmut," says the robot. His dark head doesn't even come up to my chest. I don't see any eyes set in the metallic, plastic-looking face, but there are dark bands where the eyes might be, and I have the sense he's staring at me. "My friend is Orphu of Io," he adds. The robot's voice is soft, only vaguely male, and not metallic or robot-sounding in the least. It . . . he . . . gestures toward the cracked shell that takes up fifteen or more feet of space across the room.

"Is . . . Orphu . . . alive?" I ask.

"Yes, but he has no eyes or manipulators right now," says the little robot. "But I'm conveying what we say to Orphu via radio and he says that it is a pleasure making your acquaintance. He says that if he still had eyes, you would be the first human being he has ever laid eyes on."

"Orphu of Io," I repeat. "Isn't there a moon of Saturn named Io?"

"Jupiter actually," says the Mahnmut machine.

"Well, it's nice meeting you," I say, "but we have to get out of here right now and chat later. This cow is waking up. Someone'll be looking for her in a minute or two. The gods are pretty upset right now."

"Cow," repeats the robot. He is looking down at Hera. "How droll." The robot shifts his twin searchlight beams to the door. "The barn door appears to have locked behind the cow. Do you have some means of un-locking or blowing the door off its hinges?"

"No," I say. "But we don't have to go through the door to get out of here. Give me your hand . . . paw . . . whatever it is."

The robot hesitates. "Are you planning to quantum teleport us out of here by any chance?"

"You know about QT?"

The little figure shifts the beams back to the inert crabshell that looms taller than my head. "Can you take both of us with you?"

It's my turn to hesitate. "I don't know. I suspect not. That much mass . . ." Hera is stirring and moaning at our feet—well, at my feet and at this Mahnmut's vaguely footish-looking peds. "Give me your hand," I say again. "I'll QT you to safety, off Olympos, and I'll come back for your friend."

The little robot takes another step away. "I have to know that Orphu can be saved before I go."

There are voices booming in the hall. Are they searching for me already? That's likely the case. Has Aphrodite shared her seeing-through-the-Hades-Helmet technology, or are they just fanning out and searching the space as though they were hunting for an invisible man? Hera moans and turns on her side. Her eyelids are still fluttering, but she's coming to.

"Fuck it," I say. I tear off my cape and remove the levitation harness that's part of my armor. "Give me some light here, please." Should one say please to a robot? Of course, this Mahnmut didn't say he was a robot, but a moravec. Whatever that is.

The first belt of the harness is far too short to fit around the big crab-shell, but I link all three sections of the harness together, wrapping the buckles on each end to cracks in the shell. This poor Orphu bugger looks as if terrorists have been using him for target practice for years. There are craters within craters on his vaguely metallic-looking carapace.

"All right," I say. "Let's see if this works." I activate the harness.

What must be tons of inert crabshell wobbles, bumps, but then levitates ten inches or so off the marble floor.

"Let's see if this medallion can haul this much freight," I say, not caring if the Mahnmut understands me. I hand the taser baton to the little robot. "If the cow stirs before I'm back, or if someone else comes through that door, aim and tap the baton here. It'll stop one of them."

"Actually," says Mahnmut, "I have to go fetch two things they stole from us and I might be better served by that invisibility device you were using. Might it be borrowable?" He hands me the baton back.

"Shit," I say. The voices are right outside the door now. I loosen my armor, tug off the leathery cowl, and toss it to the robot. Will Hades' little device work for a machine? Should I tell him that Aphrodite can see him even with it on? No time now. I say, "How will I find you when I come back?"

"Come to the near side of the caldera lake any time in the next hour," says the robot. "I'll find you."

The door opens. The little robot disappears.

With Nightenhelser and Patroclus, I'd simply grabbed them to include them in the QT field, although I'd been dragging the inert Patroclus with my arm around him. Now I lean against the Orphu shell, one arm thrown up over it as far as I can reach, while I visualize my destination and twist the medallion.

Bright sunlight and sand underfoot. The Orphu mass has teleported with me and now floats ten inches off the sand, which is good since there are small boulders beneath it. I don't think it's possible to emerge from QT into a solid object, but I'm glad we haven't picked today to find out.

I've come to Agamemnon's camp on the beach, but the tented area is mostly deserted this late morning hour. Despite the roiling storm clouds overhead, sunlight shafts down across the beach and across the bright tents, paints the long black boats with light, and shows me the Achaean guards jumping back in shock at our sudden appearance. I can hear the roar of battle a few hundred yards beyond the camp and know that the Greeks and Trojans are still fighting out there beyond the Achaean defensive trenches. Perhaps Achilles is leading a counterattack.

"This shell is sacred to the gods," I shout at the guards who are crouching behind their spears. "Do not touch it upon pain of death. Where is Achilles? Has he been here?"

"Who wants to know?" demands the tallest and hairiest of the guards. He lifts his spear. I vaguely recognize him as Guneus, commander of the Enienes and Peraebians from Dodona. What this captain is doing standing guard in Agamemnon's camp this day I don't know and don't have time to find out right now.

I taser Guneus down and look at the second in command, a bowlegged little sergeant. "Will *you* take me to Achilles?"

The man plants the butt of his spear in the sand, goes to one knee, and bows his head briefly. The other guards hesitate but then do the same.

I ask where Achilles is. "All this morning, godlike Achilles strode the edge of the surf, summoning sleeping Achaeans and rousing captains with his piercing cry," says the sergeant. "Then he challenged the Atrides in combat and beat them both. Now he is with the great generals, planning a war, they say, against Olympos itself."

"Take me to him," I say.

As they lead me out of the camp, I glance back toward the Orphu of Io shell—it's still floating above the sand, the remaining guards are still keeping a respectful district—and then I laugh aloud.

The little sergeant glances at me but I don't explain. It's simply that this is the first time in nine years that I've walked freely on the plains of Ilium in an unmorphed form, as Thomas Hockenberry rather than anyone else. It feels good.

Equatorial Ring

Just before they found the firmary, Daeman had been complaining about being starved. He *was* starved. He'd never gone so long between meals before. The last thing he'd eaten had been a paltry few bites of the last dried food bar almost ten hours earlier.

"There must be *something* to eat in this city," Daeman was saying. The three of them were kick-swimming their way through the dead orbital city. Above them, the glowing panes had given away to clear panels and they saw now how the asteroid and its city were slowly turning. The Earth would appear, move across their field of view above them, its soft light illuminating the empty space, floating bodies, dead plants, and floating kelp. "There has to be something to eat here," repeated Daeman. "Cans of food, freeze-dried food . . . *something.*"

"If there is, it's centuries old," said Savi. "And as mummified as the post-humans."

"If we find any servitors, they'll feed us," said Daeman, realizing that the statement was nonsense as soon as he said it.

Harman and the old woman did not bother replying. They floated into a small clearing in the wild kelpfields. The air seemed slightly thicker here, although Daeman did not lift his osmosis mask or thermskin cowl to try to breathe it. Even through the mask he could tell the little bit of cold air smelled foul.

"If we find a faxportal," said Harman, "we'll have to use it to get home." Harman's body was muscled and taut in his blue thermskin suit, but Daeman could see the beginning of wrinkles and lines around the eyes through the other man's clear mask. He looked older than he had just a day earlier.

"I don't know if there are faxportals up here," said Savi. "And I wouldn't fax again if I could.

Harman looked at her. The Earth rotated into view overhead and the soft Earthlight dimly illuminated all of their faces. "Will we have a choice? You said the chairs were a one-way ride."

Savi's smile was tired. "My code's no longer in their faxbanks. Or if it is, it's for delete purposes only. And I'm afraid the same may be true for both of you after the voynix detected us in Jerusalem. But even if your codes are viable, and even if we somehow located faxnodes here, and even if we somehow learned to operate the machinery—those are no common faxportals, you know—and I stayed behind to fax you home, I don't think it would work."

Harman sighed. "We'll just have to find another way." He looked around the dark city, frozen corpses, and swaying kelp beds. "This isn't what I expected in the rings, Savi."

"No," said the old woman. "None of us did. Even in my day, we thought the thousands of lights in the sky at night meant millions upon millions of post-humans in thousands of orbital cities."

"How many cities do you think they had?" asked Harman. "Besides this one?"

Savi shrugged. "Perhaps just one in the polar ring. Perhaps no more. My guess now is that there were only a few thousand post-humans when the holocaust hit them."

"Then what were all those machines and devices we saw coming up?" asked Daeman. He didn't really care, but he was trying to take his mind off his empty stomach.

"Particle accelerators of some sort," said the old woman. "The posts were obsessed with time travel. Those thousands of big accelerators produced thousands of tiny wormholes, which they tweaked into stable wormholes—those were the swirling masses you saw at the end of most of the accelerators."

"And the giant mirrors?" said Harman.

"Casimir Effect," said Savi, "reflecting negative energy into the wormholes to keep them from imploding into black holes. If the wormholes were stable, the posts could have traveled through them to any place in space-time where they could position the other end of the wormhole."

"Other solar systems?" asked Harman.

"I don't think so. I don't think the posts ever got around to sending probes out of the system. They seeded the outer system with intelligent, self-evolving robots long before I was born—the posts needed asteroids for building materials—but no starships, robot or otherwise."

"Where were they going then with these wormholes?" said Harman.

Savi shrugged. "I think it was the quantum work that . . ."

"God *damn* it!" shouted Daeman. He'd listened to this meaningless drivel long enough. "I'm *hungry*! I want some *food*!"

"Wait," said Harman. "I see something." He pointed up and ahead of their direction of travel.

"It's the firmary," said Savi.

She was right. They'd swum-kicked another exhausting half mile through the underwater light of the dead asteroid city, ignoring the floating gray mummies of the dead post-humans they'd encountered, until they could clearly see the rectangle of clear plastic three hundred feet or so up one of the glowing walls. Inside, stretching for hundreds of yards, were row upon row of familiar healing tanks filled with naked old-style human beings, busy servitors—Daeman almost wept at the familiar sight—and other shapes moving to and fro in the bright hospital light within the room.

"Wait," gasped Daeman. They'd been swimming and kicking through the thin, toxic air close to the ground, finding stanchions, terraces, dead trees, and other solid objects from which to kick off, but Daeman was exhausted. He'd never worked this hard.

Although visibly impatient to fly her way up to the glowing infirmary, Savi doubled back and floated near the panting Daeman. Harman looked up at the clear-walled room with something like hunger in his eyes.

Savi handed Daeman her bottle and he finished the last of the water without hesitation or asking permission. He was dehydrated and worn out.

"I promised Ada that I'd take her with us," Harman said softly.

Both Daeman and the old Jew looked at him.

"I was sure we'd be in a spaceship," said Harman with an embarrassed shrug. "I promised her I'd stop at Ardis Hall and pick her up."

"She was angry at you anyway," said Daeman between gasps for air. The osmosis mask never seemed to supply all the oxygen he needed.

"Yes," said Harman.

Savi pushed aside a chewed gray corpse that floated out of the kelp, its frozen white eyes seeming to stare at them in reproach. "I doubt very much if Ada would be all that thankful to be here right now," she said. She pointed up at the infirmary. "But you should be, Harman. This was your goal, wasn't it? To get to the infirmary and negotiate a few more years?"

"Something like that," said Harman.

She nodded toward the corpse. "It doesn't look like it's the posts you'll be negotiating with."

"Do you think the firmary is automated?" asked Harman. "That it's just the servitors who've been keeping it running, faxing us up, repairing us for our allotted five Twenties, and then faxing us back to our dull little lives these past few centuries?"

"Why don't we go up and find out?" said the old woman.

They got into the glowing, glass-sided rectangle through a white square of semipermeable wall just like the one at the airlock.

It was the firmary. It not only had light and air, it somehow had one-tenth Earth gravity. Daeman fell on his hands and knees coming through the wall, unable to adapt so quickly to the light but persistent tug of gravity. The sudden change, plus the welcome sight of the oh-so-familiar servitors, plus his terror in being back in the firmary so soon after the al-losaurus episode, made his legs too weak for him to stand even in the swimming-pool g-field.

Savi and Harman walked from tank to tank. Savi had slipped her osmosis mask down and tested the air. "Thin, but there's a terrible stench," she said, her voice sounding strange and high-pitched. "They must need air for something here, but it's too foul to breathe. Keep your masks on."

Daeman needed no more prompting; he kept the mask in place.

The servitors ignored them, tending to various virtual control panels. Clear pipelines and tubes showed green and red fluid flowing to and from the tanks. Harman stared in each ten-foot-high holding tank. The human bodies in each were, for the most part, almost perfect, but unformed, the flesh too slick, the skulls and groin areas hairless, the eyes white. Only a few of the floating forms were nearly complete, and on these, eyes with color and torpid intelligence blinked out at them.

Daeman walked behind the other two, staying farther away from the tanks. He looked at these proto-humans, remembered his hazy images from his tank time only days earlier, and he shuddered again, backing away from the tanks until he bumped into a counter. A servitor floated around him, ignoring him.

"They're evidently not programmed to deal with humans outside the tanks," Savi said. "Although if you interfered with their work enough, they'd probably do something to get you out of the way."

Suddenly a green light blinked on one of the vats holding a fully re-built body—a young woman, with blue eyes and red hair on her head and groin—and the fluid in the tank began bubbling wildly. A second later the body was gone. A few seconds after that, another body materialized in the tank—this one a pale man with staring dead eyes, and a wound on his forehead.

"They have a faxportal in each tank!" cried Daeman. Then he realized, of course they must. That's how their bodies were brought up here each Twenty, or after each serious injury. *Or death.* "We could use these faxnodes," he said.

"You might be able to," said Savi, her face close to one of the tanks. "Or perhaps not. The fax is coded for the body in the tank. The faxing machinery might not recognize your codes and might just . . . flush you."

Colored fluids flowed into the tank with the new corpse. Clusters of tiny blue worms appeared from an aperture, swam to the dead man, and burrowed into his battered skull and into his bloated, white flesh.

"Still want your extra tank time?" Savi asked Harman.

Harman only rubbed his chin and squinted down the multiple rows of glowing tanks. Suddenly he pointed. "Holy Christ," he said.

The three approached slowly, half walking, half floating in the low but no longer negligible gravity. Daeman simply did not believe what he was seeing.

A third of the tanks at this end were filled with fluid but empty of human bodies. But there were bodies—parts of bodies—on every available surface here: the floor, the tables, the tops of servitor consoles, on top of disabled servitors themselves. At first glance, Daeman thought—hoped—that these were more mummified remains of the posts, as horrible as that was, but these were no mummies. Nor were they the remains of post-humans.

The firmary was something's smorgasbord.

Lying on the long table ahead of them were human body parts—white, pink, red, moist, bloody, fresh. A dozen forms on that table, male and female, seemingly still wet from the tanks, lay eviscerated—organs scooped out, meat gnawed off bloody ribs. A human head lay under the table, blue eyes staring up in what might have been a second of shock as something or someone ate the body to which it had been attached. A small pile of hands lay in front of a tall-backed swivel chair turned away from the table.

Before any of them could speak to each other on the commline, the chair swiveled around. For a second, Daeman thought it was another human body propped up in the chair, but this one was greenish, intact, and breathing. Yellow eyes blinked. Impossibly long forearms and clawed fingers unfolded. A lizardy tongue flicked out over long teeth.

"Thou thoughtest that I was altogether such a one as theyself," said what Daeman realized had to be the real Caliban. "Thou thoughtest wrong."

Savi and Harman grabbed Daeman as they kick-flew their way up the length of the firmary, Daeman screaming into the comm the same way he'd screamed on the way up in the chair. They hit the white wall dead on, passed through it without pause—feeling the thermskins clutch them tighter as they hit the freezing near-vacuum outside the firmary—and then kicked strongly off the clear wall as they dove toward the ground three hundred feet below.

Savi and Harman released Daeman's arms as they paused on a platform sixty feet above the city floor. He had time to notice the floating mummies all around, bits of their throats and bellies bitten away with the same bite radius as the humans inside the firmary, realized that he was about to vomit into his breathing mask, and then the two on either side of him found something solid to kick from and swam toward the darkness ahead.

Daeman tugged up his mask in desperation and vomited into near-vacuum and stinking, cold air. He felt his eardrums bursting and his eyes swelling, but he tugged the mask back in place—smelling his own vomit and fear—and kicked off after Savi and Harman. He didn't want to run. He just wanted to curl up, float in a tight ball, and throw up again. But even Daeman realized that he didn't have that choice. Flailing wildly, looking over his shoulder at the glow of the firmary, Daeman swam and ran and kicked for his life.

Caliban caught them in the darkest corner of the city, where the wild-kelp beds swayed to the coriolis of the slowly turning asteroid. All of the glass walls of the city here were clear, showing them the cloud-whitened earth floating by for several minutes and then several minutes of darkness broken only by the cold stars. It was in the darkness that Caliban came.

The three huddled together in the darkness there.

"Did you see him come out of the firmary?" gasped Savi.

"No."

"I didn't see anything after we ran," gasped Harman.

"Was it a *calibani*?" gasped Daeman, realizing that he was weeping, not caring that he was. He asked the question with his last reservoir of hope.

"No," said Savi over the comm, her tone dashing Daeman's last hopes. "It was Caliban himself."

"Those bodies . . ." began Harman. "Fifth Twenties?"

"It looked like younger ones, too," whispered Savi. She had the black gun in her hand and was swiveling, peering into the darkness between the strands of swaying kelp.

"Maybe the thing used to harvest just the Fifth Twenties," whispered Harman over the comm. "But it's gotten bolder. Impatient. Hungrier."

"Jesus, Jesus, Jesus, Jesus," hissed Daeman. It was the oldest invocation known to humankind, even if they didn't know what it meant. His teeth were chattering

"Still hungry?" asked Savi. Perhaps she was attempting to calm Daeman down with some dark approximation of humor. "I'm not," she said.

"I am," said Caliban over their radio frequencies. The monster floated out of the kelp, cast his net over the three of them, batted the gun out of Savi's hand, and gathered them in like fish.

44

Olympus Mons

It felt strange to Mahnmut not to have Orphu in tightbeam range. He hoped his friend was safe.

The gods burst into the room a second after the human, who had never identified himself, quantum teleported out. Mahnmut didn't believe in invisibility other than good stealth material, but he was obviously invisible to the tall gods and goddesses who crowded into the room and knelt around Hera. Mahnmut slipped out between the bronzed legs and white togas and began retracing his way through the labyrinth of corridors. He discovered that it was very hard to walk as a biped when one is invisible—he kept checking to see where his feet were and they were nowhere—so he dropped to all fours and padded silently along the halls.

Because Orphu had slowed down the gods escorting him to his cell, Mahnmut had seen where they'd stored the transmitter and Device. The room had been down a side corridor three right turns away from the corridor where he and Orphu had been incarcerated.

When Mahnmut reached the storage room, the hallway was empty—although gods passed through the adjoining hallways and intersections frequently—and Mahnmut activated his low-wattage wrist laser to cut through the door. Even while he was cutting he realized how odd this would look to any divinity turning into this hallway—no moravec in sight, but a twenty-centimeter red beam floating by itself, slowly burning a circle into the lock mechanism of the huge door.

The laser could never have cut through the entire door, but it cut a nice five-centimeter circle above the lock—Mahnmut's hearing could detect the solid-state mechanism shifting up through subsonic frequencies—and the door swung inward. Mahnmut closed it behind him when he stepped in, hearing footsteps coming down his corridor only a few seconds later. They passed by. He tugged off the leather Hades Helmet cowl the better to see his hands and feet.

This was no empty holding cell. The room was at least two hundred meters long, half that high, and filled with bars of gold, heaps of coins, chests of precious stones, small mountains of polished bronze artifacts, marble statues of gods and men, great seashells spilling pearls onto the polished floor, dismantled gold chariots, glass columns filled with lapis lazuli, and a hundred other treasures, all gleaming from the reflected light from flames flickering in a score of gold fire tripods.

Mahnmut ignored the wealth and ran to the dull-metal squirt transmitter and slightly smaller Device. There was no way that Mahnmut could carry both things out of here—invisibility didn't keep one inconspicuous when two metal devices could be seen floating down the hallway—and he knew that he only had seconds in which to act, so he dragged the Device out of the way, found the correct jackpatch on the communicator, and triggered it with a standard low-voltage command.

The transmitter's primitive AI accepted the command and shed its nanocarbon skin to show complex devices folded in on themselves. Mahnmut backed away as the transmitter did a forward roll as gracefully as a human acrobat, extended tripod legs and Chevkovian *felschenmass* power booms, then unfurled a mesh dish eight meters wide. Mahnmut was glad he hadn't tried this in a small room.

But he was still in a windowless room, perhaps under tons of marble and granite and Martian stone, quite possibly too thick for the transmission to pass through. At any rate, there was no starfield for the dish to use for navigation or orientation. As the dish searched and whirred, Mahnmut felt anxiety build—and not just because there were more shouts from the corridors. This should be the next place the gods would search—or QT to—after making sure that Hera was alive. If the transmitter couldn't lock on here, Mahnmut's and Orphu's mission was probably over. It all depended on the sophistication of the squirt transmitter's design.

The dish wobbled, whirred, adjusted itself a final time, and locked on something about twenty degrees from vertical. A virtual control panel appeared next to the physical jackports and green lights glowed.

Mahnmut jacked in and downloaded everything in his memory banks from the entire trip—every conversation with Orphu, every piece of dialogue with Koros III, Ri Po, or the gods, every visual he'd seen and recorded from the time they left Jupiter space. With the broadband on the transmitter jackport enabled, it took less than fifteen seconds to complete the download.

Mahnmut's sensors picked up the Chevkovian antimatter energy field in the squirt transmitter building, and he wondered if the gods could sense it. One way or the other, he knew, they'd find him within minutes, if not sooner. And there was no way out of this room and the building while carrying the Device. He could trigger it now, or he could trigger it later. Either way, he'd be in the center of whatever happened.

But it wasn't the Device he had to worry about now, Mahnmut reminded himself. It was this squirt transmitter.

The communicator blinked green across a myriad of indicators, suggesting to Mahnmut that the squirt power source was now at maximum charge, the data was encrypted, and the target—probably Jupiter space, possibly even Europa—was locked. Or so he hoped.

Someone was banging against the doors.

Why don't they just quantum teleport in? thought Mahnmut. He didn't take time to figure that out. Swapping out his hands for metal leads, he found the final enable port and transmitted the actuate charge of thirty-two modulated volts.

The dish shot out a yellow beam eight meters wide. The column of pure Chevkovian energy blasted a hole in the ceiling and through three more floors before stabbing out to the stars. Then it switched off and the transmitter silently self-destructed into a molten blob.

Mahnmut's emergency polarizing filters had come on in nanoseconds during the transmission, but he was still blinded for a few seconds. When he did look up through the series of slanted, steaming holes above and saw the sky, he dared to have hope for the first time.

The gods blew the door inward and Mahnmut's end of the treasure vault filled with smoke and vapor.

Mahnmut used the few seconds of cover the smoke provided to grab the Device—which would have massed only about ten kilograms on Earth's gravity and weighed only about three here on Mars—and then he crouched, contracted the springs and actuators in his hind legs as tightly as he could, ignoring design tolerances, and then leaped up through the smoking holes, flying up and through fifteen meters of shattered marble and dripping granite.

The roof of this part of the Great Hall was flat and Mahnmut ran along it as fast as he could on two legs, exhilarated to be out in the open air, carrying the Device under his left arm.

The sky above the summit of Olympus Mons was blue, and filled with dozens of flying chariots being guided by gods and goddesses. One of the machines swooped down now and hurtled ten meters above the rooftop, evidently intent upon smashing Mahnmut under its wheels.

Too late, Mahnmut realized that he'd forgotten to pull the Hades Helmet cowl over his head. He was visible to every one of the searching gods above.

Using every bit of stored energy in his system, leaving any worry about recharging for a later date, Mahnmut coiled and jumped again, passed right through the holographic horses, and kicked the surprised goddess right in the chest. She flew backward off the chariot, white arms pinwheeling, and landed hard on the roof of the Great Hall of the Gods.

Mahnmut spent three-tenths of a second studying the virtual display holographed above the front chariot rail, and then he slipped his manipulators into the matrix and banked the chariot hard right. Other chariots and shouting gods banked and dived and climbed to cut him off. There'd be no escape from Olympos airspace, but Mahnmut wasn't planning to escape that way.

Five chariots were closing and the air was full of titanium arrows—arrows!—when Mahnmut crossed over the edge of the huge caldera lake. He grabbed the Device and jumped just as the first of Apollo's arrows struck his chariot. The machine exploded just meters above him and Mahnmut fell toward the water amidst melting gold and flaming energy cubes. The air rained microcircuits in the seconds before Mahnmut hit the surface. His deep-ranging sonar told him that the caldera under the lake's surface was more than 2,000 meters deep.

It might be good enough, thought the little moravec. Then he hit the water, activated his flippers, kept a tight hug on the Device with one arm, and dived deep.

45

The Plains of Ilium, Ilium

I feel bad about not going back for the little robot right away, but things are busy here.

The guards lead me to an Achilles dressing for combat, surrounded by the chieftains he has inherited from Agamemnon—Odysseus, Diomedes, old Nestor, the Big and Little Ajaxes—the usual crew except for the Atrides, Agamemnon and Menelaus. Can it be true, as Ares was shouting above, that Achilles has slaughtered King Agamemnon, thus depriving his wife, Clytaemnestra, of her bloody revenge and a hundred future playwrights their subject matter? Has Cassandra overnight been spared her fate?

"Who in Hades are you?" snarls the man-killer, swift-footed Achilles, when the sergeant leads me into his inner camp. Again I realize that they're looking at only Thomas Hockenberry, slump-shouldered, be-whiskered and begrimed, minus his cape and sword and levitation harness, a sloppy-looking foot soldier in dull bronze chest armor.

"I'm the man your mother, the goddess Thetis, said would guide you first to Hector and then to victory over the gods who murdered Patroclus," I say.

The various heroes and captains take a step back at hearing this. Achilles has obviously told them that Patroclus is dead, but perhaps he hasn't told all of them his plan of declaring war on Olympos.

Achilles hastily pulls me aside, further from the listening circle of weary warriors. "How do I know that you are the one of whom my mother, the goddess Thetis, spoke?" demands this young god-man. Achilles looks older today than yesterday, as if new lines have been chiseled into his young face overnight.

"I will show you by taking you where we must go," I say.

"Olympos?" His eyes are not quite sane.

"Eventually," I say softly. "But as your mother told you, first you must make peace and common cause with Hector."

Achilles grimaces and spits into the sand. "I am not capable of making peace this day. It's war I want. War and divine blood."

"To fight the gods," I say, "you must first end this useless war with Troy's heroes."

Achilles turns and gestures toward the distant battle lines. I see Achaean pennants across the defensive ditch, moving into what were Trojan lines the night before. "But we're beating them," cries Achilles. "Why should I make peace with Hector when I can have his guts on my speartip in mere hours?"

I shrug. "Have it your way, son of Peleus. I was sent here to help you avenge Patroclus and reclaim his body for funeral rites. If these things are not your will, I'll take my leave." I turn my back on him and start to walk away.

Achilles is on me so fast, throwing me to the sand and drawing his knife so quickly, that I couldn't have tasered him if my life depended on it. Perhaps it does, for now he sets the razor-sharp blade against my throat. "You dare insult *me*?"

I speak very carefully so the blade does not draw blood. "I insult no one, Achilles. I was sent here to help you avenge Patroclus. If you wish to do so, do what I say."

Achilles stares at me a moment, then rises, resheaths his knife, and offers his hand to pull me up. Odysseus and the other captains are watching silently from thirty feet away, obviously curious as hell.

"What is your name?" demands Achilles.

"Hockenberry," I say, dusting sand off my butt and rubbing my neck where the blade touched it. "Son of Duane," I add, remembering the usual ritual.

"A strange name," mutters the man-killer. "But these are strange times. Welcome, Hockenberry, son of Duane." He extends his hand and grasps my forearm so tight that he squeezes off circulation. I try to return the grip.

Achilles turns back to his captains and his aides. "I am dressing for war, son of Duane. When I am done, I shall accompany you to the depths of Hades if need be."

"Just Ilium to start with," I say.

"Come, meet my comrades and my generals now that Agamemnon is defeated." He leads me over toward Odysseus and the others.

I have to ask. "Is Agamemnon dead? Menelaus?"

Achilles looks grim when he shakes his head. "No, I've not killed the Atrides, although I bested both in single combat this morning, one after the other. They are bruised and bloody, but not so badly hurt. They are with the healer Asclepius, and although they have sworn allegiance in return for their lives, I will never trust them."

Then Achilles is introducing me to Odysseus and all the other heroes I've watched for more than nine years. Each of the men grips my forearm in greeting and by the time I've gone down the line of just the top captains, my wrist and fingers are numb.

"Godlike Achilles," says Odysseus, "this morning you have become our king and we swear our allegiance and have given our oath to follow you to Olympos if need be to win back our comrade Patroclus' body after Athena's treachery—as unbelievable as that sounds—but I have to tell you that your men and your captains are hungry. The Achaeans must eat. They have been fighting Trojans all morning after little or no sleep and have driven Hector's forces back from our black ships, our wall, and our trenches, but the men are tired and hungry. Let Talthybius there prepare a wild boar for the captains while your men and you draw back to eat and . . ."

Achilles wheels on the son of Laertes. "*Eat?* Are you mad, Odysseus? I have no taste for food this day. What I really crave is slaughter and blood and the cries and groans of dying men and butchered gods."

Odysseus bows his head slightly. "Achilles, son of Peleus, greatest by far of all the Achaeans, you are stronger than I am, and greater by not just a little with the spear, but I might surpass you in wisdom, seasoned as I am by more years of experience and more trials of judgment. Let your heart be swayed by what I say, new King. Do not let your loyal Achaeans and Argives and Danaans attack Ilium on empty bellies this long day, much less go to war against Olympos while they're hungry."

Achilles pauses before answering.

Odysseus takes Achilles' silence as an opportunity to press home his argument. "You want your heroes, Achilles, willing to die for you to a man, eager to avenge Patroclus, to meet their deaths not by battle with the immortal gods but by *starving*?"

Achilles sets his strong hand on Odysseus' shoulder, and I realize, not for the first time, how much taller the man-killer is than the stocky tactician. "Odysseus, wise counselor," says Achilles, "have Agamemnon's herald Talthybius draw his dragger across the largest boar's throat and set the animal to the spit over the hottest fire your men can make. Then slaughter as many more as there are appetites in the Achaean ranks. I will order my loyal Myrmidons to take charge of the feast. But make no initial offering to the gods this day. No firstling thrown into the fire for sacrifice. This day, we will give the gods only the business ends of our spears and swords. Let them take the hindmost for a change."

He looks around and speaks loudly so that all of the captains can hear. "Eat well, my friends. Nestor! Have your sons, Antilochos and Thrasymedes, also Meges the son of Phyleus, Meriones and Thoas, Lycoedes the son of Creon, and Melanippus too, carry the word of the feast to the very front of the fighting, so that no Achaean warrior goes without meat and wine for his midday meal this day! I will dress myself for battle and go off with Hockenberry, the son of Duane, to prepare myself for the coming war with the gods."

Achilles turns and walks into the tent where he had been dressing when I arrived, beckoning now for me to follow him.

Waiting for Achilles to get dressed for war reminds me of the times I waited for my wife, Susan, to get dressed when we were late for a dinner party somewhere. There's nothing to do to hurry up the process—all one can do is wait.

But I keep checking my chronometer, thinking of the little robot I left up there—Mahnmut was its name—and wondering if the gods have killed it, him, it, yet. But he told me to return and meet him by the caldera lake in an hour and I still have more than thirty minutes left.

But how can I return to Olympos without the Hades Helmet to hide me? I'd been impulsive in giving the leather cowl to the little robot, and now I may pay for that impulsiveness at any moment if the gods look down and spy me here. But I tell myself that Aphrodite will be able to see me anyway if I return to Olympos, Hades Helmet or no Hades Helmet, so I'll just have to QT in there fast, get Mahnmut, and QT out. What's important now is what's happening here and in Ilium.

What's happening here is that Achilles is getting dressed.

I notice that Achilles is grinding his teeth as he dresses for war—or rather, as his servants, slaves, and stewards help him dress for war. No *knight chavaliex* from the Middle Ages ever handled his weapons and armor with greater care and ceremony than does Achilles, son of Peleus, this day.

First, Achilles wraps his legs with finely formed greaves—shin guards that make me remember my days as a catcher in Little League—although these greaves aren't made of molded plastic, but are wonderfully worked in bronze with silver ankle-clasps.

Then Achilles straps the breastplate around his broad chest and slings his sword over his shoulder. The sword is also made of bronze, is polished brighter than a mirror, is razor sharp, and has a silver-studded hilt. I might lift that sword if I crouched and used both hands. Perhaps.

Then he hoists his huge, round shield, made of two layers of bronze and two layers of tin—a rare metal at this time—separated by a layer of gold. This shield is a polished and gleaming work of art so famous that its design had Homer devote a full book of the *Iliad* to it; the shield has also been the subject of many stand-alone poems, including my favorite by Robert Graves. And, surprisingly, it doesn't disappoint when seen in person. Suffice it to say that the shield design includes concentric circles of images which summarize the essence of thought in much of this ancient Greek world, beginning with the River Ocean on the outer rim and moving through amazing images of the City at Peace and the City at War near the center, culminating in beautiful renderings of the Earth, sea, sun, moon and stars in the bull's-eye center. The shield is so brightly polished that even in the shade of this tent, it gleams like a heliograph mirror.

Finally Achilles lifts his rugged helmet and sets it in place over his brows. Legend has it that the fire god Hephaestus personally drove in the horsehair crest—not only Trojans wear high-crested war helmets in this war, but also the Achaeans—and it's true that the tall golden plumes along the ridge of the helmet shimmer like flames when Achilles walks.

Fully armed now except for his spear, Achilles tests himself in his gear like an NFL lineman making sure his shoulder pads are set. The man-killer spins on his heels to see that his greaves are tightly fitted and his breastplate tight, but not so tight that he cannot turn and twist and dodge and thrust with ease. Then he runs a few paces, making sure that everything from his high-laced sandals to his helmet stays in place. Finally, Achilles lifts his shield, raises his hand over his shoulder, and pulls free his sword, all in a single movement so fluid that it looks as if he's been doing it since birth.

He resheaths the sword and says, "I'm ready, Hockenberry."

The captains follow us as I lead Achilles back to the beach where I left the Orphu shell. The guards have not gone near the huge crab-thing—which is still floating thanks to my levitation harnesses, a fact not lost on the gathering crowd of soldiers. I've decided to give a little magic show here, impressing Odysseus, Diomedes, and the other captains while earning a little more respect. Besides, I know that these other Achaeans, not blinded by fury as Achilles is, can't be very enthusiastic about going up against the immortal gods they've worshiped and sacrificed to and obeyed since they were old enough to think. Theoretically, anything I can do now to reinforce Achilles' dominion over his new army should be helpful to both of us.

"Grasp my forearm, son of Peleus," I say softly. When Achilles does so, I twist the medallion with my free hand and we blink out.

Helen had said to meet them in the foyer of the baby Scamandrius' nursery in Hector's home. I've been there, so there is no problem visualizing it and we QT into an empty room. We are a few minutes early—the changing of the guards on the walls of Ilium won't happen for four or five minutes yet. There's a window in this foyer, and we can both see that we're in the center of Ilium. The street traffic—oxcarts, horses and their clanking livery, marketplace shouts, the shuffle of hundreds and hundreds of pedestrians on cobblestones—comes through the open window as a reassuring background noise.

Achilles doesn't seem to be nonplussed by quantum teleportation. I realize that the young man's life has been full of divine magic. He was raised and educated by a *centaur,* for God's sake. Now—knowing that he's in the belly of the belly of the enemy beast in Ilium—he only sets his hand on the hilt of his sword, not drawing it, and looks at me as if to ask, "What next?"

The "what next" is a man crying out in terrible pain from the room next door, the nursery. I recognize the voice of the shouting man as Hector, although I have never heard him moan and cry like this. Women are also weeping and lamenting. Hector shouts again, as if in mortal pain.

I have no urge to go into that nursery, but Achilles acts for me, striding ahead, his hand still tight on the hilt of the half-drawn sword. I follow.

My Trojan women are all here—Helen, Hecuba, Laodice, Theano, and Andromache—but they don't even turn as Achilles and I enter the nursery. Hector is here, in dusty, bloody battle gear, but he doesn't even look up at his archenemy as Achilles stops and stares at what everyone's horrified attention is focused on.

The baby's hand-carved cradle is tipped over. Blood is splattered across the cradle wood, the marble floor, and the mosquito netting. The body of little Scamandrius, also lovingly known as Astyanax, not quite one year old, lies on the floor—hacked to pieces. The baby's head is missing. The arms and legs have been lopped off. One pudgy little hand remains attached, but the other has been severed at the wrist. The baby's royal swaddling clothes, with Hector's family crest so delicately embroidered on the breast, is sodden with blood. Nearby lies the body of the wet nurse I'd seen on the battlements and sleeping here peacefully just one night ago. It looks as if she's been mauled by some huge jungle cat, her dead arms still extended toward the overturned cradle as if she died attempting to protect the infant.

Servants are wailing and screaming in the background, but Andromache is speaking, her voice stunned but almost frighteningly calm. "It was the goddesses, Athena and Aphrodite, who did this, my lord and husband."

Hector looks up and his face under his helmet is a terrible mask of shock and horror. His mouth hangs open, spittle dangling. His eyes are wide and red-rimmed. "Athena? Aphrodite? How can this be?"

"I came to the door from my chamber just an hour ago when I heard them talking to the nurse," says Andromache. "Pallas Athena herself said to me that this sacrifice of our beloved Scamandrius is the will of Zeus. 'A yearling heifer for sacrifice slaughter' is the phrase the goddess used. I tried to argue, weeping, begging, but goddess Aphrodite willed me into silence, saying that Zeus's will on this shall not be denied. Aphrodite said that the gods were ill pleased with the way of the war and with your failure to burn the black ships last night. And that they would take this sacrifice as warning." She gestures to the butchered child on the floor. "I sent the fleetest servants to recall you from the battlefield, and called these women, my friends, to see me through my grief until you arrived, O Husband. We have not reentered this room until you came."

Hector turns his wild face on us, but his gaze passes right over the silent Achilles. I don't think he would have seen a cobra at his feet this moment. He's blind with shock. All he can see is Scamandrius' corpse—headless, bloodied, one little fist closed. Then Hector chokes out, "Andromache, wife, beloved, why aren't you dead on the floor next to the nurse, fallen likewise in an attempt to save our child from the wrath of the immortals?"

Andromache lowers her face and weeps silently. "Athena kept me at the doorway behind an invisible wall of force while their divine power did this deed," she says, tears falling on the bodice of her gown. I see now that her gown is bloodied where she must have knelt and hugged to her the remains of her slaughtered child. Irrelevant as it is right now, I think of watching television and seeing Jackie Kennedy on that distant day in November when I was a teenager.

Hector does not move to hug or console his wife. The servants' wailings rise in pitch, but Hector remains silent a minute until he raises his scarred and muscled arm, closes a mighty fist, and snarls at the ceiling, "Then I defy you gods! From this moment on, Athena, Aphrodite,

Zeus—all those gods I've served and honored, even to my life all these years—thou art my enemy." He shakes his fist.

"Hector," says Achilles.

Every head turns. Servants wail in terror. Helen throws her hands to her mouth in a perfect simulation of surprise. Hecuba screams.

Hector pulls his sword free and snarls with an expression almost resembling relief. *Here is someone to vent my fury on. Here is someone to kill.* I can read his thoughts on his face.

Achilles holds both palms up. "Hector, brother in grief. I come here today to share your grief and to offer you my right arm in battle."

Hector has tensed to rush the man-killer but now the Trojan hero freezes, his face turning into a mask of confusion.

"Last night," says Achilles, his callused palms still raised to show his empty hands, "Pallas Athena came to my tent in the Myrmidon encampment and killed my dearest friend—Patroclus dead by her hand—his body taken to Olympos to be fed to the carrion birds there."

Still holding his sword, Hector says, "You saw this?"

"I spoke to her and witnessed it myself," says Achilles. "It was the goddess. She cut down Patroclus then just as she has your son today—and for the same reasons. She told me these herself."

Hector looks down at his sword hand as if his weapon and his arm have betrayed him.

Achilles strides forward. The crowd of women parts for him. The Achaean man-killer extends his right hand so that it is almost touching the tip of Hector's sword.

"Noble Hector, enemy, brother in blood," Achilles says softly, "will you join me in this new battle we must fight to avenge our loss?"

Hector drops his sword so that the bronze echoes on the marble floor, its hilt ending up in a pool of Scamandrius' blood. The Trojan cannot speak. He steps forward almost as if attacking, but then grips Achilles' forearm fiercely—if it had been my arm, he would have torn it off—and continues gripping the other man's arm as if hanging on to keep from falling.

All through this, I confess, I keep flicking my gaze to Andromache, still weeping silently, even while the other faces register more shock and amazement.

You did this? I think at Hector's wife. *You did this to your own son to get your way on this war?*

Even as I think of it, stepping further back from Andromache in revulsion, I know it was the only way. The only way. But then I look down at the butchered remnants of Astyanax, "Lord of the City," the murdered

Scamandrius, and I take another step back. If I live to be a thousand years old, ten thousand, I will never understand these people.

At that instant, the real goddess Athena, accompanied by my Muse and the god Apollo, QT into the empty half of the nursery.

"What is happening here?" demands Pallas Athena, eight feet tall and arrogant in posture, tone, and gaze.

The Muse points to me. "There he is!" she cries.

Apollo draws his silver bow.

46

The Equatorial Ring

Caliban's lair was dark and moist and warm, hidden as it was amidst the old pipes and septic system beneath the city's surface, the grotto warmed to tropical temperatures by biotic decay and populated with scuttling eft-things and pompion plants. Caliban cracked thin ice, swam through a pipe in the asteroid's soil, emerged into a long, narrow grotto, hung his netful of captives by a hook, slashed the net, set the three stunned and unresisting humans on three rocks ten feet above a bubbling pool, and stretched out on a licheny pipe overgrown with ferns. The creature kicked both feet in the slush, and propped his chin on his huge clenched fists to inspect Savi, Harman, and Daeman.

Daeman had pissed himself when the monster seized them. The thermskin absorbed the moisture and dried itself almost immediately, leaving no stain, but his cheeks reddened even through his terror when he thought of it.

There was air in Caliban's lair, and more gravity than in the city proper, and the creature ripped off their osmosis masks so quickly, his long arm striking forward so rapidly and clawed fingers grasping with such speed that none of the three, even the last, had time to duck or back away. Their rocks rose like slimy columns above the black pool. The air around them smelled foul and thick and sewage-rich. Caliban breathed it in as if it were ambrosial, showing his yellow smile from time to time as if to taunt them. Part of the fishy smell in the grotto came from the creature itself.

Daeman had thought the *calibani* in the Mediterranean Basin were scary, but knew now that they were shadowy duplicates of the awfulness of this real and original Caliban, if that's what this thing was. This creature was no larger than the *calibani*, but was infinitely more obscene in all his toothed and testicled fleshiness. At first glance Caliban seemed ungainly, almost clumsy, but he'd swum through the cold, thin air of the dead city easily enough, using his huge webbed feet and webbed hands as effective paddles. He'd gripped the gathered end of their net in his oversized mouth, the sharp teeth there holding it fast even as Savi, Harman, and Daeman struggled and kicked against the net.

"What do you want with us?" demanded Savi as the three of them were perched on their stones above the underground pond and Caliban lay studying them. Daeman could see that she'd retrieved the gun that had fallen into the net with them and that it was in her hand, but it wasn't aimed. *Shoot it!* Daeman thought at the old woman. *Kill this thing!*

Caliban, sprawled close enough above their stone columns that his breath washed over them, redolent with the same decay as the air itself, hissed, "He creeps down to touch and tickle hair and beard. And now a flower drops with a bee inside, and now a fruit to snap at, catch, and crunch."

"He's crazy," whispered Harman over their radio link.

Caliban smiled. "He talks to his own self, howe'er he please, touching that other, whom his dam called God. Because to talk about Him, vexes—ha, could He but know! And time to vex is now."

"Who is 'He'?" asked Savi. Her voice was very calm for someone in a stinking grotto and at the mercy of a beast. "Are you speaking of yourself in the third person, Caliban?"

"He is He," whispered the monster, prone on his mossy pipe, "except when He is Setebos!" At the mention of the name, Caliban sprawled lower, spraddled and splay-footed, putting his arms over his head as if ready to ward off a blow from above. Something small and scaly scuttled and splashed in the fetid pond below them. Yellow vapors rose around them all.

"Who is Setebos?" asked Harman, obviously working to keep his voice as calm as Savi's. "Is Setebos your master? Will you go get him for us so he can let us go? We'll talk with him."

Caliban raised his head, scraped the pipe with his claws fore and aft, and barked at the roof of the grotto. "Setebos, Setebos, and Setebos! Thinketh, He dwelleth i' the cold o' the moon."

"The moon?" said Savi. "This Setebos of yours lives on the moon?"

"Thinketh, He made it, with the sun to match," purred the creature. "But not the stars; the stars came otherwise; only made clouds, winds, meteors, such as that: Also this isle, what lives and grows thereon, And snaky sea which rounds and ends the same."

"What is he talking about?" whispered Daeman to Savi on the suit comms. "Is he mad? It sounds like he's talking about some god."

"I think he is talking about a god," Savi whispered back. "His god. Or something real that he views as a god."

"Who or what created this monster? No God, certainly," whispered Daeman.

Caliban's odd, translucent ears twitched and raised at this. "Thinketh, Sycorax, my mother made me, mortal morsel. Thinketh, Prospero, the silent servant of the Quiet, made Himself servant to the servant. Thinketh, though, that Setebos, the many-handed as a cuttlefish, who, making Himself feared through what He does, looks up, first, and perceives he cannot soar to what is quiet and happy in life, but makes this bauble-world to ape yon real, These good things to match those as hips do grapes."

"This bauble-world," repeated Savi. "Do you mean the asteroid city here on the e-ring, Caliban?"

Instead of responding, Caliban crawled forward like a scaled cat ready to pounce, his yellow eyes only a yard from their heads. "Thinketh, Himself, do they know Prosper?"

"I know Ariel, the biosphere entity," said Savi. "Ariel gave us pass to Atlantis and to travel here. It's all right for us to be here. Ask Ariel."

Caliban laughed and rolled onto his back, only his claws and webbed feet keeping him from rolling off the slick pipe into the fetid water below. "Thinketh, Himself as Prosper, keeps for his Ariel a tall pouch-bill crane He bids go wade for fish and straight disgorge; also a sea beast, lumpish, which he snared, blinded the eyes of, and brought somewhat tame, and split its toe-webs, and now pens the drudge in a hole o' the rock and calls him . . . *Caliban*."

"What the *hell* is he talking about?" demanded Daeman on the commline. "The thing is mad. Shoot it, Savi. Shoot it."

"I think I . . . may . . . understand," whispered Harman. "Himself is Caliban. He does speak of himself in the third person, Savi. Your logosphere Prospero enslaved him somehow and used Ariel, the biosphere persona, to do it."

"And Caliban blinded some little sea beast, maybe a lizard like those in the pool below, and called it Caliban," said Savi. Her voice was odd—distant, almost bemused—as if the yellow-eyed thing reclining and stretching in front of them had mesmerized her. "He plays at being his master, Prospero," she said softly.

Caliban laughed and scratched his side. Daeman could see gills there, opening and closing like obscene gray mouths above his ribs and just below his armpits. "Himself, peeped late, eyed Prosper at his books careless and lofty, lord now of the isle," hissed Caliban. "Vexed, stitched a book of broad leaves, arrow-shaped, has peeled a wand and called it by a name; weareth at whiles for an enchanter's robe the eyed skin of a supple oncelot."

"Oncelot?" said Harman.

"Shoot it, Savi," hissed Daeman. "Shoot it now before it kills us."

"Caliban," said Savi, voice soothing, "what happened to the post-humans here?"

Caliban began to weep. Mucus ran from his muzzle. "Setebos," he whispered, looking again toward the roof of the grotto as if someone was listening. "Setebos bid me to give these mankins three sound legs for one, or pluck the other off, and leave them like an egg. Were this no pleasure, mind me mortal, hunting posties one by one, drinking the mash to wash down their flesh, with brain become alive, making and marring clay at will. So He. *So He!*"

"Oh, my God," breathed Savi. She slumped back on her high, rough stone. It looked as if she was considering leaping to the foul pool below.

"What?" whispered Daeman on the comm. "What?"

"Caliban did kill the post-humans," whispered the old woman. She seemed older now in this sewer light. "On this Setebos' command. Or perhaps Prospero's. Caliban seems to worship both as gods. Perhaps there is no Setebos, only his worship of the Prospero persona."

The creature quit snuffling and brightened up, his wide mouth-flap rising. "Thinketh, such shows nor right nor wrong in Him, nor kind, nor cruel: He is strong and Lord."

"Who is?" asked Savi. "Setebos or Prospero? Whom do you serve, Caliban?"

"Saith He is terrible," roared Caliban, rising on his hind legs now. "Watch his feats in proof! One hurricane will spoil six good months' hope. He hath a spite against me, that I know."

"Who has a spite against you?" asked Harman.

Daeman thought it was insane to try to talk to this insane creature. *"Shoot it,"* he whispered again to Savi. *"Kill the thing."*

Savi raised the gun a little higher but still did not aim it.

"Thinketh, Himself, that the posties brought wormholes, Setebos brought the worms," said Caliban. "Prospero made maggots into gods, and Setebos made stone into Prosper's face, and zeks to place him well. My dam said the Quiet made all things which Setebos vexed only, but then, Himself observes, who made them weak when weakness meant weakness He might vex? Had He meant other, while His hand was in, why not make horny eyes, like Caliban's, which no thorn could prick?

Or plate their scalps with bone against the snow, like thus, or overscale their flesh 'neath joint and joint like an orc's armor? Aye—spoil His sport! He is the One now: only He doth all."

"Who is the one?" asked Savi.

Caliban looked as if he was going to weep again. "My blinded beast loves whoso places fleshmeat on his nose. It pleases Setebos thus, to work, use all His hands."

"Caliban," Savi said softly, slowly, as if to a child, "we're tired and want to go home. Can you help us go home?"

The monster's eyes seemed to focus on something other than his hate and self-hate now. "Aye, Lady, Caliban knows the way and wishes you well. But you and Himself both know His ways and must not play Him off, sure of the issue."

"Tell us how . . ." began Savi.

"Doth the like himself," said Caliban, growing more agitated now, crouching on his hind legs, his long forearms hanging down, thorned knuckles scraping moss from pipe. "There is the sport; discover how or die! Please Him and hinder this? What Prosper does? Aha, if He would tell me how! Not He!"

"Caliban, if you take us home, we can . . ." began Savi. She'd raised the gun a bit.

"All need to die," shouted Caliban, tensing his thighs and scraping his knuckles. "Thinketh, Himself, Prosper brings crafty Odysseus here, but Setebos makes him wander. Prosper sends night cries to Jove in the skies, bringing the hollow men to Mars, but Setebos sets it right with false gods' rage. There is the sport; discover how or die!"

Caliban hopped to the end of the pipe, girdled the pipe with his legs, swung low, and scooped an albino lizard from the ooze. The lizard's eyes had been gouged out.

"Savi," said Harman.

"All need not die, no," cried Caliban, weeping and gnashing his teeth. "Some flee afar, some dive, some run up trees; those at His mercy—why, they please Him most when . . . when . . . well, never try the same way twice!"

"Shoot it, Savi," said Daeman loudly, not on the commline, but speaking clearly, his voice echoing in the grotto.

Savi bit her lip but raised the weapon.

"Lo!" cried Caliban. "Lieth flat and loveth Setebos! Maketh his teeth meet through his upper lip."

Caliban released the blind lizard, which leaped for the pond below but struck Savi's rock on its way to the water.

"Watch His feats in proof!" cried Caliban and leaped.

Savi fired and several hundred barbed, crystal flechettes struck Caliban in the chest, rending flesh like paper. Caliban howled again, landed on Savi's rock, wrapped the old woman in his impossibly long arms, and bit through her neck with one powerful snap of his jaws. Savi didn't even have time to scream before she was dead, neck almost severed, body gone limp in the monster's arms, gun falling from lifeless fingers to the swamp below and disappearing.

Pouring blood himself, Caliban raised his bloodied jaws and yellow eyes to the grotto walls and howled again. Then, carrying Savi's corpse under one long arm, the monster dived to the bubbling water below and disappeared beneath the scum.

Ardis Hall

It was on the morning of Hannah's First Twenty, after riding with her young friend to the faxnode and watching her be escorted into the pavilion by two servitors and a voynix, that Ada began worrying in earnest.

She'd begun to worry about Harman on the second day after he'd flown away with Daeman and Savi. She didn't really expect him to come swooping by to pick her up on a spaceship as he'd promised—that was a childish fantasy that she didn't think even Harman believed in—but she did expect the three of them back with the sonie in two or three days. After four days, her worry turned to anger. After a week, the emotion had resolved itself into worry again—a deeper, more gnawing worry than she'd ever experienced—and she began to have trouble sleeping. After two weeks, Ada didn't know what to think.

On the fourteenth morning after the trio's departure, with no word of the three from visiting friends—and hundreds upon hundreds of people were certainly visiting Ardis Hall now—Ada had a voynix take her on the short carriole ride to the faxportal, and after only a minute's hesitation—what could be harmful about faxing?—she stepped through to Paris Crater and visited Daeman's mother's domi there.

The young man's mother was beside herself with worry. Daeman stayed at parties for weeks sometimes—and had even gone butterfly hunting for a full month when he was one year short of his First Twenty—but he always got word to his mother about where he was and when he would be home. For the past two weeks—nothing.

"I wouldn't worry," consoled Ada, patting the older woman's arm. "Our friend Harman will watch over Daeman, and the woman we met—

Savi—will watch over both of them." Saying that helped Daeman's mother, but it made Ada more anxious than ever.

Now, two weeks after her visit to Paris Crater, missing Hannah already but knowing that the girl must be safe in the firmary, Ada found herself lost in thought during the carriole ride over the hills to home.

Ardis Hall had been invaded during the last month. Her return from Paris Crater two weeks ago had been at night, so this morning's ride was the first time in the past four weeks that Ada had actually seen the changes from the high road approaching the manor, and now the sight made her gasp.

Scores of colored tents surrounded the old white estate on the hill. At first, ten and twenty visitors—mostly men—had come to hear Odysseus speak in the great sloping meadow behind the house, but the dozens turned to hundreds, and by now thousands had made the fax trip. Ardis Hall had only a dozen carrioles and droshkies, and these were being worn out—as were the oddly sullen voynix—in transporting the constant stream of visitors between faxnode and house all hours of the day and night, so some of the volunteers from the first days of Odysseus' teaching took turns staying at the fax portal and urging the constant line of visitors to walk the incredible mile and a quarter to the manor. They did. And they walked back to fax out, returning days or even hours later with more visitors—again mostly men.

Now, as Ada's droshky rolled to a stop in the crowded circle lane in front of Ardis Hall, she realized that her isolated estate had become merely one part of an expanding city. The score of tents, erected by voynix but now looked after by men and women, included cook tents, eating pavilions, privy tents—Odysseus had showed the men how to dig a latrine away from the other tents—and sleeping tents. Ada's mother had visited once during this madness, had been overwhelmed by the scores of people wandering into Ardis Hall as if it were a public market, and she'd immediately faxed to her domi in Ulanbat and had not returned.

Ada accepted a cold drink from one of the permanent volunteers—a young man named Reman who was growing a beard, as so many of the disciples were—and she wandered back to the field where Odysseus spoke and answered questions four or five times a day, for ever larger crowds. Ada had half a mind to interrupt the arrogant barbarian's useless lectures to ask him—in front of everyone—why he, Odysseus, hadn't bothered to say good-bye to the young woman who worshiped him.

Last night, at Hannah's First Twenty party—the celebrations were always thrown the day before the actual birthday, the day before someone actually faxed to the firmary—Odysseus had barely made an appearance at the dinner. Ada knew that Hannah had been hurt. The young woman still thought she was in love with Odysseus, even though the man seemed indifferent to Hannah's feelings. After returning from their trip, Hannah had been Odysseus' shadow, but he barely seemed to notice. When he had eschewed Ada's hospitality and chosen to build a camp for himself in the forest, Hannah had tried to accompany him there, but Odysseus had insisted that she sleep in the big house. During the course of each day, as Odysseus ran, exercised, and, later, wrestled with his male disciples, Hannah was always nearby—running, climbing on the obstacle course ropes, even volunteering to wrestle. Odysseus never agreed to wrestle the beautiful young girl.

At the First Twenty party, each of the dozen or so guests around the table set under the giant oak had made the traditional speeches—congratulations to Hannah for her first visit to the firmary, wishes for life-long good health and happiness—but when it came to Odysseus' turn, the old man had said simply, "Don't go." Hannah had wept later in Ada's bedroom—had even considered *not* going, of somehow hiding from the servitors who even then were embroidering her ceremonial Twenty gown—but of course she had to go. Everyone went. Ada had gone. Harman had gone four times. Even the absent Daeman had been to the firmary twice—once on his First Twenty and again after the accident with the allosaurus. Everyone went.

So this morning, when Hannah had come down from her room dressed in only the ceremonial cotton robe, ornamented by just the small, traditional embroidered image of the caduceus—two blue snakes of healing twined around a staff—Odysseus had not been there to say good-bye to his young friend.

Ada had been furious as the two rode in one of Ardis's droshkies to the fax pavilion. Hannah had wept a bit, turning her face away so that Ada wouldn't see. Hannah had always been the toughest young woman Ada'd known—the artist and athlete, the risk-taker and sculptor—but this morning she'd seemed a lost little girl.

"Maybe he'll pay attention to me after I return from the firmary," Hannah had said. "Maybe I'll seem like more of a woman to him tomorrow."

"Maybe," said Ada, but she was thinking that all men seemed to be self-serving, selfish, insensitive pigs, just waiting for an opportunity to act like *greater* self-serving, selfish, insensitive pigs.

Hannah had looked so fragile as the two servitors floated out of the fax pavilion, each taking one of Hannah's arms, and led her to the faxportal. It was a beautiful day, clear blue sky, soft winds from the west, but it might as well have been raining so far as Ada's mood would have dictated. She had no idea why she had this sense of doom—she'd seen scores of friends off to their various Twenty trips to the firmary and had gone herself, remembering only hazy images of floating in a warm liquid—but Ada had wept when Hannah had raised her hand and waved in that second before the faxportal whisked her away and out of sight. The ride back to Ardis Hall alone had simply deepened Ada's anger at Odysseus, at Harman, and at men in general.

So Ada felt like anything but a loving disciple as she wandered up the hill behind Ardis Hall to listen to Odysseus' lecture to the faithful and the curious.

The short, bearded man was dressed in his tunic and sandals, sword by his side, sitting against a fallen dead tree that Odysseus had cut down himself, while all around him and stretching down the hill toward the house sat and stood several hundred men and women. Several of the men were wearing tunics similar to Odysseus now, belted by the same kind of broad leather belt. Most seemed to be growing beards, which had not been in style in Ada's lifetime.

Odysseus was answering questions at the moment. Ada knew that his usual schedule was to speak for about ninety minutes one hour after sunrise, then to go off by himself for hours, answer questions in the hour before lunch, speak again without interruption in the mid-afternoon, and entertain questions in the long twilight hour after the sun set. This was the pre-lunch gathering.

"Teacher, why must we find out who our fathers are? It's never been important before." It was a new young man who had held up his hand.

When Odysseus spoke, Ada had noticed over the past month, he usually held his hands straight out, thrusting his short, strong fingers at the air as if driving home the points of what he said. His arms and legs were tanned and powerful. For the first time, Ada noticed that some of the bearded men in the audience were also getting tanned and muscled. Odysseus had set up an obstacle course—all ropes and logs and muddy pits—in the forest up the hill, and demanded that anyone who listened to him more than twice must exercise at least an hour a day on the course. Many of the men—and some of the female disciples—had laughed at the idea the first time they tried it, but now they were spending long hours on the course, or running, each day. It made Ada wonder.

"If you don't know your father," Odysseus was answering in that low, calm, but fiercely firm voice of his that always seemed to carry as far as it had to, "how can you know yourself? I am Odysseus, son of Laertes. My father is a king, but also a man of the soil. When I saw him last, the old man was down on his knees in the dirt, planting a tree where an old giant of a tree had fallen—cut down by his hand finally— after being struck by lightning. If I do not know my father, and his father before him, and what these men were worth, what they lived for and were willing to die for, how can I know myself?"

"Tell us again about *arete*" came a voice from the front row. Ada recognized the man speaking as Petyr, one of the earliest visitors. Petyr was no boy—Ada thought he was in his fourth Twenty—but his beard was already almost as full as Odysseus'. Ada didn't think the man had left Ardis since he'd first heard Odysseus speak that second or third day, when the visitors could be counted on two hands.

"*Arete* is simply excellence and the striving for excellence in all things," said Odysseus. "*Arete* simply means the act of offering all actions as a sort of sacrament to excellence, of devoting one's life to finding excellence, identifying it when it offers itself, and achieving it in your own life."

A newcomer ten rows up the hill, a heavyset man who reminded Ada a bit of Daeman, laughed and said, "How can you achieve excellence in all things, Teacher? Why would you want to? It sounds terribly tiring." The heavy man looked around, sure of laughter, but the others on the hill looked at him silently and then turned back to Odysseus.

The Greek smiled easily—strong white teeth flashing against his tanned cheeks and short, gray beard—and said, "You can't *achieve* excellence in all things, my friend, but you have to *try*. And how could you *not* want to?"

"But there are so many things to do," laughed the heavy man. "One can't practice for them all. One has to make choices and concentrate on the important things." The man squeezed the young woman next to him, obviously his companion, and she laughed loudly, but she was the only one to laugh.

"Yes," said Odysseus, "but you insult all those actions in which you do not honor *arete*. Eating? Eat as if it were your last meal. *Prepare* the food as if there were no more food! Sacrifices to the gods? You must make each sacrifice as if the lives of your family depended upon your energy and devotion and focus. Loving? Yes, love as if it were the most important thing in the world, but make it just one star in the constellation of excellence that is *arete*."

"I don't understand the *agon*, Odysseus," said a young woman in the third row. Ada knew that her name was Peaen. She was intelligent, a skeptic of all things, but this was her fourth day here.

"The *agon* is simply the comparison of all like things, one to the other," Odysseus said softly but clearly, "and the judgment of those things as equal to, greater than, or lesser than. All things in the universe take part in the dynamic of *agon*." Odysseus pointed to the dead tree he was sitting on. "Was this tree greater than, lesser than, or simply equal to . . . *that* tree?" He pointed to a tall living tree up the hill, at the edge of the forest there. Voynix stood under the shadows of the branches. The voynix would not come close to Odysseus.

"That tree is living," called the heavy man who had spoken earlier. "It must be superior to the dead tree."

"Are all living things superior to all dead things?" asked Odysseus. "Many of you have gone under the turin cloth and seen the battle there. Is a dung merchant alive today a better man than Achilles was then, even if Achilles is dead now?"

"That's comparing unlike things," cried a woman.

"No," said Odysseus. "Both are men. Both were born. Both will die. It matters little if one still breathes and the other resides only in the impotent shades of Hades. One must be able to compare men—or women—and that is why we need to know our fathers. Our mothers. Our history. Our stories."

"Well, that tree you're sitting on is still dead, Teacher," said Petyr. This time people up and down the hill did laugh.

Odysseus joined in the laughter. He pointed to a sparrow that had just landed on one of the few branches Odysseus hadn't hacked away from the fallen tree. "It is not only *still* dead," he said, "it is *newly* dead. But already the usefulness of the tree—in usefulness terms of the *agon*—have surpassed the *agon* usefulness of that living tree up the hill. For that bird. For the insects even now burrowing into the bark of this fallen giant. For the mice and voles and larger creatures who will soon come to inhabit this dead tree."

"Who is to be the final judge of the *agon* then?" asked a serious, older man in the fifth row. "Birds, bugs, or men?"

"All," answered Odysseus. "Each in his turn. But the only judge who counts is you."

"Isn't that arrogant?" demanded a woman Ada recognized as a friend of her mother's. "Who elected *us* judge? Who gave us the right to be judgmental?"

"The universe elected you through fifteen billions years of evolution," said Odysseus. "It gave you eyes with which to see. Hands with which to hold and weigh. A heart with which to feel. A mind to learn the rules of judgment. And an imagination with which to consider the bird's and bug's—and even other trees'—judgment in this matter. And you must approach this judgment with *arete* to guide you—trust me that the bugs and birds and trees already do. They have no time for mediocrity in their world. They do not worry about the arrogance of judging, whether it is in choosing a mate, an enemy—or a home."

Odysseus pointed to where the sparrow had hopped into a hole in the fallen trunk, disappeared into the hollow there.

"Teacher," said a young man far back in the crowd, "why do you ask us men to wrestle at least once a day?"

Ada had heard enough. She took the last of her cold drink and walked back up to the house, pausing on the porch to look down the long grassy yard to where dozens more of the visitors—disciples—walked and talked together. Silk on the tents stirred to the warm breeze. Servitors shuffled from one visitor to the other, but few accepted offers of food or drink. Odysseus had asked that anyone staying to hear him speak more than once not allow the servitors to work for them, or the voynix to serve them. That had initially driven many away, but more and more were staying.

Ada looked up at the blue sky, noted the pale circles of the two rings orbiting there, and thought about Harman. She'd been so *angry* at him when he'd talked about women choosing among men's sperm months or years or decades after intercourse—it was simply not discussed, except between mothers and daughters, and then only once. And that nonsense about a moth's genes being involved, as if human women had not chosen the fathers of their allowed babies like that since time immemorial. That had been so . . . *obscene* . . . of Harman to bring that up.

But it was her new lover's statement that he wanted to be the father of Ada's child . . . not only *be* the one whose seed was chosen at some future date, but be *around*, be *known* as the father . . . that had so nonplussed and infuriated Ada that she'd sent Harman away on his harmless adventure with Savi and Daeman without so much as a kind word. In fact, with hostile words and glances.

Ada touched her lower belly. The firmary had not notified her through servitors that her time for pregnancy had arrived, but then, she had not asked to be put on the list. She was glad that she didn't soon have to choose between—what had Harman called them?—sperm packets. But she thought of Harman—his intelligent, loving eyes, his gentle and then firm touch, his old but eager body—and she touched her belly again.

"Aman," she whispered to herself, "son of Harman and Ada."

She shook her head. Odysseus' prattle the last weeks was beginning to fill her head with nonsense. Yesterday, fed up, after dark, after the scores and scores of disciples had wandered off to the fax pavilion or sleeping tents—more to the tents than to the pavilion—she had bluntly asked Odysseus how much longer he planned to stay at Ardis Hall.

The old man had smiled at her almost sadly. "Not much longer, my dear."

"A week?" pressed Ada. "A month? A year?"

"Not so long," said Odysseus. "Just until the sky begins falling, Ada. Just until new worlds appear in your yard."

Furious at his flippancy, tempted to order the servitors to evict the hairy barbarian at once, Ada had stalked up to her bedroom—her last place of privacy in this suddenly public Ardis Hall—where she had lain awake being angry at Harman, missing Harman, worrying about Harman, instead of ordering servitors to do anything about old Odysseus.

Now she turned to go into the house, but a strange motion caught at the edge of her vision made her turn back. At first she thought it was just the rings rotating, as always, but then she looked again and saw another streak—like a diamond scratching a line across the perfect blue glass of the sky. Then another scratch, broader, brighter. Then yet another, so bright and so clear that Ada could clearly see flames stretching behind the streak of light. A few seconds later, three dull booms echoed across the lawn, made strolling disciples pause and look up, and caused even the servitors and voynix to freeze in their duties.

Ada heard screams and shouts from the hill behind the house. People on the lawn were pointing skyward.

There were scores of lines marring the azure sky now—bright, flaming, roiling red lines slashing and crisscrossing, falling west to east, some with plumes of color, others with rumbles and terrifying booms.

The sky was falling.

Ilium and Olympos

The ultimate war begins here in a murdered child's nursery.

The gods must have quantum teleported down to talk with mortals this way a thousand times before—Athena, arrogant in her divinity, Apollo, secure in his power, and my Muse, probably brought along to identify the rogue scholic, Hockenberry. But this day, instead of encountering deference and awe, instead of conversing with the foolish mortals eager to be cajoled into more interesting ways of slaughtering one another, they are attacked on sight.

Apollo lifts his bow in my direction, the Muse pointing and saying "There he is!" but before the god can nock one of his silver arrows, Hector leaps, swings his sword, hacks down the bow, steps closer, and thrusts his sword deep into Apollo's belly.

"Stop!" shouts Athena, throwing up a forcefield, but too late. Fleet-footed Achilles has already stepped inside the circle of the forcefield and slashes the goddess from shoulder to hip with a single mighty swing.

Athena screams and the jet roar is so loud that most of the mortals in this room—myself included—go to one knee in pain with hands over our ears. Not Hector. Not Achilles. The two must be deaf to anything but the internal roar of their own rage.

Apollo shouts some amplified warning even as he raises his right arm—either to warn off Hector or to unleash some godly lightning—but Hector doesn't wait to discover the god's intentions. Swinging his heavy sword in a two-handed backhand that reminds me of Andre Agassiz in his prime, Hector slices off Apollo's right arm in a spray of golden ichor.

For the second time in my life, I watch a god writhe in agony and change shape—losing his godlike human form and becoming a whirlpool of blackness. From that blackness comes a bellow that sends the servants running from the nursery and drops me to both knees. The five Trojan women—Andromache, Laodice, Theano, Hecuba, and Helen—pull daggers from their robes and turn on the Muse.

Athena, her shape also quivering and unstable, stares down at her slashed breasts and bleeding belly and then raises her right hand, firing a beam of coherent energy that should have turned Achilles' skull to plasma, but the Achaean ducks with superhuman speed—his DNA is nanocell enriched, tailored by the gods themselves—and swings his sword at the goddess's legs even as the wall behind him bursts into flame. Athena levitates—rising off the floor and hovering—but not before Achilles' sword slashes through divine muscle and bone, leaving her left leg dangling in two pieces.

This time the scream is too loud to bear, and I lose consciousness for a minute, but not before I see my Muse—the terror of my days—so panicked that she forgets her power to teleport and simply runs from the room, my five Trojan women chasing her with daggers in hand.

I come to a few seconds later. Achilles is shaking me.

"They fled," he snarls. "The shit-eating cowards fled to Olympos. Take us there, Hockenberry." He picks me up with one hand, his fist tight around the strap that holds my breastplate in place, shakes me at arm's length, and sets the tip of his god-blooded sword under my chin. "*Now!*" he snarls.

I know that to resist will mean death—Achilles' eyes are mad, pupils contracted to black pinpricks—but at that moment Hector grabs Achilles' arm and forces it down until my feet touch the floor. Achilles drops me and turns toward his short-lived Trojan ally, and for an instant I'm sure that Fate will reassert itself—that fleet-footed Achilles will slaughter Hector here and now.

"Comrade," says Hector, holding his empty palm straight. "Fellow enemy of the ruthless gods!"

Achilles checks his attack.

"Hear me!" snaps Hector, every inch the field marshal now. "Our shared desire is to follow these wounded gods to Olympos and there die in glorious combat, trying to bring down Zeus himself."

Achilles' wild expression does not change. His eyes show mostly white. But he's listening. Barely.

"But our glorious deaths now will mean our peoples' destruction," continues Hector. "To avenge ourselves properly, we must rally our armies to our side, lay siege to Olympos, and bring down *all* the gods. Achilles, see to your people!"

Achilles blinks and turns to me. "You," he snaps. "Can you carry me straight back to the Achaean camp with your magic?"

"Yes," I say shakily. I see Helen and the other women returning to the death nursery, their daggers unstained by golden god-blood. Evidently the Muse has escaped.

Achilles turns to Hector. "Speak to your men. Kill any captains who resist your will. I shall do the same with my Argives and meet you in three hours at that sharp ridge that rises out of Ilium—you know the one I mean, man. You locals call it Thicket Ridge. The gods and we Achaeans think of it as the leaping Amazon Myrine's mounded tomb."

"I know it," says Hector. "Bring a dozen of your favorite generals with you to this conference, Achilles. But leave your armies a half a league behind until we agree on strategy."

Achilles shows his teeth in what could be a snarl or grin. "You don't trust me, son of Priam?"

"Our hearts are joined in boundless anger and bottomless sorrow at this moment," says Hector. "You for Patroclus, me for my son. We are brothers in madness at the moment, but three hours is enough for even the fires of common cause to cool. And you have the world's ablest tactician with you—Odysseus, whose craft and cleverness all Trojans fear. If the son of Laertes counsels you to betrayal, how will I know?"

Achilles shakes his head impatiently. "Two hours then. I'll bring my most trustworthy generals. And any Achaeans who will not follow me in war against the gods today will be shades in Hades by nightfall."

He swings away from Hector and grasps my forearm so tightly that I almost cry out. "Take me to my camp, Hockenberry."

I fumble for the QT medallion.

The wind has blown the levitating Orphu-thing a quarter of a mile down the beach and into the surf between two long black Achaean ships, and I have to leave Achilles and his captains to retrieve the Device. Because of the levitation harness, there's no friction, and I borrow a rope from the watching Greeks, hitch it around one of the levitation belts, and drag the cracked and cratered shell out of the water and back up the beach in front of the staring heroes of the *Iliad*.

It's obvious that there has been much argument in the Achaean camp. Diomedes is telling Achilles that half the men are preparing their ships for sail, while the other half are readying themselves for death. The idea of resisting the gods—much less attacking them—is not only madness but blasphemy to all these men who've seen the gods in action. Diomedes himself comes close to defying Achilles here in council.

Speaking with the fine rhetoric he's famous for, Achilles reminds them of his hand-to-hand combat with Agamemnon and Menelaus and his legal assumption of command of the Achaean armies. He reminds them of the murder of Patroclus. He praises their courage and their loyalty. He tells them that the loot of Ilium is nothing compared to the riches they'll have when they loot Olympos. He reminds them that he can and will kill all of them if they resist. All in all, it's a convincing speech but not a happy conference.

This is all screwed up. My plan had been for the heroes to defy the gods and end the war, for the Achaeans to sail home and for the Trojans to resume their lives with the great gates of their walled city open once again to travelers and merchants. I'd imagined the City at Peace as illustrated near the center of Achilles' shield. And I'd thought—hoped— that Achilles and Hector would meekly sacrifice themselves for the greater good, not enlist tens upon tens or hundreds of thousands of others in their battle.

And even my plan to get Hector and Achilles to Olympos for their fatal *aristeia* is doomed. I'd planned to take the two warriors up there one at a time, the gods all unaware that danger existed until it descended on them like a Greek and Trojan lightning storm. But the attack on Apollo and Athena in Scamandrius' nursery has lost us even this small element of surprise.

So now what?

I check my watch. I'd promised the little robot that I'd pick him up. But the Great Hall of the Gods and all of Olympos must be a hornet's nest now. The odds of my QTing in and getting out undetected seem low to zero. *What will Hector and Achilles do if I don't come back here?*

That's their problem. I reach up to lift my Hades Helmet over my head, remember that I loaned it to Mahnmut, sigh, visualize the coordinates for the west side of the Caldera Lake on the Olympian summit, and QT out.

It *is* a hornet's nest. The sky is filled with chariots zipping back and forth above the lake. I can see scores of gods standing along the shoreline, some pointing, some firing lances of pure energy into the lake. The water is boiling for miles out into the caldera. Other gods are shouting with amplified voices, declaring that Zeus commands everyone to gather in the Great Hall. No one's noticed me yet—there's too much confusion—but it's just a matter of a minute or less before someone spots a non-god on their exclusive country club turf.

Suddenly the boiling water erupts just yards from where I stand and a vague shape emerges, visible only because of water cascading off its invisible surface. Then the dark little robot snicks into view, pulling the Hades Helmet off and handing it to me.

"It would be best if we left quickly," Mahnmut says in English. After I dumbly take the leather helmet, he keeps one arm extended for me to grasp so that he can be included in the QT field. I grab his forearm and then scream and release it. The metal or plastic or whatever it is that makes up his skin is red hot. Already the palm of my right hand is red and beginning to blister.

Two chariots swoop our way. Lightning flashes. The air smells of ozone.

I grab the robot's shoulder and twist the medallion again, knowing that none of us are going to get out of this alive, but telling myself that at least I came back for the little machine as promised. At least I did that.

The Equatorial Ring

For the first two weeks, they lived on lizards in the polluted spring. Each lost so much weight that his thermskin had to contract two sizes to stay in contact with skin.

The death of Savi had so shocked Daeman and Harman that for a full minute after Caliban's departure—still carrying their friend's corpse—each man had sat stupidly on his rock pillar ten feet above the fetid water. Daeman found that only one thought had been running through his mind—*Caliban's coming back to get us. Caliban's coming back to get us.* Then Harman broke the spell by leaping feet first into the stinking water and disappearing himself.

Daeman would have howled from terror then if he'd had the energy, but all he could do is stare at the undulating scum where Harman had abandoned him. After what seemed like long minutes, Harman bobbed up, gasping and spluttering and holding three objects in his hands—their two osmosis masks and Savi's gun. He pulled himself up onto the lower shelf of rock and Daeman—finally released from his paralysis—clambered down to join him.

"It's only about ten feet deep here," gasped Harman, "or I never would have found this stuff." He handed Daeman his osmosis mask and slipped his own on over his thermskin cowl, not securing it over his face. Then Harman had hefted the gun.

"Does it work?" asked Daeman, his voice shaking. He was afraid to be so close to the water, certain that Caliban's long arm would snake up at any second to pull him down. Daeman kept remembering the obscene *snap* as the monster's jaws bit through Savi's throat and spinal cord.

"One way to find out," whispered Harman. The older man's voice was also shaking, although from the cold water or terror, Daeman couldn't tell.

Harman aimed the weapon the way he'd seen Savi fire it, slipped his finger into the trigger guard, and squeezed. A circle of water near the far wall erupted in an irregular fountain three feet high as hundreds of flechettes ripped the surface.

"Yes!" screamed Daeman, his voice echoing back to him in the small grotto. *Fuck Caliban!*

"Where's Savi's pack?" whispered Harman.

Daeman pointed to where it had fallen behind and below her rock column. The two men scrambled to it and pawed through the contents. The flashlight still worked. There were three more clips of flechettes, each clip holding seven plastic packs of darts. Harman found the way to release the current ammunition clip and count the remaining flechette charges there. Two.

"Do you think he . . . it . . . is dead?" whispered Daeman, glancing over his shoulder at both points where the underground stream entered the small grotto. The rocky space was illuminated only by fungal glow. "Savi shot it straight in the chest from just a few feet away. Maybe it's dead."

"No," said Harman. "Caliban's not dead. Tug your mask down. We have to find a way out of here."

The underground stream ran from grotto to grotto, then grotto to cavern, each space larger than the last. The top layers of the asteroid under the crystal city seemed to be honeycombed with caves and pipes. They found blood spattered on rocks in the second grotto they surfaced in.

"Savi's or Caliban's?" whispered Daeman.

Harman shrugged. "Maybe both." He swung the flashlight around the flat rock stretching away to shadows ten yards on either side of the foul stream. Rib cages, tibias, pelvic bones, and a skull stared back.

"Oh, God, Savi," gasped Daeman. He tugged his mask down in a hurry and prepared to jump back into the underground stream.

Harman stopped him with a firm hand on his shoulder. "I don't think so." He walked closer to the bones and shifted the flashlight beam to and fro. More skeletal remains were scattered on all the rock ledges on either side of the stream. "These are old," said Harman. "Months or years— maybe decades." He picked up two ribs and held them in the light, the bones shockingly white against his blue thermskin glove. Daeman could see the gnaw marks there.

Daeman began shaking again. "I'm sorry," he whispered.

Harman shook his head. "We're both in shock and starved. We've eaten almost nothing for more than two days." He lay prone on a rock near the edge of the water.

"But maybe there's food in the city . . ." began Daeman.

Harman's hand shot down into the water and there was a wild thrashing. Daeman jumped away, sure it was Caliban returned, but when he looked back over his shoulder, the older man had an albino lizard in both hands. This one was not eyeless like the one who selected Savi—its beaded eyes were pink.

"You're kidding," said Daeman.

"No."

"We don't want to waste flechettes on killing this . . ." began Daeman.

Harman grasped the lizard firmly above its hind legs and bashed its brains out against a rock.

Daeman flipped up his osmosis mask, sure that he was going to throw up again. He didn't. His stomach rumbled and cramped.

"I wish Savi had a knife in her pack," muttered Harman. "Remember that nice skinning knife Odysseus always carried with him at the Golden Gate Bridge? We could sure use that now."

Daeman stared back, appalled beyond nausea as Harman found a fist-sized rock amongst the human bones and began chipping away one edge of it. When he had a crude point, he chopped the dead lizard's head off and began pealing away the amphibian's white skin.

"I can't eat that," gasped Daeman.

"You said yourself there's no food up in the city," said Harman, crouched over his work. Skinning a lizard, Daeman saw, was a relatively bloodless process.

"How do we cook it?"

"I don't think we can. Savi didn't bring any matches, there's no fuel to burn down here, and no air in the city above," said Harman. He ripped red flesh from the lizard's upper thigh, dangled it a minute in the flashlight beam, and then popped it in his mouth. Then he scooped up some stream water in Savi's bottle and washed the morsel down.

"How is it?" asked Daeman, although he could answer that himself based on the expression on Harman's face.

Harman ripped a thinner strip and handed it to Daeman. It was a full two minutes before Daeman slipped it into his mouth and chewed. He didn't vomit. It tasted, he thought, like salty, fishy mucus. His stomach cramped for more.

Harman handed him the flashlight. "Lie at the edge of the stream. The light attracts the lizards."

And Caliban? thought Daeman, but he lay prone at the edge of the water, shining the light into the deep pool with his left hand and preparing to grab at the white, swimming lizards when they wriggled closer.

"We'll turn into Caliban," murmured Daeman. He could hear Harman ripping flesh and chewing in the fungal darkness behind him.

"No," said Harman between bites. "We won't."

They emerged from the caverns two weeks later—two pale, bearded, emaciated, and wide-eyed men—swimming up through the proper pipe, cracking through the skim of ice on the pond above, and floating into the comparative brightness of the crystal city.

It was, strangely enough, Daeman who insisted that they go up.

"It's easier to defend against Caliban down here," argued Harman. He'd rigged a sort of holster out of part of Savi's pack and the gun was in it. They took turns sleeping against one cave wall or the other, and while one dozed the other sat watch with the flashlight and weapon.

"It doesn't matter," said Daeman. "We have to get off this rock."

"Caliban might be dying from his wounds," said Harman.

"He might be healing from them," said Daeman. The two of them looked more alike now that Daeman had lost all of his pudginess and both had grown beards. Daeman's beard was a bit fuller and darker than Harman's. "It doesn't matter," he said again. "We have to find a way off."

"I can't go back to the firmary," said Harman.

"We may have to. Those may be the only faxportals in the orbital ring."

"I don't care," replied Harman. "I can't go in that slaughterhouse again. Plus the faxportals there are for the bodies going up and down after their repair. The nodes must be coded to those people."

"We'll change the codes if we have to," said Daeman.

"How?"

"I don't know. We'll watch the servitors fax people back down and do what they do."

"Savi said she didn't think our codes were fax-viable any longer," said Harman.

"She didn't know. She'd been out of the fax loop for more than a millennium. But at the very least, we have to explore the rest of the posthuman's city up there."

"Why?" asked Harman. The older man had more trouble sleeping that Daeman did and his morale was low.

"There might be a spaceship stored somewhere," said Daeman.

Harman began laughing then, softly at first but then so uncontrollably that he began to weep. Daeman had to pinch his upper arm to get his attention.

"Come on," said Daeman. "We know the pipe that goes to the surface. Follow me. I'll shoot our way through the surface ice if I have to."

They explored the rest of the city over the next two weeks, finding cubbies and closets in which to sleep, one always standing watch while the other slept. Daeman always dreamed that he was falling and jerked awake, legs and arms struggling against the zero-g. He knew that Harman had the same dreams because the other man dozed even shorter periods of time before gasping and flailing awake.

The crystal city was uniformly dead, although the towers on the far side of the mile-long rock were more elaborate, with more terraces and enclosed spaces. Everywhere floated the mummified, half-chewed remains of the post-human women. The two men were always hungry themselves, although Savi's pack was filled with skinned and sliced water lizards, and sometimes Daeman's belly growled at the sight of some of these meaty mummified remains. It was water, they knew, that would drive them back to one of the frozen pools every third day or so.

Although they expected to encounter Caliban at every kick or turn, they found only occasional floating spheroids of blood that might be his. On their third day out of the caverns, with their eyes just then adjusting to the brighter Earthlight through clear panels above, they found a wrist and hand—floating like a pale spider outside the thickest kelp beds—that they thought might be Savi's. That night—"night" being what they called the brief twenty-minute periods where the Earth wasn't illuminating the clear panes above—they both heard a terrible, Calibanish howl from the direction of the firmary. The noise seemed to be transmitted more through the ground of the asteroid and the exotic material of the towers around them than through the thin air.

A month after their arrival in this orbital hell, they'd explored all of the city except for two areas—the far end of the firmary beyond where they'd first encountered Caliban, and a long dark corridor right at the point where the city curved sharply around the north pole of the asteroid. This narrow corridor, no more than twenty meters across, was windowless and filled with swaying kelp—a perfect hiding spot for a recovering Caliban—and on their first trip around the moonlet, they'd both voted to stay out of that dark place in favor of checking out the rest of the post-humans' city. Now the rest of the city had been checked—no spaceships, no other airlocks, no control rooms, no other firmaries, no storage rooms filled with food, no other sources for water—and they had the choice now of returning to the caverns to stock up on lizards since they were down to their last rotting lizard corpse, or going back to the firmary to try the tank faxnodes there, or exploring the dark, kelp-filled corridor.

"The dark place," voted Harman.

Daeman only nodded tiredly.

They kicked their way down through the tangling kelp while keeping one hand on the other's arm so as not to be separated. Daeman had the gun this day and he swept it from side to side at every spectral movement of the kelp. Without windows or reflected glow from the central city core, only Savi's flashlight showed the way. Both men wondered about the flashlight's charge, but neither spoke their worry aloud. Daeman reassured himself by remembering the dim fungal glow in most, not all, of the caverns below, enough to hunt lizards by, with luck, but the truth was that he didn't want to go back down to those charnel hunting grounds ever again. He'd asked Harman about the near vacuum around them just two nights earlier.

"What do you think would happen if I took my osmosis mask off?"

"You'd die," said Harman without emotion. The older man was ill—not a condition humans had encountered often, since the firmary dealt with such things—and he was shaking with cold, despite the thermskin's preservation of all his body heat. "You'd die," he repeated.

"Quickly?"

"Slowly, I think," said Harman. His blue thermskin was filthy from river mud and lizard blood. "You'd asphyxiate. But it's not pure vacuum here, so you'd struggle for quite a while."

Daeman nodded. "What if I took my thermskin off but left my mask on?"

Harman thought about this. "That would be quicker," he agreed. "You'd freeze to death in a minute or less."

Daeman had said nothing and he'd thought Harman had drifted back to sleep, but then the older man whispered over the comm, "But don't do it without telling me first, all right, Daeman?"

"All right," said Daeman.

The corridor was so thick with wild kelp that they almost had to turn back, but by having one of them twist and shove the floating growth aside while the other fought his way through, they were able to wiggle and kick and pull their way the two hundred yards or so of the dark length of the windowless column. There was a wall at the end—just what both men expected after their troubles—but Daeman kept moving the flashlight beam past the kelp, and suddenly they could just barely make out a white square set in the dark bulkhead of exotic material. Daeman had the gun so he went through the semipermeable membrane first.

"What do you see?" called Harman on the commline. He hadn't come through yet. "Can you see anything?"

"Yes." It was Daeman's thermskin suitcomm answering, but not Daeman's voice. "He can see wonderful things."

Ilium

"Tell me again what you're looking at," said Orphu, speaking not over the tightbeam but via k-link cable. Mahnmut was riding on the Ionian's back like a jockey on a floating elephant. The k-link had given them enough broadband for Orphu to upload the entire Greek language and *Iliad* databases in a few seconds.

"The Greek and Trojan leaders are meeting on this ridgetop," said Mahnmut. "We're just behind the Greek contingent—Achilles, Hockenberry, Odysseus, Diomedes, Big and Little Ajax, Nestor, Idomeneus, Thoas, Tlepolemus, Nireus, Machaon, Polypoetes, Meriones, and a half dozen other men whose names I didn't catch during Hockenberry's quick introductions earlier."

"But no Agamemnon? No Menelaus?"

"No, they're still back in Agamemnon's camp, recovering from their single combat with Achilles. Hockenberry told me that they're being cared for by Asclepius, their healer. The brothers have broken ribs and cuts and bruises—Menelaus has a concussion from where Achilles brained him with a shield—but nothing life-threatening. According to the scholic, both of them will be able to walk in a day or two.""

"I wonder if Asclepius could give me my eyes and arms back," rumbled Orphu.

Mahnmut had nothing to say to this.

"What about the Trojans?" asked Orphu, his voice eager. He sounded the way Mahnmut always imagined a human child would sound—happy, enthusiastic, almost gleeful. "Who's here representing Ilium?"

Mahnmut got to his feet on the cracked shell, better to see across the plumed heads of the Achaean heroes into the ranks of the Trojans.

"Hector leads the contingent, naturally," said Mahnmut. "His red horsehair plume and bright war helmet really stand out. He's wearing a red cape as well. It's as if he's defying the gods to come down and fight."

Mahnmut had already relayed to Orphu the scene described by Hockenberry from earlier that afternoon when Hector and his wife, Andromache, had walked among the massed thousands of warriors from Ilium, holding high the mutilated body of their dead son—Scamandrius—still dressed in blood-stained royal linen, holding up the corpse for all the Trojans to see. Hockenberry reported that there were thousands of Achaeans still contemplating flight to the high seas in their black ships, but after Hector's and Andromache's grim procession, all of the Trojans and their allies were ready to fight the gods, hand to hand if need be.

"Who's here for Ilium besides Hector?" asked Orphu.

"Paris stands next to him. Then the old counselor, Antenor, and King Priam himself. The old men stand slightly apart, not interfering with Hector."

"Antenor's two sons, Acamus and Archelochus, have been killed already, I think," said Orphu. "Both by Telemonian Ajax—Big Ajax."

"I think that's right," said Mahnmut. "It must make it hard for them to be clasping forearms in truce the way they are now. I see Big Ajax talking to Antenor as if nothing's happened."

"They're all professional soldiers," said Orphu. "They know they raise their sons for battle and possible death. Who else do you see in Hector's contingent?"

"Aeneas is there," said Mahnmut.

"Ah, the *Aeneid*," sighed Orphu. "Aeneas is . . . *was* . . . destined to be the only survivor of the royal house of Ilium. He's destined . . . *was* destined—to escape the burning city with his son, Ascanius, and a small band of Trojans, where their descendants will eventually found a city that will become Rome. According to Virgil, Aeneas will . . ."

"Let's not get ahead of ourselves here," interrupted Mahnmut. "As Hockenberry says, all bets are off now. I don't think there's any part of this *Iliad* you uploaded to me where the Greeks and Trojans become allies in a doomed crusade against Olympos."

"No," said Orphu. "Who else is standing there with Hector besides Aeneas, Paris, old Priam, and Antenor?"

"Othryoneus is there," said Mahnmut. "Cassandra's fiance."

"My God," said Orphu. "Othryoneus was destined to be killed by Idomeneus this evening or tomorrow. In the battle for the Greek ships."

"All bets are off," repeated Mahnmut. "It looks as if there isn't going to be any battle for the ships tonight."

"Who else?"

"Deiphobos, another son of Priam, is there," said Mahnmut. "His armor is polished so bright I have to drop more polarizing filters in place just to look at him. Next to Deiphobos is that fellow from Pedaeon, Priam's son-in-law, whatshisname . . . Imbrius."

"Oh my," said Orphu. "Imbrius was destined to be killed by Teucer in just a few hours . . ."

"Stop that!" said Mahnmut. "Somebody's going to overhear you."

"Overhear me on tightbeam or k-link?" said Orphu with a rumble. "Not likely, old friend. Unless these Greeks and Trojans have a bit more technology than you've told me about."

"Well, it's disconcerting," said the smaller moravec. "Half the people standing up there on Thicket Ridge are supposed to be dead in a day or two, according to your stupid *Iliad*."

"It's not *my* stupid *Iliad*," rumbled Orphu. "And besides . . ."

"All bets are off," finished Mahnmut. "Uh-oh."

"What?"

"The negotiations are over. Hector and Achilles are stepping forward, grasping each other's forearms now . . . good God!"

"What?"

"Can you hear that?" gasped Mahnmut.

"No," said Orphu.

"Sorry, sorry," said Mahnmut. "I'm sorry. I didn't mean that literally. I just meant . . . I mean . . ."

"Get *on* with it," snapped the Ionian. "What didn't I hear?"

"The armies—Greek and Trojan both—are roaring now. Good Lord, it's an overwhelming sound. Hundreds of thousands of Achaeans and Trojans combined, cheering, waving pennants, thrusting their swords and spears and banners into the air . . . the cheering and yelling mob goes all the way back to the walls of Ilium. The people on the walls there—I can see Andromache and Helen and the other women Hockenberry pointed out—they're all shouting as well. The other Achaeans—the ones who were undecided, waiting by their ships—they've come out to the Greek trenches and are cheering and screaming as well. What a noise!"

"Well, you don't have to shout as well," Orphu said drily. "The k-link works just fine. What's happening now?"

"Well . . . not much," said Mahnmut. "The captains are all shaking hands up and down the ridge. Bells and gongs are ringing out from the walled city. The armies are milling around—regular foot soldiers from each side crossing the no-man's-land to clap each other on the shoulder and exchange names or whatever—and everyone looks like they're ready to fight, but . . ."

"But there's no one to fight," said Orphu.

"Right."

"Maybe the gods won't come down to fight," said the Ionian.

"I doubt that," said Mahnmut.

"Or maybe the Device will blow Olympos into a billion pieces," said Orphu.

Mahnmut was silent at the thought of this. He had seen the gods and goddesses up there, sentient beings by the thousands, and he had no wish to be a mass murderer.

"How long until your jury-rigged timer activates the Device?" asked Orphu, although he must have known himself.

Mahnmut checked his internal chronomoter. "Fifty-four minutes," he said.

Overhead, dark clouds suddenly boiled and roiled. It appeared that the gods were coming down after all.

When Mahnmut had dived into the Caldera Lake atop Olympus Mons, he had little hope of escape. He needed a minute or so to prep the Device for triggering—for detonation?—and he thought some depth and pressure might give him that time.

It did. Mahnmut dove to 800 meters, feeling the familiar and pleasant sensation of pressure pushing on every square millimeter of his frame, and found a ledge on the west side of the steep caldera wall where he could rest, secure the Device, and ready it. The gods did not pursue him into the water. Whether they didn't like to swim or foolishly thought that their lasering and microwaving of the surface would drive him up, Mahnmut didn't know or care.

He'd been negligent in not configuring a remote triggering mechanism before he and Orphu began their short-lived balloon trip, so he did so now, 800 meters down in the dark lake, his chestlamps illumating the ovoid macromolecular Device. Removing the access cover of its transalloy shell, Mahnmut cannibalized bits of himself—one of his four power cells to provide the necessary 32-volt trigger signal, one of his three redundant tightbeam/radio receivers arc-welded to the trigger plate by his wrist laser, and a timer made from his external chronometer. Finally, he'd attached a crude motion-contact sensor rigged from one of his own transponders, so the Device would auto-trigger at this depth if anyone other than he touched it.

If these ersatz gods come down for me now, I'll trigger the thing manually, he'd thought as he sat on the ledge 800 meters below the lake surface. But he didn't want to destroy himself—if destruction was, indeed, the Device's purpose—and he didn't want to hide underwater all day. But the Hockenberry human had promised to QT back for him, so he'd wait. He wanted to see Orphu again. Besides, their mission—the late Koros III's and Ri Po's mission, actually—was to deliver the Device to Olympus Mons and transmit its arrival via the communicator. Both these objectives had been met. In a sense, Mahnmut and the Ionian had completed their mission.

Then why am I hiding 800 meters under the surface in this impossible Caldera Lake? He thought of the water boiling above him as the gods poured their anger and heat-rays into the lake and had to chuckle in his moravec way—this water should be boiling away anyway, since the top of Olympos Mons should be in near-vacuum.

Then the time had come for the human named Hockenberry to return to rescue him, and, amazingly, he did.

"Describe Earth," said Orphu on Thicket Ridge. Mahnmut had slid down from the shell and was leading his friend by the rope leader he'd looped around the levitation harness. "And are you sure we're on Earth?" Orphu added.

"Pretty sure," said Mahnmut. "The gravity is right, the air is right, the sun looks the right size, and the plant life matches the images in the databanks. Oh, so do the human beings—although all these men and women seem to have memberships in the solar system's best health and exercise club."

"That good-looking, huh?" said Orphu.

"As humans go, I think so," said Mahnmut. "But since these are the first Homo sapiens I've met in person, who knows? Only Hockenberry of all the men I've met here looks as ordinary as the men and women in the photos and vids and holos you and I have in our data banks."

"What do you think . . ." began Orphu.

Sshhh, said Mahnmut on the tightbeam. He'd pulled the k-link so he didn't have to ride on Orphu's shell any more. The clouds continued to swirl above the battlefield. *Achilles is addressing the troops—both Trojans and Achaean.*

Can you understand him?

Of course I can. The files downloaded just fine, although some of the colloqialisms and cuss words I have to guess from context.

Can the other humans hear him without a public address system?

The man's got lungs of iron, said Mahnmut. *Metaphorically speaking. His voice must be carrying all the way to the sea in one direction and all the way to the walls of Troy in the other.*

What's he saying? asked Orphu.

I defy you, gods . . . blah, blah, blah . . . and now cry havoc and unleash the dogs of war . . . blah, blah, blah . . . recited Mahnmut.

Wait, said Orphu. *Did he really use that Shakespeare quote?*

No, said Mahnmut. *I'm loosely translating.*

Whew, said the Ionian on the tightbeam. *I thought we had an amazing bit of plagiarism there. How long until activation of the Device?*

Forty-one minutes, said Mahnmut. *Is there something wrong with your . . .* He stopped.

What? said Orphu.

In the middle of Achilles' defiant *cri de coeur* against the gods, the King of the Gods appeared. Achilles stopped speaking. Two hundred thousand male faces and one robot face turned skyward on the plains of Ilium.

Zeus descended from the roiling black clouds in his golden chariot, pulled by four beautiful holographic horses.

The Achaean master-archer, Teucer, standing close to Achilles and Odysseus, took aim and launched an arrow skyward, but the chariot was too high and—Mahnmut was sure—surrounded by a powerful forcefield. The arrow arced and fell short, dropping into the thickets of brambles along the base of the ridge where the generals stood.

"**YOU DARE TO DEFY ME?**" boomed Zeus's voice across the length and breadth of the fields and shore and city where the armies were gathered. "**BEHOLD THE CONSEQUENCE OF YOUR HUBRIS!**"

The chariot swung higher and then accelerated toward the south, as if Zeus were leaving the field in the direction of Mount Ida just visible on the southern horizon. Perhaps only Mahnmut, with his telescopic vision, saw the small silver spheroid Zeus dropped from the chariot when it was about fifteen kilometers south of them.

"Down!" roared Mahnmut on full amplification, shouting the word in Greek. "For your lives, get down now!! Don't look to the south!!"

Few obeyed his command.

Mahnmut grabbed Orphu's halter and ran for the slight shelter of a large boulder on the ridgetop thirty meters away.

The flash, when it came, blinded thousands. Mahnmut's polarizing filters automatically went from Value 6 to Value 300. He didn't pause in his wild running, tugging Orphu along behind him like a giant toy.

The shock wave hit seconds after the flash, rolling up from the south in a wall of dust and sending visible stress waves rippling through the atmosphere itself. The wind speed went from five kilometers per hour out of the west to a hundred klicks per hour from the south in less than a second. Hundreds of tents were ripped from their moorings and flown into the sky. Horses whinnied and fled their masters. The whitecaps blew out away from the land.

The roar and shock wave knocked everyone standing—everyone except Hector and Achilles—to the ground. The noise and shattering overpressure were overwhelming, vibrating human bones and moravec solid-state innards, as well as setting Mahnmut's organic parts quivering. It was as if the Earth itself was roaring and howling in anger. Hundreds of Achaean and Trojan soldiers two kilometers or so to the south of the ridge burst into flame and were thrown high into the air, their ashes falling on thousands of cowering, fleeing men running north.

A section of the south wall of Ilium crumbled and fell, carrying scores of men and women with it. Several of the wooden towers in the city burst into flame, and one tall tower—the one from which Hockenberry had watched Hector saying good-bye to his wife and son just days ago—fell into the streets with a crash.

Achilles and Hector had their hands to their faces, shielding their eyes from the terrible flash that threw their shadows a hundred meters behind them on Thicket Ridge. Behind them, great boulders that had stood firm high on the Amazon Myrine's mounded tomb vibrated, slipped, and fell, crushing running Achaeans and Trojans alike. Hector's polished helmet stayed on his head, but his proud crest of red horsehairs were torn off in the high winds that followed the initial shock wave.

Has something happened? tightbeamed Orphu.

Yes, whispered Mahnmut.

I can feel some sort of vibration and pressure right through my shell, said Orphu.

Yes, whispered Mahnmut. The only reason the Ionian hadn't tumbled away on the winds and blast was that Mahnmut had lashed the rope around the largest rock he could find on the lee side of their sheltering boulder.

What . . . began Orphu.

Just a minute, whispered Mahnmut.

The mushroom cloud was rising through ten thousand meters now, smoke and tons of radioactive debris lifting toward the stratosphere. The ground vibrated so fiercely to aftershocks that even Achilles and Hector had to drop to one knee rather than be thrown down like the tens of thousands of their men.

This atomic mushroom cloud resolved itself into a face.

"**YOU WANT WAR, O MORTALS?**" bellowed the bearded face of Zeus in the rising, roiling, slowly unfurling cloud. "**THE IMMORTAL GODS WILL SHOW YOU WAR.**"

The Equatorial Ring

Prospero sat there in a long, royal-blue robe covered with brightly colored embroidery showing galaxies, suns, comets, and planets. He held a carved staff in one age-motttled right hand and there was a foot-thick book under the palm of his left hand. The carved chair with the broad armrests was not quite a throne, but close enough to impart a sense of magisterial authority reinforced by the magus's cool stare. The man was mostly bald, but a mane of vestigial white hair poured back over his ears and fell in curls to the blue of his robe. The once-grand head was now perched on an old man's withered neck, but the face was iron-firm with character, showing coolly indifferent if not actively cruel little eyes, a bold beak of a nose, a forceful declaration of a chin not yet lost in jowls or wattles, and a sorcerer's thin lips turned up in ancient habits of irony. He was, of course, a hologram.

Daeman had watched Harman burst through the semipermeable membrane and fall to the floor under the unexpected gravity, just as Daeman had done. Then, seeing Daeman sitting in a comfortable chair with his osmosis mask off, Harman had peeled his own mask off, breathed in the fresh air deeply, and then staggered to the other empty chair.

"It's only one-third Earth gravity," said Prospero, "but it must seem like Jupiter after a month in near zero-g."

Neither Harman nor Daeman replied.

The room was circular, about fifteen meters across, and essentially a glassed-in dome from the floor up. Daeman hadn't seen it while they were approaching the crystal city on the chairs because they'd come in at the asteroid's south pole and this was the north pole, but he imagined it must look like a long, slender metal stalk with this glowing mushroom at its end. The only light in the room came from the soft glow of a circular virtual control console in the center of the space, behind Prospero, and the earthlight and moonlight and starlight flooding in above and around them. It was bright enough that Daeman could see the careful workings on the magus's embroidered robe and the hand-oiled carvings on his staff.

"You're Prospero," said Harman, his chest rising and falling quickly under the blue thermskin. The fresh air in the room had been a shock to Daeman as well. It was like breathing a rich, thick wine.

Prospero nodded.

"But you're not real," continued Harman. The man *looked* solid. The robe fell in beautiful but dynamic folds and wrinkles in the one-third gravity.

Prospero shrugged. "This is true. I'm nothing more than a recorded echo of a shadow of a shade. But I can see you, hear you, talk with you, and sympathize with your travails. It's more than some real beings are capable of doing."

Daeman looked over his shoulder. He was holding the black gun loosely in his lap.

"Will Caliban come here?"

"No," said Prospero. "My former servant fears me. Fears this speaking memory of me. If the blue-eyed hag who bore him was here on this isle, that damned quantum-witch Sycorax, she'd be on you here in a minute, but Caliban fears me."

"Prospero," said Daeman, "we need to get off this rock. Back to Earth. Alive. Can you help us?"

The old man leaned his staff against his chair and held up both mottled hands. "Perhaps."

"Just perhaps?" said Daeman.

Prospero nodded. "As an echo of a recorded shadow, I can *do* nothing. But I can give you information. You can act if you will, and if you *have* the will. Few of your kind do anymore."

"How do we get out of here?" asked Harman.

Prospero passed his hand over the book and a hologram rose above the center of the circular console behind him. It was the asteroid and the crystal city as seen from some miles out in space, the gold-glassed towers turning slowly beneath the vantage point as the asteroid turned on its axis. Daeman glanced at the bold blue and white of the Earth coming into view outside the windows and realized that the image was synchronized—it was a real-time view from somewhere out there.

"There!" cried Harman, pointing. He tried to jump out of his chair, but the gravity made him stagger and grab the armrest for support. "There," he said again.

Daeman saw it. On an outside slab of terrace five or six hundred feet up that first tall tower where they'd entered, its metal shell glowing now in Earthlight—a sonie. "We searched the city," said Daeman. "We never thought that there might be a vehicle parked *outside* the city."

"It looks like the sonie we took to Jerusalem," said Harman, leaning forward the better to see the holographic display.

"It *is* the same sonie," said Prospero. He moved his palm again and the image disappeared.

"No," said Daeman. "Savi told us that sonies couldn't fly to the orbital rings."

"She didn't know they could," said the old magus. "Ariel freed it from the voynixes' stones and programmed it to come up here."

"Ariel?" Daeman stupidly repeated. He was so, so hungry, and so very tired. He sorted through his memory. "Ariel? The avatar of the biosphere below?"

"Something like that," said Prospero with a smile. "Savi never really met Ariel. All their communications were through the allnet. The old woman always thought that Ariel's persona was male, when most frequently the sprite chooses a female avatar."

Who gives a shit? thought Daeman. Aloud, he said, "Can we take the sonie back to Earth?"

"I would think so," said Prospero. "I think Ariel sent it preprogrammed to return the three of you to Ardis Hall. Another deus ex machina. I'm not happy with the machine being here."

"Why not?" said Harman, but then he nodded. "Caliban."

"Yes," said Prospero. "Even my erstwhile goblin would grind his joints with dry convulsions and shorten up his sinews with aged cramps should he try hard vacuum without a suit or thermskin. But he forgot, and bit through poor Savi's."

"There were two more suits he could have had the last month," said Daeman, his voice so low it fell below the whisper of ventilation. The room left the curve-slice of Earth above and rotated into starlight. There was a half-moon rising above Prospero.

"And he would have, but Caliban is no god," said the magus. "Savi did not kill the beast with her full salvo of flechettes to its chest, but she hurt it sore. Caliban has been bleeding and recovering, gone deep sometimes to his deepest grotto where he packs the wounds with mud muck and drinks lizard blood for strength."

"We've been drinking and eating the same," said Daeman.

"Yes," said Prospero, showing an old man's yellow smile. "But you don't *enjoy* it."

"How do we get to the sonie?" asked Harman. "And do you have food in here?"

"No, to your second question," said Prospero. "No one but Caliban has eaten here on this stony isle for the last five hundred years. But yes to your first. There is a membrane on the tower glass high up that will let you pass out to the launch terrace. Your suits may . . . may . . . protect you long enough to charge up the sonie and activate its guidance program. Do you remember how to fly the thing?"

"I think . . . I watched Savi . . . I mean . . ." stammered Harman. He shook his head as if brushing away cobwebs. His eyes looked as weary as Daeman felt. "We'll have to. We will."

"You'll have to pass the firmary and Caliban again to reach the far tower," said Prospero. The old man's little eyes moved from Harman to Daeman and the gaze was judicial. "Do you have anything else you must do before you flee this place?"

"No," said Harman.

"*Yes*," said Daeman. He managed to stand and stagger over to the curved window-wall. The reflection there was thin, gaunt, and bearded, but there was something new in its eyes. "We have to destroy the firmary," he said. "We have to destroy this whole damned place."

Ilium and Olympos

For some reason, I flee with the Trojans on Thicket Ridge toward and through the smaller man-gates of the Scaean Gates, main entrance to Ilium. The wind still howls and we're all partially deaf from the nuclear explosion to the south. My last glimpse of the mushroom cloud before entering the city with the shoving mob of Trojan soldiers shows me that the column of smoke and ash is already beginning to bend southeast with the prevailing wind. There's still a hint of Zeus's face in the coiled cloud at the top, but the wind and the cloud's own infolding is breaking up that visage as well.

Scores are crushed at the man-gates, so Hector orders the guards to throw wide the central Scaean Gates, something that hasn't been done for more than nine years. The thousands flock inside.

The Argives have run for their ships. Just as Hector is trying to rally his panicked troops here, I catch a glimpse of Achilles trying to hold back the fleeing Greeks. In the *Iliad*, in Achilles' rampage after Patroclus' death, Homer tells of the man-god fighting a flooding river—and winning, damming it with the bodies of his Trojan enemies—but now Achilles can't stop this tsunami of fleeing Achaeans without killing hundreds, and this he will not do.

I'm swept into the city, already sorry that I ran. I realize that I should have fought my way through the milling mob on the ridge to where I saw the little robot, Mahnmut, sheltering behind the boulders atop the Amazon Myrine's mounded tomb. Does the robot—what did he call his type? moravec?—does the moravec know that Zeus's weapon was nuclear, possibly thermonuclear? Suddenly a memory emerges from my other life, as so many have in the past week or so—Susan trying to drag me to a talk at IU's science hall during some multidisciplinary week at the university. A scientist named Moravec was speaking about his autonomous artificial intelligence theories. Fritz? Hans? I hadn't gone, of course—of what interest would some scientist's theories be to a classical scholar?

Well, it doesn't matter now.

As if to underline this point, five chariots appear from the north—I know the QT point they translated in through up there—and begin circling the city at an altitude of three or four thousand feet. Even with optical amplification, I can't make out the little figures in the gleaming machines, but it looks as if there are both gods and goddesses up there.

Then the bombardment begins.

The shafts scream down into the city like slender, silver, ballistic missiles, and where each one strikes, there is an explosion, dust and smoke rising, screams. Ilium is a large city by ancient standards, but the arrows come fast—from Apollo's bow, I realize, although I think I can make out Ares doing the shooting when the chariot swoops low to assess the damage—and soon the explosions and screams are coming from every quarter of the walled metropolis.

I realize that I've not only lost control of everything, I've lost sight of everyone I should be talking to, helping, conferring with. Achilles is probably three miles away down the hill already, back with his men, trying to keep them from sailing away in panic. Hearing more explosions— conventional, not nuclear—coming from the direction of the Achaean camp, I don't see how Achilles can succeed in rallying his men. I've also lost sight of Hector, and see that the huge Achaean Gates have been swung shut again—as if that can keep out the gods. Poor Mahnmut and his silent pal, Orphu, are probably destroyed out there on the ridge already. I don't see how anything can survive this bombardment.

More explosions from the central marketplace. Red-crested Trojan soldiers rush to reinforce the walls, but the danger's not outside the walls. The golden chariot swings above again, outside of even archer shot, and five silver arrows rain down like Scud missiles, exploding near the south wall, near the central well, and apparently right on Priam's Palace. This is beginning to remind me of CNN images from the second war with Iraq right before I became ill with cancer.

Hector. The hero is probably rallying his men, but since there's nothing to rally them for except to duck and cover, it's possible that Hector has gone to his home to check on Andromache. I think of that empty, bloodstained nursery and grimace even here in the smoke and noise of the bombed city street. The royal couple hasn't had time to bury their baby yet.

Jesus, God, is all this my doing?

A flying chariot swoops low. An explosion breaches the ramparts along the main wall and throws a dozen red-caped figures into the air. Body parts rain into the streets and patter on rooftops like fleshy hail. Suddenly another memory returns, a similar horror, three thousand two hundred years in this world's future, two thousand and one bloody years after the birth of Christ. In my mind's eye, I see bodies hurling down into the street and a wall of dust and pumice chasing the fleeing thousands, just as I see down Ilium's main street this moment. Only the buildings and modes of dress are different.

We'll never learn. Things will never change.

I run for Hector's home. More missiles rain down, blasting the plaza just inside the gate from where I've just come. I see a small child staggering into the street from rubble that was a two-story home just minutes before. I can't tell if the toddler's a little boy or girl, but the child's face is bloody, its curly hair covered with plaster dust. I stop running and go to one knee to gather the child in—where can I take it? There's no hospital in Ilium!—but a woman with a red scarf over her head runs to the infant and scoops it up. I wipe rivulets of sweat out of my eyes and stagger on toward Hector's house.

It's gone. The whole of Hector's palace is missing—just rubble and a series of holes in the ground. I have to keep mopping sweat out of my eyes to see, and even when I see I can't believe. This whole block has been pounded by the missiles raining down. Already, Trojan soldiers are digging through the rubble with their spears and makeshift shovels, their proud red-crests turned gray by the dust in the air. They create a human chain to hand bodies and body parts back to the waiting crowds in the street.

"Hock-en-bear-eeee," says a voice. I realize that someone's been saying my name over and over, but now has begun tugging at my arm. "Hock-en-bear-eeee!"

I turn stupidly, blink away sweat again, and look down at Helen. She's dirty, her gown is bloodied, and her hair is unkempt. I've never seen anyone or anything so beautiful. She hugs me and I gather her in with both arms.

She pulls apart. "Are you badly hurt, Hock-en-bear-eeee?"

"What?"

"Are your injuries severe?"

"I'm not hurt," I say. She touches my face then and her hand comes away red with blood. I raise my hand to my temple—a deep cut there, another in my hairline—see the bloody fingers on both of my hands, and realize that I've been wiping blood away, not sweat. "I'm fine," I say. I point to the smoking rubble. "Hector? Andromache?"

"They weren't there, Hock-en-bear-eeee," Helen shouts over the screams and babble. "Hector sent his family to Athena's temple. The basement is safe there."

I look through the smoke and see the tall roof of the temple standing. *Of course,* I think. *The gods aren't going to bomb their own temples. Too much fucking ego.*

"Theano is dead," says Helen. "And Hecuba. And Laodice."

I repeat the names stupidly. Athena's priestess, the woman with the cold blade at my balls just hours ago. And Priam's wife and daughter. Three of my Trojan Women dead already. And the bombardment's just begun.

Suddenly I whirl around in panic. The noise is wrong. The blasts have stopped.

Men and women in the streets are pointing skyward and shouting. Four of the five chariots have already disappeared and now the fifth, Ares' bombardment chariot, I think, flies north and winks out of existence, obviously QTing back to Olympos. All this damage—I look around at the tumbled buildings, smoking craters, bloodied bodies in the streets—from just one god's attack with one bow and a few of Apollo's arrows. What next? Biological attack? The Shining Archer—probably recovering up there in the healing tanks right now—is famous for firing plague into the people below.

I grab the medallion at my neck. "Where's Hector?" I ask Helen. "I have to find Hector."

"He went back out through the Scaean Gate with Paris, Aeneas, and his brother Deiphobus," says Helen. "He said he has to find Achilles before all hearts flag."

"I have to find him," I repeat. I turn toward the main gate, but Helen pulls me back and around.

"Hock-en-bear-eeee," she says, and pulls my face down to hers and kisses me there in the shoving, screaming street. When her lips leave mine, I can only blink stupidly, still bent to her kiss. "Hock-en-bear-eeee," she says again. "If you must die, die well."

Then she turns and strides back up the street without once looking back.

The Equatorial Ring

Daeman was only a little surprised to see that the Prospero hologram can stand and walk. The magus picked up his staff and walked slowly to the dome-window of the room. When he lifted his face to watch the stars march by, the pale light emphasized the wrinkles on his throat and cheeks. All this onslaught of old age in recent days made Daeman queasy—and even queasier considering what they're discussing at that moment. He tried to imagine a world in which his friends and he—his mother!—grew old like Savi, like this mottled and wattled hologram. The horror of it made him shudder.

Then he remembered the horror of the tanks, the blue worms, and Caliban's dining table.

Wouldn't it be easier just to kill the monster? Leave the firmary intact?

No, Daeman realized through his hunger and fatigue. This place was an obscenity any way one looked at it. The entire belief system of the Five Twenties was based on the conviction that people went to the rings after one hundred years, joining the post-humans up here in comfort and immortality. Daeman thought of the gray, half-eaten corpses floating out there in the thin, stale air, and could only snort a laugh.

"What is it?" asked Prospero, half turning from the view.

"Nothing," said Daeman. He felt like weeping or breaking something. Preferably the latter.

"How can we destroy the firmary?" asked Harman. The taller, older man was shivering from his illness. His face was even paler than Daeman's and sheened slick with sweat.

"How indeed?" asked Prospero. He leaned on his staff and looked at them. "Did you bring explosives, weapons—other than Savi's silly little pistol—or tools?"

"No," said Harman.

"There are none up here," said Prospero. "The post-humans had evolved themselves far beyond wars and conflicts. Or tools. The servitors did all work up here."

"They're still working," said Daeman.

"Only in the firmary," said the magus. He crossed slowly back to the center console. "Have you given thought to the hundreds of human beings floating helpless in the firmary tanks?"

"My God," whispered Harman.

Daeman rubbed his cheek, feeling the beard there. It was an oddly satisfying sensation. "We can't use the faxnodes in the healing tanks to get back to Earth," he said, "but presumably those people already in the tanks could be faxed back to the portals from which they came."

"Yes," said Prospero. "If you can convince the servitors to do so. Or if you were to take over the fax controls yourselves. But there's a problem with that."

"What?" said Daeman, but even as he asked the question he saw the problem clearly.

Prospero smiled grimly and nodded. "For those who've just been faxed up to the tanks, or those finished with their blue-worm healing process, fax return is possible. But for those hundreds midway in the healing process . . ." His silence said everything.

"What can we do?" asked Harman. "There will be new people faxing in and healed ones faxing out, hundreds in the process."

"If Prospero's right and we can take over the fax controls," said Daeman, "we could shut off the incoming, then continue to fax down the healed as the process is finished, until all the tanks are empty. We've both been in the tanks. How long does the Twenty healing usually take—twenty-four hours? Forty-eight for serious injuries like being eaten by an allosaurus?"

"You weren't being 'healed' for that," said Prospero. "They were rebuilding you from scratch, using your updated memory codes from the fax grid banks, stored DNA, and organic spare parts. But you are correct, even the slowest healing cases require no more than forty-eight hours."

Daeman opened his hands and looked at Harman. "Two days from the time we take over the firmary."

"If we *can* take over the firmary and control the fax process," Harman said doubtfully.

The magus leaned on the back of his chair. "I can *do* nothing, but I can give information," said the old man. "I can tell you how the fax controls work."

"But we won't be able to fax down ourselves?" Harman asked again. Obviously the thought of using the sonie worried him.

"No," said Prospero.

"Can we reprogram the servitors to handle the faxing?" asked Daeman.

"No," said the magus. "You will have to destroy or disable them. But they are not programmed for conflict."

"Neither are we," laughed Harman.

Prospero stepped around his chair. "Yes," he whispered. "You *are*. With human beings, no matter how *civilized* you may appear, it is just a matter of reawakening old programming."

Daeman and Harman looked at one another. Harman shivered again in his blue thermskin suit.

"Your genes remember how to kill," said Prospero. "Come, let me show you the instrument of destruction."

Prospero's hologram couldn't manipulate the virtual controls in the center console himself, but he showed Daeman and Harman how to use their hands on and in the complex glowing toggles, shunts, slides, switches, and manipulators.

An image misted into solidity above the console, then rotated in three dimensions for their inspection.

"It's one of those big e-ring devices we saw on the way in," said Daeman.

"A linear accelerator with its wormhole collection ring," said Prospero. "The post-humans were *so* proud of these things. As you saw, they made thousands."

"So?" said Harman. "Are you saying that the fax system on Earth is controlled by these things?"

Prospero shook his brow-heavy head. "Your fax system is terrestrial. It doesn't move bodies through space and time, only data. But these wormhole collectors are the spiders in the center of the post-humans quantum teleportation web."

"So?" said Harman again. "We just want to go back to Earth."

"Grip that green controller and squeeze the red circle twice," said Prospero.

Daeman did so. On the holographic display of the orbital linear accelerator, a small quad of engine thrusters pulsed twice, sending a tiny silver cone of crystallized exhaust into space. The long array of girders, tanks, columns, and rings began to rotate ever so slowly. Counterthrusters fired just as briefly, and the long accelerator stabilized. The fifty-meter-wide shimmering wormhole at its end, centered within the huge and gleaming collection ring, had not turned with the accelerator. Daeman leaned close to the holographic image of the accelerator and saw that the collection ring was on gimbals. He reached a finger into the image, touched different elements, and saw the vid image shift into diagrams and descriptive lettering—*return line, injector, quad thrusters.* He removed his hand and the real-time image reappeared. The words had, of course, meant nothing to him.

"Attitude control, orbital translation thrusters," said Prospero. "This asteroid is in stable orbit—it would be a possible species-extinction event if it fell onto the Earth—but the wormhole collecting accelerators and the Casimir mirrors were constantly being moved around."

"From here," said Daeman.

Prospero nodded. "And from the other asteroid cities."

Harman and Daeman looked at each other again. "There are more post-human cities?" asked Harman.

"Three more," said the magus. "One other on this equatorial ring. Two on the polar ring."

"Are there living post-humans there?" asked Daeman. He suddenly saw an alternative to all this destruction and the end of the Five Twenties way of life.

"No." Prospero sat in his high-backed chair. "And there are no other firmaries, either. This city was the only one that bothered itself with the affairs of you modified old-styles down there." He waved a mottled hand toward the Earth rising on the right curve of the dome. The room was suddenly brightened again by Earthlight.

"All the posts are dead," repeated Daeman.

"No, not dead," said Prospero. "Gone elsewhere."

Daeman looked at the limb of the Earth rising and the blackness of space above the shimmering curve of atmosphere. "Gone where?"

"Mars, to begin with," said the magus. He looked at their quizzical expressions and chuckled. "Do either of you modern men have any idea where Mars is? *What* Mars is?"

"No," said Daeman without embarrassment. "Will the posts be coming back from there?"

"I think not," said Prospero, still smiling.

"Then it doesn't matter, does it?" said Harman. "Prospero, were you suggesting we could use this . . . particle accelerator wormhole thing . . . as a weapon?"

"As the ultimate weapon against this city," said Prospero. "Common explosives or weapons would have little effect on the crystal city or its asteroid. These towers are made to withstand actual meteor impact. But three kilometers and more of heavy-mass exotic materials with a wormhole on its snout, under thrust, will have a definite impact, especially if you target it directly on the firmary."

"Will Caliban survive?" asked Daeman.

Prospero shrugged. "His tunnels and grottoes have saved him before. But perhaps such a collision will provide a Caliban-species extinction event here of its own."

"Can he escape before it hits?" asked Harman.

"Only if he learns of the sonie and takes possession of one of your thermskin suits," said Prospero. Then he smiled disconcertingly, as if such a prospect was not totally improbable.

"How long will it take for this accelerator-monstrosity to get here?" asked Daeman. "Until impact?"

"You can program it to arrive as quickly or slowly as you wish," said the magus, rising and walking *into* the center console, his lower body disappearing into the metal and virtual panels. He raised one arm, the robe slid back a bit, and the skinny forearm and bony finger pointed to the end of the accelerator away from the wormhole ring. "Right here," said Prospero, "are the plane-change thrusters—the most powerful engines. I'll show you how to activate them and to aim this weapon."

The two followed his instructions on rotating the accelerator and programming what Prospero called its trajectory coordinates and delta-v. Daeman's finger hovered above the *initiate* virtual button. "You didn't tell us how long we have until impact," he said to Prospero.

The hologram steepled its fingers. "Fifty hours sounds right. An hour for you to get to the firmary and take control. Forty-eight hours to allow the new arrivals to heal and to fax them all back intact. An hour then to find your way to the sonie and escape before this little world ends."

"No time to sleep?" said Harman.

"I would advise against it," said Prospero. "Caliban will probably be trying to kill you every minute of that time."

Harman and Daeman exchanged glances. "We can take turns napping and eating and keeping watch at the controls there," said Daeman. He hefted the pistol and then set it back in Savi's pack. "We'll keep Caliban at bay."

Harman nodded doubtfully. He looked very, very weary.

Daeman looked at the real-time image of the linear accelerator again and set his thumb above the *thruster initiate* button again. "Prospero, you're sure this won't end all life on Earth or anything?"

The magus chuckled. "All life as you know it, yes," he said. "But no flaming asteroid from the sky species-extinction event. At least I don't believe so. We'll have to see."

Daeman looked at Harman, whose own hands were wrist-deep in the virtual panel. "Do it," said Harman.

Daeman pushed the button. On the display above the holographic projector, eight huge thrusters at the end of the linear accelerator lit up with solid, continuous pulses of blue-ion ignition. The long structure shuddered slightly and began to move slowly—directly toward Daeman's and Harman's faces.

"Good-bye, Prospero," said Daeman, grabbing Savi's pack and turning toward the semipermeable exit.

"Oh, no," said Prospero. "If you make it to the firmary, I'll be there. I wouldn't miss the next fifty hours for the world."

54

The Plains of Ilium
and Olympos

I leave the burning city in search of Achilles and see chaos stretching all the way to the sea. Trojans and Achaeans alike are pulling bodies from smoking craters from the Scaean Gates to the surf's edge, and everywhere confused men are helping their wounded comrades back to Ilium or across the defensive trench into the Greek camps. As with most aerial bombardments in my era, the effects of the attack were more terrifying than the results. I imagine that there are several hundred dead—Trojan and Achaean warriors and civilians in Ilium all included—but most escaped unharmed, especially out here away from falling walls and flying masonry.

As I'm clambering over the lowest part of Thicket Ridge, I see the little robot coming toward me, tugging along his floating crabshell friend like a little boy pulling an especially large Radio Flyer wagon. For some reason, I'm so pleased to see them alive—although "still in existence" might be a better term—that I come very close to crying.

"Hockenberry," says the robot, Mahnmut, "you're injured. Is it bad?"

I touch my forehead and scalp. The bleeding has almost stopped. "It's nothing."

"Hockenberry, do you know what that large blast was?"

"Nuclear explosion," I say. "It could have been thermonuclear, but for all its roar, I suspect it was just a fission weapon. A little larger than the Hiroshima bomb, perhaps. I don't know much about bombs."

Mahnmut cocks his head at me. "Where are you from, Hockenberry?"

"Indiana," I reply without thinking.

Mahnmut waits.

"I'm a scholic," I say to him again, knowing that he's passing all this along to his silent friend via the radio link he called tightbeam earlier. "The gods rebuilt me out of old bones and DNA and some sort of memory fragments they extracted from the bits they found on Earth."

"Memory from DNA?" said Mahnmut. "I don't think so."

I wave my hands impatiently. "It doesn't *matter*," I snap. "I'm the walking dead. I lived in the second half of the Twentieth Century, probably died in the first part of the Twenty-first. I'm hazy on dates. I was hazy on everything in my past life until recent weeks, when memories started flooding back." I shake my head. "I'm a dead man walking."

Mahnmut continues looking at me with that dark metallic strip instead of eyes. Then he nods judiciously and kicks me—rather viciously—in the left shin.

"God *damn* it!" I cry, hopping on the other leg. "Why'd you do that?"

"You seem alive to me," says the little robot. "How did you come here from the Twentieth or Twenty-first Lost Age century, Hockenberry? Most of our moravec scientists are fairly sure that such time travel is impossible unless you're whipping around near the speed of light or swimming too close to a black hole. Did you do either of those things?"

"I don't *know*," I say. "And surely it doesn't *matter*. Look at all this!" I gesture toward the smoking city and the chaos on the plains of Ilium. Already, some of the Greek ships are putting to sea.

Mahnmut nods. For a robot, his body language is oddly human. "Orphu wonders why the gods broke off their attack," he says.

I glance at the huge battered shell of a thing behind him. Sometimes I forget that there's reportedly a brain in there. "Tell Orphu that I don't know," I say. "Perhaps they just want to enjoy the fear and chaos down here for a while before administering the coup de grâce." I hesitate a second. "That's French for . . ." I begin.

"Yes, I know French, unfortunately," says Mahnmut. "Orphu was just quoting some fairly irrelevant Proust to me in French during the bombardment. What are you going to do next, Hockenberry?"

I look toward the Achaean encampment. Tents are burning, wounded horses are running in panic, men are milling, ships are being outfitted for sea, others already are moving out away from the coast, their sails catching the wind. "I was going to find Achilles and Hector," I say. "But it may take me hours in all this mess."

"In eighteen minutes and thirty-five seconds," says Mahnmut, "something is going to happen that may change everything."

I look at him and wait.

"I planted a . . . Device . . . up there in the Caldera Lake," says the little robot. "Orphu and I brought it all the way from Jupiter space. Putting that thing up there was the main goal of our mission, actually, although we weren't supposed to be the ones delivering it to . . . well, that's another story. At any rate, in seventeen minutes, fifty-two seconds, the Device triggers itself."

"It's a bomb?" I say hoarsely. Suddenly my mouth is absolutely dry. I couldn't spit if my life depended on it.

Mahnmut shrugs in that oddly human way of his. "We don't know."

"You don't *know!?*" I bellow. "You don't *know??* How could you plant a . . . a . . . Device up there and set a timer if you don't know what it's going to do? That's ridiculous!"

"Perhaps," says Mahnmut, "but it's what we were sent here to do. . . well, sent *there,* actually . . . by the moravecs who planned this mission."

"How long, did you say?" I ask, grabbing the apparent leather bracelet on my wrist that serves as my own covert chronometer. The bracelet has microcircuits and small holographic projectors for when I need to know the time.

"Seventeen minutes and eight seconds," says the little robot. "And counting."

I set the timer on my watch and leave the little holographic display visible. "Shit," I say.

"Yes," agrees Mahnmut. "Are you QTing back up there, Hockenberry? To Olympos?"

I'd set my hand on the QT medallion at my throat, but only because I was thinking about saving a few minutes by teleporting straight into the Achaean camp to find Achilles. But Mahnmut's question makes me pause and think.

"Maybe I should," I say. "Someone needs to see what the gods are up to. Perhaps I could play spy one last time."

"And then what?" asks the robot.

It's my turn to shrug. "Then I come back for Achilles and Hector. Then maybe, say, Odysseus and Paris. Aeneas and Diomedes. Carry the war to the gods, shuttling these heroes up there two by two, like animals on Noah's Ark."

"That doesn't sound too efficient as military campaign logistics go," says Mahnmut.

"Do you know military strategy, little robot person?"

"No. Actually, all I really know anything about is a submersible that sank on Mars and Shakespeare's sonnets," says Mahnmut. He pauses. "Orphu just told me that I shouldn't include the sonnets in my resumé."

"Mars?" I say.

The shiny metallic head turns up toward me. "You didn't know that

Olympos is really the volcano Olympus Mons on Mars? You've lived there for nine Earth years, haven't you?"

For a second, I'm dizzy enough that I have to stagger over to a low boulder and sit or I'm afraid I'll wake up on the ground. "Mars," I repeat. *Two moons, the huge volcano, the red soil, the reduced gravity that I was always so happy to return to after a long day on the plains of Ilium.* "Mars." *Fuck me.* "Mars."

Mahnmut says nothing, perhaps knowing that he's embarrassed me enough for one day.

"Wait a minute," I say. "Mars doesn't have blue skies, oceans, trees, air to breathe. I watched the first Viking lander touch down in 1976. I watched on TV years later, decades later, when that little Sojourner buggy thing trundled down and got stuck on a rock. There were no oceans. No trees. No *air*."

"They've terraformed it," says Mahnmut. "And rather recently, too."

"*Who's* terraformed it?" I say, hearing the defensive anger in my voice.

"The gods," says Mahnmut, but I can hear the slight hint of a question mark in his smooth robot voice.

I look at my watch. Fifteen minutes thirty-eight seconds. I tap the virtual chronometer display in front of the little robot's cameras or eyes or whatever's behind that sunglass strip on his face. "What's going to happen in fifteen minutes, Mahnmut? Don't tell me you and Orphu don't know."

"We don't know," says Mahnmut.

"I'm going up there to see what's going on," I say, grabbing the medallion.

"Take me," says Mahnmut. "I set the timer. I should be there when the Device activates."

I pause again, looking at the huge shell behind Mahnmut. "Are you going to defuse it?" I ask.

"No. That was my mission—to deliver and activate the Device. But if the timer doesn't trigger it, I should be there in person to set it off."

"Are we talking . . . even as a low-priority probability . . . the end of the world here, Mahnmut?"

The robot's hesitation tells me everything.

"You should stay with Orphu another . . . ah . . . fourteen minutes thirty-nine seconds," I say. "The shape the poor guy's in, the world might end and he wouldn't know it unless you told him."

"Orphu says that you're pretty funny for a scholic, Hockenberry," says Mahnmut. "I still think I should go with you."

"One," I say, "you're using up all our goddamned time talking. Two, I only have one Hades Helmet and I don't want to be caught because the gods see a robot walking with invisible me. Three . . . good-bye."

I pull the Hades Helmet cowl down over my head, twist the medallion, and go.

I QT right into the Great Hall of the Gods.

It looks like they're all here except for Athena and Apollo, whom I suppose are floating in the healing tanks with green worms in their eyes and armpits about now. In the few seconds I have before the baklava hits the fan, I see that the gods are armored and armed for war—the hall is resplendent with gold breastplates, shining spears, tall helmets with feathered plumes, and polished, god-sized shields. I see Zeus standing by his blazing chariot, Poseidon in dark armor, Hermes and Hephaestus armed to the teeth, Ares carrying Apollo's silver bow, Hera in gleaming bronze and gold, and Aphrodite pointing my way . . .

Shit.

"**SCHOLIC HOCKENBERRY!**" bellows Zeus himself, looking right at me across the crowded hall. "**FREEZE!**"

It's not just Zeusian advice. Every muscle and tendon and ligament and cell in my body freezes. I feel the cold stop my heart. Brownian motion ceases in me. My hand doesn't make it an inch toward the QT medallion before I'm a statue.

"Take the Hades Helmet, the QT device, and everything else from him," commands Zeus.

Ares and Hephaestus spring forward and strip me naked in front of gods and goddesses. The leather helmet is tossed to a glowering Hades, and, dressed as he is in black chitinous armor of exotic design, he looks like a terrible, glowering beetle. Zeus steps forward and grabs up my QT medallion from the floor, staring at it and glowering as if he's going to crush it in his giant fist. They two gods finish ripping my clothes off and don't even leave me my wristwatch or underpants.

"Unfreeze," says Zeus. I collapse onto the marble floor and pant, holding my chest. My heart aches so much as it begins beating again that I'm sure I'm having a coronary. It's everything I can do just not to piss myself in front of everyone.

"Take him away," says Zeus, turning his back on me.

The eight-foot-tall Ares, god of war, grabs me by the hair and drags me away.

55

The Equatorial Ring

"Thinketh, Himself," hissed Caliban's voice from the shadows of the firmary, "would teach the reasoning couple what 'must' means! Doth as he likes, or wherefore Lord? So He."

"Where the hell's that voice coming from?" snapped Harman. The firmary was mostly dark, light coming from the glowing tanks that were emptying one by one, and Daeman roamed from the semipermeable wall to the cannibal table, trying to find the source of the whispers.

"I don't know," said Daeman at last. "Air vent. Some entrance we haven't found. But if he comes into the light, I'll kill him."

"You may shoot him," said the Prospero hologram standing against the counter near the healing tank controls, "but it is not certain that you will kill him. Caliban—a devil, a born devil, on whose nature nurture can never stick; on whom my pains humanely taken—all, all lost, quite lost!"

For two days and nights, forty-seven and a half hours, one hundred forty-four revolutions of the asteroid from Earthlight to starlight, the two men had overseen the faxing out of the healing tanks until only a dozen or so bodies were left. They knew now how to call up external holos of the linear accelerator accelerating in a most linear fashion directly toward them. They could see the huge thing now, approaching wormhole first, visible and awful in the clear overhead firmary panels, thrusters burning blue behind. Prospero and the virtual readouts assured them that they had almost ninety minutes left before impact, but instinct and their vision told them otherwise, so both men quit looking up.

Caliban was somewhere near. Daeman kept his thermskin mask down for the light-augmenting lenses, but also used Savi's flashlight, playing it under the cannibal table, light glinting on white bones there.

They'd thought the trip from the domed control room was the worst—the long swim-kick through kelp and half-light, waiting for Caliban to attack at any minute—but although twice something green-gray moved in the shadows, and twice Daeman had fired Savi's gun at the movement, once the shadow-thing swam away, and the next time it tumbled out, dead, flechettes glinting in its gray flesh. A post-human corpse in the kelp. But now, after forty-seven and a half hours more without sleep and eating only rancid lizard flesh, there was no worst. This last hour was the worst. At least they'd stopped by the entrance to the grotto, pounded the ice-skim with their boots and gun butt, until they could refill their single bottle with spheroids of vile, scummed, much-lusted-after water. At least they'd done that. But now the water was gone and neither man could leave his post and leave the firmary to go for more. Besides, they'd taken plastic sheets from the tops of the tanks and nailed them up over the semipermeable entrance membrane so that they'd be warned by the ripping if and when Caliban entered the firmary that way, so they couldn't easily go out that way if they wanted. Now both men's tongues were swollen and their heads ached abominably from thirst and fatigue and the bad air and fear.

They'd had little problem with the dozen firmary servitors. Several were allowed to continue to work at their tasks of faxing out the healed bodies, while others—whose duties got in the men's way—were incapacitated. Daeman had fired the gun at one, but that was a mistake. The flechettes tore paint and metal fragments from the servitor, and shattered one manipulator arm and ripped off an eye, but did not destroy it. Harman solved the problem by finding a heavy piece of pipe in the tank farm, wrenching it free—allowing liquid oxygen to steam into the already cold air—and bashing the servitor into immobility. The remaining servitors went into retirement the same way.

Prospero arrived when they powered up the holographic comm sphere atop the control panel, and the magus made sure their adjustments were correct on the tank voidings. First, they shut off the incoming faxnodes. Then they immediately faxed the arriving Twenty-somethings back to their Earthly nodes before any repair was started. Prospero said that there was no way to hurry the work of the blue worms and the orange fluid, so they left those tanks to cycle. The humans floating naked who were near the end of their healing were faxed back early. Of the six hundred and sixty-nine tanks in the firmary, all but thirty-eight were empty now—thirty-six of those were extensive repairs and two were regular Twenties who had faxed in and begun normal repair just before Harman and Daeman had managed to shut off the fax computers.

"Also, it pleaseth Setebos to work," hissed the unseen Caliban's voice.

"Shut up!" shouted Daeman. He moved between the glowing tanks, trying not to float in the low but appreciable gravity there. Shadows danced everywhere but none of them were solid enough to shoot.

"Falls to make something: piled yon pile of turfs, and squared and stuck there squares of soft white chalk," whispered Caliban from the dark. "And, with a fish tooth, scratched a moon on each, and set up end-wise certain spikes of tree, and crowned the whole with a sloth's skull atop, found dead i' the woods, too hard for one to kill. No use at all i' the work, for work's sole sake; Shall someday knock it down again: so He."

Harman laughed.

"What?" Daeman walked and floated back to the virtual controls where the holosphere allowed Prospero to stand. Parts and pieces of servitors were everywhere underfoot, mimicking the cannibal table farther back in the shadows.

"We have to get out of here soon," said Harman, rubbing his reddened eyes. "The monster's beginning to make sense to me."

"Prospero," said Daeman, moving his eyes from shadow to shadow in the shadowy forest of softly glowing tanks. "Who or what is this Setebos that Caliban keeps going on about?"

"Caliban's mother's god," said the magus.

"And you said that Caliban's mother is out there somewhere as well." Daeman held the gun in one hand and rubbed his eyes with the other. The firmary was all blurry, and only partially because of the drifting steam from the spilled liquid oxygen.

"Yes, Sycorax still lives," said Prospero. "But not on this isle. No longer on this isle."

"And this Setebos?" prompted Daeman.

"The enemy of the Quiet," said Prospero. "Like both his congregation of two, a bitter heart that bides its time and bites."

Buzzers went off above the console. Harman activated virtual controls. Three more healed humans—almost healed, at least—were faxed away. Thirty-five remained.

"Where'd this Setebos come from?" asked Harman.

"Brought in from the dark with the voynix and other things," said Prospero. "A minor miscalculation."

"Is Odysseus one of those other things brought in from the dark?" asked Daeman.

Prospero laughed. "Oh, no. That poor fellow was sent here by a curse, from that crossroads where most of the post-humans have fled. Odysseus is lost in time, made to wander longer by a wicked, wicked lady whom I know as Ceres, but whom Odysseus knew—in every sense—as Circe."

"I don't understand," said Harman. "Savi said she discovered Odysseus only a short time ago, sleeping in one of her cryo couches."

"That was true," said Prospero, "but a lie as well. Savi knew of Odysseus' voyage and where he seeks to go. She used him as surely as he used her."

"But he *is* the Achaean from the turin drama?" asked Daeman.

"Yes and no," said Prospero in his maddening way. "The drama shows a time and tale that's cleft. This Odysseus is from one of those branchings, yes. He's not the Odysseus of all the telling, no."

"You still haven't told us who Setebos is," said Harman. His temper was short. Six more humans faxed out of their tanks, finished and healed. Only twenty-nine remained. It was twenty minutes until the time they'd set to make a run for the sonie. The linear accelerator was close enough to see out the window now with no amplification. The wormhole was a sphere of shifting light and dark.

"Setebos is a god whose hallmark is pure, arbitrary power," said Prospero. "He kills at random. He spares at a whim. He murders vast numbers, but with no pattern or plan. He's a September eleven god. An Auschwitz god."

"What?" said Daeman.

"It doesn't matter," said the magus.

"'Saith," hissed Caliban from the darkness down by the cannibal table, "He may like, perchance, what profits Him. Ay, himself loves what does him good; but why? Gets no good otherwise."

"God *damn* it!" roared Daeman. "I'm going to find that bastard." He took the gun and bounced down toward the darkness. Five more human bodies faxed away and their tanks emptied with a whoosh. *Twenty-four remaining.*

There were bodies on the floor here, bodies on the table, parts of bodies on the chair. Daeman held Savi's flashlight in his left hand, her gun in his right, his cowl and night lenses in place, but still the darkness through shadows. He watched and waited for movement out of the corner of his eyes.

"Daeman!" called Harman.

"In a minute," shouted Daeman, waiting, using himself as bait. He wanted Caliban to leap. There were five flechette rounds in the gun right now and he knew from experience that they would fire rapidly if he held the trigger down. He could put five thousand crystal darts into the murdering son of a bitch if . . .

"Daeman!"

He turned back to Harman's shout. "Do you see Caliban?" he shouted back at the lighted control area.

"No," said Harman. "Something worse."

Daeman heard the pressure valves roaring and the soft alarms then. Something was wrong with the tanks.

Harman pointed to various virtual readouts flashing red. "The tanks are draining *before* the last bodies are healed."

"Caliban found a way to interrupt the nutrient flow from outside the firmary somewhere," said Prospero. "These twenty-four men and women are dead."

"Damn!" roared Harman. He pounded his fist against the wall.

Daeman walked into the tank forest, shining the flashlight into the draining tanks.

"The fluid level's dropping fast," he called to Harman.

"We'll fax them out anyway."

"You'll be faxing corpses home with blue worms boiling in their guts," said Daeman. "We have to get out of here."

"That's what Caliban wants," shouted Harman. Daeman couldn't see the control console now. He was deep in the rearmost row of tanks, in the dark places where he had been afraid to go before. The gun was heavy in his hand. He continued to shine the light from tank to tank.

Prospero was droning on in his old-man's voice—

> "You do look, my son, in a moved sort,
> As if you were dismayed. Be cheerful, sir.
> Our revels now are ended. These, our actors,
> As I foretold you, were all spirits and
> Are melted into air, into thin air;
> And—like the baseless fabric of this vision—
> The cloud-capped towers, the gorgeous palaces,
> The solemn temples, the great globe itself,
> Yea, all which it inherit, shall dissolve,
> And like this insubstantial faded,
> Leave not a rack behind. We are such stuff
> As dreams are made on, and our little life
> Is rounded with a . . ."

"Shut the fuck up!" shouted Daeman. "Harman, can you hear me?"

"Yes," said the older man, slumped over the control panel. "We have to go, Daeman. We lost these last twenty-four. There's nothing we can do."

"Harman, *listen to me*!" Daeman was standing in the back row of the tanks, flashlight beam steady. "In this tank . . ."

"Daeman, we have to go! The power's dying. Caliban is cutting the power."

As if to prove Harman's point, the holosphere faded and Prospero winked out of existence. The tank lights went off. The glow of the virtual control panel began fading away.

"Harman!" shouted Daeman from the shadows. "In this tank. It's Hannah."

56

The Plains of Ilium

"I have t⊙ ⊙ind Achilles and Hector," Mahnmut said to Orphu. "I'm going to have to leave you here on Thicket Ridge."

"Sure. Why not? Maybe the gods will mistake me for a gray boulder and not drop a bomb on me. But will you do me two favors?"

"Of course."

"First, keep in tightbeam touch. It gets sort of lonely here in the dark when I don't know what's going on. Especially with only a few minutes left before the Device goes off."

"Sure."

"Second, tie me down, will you? I like this levitation harness stuff—although I'm damned if I can figure out how it works—but I don't want the breeze to blow me into the sea again."

"Already done," said Mahnmut. "I've got you tied to the biggest rock on the leaping Amazon Myrine's mounded tomb up here on the ridge."

"Great," said Orphu. "By the by, do you have any idea who this leaping Amazon Myrine was and why she has a tomb here just outside the walls of Ilium?"

"Not a clue," said Mahnmut. He left his friend behind and began running on all fours across the plains of Ilium toward the Achaean camp, receiving a few curious stares from the milling Greeks in the process.

He didn't have to search the beach for Achilles and Hector. The two heroes had just crossed the trench bridge and were leading their captains and two or three thousand fighters with them toward the middle of the old battlefield. Mahnmut decided to be formal and rose to his hind legs for the greetings.

"Little machine," said Achilles, "where is your master, the son of Duane?"

It took Mahnmut a second to process this. "Hockenberry?" he said at last. "First of all, he's not my master. No man is my master and I'm no man. Secondly, he's gone to Olympos to see what the gods are up to. He said he'd be right back."

Achilles showed his white teeth in a grin. "Good. We need intelligence on the enemy."

Odysseus, standing between Hector and Achilles, said, "It didn't work too well for Dolon." Diomedes, behind the heroes, laughed. Hector scowled.

Dolon was Hector's scout last night when things looked so bad for the Greeks, sent Orphu. Even though Mahnmut understood Greek now and could speak it after the download from Orphu, he was still sending the whole dialogue to his friend via subvocals. Orphu's message wasn't finished—*Diomedes and Odysseus captured Dolon when they were going out on a night raid, and after promising the Trojan that they wouldn't hurt him, they got all the information they could from him and then Diomedes cut off his head. I think that Diomedes mentioned it because he still doesn't really trust Hector as an ally and . . .*

"Shelve it," said Mahnmut, forgetting to subvocalize. He switched frequencies. *I need to concentrate here.* Mahnmut thought he was capable of multitasking as well as any other moravec, but Orphu's history lesson was interfering with his real-time concentration.

"What did you just say?" demanded Hector. The Trojan hero was not happy. Mahnmut remembered that the man's mother and half-sister had just been killed in the aerial bombardment, although he wasn't sure that Hector knew that yet. Perhaps Hector was just in a bad mood.

"Just a brief prayer to my own gods," said Mahnmut.

Odysseus had dropped to one knee and was feeling Mahnmut's arms, torso, head, and protective shell. "Ingenious," said the son of Laertes. "Whichever god crafted you, it was a fine job."

"Thank you," said Mahnmut.

I think you've stepped into a Samuel Beckett play, sent Orphu.

"Shut up," Mahnmut said and sent in English. "Damn it, I keep forgetting to set the tightbeam for subvocal only."

"He prays still," said Odysseus, getting to his feet. "But I like the part where he said that his name was No Man. I'll remember that."

"Fleet-footed Achilles," said Mahnmut in the proper Greek, "may I ask your intentions now?"

"We go to challenge the gods to come down for single combat," said Achilles. "Or their army of immortals against our army of men—whichever they prefer."

Mahnmut looked at the few thousand Greeks—many of them blood-ied—who'd followed Achilles out from the camp. He turned his head and saw a thousand or fewer Trojans coming over the ridge to join Hector. "This is your army?" asked Mahnmut.

"The others will join us," said Achilles. "Little machine, if you see Hockenberry, son of Duane, tell him to come to me at the center of the field."

Achilles, Hector, and the Achaean captains strode off. The moravec had to dodge quickly or be trampled by the men and shields following.

"**WAIT!**" called Mahnmut. He'd used more amplification than he'd planned.

Achilles, Hector, Odysseus, Diomedes, Nestor, and the others turned. The men between Mahnmut and the heroes made a space.

"In thirty seconds," said Mahnmut, "something's going to happen."

"What?" demanded Hector.

I don't know, thought Mahnmut. *I don't even know if we'll feel the effects here. Hell, I don't even know if my timer-trigger is going to work at that depth in the Caldera Lake.*

You're subvocalizing, you know, sent Orphu.

Sorry, sent Mahnmut. Aloud, he said in Greek, "Wait and see. Eighteen seconds now." The Greeks didn't use minutes and seconds, of course, but Mahnmut thought he'd got the units translation right.

Even if the device blows Mars to bits, said Orphu, *I don't think this Earth is in that time or universe. But then again, the so-called gods have connected this place—wherever it is—to Olympos Mons via a thousand quantum tunnels.*

"Nine seconds," said Mahnmut.

What would an exploding Mars look like, in daylight, from this point in Asia Minor? sent Orphu. *I could do a quick simulation.*

"Four seconds," said Mahnmut.

Or I could just wait to see. Of course, you'll have to see for me.

"One second," said Mahnmut.

Olympos

I don't remember Ares or Hephaestus QTing as they dragged me out of the Great Hall, but obviously they did. The room they've thrown me into—my holding cell—is on the upper floor of an impossibly tall building on the east side of Olympos. The door was sealed behind them and there are no windows as such, but another door opens onto a balcony that hangs hundreds of feet above nothing except the slopes of Olympos right where they drop down to the vertical cliffs of Olympos. To the north is the ocean, a burnished bronze in this afternoon light, and far, far to the east are the three volcanoes I realize now are Martian volcanoes.

Mars. All these years. Mother of Mercy . . . Mars.

I shiver in the cold air. I see the goose bumps on my naked arms and thighs and can imagine them on my bare butt. The soles of my feet are ice cold against the chilly marble. My scalp hurts from being dragged and my pride hurts from being caught and stripped naked so easily.

Who did I think I was? I've been watching gods and superheroes so long that I forgot I was just an ordinary guy when I was real. Less now.

The toys went to my head, I think—the levitation harness and impact armor and morphing bracelet and QT medallion and shotgun mike and zoom lenses and taser baton and Hades Helmet. All that nifty Sharper Image crap. It allowed me to play superhero for a few days.

No longer. Daddy took my toys away. And Daddy's angry.

I remember Mahnmut's bomb and, out of old habit, lift my bare wrist to check the time. *Shit.* I don't even have my watch. But it has to be only a few minutes until the robot's Device is supposed to detonate. I lean out from the balcony, but this side of the building looks away from the caldera lake, so I guess I won't see the flash. Will the shock wave knock this building off the top of Olympos, or merely set it afire? A new memory swims up—TV images of doomed men and women jumping from burning towers in New York—and I close my eyes and squeeze my temples in a vain attempt to get rid of these unbidden visions. It only makes them more vivid. *Hell,* I think, *if they'd let me live another few weeks—if* I'd *let me live just by not screwing around with my toys and the fates of so many—I might have remembered all of my previous life. Maybe even my death.*

The door crashes open behind me and Zeus strides in alone. I turn to face him, walking back into the bare room.

Do you want a recipe for losing all self-esteem? Try being naked and barefoot, facing the God of All Gods who's dressed in high boots, golden greaves, and full battle armor. Besides that obvious disparity, there's the height thing. I mean, I'm five feet nine inches tall—not short, I used to remind people, including my wife Susan, but "average height"—and Zeus has to be fifteen feet tall this afternoon. The damned door was made for NBA stars carrying other NBA stars standing on their shoulders, and Zeus had to duck when he came in. Now he slams the door behind him. I see that he's still carrying my QT medallion in his massive hand.

"Scholic Hockenberry," he says in English, "do you know what trouble you've caused?"

I try to make my stare defiant, but I settle on not allowing my bare legs to shake uncontrollably. I can feel my penis and scrotum contracting toward baby-carrot and marble size from cold and fear.

As if noticing, Zeus looks me up and down. "My God, you old-style humans were ugly to look upon," he rumbles. "How can you be so scrawny your ribs are showing and *still* have a paunch?"

I remember that Susan used to say that I had a butt like two BB's, but she used to say it with affection.

"How do you know English?" I ask, voice quavering.

"**SHUT UP!**" roars the Father of the Gods.

Zeus brusquely gestures me onto the balcony and follows me out. He's so huge that there's barely room enough for me out here beside him. I back into a corner, trying not to look down. All this angered god of gods has to do now is lift me in one hand and fling me over the railing to get his revenge. I'd be flapping and screaming for five minutes on the way down.

"You harmed my daughter," growls Zeus.

Which one? I think desperately. I'm guilty of conspiring to kill Aphrodite *and* Athena, although I suspect it's Athena he's talking about. He's always been fond of Athena. I suspect it doesn't matter. Conspiring to harm any god—much less to overthrow the gods in general—has to be a capital offense. I peer over the railing again. I see the crystal escalator snaking down into the mists at sea level directly below, although my old scholic barracks, burned to the ground as it is, is too small to see with regular vision. Good Christ, that's a long way down.

"Do you know what's going to happen today, Hockenberry?" asks Zeus, although I assume the question is rhetorical. He extends his arms straight down and sets his fingers—each half as long as my forearm—on the stone railing.

"No," I say.

He turns to look down at me. "That must be disturbing after all these years of scholic-wisdom," he rumbles. "Always knowing what's going to happen next even when the gods do not. You must have felt like Fate himself."

"I felt like an asshole," I say.

Zeus nods. Then he points toward chariots rising off the summit of Olympos one after the other. There are hundreds of them. "This afternoon," says Zeus, "we are going to destroy mankind. Not just those posturing fools at Troy, but all human beings, everywhere."

What can you say to that? "That seems a bit excessive," I manage at last. My bravado would be more satisfying if my voice weren't still shaking like a nervous boy's.

Zeus looks out at the rising chariots and at the mass of golden-armored gods and goddesses still waiting to mount their cars. "Poseidon and Ares and others have been after me for centuries to eliminate humankind like the virus it is," says Zeus, rumbling more to himself than to me, I think. "We all have concerns—this Age of Man Heroic you see at Ilium would concern any race of gods, too much inbreeding between their race and ours—you must know the amount of DNA nano-engineering that we've passed down to freaks like Heracles and Achilles through our libidinous fucking with mortals. And I mean that literally."

"Why are you talking to me about this?" I ask.

Zeus really looks down at me now. He shrugs, those huge shoulders eight feet above my head. "Because you're going to be dead in a few seconds, so I can talk freely. On Olympos, Scholic Hockenberry, there are no permanent friends or trustworthy allies or loyal mates . . . only permanent interests. My interest is in remaining Lord of the Gods and Ruler of the Universe."

"It must be a full-time job," I say sarcastically.

"It is," says Zeus. "It is. Just ask Setebos or Prospero or the Quiet if you doubt me. Now, do you have any last questions before you go, Hockenberry?"

"I do actually," I say. To my amazement, the quaver is gone from my voice, the quiver gone from my knees. "I want to know who you gods really are. Where are you from? I know you're not the *real* Greek gods."

"We're not?" says Zeus. His smile, sharp white teeth glinting from his gray-silver beard, is not paternal.

"Who *are* you?" I ask again.

Almighty Zeus sighs. "I'm afraid we don't have time for the story right now. Good-bye, Scholic Hockenberry." He takes his hands off the railing and turns toward me.

As it turns out, he's right—we don't have time for the story or for anything else. Suddenly the tall building shakes, cracks, moans. The very air above the summit of Olympos seems to thicken and ripple. Golden chariots stagger in flight and I can hear the shouts and screams from gods and goddesses on the ground far below.

Zeus staggers back against the rail, drops the QT medallion on the marble floor, and reaches out a huge hand to steady himself against the building even as the tall tower shakes on its foundations, vibrating back and forth in a ten-degree arc.

He looks up.

Suddenly the sky is full of streaks. I can hear sonic booms as line after line of fire slashes across the Martian sky. Above Olympos, above our heads, several huge, spinning spheres of space-black and magma-red are opening against the blue. They are like holes punched into the sky itself and they're spinning lower.

Lower down, much farther down, I see more of these jagged circles, each one with the radius of a football field at least, spinning at the base of Olympos. More appear out above the ocean to the north, some slicing into the sea itself.

Ants are coming through the land-based circles by the thousands, and then I realize that the ants are men. Human men?

The sky is filled now not only with golden chariots, but with sharp-edged black machines, some larger than the chariots, some smaller, all carrying the lethal, inhuman look of military design. More fiery streaks fill the upper atmosphere, lashing down toward Olympos like ICBMs.

Zeus raises both fists toward the sky and bellows at the little god-figures far below. "**RAISE THE AEGIS!**" he roars. "**ACTIVATE THE AEGIS!**"

I'd love to stay around and see what he's talking about and what happens next, but I have other priorities. I throw myself headfirst between Zeus's mighty arch of legs, slide on my belly across the bouncing marble floor, grab the QT medallion in one hand and twist its dial with the other.

The Equatorial Ring

At first they couldn't get Hannah out of the tank. The heavy piece of pipe wouldn't dent the plastic glass. Daeman fired off three rounds from Savi's gun, but the flechettes barely knicked the tank's surface before ricocheting around the firmary, smashing fragile things, ripping into already decommissioned servitors, and barely missing both men. Finally Harman found a way to clamber to the top of the tank and they used the pipe as a lever to first lift and then rip off the complicated lid. Then Harman pulled his thermskin visor lower, tugged on the osmosis mask, and leaped down into the draining fluids to pull Hannah out. With the main power out, lights off, and tank glow fading to nothing, they worked mostly by the light of the single flashlight.

Naked, wet, hairless, her skin looking raw and new, their young friend looked as vulnerable as a baby bird as she lay on the wet firmary floor. The good news was that she was breathing—gaspingly, shallowly, alarmingly rapidly—but definitely breathing on her own. The bad news was that they couldn't wake her.

"Is she going to live?" demanded Daeman. The other twenty-three men and women in the tank were obviously dead or dying and there was no way to get to them in time.

"How do I know?" gasped Harman.

Daeman looked around. "Temperature's dropping in here without the power to heat things. Another few minutes, it'll be below zero, just like outside in the main city. We have to find something to cover her with."

Still carrying the gun but mostly heedless, not looking for Caliban, Daeman ran through the darkening firmary. There were human bones, haunches of decaying flesh, motionless servitors, bits and pieces of beakers and tubes and pipes, but not so much as a blanket. Daeman ripped a square sheet of clear plastic from the covering they'd already torn to seal the semipermeable entrance and returned.

Hannah was still unconscious but shivering uncontrollably. Harman had his arms around her and was rubbing her flesh with his bare hands, but it didn't seem to be helping. The plastic folded awkwardly around her thin, white body, but neither man thought it was holding in any body heat.

"She's going to die unless we do something," whispered Daeman. From the shadows of the now-dark healing tanks, there came a sliding sound. Daeman didn't even bother to raise his gun. Steam from the liquid oxygen and other spilled fluids was filling the firmary.

"We're all going to die soon anyway," said Harman. He pointed toward the clear panels above them.

Daeman looked up. The white star that was the two-mile-long linear accelerator was closer—much closer. "How much time left?" he asked.

Harman shook his head. "The chronometers disappeared with the power and Prospero."

"We had about twenty minutes to go when the problems began."

"Yes," said Harman. "But how long ago was that? Ten minutes? Fifteen? Nineteen?"

Daeman looked up. The Earth was gone and only stars—including the bright shape rushing at them—burned cold in the clear panels. "The Earth was still visible when this crap started," he said. "Can't be much more than twenty minutes ago. When the earth reappears . . ."

The blue and white limb of the planet moved into sight among the lower panes. "We have to go," said Daeman. There were more crashes and slidings in the dark behind them. Daeman whirled with the gun high, but Caliban did not emerge. The firmary gravity was failing now as well; pooled fluids were lifting themselves from the floor and trying to float, accreting themselves into amoeba shapes, seeking to become spheres. Savi's flashlight reflected back from slick surfaces everywhere.

"How do we go?" asked Harman. "Leave her behind?" Hannah's eyelids were not quite closed, but they could see only the whites of her eyes. Her shaking was lessening, but this seemed ominous to Daeman.

Daeman had tugged up his mask—there was just enough air in the firmary to breathe, although it still smelled like a meat locker with the power off—and now he rubbed his beard. "We can't get her to the sonie with only two thermskins. She'd die of exposure in the city, much less in space."

"There's the sonie forcefield and heater," whispered Harman. "Savi had them on when we were flying high." He'd tugged his own mask up again, and his breath fogged in the cold air. There were icicles in his beard and mustache. His eyes looked so tired that it hurt Daeman to look at them.

Daeman shook his head. "Savi told me all about how cold and hot it was in space, what vacuum does to the body. She'd be dead before we got the forcefield powered up."

"Do you remember how to power it up?" asked Harman. "How to fly the damned thing?"

"I . . . don't know," said Daeman. "I watched her fly it, but I never thought I'd have to. Don't you remember how?"

"I am so . . . tired," said Harman, rubbing his temples.

Hannah had quit shaking and now looked dead. Daeman peeled his thermskin glove back and put his bare palm on her chest. For a second he was sure she was gone, but then he felt the faint, bird-rapid beat of her heart.

"Harman," he said, voice strong, "get out of your thermskin."

Harman looked up at him and blinked. "Yes," he said stupidly, "you're right. I've had my five Twenties. She deserves to live more than . . ."

"No, you idiot." Daeman began helping him tug off his suit. The air was already turning Daeman's exposed face and hands to ice; he couldn't imagine being naked in this cold. The air was thinning as they spoke, their voices sounding higher and fainter. "Share the thermskin with her. Count to five hundred, then peel it off her and warm yourself. Keep swapping unless she dies."

"Where are you going to be?" gasped Harman. He'd tugged the thermskin off and was trying to pull it on the unconscious girl, but his hands and arms were shaking so badly from the cold that Daeman had to help him. Immediately the thermskin adapted itself to Hannah's body and she began shaking again, although the suit was holding in almost 100 percent of her body heat now. Harman set his osmosis mask over her face.

"I'm going for the sonie," gasped Daeman. He handed Harman the gun, but had to lift his own osmosis mask to make himself heard since the other man wasn't on suitcomm any longer. "Here. You keep this in case Caliban comes for you two." Daeman lifted the four-foot-long length of pipe they'd used as a crowbar.

"He won't," said Harman between racking breaths. "He'll go for you. Then he can eat us all at his leisure."

"Well, I hope we give him a bellyache," said Daeman. He pulled down his osmosis mask and kicked and ran and floated toward the exit membrane.

It was only after Daeman had used the sharp end of the pipe to rip and tear a man-sized hole in the membrane, kicking through into the even lower gravity and deeper cold and dark outside the firmary, that he realized that he hadn't told Harman that his plan was to come *back* with the sonie—to somehow get it through the window wall to pick them up. *Well, too late to go back to tell him now.*

Daeman had always had trouble keeping up with Savi and Harman when the three of them were first swim-kicking their way through the crystal city a month ago—an eternity ago—but now Daeman swam through the thin air like some low-gravity sea creature, a crystal-city otter, always finding the perfect place from which to kick off at just the right instant, paddling through the air with his three free limbs with pure economy of effort, somersaulting and pirouetting with perfect timing to find the next strut or table or even the next post-human corpse to kick off from for his next leg of the trip.

It still wasn't fast enough. He could feel time winning this race, even as he looked up at the panels of the crystal city—the panels showing their dying glow, bringing an even deeper darkness to the kelp beds and body-strewn terraces where he kicked and swam—but there were no clear panels here through which he could see the onrushing linear accelerator. *Will I hear it when it crashes through the crystal roof, or is the air too thin for sound?*

He shook the question out of his head. He'd know when it arrived.

Daeman almost passed the crystal tower headed south when he looked up and saw that he was already directly under the hundreds and hundreds of stories of air rising into darkness above him.

He landed on the asteroid, held the pipe in both hands, swiveling, using only his thermskin lenses to penetrate the darkness. Humanoid shapes floated out there, some close, but their purposeless tumble suggested they were probably post-corpses, not Caliban. *Probably.*

Daeman tucked the pipe under his arms, crouched low, remembered Caliban's long-armed squat, imitated it, and shoved off with all the remaining energy in his legs and arms. He floated upward, but slowly, far too slowly. He felt like he was barely moving by the time he got to the first extruded terrace some seventy or eighty feet up, and realized how weak he was as he used the terrace railing to push himself upward again, watching the shadows as he rose.

There were too many shadows. Caliban could leap at him from any of those darkened terraces, but there was nothing Daeman could do about it—he had to stay close to the wall and the terraces to keep pushing off, always moving, floating upward—quickly at first, then with dying speed until he chose the next terrace—feeling like a frog jumping from one stone and metal lily pad to the next.

Suddenly Daeman laughed out loud. His thermskin, beneath the dirt and mud and blood and grime, was green. He *did* look like some awkward, scrawny frog, squatting to push himself off vertically at every tenth railing of every tenth terrace. His laugh echoed hollowly through his commpads over his ears and shocked him back into silence except for his tortured breathing and grunts.

With a stab of fear, Daeman paused and did a somersault even as he floated higher. *Have I passed the level where the sonie's parked outside?* The distance to the floor below seemed impossible—a thousand feet of empty air, at least—and the sonie was only . . . *How many stories up?* His heart pounding with panic, Daeman tried to remember the holo image in Prospero's control room cell. Five hundred feet or so up? Seven hundred?

Sick with terror at having lost his way, Daeman floated out further from the wall and checked the panels of glass. Most glowed that sickly, ever-weakening orange. Some were clear this far up, silver with earthlight. None showed the white mark of the semipermeable membranes at the first airlock and Prospero's door. *Did I see such a window mark on the holo, or just assume there'd be one visible from the inside?*

Floating almost to a halt now at the apogee of his last leap, Daeman wrenched his osmosis mask loose. He was going to vomit.

You don't have time for that, idiot. He tried to breathe in the air up here, but it was too thin, too cold, too rank. Only semiconscious, Daeman pulled the mask back down. *Why didn't I bring the flashlight? I thought Harman might need it to tend to Hannah or to shoot at Caliban, but now I can't make out the fucking windows.*

Daeman forced himself to slow his breathing and to calm down. Before the gravity began pulling him down again toward that dark floor hundreds of feet below, he kicked and paddled his way farther out from the wall, rolling over onto his back like a swimmer looking up at the stars.

There. Another fifty feet up, on this wall. The white square on an opaque window panel.

Daeman did a pirouette, clasped the pipe between his chin and chest, and used both arms and his gloved hands in a powerful breaststroke. If he couldn't get to that closest terrace now, he'd lose two hundred or more feet of altitude, and he didn't think he had the strength to fight his way back up again.

He reached the terrace, grabbed the pipe with his left hand, and kicked his way vertical, timing it so perfectly that he slowed to a stop just as he reached the white-marked panel. Panting, his vision dimmed with sweat, Daeman extended his right arm—his hand and forearm passed through the membrane as if it were slightly sticky gauze.

"Thank you, God," gasped Daeman.

Caliban hit him then, leaping out of the shadowed recesses under the next terrace up, long arms and longer legs wide and grasping, teeth glinting in earthlight.

"No," grunted Daeman just as the monster struck, wrapping arms and legs and long fingers around the man, teeth snapping for Daeman's jugular. The human managed to get his right forearm up to protect his throat—Caliban's teeth ripping through flesh and meeting on bone—while the two forms, entangled and thrashing, blood fountaining in low-g around them, fell together through the thin air down to the next terrace, crashing into glass and plastic and wood and frozen post-human flesh as they tumbled into darkness there.

59

The Plains of Ilium

Mahnmut may have been the first to notice what was happening in the sky, sea, and earth around Ilium, but that was because he was expecting it. He hadn't known *what* he was expecting . . . but certainly not what he saw now.

What do you see? asked Orphu on the tightbeam.

Ah . . . gasped Mahnmut.

A rotating sphere some hundreds of meters across had appeared in the sky several thousand feet above Ilium. Then a second one rotated into view just above the battlefield, centered between the city and Thicket Ridge. Mahnmut turned quickly and saw a third sphere pop into existence above the Achaean encampments, then a fourth one suddenly appearing several miles out to sea immediately in front of the scores of fleeing Achaean ships. A fifth one appeared to the north of the city; a sixth one to the south.

What do you see? demanded Orphu.

Uh . . . said Mahnmut.

All of the spheres showed flashing colors but were suddenly filled with stabbing fractal designs; then all resolved themselves into multiple images of Olympus Mons, seen from different distances, viewed from different angles, and framed by different perspectives; now all showed the Martian volcano and the blue Martian sky. One of the spheres settled into the plains of Ilium ahead so that the Martian ground in the hundred-meter-wide circle extended smoothly from the Trojan soil. The huge sphere to the west flattened to a circle in the sky and then sank until the Martian ocean was level with the Mediterranean Sea. Water surged back and forth between the two worlds. The Achaean ships tried to drop their sails, men quit rowing, but the high-beaked ships could not stop in time and sailed through the circle of boiling turbulence into the Martian northern ocean, with white-sloped Olympus Mons looming in the background. No matter which direction Mahnmut looked, he could see the Martian volcano, even through the spheres now resolving themselves into circular portals high in the sky over Ilium.

What's going on? shouted Orphu over the tightbeam.

Ah . . . said Mahnmut again.

Scores of black flying objects hurtled through the circular portals in the sky, out of the circle slicing into the sea behind Mahnmut, even through the ground-level portal—more arch now than circle, since its base was under Trojan soil—opening less than a hundred meters in front of Achilles and Hector and his men. The flying objects threw themselves through the sky like giant hornets and Mahnmut noticed that they were black, barbed, sharp-planed, not much larger than Orphu, and powered by visible pulse-engines in their bellies, sides, and sterns. The machines had bulbous, black-glassed cockpits and were festooned with whip comm antennae and what looked to be weapons—missiles, guns, bombs, ray projectors. If these were new-generation chariots from the gods, they'd gone high-tech industrial in a hurry.

Mahnmut! bellowed Orphu.

Sorry, said the little moravec. Almost stuttering, he hurried to describe the chaos in the skies, seas, and fields around them. He had trouble catching up to real time.

What are Achilles and Hector and all the other Greeks and Trojans doing? asked Orphu. *Running?*

Some are, said Mahnmut. *But most of the Achaeans around me and the Trojans near your ridge are running into the closest circle-portal.*

Running into it? repeated Orphu of Io. Mahnmut had never heard his big friend sound flabbergasted before.

Yeah. Achilles and Hector started it—they shouted, bellowed something, held their spears and shields high, and just . . . well . . . rushed into it. I guess they see Olympus Mons and know what it is and just . . . attacked.

Attacked a Martian volcano? repeated Orphu. He sounded even more thunderstruck.

Attacked Olympos, the home of the gods, said Mahnmut, sounding pretty stupefied himself. *Oh, my!*

What "Oh, My"? demanded Orphu.

The circle-portal-thing behind us, stammered Mahnmut. *Dozens of Greek ships went through it . . .*

Yeah, you said that.

But there are hundreds *of ships visible through the portal.*

Greek ships? asked the Ionian.

No, said Mahnmut. *Most of them are LGM ships.*

Little green men? Orphu sounded like a poorly engineered voice-synthesis device, sounding each word out as if he'd never heard it before.

Thousands of LGM. On hundreds of ships.

Feluccas? said Orphu.

Feluccas, those big barges they used to transport the stones for heads, larger sailing ships, smaller ships . . . they're all sailing toward Olympos Mons, mixed in with the Achaean ships now.

Why? asked Orphu. *Why are the zeks sailing toward Olympos?*

Don't ask me! shouted Mahnmut. *I just work here . . . uh-oh.*

Uh-oh?

The sky's full of fiery streaks now, like meteors flaming down from space.

The gods resuming their bombardment? asked Orphu.

I don't know.

Which direction?

What? said Mahnmut. If he had been designed with a jaw, it would be dropping now. The sky was a latticework of fiery streaks, with the circular portals showing Olympos Mons in a dozen places around Ilium and the sky filled with black barbed machines jetting back and forth at increasingly lower altitudes. Thousands more Achaeans and Trojans had rushed into the first portal after Achilles and Hector, while tens of thousands more Trojans and their allies were taking up defensive positions on the walls of Ilium and on the plain just outside the Scaean Gates. Gongs rang out. Drums beat. The air sizzled with energy and echoed with roars. Achaeans ran to defensive positions on their trenches, sunlight glinting on polished armor. A thousand Trojan archers on the Ilium ramparts went to full pull on their bows, arrows aimed skyward. A score more of black ships put out to sea from the Achaean camp. Mahnmut couldn't pivot fast enough to take it all in.

Which direction are the meteor trails going? said Orphu. *West to east, east to west, north to south?*

What the hell does it matter which direction? snapped Mahnmut. *No, wait, sorry. They're coming from all parts of the sky. Making cross-hatches against the blue.*

Any of them heading for Ilium? asked Orphu.

I don't think so. Not directly. Wait, I can see something at the end of one of those trails now . . . I'm zooming in . . . good heavens, it's a . . .

Spaceship? said Orphu.

Yes! breathed Mahnmut. *Fins, hull, roaring engine . . . it looks like a car-*

toon of a spaceship, Orphu. It's hovering on a column of yellow energy. The other meteors are also ships . . . some hovering . . . one coming down. Uh-oh.

Uh-oh again? said Orphu.

That hovering spaceship appears to be landing, said Mahnmut. *So are four or five of the smaller black flying machines.*

Yes? said Orphu. The Ionian sounded calm, perhaps even amused.

They're landing on the ridge near you! *Almost right on top of you, Orphu! Stay put, I'm coming!* Mahnmut began running on all fours at top speed for the ridge where the yellow spacecraft exhaust was kicking dust and small rocks a hundred feet into the air. He couldn't see Orphu through the dust as the various machines set down next to the amazon's tomb. The barbed flying machines were extending a complicated tripod landing gear. The weapons on the landing hornet ships were swiveling, targeting Orphu. Mahnmut saw this just before he lost sight of everything as he galloped into the dust storm.

I'm not going anywhere, sent Orphu. *But don't sprain a servomechanism hurrying, old friend. I think I know who these guys are.*

60

The Equatorial Ring

Rolling in the terrace darkness with Caliban, it felt to Daeman as if the monster were trying to tear his arm off. Indeed, the monster *was* trying to tear Daeman's arm off. Only the metallic fibers in the thermskin and the suit's automatic response to seal all rends kept Caliban's teeth from ripping the meat off Daeman's arm and then tearing the bones one from the other. But the suit wouldn't save Daeman for much longer.

The man and man-beast crashed into tables, rolled among post-human corpses, bounced off a girder, and rebounded in microgravity from a glass wall. Caliban would not release his grip and hugged Daeman tightly to him with long fingers and prehensile webbed toes. Suddenly the creature relaxed its bite, pulled its slavering head back, and lunged for Daeman's neck again. Daeman blocked the lunge with his right forearm again, was bitten to the bone again, and moaned aloud as they bounced back to the terrace railing. In spite of the suit's automatic closing, blood jetted out in discrete spheres, bursting on impact with Daeman's suit or Caliban's scaly hide.

For a second they were wedged against the terrace railing and Daeman was staring into Caliban's yellow eyes, only inches from his own. He knew that if his punctured forearm wasn't in the way, Caliban would bite through his osmosis mask and rip his face off in a second, but what really passed through Daeman's mind at this moment was a simple phrase and an astounding fact—*I'm not afraid.*

There was no firmary standing by to fax his dead body away and fix it in forty-eight hours or less, no blue worms waiting for Daeman now—whatever happened next was forever.

I am not afraid.

Daeman saw the animal ears, the slavering muzzle, the scaly shoulders, and he thought again how physical and fleshy Caliban was. He remembered from the grotto the obscene pink of the animal-thing's bare scrotum and penis.

As Caliban pulled his teeth free to lunge again—even while Daeman knew that he couldn't block the lunge toward his jugular a third time—the man reached down with his free left hand, found yielding globes, and squeezed as hard as he'd ever squeezed anything in his life.

Instead of lunging, the monster jerked its head far back, roared so loudly into the thin air that the noise echoed in the almost airless space, and then the beast struggled to break away. Daeman ducked low, shifted both hands lower—his right arm bled, but the fingers on that hand still worked—and squeezed again, hanging on and being dragged behind as Caliban writhed and kicked to break free. Daeman imagined pulping tomatoes with his powerful hands, his human hands, he imagined squeezing the juice out of oranges, of bursting pulp, and he hung on—the world had receded to the will to hang on and squeeze—and Caliban roared again, swung his long arm, and struck Daeman hard enough to send him flying.

For several seconds, Daeman was not conscious enough to defend himself or even to know where he was. But the creature did not use those seconds—he was too busy flailing and howling and holding himself, his scaly knees flying high as Caliban tried to crouch and hunch in midair. Just as Daeman's vision began to clear, he saw the monster flail his way back to the terrace, grab the railing, and fling himself the fifteen feet between him and Daeman. The long arms and claws were already halfway to him.

Daeman groped blindly amidst the chairs and tables around him, found his iron pipe where it had bounced, lifted it to his shoulder with both hands, and savagely swung the metal into the side of Caliban's head. The sound was most satisfying. Caliban's head snapped aside and his flailing arms and tumbling torso crashed into Daeman, but the man flung the beast to one side—feeling his own right arm going numb now—and he dropped the pipe, leaped for the terrace railing, and then kicked up toward the semipermeable exit thirty feet above.

Too slow.

More used to the low-gravity, powered by hate now beyond human measurement, Caliban used hands, feet, legs, and momentum to rebound off the terrace wall, catch the railing with his toes, crouch, spring, and beat Daeman through the air to the marked panel above them.

Seeing that he wouldn't win the race to the glass, Daeman grabbed a girder protruding fifteen feet from below the marked panel and arrested his movement. Caliban landed on the ledge, arms out, blocking the approach to the white square. Daeman saw that there was no way that he could get around or past those wide arms, those raking claws. He suddenly felt the pain from his torn and punctured arm hitting his mind and torso like an electric shock, then felt the growing numbness there as warning of the weakness and shock that must soon follow.

Caliban threw his head back, roared again, showed his teeth, and chanted—"What I hate, He consecrates—what I ate, He celebrates! No mate for thee—more meat for me!" Caliban was ready to spring after Daeman as soon as the human turned to flee.

Seeing the raw scars on Caliban's chest, Daeman found himself smiling grimly. *Savi hurt him with her shot. She didn't die without a fight.*

Neither will I.

Instead of turning to flee, Daeman pulled himself horizontal on the girder, squatted, gathered his remaining energy in his legs, put his head down, and launched himself straight at Caliban's chest.

It took Daeman two or three seconds to cross the space between them, but for an instant the monster seemed too surprised to react. Food was not supposed to act in this impertinent manner—prey was not supposed to charge. Then the creature realized that his dinner was coming to him—wearing the thermskin he desired—and Caliban showed all of his teeth in a smile that became a snarl. The beast threw his arms and legs around the incoming human in a grip that Daeman knew the monster would not release until the man was dead and half-eaten.

They went through the membrane together, Daeman feeling the sensation of tearing through a curtain of sticky gauze, Caliban bellowing into thin air one second and into cold silence the next. Together, they tumbled into outer space, Daeman hugging Caliban as fiercely as the monster was clutching Daeman, the human's left hand pressed up against the monster's underjaw, trying to keep those teeth away for the eight or ten seconds he thought he needed.

The thermskin suit reacted immediately to vacuum—tightening fiercely into Daeman's flesh, constricting until it acted as a pressure suit, sealing off even molecular gaps that would bleed air or blood or heat into space. The osmosis mask inflated the clear visor and switched the movement and purification of the man's recycled breath to 100 percent. Cooling tubules in the thermskin let Daeman's natural sweat flow quickly through channels, cooling his sunward side even as body heat was transferred to the part of his body in minus-two-hundred-degree shadow. All this happened in a fraction of a second and Daeman did not even notice. He was too busy thrusting Caliban's jaw and muzzle upward, keeping those teeth away from his throat and shoulder.

Caliban was too strong. He shook his head, freed it from Daeman's weakening pressure, and then threw open his mouth to bellow before ripping the man's throat out.

Air rushed out of Caliban's chest and mouth like water from a punctured gourd. Saliva froze even as it spewed into space. Caliban clapped his long-fingered hands over his ears, but not in time—blood globules spewed into space as the creature's eardrums exploded. The blobs of blood began to boil in vacuum and, barely more than a second later, the blood in Caliban's veins began to boil as well.

Caliban's eyes started to swell and more blood spurted from his tear ducts. His muzzle moved up and down as his mouth worked like a fish's, wheezing silently in vacuum, gasping for air, but no air came. The surface of Caliban's bulging eyes began to freeze over and cloud white.

Daeman had wrenched himself free, tumbled across the outside terrace—almost floated helplessly off into space, but caught the metal-mesh railing—then hauled himself hand over hand to where the familiar sonie was tethered to the metal surface. He didn't want to run. He didn't want to turn his back on Caliban. He wanted to stay and kill the thrashing monster with his gloved hands.

But one of those hands wasn't working now—his torn right arm now hung useless as he kicked the final ten feet to the low vehicle. *Harman. Hannah.*

A human would be dead by now, unprotected in space—knowing so little about anything, Daeman instinctively knew that—but Caliban was not human. Spewing blood and frozen air like some horrible comet boiling away its own surface as it approached the sun, Caliban tumbled, flailed, found purchase on the gridded metal of the terrace, and kicked his way back through the semipermeable wall, back into air and relative warmth.

Daeman was too busy to watch. Pulling himself down prone into the driver's cushions, he turned his gaze to the metal shelf where the virtual control panel should be. It was off.

How do I activate it? What do I do if I can? How did Savi start it up?

Daeman's mind was blank. His vision narrowed as black dots danced in his field of view. He was hyperventilating and close to passing out as he worked frantically to recall the image of Savi flying the sonie, activating the controls. He couldn't remember.

Calm down. Easy. Easy. It was his voice, but not his—an older voice, steady, amused. *Take it easy.*

He did, forcing first his breathing back to a sane rate, then willing his heartbeat to slow, then focusing his vision and his mind.

Didn't she use some voice command? That wouldn't work here in space. No air, no sound—Savi had told them that. Or perhaps Harman had. Daeman was learning from everyone these days. *How then?* He forced himself to relax a step further, and then closed his eyes and tried to recall the image of Savi flying them all away from the iceberg that first night flight.

She passed one hand under this low cowl, near the handgrip, to activate things.

Daeman moved his left hand. A virtual control panel flashed into existence. Able to use only his left hand, closing his eyes when he had to remember more clearly, Daeman moved his fingers through control sequences on the multicolored virtual panel. The forcefield flicked on and pressed him down against the cushions. A second later, a roar startled Daeman into looking up, but it was only air flooding into the secured space, just as he'd commanded with his fingers. With the air, came a voice, "Manual or autopilot mode?"

Daeman tugged his osmosis mask up a bit, almost wept as he breathed in the first sweet air he'd tasted in a month, and said, "Manual."

The control grip flicked into place, surrounded by a virtual aura. The stick felt solid in Daeman's left hand.

Forgetting the tie-downs until he saw the elastic bands rip free and fly into space, Daeman lifted the sonie ten feet above the metal terrace, twitched the stick, fed power to the rear thrusters, went off course, quickly realigned before smashing into metal instead of window, and hit the semipermeable square doing thirty or forty miles per hour.

Caliban was waiting on the ledge inside. The monster leaped for Daeman's head and his trajectory was perfect, but the forcefield was on. Caliban bounced off and tumbled into the empty air at the center of the tower.

Daeman made a wide turn, getting used to the steering, twisted the control stick to add more power. The sonie was doing sixty or seventy miles per hour when Caliban looked up, the beast's bleeding eyes went wide, and the bow of the sonie plowed into the monster's midsection, sending him flying across the open tower space and crashing into girders and glass on the far side.

Daeman would have loved to stay and play—the *want* of it ached more in him that the screaming pain from his right arm—but his friends were dying below. He banked the sonie and dived straight down toward the city floor more than ninety stories below.

He almost didn't pull up in time—the sonie sheered turf, cut through kelp, and sent dead grass flying—but then Daeman got the thing flying level and cut back on the speed a bit. His twenty-minute flailing trip from the firmary took him three minutes on the flight back.

The entrance wall was not quite wide enough for the sonie. Daeman backed the hovering machine up, gave it more throttle, and made the semipermeable entrance permanently permeable. Shards of glass and metal and plastic followed the sonie as Daeman flew it between dark, empty healing tanks. He winced as he caught a glimpse in some of those tanks of the dead white bodies of those humans they hadn't saved in time. Then he was stopping the sonie, killing the forcefield, and jumping out next to two more bodies on the floor.

Harman had left the blue thermskin suit on Hannah, keeping only the osmosis mask for himself in the final minutes. The man's naked body looked bruised and pale in the reflected light from the sonie's headlights. Hannah's mouth was open wide, as if in a final, futile effort to force more air into her lungs. Daeman didn't waste time to see if they were alive. Using only his left arm, he scooped each of them up and laid them in the two couches on either side of his own. He paused only to jump out again, throw Savi's pack in the back couch, and to toss the gun onto the armrest of his own couch before he was back in place and activating the forcefield.

"Pure oxygen," he said to the sonie as the air-rush began. The clean, cold air became thicker, making Daeman's head swim it was so rich. He fumbled in the virtual control panel, setting off several caution alarms before finding the heat. Warm air radiated from the console and various vents.

Harman began coughing first, then Hannah a few seconds later. Their eyes flickered, opened, finally focused.

Daeman grinned stupidly at them.

"Where . . . where . . ." gasped Harman.

"Take it easy," said Daeman, slowly moving the sonie toward the firmary exit. "Take your time."

"Time . . . the time . . ." gasped the older man. "The linear . . . accelerator."

"Oh, fuck," said Daeman. He'd forgotten about the onrushing structure, never once looked up or over his shoulder in space to see it coming.

Daeman twisted the sonie's throttle full open, slammed through the hole where the membrane had been, and accelerated toward the tower exit.

There was no sign of Caliban in the tower. Daeman slewed a wide curve, threaded the needle through the tower exit pane, and climbed from the outside terrace into space.

"Oh, Jesus Christ," breathed Harman.

Hannah screamed—the first sound she'd made since being fished out of the healing tank.

The two-mile-long linear accelerator was so close that the wormhole collection ring at its bow filled two-thirds of the sky above them, blotting out sun and stars. Thrusters were firing in quad-pods all along its absurd length, making final course corrections before impact. Daeman didn't know the names of everything at that moment, but he could make out every detail of the gleaming cross-braces, polished rings now cratered with countless micrometeorite strikes, racks of cooling coils, the long, copper-colored return line above the main accelerator core, the distant injector stacks, and the swirling, earth-and-sea-colored sphere of the captured wormhole itself. The thing grew larger as they watched, blotting out the last of the stars above, and the shadow of it fell across the mile-long crystal city beneath them.

"Daeman . . ." began Harman.

Daeman had already acted, twisting the throttle ring full over and looping up and over the tower, the city, the asteroid, diving for the great blue curve of the Earth even as the linear accelerator covered the last few hundred meters behind them.

For an instant the city towers were above them as the sonie looped, and then just slightly behind when the hurtling mass struck the city and the asteroid, the wormhole sphere crashing into the towers and the long city a second or two before the exotic-metal structure of the accelerator itself. The wormhole silently collapsed into itself and the accelerator seemed to accordion neatly into nothing, but then the full force of the impact became apparent as all three of the humans turned in their couches and craned their necks to see behind them.

There was no sound. That struck Daeman the hardest—the pure silence of the moment. No vibration. None of the usual earthly clues that some great cataclysm was taking place.

But taking place it was.

The crystal city exploded into millions upon millions of fragments, glowing glass and burning gas expanding outward in all directions.

Great, ballooning balls of flame bulged outward a mile, two miles, ten miles, as if trying to catch the diving sonie, but then the huge fires seemed to fold inward—like a video image running in reverse—as the flames consumed the last of the escaping oxygen.

The city on the opposite side of the asteroid from the impact was propelled off the surface of the stony worldlet, coming apart in a thousand discrete trajectories as the glass and steel and pulsing exotic materials flew and blew apart, most sections celebrating their own separate orgies of destruction, punctuated everywhere with more silent explosions and self-consuming fireballs.

A second after the first impact, the entire, mile-long asteroid shuddered, sending concentric waves of dust and gas into space after the city debris. Then the asteroid broke apart.

"Hurry!" said Harman.

Daeman didn't know what he was doing. He'd dived the ship toward Earth at full velocity, staying just ahead of the flames and debris and waves of frozen gases, but now various red and yellow and green alarms were showing all over the virtual control board. Worse than that, there was sound outside the sonie at long last—a suspicious hiss and crackle growing in seconds to a terrifying roar. Worst of all, an orange glow around the edges of the sonie was quickly turning into a sphere of flame and blue electrical plasma.

"What's the matter?" shouted Hannah. "Where are we?"

Daeman ignored her. He didn't know what to do with the throttle and attitude control. The roar rose in volume and the sheath of flames thickened around them.

"Are we damaged?" shouted Harman.

Daeman shook his head. He didn't think so. He thought perhaps it had something to do with coming back into the Earth's atmosphere at such speed. Once, at a friend's house in Paris Crater, when Daeman was six or seven, despite his mother's admonitions not to do so, he'd slid down a long banister, popped off onto the floor at high speed, and then slid on his bare hands and knees along his mother's friend's thick carpet. It had burned him badly and he'd never done that again. This friction felt something like that to Daeman.

He decided not to tell Harman and Hannah his theory. It sounded a little silly, even to himself.

"Do something!" shouted Harman over the roar and crackle all around them. Both men's hair and beards were standing on end in the center of all this electrical madness. Hannah—bald, even her eyebrows gone—stared around her as if she'd wakened to madness.

Before the noise drowned out everything else, Daeman shouted at the virtual controls, "Autopilot!"

"Engage autopilot?" The sonie's neutral voice was almost inaudible under the entry roar. Daeman could feel the heat through the forcefield and knew that couldn't be good.

"Engage autopilot!" shouted Daeman at the top of his lungs.

The forcefield fell in on the three humans, squeezing them tightly to their couches as the sonie flipped upside down and the stern engines fired so fiercely that Daeman thought his teeth were going to rattle out of his head. His arm hurt terribly under the deceleration pressure.

"Re-enter on pre-programmed flight path?" the sonie asked calmly, speaking like the idiot savant it was.

"Yeah," shouted Daeman. His neck was aching from the terrible pressure and he was sure that his spine was going to snap.

"Is that an affirmative?" asked the sonie.

"Affirmative!" screamed Daeman.

More thrusters fired, the sonie seemed to bounce like a thrown rock skipping off a pond's surface, was wrapped twice more in reentry fire, and then somehow straightened itself out.

Daeman raised his head.

They were flying—flying so high that the edge of the Earth was still curved ahead of them, so high that the mountains far beneath them were visibly mountains only by the white snow texture against the brown and green earth colors—but flying. There was air out there.

Daeman cheered, reached over and hugged Hannah in her blue thermskin suit, then cheered again, raising his fist toward the sky in triumph.

He froze with his fist and eyes raised. "Oh, shit," he said.

"What?" said Harman, still naked except for the osmosis mask now dangling around his neck. Then the older man looked up, following Daeman's gaze. "Oh, shit," he said.

The first of a thousand fireballs—debris from the city or the linear accelerator or the broken asteroid—roared by them less than a mile away, trailing a vertical wake of flame and plasma ten miles behind it, almost flipping the sonie over with the violence of its passage. More meteors roared down at them from the burning sky above.

61

The Plains of Ilium

Mahnmut arrived on the Thicket Ridge just as nine tall black figures stepped out of the spacecraft that had landed amidst the hornet fliers, all nine striding down the ramp into the swirling dust storm created by their landing. The figures were humanoid by way of insectoid, each about two meters tall, each covered with shiny, chitinous duraplast armor and a helmet that reflected the world around them like polished onyx. The individuals' arms and hands reminded Mahnmut of images he'd seen of a dung beetle's appendages—painfully curved, hooked, barbed, and blackly thorned. Each carried a complex, multibarreled weapon of some sort that looked to weigh at least fifteen kilograms. The figure in the lead paused in the swirling dust and pointed directly at Mahnmut.

"You there, little moravec, is this Mars?" The amplified voice spoke in inter-moon Basic English and arrived via both sound and tightbeam.

"No," said Mahnmut.

"It's not? It's supposed to be Mars."

"It's not," said Mahnmut, sending all this to Orphu. "It's Earth. I think."

The tall soldierly form shook its helmeted head as if this was an unacceptable answer. "What kind of moravec are you? Callistan?"

Mahnmut drew himself up to his full bipedal height. "I'm Mahnmut from Europa, formerly of the exploration submersible *The Dark Lady*. This is Orphu of Io."

"Isn't that a hard-vac moravec?"

"Yes."

"What happened to his eyes, sensors, manipulators and legs? Who cracked his shell like that?"

"Orphu is a war veteran," said Mahnmut.

"We're supposed to report to a Ganymedan named Koros III," said the armored form. "Take us to him."

"He was destroyed," said Mahnmut. "In the line of duty."

The tall black figure hesitated. It looked at the other eight onyx warriors and Mahnmut had the idea they were conferring via tightbeam. The first soldier turned back. "Take us to the Callistan Ri Po then," he ordered.

"Also destroyed," said Mahnmut. "And before we go any further, who are you?"

They're rockvecs, sent Orphu on his private tightbeam channel. "Aren't you rockvecs?" the Ionian asked on the common tightbeam wavelength. It had been so long since Orphu had communicated with anyone except Mahnmut that the smaller moravec was shocked to hear his voice on the common band.

"We prefer to be called Belt moravecs," said the leader, turning to address Orphu's shell. "We should medevac you to a combat repair center, Old Timer." He gestured to some of the other combat moravecs and they began moving toward the Ionian.

"Stop," commanded Orphu, and his voice held enough authority to freeze the tall forms in their booted tracks. "I'll decide when to leave the field. And don't call me Old Timer, or I'll have your gears for garters. Koros III was in charge of this mission. He's dead. Ri Po was second in command. He's dead. That leaves Mahnmut of Europa and me, Orphu of Io, in command. What's your rank, rockvec?"

"Centurion Leader Mep Ahoo, sir."

Mep Ahoo? thought Mahnmut.

"I'm a commander," snapped Orphu. "Is the chain of command clear here, trooper?"

"Yes, sir," said the rockvec.

"Brief us on why you're here and why you think this is Mars," said Orphu in the same tone of absolute command. Mahnmut thought his friend's voice on tightbeam was dipping into the subsonic the bass was cranked so deep. "*Immediately*, Centurion Leader Ahoo."

The rockvec did as he was told, explaining as quickly as he could while more hornet fliers buzzed overhead and hundreds of Trojan warriors came out of the city and slowly advanced up the ridge toward the landing party, shields raised, spears poised. At the same moment, hundreds more Achaeans and Trojans were flowing through the circular portal a few hundred meters to the south, all of them running toward the icy slopes of Olympos visible through the slice taken out of the sky and ground.

Centurion Leader Mep Ahoo was succinct. He confirmed Orphu's earlier statement to Mahnmut—from their discussion when they'd been passing over the Asteroid Belt on their way to Mars—that sixty e-years ago the Ganymedan Koros III had been sent to the Belt by the Pwyll-based moravec Asteague/Che and the Five Moons Consortium. But Koros's mission had been as a diplomat, not as a spy. Spending more than five years in the Belt, hopping from rock to rock and losing most of his Jovian-moravec support team in the process, Koros had negotiated with the belligerant rockvec clan leaders, sharing the Jovian-space moravec scientists' concerns about the rapid terraforming of Mars and the early signs of quantum tunneling activity just detected there. The rockvecs wanted to know who was doing this dangerous QT tunneling—post-humans from Earth? Koros III and the Belt moravecs agreed on the acronym UME's—Unknown Martian Entities.

The rockvecs were already concerned, although more about the visible—and impossible—rapid terraforming of Mars than about the quantum activity, which their technology could not easily detect. Confrontational and bold by nature, the Belt moravecs had already dispatched six expeditionary fleets of spacecraft on the relatively short hop to Mars. None of their ships had returned or survived translation to Mars orbit. Something on the Red Planet, or on what had been the Red Planet until recently—the rockvecs had no idea what—was destroying their fleets before arrival.

Through diplomacy, guile, courage, and some single combat, Koros III had earned the rockvec clan leaders' trust. The Ganeymedan explained the Five Moons Consortium's plan—first, the rockvecs would design and biofacture dedicated warrior-vecs over the next fifty years or so, using their already tough rockvec DNA as a breeding base. The rockvecs would also be responsible for designing and constructing advanced space and atmospheric fighting vehicles. Meanwhile, the more advanced Five Moons moravec scientists and engineers would divert cutting-edge technology from their interstellar program to the building of a quantum-tuneler and wormhole stabilizer of their own. Second, when the time was right and the quantum activity on Mars reached alarming levels, Koros himself would lead a small contingent of moravecs from Jupiter space, its goal to arrive undetected on the Red Planet. Third, once on Mars, Koros III would place the quantum-tuneler at the vertex of the current QT activity, stabilizing not only those quantum tunnels already in use by the UME's, but opening new tunnels to the Asteroid Belt, where other Five Moons'-designed tunneling devices would be waiting for his maser signal before activating.

Fourth, finally, the rockvecs would send their fleets and fighting men through these quantum tunnels to Mars, where they would confront, identify, overpower, subdue, and interrogate the Unidentified Martian Entities and eliminate the threat to the solar system from the excessive quantum activity.

"It sounds simple," said Mahnmut. "Confront, identify, overpower, subdue, and interrogate. But in reality, your group didn't even make it to the right planet."

"Navigating the quantum tunnels was more complicated than expected," said Centurion Leader Mep Ahoo. "Our groups obviously connected to one of the UME's existing tunnels and overshot Mars, arriving . . . here." The chitinous onyx figure looked around. His troopers were raising their heavy weapons as a hundred or so Trojans came onto the crest of the ridge.

"Don't shoot at them," said Mahnmut. "They're our allies."

"Allies?" said the rockvec soldier, his shiny visor turned toward the advancing wall of shields and spears. But in the end he nodded, tight-beamed his troopers, and the complex weapons were lowered.

The Trojans did not lower their weapons.

Luckily, Mahnmut recognized the Trojan commander from the long introductions of captains earlier in the day. In Greek, Mahnmut called out, "Perimus, son of Megas, do not attack. These black fellows are our friends and allies."

The spears and shields stayed high. Archers in the second row had their bows lowered but arrows nocked and the bows at half-pull, ready to lift and fire on command. The rockvecs might feel secure from meter-long barbed arrows dipped in poison, but Mahnmut didn't want to test the strength of his own integument that way.

" 'Friends and allies,' " mocked Perimus. The man's polished bronze helmet—noseguard, cheek flaps, round eyeholes, and low ridge in the back—showed only Perimus' angry gaze, narrow lips, and strong chin. "How can they be 'friends and allies,' little machine, when they aren't even men? For that matter, little toy, how can *you*?"

Mahnmut didn't have a good answer for that. He said, "You saw me with Hector this morning, son of Megas."

"I saw you with man-killing Achilles as well," called the Trojan. The archers had raised their bows now and there were at least thirty arrows aimed at Mahnmut and the rockvecs.

How do I win this guy's trust? Mahnmut tightbeamed Orphu.

Perimus, son of Megas, mused the Ionian. *If we'd let things go the way the* Iliad *said they should, Perimus would be dead in two days—killed by Patroclus along with Autonous, Echeclus, Adrestus, Elasus, Mulius, and Plyartes in one wild melee.*

Well, sent Mahnmut, *we don't have two days, most of the Trojans you mentioned—Autonous, Mulius, and the rest—are standing there right now with shields raised and spears poised, and I don't think Patroclus is going to help us out here, according to Hockenberry, unless Achilles' friend has been swimming back from Indiana. Any ideas on what we can do* now?

Tell them that the rockvecs are attendants, *forged by Hephaestus and summoned by Achilles to help win the war against the gods.*

"Attendants," Mahnmut said, repeating the word in Greek. *I don't know that particular form of the noun—it doesn't mean "servant" or "slave" and . . .*

Just say it, growled Orphu, *before Perimus has them put a shaft through your liver.*

Mahnmut didn't have a liver, but he understood the thrust of Orphu's suggestion.

"Perimus, noble son of Megas," called Mahnmut, "these dark forms are *attendants,* forged by Hephaestus but brought here by Achilles to help us win this war against the gods."

Perimus glowered. "Are you then also an *attendant*?" he demanded.

Say yes, sent Orphu.

"Yes."

Perimus barked at his men and the bows were lowered, the arrows unnocked.

According to Homer, sent Orphu, *"Attendants" are sort of androids created in Hephaestus' forge from human parts and used like robots by the gods and some mortals.*

Are you telling me that the Iliad *has androids and moravecs in it?* demanded Mahnmut.

The Iliad *has everything in it,* said Orphu. To the rockvec leader, Orphu barked, "Centurion Leader Ahoo, did you bring forcefield projectors with you in that ship?"

The tall onyx rockvec clicked to its full height. "Yes, Commander."

"Send a squad into the city—that city, Ilium—and set up a full-strength forcefield to protect it," ordered Orphu. "Set up another to protect the Achaean encampment you see along the coast."

"Full-strength field, sir?" asked the centurion leader. Mahnmut knew that it would probably take the spacecraft's entire fusion reactor's output to power such a field.

"Full-strength," said Orphu. "Able to repel lance, laser, maser, ballistic, cruise, nuclear, thermonuclear, neutron, plasma, antimatter, and arrow attack. These are our allies, Centurion Leader."

"Yes, *sir*." The onyx figure turned and tightbeamed. A dozen more troopers descended the ramp carrying massive projectors. The dark troopers jogged double-time in both directions from the ridge until only Centurion Leader Ahoo remained there next to Mahnmut and Orphu. The landed hornet fliers buzzed into the air and circled, weapons still swiveling.

Perimus walked closer. The crest on the man's polished but battered helmet barely came up to Centurion Leader Ahoo's chiseled chest. Perimus lifted his fist and rapped on the rockvec's duraplast breastplate with his knuckles. "Interesting armor," said the Trojan. He turned back to Mahnmut. "Little attendant, we're going to go join Hector in the fight. Do you want to join us?" He pointed to the huge circle bitten out of the sky and ground to the south. More Trojan and Achaean units were marching—not running, but marching in orderly fashion, chariots and shields gleaming, banners flying—through the quantum portal, their speartips catching Earth's sunlight on this side of the slice, Martian light on the other.

"Yes," said Mahnmut, "I want to join you." To Orphu he tight-beamed, *You going to be okay here, Old Timer?*

I have Centurion Leader Mep Ahoo to protect me, sent the Ionian.

Mahnmut marched next to Perimus down the slope—the thickets there trampled almost flat now by nine years of the ebb and flow of battle—leading the small contingent of Trojans to join Hector. At the bottom of the hill, they paused as an odd figure staggered toward them—a naked, beardless man with mussed hair and slightly wild eyes. He was walking gingerly, picking his way over the stones on bloody feet, and wore only a medallion.

"Hockenberry?" said Mahnmut in English. He doubted his own visual-recognition circuits.

"Present and accounted for," grinned the scholic. "Howdy, Mahnmut." In Greek, he said, "Good afternoon, Perimus, son of Megas. I'm Hockenberry, son of Duane, friend of Hector and Achilles. We met this morning, remember?"

Mahnmut had never seen a live human being naked before this minute, and he hoped it would be a long, long time until he saw a second one. "What happened to you? To your clothes?" he asked.

"It's a long story," said Hockenberry, "but I bet I could condense it and finish it before we march through that hole in the sky over there." To Perimus, he said, "Son of Megas, is there any chance I could get some clothes from your group?"

Perimus obviously recognized Hockenberry now and remembered

how both Achilles and Hector had deferred to him earlier at their inter-rupted captains' conference on Thicket Ridge. He turned and snarled at his men, "Clothes for this lord! The best cape, the newest sandals, the best armor, the most polished greaves, and the cleanest underwear!"

Autonous stepped forward. "We don't have any extra clothes or armor or sandals, noble Perimus."

"*Strip and give him your own immediately!*" bellowed the Trojan com-mander. "But kill the lice first. That's an order."

Ardis

The sky continued to fall all that late afternoon into evening.

Ada had rushed out onto Ardis Hall's long lawn to watch the bloody streaks slash the sky—sonic booms crashing and re-crashing across the wooded hills and river valley—and just stood there as the guests and disciples screamed and overturned tables and ran down the road toward the distant fax pavilion in their panicked eagerness to escape.

Odysseus joined her and they stood there on the grass, a two-person island of immobility in a sea of chaos.

"What is it?" whispered Ada. "What's happening?" There were never fewer than a dozen fiery streaks in the sky, and sometimes the evening sky was all but occluded by the meteors.

"I'm not sure," said the barbarian.

"Does it have something to do with Savi, Harman, and Daeman?"

The bearded man in the tunic looked at her. "Perhaps."

Most of the burning trails scorched the sky and disappeared, but now one—brighter than the others and audible, screeching like a thousand fingernails dragged across glass—burned its way to the eastern horizon and struck, throwing up a billowing cloud of flame. A minute later a terrible sound rolled over them—so much louder and deeper than the fingernail scraping of the meteor's passage that the rumble made Ada's back teeth ache—and then a violent wind came up, knocking leaves off the ancient elm and tumbling most of the tents that had been set up in the meadow just beyond the driveway turnaround.

Ada gripped Odysseus's poweful forearm and clung to it until her fingernails drew blood without her noticing or Odysseus saying anything.

"Do you want to go inside?" he said at last.

"No."

They watched the aerial display for another hour. Most of the guests had fled, running down the road when they could find no available droshky or carriole or voynix to pull them, but about seventy disciples had stayed, standing with Ada and Odysseus on the sloping yard. Several more objects struck the earth, the last one more violent than the first. All of the windows on Ardis Hall's north side shattered, shards raining down in the evening light.

"I'm so glad that Hannah is safe in the firmary right now," said Ada.

Odysseus looked at her and said nothing.

It was the man named Petyr who came out of the manor at sunset to tell them that the servitors were down.

"What do you mean, 'down'?" demanded Ada.

"Down," repeated Petyr. "On the ground. Not working. Broken."

"Nonsense," said Ada. "Servitors don't break." Even with the meteor shower brighter now with the sun setting, she turned her back on the view and led Odysseus and Petyr back into Ardis Hall, stepping carefully across the broken glass and shattered plaster.

Two servitors were on the floor of the kitchen, one more in the upstairs bedroom. Their communicators were silent, their manipulators limp, the little white-gloved hands dangling. None responded to proddings, commands, or kicks. The three humans went out back and found two more servitors where they had fallen on the yard.

"Have you ever seen a servitor fail?" asked Odysseus.

"Never," said Ada.

More disciples gathered. "Is this the end of the world?" asked the young woman named Peaen. It wasn't clear who she was addressing.

Finally Odysseus spoke over the sky roar. "It depends on what's falling." He pointed his powerful, stubby finger at the e- and p-rings just visible behind the meteor storm pyrotechnics. "If it's just some of the big accelerators and quantum devices up there, we should survive this. If it's one of the four major asteroids where the posts used to live . . . well, it could be the end of the world . . . at least as we know it."

"What's an asteroid?" asked Petyr, ever the curious disciple.

Odysseus shook his head, waving the question away.

"When will we know?" asked Ada.

The older bearded man sighed. "A few hours. Almost certainly by tomorrow evening."

"I never really thought about the world ending," said Ada. "But I certainly never imagined it ending by fire."

"No," said Odysseus, "if it ends for us, it'll end by ice."

The circle of men and women looked at him.

"Nuclear winter," muttered the Greek. "If one of those asteroids—or even a big enough chunk of one—hits the ocean or land, it'll throw enough garbage in the atmosphere to drop the temperature by sixty or seventy degrees Fahrenheit in a few hours. Maybe more. The skies will cloud over. The storm will start as rain and then turn to snow for months, maybe centuries. This planetary tropical hothouse you've grown accustomed to in the last millennium and a half will become a playground for glaciers."

A smaller meteor ripped low in the northern sky, striking somewhere in the forests there. The air smelled of smoke and Ada could see distant flames in all directions. She took a second to think about how unknown this whole world was to her. What was north of Ardis Hall in the forests there? She'd never walked more than a few miles from Ardis or any other faxnode, and then always with an escort of voynix for protection.

"Where are the voynix?" she asked suddenly.

No one knew. Ada and Odysseus circled Ardis Hall, checked the outer fields and driveway and lower meadow where the voynix usually stood waiting or walking perimeter duty. None were there. Nobody in the small group on the lawn remembered seeing any even before the meteor shower began.

"You finally frightened them away for good," Ada said to Odysseus, trying to make a joke.

He shook his head again. "This isn't good."

"I thought you didn't like voynix," said Ada. "You cut one of mine in half your first day here."

"They're up to something," said Odysseus. "Their time may have come 'round at last."

"What?"

"Nothing, Ada *Uhr*." He took her hand and patted it. *Like a father*, thought Ada and, stupidly, shockingly, began to cry. She kept thinking about Harman and how confused and angry she'd been when he'd told her he wanted to help her choose him as a father for her child, and how he wanted the child to *know* that he was the father. What had seemed an absurd idea—almost obscene—now seemed so very, very sensible to Ada. She gripped Odysseus' hand tightly and wept.

"Look!" cried the girl named Peaen.

A less brilliant meteor was descending right toward Ardis, but at a shallower angle than all the others. It still trailed a fiery trail against the darkening sky—the sun had finally set—but this meteor tail looked more like real flames than screaming, heated plasma.

The glowing object circled once and seemed to fall out of the sky, crashing with audible impact somewhere beyond the line of trees above the upper meadow.

"That was close," said Ada. Her heart was pounding.

"That wasn't a meteor," said Odysseus. "Stay here. I'm going to walk up there and check it out."

"I'm going with you," said Ada. When the bearded man opened his mouth to argue, she said simply, "It's my land."

They walked up the hill together into the deepening twilight, the sky above them still alive with silent flame.

The flames and smoke were visible just beyond the edge of the upper meadow, just past the line of trees, but Ada and Odysseus didn't have to go searching in the darkness there. Ada saw them first—two bearded, emaciated men walking toward them from the forest. One of the men was naked, skin glowing palely in the dim twilight, ribs visible from fifty feet away, and he appeared to be caring a bald, blue-suited child in his arms. The other skeletal, bearded man was dressed in what Ada immediately recognized as a green thermskin suit, but the suit itself was so torn and filthy she could barely see the color of the material. This man's right arm hung uselessly at his side, palm forward, and his bare wrist and hand were dull red with blood. Both men were staggering, struggling to stay upright and to keep moving.

Odysseus drew his short sword halfway from its scabbard on his belt.

"No," cried Ada, pushing Odysseus' hand and sword down. "No, it's Harman! It's Daeman!" She ran toward them through the high grass.

Harman started to pitch forward as she approached and Odysseus sprinted the last twenty paces, catching Harman's burden as the man fell forward. Daeman also went to his knees

"It's Hannah," said Odysseus, laying the semiconscious young woman in the grass and setting his fingers on her neck to find her pulse.

"Hannah?" repeated Ada. This woman had no hair or eyelashes, but the eyes under flickering eyelids were Hannah's.

"Hi, Ada," said the girl on the ground.

Ada went to one knee and crouched next to the fallen Harman, helping him roll over onto his back. He tried to smile up at her. Her lover's face was bruised and cut under the whiskers, his cheeks and forehead all but covered with caked blood. His eyes were sunken, skin an unhealthy white, and his cheekbones too sharp above his beard. Harman shivered with fever and his eyes burned at her. His teeth chattered when he spoke. "I'm all right, Ada. God, I'm glad to see you."

Daeman was in worse shape. Ada couldn't believe that these two battered, bloodied, emaciated men were the same two who had set forth so casually a month earlier. She put one arm under Daeman's arm to keep him from pitching facefirst into the ground. He swayed on his knees.

"Where's Savi?" asked Odysseus.

Harman shook his head sadly. He seemed too tired to speak again.

"Caliban," said Daeman. His voice sounded twenty years older to Ada's ear.

The worst of the meteor storm had abated, the audible impacts and more fiery falls having moved off to the east. A few dozen minor streaks crossed the zenith west to east almost gently, looking more like August's annual Perseid showers than the violence of earlier in the evening.

"Let's get them back to the house," said Odysseus. He stood, lifted Hannah easily in both arms, and gave his right shoulder to Daeman to lean on as he rose. Ada helped Harman to his knees and then to his feet, putting his right arm over her shoulder and holding much of his weight as they all headed down the darkened meadow toward the lights of Ardis Hall where Odysseus' disciples and Ada's friends had lighted candles.

"That arm looks bad," Odysseus said to Daeman as the four of them and the unconscious girl descended. "I'll cut the thermskin off and take a look at it when we get in the light."

Ada used her free hand to reach and gently touch Daeman's bloodied arm, and the gaunt man moaned and almost swooned. Only Odysseus' strong shoulder and Ada's right hand slid quickly to the small of his back kept Daeman upright. The young man's eyelids fluttered for a few seconds, but then he focused, smiled at her, and kept walking.

"These are serious injuries," said Ada, feeling close to tears for the second time that evening. "You should both be faxed to the firmary."

She didn't understand at all when both men started laughing, hesitantly and painfully at first, more coughing than laughing for a moment, but then the barking changing to pure laughter, increasing in volume and sincerity until the two battered, bearded men sounded almost irritatingly drunk in the throes of their own private amusement.

63

Olympos

Olympus Mons, the tallest volcano on Mars, rises more than seventeen miles above the surrounding plains and above the new ocean at its base. The volcano, at its base, spreads more than 400 miles in diameter. With its green summit peaking above 87,000 feet, Olympus Mons is almost three times the height of Mount Everest on Earth. The sides of the mountain, white from snow and ice in the daytime, are glowing almost blood red this evening from the glare of the setting Martian sun.

The ragged cliffs here at the northeast base of Olympus Mons sweep up vertically for 17,000 feet. On this particular Martian evening, the long shadow of the volcano stretches east almost to the line of the three Tharsis volcanoes on the hazy horizon.

The high-speed crystal elevator that used to snake its way up this side of Olympos has been sliced in two not far above the cliffs, and sliced as cleanly as if cut by a guillotine. A powerful seven-layer forcefield generated by Zeus himself—the *aegis*—shields the entire Olympus Mons massif from attack and shimmers now in the red light of evening.

Just beyond the cliffs, near where the base of Olympos comes close to the northern ocean terraformed here just a century and a half earlier, a thousand or more gods have come down to gather for war. A hundred golden chariots, each powered by invisible forces but visibly pulled by powerful steeds, fly air cover thousands of feet above the masses of gods and golden armor assembled on the high plains and shingled beaches below.

Zeus and Hera are at the forefront of this immortal army, each figure twenty feet tall, husband and wife both resplendent in armor and shields and weapons hammered into shape by Hephaestus and other craft-skilled gods; even Hera's and Zeus's high helmets are forged of pure gold, laced with microcircuits, and reinforced by advanced alloys. Athena and Apollo are temporarily missing from the forefront of this divine phalanx, but the other gods and goddesses are here—

Aphrodite is here, still beautiful in her war gear. Her war helmet is studded with precious stones; her tiny bow is made to shoot crystal arrows with hollow tips filled with poison gas.

Ares is here, grinning beneath the brow of his red-crested war helmet, happy in anticipation of the unprecedented bloodletting soon to come. He carries Apollo's silver bow and a quiver full of heat-seeking arrows. Any target he shoots at, he will kill or destroy.

Poseidon is here—the Earth-Shaker, huge and darkly powerful, dressed in war gear for the first time in millennia. Ten men, even including Achilles, could not lift the massive axe Poseidon carries in his left hand.

Hades is here—darker in countenance, mood, and armor than even Poseidon, his red eyes gleaming from the depths of his battle helmet's deep sockets. Persephone stands by her lord, armored in lapis lazuli, a barbed titanium trident held firm in her long, pale fingers.

Hermes is here—thin and deadly, wrapped in his red-insect's armor, poised to quantum teleport into battle, kill, and leap away before mortal eye can record his arrival, much less the carnage he will leave behind.

Thetis is here, her divine eyes red from weeping, but dutifully clad in full-scaled war gear, ready to kill her son, Achilles, if and when Zeus wills it so.

Triton is here—bold in layers of green-black armor; this is the forgotten Satyros of the old worlds—terror of the conch-horn and rapist of girls and boys, the god who took pleasure in discarding children's bodies in the depths after he'd had his pleasure with them.

Artemis is here—gold-armored goddess of the hunt, her war-bow in her hand, ready and eager to spill gallons of human blood as the first step toward avenging the injury to her beloved brother, Apollo.

Hephaestus is here—armored in flames and ready to bring the torch to the mortal enemy.

All the gods except healing Apollo and healing Athena are here—row upon row of giant armored silent figures drawn up beneath the shadows of the cliffs. Above them, more gods and goddesses circle in their flying chariots. Above everything, the shimmering *aegis*—both offensive and defensive weapon—shimmers and builds its energies.

In the no-man's-land beyond the gods, just beyond where the *aegis* shimmer slices into soil and stone and continues downward, curving in a sphere deep toward the center of Mars, the bodies of the two cerberids lie. Two-headed dog-things more than twenty feet long with teeth of chrome steel and gas chromatograph mass spectrometers in their snouts, the cerberids sprawl dead where Achilles and Hector each killed one upon the heroes' arrival at Olympos only hours earlier.

A hundred feet beyond the cerberids are the burned remnants of the old scholic barracks. Beyond the barracks are the armies of humankind, a hundred and twenty thousand strong this evening.

Hector's forces are drawn up in ranks and rows on the inland side, forty thousand of Ilium's boldest fighters. Paris has been ordered to stay behind in Ilium, tasked by his older brother with the heavy responsibility of protecting their homes and loved ones in the ancient city—domed now by the moravec forcefield, but more securely protected, Hector has said, by bronze spearpoints and human courage. But the other captains and their contingents are here.

Near Hector stands the Trojan supreme commander's trusted brother, Deiphobus, in charge of ten thousand handpicked spearmen. Nearby is Aeneas, forging his new destiny here, no longer favored by the Fates. Behind Aeneas' contingent of fighters is noble Glaucus, at the head of his ranks of chariots and 11,000 wild Lycians ready to fight.

Ascanius from Ascania, co-commander of the Phrygians, is here, the young captain fully clad in bronze and leather and eager for glory. His 4,200 Ascanians are eager to spill immortal ichor, if immortal blood is not available.

Behind the Trojan fighters, too old and too valued to lead men into combat but dressed in battle gear this day and ready to die if such is the universe's will, are clustered the kings and counselors of Ilium—first King Priam himself, wearing legendary armor hammered from the metal of an ancient meteor, then old Antenor, father of many Trojan heroes—most of whom have already fallen in battle.

Near Antenor stand Priam's honored brothers Lampus and Clytius, and gray-bearded Hicetaon—who until this day had honored Ares, the god of war, above all other beings—and behind Hicetaon those most respected of Trojan elders, Panthous and Thymoetes. Standing with these old men today, eyes always on her husband, dressed in red as if she's become a living banner of blood and loss, is beautiful Andromache, Hector's wife, mother of the murdered Scamandrius, the babe known to the loving residents of Ilium as Astyanax—"Lord of the City."

At the center of this three-mile-long human battle line, commanding more than 80,000 battle-tested Achaeans, towers golden Achilles, son of Peleus, killer of men. He is said to be—save for one secret weakness—

invulnerable. This evening, in full battle dress and flushed with the superhuman energy of almost inhuman rage, he looks immortal. The spot
to Achilles' right has been left empty to honor the memory of his dearest friend and battle-comrade, Patroclus, said to have been savagely
murdered by Pallas Athena less than twenty-four hours earlier.

Behind and to the right of Achilles is the surprising troika of
Agamemnon, Menelaus, and Odysseus. The two sons of Atreides are
still bruised from their single combat with Achilles, and Menelaus' left
arm is too injured for him to carry a shield, but the two deposed leaders
have found it necessary to be with their captains and men on this day.
Odysseus, apparently lost in thought, is looking out over the human and
immortal battle lines and scratching his beard.

Spread through the rest of the Achaean ranks, in chariots and on foot,
always at the head of their men, are the surviving Greek heroes of nine
years of bitter war—Diomedes, still dressed in his lion's skin and carrying a club larger than most men; Big Ajax, bulwark of the Achaeans, towering over his entire line of warriors, and Little Ajax, leading his
professional killers from Locris. Within a rock's throw of these heroes
stands the great spearman, Idomeneus, at the head of his legendary Cre-
tan warriors, and nearby, tall in his chariot, Meriones, eager to ride into
combat next to Big Ajax's half-brother, the master archer Teucer.

On the Achaeans' right flank, nearest the ocean, row upon row of armored men turn their crested helmets to look to their leader and the oldest Achaean captain present this day, wily Nestor, breaker of horses.
Nestor has placed himself out ahead of all others there on the right flank,
red-caped and visible in his four-horsed chariot, so he will be the first on
this flank to fall or the first to fight his way through the battle line of the
immortals. In nearby chariots, obviously eager to ride into combat with
their father, are Nestor's sons, Antilochus—Achilles' good friend—and
Antilochus' taller and more handsome brother, Thrasymedes.

A hundred more captains are here this day, each carrying his proud
name and his father's proud name, together leading tens of thousands
more men, each of those men holding noble names and complex histories, each man carrying their fathers' proud names into battle to glory
and life, or taking those names down with them to the House of Death
this day.

To the right of the massed Achaeans, spread out along the shore in no
particular order, standing silent and green, are several thousand zeks—
Little Green Men who have poured out of their barges and feluccas and
flimsy sailing ships from Ocean Tethys and the Valles Marineris Inland
Sea and who stand witness here this day for reasons known only to

themselves, and perhaps to their avatar Prospero or the unmet god called Setebos. They stand mute along the softly crashing line of surf, and neither the Greeks nor the Trojans nor the immortal gods have yet interfered with them.

A half mile or so out to sea behind the *zeks*, sails catching the rosy Martian sunset and oars reflecting the golden sea glow, range more than a hundred Achaean ships of the line. Now the sails are slackened, the oars are shipped, and shields and spears line the ships' sides. Crests of yellow, red, purple, and blue and the gleaming tops of helmets are all that can be seen of the more than 3,000 Achaean fighters on those ships. In the space between the massed ships, barbed black fins are cutting through the sun-gilded seas. Hinted at now only by their periscopes and the tops of their black-metal sails, three Belt moravec ballistic missile submarines cruise through the Martian sea.

Spread thinly for two miles behind the Trojans and Achaeans on land are massed the Belt moravec infantry—27,000 black-armored, beetle-armed ground troopers carrying weapons both heavy and light. Energy and ballistic rockvec artillery batteries are arrayed as far back as fifteen kilometers behind the front lines, their projectors and tubes aimed at Olympos and the massed immortals. Above all the human and moravec lines circle and dart 116 hornet-fighter aircraft, some tuned to stealth, others still as boldly black as when first sighted earlier in the day. In orbit overhead, so the Belt moravecs have reported, are 65 combat space-craft circling Mars in orbits ranging from just a hair above the Martian atmosphere to several million miles out beyond hurtling Phobos and Deimos. The Belt moravec military commander on the ground has re-ported to the Europan moravec Mahnmut, who has translated to Achilles and Hector, that all grades of bombs, missiles, forcefields, and energy weapons on all these ships are cocked and locked. The report means nothing to the heroes and they have disregarded it.

On the same flat area near Achilles, to the right of Odysseus and the Atrides but standing apart, are Mahnmut, Orphu, and Hockenberry. Mahnmut had taken one look at the gathering armies earlier in the af-ternoon and, with the Trojan commander Perimus' help, immediately commandeered a chariot with which to fetch Orphu through the quan-tum tunnel slice, dragging the levitated Ionian behind the chariot—in Orphu's own words—like a "dinged-up U-Haul trailer." Mahnmut didn't know what that was exactly—his Lost Age colloquial data banks were not as obsessively overflowing as Orphu's—but he promised him-self he'd look it up someday. If he survived.

Scholic Thomas Hockenberry, Ph.D., is dressed in a Trojan captain's cape, armor, and clothes, and although he seems thrilled to be witnessing all this, he also appears to have some trouble standing still. While the thousands of warriors up to the level of noble Achilles wait almost motionless for the final stragglers in each army—human and immortal—to assemble, Hockenberry is shuffling from foot to foot.

"Something wrong?" whispers Mahnmut in English.

"I think something's crawling in my shorts," Hockenberry whispers back.

The armies are assembled. The silence is uncanny—there is no noise from either side except for the slow hiss of distant waves rolling in to the pebbled beach, the occasional whinny of a horse harnessed to a battle chariot, the soft sound of Martian breeze through the cliff rocks of Olympos, the air-hiss of flying chariots circling and the higher buzz of hornet fighters, the occasional inadvertent soft clank of bronze on bronze as some soldier shifts position, and the powerful, omnipresent negative sound of tens of thousands of anxious men trying to remember to breathe normally.

Zeus steps forward, passing through the *aegis* like a giant stepping through a rippling waterfall.

Achilles walks out into no-man's-land to face the Father of the Gods.

"DO YOU HAVE ANYTHING TO SAY BEFORE YOU AND YOUR SPECIES DIE?" says Zeus, his tone conversational but so amplified that it carries to the farthest reaches of the field, even to the men on the Greek ships at sea.

Achilles pauses, looks over his shoulder at the masses of men behind him, turns back, looks past Zeus toward Olympos and the masses of gods in front of him, and then crooks his neck to look up again at towering Zeus.

"Surrender now," says Achilles, "and we'll spare your goddesses's lives so they can be our slaves and courtesans."

64

Ardis Hall

Daeman slept for two days and two nights, waking fitfully only when Ada fed him broth or Odysseus bathed him. He woke again briefly the afternoon that Odysseus shaved him, drawing a straight razor through his lathered beard, but Daeman was too tired to speak or listen to language. Nor did the sleeping man pay any attention to the roars in the sky as the meteors returned the next night and then the next. He didn't wake when a small bit of something traveling several thousand miles per hour plowed into the field behind the house, exactly where Odysseus had taught for weeks. The impact excavated a crater fifteen feet across and nine feet deep and broke every remaining window on Ardis Hall.

Daeman awoke mid-morning of the third day. Ada was sitting on the edge of his bed—her bed, it turned out—and Odysseus was leaning against the door frame, arms crossed.

"Welcome back, Daeman *Uhr*," Ada said softly.

"Thank you, Ada *Uhr*," said Daeman. His voice was hoarse and it seemed to him that he had to use an inordinate amount of energy just to croak a few words. "Harman? Hannah?"

"Both better," said Ada. Daeman had never noticed how perfectly green the young woman's eyes were. "Harman is out of bed and downstairs eating this morning, and Hannah is learning to walk again. Right now she's on the front lawn, in the sun."

Daeman nodded and closed his eyes. He had the overwhelming urge to keep them closed and to drift back into dreams and sleep. It hurt less there and right now his right arm ached and burned terribly. Suddenly he opened his eyes and pulled the covers off that arm, filled with a terrible certainty that they had amputated the limb while he slept and that all he was feeling was phantom pain from a phantom limb.

The arm was red, swollen, scarred, the wound from Caliban's terrible bite stitched together with heavy thread, but the arm was there. Daeman tried to move it, to wiggle his fingers. The pain made him gasp, but the fingers had moved, the arm had lifted a bit. He dropped it back onto the sheet and gasped for a while.

"Who did that?" he asked a moment later. "The stitches? Servitors?"

Odysseus walked closer to the bed. "I did the stitching," said the barrel-chested barbarian.

"The servitors don't work anymore," said Ada. "Anywhere. The faxnodes still operate, so we're hearing from everywhere—servitors out of order, the voynix gone."

Daeman frowned at this, trying to understand and failing. Harman entered the room, using a walking stick as a cane. Daeman saw that the older man had kept his beard, although it looked as if he'd trimmed it. He sat on a chair next to the bed and gripped Daeman's left arm. Daeman closed his eyes for a minute and just returned the tight grip. When he opened his eyes, they were watering. *Fatigue,* he thought.

"The meteor storm is letting up, a little less fierce each evening," said Harman. "But there have been casualties. Deaths. More than a hundred people died in Ulanbat alone."

"Deaths?" repeated Daeman. The word had not held real meaning for a long, long time.

"You people had to learn about burials again from scratch," said Odysseus. "No faxing up to a happy eternity as immortal post-humans in the e- and p-rings any longer. People are burying their dead and trying to tend to the injured."

"Paris Crater?" managed Daeman. "My mother?"

"She's well," said Ada. "That city wasn't hit. We have runners coming every day with news. She sent a letter, Daeman—she's afraid to fax until things settle down. A lot of people are. With servitors and voynix gone and the power off everywhere, most people don't want to travel unless they absolutely have to."

Daeman nodded. "Why is the power off but the faxnodes still working? Where are the voynix? What's going on?"

"We don't know," said Harman. "But the meteor shower didn't include . . . what did Prospero call it? . . . a Species Extinction Event. We can be glad for that."

"Yes," said Daeman, but what he was thinking was—*So Prospero and Caliban and Savi's death were real—it wasn't all a dream?* He moved his right arm again and the pain answered the question.

Hannah came in wearing a simple white shift. There seemed to be a slight fuzz on her scalp. Her face looked more human and alive in every way. She moved to Daeman's bedside, took care not to touch his arm, and bent over and kissed him firmly on the lips. "Thank you, Daeman. Thank you," she said when the kiss was finished. She handed him a tiny forget-me-not she'd picked in the yard and he took it clumsily in his left hand.

"You're welcome," said Daeman. "I liked that kiss." He had. It was as if he—Daeman, the world's most eager womanizer—had never been kissed before.

"This is interesting," said Hannah, unballing a turin cloth from her other hand. "I found it down by the old oak table, but it doesn't work anymore. I tried two others. Nothing. Even the turins don't work now."

"Or maybe the Greek and Trojan battle drama is finished," said Harman, holding the embroidered circuits on the cloth to his forehead and then tossing the cloth aside. "Perhaps the turin's story is over."

Odysseus was looking out the window at the blue sky and green lawn, but now he turned back toward the little gathering. "I don't think so," he said. "I suspect that the real war has just begun."

"Do you know anything about the turin drama?" asked Hannah. "I thought you said you never went under the cloth."

Odysseus shrugged. "Savi and I distributed the turin cloths almost ten years ago. I brought the prototype from . . . far away."

"Why?" asked Daeman.

Odysseus opened his hand. "The war was coming. Human beings here on earth had to learn something about war, its terror and its beauty. And they had to learn something about those people in the tale—Achilles, Hector, the others. Even me."

"Why?" asked Hannah.

"Because the war *is* coming," said Odysseus.

"We're not a part of it," said Ada.

Odysseus folded his arms. "You will be. You're not on the front lines yet, but those battle lines are coming this way. You'll be part of this conflict whether you want to be or not."

"How can we take part?" asked Ada. "We don't know how to fight. Or even want to learn how."

"About sixty of the young men and women who've stayed here will know a bit about fighting in a few weeks time," said Odysseus. "Whether they want to fight when the time comes will be up to them. As it always is." He pointed to Harman. "Believe it or not, your sonie's fixable. I've been working on it and may have it in the air in a week or ten days."

"I don't want to see fighting," said Ada. "I don't want to be in a war."

"No," said Odysseus. "You're right not to."

Ada lowered her face as if to fight back tears. When she put her closed hand on the bed, Daeman set his fingers next to hers and handed her Hannah's forget-me-not. Then he drifted off to sleep.

He awoke in darkness and moonlight with a shape sitting next to the bed. *Caliban!* Daeman instinctively lifted his right arm, folding his right hand into a fist, and the pain set off lights behind his eyes.

"Easy," said Harman, leaning across him to straighten the bandaged arm. "Easy, Daeman."

Daeman was gasping, trying not to vomit from the pain. "I thought you were . . ."

"I know," said Harman.

Daeman sat up in bed. "Do you think he's dead?"

The shadow-man shook his head. "I don't know. I've been wondering . . . thinking about it. About both of them."

"Both of them?" said Daeman. "You mean Savi as well?"

"No . . . I mean, yes, I think about her a lot . . . but I was thinking about Prospero. The hologram of Prospero who said it was only an echo of a shadow or whatever."

"What about it?"

"I think it *was* Prospero," whispered Harman. He leaned closer. "I think he was imprisoned somehow on the post-humans' asteroid city—what the Prospero holo called 'my isle'—just as Caliban was imprisoned there."

"By whom?" said Daeman.

Harman sat back and sighed. "I don't know. These days I don't know a damned thing."

Daeman nodded. "It took us a long time to learn enough to realize that none of us knows a damned thing, didn't it, Harman?"

The older man laughed. But when he spoke again, his whispered tone was serious. "I'm worried that we freed them."

"Freed them?" whispered Daeman. He'd been hungry a second before, ravenous, but now his belly felt filled with icewater. "Caliban and Prospero."

"Yes."

"Or maybe we killed them," said Daeman, voice hard.

"Yes." Harman rose and clasped the younger man's shoulder. "I'm going to go and let you get some sleep. Thank you, Daeman."

"For what?"

"Thank you," repeated Harman. He left the room.

Daeman lay back on the pillows, exhausted, but sleep didn't come. He listened to night sounds coming through the broken window—crickets, night birds he couldn't name, frogs croaking in the small pond behind the house, the rustle of leaves in the night breeze—and he found that he was grinning.

If Caliban's alive, it's a damned shame. But I'm alive as well. I'm alive.

He slept then, a clean and dreamless sleep that lasted until Ada awoke him an hour after dawn with his first real breakfast in five weeks.

Four days later and Daeman was walking in the gardens alone on a cool but beautiful evening when Ada, Harman, Hannah, Odysseus, Petyr, and the young woman named Peaen came down the hill to find him.

"The sonie's fixed," said Odysseus. "Or at least it can fly. Want to watch its test flight?"

Daeman shrugged. "Not especially. But I do want to know what you're going to do with it."

Odysseus glanced at Petyr, Peaen, and Harman. "First, I'm going to do some reconnaissance," he said. "See what the meteor damage is in the surrounding area, see if the machine will carry me all the way to the coast and back."

"And if it doesn't?" asked Harman.

Odysseus shrugged. "I'll walk home."

"Where's home?" asked Daeman. "And how long will it take for you to get there, Odysseus *Uhr*?"

Odysseus smiled at that, but there was great sadness in his eyes. "If you only knew," he said softly. "If you only knew." Trailed by his two young disciples and Hannah, the barbarian walked back up the hill toward the house.

Harman and Ada strolled with Daeman.

"What's he up to?" Daeman asked Harman. "Really?"

"He's going to find the voynix," said Harman.

"And then what?"

"I don't know." Harman didn't need a cane any longer, but he'd said that he'd gotten used to the walking stick and now he used it to whack a weed growing among the flowers.

"Servitors used to weed the garden," said Ada. "I try, but I'm so busy with the meals and laundry and everything . . ."

Harman laughed. "It's hard to get good help these days," he said.

Harman put his arm around Ada's waist. The young woman looked at him with a gaze that Daeman couldn't interpret, but knew was important.

"I lied," Harman said to Daeman. "You know and I know that Odysseus is going to attack the voynix, stop them from doing whatever they're planning to do."

"Yes," said Daeman. "I know."

"He'll use that war to prepare his disciples for what he considers the real war," said Harman, looking up at the white manor house on the hill. "He's trying to teach us how to fight before the real battle arrives. He says we'll know it—that the war will come like whirling spheres, opening holes in the sky, bringing us to new worlds and new worlds to us."

"I know," said Daeman. "I've heard him say that."

"He's crazy," said Harman.

"No," said Daeman. "He isn't."

"Are you going to war with him?" asked Harman, sounding as if he'd asked himself this question many times.

"Not against the voynix," said Daeman. "Not unless I have to. I have another battle to fight first."

"I know," said Harman. "I know." He kissed Ada, said, "I'll see you up at the house," and walked up the hill alone, still limping slightly.

Daeman found himself suddenly out of energy. There was a wooden bench here with a view of the lower lawn and the evening-shadowed river valley, and he sat on it with relief. Ada sat next to him.

"Harman understood what you were talking about," she said, "but I don't. What battle do you have to fight first?"

Daeman shrugged, embarrassed to talk about it.

"Daeman?" Her voice suggested that she was going to sit here on the bench until he spoke, and he didn't have the energy to stand up and walk away at the moment.

"There's a blue searchlight rising into the night at a place called Jerusalem," he said at last, "and in that light are trapped more than nine thousand of Savi's people. Nine thousand Jews. Whatever Jews are."

Ada looked at him, not understanding. Daeman realized that she'd not heard this part of their story yet. They were all slowly relearning the fine art of storytelling—it filled the candlelit evenings with something other than washing dishes.

"Before Odysseus' promised war gets here," said Daeman, his voice soft but determined, "before I have no choice but to fight in some huge struggle I don't understand, I'm going to go get those nine thousand people out of that goddamned blue light."

"How?" asked Ada.

Daeman laughed. It was an easy, unselfconscious laugh, something he'd learned in the last two months. "I have no fucking idea," he said.

He struggled to his feet, allowed Ada to steady him, and they walked side by side up the hill toward Ardis Hall. Some of the disciples were lighting the lanterns at the outside table already, although it was still an hour before their evening meal. It was Daeman's turn to help cook tonight, and he was trying to remember what course he was in charge of. Salad, he hoped.

"Daeman?" Ada had stopped and was looking at him.

He stopped and returned her gaze, knowing that the young woman would love Harman forever and somehow feeling happy about it. Maybe it was the wounds and fatigue, but Daeman no longer wanted to have sex with every female he met. Of course, he realized, he hadn't met many new females since the meteor storm.

"Daeman, how did you do it?" asked Ada.

"Do what?"

"Kill Caliban."

"I'm not sure I killed him," said Daeman.

"But you *beat* him," said the young woman, her voice almost fierce. "How?"

"I had a secret weapon," said Daeman. He saw the truth of what he was saying even as he said it.

"What?" asked Ada. The evening shadows were long and soft on the sloping lawn around them, the evening sky gentle above Ardis Hall, but Daeman could see dark clouds gathering on the horizon behind her.

"Rage," he said at last. "Rage."

Indiana, 1200 B.C.

About three weeks after the start of the war to end all wars—no kidding—I use my gold medallion to QT to the opposite side of the world. I had promised Nightenhelser I'd come back for him and I like to keep my promises when I can.

I'd left in the middle of the night Ilium–Olympos time, stepping out of a conference in one of the new blastproof tents where Achilles now meets with his surviving captains, and then just QTing away on a whim—knowing that all such personal quantum teleportation will be a memory soon—and it's a shock when I pop onto a grassy hillside on a sunny morning in prehistoric North America. There isn't much grass growing around Ilium these days and none on the bloody plains of Mars.

I wander down the hill to the stream, then cross over into the woods, blinking at the sunlight and relative silence here. There are no explosions, no shouts of dying men, no gods teleporting in amid the violence of screaming men and horses. For a minute or so, I worry about any Indians that might be around, but then I laugh at myself. I don't boast impact armor these days, nor do I have a magical Hades Helmet or a morphing bracelet, but the bronze and duraplast armor I'm wearing has been tested. And I know how to use the sword on my belt and the bow over my shoulder now. Of course, if I meet Patroclus, and if he's managed to arm himself, and if he holds a grudge—and which of these Achaean heroes doesn't?—I wouldn't wager a lot of money on my chances.

Fuck it. As Achilles—or maybe it's Centurion Leader Mep Ahoo—likes to say, "No guts, no glory."

"Nightenhelser!" I shout into the forest. "Keith!"

For all my bellowing, it takes me an hour to find him, and I do so only by blundering into the Indian village in a clearing about half a mile from where I'd QT'd in. There are no tipis in this village, only rough huts made of bent branches, leaves, and what looks to be sod. A campfire is burning in the center of the six-wigwam village. Suddenly dogs are barking, women are shouting and scooping up kids, and six male Native Americans are drawing primitive bows and nocking arrows at me.

I draw my beautiful cedar bow, handcrafted by artisans in distant Argos, nock my beautiful handmade arrow in one fluid, well-practiced move, and aim at them, ready to bring them all down with my shafts in their livers while their silly sharpened sticks bounce off my armor. Unless they get me in the face or eye. Or throat. Or . . .

The ex-scholic Nightenhelser, dressed in the same animal skins as the leaner Indian warriors, rushes between us and shouts syllables at the men. The Indians look sullen but lower their bows. I lower mine.

Nightenhelser stalks up to me. "God damn it, Hockenberry, what do you think you're doing?"

"Rescuing you?"

"Don't move," he orders. He barks more odd syllables at the men and then says to them in classic Greek, "And please wait for me before serving the roast dog. I'll be back in a minute."

He takes my elbow and walks me back toward the stream, out of sight of the village.

"Greek?" I say. "Roast dog?"

He answers only the first part of the question. "Their language is complex, hard for me to learn. I'm finding it easier to teach them all Greek."

I laugh then, but mostly at the sudden image I have of archaeologists three or four or five thousand years from now, digging up this prehistoric Native American village in Indiana and finding potsherds with Greek images from the Trojan War etched on them.

"What?" says Nightenhelser.

"Nothing."

We sit on some less-than-comfortable boulders on the far side of the stream and talk for a few minutes.

"How goes the war?" asks Nightenhelser. I notice that he's lost some weight. He looks healthy and happy. I realize that I must look as tired and grimy as I feel.

"Which war?" I say. "We have a whole new one."

Always a man of few words, Nightenhelser raises his eyebrows and waits.

I tell him a bit about the ultimate war, leaving out some of the worst things. I don't want to cry or start shaking in front of my old fellow scholic.

Nightenhelser listens for a few minutes and then says, "Are you shitting me?"

"I shit thee not," I say. "Would I make this up? *Could* I make this up?"

"No, you're right," says Nightenhelser. "You've never shown the imagination to make up something like this."

I blink at that but stay quiet.

"What are you going to do?" he asks.

I shrug. "Rescue you?"

Nightenhelser chuckles. "It sounds like you need rescuing more than I do. Why would I go back to what you just described?"

"Professional curiosity?" I suggest.

"My specialty was the *Iliad*," says Nightenhelser. "It sounds as if you've left all that far behind." He shakes his head and rubs his cheeks. "How can anyone lay siege to Olympos?"

"Achilles and Hector found a way," I say. "I need to get back. Are you coming with me? I can't promise I'll ever be able to QT this way again."

The big scholic shakes his head. "I'll stay here."

"You realize," I say slowly, shifting to Greek in case his English has gotten rusty, "that you're not safe here. From the war, I mean. If things go badly, the entire Earth will . . ."

"I know. I was listening," says Nightenhelser. "I'll stay here."

We both stand. I touch the QT medallion, then drop my hand. "You've got a woman here," I say.

Nightenhelser shrugs. "I did a few tricks with my morphing bracelet, the taser, and other toys. It impressed the clan. Or at least they pretended to be impressed." He smiles in his ironic way. "It's a small group here and a big empty country, Thomas. No other bands for miles and miles. They need new DNA in their little gene pool here."

"Well, go to it," I say and clap him on the shoulder. I touch the medallion again but think of something else. "Where *is* your morphing bracelet? The taser baton?"

"Patroclus took all of that stuff," says Nightenhelser.

I actually look over my shoulder and set my hand on the hilt of my sword.

"Don't worry, he's long gone," says Nightenhelser.

"Gone where?"

"He said something about heading back to Ilium to join his friend Achilles," says Nightenhelser. "Then he asked me which direction Ilium was. I pointed east. He walked off in that direction . . . and let me live."

"Jesus," I whisper. "He's probably swimming the Atlantic as we speak."

"I wouldn't put it past him." Nightenhelser holds out his hand and I take it. It's strange to shake hands palm to palm with a man, after these intense weeks of forearm grips. "Good-bye, Hockenberry. I don't expect we'll meet again."

"Probably not," I say. "Good-bye, Nightenhelser."

My hand is on the QT medallion, ready to turn its dial, when the other scholic—ex-scholic—touches my shoulder.

"Hockenberry?" he says, pulling his hand away quickly so that he doesn't accidentally teleport with me if I QT away. "Does Ilium still stand?"

"Oh, yes," I say, "Ilium still stands."

"We always knew what was going to happen," says Nightenhelser. "Nine years and we always knew—within a small margin of error— what was going to happen next. Which man or god would do what. Who was going to die and when. Who was going to live."

"I know."

"It's one of the reasons I have to stay here, with her," says Nightenhelser, looking me in the eye. "Every hour, every day, every morning, I don't know what's going to happen next. It's wonderful."

"I understand," I say. And I do.

"Do you know what's going to happen next there?" asks Hockenberry. "In your new world?"

"Not a clue," I say. I realize that I'm grinning fiercely, joyously, and probably frighteningly, all signs of a civilized scholic or scholar in me gone now. "But it's going to be damned interesting to find out what happens next."

I twist the QT medallion and disappear.

Dramatis Personae for *Ilium*

ACHAEANS (Greeks)

Achilles   son of Peleus and the goddess Thetis, most ferocious of the Achaean heroes, fated at birth to die young by Hector's hand at Troy and receive glory forever, or to live a long life in obscurity.

Odysseus   son of Laertes, lord of Ithaca, husband of Penelope, crafty strategist, a favorite of the goddess Athena

Agamemnon   son of Atreus, supreme commander of the Achaeans, husband of Clytemnestra. It is Agamemnon's insistence on seizing Achilles' slave girl, Briseis, that precipitates the central crisis of the *Iliad*.

Menelaus   younger son of Atreus, brother of Agamemnon, husband to Helen

Diomedes   son of Tydeus, captain of the Achaeans, and such a ferocious warrior that he receives *aristeia* (a tale within the tale showing individual valor in battle) in the *Iliad*, second only to Achilles' final wrath

Patroclus   son of Menoetus, best friend to Achilles, destined to die by Hector's hand in the *Iliad*

Nestor   son of Neleus and the oldest of the Achaean captains, "the clear speaker of Pylos," given to long-winded rants in council

Phoenix son of Amyntor, older tutor and longtime comrade of Achilles, who inexplicably has a central role in the important "embassy to Achilles"

TROJANS (defenders of Ilium)

Hector son of Priam, leader and greatest hero of the Trojans, husband to Andromache and father to the toddler Astyanax (the child also known as "Scamandrius" and "Lord of the City" to the citizens of Ilium)

Andromache wife of Hector, mother of Astyanax; Andromache's royal father and brothers were slain by Achilles

Priam son of Laomedon, elder king of Ilium (Troy), father of Hector and Paris and many other sons

Paris son of Priam, brother of Hector, gifted as both fighter and lover; it is Paris who brought about the Trojan War by abducting Helen, Menelaus' wife, from Sparta and bringing her to Ilium

Helen wife of Meneleus, daughter of Zeus, victim of multiple abductions because of her fabled beauty

Hecuba Priam's wife, queen of Troy

Aeneas son of Anchises and Aphrodite, leader of the Dardanians, destined in the *Iliad* to be the future king of the scattered Trojans

Cassandra daughter of Priam, rape victim, tortured clairvoyant

GODS ON OLYMPOS

Zeus king of the gods, husband and brother to Hera, father to countless Olympians and mortals, son of Kronos and Rhea—the Titans whom he overthrew and cast down into Tartarus, the lowest circles of the world of the dead

Hera wife and sister of Zeus, champion of the Achaeans

Athena daughter of Zeus, strong defender of the Achaeans

Ares god of war, a hothead, ally of the Trojans

Apollo god of the arts, healing, and disease—"lord of the silver bow"—and prime ally of the Trojans

Aphrodite goddess of love, ally of the Trojans, a schemer

Hephaestus god of fire, artificer and engineer to the gods, son of Hera; lusts after Athena

OLD STYLE HUMANS

Ada a few years past her First Twenty, mistress of Ardis Hall

Harman ninety-nine years old and thus one year away from his Final Twenty; the only man on Earth who knows how to read

Daeman approaching his Second Twenty, a pudgy seducer of women and a collector of butterflies

Savi the Wandering Jew, the only old-style human not gathered up in the final fax 1,400 years earlier

MORAVECS*

*(*autonomous, sentient, biomechanical organisms seeded throughout the outer solar system by humans during the Lost Age)*

Mahnmut explorer under the ice-capped seas of Jupiter's moon Europa; skipper of *The Dark Lady* submersible; amateur scholar of Shakespeare's sonnets

Orphu of Io eight-ton, six-meter-long, crab-shaped, heavily armored hard-vac moravec who works in the sulfur-torus of Io; Proust enthusiast

Asteague/Che	Europan, prime integrator of the Five Moons Consortium
Koros III	Ganymedan, buckycarbon-sheathed, humanoid in design, fly's eyes, commander of the Mars expedition
Ri Po	Callistan, non-humanoid in design, ship's navigator

Centurion Leader
Mep Ahoo	Rockvec soldier from the Asteroid Belt

OTHER ENTITIES

Voynix	mysterious bipedal creatures, part servants, part watchdogs, not of Earth
LGM	Little Green Men, also known as *zeks*; chlorophyll-based workers on Mars, tasked with erecting thousands of Great Stone Heads
Prospero	avatar of the evolved and self-aware Earth logosphere
Ariel	avatar of the evolved and self-aware Earth biosphere
Caliban	Prospero's pet monster
calibani	lesser clones of Caliban, guardians of the Mediterranean Basin
Sycorax	a witch, Caliban's mother; according to Prospero, she is also known as Circe
Setebos	Caliban's violent, arbitrary god, the "many-handed as a cuttlefish," not from Earth's solar system
The Quiet	Prospero's god (maybe), Setebos' nemesis, an unknown entity